Kip Manley

CITY *of* ROSES

VOL. 2

THE DAZZLE *of* DAY

Supersticery Press
Manley, Kip
City of Roses Vol. 2: The Dazzle of Day / Kip Manley
ISBN 978-1-7349452-1-8

Originally published as individual chapbook nos. 12 – 22 from 2011 – 2014.

Art is a Gift

www.thecityofroses.com

A Duel

Jo stoops, her sword still in one hand, and begins to gather up the duffel and the box. She stops when the point of Roland's sword presses against the bag before her, then lifts, slowly, toward her face. She lets go of the bag and stands, slowly, and his sword follows her up. "Princess," he says. "I can still defeat your champion. Take up the keeping of you, once again."

"You might try," says Ysabel. "You'll lose. I've seen it."

"Do *you* think I'll lose?" says Roland to Jo. "A month with even the notorious Erne is hardly enough to make you a creditable swordsman."

Jo spares a glance over her shoulder for Ysabel in the shadows, then takes the hilt of her sword in her hand. Steps back, and back again. "All right," says Roland, "a single pass, as I proposed," as she yanks the scabbard from her blade and settles in a stance sidelong to him, the scabbard in her left hand held behind, her blade up and at an angle before. His left hand tucked against his chest leaning back just, his sword arm canted up the blade angled down a little and a little to the left and sliding his foot forward kicking the duffel to one side his sword-tip lazily swinging toward her when he flicks his wrist and it leaps up and over her blade a looping cut she catches with a jerk of a parry, clang. "There," he says, and steps back, lowering his blade. "Put up." Shaking out his left hand. "You've fought for her, and we can both agree I've won. Honor's satisfied." And then, "Gallowglas."

Jo's blade's still there between them, up, and at an angle.

"I would not hurt you, Jo Maguire," says Roland.

"You're gonna have to," says Jo. Her hand settling and resettling itself about the hilt.

"You can't win," says Roland. Lifting his sword somewhat. "Put up your blade."

"If you were in my shoes," says Jo, and she takes a deep breath, "would you?"

And behind her, in the darkness, leaning against the railing over the water, Ysabel is smiling.

A DUEL

the TABLE *of* CONTENTS

PREVIOUSLY

ONCE UPON A TIME, a young woman named Jo lived in a small apartment in Portland, the City of Roses. She was employed as a telemarketer, and had recently broken off relations with a rather hapless young man.

One day Jo's friend, Becker, was promoted, and Jo went with her co-workers to a bar to celebrate. An argument erupted at the next table, and Jo leapt to what she thought was the defense of a woman unchivalrously pressed by her companion. The woman, Ysabel, invited Jo to a party on the other side of the freeway where the music was loud, the dancing furious, and Jo insulted Ysabel's companion, a man known as the Chariot. He challenged her to a duel, and Jo went along till it became quite clear it wasn't some mad prank. She dropped her sword, ceding the fight, and the Chariot, stung by another insult, stabbed her in the back.

Jo was taken to Ysabel's house, where she was healed by the Gammer and told that, having thus beaten the Chariot, she now had the keeping of the Princess, Ysabel. She would be brought before the Queen and offered a chance to give it up. Before the audience, Jo received a call from Becker, who didn't remember the party, or the duel, and wanted to know why she wasn't at work. Jo then met the Chariot once more: he sneered at her presumption; she refused to relinquish what she'd won.

Jo brought her new roommate to work, telling Becker that Ysabel was fleeing a dangerous ex, and could not stay alone. Meanwhile, news spread quickly of Ysabel's new circumstance, and two knights banneret, the Stirrup and the Mooncalfe, presented the Duke of Southeast with a simple plan to seize Ysabel from her new guardian and wed her, thus cementing his claim to the Throne. They struck as Jo and Ysabel left work, chasing them to the steps of a church. Before Ysabel could give herself up, the Chariot appeared, drawing his sword to fight Stirrup and Mooncalfe at once. But Jo stepped onto the sidewalk just as the Chariot struck the Duke's boon companion, Tommy Rawhead, and thus she learned of her terrible power: as a gallowglas, her mere presence on a field of battle made blows mortal. Tommy Rawhead was destroyed.

Furious, the Duke planned revenge: he proposed a hunt in honor of the Bride, a hunt for a monstrous boar, to be held within the Lloyd Center Mall in Northeast, demesne of the outcast sister of the Queen. As the Bride's champion, Jo was expected to participate, and it fell to the Chariot to determine whether she could. He took her to Vincent Erne, who taught stage actors how best to fight with mock swords. The Chariot arranged for the Axe to stay with Ysabel while Jo was training, and Ysabel and the Axe took the opportunity to resume their relationship, even as Ysabel began to work on the phones alongside Jo.

The Stirrup and the Mooncalfe, to make amends, assisted the Duke by kidnapping Jo's ex, Frankie. The Queen determined Jo shouldn't participate in the hunt; the Mooncalfe, acting for the Duke, picked a fight with the Anvil, Southwest's champion. Thus, the Chariot and the Axe stepped up, along with the Duke's chosen champion: Frankie. The hunt was interrupted by the Queen's sister, who threatened Frankie, and was threatened by Jo in turn. She laughed; the boar escaped.

Mr. Charlock, and Mr. Keightlinger, two men who had been surveilling Ysabel and Jo, were tasked by their employer, Mr. Leir, with hiding the monstrous boar. The Duke was tasked with destroying the boar, as he'd promised, by the mysterious man in grey. He called up two of his own knights, the Dagger and the Helm, and waylaid Jo and Ysabel, along with the Axe, to join him on this hunt. They rode to a point on the freeway where the boar might be driven to them, and the boar threw the Duke from his horse, breaking his leg, before succumbing to its wounds. The Dagger, furious at the Bride's dalliance with the Axe, made to strike the Axe from behind, and was fought off by the Chariot.

Jo, in a foul temper, left work early one night with Ysabel to visit the site where the boar'd fallen. On their way back they were attacked by mysterious hollow men, and Jo fought them, defending Ysabel. The Queen was forced to recognize her heroism by creating Jo a knight. At the dinner where this was announced, the Axe tried to break up with Ysabel, only to be rejected in turn. Ysabel was then approached by the mechanicals, to attend one of their union meetings, where she met with their leader, the Soames. Ysabel gave them the last of her dust, and was given a vial of dew in return. Becker and Guthrie, at the behest of the Thrummy-Cap's oracular warnings, crashed the meeting with the Anvil, just as it was assaulted by the Dagger and the Helm with a flotilla of ghost bicycles. Jo was able to lay the ghosts to rest, and the Anvil destroyed the Dagger.

Ysabel convinced Jo to go shopping by herself one night, and took advantage of her solitude by trying to turn the dew she'd been given by the mechanicals. Jo encountered the Mooncalfe at the grocery store, and he drew his sword on her, but she was able to win past him, and ran back to her apartment only to find Ysabel fallen and unresponsive. Frantic, Jo called to the Chariot for help, and he determined Ysabel'd drunk the dew, and it was churning in her. He cut it out, and gave Jo dust to heal the wound he'd made.

The Axe, in a bid to win back Ysabel, told Jo she would challenge her to a duel at her dubbing. The Mooncalfe, one eye now lost, kidnapped Frankie. The Duke found a strange briefcase somehow linked to the mysterious hollow men. The Chariot took it upon himself to execute the Soames for giving the dew to Ysabel. Becker had to let Jo and Ysabel go from their jobs at the end of a run of surveys, and because Ysabel was considered her roommate, Jo was to lose the assistance she received for rent. But her dubbing as a knight was a glorious spectacle, and before the Axe could challenge her, a mysterious knight wearing the Huntsman's mask challenged the Axe.

At the party afterwards, Ysabel danced with the Axe, Becker laughed with the Anvil, and Jo kissed the Duke, who gave her an unlimited bank card. The Chariot drew his sword on the Axe, who drove hers into the floor and walked away. Ysabel asked Jo if she loved her, and Jo, confused, apologetic, said no, and it started to rain.

Jo bought a number of new things with the card before Ysabel asked if she knew where the money came from, or where it went. They confronted the Duke in his demesne, and he took them with him on his rounds about the city as he portioned out the last of his dust to some of his subjects, but not others. They were followed by Mr. Charlock and his old friend from the Army, Bottle John Wesson, while Mr. Keightlinger tried to find who'd been interfering with the construction of new condominiums in Southwest with the help of someone who might or might not have been Bottle John's brother, Ezra. Their various paths all converged on the Next Thursday Teahouse, a folly built by the river in Sellwood, where Bottle John drew a gun on Mr. Charlock, Ezra summoned what looked like an angel, Ysabel kissed Jessie, the Duke's driver, and the Duke told Jo where the money came from, and then disappeared.

Our story resumes as Jo closes her eyes.

Portland, Oregon
2011 – 2014

Dreams vary according to where you are, what area and what street, but above all according to the time of year and the weather. Rainy weather in the city, in its thoroughly treacherous sweetness and its power to draw one back to the days of early childhood, can be appreciated only by someone who has grown up in the big city. It naturally evens out the day, and with rainy weather one can do the same thing day in, day out—play cards, read, or engage in argument—whereas sunshine, by contrast, shades the hours and is furthermore less friendly to the dreamer.

—Walter Benjamin

After the clangor of organ majestic, or chorus, or perfect band,
Silent, athwart my soul, moves the symphony true.

—Walt Whitman

NO. 12
INNOCENCY

A SMALL ROOM lined with books from floor to ceiling on dark wooden shelves lit by unobtrusive spots. More books in roughly neat piles on rugs by a couple of wing chairs and narrow end tables bearing up under the weight of yet more unshelved books, leather-bound and dust-jacketed some wrapped in clear plastic, paperbacks tucked here and there and some books blankly featureless in wraps of plain brown paper. A stretch of rug, ankle-deep arabesques where it isn't cluttered by more stacks of books ragged and angled and tumbled into a wave that's broken against the broad high oxblood back of a tufted leather sofa pulled before the dying flicker of a fireplace. A bare foot edges up above the back of that sofa, toes pointed, clenched, the bottom of it dark with grime, a gasp and a grunt and it shivers toes unfurling with a glottal, a guttural, a long low groan that judders into a word, " – *God* – " and then relaxes, lowering, settling, the heel of it hooked over the back of the sofa, the nail of the big toe a dead grey ridge.

"Yeah?" says someone, a man. A rustle, a squeak of skin on leather, a sigh. A woman laughs, "That's, that was," and then she gasps and her foot on the back of the sofa jerks up and draws back lifting her shin her quivering calf, "sorry," she says, and "aftershock." More squeaking and rustling that's her head there against the arm of the sofa short brown hair dark in the fire-light. She's looking off to the side, her foot braced for leverage,

1

she's tugging something. "Wait," says the man. "Jo, just," and, more rustling, "leave it," he says.

She says, "I need a minute," and he says, "I want to look at you," and she says, "don't," but the rustling stops.

"What is this?" he says.

At the other end of the sofa in his soft brown vest the Duke's leaning over on his elbows his shoulder under Jo's upraised thigh his arm about her hip his hand splayed over her belly, stroking the harsh, green-black lines of a tattoo along the swell of it from navel to the edge of dark curled hair, an angular thing, abstract, a suggestion of beak and eyes.

"A tattoo," says Jo. Lying back looking down the length of herself at him. Soft heathery dress drawn in rumpled waves up past her hips up baring her belly up to lap under her breasts, straps askew, black bra still in place beneath. One arm tangled in the folds of it not tugging it down. "Well, yes, a tattoo," says the Duke. He kisses it. "What's it of?"

"It's, a reminder," says Jo. She sits up, she scoots back, she pulls her foot down from the back of the sofa. "Wait," says the Duke, sitting back, as her dress falling into her lap she takes his face in her hands and kisses him. "Oh," he says. On the floor by the hearth a cane topped by a rough-hewn hawk, a sword in a plain black scabbard, a tossed-off red and brown striped jacket, a wadded pair of grey boxer briefs. "That was," says Jo, and then she kisses him again. His hand on her knee, his hand on her hip under her dress. "It's been a while," says Jo. "I can't believe I'm asking you this. But tell me you have a rubber in your pocket."

"In my," says the Duke.

"A condom," says Jo.

"I know what," says the Duke, "you have to trust me, Jo, I could no more get you with child than I could bring you down the moon."

"That's not," says Jo, "that's not all I'm." She's frowning. "The music."

"There's no," says the Duke, and Jo says, "It stopped." Reaching down for the hilt of the sword when from somewhere else in the house a great crack of sound that shakes the sofa and tumbles the books piled all about them. Someone's screaming. Jo stands abruptly banging into the picnic table rattling the liquor bottles lined across it, five or six of them round and square, clear glass and green glass and deep deep brown. In her satiny black slip, her skinny black jeans, her hands splayed flat on rainbowed graffiti. "Duke?" she says. "Leo?" Someone screams.

"Shit." Jo jerks herself free of the picnic table, toppling a bottle. Whisky slops to the floor. "Is anyone," comes a call from deeper, further in, "is anybody, where's, is anyone? Here?"

"Jessie?" calls Jo down the cramped hall lit by ropes of white lights.

"Hello? Who's that?"

"Hang on," says Jo, "I'm coming," but behind her something thumps and someone gruffly says "Hey!" and Jo catches herself as white lights clatter with the heavy footsteps behind her. "Hey, lady!" Jo turns arms wrapped tightly about herself in a puffy ski jacket some filthy color impossible to name in those shadows under the bridge. One arm of it slashed leaking tufts of white down fill. "Where else am I gonna go?" she's saying. "Huh? Tell me that."

"Anywhere," says the man in the long dark coat, more of a boy, narrow shoulders hunched up around his ears. "Anywhere but here." A truck booms over the bridge above and he scowls up and waits until it's passed. "They weren't all out looking for you they'd be here. They'd be drawing you a circle in the dirt."

"But not you, huh, Christian?" She sniffs, she gulps. Her hair's long, dark, the tips of it stiff with dirt patter the shoulders of her jacket as she shudders. "Smart enough to know I'd come back here." Her Chuck Taylors digging into the gravel, scuffed white toe half torn away, the sock within spotted dark. "I been taxed," says Jo. "What else she gonna do to me?"

"Lady, what the hell. You hear me? You okay?"

One hand braced against a bare wood rafter Jo's frowning at the man in the grey suit and the white shirt buttoned all the way up to his throat. He's got her wrist in one hand and a gun in the other, a snub-nosed revolver pointed at the floor between them. "Let go," she says, and he does. "Leir," he says. "I'm looking for Leir."

"Damned if I know," says Jo, taking a step back. He takes a step forward. Strings of light clatter. She's looking at the gun still pointed at the floor and takes another step back. "I ain't gonna shoot you," he says, taking another step toward her. "This is for him." Another step, boards creaking, lights clattering. "Ain't neither of us got time for this."

"I don't *know*," says Jo, taking another step back. He doesn't. He isn't looking at her, he's blinking rapidly, his gaze jerks about, gun-hand dangling. Jo steps toward him, bending low, looks up at his dark face. He's mumbling something turning his head chin brushing the shoulder of his suit. Her eyes on the gun now forgotten in his fist. His face jerks tendons in his throat jumping like he's yelling at something far away. "Jo?" cries someone from further, deeper in. "Oh God are you gone too?" and the man in the grey suit shudders and blinks and Jo cringes, the hand that was reaching for the gun closing in a fist stepping back and back again she turns on down the hallway stumbling through a door down the one low step beyond crashing to all fours on the rugs laid one over another on the unfinished planks. Lifting herself and starting back suddenly one hand still on the floor the other over her mouth. Not looking away from the puddle of puke on the black-and-white tiles between her bare knees.

Chairs scrape back. "Oh *God*," says someone, a blond girl at a desk beside her. Jo looks up to see all of them staring at her and at the end of the aisle of desks before the whiteboard a man in an argyle sweater, cheeks reddening over his thick brown beard.

"What have you *done* to me," says Jo Maguire.

CROUCHING NAKED — MR. KEIGHTLINGER REFUSES

CROUCHING NAKED under thick white smoke that's rapidly ceiling the room he flips open the scorched grey jacket and the yellowed shirt inside collapses white ash soughing from placket and collar and the blackened bow tie and he's saying "No, no," poking the ash-dusted skull, "how could you, how," as flames rush up the curtain over across the bed and billow the smoke that's hung above the upended table. He slaps the skull clenches his face runs his hands over and over his bare bald head until the curl of lank grey hair that's left is standing stiffly straight. "It's not, it wasn't, it shouldn't have *done* that." He stands, fingertips digging in the corners of his eyes. "Stupid, *stupid*. What were you after what were you even *doing* here you dumb sonofabitch." Bumping into the bed behind him he sits heavily. Over behind him one of the table legs falls in a splash of flame. The armchair in the corner's smoking. "You blew up," says Mr. Charlock, jerking to his feet again, "you stupid motherfucker, you *blew up!*" and he kicks the skull tearing it loose from a blackened patch of carpet rolling wobbling clacking against the night-table between the beds its jaw askew.

"You blew up," he says.

Outside the smoke-smeared window there's movement, shadows. A pounding on the door. Mr. Charlock stands and steps carefully over the body, stoops to pick up the skull. "*You* blew up," he says, jabbing his middle finger into an eye-socket, wiggling it, poking, pulling it out, thumbing his fingertip clean of nothing but a little soot. Turning the skull over in his hands. Someone's yelling "Hey! Anybody in there?" Fire sprouts in a corner of the armchair and rapidly blooms.

"You been dead a while," says Mr. Charlock to the skull in his hands. "Hadn't you. Here's me thinking it was you fucking with my old buddy and all along it was him. *He's* the one." He closes his eyes and kisses the top of the skull lightly, then sets it down in the middle of the smoking bed. Steps back over the scorched grey suit on the floor past the beds towards the alcove in the back, the sink, the overturned wheelchair. Someone outside's still pounding on the door. He stops in the doorway to the bathroom, one hand resting on his hard round belly, the hair furring his arm, his belly, hanks of it at the tops of his skinny thighs all gone a ghost grey in the bright clean slash of light. "For what it's worth," he says, looking back, "I'm sorry." He steps into the bathroom and gently closes the door. The flames in the corner have reached the ceiling now and the smoke there boils away. Outside a siren's wailing, coming closer.

The black car growls too quickly down the narrow residential street, jerking to a stop at the corner with a yelp from its tires. The driver's door's yanked open with a popping squonk and Mr. Keightlinger's shaggy brown head pops up, looks left, looks right over the roof of the car lined with hand-painted cramped white shapes like letters. Quiet streets lined with parked cars and houses lit up against the deepening night and nothing moving, no sound, not even rain. "Yeah?" says Mr. Keightlinger, falling back into the driver's seat. "Vacant lot, vacant lot by the river, where'd the river go." He leans out over the pavement, hawks and spits. Patting his lips and his beard he looks down at the whitish blot gleaming in the streetlight, a tendril spattered away to the left. He slams his door, guns the motor. The black car wheels neatly to the left and leaps away.

The next corner's much the same as the last. He's about to open the door but looking off to the right he doesn't. It's bright down that way, wet pavement gleaming in a warm and yellow light. "Huh," he says, spinning the wheel, working the gearshift and clutch.

It fills a simple intersection, the pavement of it painted in a great circle stretching from corner to corner in yellows and whites a sunflower burning bitterly in all that light, light glaring from the blankened windows of the houses that sit at three of the corners, sunlight gushing from a jagged hole in the night air filled with feathers and eyes, wings lapping wings unfolding and lazily flapping, wings shivering, stretching, eyes that blink and look about, eyes the color of shadowed earth and polished wood and dead dry grass and the high white blue of desert skies. The black car sails under that hole, the spidery white lines of the letter-shapes whorling its hood and roof flaring with a coldly furious light of their own. It squeals to a stop before the fourth corner, where instead of a house there's a high red gate freshly painted and old paned windows suspended to either side. The driver's door opens with a popping squonk and Mr. Keightlinger climbs out, scuffing the old yellow and white paint with a black shoe. "Fortuitous," he says. "Nothing to see here." Putting on a pair of classic black sunglasses. "Nothing to see here, nothing to see." Stamping one foot, then the other, shaking out his arms. The left lens of his sunglasses covered with spidery words painted in white ink. All those wings and eyes towering above him shudder and pull together like a great breath taken in and then there is a sound, a monstrous blare of eagle-screams, of lions, of a phalanx of trumpets as they surge toward the gate, the car, only to be brought up short by Mr. Keightlinger standing there unmoved arms up crossed before his face two fingers extended from either hand.

"Oh I don't think so," he says.

"Shit," says Mr. Charlock, sitting up abruptly in the back seat face in his hands. "Oh fucking *fuck* me hell I do *not,*" rolling up onto his knees, heels of his hands tight against his eyes, sobbing for breath slumping against the back of the driver's seat. "Have *time* for this," he whispers. Trembling reaching for the black suit laid out on the seat fists knotting the pants and dragging them out from under himself, working them open belt buckle jangling, wailing once as he sits back, a high thin keening through clenched teeth as he lifts his outsized feet toes curled knobby knees jack-knifed and jams them all at once into the pants legs. *"God!"* Chest heaving belly bouncing with fast shallow breaths. Hands clumsily fumbling with zipper and button and belt. *"Fuck!"* He pounds the back of the driver's seat and again, and again. Pounces on the black jacket, rips it open, roots in the buttoned white shirt beneath it, yanks out a sleeveless T-shirt and fights his way into it.

Mr. Charlock falls out of the orange car to his hands and bare feet scrabbling on the damp pavement pushing himself up into a stumbling headlong run out into the intersection painted with a great circle of yellows and whites dulled by weather and traffic a sunflower barely visible in the darkness lit only by streetlights at three of the corners. "No," he's saying, "no, no, *no!*" Spinning in the middle of the intersection running his hands over and over his bare bald head. More steadily now he heads for the dark fourth corner, the high red gate, the empty paned windows, the dark vacant lot behind it filled with trees and junk, bare wood, discarded doors, sheets of tin and translucent plastic. "Already gone," he's saying to himself, "already fell out of the fucking *god*damn hell." Wiping his mouth with the back of one hand. "Oh this is gonna. Oh I am gonna take someone apart joint by joint for this."

Over across the intersection a yapping there's a dog a little shaggy thing tugging at a leash a woman in sweatpants and a raincoat peering at him. "What?" snarls Mr. Charlock. "The fuck *you* looking at?" Slapping his feet against the sidewalk, clapping his hands. "Fucking pants for no fucking reason," he mutters, and then he throws back his head eyes wide and bellows, "Wissenkunst, motherfucker! Four walls can't hold *me!*"

A jangle of belt buckle, a flutter of white. The woman in the raincoat frowning lets the little dog tug her out into the intersection, across it, toward that dark corner, the red gate. There on the sidewalk a pair of black pants, a white T-shirt, crumpled, empty. The little dog sniffs at them and starts back, growling.

"I DON'T KNOW HOW MUCH LONGER IT'LL HOLD"
JASMINE REFUSES – A JUMP; A LANDING

"I DON'T KNOW HOW MUCH LONGER IT'LL HOLD," says the gaunt man sitting at one end of the long low sofa.

"And then it'll start happening again?" says the man with the gun, standing in the low wide doorway to the porch. Outside the wind's a low and constant wash of sound unbroken by any patter of rain. The woman huddled at the other end of the sofa says, "What was it you said you had parked outside?" Her shoulders bare she's wrapped in a particolored quilt, her long hair straight and black and loose.

"An angel," says the man with the gun, and Jessie says "Oh God." She's sitting on the floor to one side of the doorway under stained and faded snapshots of various angles and corners of the room about them, each one hazed by wisps and tendrils of smoke that seem to eddy in the uncertain light. Her grey chauffeur's jacket unbuttoned, sagging open, a scrap of black lace stuffed in one clenched fist. "Ain't about you," says the man with the gun. "We here for the sorcerer. Soon as I get him, soon as we're gone."

"He isn't here," says Jo. Still in her satiny black slip and her black jeans by the porch railing, leaning against one of the peeled and polished branches that serve as columns, arms wrapped about herself.

"He *is*," says the man with the gun. "You." He waves at the gaunt man on the sofa, who says "Michael St. John Lake."

"Okay. You his wife?" waving it at the woman at the other end of the sofa.

"No," she says, and the gaunt man says "I'm not married."

The man with the gun says, "This your place?" to Michael.

"Yes."

"The fuck *is* it? What did it do to me?" His arms folded now, the gun in his hand tucked away under an armpit, grey jacket rucked open over the white shirt buttoned all the way up to his throat. "To us, right? I mean you saw, we all saw," looking around the room.

"It's a teahouse," says Michael. "A place to be alone with your memories. Or make new ones, with friends."

"That wasn't no memory," says the man with the gun.

"Your – rather *precipitous* arrival, unbalanced things," says Michael.

"An *angel*." The woman at the end of the sofa snorts.

"Oh," says Jo, gripping the porch railing. "We're there. We aren't here anymore."

"I would take great care in putting names to things," says Michael. He takes in a deep breath, stroking his forehead under the cuff of his black watch cap. "This house was always – perched." His hands in black knit gloves with the fingertips removed. "Now, for want of a better word, we're falling."

"Falling," says the man with the gun.

"The gate," says Michael. "The piazza. They're still there. Here. But your angel's stopped that up."

"So give me Leir," says the man with the gun, as Jessie blurts "Leo!" and then, huddled back against the wall, "Ysabel." Not looking at the man with the gun. "Where are they?"

"And our Lauren," says the woman at the other end of the sofa.

"Out there," says Jo.

"I suppose they're falling, too," says Michael, "further," and he shakes his head suddenly, "up, further in. For want of better words."

"Shut *up*," says the man with the gun. "Already. Dammit." His cheeks gone ashen, yellowed, held tightly stiff, as if his face might break. "You're a wizard," he says to Michael.

"A poor one, if at all," says Michael. "I was once an architect. The best word for me now, perhaps, is host?" He looks up at the man with the gun. "I know of Mr. Leir, but only by reputation. He's never set foot in this house, I can assure you."

"That was no. *God*damn. Memory," says the man with the gun, and he's pulled it out, he's pointing it now at Michael. "I saw my brother being put in the *ground*." The gun dips. He lifts it again. "In a goddamn wooden *box*. We are about the Lord's work. *All* the signs pointed to here. *Here*. He *called* that angel down, his own. Damn. Self. So tell me! How come it's *there*, if he's dead and buried? How could it be?"

The sound of the wind hasn't changed at all.

"I don't know, John," says Michael, looking down. His hollowed cheeks salted with stubble. "If it wasn't a memory, it has nothing to do with this house."

"Sinjin," says the woman at the other end of the sofa.

"Not now, Jasmine," says Michael. The gun's wavering jerking toward her, then him, back to her again. "On me, John. Tell me more about Ezra."

"Ezra," says Bottle John, and the gun swings back from Jasmine past Jo to point again at Michael. "How did you know that. Ezra."

"A poor wizard indeed who couldn't hear it," says Michael. At the other end of the sofa Jasmine's getting to her feet, the quilt clutched tightly about herself. "Take it away from him, Sinjin," she says. "We haven't the time."

"She doesn't have anything to do with us, John," says Michael, sitting up, standing slowly. "None of them do. On me, John. Just you and me." His hands in those black knit gloves held out to either side, his spindly arms swallowed by the wide loose sleeves of his pullover. Jasmine's stooping, one hand holding the quilt in place, scooping something up from the floor, a T-shirt dress, a blond Batgirl printed on it, purple and grey. She lets it fall. Bottle John's saying "No, wait" and the gun jolts from Michael to Jasmine her quilt dragging on the bare plank floor as she walks up to Jo by the railing and the blank dark beyond and the hissing wind.

"John, John don't," says Michael, stepping along the sofa, putting himself between the gun and Jasmine. "On me, John." At Bottle John's feet Jessie's drawing her feet under herself, leaning, pushing herself down the wall under those snapshots away from him as he lowers the gun in fits and starts. "Leir," he's saying. Wiping his eyes roughly with his free hand. "Give the sorcerer to me. The angel's satisfied and this is over."

"We'll talk about that, John," says Michael. "I promise."

Jasmine's gripping the porch railing, giving it a shake. It's solid. She's thickset, short, a head or so shorter than Jo. Jo's back is to the railing, watching as Jessie slowly, carefully stands, rustling those snapshots behind her.

"Will you let the others leave?" says Michael, his hands still out to either side, his voice gentle, calm, loud enough just to be heard over the wind. Bottle John's wiping his eyes again with his thumb, his gun now pointed at the floor. "Jasmine," says Michael. "Take the girls. Head back to the Heart. Wait there."

"No," says Jasmine.

"On me, John, on me," says Michael as the gun comes up. "Please, Jasmine, for their sake – "

"I am not going to huddle away somewhere while you try to save whatever you can reach, Sinjin." She aims a small sly smile at Jo beside her. "What do you think? Shall we go get our neighbors?"

Before Jo can answer, Michael says, "You'll lose yourselves."

"And you can't say how long this house will hold," says Jasmine. The wind tugs at the quilt down by her ankles. Her calves streaked with dark hair.

"The sorcerer!" roars Bottle John. "Give me Leir! And all this ends!" Jasmine's grabbed Jo's hand in hers, and Jessie's shrinking back against that wall, and "Keep it on me!" cries Michael, coughing. "I'm completely at your mercy," he says when he catches his breath. "Let them go. Keep the gun *on me.*"

The gun's pointing squarely at his chest.

"All right," says Bottle John.

"Girl," says Jasmine after a moment. She's looking up at Jessie. "Come on over here." Jessie's looking at Jo, and Jo her hand still in Jasmine's nods quickly, jerkily. Jessie takes a slow small step away from the wall and another, longer, and another, faster, and another, half-running by the time she makes it to the railing. Bottle John doesn't watch her go. He doesn't look away from Michael. Michael doesn't look away from Bottle John.

"What's going to happen?" says Jessie, taking Jo's other hand.

"I don't know," says Jo to Jessie.

"Three of us, three of them," Jasmine's saying. "Those are good numbers." Still holding Jo's hand in hers she tugs the quilt loose from about her shoulders and unwinds it. The wind hauls it up in her grip like a flag snapping over the railing. She lets it go.

Yanked and fluttering dropping tumbling rising up again it falls away from them further and further into that hissing darkness. Jo one hand in Jasmine's one in Jessie's mouth open watches it, a scrap of color beating like a moth against the black.

"Well?" says Jasmine. One hand on the railing pulling a leg up to balance awkwardly sitting on it still holding Jo's hand in hers. Jessie's looking back at the low wide doorway, at Bottle John standing in it, blowing great bullish breaths in and out through his nose. "My shoes," she says, looking down at her bare feet.

"Leave 'em!" cries Jasmine over the wind. "Take nothing you can't stand losing!" Jo's already kicked a leg up and over the railing, sits a-straddle, black boot dangling over the edge. "Come on," she says to Jessie.

But Jessie's leaning back toward the sofa, toward Michael and John, and she opens the fist she's clenched about the scrap of black lace, and she tosses the underwear onto the T-shirt dress left crumpled on the bare plank floor, Batgirl's face smiling up from a wrinkle. She turns and sits up on the railing, still holding Jo's hand.

"Come back," says Michael Lake.

"Keep the lights burning," says Jasmine, and she jumps, and Jo jumps, and Jessie jumps.

The drop of light far off shapes a sound, the sound shapes a shout, a letter, the letter a mouth, the mouth stretched wide and straining shapes a face, a pale face, squinted eyes glinting among the wrinkles crimping the bridge of its nose, a single curl of lank grey hair sprung atop the empty furrows of its forehead. That face drags in its wake a body small and sinewy arms spread wide fingertips fluttering in the wind of his passage falling flying head-long down the length of a narrow residential street past cars all unremarkable, grey sedans parked in shadows before houses with dim white walls and the same blank windows over and over and over again, and the light grows about him bright and white and his shout is answered by a blast of trumpets and the roar of a host of soldiers saluting the dawn. He draws his arms in tight against the force of his fall and tumbling rolls over into himself, covering his shout with his hands.

The freshly painted red gate rings and quivers like a bell setting the old paned windows hung to either side of it a-sway and something falls to the brush at its base with a howl and a thump.

"Huh," grunts Mr. Keightlinger, standing still by the black car, arms still held up crossed before his face upturned in the glare from all those feathers and eyes hanging ponderously above him. Sprigs of hair have worked loose from the club of his ponytail and float gently about his head in the still air. His sunglasses still in place. He doesn't look to see what fell.

Mr. Charlock lurches to his feet staggers to one side then the other fetching up against a gatepost clinging to it with one hand clutching his head. "My *skull*," he bellows. Mr. Keightlinger's black shoe scuffs gravel against pavement as he shifts his stance. The only other sound the far-off hiss of rushing wind. "Fucking *tectonic,"* says Mr. Charlock, pushing off the gate to blunder onto the path beneath it. He is quite naked. Swaying a little blinking thickly at Mr. Keightlinger's back. "Hello to you too," he snorts.

The cords stand out in Mr. Keightlinger's neck. Inside his beard his lips part and he ducks his head with the effort.

"No, no, don't mind me," snaps Mr. Charlock. "Can't even manage to keep it together until I get back here, third fucking jaunt in ten minutes and *this* one – you have *any* idea how cold it gets out there?"

"Hello," growls Mr. Keightlinger.

"You? Were right, by the way." Mr. Charlock brushes a leaf from his shoulder. "John Wesson *did* have a brother. So I forgot." Stretching, working his head back and forth. "But he's been dead for years so I'm still gonna have to call that one for me. On a technicality." Turning on wobbly feet to look back through the gate. A luxurious confusion has gathered itself from windows and doors and polished wood, roofs of gleaming tin and glass lit up by dozens of warmly gold lamps, trees winding in and out of the rooms built around them. "Whoa," says Mr. Charlock.

Mr. Keightlinger's shifted back another inch or so more toward the car with another gravelly scrape.

"So he went in there, right?" says Mr. Charlock. "Bottle John. After something, something he could find quick, because Junior here," jerking a thumb over his shoulder, "is primed to wipe this place off the map. Something quick, something obvious, something that wasn't anywhere else we went today…" He shrugs. "Fucked if I know."

"Pants," spits Mr. Keightlinger.

"Well I couldn't fucking bring them *with* me, c ould I?" says Mr. Charlock. "Or my glasses neither. I gotta go in there shorn of arms and armor, *I'm* the one has to rescue the Bride so our boss doesn't eat us for breakfast, I gotta go tell an old friend I accidentally killed his dead brother, and all you have to do is wrestle with this sorry excuse for an angel." He stalks toward the open door of the teahouse. "Have a little sympathy, would you?"

Groaning with the effort Mr. Keightlinger forces one foot forward an inch or so, leaning into the step as the angel above shrinks back eyes rolling. "Collar," he manages to say. Hanging his head shaking it turning to spare a glance over his shoulder he says it again, "Collar," but Mr. Charlock's already inside.

WHEN THE ALARM CLOCK BUZZES – HOW IT IS
WHAT SHE SHOULDN'T HAVE DONE – THE WRONG DAMN HATCH

WHEN THE ALARM CLOCK BUZZES the rumpled blankets jerk and twist and spit out a hand. It fumbles about and finds the clock and slaps the snooze button. A head pops out, blinking, befuddled. Mousy brown hair maybe down to the shoulders, tangled with sleep. She kicks herself free of the thick down comforter half-tumbling naked from off the big broad bed to stand there a moment, scratching herself under her breasts. Sunlight shines vaguely behind the drawn curtains. The sound of a shower running somewhere down the hall.

The kitchen's long and narrow, empty, dim. She's pouring steaming water from a kettle into a carafe of ground coffee. She's pulled on a faded yellow work shirt with the sleeves rolled up and only a couple-three buttons fastened. She sets the kettle on the gleaming white stovetop and picks up a plunger, fits it to the top of the carafe. Looks up at the round clock over the stainless steel refrigerator, toying with one of the undone buttons on her shirt. Quarter of nine.

There are two doors at the other end of the kitchen.

One of them stands open, a small dark room beyond, coats on the wall, a couple bicycles leaning together, the corner of a clothes-dryer stacked on top of a washing machine. A pair of rubber boots. The other door is closed. Like the first it's tall, skinny, paneled and painted white. She walks toward them, bare feet pale against the red and black whorls of the linoleum, reaching for the closed door, its crystal knob set in old greened brass.

"Coffee?"

Jo spins, hand to her mouth. "Jesus, Duke," she says. He's by the sink in a long dressing gown crowded with paisleys of purple and maroon and gold and brown. He stops drying his hair with a towel, head tocking back, struck by a little smile. "You haven't called me that in a while," he says. Draping the towel about his neck. "Is there coffee?"

The clock says five of nine. "Oh hell," says Jo, rushing back down the length of the kitchen. "I don't know what happened – "

"It's okay," says the Duke.

"It's only been ten minutes, it should be okay," she's saying, grabbing the plunger, leaning on it, pressing down into the carafe, and "Not so hard," says the Duke, "you don't want to," leaning over, peering around her, "pop it, like last time," as Jo says, "It's not gonna break." Hiking up on her toes to force the plunger down. "You want to get down a couple of cups?"

"I dunno," says the Duke close behind her. One arm snaking about her waist. One hand on her bare hip under her shirt. "Maybe I don't need the coffee."

"Leo," she says, letting go of the plunger as he kisses her neck. "That's it," he says, both hands on her hips now, bending his knees a little leaning back. "Jesus, Leo, not so – " and her eyes get wide and she takes a quick sip of air and grips the counter.

"Well?" says the Duke, leaning forward over her back, kissing her neck again, her ear. "Go on," she says, still gripping the counter, "if you're gonna, go on," and ducking bracing himself hands on her hips again his dressing gown falls open towel slipping from his shoulders belly tight against her ass bared shirt ridden up to the small of her back slapping as he rocks back and forth and she winces hand slapping grabbing the rim of the sink face clenched she bites her lip "Jesus" she says, "Leo – "

A rattling bang his knees against the cabinets and "Shit," he says, faltering. "Oh," says Jo, "hey," and he leans back jerking her hips back bucking against her again and again a bang. "Fuck!" says the Duke, "hang on," but Jo's leaning forward against the sink pushing him back a step and then another staggering vaguely confused his gown slipping from his shoulders his cock bobbing, foreskin drawn back, the swollen purple head of it glistening. "No I can," he says, reaching for her, but she's swarming over him grabbing his face her mouth glued to his and

16

they spin about her hair swinging his wet hair pasted to the back of his neck. She pushes him down and down to his knees still kissing him down and back to sit on the floor as she straddles his lap. "There," she says, one hand on his shoulder, one hand down between them as she settles herself, and "Oh," he says, "oh that works too." A phone's ringing.

"I guess it has, hasn't it," says Jo, sitting in a low flat armchair, a glassy black phone to her ear. "We've been busy." In her faded yellow work shirt and a pair of brown jeans. "Well there's a lot to do, you know? A lot of things to do."

It's a wide white room filled with blue shadows, wheat-colored drapes drawn over an enormous picture window. At one end a big white unadorned fireplace, cold and dark, the wall above it darkened by old smoke. There's an orange couch, long and low on spindly aluminum legs. "I want you to meet him too," says Jo. Hanging over the couch a sword slung from a red leather strap, the scabbard plain and black with a beaten metal throat and chape the color of thunderclouds, the hilt of it simple and straight, wrapped in dulled wire, swaddled in a basket of wiry strands. "He's a, well, there's a lot of things he does. I guess you could say he's an entrepreneur. But that's what I mean, he's always, there's always – " Jo leans forward, one leg drawn up, her foot resting on the cushion. "Well, openings, things like that, going out to support this or – " Rolls her eyes. "I don't really need one anymore. Actually, I'm thinking of going to school." Leans back a little. "Yeah. I was thinking maybe art history or – well it doesn't – well it doesn't have to be – it doesn't *have* to be practical, Mom." Leaning forward again, elbows on her knees, both feet swallowed by the thick white carpet. "That's just how it is." Anger flashes across her face. "Well, I did." She squeezes her eyes shut, dips her head. "What, I was gonna keep Dad's name? That would have made you happy?" She leaps to her feet. "Well I did, it's done. Okay? It happened. It's done." Listening, her eyes shutting again, shaking her head. "Mom." With aimless steps she walks away from the chair, past the front door white in a white frame, high windows filled with reflected white light. "Well – " she says, biting off the word with stern lips set in a grimace that shivers, softens, melts into something almost concerned, almost a smile. She leans in the doorway to the dim narrow kitchen. "We both said stuff we didn't – " Ducking her head again, tucking a wave of hair up behind her ear. "Well I'm – I'm – well, I, I'm – thanks, Mom. Thank you." Turning in the doorway, folding her free arm about herself. "I'm, I'm sorry, too, Mom."

There are two doors at the other end of the kitchen.

"What?" Frowning, blinking. Stepping into the kitchen. "I, I missed that. What – "

One of them standing open, a small dark room beyond, coats, a couple bicycles, washer and dryer and a pair of rubber boots. The other door is closed. Jo's walking toward them both her bare feet pale against the red and black whorls of the linoleum. "I'm sorry, Mom, can you hang on just a – " Reaching for the closed door, its crystal knob set in old greened brass. From the front of the house a pounding, a doorbell bonging, and again.

"Mrs. Barganax?"

"What," says Jo, the door opened just a crack between them.

"Joliet Kendal Barganax?" says the one with the shock of pinkish orange hair. He's holding up a badge in a brown leather wallet. "I'm Detective Fox." Tucking the badge back into his black leather jacket, nodding at the man next to him, both hands in the pockets of his black wool greatcoat. "This is Detective Tassick. We have some questions for you, if we could come inside?"

"Here's fine," says Jo, lifting a cigarette to her lipsticked mouth. Blowing smoke past them. The little entryway screened by a high green hedge.

"Bit chilly," says Fox, shrugging. He pulls a manila envelope from his jacket. "You know a Jasmine Chavda?" Showing her a black and white photo, a woman looking away from the camera, a strong nose, long hair straight and black and loose.

"No," says Jo, letting the door open a little more. She's wearing a brief black slip with simple ribbon straps and her hair's done up in curlers, pink and minty green and baby blue. Her toenails painted red and black, except the dead grey ridge on the big toe of her left foot.

"Lauren Yallowshot?" says Fox. "Jessie Vitaly?" More photos, a teenaged girl laughing, one hand on the oversized headphones she's wearing, a blond woman in a white T-shirt staring expressionless at the camera.

"Jessie, yes," says Jo. "She used to work for my husband."

"You know she's an exotic dancer," says Tassick. His voice is deep and roughly worn. He wears a salt-and-pepper Van Dyke, neatly trimmed.

"I didn't know she'd gone back to it," says Jo.

"But she and your husband, had a relationship?" says Fox.

"So?" says Jo.

"You said she *worked* for him," says Tassick.

"Guys," says Jo, "if everybody with a, a stripper for an ex in this city's suddenly police business, I mean, *damn.*"

"We have reason to believe these women are involved in a matter of notional security," says Fox, reaching into his jacket again. "If you see any of them, or hear from Ms. Vitaly at any point, in the next few days, Mrs. Barganax," he's handing her a card, "we'd appreciate a call?"

She takes the card in her free hand, saying, "My name's Jo – " Looking down, past the card, her feet in mismatched Chuck Taylors, one of them black, one of them white, the toe held on with duct tape. "This is bullshit," she says, and lets the card drop from her fingers.

"Mrs. Barganax," says Tassick.

"I didn't get married!" screams Jo, and for a moment no one says anything, the detectives outside, Jo clinging to the door. "I'm not the one getting married," she says, and she ducks back into the house. "Mrs. Barganax!" calls Fox, and Tassick shoves him.

There are two doors at the other end of the kitchen.

Jo cigarette in her hand marches down the length of the kitchen and puts her hand on the crystal knob set in old green brass. "Please," she whispers, and she opens the door.

A gleaming white bathroom lit by coiled fluorescent bulbs around a mirror over the sink the floor of tiny black and white hexagonal tiles stretching the length of it to a clawfoot tub ringed by clear plastic curtains.

"Ysabel?" says Jo, setting her cigarette on the edge of the sink.

Through the curtains blurry vague the tub's filled almost to the brim with filthy water clouded brown and grey a greasy sheen to it jackknifed knees upright at one end a hand floating limply thumb just breaking the surface. "Oh God" says Jo, ripping the curtains open hooks ringing, "oh God no," plunging heedless hands into the tub pulling splashing slippery torso an arm flopping a chin a woman's face foul water the color of old blood pouring from the slackly open mouth black hair heavy a thickly soaking sheet of it clinging to shoulders breasts as Jo hauls twisting falling back one arm wrapped about the weight of the body half out of the tub now, "Ysabel," she says, sluicing black hair from that face, "Ysabel!" the half-open mouth, the green eyes dull in the harsh flat light.

"Jo," says someone, the Duke, a flat question. Ysabel in her arms she turns halfway to see him in the mirror over the sink, his red and brown striped jacket, his face obscured by a streak of something smeared across the glass. "I wish you hadn't done that." A drift of grey ash falls from the smoldering cigarette to mar the white bowl of the sink. A tearing retching gasp and Ysabel begins to breathe heaving in Jo's arms sloshing water from the tub squeaking one arm caught in the shower curtains pulling rings popping ripping loose as Ysabel slips from the tub and they fall back to the tiles hacking coughing spitting rustling in all that clear plastic. "Ysabel?" Jo's saying. "Ysabel are you okay? Are you there?" and Ysabel, slowly, nods.

Gasping, laughing, Jo pulls her close, "Oh God," she's saying, Ysabel clinging to her still nodding, still coughing, and Jo scrapes away more hair to find her mouth her eyes her forehead which she kisses, holding Ysabel calming gentling to her. "Hey," says Jo then, "Leo." Struggling with the plastic. "A little help here? Leo?"

He's standing in the doorway, leaning on his cane, the rough-hewn hawk at its head caged in his fingers. Staring at the tub, the wall beyond, his brow faintly creased by some quizzical concern.

"Christ," mutters Jo, kicking at the plastic. "Ysabel," fighting her way upright, "are you, can you," and Ysabel curled on her side lifts a hand weakly shaking her head, then nods, pushes herself up to her hands and knees, shivering. Jo to her feet now grabs the Duke by his lapels. "Hey!" She slaps him. Blinking, his mouth working, he lifts a hand to his cheek. "You in there?" says Jo.

"Of course," says the Duke.

"Well fucking help then or get out of the way," says Jo, pushing past him, wet shoes slapping the kitchen floor.

In the bedroom she hauls open the frosted glass doors of the closet at the foot of the big broad bed to find a row of red and brown striped jackets and little black dresses one after another all the same. Hangers rattle as she shoves them back and forth. "This has got to be *your* dream house," she mutters, pulling out one of the jackets free, turning to the bed. Shoving the down comforter to the floor she yanks a woven blanket loose and bundles it with her.

In the living room Ysabel's crouching on the carpet wrapped in the Duke's red and brown striped jacket. The Duke in his cream-colored vest propped on his cane leans over her. Jo looks at the red and brown striped jacket in her hands, shrugs, tosses it to him, then kneels by the shivering Ysabel, wrapping her in the blanket. "I have other clothes, you know," says the Duke, pulling on the jacket.

"Not here you don't," says Jo. Ysabel's squeezing water from her hair with a corner of the blanket.

"You should pay more attention."

"*I* should," snaps Jo. "Where'd you get the idea I'd be wearing slinky little cocktail dresses?"

"We need," says Ysabel, "to *go.*"

"Couldn't agree more," says Jo, getting to her feet.

"Jo, no," says the Duke, as she heads to the front door, "not that way," as she pulls it open. The entryway's gone. The doorway's walled off by the high thick hedge. "Shit," says Jo, shutting the door, heading for the wheat-colored drapes. "Jo, don't," says the Duke, we have to, don't!" as she yanks them open.

The Duke's gently pushing her back from the window, pulling the drapes shut without looking. The hissing rush of sound dies away. "It's pretty raw," he says.

"How do we," says Jo, shuddering, "is there, what, a back door?"

"We need to go up," says Ysabel, standing now, wrapped in the jacket and the blanket.

"Or down," says the Duke. He lifts a hand but doesn't brush her cheek.

"Up's good," says Jo, pointing back toward the bedroom. "I think this place has an attic."

"Lead on," says the Duke, and limping after her offers an arm to Ysabel. They follow her into the hall.

Then Jo jogs back into the living room jumps onto the orange couch grabs the sword hanging there. Wet shoes on the orange cushions she takes the scabbard in her left hand and the hilt in her right and tugs free half a foot of blade. The surface of it polished but within deep waves of dark and light steel chase the spine of it. "Okay," says Jo, sheathing it with a whisp and a snick, slinging the red strap over a shoulder, stepping down off the couch.

In the hall the Duke's unfolding a stepladder from a trapdoor in the ceiling, Ysabel beside him, huddled in the blanket. "So what's up there?" says Jo.

"The attic?" says the Duke, his hand on one of the rungs. "Let's go find out," he says, limping around to the foot of the ladder, tucking his cane under an arm. "No, no," says Jo, "let me go first," a hand on the other side.

"Barganax," says Ysabel.

"You need to help the Princess," says the Duke, pushing gently but firmly against Jo, and "Dammit, Leo," says Jo, pushing back.

"Gallowglas!" says Ysabel sharply. "Southeast!" They both stop and turn to look at her. She's resettling the blanket about her shoulders. "Jo, you go first. Duke, I'll follow after you."

"Princess," says the Duke, stepping back. "This is hardly the time for modesty." Jo starts up the ladder.

"Your leg, Barganax," says Ysabel. "This is no time for pride."

The Duke looks down, puts a foot on a rung. "No need to be so formal."

Jo puts her head up through a hatch, works a shoulder then another up and through shimmying to get her elbows up on the floor of a small room framed and paneled in dark wood. Her sword thumping as she hauls it up. Two other hatches open in the floor, one to either side. Oil lamps sway from slender chains. In the corner there is Jasmine, sitting on a pile of folded cloth, robes in richly clashing colors folded one atop another. She's wearing a greyly black wetsuit, her hair pulled back in a long tight braid. She's cradling a girl in her lap, all knees and elbows in a school-girl's sailor suit, her face screwed up and ugly red with weeping. "You made it," says Jasmine. Snuffling the girl looks up.

"Yeah," says Jo, and from beneath her the Duke's voice, muffled, "You okay? What's up there?" Jo shifts, trying to peer down through the narrow hatch, "I don't know," she calls, pulling herself up and out. "Not an attic."

Almost immediately a hand grips the edge of the next hatch over, another hand hoisting up a wooden cane, a stern, rough-hewn hawk at its head. Grimacing the Duke's pulling himself out of the hatch on the far side of that small room, and "The fuck," Jo's saying, "Leo, Christ, that's the wrong damn hatch – "

"The hell are you," grunts the Duke in his red and brown striped jacket, sitting himself on the edge of his hatch, rubbing his thigh. "It's the only one – " He stops, seeing her hatch beside his, the hatch beyond, at Jasmine's feet.

"Can I come up?" says Ysabel somewhere below.

The Duke's lifting his legs out of the hatch as Jo scrambles over to him, grabbing his shoulder. "Are you you?" She jerks him around to face her. "How do I know it's you?"

"What kind of question is that?" says the Duke.

"Where is she?" says the girl in Jasmine's lap.

A wadded-up blanket's pushed up through the middle hatch, followed by Ysabel in her red and brown striped jacket, her damp dark head turning to take in the hatches, Jasmine and the girl, the pile of robes, the Duke and Jo.

"Where *is* she?" says the girl, sitting up.

"*You* found both the Duke and the Princess?" says Jasmine.

"I," says Jo, leaning over to grab the blanket, "yes." Wrapping it about Ysabel's shoulders. "Yes I did." Watching the Duke all the while, leaning on his cane now in the corner. "Where are we? Back in the teahouse?"

"We'll *never* get back!" wails the girl in Jasmine's lap, and "Hush, Lauren," says Jasmine, stroking her hair.

"I think we're on a ship," says the Duke.

"Never?" says Ysabel.

"What?" says Jo.

"A ship," says the Duke, pointing to the swaying lanterns.

"We're somewhere between," says Jasmine. "It will be much harder to move on, without all three of us."

"Between, between what," says Jo.

"Here," says Jasmine, "and, well, there."

"You never," says Lauren, as Ysabel says "No," and the Duke says "Well, there are nuances – Jo, dammit, *wait* – "

Jo's leaning over the hatch at his feet. "What?" she says. "Three hatches, three of us." Swinging herself around, her feet a-dangle. "You came out of that one, right?" she says to Jasmine and Lauren, pointing to the hatch on the far side of the small room.

"Yes," says Jasmine, and Lauren, wide-eyed, nods.

"And we came up out of the middle one," says Jo, turning to the Duke, "and you came up out of this one. Alone. I think she's down here."

"Wait," says the Duke.

"For what?" says Jo. "I'm just gonna take a look. What'll happen if I go down there?"

"I don't know," says the Duke.

"Anybody?" She looks around at them all in that small room. "Ysabel? Can anybody tell me what'll happen if I go down there?"

"No," says Jasmine.

"We need her," says Lauren.

"Okay then," says Jo, and she pushes off the edge and drops through the hatch and is gone.

"Oh," says the Duke, "I wish she hadn't done that."

"Well, she did," says Ysabel, and then someone raps on the door. "Are ye ready?" says a rough voice, hushed, trying to be heard through that door but not much further. The Duke looks at Ysabel, Ysabel looks at the Duke, and Jasmine looks at them both. Lauren's looking at the door.

"Well?" says whoever it is. "It's almost time!"

TINNY MUSIC – A KNIFE IN THE BACK – ONE GOES ALONE
FILLED TO THE BRIM WITH GIRLISH GLEE – HOW IT SHOULD BE

TINNY MUSIC from the speaker of a shortwave radio lashed to the beam above them with an orange bungee cord, a carillon peal of notes plucked from a guitar, a man's voice rendered thin and reedy, Tu m'as manquer mon amour, ne ni cherie willila kan be tama yala en sera Ouagadougou, and Bottle John's saying "I can't explain it to somebody who wasn't there."

"But I am there, John," says Michael. "I have been all along. Can I show you something? It's in my pocket."

Bottle John's shoulders shift but he doesn't look up. They're sitting side by side on the bare plank floor by the porch railing, their backs to all that wind. Bottle John's hands are in his lap and the gun rests small and dull in his hands. Michael's pulling a small flat plastic baggie from a pocket in his loose sweatpants. He holds it out between them lying limply on his black-gloved palm, a corner of it weighted by a smidge of dust. "What is that," says Bottle John, putting a hand to his chest, his white shirt buttoned all the way up to his throat.

"Leo brings it to me, from time to time," says Michael. "I take a pinch of it every couple of days. Have for the last four years." Bottle John's hand sliding up to his shoulder there under his grey suit jacket. Michael closes his hand over the almost empty baggie. "I was going to tell him tonight that enough was, was enough. That I wanted to stop. That I was *tired.*" Leaning back Michael reaches through the railing between them and Bottle John lurches back, watching intently hand on his neck as Michael tips the baggie over pinched between thumb and forefinger shaking the dust loose and out and away. As it falls away from them the dust becomes sparks, the sparks become drops of light, the drops grow brighter and brighter, stars ripped loose from their moorings, tumbling about them. "Open your shirt for me, John," says Michael, letting the empty baggie flutter away.

Bottle John pushes away, to his feet, one hand wrapped around the barrel and the trigger guard of the gun. "It's too clear out here," he says, and then, "too cold."

"You don't need to hide anything from me," says Michael, still sitting by the railing. Behind him the stars settling now into lines and shapes that tremble and jump and freeze and tremble again. "Tell me how your brother died, and then open your shirt for me. You shot him, didn't you."

Bottle John's taken a step or two back toward the sofa, away from the railing. "He asked," he says. "The pain was too much for him."

"And then you went to the ice."

"I can't talk about that."

"Look, John. Look." Michael's standing, leaning on the railing, pointing out at the stars that have fixed themselves against the blackness in regular rows and lines that limn blocks and towers, sparks of light caught in the corners of a thousand thousand windows all about them. "It's almost time. I'm doing what I can – " Swooping arcs and nets of light define bridge after bridge marching along the river each grander and more glorious than the last. The radio above him squawks and the chiming guitar dissolves into static and someone, a rich contralto says estoy defendiendo la apuesta de una persona and then a banjo, someone, a couple of adenoidal voices sing a path the blind can use to return, for now the way's blocked by an inferno, everything's on fire and I don't think it rains – Michael reaches up to snap the radio off. "It's your angel, John. It pushes us further and further away as it tries to get in. I'll lose my grip soon. They'll never find their way back," and Bottle John still not looking back is shaking his head, "No," he's saying, "no," and Michael says, "but you can help us all."

"We are about the Lord's work," says Bottle John, looking at the gun in his hand.

"You can set it aside now. You came here looking for help."

"No," says Bottle John.

"You came here looking for a doctor. Doctor Cee. Charley. Charley Leir?"

"No, no," says Bottle John, looking back, "Charley, he's no doctor. That's just what we called him in the service. I thought, I thought maybe he could help."

"It doesn't want that, does it," says Michael, as Bottle John turns away again. "It gave you back your brother, but it's asking for something, and you, you're still saying no, John. Open your shirt."

"He's a good man, Charley," says Bottle John, stooping to set the gun down on the long low sofa. "He don't know what he's doing, working for Leir."

"And Leir's a bad man," says Michael.

"The worst," says Bottle John, undoing the first button of his shirt.

"What's he done, John?" says Michael. Bottle John ducks his head and undoes the next button, and the next. "Open your shirt," says Michael, stepping away from the railing, and Bottle John does. Whatever it is it's barely there at all, a glistening streak against his dark skin, a swath gone indistinct, out of focus. "It's almost over," says Michael, stepping closer to Bottle John.

"What are you," says Bottle John, swallowing, throat jumping, his jacket and his shirt sliding from a blurred and indistinct shoulder.

"I'm going to take it from you," says Michael, hooking his fingers, pressing them against the stuff. Grunting. "It came from the ice, didn't it." His face set with the effort. "I'll give it to the fire, and your angel – will be *satisfied* – " Michael tugs and Bottle John looks up and howls. In and among the glittering towers lights swoop and slide, and something very like a zeppelin looms, nosing its way toward the ziggurat at the top of one of the smaller towers.

"What is that," says Bottle John, eyes lidded, runnels of sweat pasting his shirt to his skin.

"Very old," says Michael, looking at the cloudy nothing in his hands. "Let's go. It's time."

"Cute gun," says someone else.

Behind the sofa in the low wide doorway to the porch stands Mr. Charlock, barefoot, wrapped in a white trench coat, one hand lifted, thumb cocked, two fingers curled back, two fingers pointed at Bottle John and Michael. He's looking down at the snub-nosed revolved in his other hand. "What's it loaded with? Silver hollow-points?" Sniffing the cylinder. "Ampoules of holy water? Did you dip it in mistletoe oil? Smudge it with sage? Christ, John, you going Catholic on us?" He points the gun at them alongside his fingers. "Shoulda played more D and D growing up. All it takes is a knife in the back to seriously cramp any wizard's style."

"Don't," says Michael, wobbling, staring intently at his trembling hands full of glistening nothing.

"Sorry, man," says Mr. Charlock. "Sorry about your brother." He uncocks his thumb and lowers his empty hand. "Sorry about what went down with Echo. Wish I coulda been there. Woulda told you fucks to run like hell." The gun's still pointed at Bottle John, who shivering closes his eyes and nods.

"Stop," says Michael, "I've already pulled it – "

Three gunshots, loud flat cracks that punch neat little holes in Bottle John's grey jacket, his white shirt, his wet dark chest. "What?" says Mr. Charlock, lowering the smoking gun as Bottle John sits heavily, slumps, falls over on his side. "Already pulled what?"

Michael's looking at the last thready wisps of nothing wafting from his empty hands. "You goddamn fool," he says.

Wet shoes squelching Jo steps carefully through darkness bare sword in one hand scabbard in the other. Up ahead a pool of light, a low-hanging lamp over an overstuffed armchair, a low table, a hand reaching out to set down a steaming mug. The sound of a jangling piano, a man's voice pattering through it's wining and dining me, with memory and love the only clothes I let confine me, and break the rules of anyone who thinks they're really signing me, it's time again, time again, time again, time again –

"Jessie?" says Jo.

Kicking the tombstones from the middles of my eyes, out to the corners where and the song's cut off with a heavy click. A blond head peers around the side of the armchair, dark eyes framed by narrow square-lensed glasses. "Jo?" says Jessie. "Your hair. You grew it out?"

28

"Yeah, well," says Jo, hurrying up to the pool of light, pausing careful of the sword to fit the tip of it to the throat of the scabbard. Driving it home. The chair's surrounded, the edges of that pool of light walled in by stacks and piles of books, cheap mass-market paperbacks with curled white-wrinkled spines stacked atop bulwarks of trade paperbacks and here and there foundations laid from thicker, broader hardbound books. There are books splayed open on either thick round arm of the chair, and books piled on the knitted afghan laid over Jessie's tailor-fashioned lap. A book's closed about her left index finger holding its place and a book's held open in her right hand. Her T-shirt says Book Lovers Never Go To Bed Alone. "Let's go," says Jo.

"Where," says Jessie.

"Back," says Jo, holding out a hand. "C'mon."

"You go," says Jessie, looking back down at her book. "I think I'll stay."

"You," says Jo, "you can't, it doesn't, it doesn't work like that."

"Why not," says Jessie, turning a page.

"We all," says Jo, "we went in after them, and we all have to – "

"Three from the circle," says Jessie, not looking up, "three from the track. Anyone missing? Leo? Ysabel? Whatshername from Seattle, or Lake's little girlfriend?"

"What?" says Jo, and then "No, we're all, we're stuck, getting back. The Duke thinks we're on a ship or something."

"The Duke," says Jessie.

"We all need to go back together, or we won't – "

"Five shall return," says Jessie, "and one go alone. You ever read Susan Cooper?"

"I," says Jo, "no. Come on, Jessie."

"You ever read any fantasy? Ever?" Jessie turns another page.

"What?" snaps Jo. "I read, whatsit. Earthsea? And some of those dragon books. I read Dune."

"That's not," says Jessie, "that's science fiction, not fantasy – "

"It's got dukes and barons and witches – "

"It's got spaceships, Jo."

"That fly with magic spice-powers, what is this? We've got to go, Jessie."

"There's always a sacrifice." Jessie sets the one book on the arm of the chair, splays the other open on the table by the steaming mug. "In this sort of thing. Has to be."

"One goes alone," says Jo.

"Might as well be me."

"Jessie," says Jo. "Fuck the books for a minute. The others, the ones who actually live with this shit, they won't say it but they're scared out of their minds." The scabbard of her sword gripped tightly in both hands. "You have got to come back with me, Jessie. We all have to go back together."

"Did they *tell* you that?" says Jessie, her voice rising sharply. "Did they tell you that, exactly that?"

"Jessie – "

"Did they say to you, Jo, you must bring her back, she's our only hope?" Jessie picks up the splayed book from the table. "Because I gotta tell you Jo, these people?" Turning a page and then another with quick sharp jerks. "Who live with this shit? Hang out with them long enough and you figure out they know a hell of a lot less about it all than they let on."

Jo turns away abruptly. Shadows and hints of reflections hung before the chair suggest an enormous window stretching away off and up into the darkness. Jessie slaps her book closed, tosses it to the floor. Plucks up another from her lap. The White Tyger, says the bent spine. "Shouldn't you be getting back?" she says, flipping through to find the first page.

"This is pretty nice," says Jo. "You've got books, you got tea, you got a view." Somewhere out on the other side of the glass lights like stars begin to pick out the edges of blocks, of towers, and sparks glint in the corners of a thousand thousand windows. "You know where I was?" Jo turns back to Jessie, who isn't looking down at the book in her lap. "Some anonymous ranch house somewhere in deep Southeast. I don't know. I never got outside of it. I was, married, to the Duke."

"You love him," says Jessie, flatly, and Jo lets out a bark of laughter. "No," she says. "Christ no. I *like* him, but, I never left the house, Jessie. I spent all day just, waiting around, for him to come home from wherever it was he was, you know? I was putting my hair in curlers, for fuck's sake. I was, painting my toenails." Outside the light is shifting, growing, firming up into a softly greyish whitely glow of mist that laps about the buildings below, wisps of it flaring with orange and gold and smoldering into red. "I was bored out of my mind. *You* were supposed to find the Duke, Jessie. I went in for Ysabel."

"So you love her," says Jessie.

"I don't love anybody," says Jo. She looks down at the sword in her hands. Far off beyond the wakening city a great sharp tooth of a mountain rears itself above the mists, its snows blushed rose and gold and palest blue and a hint here and there of faint green light. "I made a promise," says Jo. "I will keep that promise. I found her," looking up at Jessie now, "and I got her out of – " She looks down again. "She's not going back there."

Jessie's looking away, at the cup of tea still steaming, at the little cassette player on the table beside it. At the books ringed all about her. "You get to have them both," she mutters.

"I don't *have* anybody," says Jo. "Jessie, please." She holds out a hand. "We need you." The light filling the window doesn't touch the darkness behind the chair, but away off back there up in what might be the ceiling there's a small oblong of warmly glowing light, a trapdoor, a hatch.

A scrape of gravel, a black shoe shifting, pressed against denting the rubber of a tire. A black pants leg quivering with effort, a grunt. Mr. Keightlinger's arms crossed before his blank black sunglasses fists clenched tightly as feathers straining bulging eyes press down against him and the very light that soaks the air is trembling at the point where they don't touch. Mr. Keightlinger suddenly lurches back as the angel surges toward him. He's pressed against the car, the powerful black car whorled over hood and roof with meticulous lines of spidery hand-painted letters glaring with a chilly blue light. Mr. Keightlinger blows a long sigh from his bushy beard and shifts his arms holding one upright before his face and drawing the other back, "This," he grunts, "will hurt me,"

that arm drawn back the hand beside his face unfolding from a
fist, held flat, rock-steady, "far more," and grimacing he curls that
hand back into a fist, "ah, fuck it." He throws a punch into the
enormous dust-brown slit-pupiled eye before his face.

The eye collapses wings snap open scudding yanking the angel
back and up into the air away from Mr. Keightlinger buffeted by
the sudden winds. Howling shrieking the angel throws its wings
all wide and falling from the air on him as ducking he pulls himself over the hood of the car through thickening curtains of cold
blue light. Sparks erupt white and blue as he falls onto the other
side showering bouncing splashing about him as he scrambles for
the freshly painted gate. Behind him the groaning shriek of twisting metal and the pop and clatter of breaking glass and the ripping
whump of gasoline igniting.

"Well, hell," says Mr. Keightlinger, bulling his way through
the front door of the teahouse.

In its scabbard a sword's thrust up through the middle hatch
of three in a row in a small wood-paneled room. It wobbles and
topples over in Jo's hand and she lays it on the floor her elbow
shoulder brown-haired head following it up and out. "Can you,"
she says, squirming her other arm free, hanging a moment there
half in, half out, looking at the hatches to either side. There's no
one else in the room.

"Jo?" says Jessie's voice muffled from below, "Jo, could you,"
and Jo says "Yeah, yeah," pushing herself up and out of the hatch,
then crawling thump-dragging the sword to the far hatch as
Jessie's calling "Jo! Jo! Where are you – " Jo leans over, reaching
down, inside. "Oh," says Jessie, her hand in Jo's, coming up into
the small wood-paneled room. "Why'd you – "

"Don't ask," says Jo.

"Where is everyone?"

"Working on it," says Jo, crouching, headed back along the line
of hatches to the other side of the room. The stack of robes is gone.
Jessie's looking down the middle hatch. "They didn't go that

way," says Jo, and there's a thump of a drum outside somewhere, a thinly dervished skirl of fiddles and flutes and a low round horn of some sort struggling to keep up. Stepping over the hatch Jo listens at the door to the room as the music settles into a thumping melody and there's muffled laughter and applause, a whoop of delight. "Come on," says Jo, opening the door.

A low short narrow hallway paneled in white-painted wood, a door opposite, doors at either end. To the left the doors have high-set panes of clouded glass. Jo in her satiny black slip and her mismatched Chuck Taylors, one hand on the throat of her scabbarded sword, one hand reaching back, tugging Jessie in her wake, Jessie in her T-shirt and sweatpants, her flip-flops, her narrow square-lensed glasses. Falsetto voices roughly singing three little maids who, all unwary, come from a lady's seminary, freed from its genial tutelary –

Jo opens the doors.

On the deck below them lit by smoking torches empty wooden chairs in haphazard rows pushed this way and that under a towering mast, a tautly strung welter of rigging and shrouds. "Three little maids from school," sing Ysabel and Lauren and the Duke in stumbling off-beat high-pitched trills, "three little maids from school," wrapped in richly clashing robes, kimonos loosely belted, and the Duke bouncing steps up to the rail singing, "One little maid is a bride, Yum-Yum," and to either side Ysabel and Lauren bounce up beside him, singing to those empty chairs, "Two little maids in attendance come," and off to the side sits Jasmine on a stool under an oil lamp, sawing away at the fiddle tucked under her chin. "Three little maids is the total sum – " and Jasmine looks up to see Jo and Jessie and the fiddle squawks and she nearly falls from her stool and turning fluttering faltering Ysabel and Lauren and the Duke, "three little maids – "

"The hell?" says Jo.

"It is," says Jasmine, the fiddle in her lap, "the latest from Mr. Gilbert and Mr. Sullivan. We thought it might prove entertaining to have the boys done up to sing some selections – "

"Snap 'em out of it," says Jo to Jessie, hurrying down the short flight of steps to the deck, past the empty chairs to the high broad gunwale. "If we have offended – " cries the Duke after her, and Jessie moving to stand between them trying to catch his eye says "Leo, Leo – "

Dark water below and no gangway or dock or boat. Away beyond the great dark bulk of the shore a bluff looming the pulsing rustle of trees in a low wind and above and beyond and around all that buildings and towers sketched in light, windows gleaming, the arcs of bridges busy with teeming crowds of light passing back and forth, all of it under a lowering red-black sky. Jo her free hand up to shade her eyes points with the hilt of her sword, "There!" she cries. "Look!" Flickers of warm lamplight up there, back among the dark tree-shapes. A porch, a railing of peeled and polished branches. "The teahouse. That's the teahouse, right?"

"Leo," Jessie's saying, "Leo, please," and he's standing not quite looking at her as he says "We should resume, sir, we shouldn't like to disappoint the gentlemen from Oregon City," and Jessie grabs him her hands on either side of his face trying to look him in his eyes that keep sliding away. "Jo!" she cries. "Jo, he's not – "

"Slap him!" says Jo, crossing the deck between rows of empty chairs. "Kiss him! Do something!"

Jessie slaps the Duke, lightly, and then draws her hand back and slaps him again, a loud crack as Lauren shrieks and Ysabel starts forward. Jasmine drops her fiddle with a twang and a crunch. Blinking the Duke looks at Jessie, looks her in the eye, and with a sobbing laughing gasp she pulls him to her and kisses him. The Duke's hands spring up but he does not push her away. "Oh," he says as she draws back. "That's where I left you." Jessie turns with another half-gasping laugh and grabs Ysabel's hand. "Rain," says Ysabel as Jessie pulls her close, "it's okay, I'm here, it's me," as Jessie wraps her arms about her, as Jessie kisses her, and kisses her again.

Jasmine steps up to the railing, her greyly black wetsuit gleaming in the torchlight. "That was," she says to Jo coming up the steps, "unpleasant."

"That's the teahouse, right?" says Jo, pointing. "I think we're just anchored or whatever in the river."

"Yes," says Jasmine, "yes, I think it is." Lauren beside her twirling with the force of trying to whip her kimono from her arms. "He kept them lit. All right then." Jasmine heads for the steps.

"There's no way off this boat," calls Jo.

"Yes there is," says Jasmine, as Lauren hurries down the steps after her.

"You're gonna swim?" says Jo.

"I'll swim, I'll climb, I'll hack my way through the underbrush." Jasmine grips the gunwale, gives it a shake. It's solid. "If we stay, I think you'll shortly end up a gentleman from Oregon City. And we'll all be spellbound by your Duke's rendition of the sun, whose rays are all ablaze." She takes Lauren's hand.

"I'd rather we didn't," says Ysabel, her forehead against Jessie's. "If it's all the same to you."

The Duke's taking off his kimono. "It's chilly," he says, offering it to Jo, who's watching Jasmine help Lauren up onto the gunwale. "What?" says Jo. "I hadn't noticed." She doesn't take the kimono. She's still holding the sword. He drapes it over her shoulders. "Hey," he says, leaning over her, and she turns to look up at him, and he kisses her. "Thanks," he says.

"Sure," she says.

And then as Ysabel and Jessie hand-in-hand head down the steps, and the Duke before her follows them, she says, "Wait."

"Jo?" says the Duke.

Clutching the kimono about her shoulders with one hand looking down, away at the sword, then back up at the Duke, she says, "I, should go with Ysabel. You should go with Jessie."

Jessie and Ysabel stop there on the steps, looking back at her, the Duke's frowning. "Let's go," calls Jasmine from the gunwale.

"I mean," says Jo, "it's how we went in. After you. With the, the hatches and everything." Looking down at her sword, then back up again. "We should go back the same way."

"No," says the Duke, "she's right, she's right, that actually," as he's turning back to head toward the steps, but Jo grabs his red and black sleeve the kimono slipping from her shoulders pulling him to her for a kiss, and after a startled moment he settles into it his arms wrapping about her. "I'm sorry," she says to him, as he kisses her cheek, her jaw, her throat. "I made her a promise."

"But," he says in her ear, "it's me you're kissin' on."

"Something like that," she murmurs, and she kisses him again, and he stoops to pick up the kimono and then he drapes it about her shoulders again.

Jasmine and Lauren sitting on the broad gunwale, Jo handing up her sword to Lauren, hoisting herself up beside them. The Duke in his red and brown striped jacket hands up his cane to her, and Jo takes his hand as Jessie's pushing up from below. Grunting, gasping, he folds himself over the gunwale and rolls over, sitting up, rubbing his thigh. Jessie pulls herself up beside him, and Jo's reaching down for Ysabel's hand. "Shoes," says Jasmine. "And jackets." Lauren's standing carelessly balanced on the gunwale beside her as she undoes the girl's skirt. Her stockings and shoes already kicked to the deck. Jessie lets her flip-flops fall from her feet, then leans over trying to open the Duke's jacket. "Nuh-uh," he says, and she reaches for his cane and he holds it away. "If I'm drowning," he says, "I'm gonna do it with my sixty-dollar Nunn Bushes on."

"Leo," says Jessie.

"We're not going into the drink," says the Duke.

"Oh?" says Jasmine.

"Seven to three," says the Duke. "Any stakes you care to hazard." He points to the lights up there in the trees. "We're walking on air the whole way."

"Suit yourself," says Jasmine, unbuttoning Lauren's jacket.

"What," says Jo to Ysabel, who's watching, eyebrow cocked, as Jo ties the laces of her mismatched Chuck Taylors together. "I left these in the bathroom of that damn Starbucks," says Jo. "I'm not losing them again."

"Ready?" says Jasmine, hoisting herself to her feet, taking Lauren's hand in her own. Lauren shivering in a thin pink camisole and underwear dotted with cartoon hearts.

"I'm not standing," says the Duke, tucking his cane under his arm. "We can just, you know. Push off," he says to Jessie.

"Well?" says Jo to Ysabel, who's still wearing the kimono over the red and brown striped jacket.

"I agree with the Hawk," says Ysabel.

"We're gonna walk on air, huh?" says Jo.

Ysabel shrugs. "Besides. It's a nice robe."

"Let's hope we do," Jasmine's saying. "We still have to deal with the thug, and the angel, when we get back."

"The what?" says the Duke, but they're jumping, they're jumping, they're jumping –

"WHERE ARE THEY?" – WHITE FEATHERS IN HER HAIR

"WHERE ARE THEY?" screams Mr. Charlock in that white trench coat, brandishing the gun up over his head.

"Shoot me or put it away," says Michael, squatting by Bottle John laid out on the bare plank floor. "I'm out of patience for threats."

"He's dead," says Mr. Charlock, lowering the gun.

"Dead as his brother."

"He was dead when I got there," says Mr. Charlock. "Hell, he was dead before they even showed up."

"I was starting to piece it together. You're not Leir, are you."

"What? No," says Mr. Charlock.

"So you're Doctor Charley. Only you're no doctor." Sitting back on his heels Michael's looking up at Mr. Charlock. "The aloosh? Duende? Echo Force. But you didn't go to the ice – "

"Hey," says Mr. Charlock, his empty hand up, two fingers pointed at Michael. "That's a terrible fucking idea."

"Shoot," says Michael, pushing himself to his feet, "or put it away."

After a moment Mr. Charlock shakes out his hand. "Okay," he says. Tossing the gun onto the long low sofa. "Wrong foot. We got ourselves a situation that's rapidly approaching the point of oh my fucking God, so it behooves us maybe to put our cards on the table, see what game it is we're playing. He told you what he was after."

"Leir," says Michael.

Mr. Charlock whistles. "No shit. And the thing you pulled off him?"

Michael shakes his head, his face impassive. "Something qlipothic. Scale of Thamiel, maybe. I was going to feed it to the angel."

"That thing out there?" Mr. Charlock points back over his shoulder. "Don't worry about it." Footsteps are clomping somewhere up away behind him. "My partner's got that," turning to look back up that way as there's a rattle of clattering strings of light, "covered – " The black-suited form of Mr. Keightlinger bursts into the low wide doorway to the porch, his hair undone in a frizzy halo about his head, sunglasses clutched in one hand. He coughs into the crook of his elbow. "Tell me," says Mr. Charlock, "tell me that damn thing's upped and gone."

"The," says Mr. Keightlinger, coughing again, "car – "

"Christ you let it eat the *car?*" shrieks Mr. Charlock, and Mr. Keightlinger shrugs.

"That isn't enough, is it," says Michael, looking down at his hands in their black knit gloves.

"Fuck no," says Mr. Charlock, running a hand over and over his bare bald head. "Not if that thing's gunning for a wizard. You couldn't hold it off just a little bit longer, could you?" he says to Mr. Keightlinger. "Fucking apocalypse breathing down our necks, *again,* just you and me to hold it all together, *again,* only I'm fresh out of baling wire this time you sonofawhat are you looking at?"

Mr. Keightlinger's arm's coming up, pointing away past Mr. Charlock out past the sofa the railing out into the hissing darkness where bright light picks out figures, six of them hanging motionless, arms outstretched, a sword, a walking stick with a stern hawk at its head, a red and brown jacket, kimonos fixed mid-flutter. "That's," says Mr. Charlock, stepping heavily past the long low sofa, "you," past Michael, and Bottle John's body, "that's what you, that's," across the porch, up to the railing, "you, you let the Bride, of the King Come Back, you let her *jump* out into the goddamn *void."* He throws his hands in the air. "Well hell," turning, rounding on Mr. Keightlinger, "we might as well march out the front door right the hell now, because that thing up there's got a fuckton of mercy compared to what Leir will have in – " He stops dead looking up past Mr. Keightlinger at the bare wood wall by the low wide doorway.

"What?" says Mr. Keightlinger.

"Wasn't that wall like, covered in old photographs and shit?"

One end of the sofa collapses in a cloud of dust. A twang of metal a whipping of loose cord a black and silver radio falls to the floor cracking open an empty plastic husk as rattling clattering echoing all around white strings of light stretched taut jump loose fall to the floor go dark with pops and fusillades of sparks. Mr. Charlock scuttles over to Bottle John's body, pokes it with a bare foot. The tin roof above them shivers. Mr. Keightlinger flips open his sunglasses and jams them on, looking about, then with long lumbering steps down the length of the sofa he hurls himself on Mr. Charlock knocking them both to the floor as one of the porch poles lurches listing bursting in a shower of splinters bouncing and a squeal of tearing metal. There is a sound –

Riding the crest of that rippling crash Jasmine hurtles into the room trying to get her feet under herself as she careens into the sofa turning managing just to catch Lauren before the girl flies headlong over the back of it. Jo and Ysabel hit the sofa side by side Jo's arms upflung the sword still in her hands. Jessie's feet clip the railing the Duke reaching for her twisting brushing the floor rolling arms flopping stick flying loose slamming into the base of the sofa as Jessie pinwheels end over into the settling clouds of tufts of down. A clatter of falling boards. Wrenching squawks of twisted metal. Pops and fizzles here and there as lightbulbs explode in the spitting fitful rain.

In the darkness groaning Mr. Keightlinger shifts and lifts himself brushing splinters clattering to the floor. Reaching down he helps Mr. Charlock to his feet as the Duke sits up abruptly and says "Oh, hey." Wiping down and rain from his face. Mr. Keightlinger's carefully heading for the doorway but Mr. Charlock grabs his arm. "His shoulders," says Mr. Charlock. "Get his damn shoulders!" Pointing to Bottle John. Jessie's moaning as Ysabel pushes her up and over and Jo's struggling in the drifts of down to pull herself free the sword still in her hands. "Okay," the Duke's saying. "The angel. Lemme at 'im."

"It wasn't no goddamn angel!" snaps Mr. Charlock as he backs up out of the room, Bottle John's feet clamped under his arms.

"Michael?" says Lauren. "Are we there? Michael?"

"Sinjin?" says Jasmine.

"Who the hell are you?" says Jo, twisted around on the sofa, spitting white feathers from her mouth. In the low wide doorway Mr. Keightlinger and Mr. Charlock pause, Bottle John in his grey suit slung between them. "Nobody," says Mr. Charlock. "It's gone, okay?" He spares a glance for the ruined porch, the rain coming down, the trees outside black against the red-black sky. "It weren't, you wouldn't be here."

"Where," says Jasmine, standing, looking about the room, "is Michael St. John Lake?"

Mr. Charlock hunched over in that white coat looks at Mr. Keightlinger, who shrugs. Mr. Charlock opens his mouth to say something but shakes his head instead. "Lady," he says, "I do not have the time."

And Lauren begins to wail.

The car's a reddish brown, a black stripe down the side, pulling up to the sidewalk before the apartment building. Behind the glass a harsh-lit lobby, imposing blocks of mail lockers. The driver's door opens and Jessie gets out, her chauffeur's cap on her long blond hair, her T-shirt, her sweatpants. Her feet bare. Before she can reach in to lever the seat back up Jo's worming her way out, wrapped in a purple and black kimono, her sword in one hand. Jessie stands back and lets Jo past, then reaches a hand in for Ysabel climbing out, a pink and green and yellow kimono wrapped about a red and brown striped jacket, white feathers still caught in her long black hair, limply damp. She smiles at Jessie and lightly kisses her knuckles and then her mouth.

"Hey," says Jo, leaning against the passenger door. The Duke cranks down his window. "You're sure I can't talk you into it," he says.

"Nah," she says, looking up at the windows towering above her. Closing her eyes against the misting rain. "We need, I need someplace – stable. Safe. After all that."

"Call me," says the Duke.

Jo turns, leans into the open window. "I gotta get a new phone," she says. "I left my old one in the pocket of some pants I've never seen before."

"Look in the coat Ysabel's wearing," says the Duke. "I saw it on the couch, in that house? While you were getting a blanket."

Jo's looking at her sword, her mismatched shoes. "This is getting fucking spooky," she mutters.

"Call me," says the Duke.

"Sure," says Jo, "if the phone bill out of limbo doesn't break me." He's leaning up a little and she leans down and then she kisses him, and then kisses him again.

"I thanked you," he says, a smile on his face. "I owe you a favor. That's a dangerous place for you to be." Jo starts up, looking at him. He's still smiling. "I like your hair like this," he says.

"What?" says Jo, but he's cranking up the window, Jessie's climbing into the car, the engine's growling. Ysabel's by her side. "Let's get in out of the rain," she says.

Jo presses the button for the elevator. "So. He's, well. He's dead, huh."

"I think," says Ysabel, "it'll turn out he was dead for a while. And the teahouse never was built. Or never was as – beautiful, as it was. And it blew down in a storm. And we'll all forget."

"Forget?" says Jo.

"Do you remember your dreams?" says Ysabel, taking Jo's hand in hers.

"Sometimes? Ysabel – "

"Like that, then," says Ysabel, pulling Jo close to her.

"Ysabel, I – "

"Just hold me, Jo," says Ysabel. "Please. Just hold me."

The sword still in one hand Jo puts her arms about Ysabel and Ysabel pulls them together, tightly, those richly clashing kimonos folding one over the other, Ysabel's face buried in Jo's shoulder, Jo leaning her head against Ysabel's, eyes closed, and then, after a bit, the elevator behind them softly dings.

And there's no waiting worth the misery
And there's no wanting worth the tears
And there's no searching for a mystery
And there's no innocence at the heart of me

—*Martin Swan*

NO. 13
CHANGEL

I T'S A BEAUTIFUL GUITAR, AND EXTRAVAGANT, a second soundbox like a swan's neck swooping above the fretboard for another ten strings or so, and the red-headed man's right hand leaps up to strike shimmering sheets from them to punctuate the rollicking tumult hammered and plucked from his left and right hands, notes sharp and clear as peals rung from bells tumbling out of the small black speakers on the stands to either side. Green fluorescent ink on a glassy black board at his feet says Live Music Every Night the Guitarp Stylings of John Wharfinger. Beside it a balloon snifter with a handful of change and some limp dollar bills. A woman all in black, a black apron about her waist, a loaded tray up above her head, a plate of pasta, a couple of burgers, the fish, squeezes between him and a table full of raucous laughter, one of them reading something from the phone in the palm his hand. The red-headed man chases the melody up the fretboard ringing and chiming until it suddenly, irrevocably ends, and his hands leap away, his head down, a long flop of hair hanging over the guitar. The table before him's still laughing. A desultory flutter of clapping here, there, over in the back. His hands settle on the guitar again, his left hand curled about the neck, his right hand hovering over the soundbox, fingers wiggling. They strike a chord and another, letting it ring, then a third, and someone by the bar drops a tray of glasses with a shattering crash. The room erupts in applause and whoops and laughter.

Later, as he's wrapping the guitar in a soft brown leather case, a woman scrapes a chair up by his side. She sits in it heavily, her bulk wrapped in an enormous black coat, a little grey snap-brim fedora at a jaunty angle on her head. "New gig?" she says.

"You have me," he says, working one end of the case carefully around the shoulder of the harp, "at a disadvantage."

"Really?" she says. "I thought everybody knew me." He starts zipping the case closed around the guitar's elaborate shape. "Anne Thorpe," she says, "I write for Anodyne? Among others?" and the zipper stops for a moment. "You know *of* me, anyway," she says.

"I don't have anything to say," he says, tugging the zipper closed, securing a couple of velcro straps.

"Not even hello? How's it going? Sure I'll let you buy me a drink?"

He sets the case to one side of the stool, frowning.

"That means I'd buy you a drink," she says. "Because you'd be the one? Saying sure, I'll let you – anyway. Not a gift, mind. Strictly tit for tat."

"But I have nothing to offer in return," he says with a shrug.

"It's not a story," she says, "if that's what you're worried about. I'm nowhere near a story yet. I just have to know, you know?"

He shrugs again.

"You guys," she says. She rolls her eyes. "You bow with a blast at the Acme like a month ago and suddenly it's all anybody can talk about, this album y'all are gonna do that nobody's heard anything from. You start racking up high-profile gigs at a rate I've never seen before in this town, all on good will and word of mouth, until bam!" She slaps one black-draped knee, and the hat slips from her head with the force of it. "Three shows, the last ten days or so. Nocturnal, the Woods, La Luna." She settles the hat back on her head, her dark hair short and swept back, shot through with grey and white. "Y'all no-show all three, nobody's calls get returned, nobody's emails, and here you turn up playing a brewpub on Powell. And Deke," she jerks a thumb at the bar behind her, careful of her hat, "has no idea he's got the fiddler from Stone and Salt serenading his dinner rush."

"Multi-instrumentalist," he says, looking at the case at his feet.

"What?"

"I don't just fiddle."

She sits back in her chair, looks over at a busser clearing one of the last tables. Looks back at him. "What the hell happened, man? You've got something to say, all right, and it's worth at least a couple shots of Macallan, you know?"

"Redbreast," says John Wharfinger with a wry smile.

"What?"

"It's Redbreast you'd be buying," he says, "but I'll tell you for free. Sometimes, these things? They just don't work out." He stands, tugging his long green coat into place. "Don't," she's saying, "don't, don't do me like this. Don't send me back out into the rain with nothing but a measly scrap like that."

"What do you want from me?" says John Wharfinger, scooping the money up out of the glass. "It's November."

"You cut your hair!" — Who were Those Guys?
the Rain beneath her — what It (he) did

"You cut your hair!" cries the Duke as he opens his white door.

"Well, yeah," says Jo, standing there hand-in-hand with Ysabel, Jo in a black leather reefer jacket, Ysabel in a short white parka lined with thick white fur. Jo's hair cropped very short and dyed a deep wine red.

"Your coats?" says the Duke. From down the dark hall behind him a burst of music, someone singing wake at night always the same, I call your name but you sleep right through and love is the light in your face!

"Why don't you go find Jessie?" says Jo to Ysabel. Letting go of her hand.

"As you wish," says Ysabel, slipping out of her parka.

"Huh," says the Duke, watching her head down the hall, her grey cardigan dress quite short and tight, her matching thigh-high socks.

"Yeah," says Jo, taking off her jacket. "She's loaded for bear."

"It's a look," says the Duke, turning back. "Whoa." Jo's in a bright red strapless dress also quite short over black leggings. "You're, ah," says the Duke. "You're wearing lipstick."

"I figured ducal function meant formal," says Jo. "Ysabel picked out the dress."

"Well, there's formal," says the Duke, "and there's, well." His blousy pyjama pants paisleyed in purples and browns and greens and a very pointed pair of Persian slippers and a silk shirt in some nameless harvest color. "C'mon. Let me get you a drink." Jo heads down the hall and he follows, their coats draped over an arm. "Did I, did I mention I like your shoulders?" he says. "Because I like your shoulders." Jo's smiling.

The big room lit by rows of dim red-shaded ceiling lamps and the flicker of torchlight from outside through the high narrow windows, and all the vicious games we play, sings a woman's voice from speakers here and there, they mean nothing to me, all I know is your touch and the way love should be. A makeshift bar, mismatched wineglasses and tumblers and bottles spread along a couple of folding tables and some crates, a boy in a brown leather jacket and an enormous set of headphones setting up a fresh album on the turntables, people here and there dancing, talking over the music, laughing, falling silent, turning to watch as Ysabel marches across the floor toward the corner by the windows where three men are laughing at something that Jessie has said, her yellow hair swept back in a mane. As her smile falls away and she looks beyond them with shining eyes they turn, the three of them, they bow deeply, they step back, and Ysabel sweeps up to take Jessie's hands in her own, smiling at her gown, a fall of sequins in golds and browns draped from either shoulder, tied at her hips with brown ribbons. "For me?" says Ysabel.

"You see anyone else?" says Jessie.

"Can I have," Jo's saying, "another one of," twirling the tumbler in her hand, "ah, whatever, this, was?" The bartender eyes the red streaks clinging to the melting ice. "You're drinking with his grace," he says. "A Negroni." His face is fleshy, his brick-red hair flops from a high widow's peak. He scoops ice into a tall straight glass and pours gin and dark vermouth. "You're the gallowglas," he says. The music a swirl of strings over rattling percussion. "Yeah," says Jo.

"It was nothing personal," he says, pouring thick red Campari.

"What?"

"Nothing personal!" Shaking a couple of drops of bitters. He stirs the drink with a long gold pick. "I just wanted you to know."

"What wasn't personal?" says Jo.

"When we went after you!" he says, straining the drink into a glass of fresh ice. "I didn't think you'd care."

"Holy shit!" says Jo. "You're that, that guy! You're one of those guys!"

"The Stirrup," he says, twisting a sliver of orange peel over her drink, letting it drop.

"Stirrup?"

"Gaveston!" He hands her the glass.

"Well," she says, hoisting it, "nice to meet you, Gaveston!"

At the edge of the dance floor leaning against each other laughing Ysabel tugging up one of her long long socks and Jessie wiping sweat-damp hair from her face and "Oh," says Ysabel, straightening, "now where did you get that." Held up close between them in Jessie's hand a glass vial no bigger than a little finger, inside a slender thread of golden dust.

"Leo said you'd like it," says Jasmine.

"How generous of him," murmurs Ysabel under the thumping beat. Someday baby, an old deep voice is singing, you ain't gonna trouble me, anymore. Ysabel brushes the vial, and Jessie's fingers. "Ever played with it before?"

"It's," says Jessie, "it does different things, every time."

"I think," says Ysabel, "Rain," plucking the vial from her hand, "we both know what it will do to us tonight," and Jessie smiles, and Ysabel laughs. "Go get some vodka for us. Neat."

Jessie leans in and kisses Ysabel. "I should," she says, and, "my," and then, "it's Jessie. My name's Jessie. Not Rain."

The vial in one hand one hand on Jessie's hip Ysabel closes her eyes and kisses Jessie. "All right," she says. "Jessie. Go get the vodka."

"I know I've seen the one guy before," Jo's saying. She's sitting on the broad flat arm of the Duke's chair. Had a good time, got beat pretty good, runs the rap over the chugging guitar.

"What, the one stole Ysabel's coat?" says the Duke, picking up his drink from the low brass table before them. Had a good thing going got more than you gave, goddammit now, give it to you, girl you got game.

"No, the other one. I'm pretty sure."

"That was weird, the thing with the coat."

"You didn't poke around?" Jo drains her glass and leans over to set it on the table. "Ask anybody who they are or what they're doing?"

"Did you?"

"You're the one with people," says Jo. The Duke chuckles. She reaches down to grab his hand before he can lift his glass for another sip, and reddened ice clinks. "They could have seriously fucked things up," she says. "They could have gotten us killed."

"They did fuck things up," says the Duke. He gently works his glass free. "They did get people killed."

"Well," says Jo, "yeah. So." Whoops and a smattering of applause away off over the dance floor.

"They're contract players," says the Duke, and he tosses back the rest of his drink. "The two of them, anyway. Work for a guy who operates in a, a consulting capacity, for various downtown developers. Pinabel," and he looks up at Jo leaning over him, takes her hand in his, "the Axehandle, I mean, not the Hound himself, has been trying to get this guy to go exclusive." He kisses her hand, then shifts, sitting back against the other arm of the chair. "Sum total of what is known to me. Other guy, their friend? The first one? Utter mystery."

"He wanted Leir. Thought we were hiding him or something."

"Leir?" says the Duke, frowning. "That's the consultant."

"Said he was a sorcerer."

"Tomato, tomahto," says the Duke. "As ever, I know even less than I thought." Wincing he pushes himself to his feet, rubbing his thigh. "Let me freshen these up and when I get back let us speak of other things." He limps away toward the bar. The music a pounding strut now stabbed by synthesized horns. "Two more," he calls to the Stirrup, and he turns leaning against the bar looking back over the dance floor, at all the people here and there milling and talking and laughing and dancing, all the way back to the chair by the low brass table, and Jo draped over the back of it, smiling back at him.

Turning back to the bar where the Stirrup's stirring the cocktails he reaches into a pocket of his pyjama pants and pulls out a small tin box dotted with chipped enameled flowers in pink and gold. Sozodont Powder, it says, For Cleansing The Teeth. He thumbs it open. Inside a spill of golden dust glitters barely in the dim red light.

"What," says Jessie, laughing, "are you doing?" as Ysabel leads her to a chair over by the windows. "Sit," says Ysabel, kissing her. "Sit." Pushing her into the chair. "Ysabel!" cries Jessie, hands leaping to resettle her gown in her lap, over her breasts. Ysabel tocking her hips to the strutting beat, dans les mouvements d'épaules, sings a forceful laughing voice, a plat comme un hiéroglyphe Inca de l'opéra! She leans over bending at the waist and runs her hands up Jessie's thighs and down again, then straightens and spins and kicks up a foot, planting it on the chair between Jessie's bare knees. "Take it off," she says, and Jessie takes Ysabel's foot in her hands and works the knot in the laces loose and peels the low grey boot open and off. Ysabel spins again and kicks up her other foot and Jessie takes that boot off, and Ysabel hands braced on the back of the chair over Jessie's head hikes herself up, over Jessie, against Jessie, letting her body slip down and down along Jessie's body until she's kneeling on the ground before her, tight cardigan rucked up about her hips, and a man in a tuxedo whistles and claps. Pushing up turning around Ysabel tugs her cardigan back down, smiling at a man in a peach-colored Nudie suit dappled with rhinestones. She sits herself sideways in Jessie's lap, lifting a leg and then peeling the long grey sock down and down her thigh, over her knee, bunching it bending her leg down her calf, working the thick sock awkward a moment over her ankle, face impassive, mouth a moue of vague amusement, as Jessie watches and giggles and a big man, shirtless, frowns over the shoulder of a woman in a long diaphanous gown of uncertain color. "Well?" says Ysabel to Jessie, letting her empty sock dangle from her hand. "How'm I doing?"

"Not bad," says Jessie. "About a forty-dollar dance."

"Forty!" cries Ysabel, letting the sock drop. "For five minutes' work?"

"You have to split your take with the house," says Jessie, "but I might tip a little extra, you know? For a little somethin-somethin?"

"So what should my name be?" says Ysabel, lifting her still-socked leg, running her hands along it. "Princess? Or is that too cliché?"

"Lady," says a man stepping out of the little crowd around them, and Ysabel shakes her head. "Goodness, no!" she says. "Cliché *and* generic."

"Lady, please." His shoulders broad under a tight brown T-shirt, his hair a dark black cap. He offers up a hand, his fingers thick and stubby, a leather thong tied loosely about his wrist. "Luys," says Jessie, and "Oh, the Mason!" cries Ysabel. "I *knew* you seemed familiar."

"The Duke has many rooms, Lady," he says. "Perhaps you might both wish to retire to one?"

"Oh?" says Ysabel, leaning back against Jessie, looking pointedly across the room to the Duke and Jo, swaying together much too slowly for the beat. "His grace doesn't seem to mind."

"Lady," says the Mason again. "Let 'em alone!" calls someone from the crowd, and "Go on!" and "Take it off!" The Mason turns to look at them all, saying, "Go on yourselves, go drink, go dance. Enjoy the party."

"I think," says Ysabel loudly to Jessie, "*he* thinks dallying with the Duke's doxy is beneath me. Are you beneath me, Rain?" Looking up at her. "Well I am in your lap. Would you rather I were beneath her?" she says to the Mason. "We are quite flexible."

"Perhaps, Mason," says the man in the peach-colored suit, "you should go get yourself a drink."

"Cater," says the Mason. "You object?"

The man in the peach-colored suit with a glitter of rhinestones sweeps an arm to encompass the little crowd. "Not a one of us would quarrel with a countercheck, Mason. Yes." He draws himself up fringe rustling his arms akimbo. "If you say, these women should remove themselves, then yes. I would object. Directly."

"Then I will oblige, and call for steel," says the Mason, and Cater smiles. "Blades!" cries the Mason, turning away, pushing through the crowd, the Cater unzipping his jacket as he follows. "I would toy with this knight!"

"Come on," says Ysabel to Jessie, grabbing her hand. "Let's go." Clambering out of her lap. Jessie shaking her head tries to pull her hand back, "What?" she's saying, and "No, wait – stop – " as Ysabel takes her face in both her hands and kisses her hard. Leaning her forehead against Jessie's she murmurs, "If your fingers aren't inside me within the minute I will explode."

"Oh," says Jessie.

"Shit," says the Duke, as the Mason marches into the middle of the dance floor followed by the Cater, his jacket slung over one bare shoulder. "Blades, your grace!" cries the Mason, and "Sweetloaf!" bellows the Duke. "See to the man!" The boy in the brown leather jacket at the turntables looks up, looks over, bends down, lifting a long bundle draped in dark red cloth. "Come on," says the Duke to Jo.

"What?" says Jo, swaying a little, half-finished drink in her hand. The Duke seizes her other hand and drags her in his wake, toward an anonymous door at the end of the room, until she plants her feet, pulling back. He comes in close to her and kisses her and says, "I'm getting you off the damn floor."

"Off," says Jo.

"Lest a fatal misstep lose me yet another knight," he says. She leans back shaking her head, "I wouldn't," she starts to say, and smiling he says, "I mean we're also gonna fuck our brains out. Might as well kill two birds while we're stoned, right?"

"Gloriosky," says the Duke, blowing the word out like a candle.

"Oh," says Jo. "Def, definitely."

And after a moment he rolls over away from her, dragging the dark brown sheet off her, and she doesn't try to pull it back, her arms at her sides knees up head lolled back on the mattress. He tugs at something, reaches out from under the sheet, a pinkly gravid condom dangling from his fingers. He lays it carefully on a saucer on the floor by the wide low bed in the middle of that dark room, lit only by the low white lamps to either side. "For you," he says, his voice rough, "I girded my loins."

"Worth it?" sys Jo, stroking the angular tattoo on her belly.

"Not done yet," he says, rolling back over winding the sheet about himself, kissing her and kissing her again, his hand at her chin, her throat, her breast, tangled momentarily with her hand on her belly, and down and again and down between her thighs and she sucks in a breath around their kiss and shakes her head loose, "No," she says. "It's okay, you don't," and "Yes," he's saying, and "I must," and she bites her lip and looks away, and he kisses her throat and then "Oh" she says and "There, right there – "

Naked he sits up to one side of the wide low bed against a mound of pillows, red and brown. Over across the bed wrapped in the sheet she's curled on her side her back to him. "If you think about it," he's saying, and "I *am* thinking about it," she says. "I *have* to think about it."

"If you think about it," he says. "It makes the most sense." He leans back, looks over at her wine red hair against those dark browns, and he brushes her bare shoulder with his fingertips. She takes his hand in hers and squeezes it. "Sense doesn't even figure," she says. "I barely know you. I only just, slept with you. Just now." She lets go of his hand. "You're asking me to move in with you."

"It's not so much asking as suggesting," says the Duke, "and it's not as if you'd be, I mean, you'd have your own suite. Your own apartment, practically. It's a flexible space. Best that way anyway, for the sake of appearances."

"Right," says Jo, hiking up on one elbow to pick up her glass from the floor by her tights and her puddled red dress. "Can't be living with your mistress when you're marrying a princess." She drains the last of her drink. The ice in it long since melted away.

"No," says the Duke, and then, "okay, yes, but the Queen will be displeased no matter what is done. Still. We should strive to give her as few legitimate legs to stand upon as possible. If it's an open agreement, with fair compensation, that's much better than if it seems I'm in your debt, or putting you in mine."

Jo rolls over on her back. "This is about how it's dangerous, if you owe somebody." Resting her glass on her belly.

"It's mostly about how you're soon to be evicted," says the Duke.

"You said you could fix that." The bottom of that glass streaked with sticky redness that glimmers weirdly in the sharp bright light of the lamp.

"I said I'd have a word," says the Duke.

"And?" Tilting the glass she peers at the stuff, pokes at it with a finger.

"I'm not so persuasive as I might have been, were you living this side of the river."

"Can't you just," says Jo, peering at her ruddied fingertip in the light.

"Just?" says the Duke. "Just what? Jo? Just what?"

There in the whorls of it small grains of dust quite golden in all that red. "You know," she says, "I know what this stuff does when you're hurt, and I know if a bunch of you hold it up and sing it lights up a whole damn block. What I *don't* know is what happens when you put it in somebody's drink." She rubs her fingertip against her thumb and folds her fingers together and closes her hand in a fist. "Well?"

"Jo," says the Duke, "just, hold on a – "

"No, Leo. Tell me." Looking him in the eye now. "What the fuck did it do?"

The elevator doors open and Jo bursts from it in her black leather reefer jacket, her legs bare beneath her quite short bright red dress. Ysabel stumbles after in her white parka and her grey cardigan dress only somewhat buttoned, her long socks bunched below her knees. "Wait," says Ysabel, "not so fast,"

tugging back against Jo's hand until Jo stops suddenly, grunting as Ysabel runs into her, catching her by the shoulders. Ysabel clings to Jo's lapels. "Just a, just a minute," she says.

"Come on," says Jo. "We're almost home."

"Not one step. No. Not until." Ysabel leans back, settles herself, smoothing Jo's jacket. "I was warm. I was comfortable. I was curled up, with some I wanted to be curled up with, for the first time in," and she frowns, biting her lip, "a while, and then you came in and dragged me out and not a word, and I am not taking one step more until you tell me. Why."

"You are blitzed," says Jo.

"That too," says Ysabel, with a wide wide smile.

"You need a bath."

"Oh stars above a long one, and hot as I can stand."

"So come on."

"No."

"What happened," says Jo, "to as you wish?"

"Why," says Ysabel, her smile smaller now, and tight. "What was it. The Duke? What did he – "

"He drugged me," says Jo, quiet and quick, looking down at that awful orange carpet.

"He," says Ysabel, blinking, "what?"

"He drugged me," says Jo, "and then he fucked me, and that is not something I'm gonna stick around, okay?" Stepping back away from Ysabel, pulling a ring of keys from her jacket.

"Jo," says Ysabel, "Jo, was it, did he," as Jo's unlocking the door, "look, we'll get in, out of these clothes, you can have the first bath, please, I insist, we can talk about it or," as Jo's opening the door, "we can sleep on it, whatever, in the morning I think – what? Jo? What is it?" Ysabel steps up behind Jo still standing in the doorway staring at the apartment beyond. "Jo?"

The floor of the little hallway kitchen littered with dead leaves and shards of broken crockery and glass. Curtains billow in the main room beyond where the glass-topped café table's over on its side in drifts of clothing, T-shirts, skirts, dresses, more dead leaves, shreds of stocking dangling from a spindly wrought-iron chair, all of it lit by a weird blue light. "What," says Ysabel, and Jo shushes her, reaching back for her hand. Something's rustling, something that isn't the curtains, something around the corner. Stepping carefully through the debris Jo leads Ysabel slowly through the little hallway kitchen. A knife and a couple of forks have been driven into the wall by the bathroom door at about knee height. Something dark's smeared on the wall over the head of the futon. More dark smears on the wall along the side of the futon, and postcards and post-it notes and pages from magazines ripped from the wall litter the rumpled blankets, and everything lit by the blue light shining from the flat-screen television tuned to the auxiliary channel. Something's under the blankets, something rolling over, rustling, something sitting up, short and stubby, a big head. "The fuck are you doing in my apartment," says Jo.

"Mommy?" it chirps, lifting stubby arms, "Mommy?" its voice rising, arms shaking, bouncing, a shriek, a wail, *"Mommy!"*

PUSHING A DEAD LAWNMOWER – A SOUND SLEEPER
CABBAGES & STORK

PUSHING A DEAD LAWNMOWER along the verge of a rolling field of dying grass an older man in a charcoal-stripe three-piece suit unbuttoned over a sunken bare chest, his head quite bald, the skin of him dark with old grime. The only sound the rustle of the grass and the squeak of the lawnmower's wheels. Up ahead in the darkness a cul de sac, a crumbling concrete pad under a broad flat gas station awning, a big roadside sign whose unbroken panel says Leathers Fuels. An old maroon sedan on four flat tires.

He stops pushing the lawnmower, steps around it, minces carefully toward that sedan arms out hands a-dangle, his last few steps a sudden waddling rush until he's squatting by the trunk. The maroon of the sedan is scaled with rust, orange and white and grey, mottled with moss and lichen, grey and green. The windows dark where they aren't streaked with green and blackish red. His back to it he scoots along careful with his bare feet toenails long and jagged sharp, clicking absently against the gravel. The handle

of the passenger door is clean and almost gleaming, but he's looking past it at the knob of the door lock just visible through the
smeared glass. He lifts a hand to brush aside his collar and touch
the polished silver torc that's clamped about his knobby neck.

He stares at that lock.

He stares at it wide eyes buckling under his heavy brow, his jaw
and throat, his shoulders trembling, his whole frame quivering
with some motionless effort, staring at it until with a click the
door lock pops up and he catches himself, doesn't fall, one hand on
concrete, one hand on the door. He pounds the concrete once and
lifts his hand closed about the handle of a push dagger, the wide
stubby blade of it sprouting from his curled fingers. He gently,
gently pulls the door open.

Inside both front seats laid back as far as they might go. A man
asleep in the passenger seat wrapped in a blue tarp and a felt furniture pad over a grimy blue windbreaker. A woman in the
driver's seat asleep on her side naked, her flesh a chilly bluish
white but for splashes of some dried mud in tannish, beigeish
streaks that flake over the cracked vinyl seat. Gleaming about
her neck a polished silver torc.

The man in the suit lifts his push dagger to his lips but frowns
before he kisses the tip of the blade. He looks down. Grunts in surprise. There's a hand wrapped around his ankle, a small pale
hand, knuckles rough and dark. The hand tightens, pulls, he topples forward foot yanked under and twisting scrabbling on the
concrete he's trying to pull himself free, whining then shrieking as
slavering gnawing sounds erupt and he's jerked and pulled inch by
scraping inch deeper under the belly of the sedan. "Christ," the
man in the passenger seat's saying, "fucking hell, oh, fuck," tangled
in the tarp and the thick felt pad. "Linesse," he's saying. "Linesse!"
The sedan shakes as the driver's door's wrenched open.

Planting his free foot against a tire the man in the suit's pushing
himself back out and with a gasp and a roar of frustration he pops
free rolling away from the sedan dragging the one foot behind him
a mangled wreck, shining wet and twisted, the leg of his pants in
shreds, holding his dagger up before him pointed at the thing
crawling out from under the sedan, a little man with small,

rough-knuckled hands, his wet smile full of very long teeth that snag the dim light about them. "I advise you," says the man in the suit voice ragged with pain and effort, "to restrain your advances," and the little man opens that mouth much too wide around those teeth and leaps.

With a sound like an axe in oak the woman's pale bare foot hits the little man's head knocking him out of the air pinwheeling across the concrete pad. "Stay put," she snarls at the man in the suit, in her hand a short sword pointed at him, short and broad, a battered round guard rattling loosely about the hilt. She's striding toward the little man who's up on his hands and knees now, shaking his head, dazed. "Cearb," she says, "I told you. Keep away."

"Assassins," pants Cearb, "come in the middle of the night," he coughs, "and who keeps safe the gallowglas?"

"Dear Linesse," says the man in the suit, his voice stretched taut, "you must be wrung out, emotionally, morally, from the effort of keeping that mortal *thing* in meat and drink. I find in general it is better to beg forgiveness than ask permission, but if I must, I shall – please, please permit me the signal honor of putting you out of its misery. For all our sakes."

"Chazz," she starts to say, looking back along her sword at the man in the suit, and then she shakes her head. "Frankie!" she calls. "Frankie, step out of the car."

"You sure?" says the man still tangled in the blue tarp in the passenger seat of the sedan.

"Frankie, set foot upon the field," she says, and then as he fights his way out of the sedan, "gentlemen, in a half-minute's time I intend to lay about with my blade. If either of you remains in reach, so be it."

Cearb's already scrambling off the concrete pad. Chazz begins to drag himself away toward his lawnmower. "What holy justice have I wronged?" cries Cearb. "Shut *up,*" says Linesse, watching them both go. Cearb calls out, his voice falling away in the night, "In our wretchedness, why should we still look up to the stars? Which one am I to invoke, when my reverence is so easily disabused?"

Chazz is pulling himself upright on the lawnmower his foot dangling, a useless wreck. "I'll be some little time," he says, "recovering from this indignity. Use it wisely — as I hope I might — consider carefully what you would gain, by granting my request." And he hops away, leaning on the lawnmower, wheels squeaking in the darkness.

"You can't stay," says Linesse to Frankie, half in and half out of the sedan, and she starts walking away, off the concrete pad, out into the cul de sac, her bare feet heedless of the gravel.

"I can't," says Frankie, "I don't *want* to stay, I never," turning, stuffing the tarp and the pad into a couple of shopping bags on the floorboard that say Thriftway and Trader Joe's. "Linesse, hey, wait up! Some clothes? Maybe? This time?" Half-running as he leaves the sedan, shopping bags in either hand bouncing against his legs. "Linesse! Who was that? What the fuck was that about?"

She stops and turns to look back, at him, the sedan, the abandoned gas station, the big broken sign. "Once," she says, "before? He was the Devil."

"Seriously," says Frankie, catching up with her. "Seriously?"

Threads of smoke drift up from the cigarette by Ysabel's knee, a half-inch of ash dangling from its tip. She's sitting in a cleared spot on the floor by the windows in an oversized sweatshirt that says Brigadoon! The wrack of torn and shredded clothing has been mostly pooled before the bulky blond armoire in the corner. The glass-topped café table now upright. In the stir of blankets on the futon Jo lies back in the ruins of her red dress eyes closed, mouth open in a gentle snore. Her cheeks criss-crossed with welts, a bruise darkening a temple. Curled against her side a young boy maybe two, maybe three, swaddled in a Spongebob Squarepants towel, his head a tangled thicket of mud-brown curls. One short arm's flopped over her chest. In his chubby fist a tatter from her dress.

Ysabel sighs and taps the ash into a butt-filled saucer at her feet. "She sleeps pretty soundly, you know," she says, and she takes one last drag, then stubs out the cigarette. "So we can talk." Standing, stretching. "Assuming you can do more than shriek." Jo still lightly snoring. The red tatter still clenched in the boy's fist. "You worked us over pretty well," says Ysabel, rubbing her face. The walls over the futon still stained were something dark and wet's been scrubbed away. "But she's asleep for now, and we both know I know you aren't what you are." Jo's breath hitches, she turns her head to one side then the other, settling back into her snore. The little fist on her chest doesn't move.

"Okay," says Ysabel.

Fluorescent lights flicker to life in the little hallway kitchen and careful of the cardboard box filled with swept-up debris Ysabel's opening drawers, cabinets, rattling dishes and utensils. "Coffee," she says to herself. Opens the refrigerator, closes it. Opens it again. Opens the freezer.

She lays an awkward armload of stuff on the glass-topped table, a bowl with an egg in it, a coffee cup half-filled with water, a box of matches, a couple of spoons, some tongs, a red can that says Hills Bros. Coffee with a drawing of a man in a turban and yellow robes. Kicking through the pile of clothes she comes up with a short red crumpled candle. Sitting in one of the spindly wrought-iron chairs, hands hovering indecisively over all these various things.

She lights the candle with a match.

She plucks the egg from the bowl and then timidly taps it against the table. Looks at it. Taps it again. Tries tapping the narrow end lightly against the table. "Shit," she says, bringing the egg up higher hand trembling then slamming it down and the egg's smashed, splattering yolk and albumen and bits of shell along the glass, her hand, her sweatshirt. "Shit," she says again.

She sits back down with some paper towels and two more eggs and mops up the slime and shell. She takes one of the eggs and holding it carefully between thumb and forefinger taps it gently against the edge of the table, and a again, a little harder. It cracks.

She holds it gingerly over the bowl, eyeing the clear slug oozing down its side, and pries it open, wincing as it cracks apart and the yolk plops out. She shakes out the last of it, then sets the smaller-butt end down and picks up the tongs. She clamps them carefully on the jagged rim of the longer narrow half of shell, then scoops up some water from the coffee cup and holds it over the candle flame. When the water starts to bubble, she pours it back into the coffee cup. She scoops up some more, holds it over the flame again. And again. And again.

"What are you doing," says a small and piping voice.

Ysabel smiles, watching the water in the eggshell as it starts to bubble. She pours it into the coffee cup, scoops up some more. "I'm making coffee for Mommy." She looks over at him sitting up on the futon, big eyes blinking, his little hands on Jo's hip. "Want to be a big boy and help?"

"Hey." Ysabel sitting on the futon by Jo stroking her scratched cheek with the back of her hand. "Hey, wake up." Smoothing the flaps of the torn red dress. "Wake up, Jo."

"Boobies," says the boy. He's standing naked on a spindly wrought-iron chair, using the tongs to hold an eggshell full of water over the candle flame.

"Coffee ready yet?" says Ysabel, pulling a blanket up over Jo's breasts.

"Toil! Trouble!" says the boy, pouring water into the cup, peering at it. "No damn bubble." Scooping more out to hold over the flame.

"Come on, Jo," says Ysabel, and she starts to lean down, then does, over Jo, closing her eyes, softly kissing Jo's cheek. "Kissy kissy Mommy kissy," sniggers the boy. "Wake up," says Ysabel in Jo's ear, and Jo opens her eyes. "Ysabel?"

Ysabel sits up.

"He's still here, isn't he," says Jo.

Ysabel nods.

"I have a kid," says Jo.

"I wouldn't put it – "

"Make out!" yells the boy. The water in the eggshell's starting to bubble. Jo starts to sit up but Ysabel pushes her gently back down, lying down next to her, "It's busy," she says. "It's okay. Just – "

"Get me a shirt," says Jo, wrestling with the ruins of her dress.

"It's *okay*," says Ysabel, trying to still Jo's hands. "We need to take a – "

"Just get me a damn shirt?" says Jo.

Ysabel rolls over to crawl down the futon, and "London! France! Underpants!" cries the boy.

"What?" says Jo, twisting her dress around to get at the zipper. It's stuck. "Shut up, you little troll." Yanking the zipper apart until it rips loose, then working the red rags over her head and off. *"Mommy's naked, Mommy's naked,"* sing-songs the boy. "Shut *up,*" snaps Jo.

"Don't egg it on," says Ysabel, rummaging through the clothing heaped around the blond wood crates under the dark flat-screen television. One corner of the screen's now webbed with cracks, a crooked line jagging all the way up to the top. She sniffs a black T-shirt, drops it, sniffs another one, tosses that one at Jo.

"The fuck is he doing?" says Jo, working the shirt over her head. A wide-eyed anime girl with pink hair drawn upside-down across it, surrounded by bits of armor cracking open like a carapace.

"Making coffee," says Ysabel.

"Mommy likes *stupid* coffee," says the boy. "Stupid stupid coffee."

"It's not breaking anything." Ysabel scoots back up the futon. "It's not smearing shit and snot all over the place. It's not kicking the hell out of you. Or me. Let's take what we can get." Jo's shaking out a cigarette, then hands the pack to Ysabel. "We need to figure out how it got here."

"Cabbages in the celery patch!" cries the boy. "A stork's as good in a pinch through the window."

"It's obvious," says Jo, striking a match, lighting her cigarette. "The Duke." Shaking out the match she hands the matchbook to Ysabel, who shakes her head, taking Jo's hand in hers, her cigarette in her mouth. She leans forward to light it from the coal at the end of Jo's. "Kissy kissy!" chirps the boy, and Jo scowls. Ysabel takes a drag, shakes her head, "Too *weird,*" she says. "The Duke prefers his vengeance raw and right away, or very, very, *very* well-done."

"Vengeance?" says Jo. "First of all, anybody gets to be pissed in this situation, it's *me*. At him."

"Jo," says Ysabel, "I tried to explain, it's – " and then she stops. "Never mind," she says. "Number two."

"Number two?"

"You said first of all." Ysabel lies back on the futon. "I assumed you had a second point?" Blowing smoke at the ceiling.

"Yeah," says Jo. "Right." Lying back next to Ysabel. "Well. We had sex."

"So I gathered," says Ysabel. "I'm doing it! I'm doing it!" The boy's dumping another eggshell of bubbling water into the cup, scooping up more.

"Not tonight," says Jo. "I mean, yes, tonight, but what I mean is, last week. When we were at the teahouse? When we were," and her hands come up, searching in the wisps of smoke above them for the right word, *"there,"* she says, "we, well, him and me, we – "

"Had sex," says Ysabel.

"A *lot* of sex," says Jo. "I think. It was, like a dream. You know?" The boy's chanting "The worm goes in, the worm goes out, the worm goes in and out and in and out!" and Jo says, "Jesus. Anyway." Looking over at Ysabel beside her. "If we, I mean *because* we did it there, could he have – "

"It," says Ysabel, "and no, I don't think that's how it works – "

"Billy!" says the boy, and Jo sits bolt upright. "What about him," she says.

"Billy Billy Billy Billy Billy," says the boy.

"Who's Billy?" says Ysabel, sitting up on her elbows next to Jo.

"That's my name," says the boy. "Billy Billy Billy Bill."

"The hell it is," says Jo, not looking away from the boy as he pours another eggshell of water into the cup.

"Jo," says Ysabel. "Listen to me. Jo." Her hand on Jo's shoulder. "This, *thing,* was sent to us. *By* somebody. Has nothing to do with you and the Duke. We really should start trying to figure out who, and why."

"Billy Billy Billy," says the boy.

"We gotta do that to get rid of it?" says Jo.

After a moment, Ysabel says, "No."

"Then fuck it," says Jo.

"I'm Billy," says the boy.

"Such a nothing time" – Drawing the Circle
What's left Behind – a Coat to a Cobbler

"Such a nothing time," says Becker, "three in the morning." He snaps the little phone shut and lays it carefully in the worn leather shoe on the floor by a discarded pair of jeans and a big plaid empty shirt. "You stay up till one, sure," he says, sitting up in the dimly greenish streak of light from the louvered windows lining one long wall of the narrow room. "Two, even, you can go back to sleep for three or four hours. That's like a full cycle. Enough to keep you going." His knees tenting the crazed tangle of quilts and blankets and sheets. He scratches the dark hair scattered sparsely across his chest. "Four o'clock, you can give up, get up, go make some coffee." Folding his hands behind his head. "But what the fuck can you do with three in the goddamn morning?"

Pyrocles his head laid on one arm folded like a wing eyes closed smiles sleepily beneath his crookedly drooping mustaches. "You can keep everyone else around you awake."

Becker shifts on his side, looking down at Pyrocles. "It's not insomnia," he says. "It's not misery loving company. I just don't want to miss any of this."

"I know," says Pyrocles.

"When I was a kid," says Becker, and then, "a kid, ha, in high school, which was *so* long ago – I was obsessed with this idea. I would try, I would do everything I could not to fall asleep." He worms his way a little deeper under the blankets, closer to Pyrocles, hands tucked under his chin. "Because, sure, I'd wake up in the morning, but it would be a, a *new* me. Like rebooting a computer. As soon as I closed my eyes and let go, that would be it, for this me." He taps his forehead. "Like blowing out a candle. Doesn't matter to the flame that the candle can be relit later."

Pyrocles hikes himself up on an elbow, a quilt of blues gone black and grey in the dim light falling from his bare shoulder. He leans over to kiss Becker's forehead. "I did not take too well to sleep at first myself," he says. "But there are dreams. The candle gutters, but it's not extinguished."

"I don't," says Becker, rolling onto his back, "I don't really remember my dreams. Once in a blue moon. But yeah, that's sort of what I ended up telling myself. There's like a pilot light. I was obsessed, yeah, but I was also in high school. I was worried sick about reports and tests and grades and getting into a good college, ha, look what *that* got me." Running a hand through what little of his hair is left. "And worrying about whether Brian Peake had any idea how gay I was for him. I couldn't possibly not sleep. And I was way too chickenshit for drugs." He squeezes his eyes shut, squeezes his whole face shut, shivering. "I should have gone home," he says. "I shouldn't have stayed. I'm gonna wake up in the morning, I'm not gonna remember who you are, I'm gonna think I got too drunk again, hooked up again," and he rolls over on his side again and there's Pyrocles, head still pillowed on his folded arm, blue eyes half-open, his smile sleepy and sad behind those mustaches. "I'll run out of here again," says Becker, "like an idiot. And make excuses at work again." A hand on Becker's shoulder Pyrocles draws him close. "And you'll have to," says Becker, "come find me, again," and they kiss. "Maybe you shouldn't," says Becker.

"Shouldn't?"

"Maybe you shouldn't come find me again," says Becker. "Maybe you should just let me go, on my merry, oblivious way. Maybe you shouldn't start this up again, and again and again – " and then Pyrocles kisses him again, and again.

"If I thought," says Pyrocles in his deep rough voice gone soft with sleep, "this was you, asking me this, and not three in the morning, I would do my best to do as you ask. But Becker, you must know that I am weak. The light that shines in your eyes, the way you blush, and duck your head, every time you see me, for the first time – forgive me, Becker. I could not help but seek you out, for another glimpse of that."

Becker sighs and closes his eyes, and then after a long long moment opens them again. "Not yet," he says. "Not just yet."

It's not rain so much as haze too heavy and wet to be fog, blurring streetlights, drifting slowly down about them. When they stop under the bridge Jo heaves the big duffel bag from her shoulder and sets it gently on the ground, then brushes water from her forehead and the sleeves of her leather jacket. Ysabel in a yellow slicker shakes out her big clear umbrella, then furls it, wiping her eyes. There's a long narrow cardboard box strapped to the side of the duffel, and it rattles and thumps as the duffel rustles. There's a muffled whine. Jo looks over at Ysabel.

"That way," says Ysabel, pointing past the railroad tracks, down the long dark aisle of pillars holding the bridge up above them. "Further in."

Jo stoops and hauls up the duffel, careful of it and the skinny box, and follows Ysabel into the darkness under the bridge. Buildings shoulder close to either side of the bridge as it slopes gradually to the ground ahead. There are things painted on the pillars about them, a hermit holding aloft a lantern shining sketchily, a black-faced lion awkwardly savaging an antelope under criss-crossed branches, a chalky bird perched on the enormous nose of a face grown from the scraggled outline of a tree, that same bird or one very like it with an elaborate tail sitting on a drawn plinth that says God Is Love, and a scroll beneath that says Light Hope Truth April 7 1948. Something large, a truck booms by overhead. "Ysabel," says Jo. "Ysabel. How much further. We're running out of, out of – bridge – " Ahead the shortening pillars stop as the deck of the bridge above meets a thick blank concrete wall.

"I thought it would be enough," says Ysabel, looking about.

"I can't exactly open this damn thing if we're still here," says Jo.

"I know, I know," says Ysabel.

"Oh, I think – I think I have an idea."

Jo kneels by the duffel as it rustles again and opens one end of the cardboard box. Reaches inside with one hand, both hands, tugs and yanks then pulls with a ringing scrape of metal free her sword. She steps back away from the duffel, out into the space between the last of the pillars and the wall, her sword-tip pointed at the dirt, but she stops before she touches the ground, and lifts it, a little. "I wouldn't," says Ysabel.

"Yeah," says Jo. "I get that." Overhead a car passes a bit of something popping under its tires quite loudly in the stillness. "Get him out of there."

Ysabel kneels by the duffel and begins unknotting the strings that hold it shut. "I think drawing your blade was enough," she says, looking up at the bridge now silent above them.

Jo's shaking her head. "We need a circle," she says. She starts to drag the duct-taped toe of her white Chuck Taylor after her through the dirt and the muck.

"You've done this before."

"No," says Jo. "Not this."

Ysabel tugs the duffel open and down. The boy's head pushes up those curls flopping as he twists his head back and forth, stretches his neck. There's something, a washcloth wadded in his mouth, tied in place with a white terrycloth belt. Jo still dragging out the circle says, "Undo it."

"I am," says Ysabel, working the duffel down past the boy's shoulders.

"The gag," says Jo. Ysabel looks up at her. "No one's gonna hear now," says Jo. "Right?"

Frowning Ysabel unties the belt and pulls the cloth from his mouth and he hacks up a cough or two and spits and says, "Mommy, Mommy! Mommy!" and "Shut up," says Ysabel, working the duffel down his chest swathed in plastic wrap, his arms pressed tight against him folded in front of him and tightly wound about with layers of the stuff. "Mommy!" he calls, twisting around in the duffel bag, and Ysabel cuffs his head, "Shut *up*," she says.

"Ysabel," says Jo.

"You wanted it undone," says Ysabel.

"Don't hit him."

"No no," says the boy, "no, no no, not again, I gave at the office."

"Just," says Jo, and "What," says Ysabel, "what?" Jo's stepping away from the half-done circle, into it, toward Ysabel and the boy in the bag, and Ysabel stands, backs away. "Just let me," says Jo, stooping.

"Mommy," says the boy.

"Shut up," says Jo. "Hold still. Hold very still." Holding her sword both hands on its blade one of them gingerly close to the tip she pierces the plastic wrap and pushes and twists until it pops and starts to rip. "Oh no it's time to go," the boy's muttering. "I hate to leave you'll make me though." Jo the sword laid across her lap tears the plastic wrap away until he can wriggle his arms loose and crawl half out of the duffel bag. "Hold still," says Jo, wrenching the plastic wrapped around his legs down and off.

"Jo, what are you," Ysabel starts to say.

"Go on," says Jo, as the boy crawls all the way out of the duffel. "Get out of here."

"You can't, Jo, you can't," says Ysabel.

"It's dark," says the boy, squatting in the dirt by the duffel, arms folding about himself.

"Where's it going to go?" says Ysabel.

"It's cold, Mommy," says the boy.

"I don't care," says Jo. "Just get out of here."

"You don't care you don't care," the boy's saying, "you don't care," as Ysabel says, "It doesn't have anywhere else to go, Jo. It can't go anywhere else. It's not a kid, it's a, a thing, a monster that was set upon us, by somebody, and if you let it go it will just – come back – "

"You don't care, Mommy," says the boy.

"What, Ysabel," says Jo, looking from the boy to her in her yellow slicker, the clear umbrella planted like a walking stick, shaking her head a little, her mouth open around something she's almost about to say. *"What,"* says Jo.

"Something," says Ysabel, tilting her head, "something my Gammer said to me, the very first night we met. I didn't think it meant anything at all at the time. Just her – babble – "

"I want to go home," says the boy. "Shut up," says Jo. "What was it. What did she say."

"Jo," says Ysabel. "Who's Billy?"

"Billy," says the boy, "Billy, I'm Billy," and Jo slaps him. Then puts her hand to her mouth and closes her eyes. Lifts her hand away. "My father," she says.

"No," says Ysabel.

"The hell he isn't!" snarls Jo, standing, taking her sword in her hand. "Bill fucking Maguire, you ask him – "

"Bill," says Ysabel. "Not Billy."

"*I'm* Billy," says the boy.

"I," says Jo. "Ysabel. Don't. Ask me that. I can't, I can't tell you – "

"Yes you can," says Ysabel. "Billy. That's how it was fixed on us." Stepping closer, taking Jo's free hand in hers. "Please. Tell me who he is."

"You don't know what you're asking," says Jo.

"I want to go home," the boy's saying, and Ysabel says, "Yes, I do."

"No," says Jo. "You really don't. I can't tell you, Ysabel. It would change – a lot – "

"You can trust me," says Ysabel, pressing Jo's hand to her breast.

"That's not," says Jo, tugging her hand back, "that's not what I'm – "

"I want to go *home,* Mommy," says the boy, "it's cold," and wailing Jo turns and steps and lunges punching a hole through his chest. The edges of that wound flutter about the blade as his head lurches back and he opens his mouth, letting out a long sighful of breath arms up fingers wigging legs wobbling his head collapsing and his torso in on itself slithering off the sword as shivering he sinks down and down to the mud. Jo stands there over what's left sword unmoving. Rubbery folds of skin, an empty hand, a foot stuck upright at an angle drooping, that curly mop of hair.

"Jo?" says Ysabel after a moment.

"Don't," says Jo. Stepping back. Pulling in her sword, lowering the tip of it. Something large, a truck booms by overhead. A car alarm's blaring and whooping somewhere blocks away. On the ground before her in the darkness a little stir of something, garbage, a screwed-up twist of greasy paper, a burger wrapper, a yellow dish glove ripped half inside-out, the fingers of it flopped at odd and broken angles, a scrap of some threadbare old stuffed animal with hanks of tangled, curly fur.

"Leave it," says Ysabel.

"Oh, yeah," says Jo, shaking her head. "Hell yeah." Kneeling by the duffel she works the sword back into that narrow cardboard box and drives it home. "I could eat a horse," she says.

The storefront's lit up yellow and warm in the blue-grey dawn. George's, it says in red and yellow letters in a curve across the big front window. Shoes Repaired. Inside a half-dozen or so men and women in the little space between the front door and the counter and as many again in the marginally larger space beyond, bounded by a worktable mounded high with shoes of every shape and color, jogging shoes and sneakers in every garish color lapped open, laces undone, hightop basketball shoes and boat shoes, brogues and wingtips, pumps and slippers in jeweled dye jobs and faded dusty blacks, lurking stilettos, slingbacks and cork-soled clogs, monk and gladiator sandals, spectators and Oxfords, flats and mules and flip-flops printed with the filthy soles of bare feet long since gone, stern little Mary Janes, galoshes and Uggs, jackboots and hiking boots and chukkas and Chelseas, winklepickers, shitkickers, a long black shining knee-high vinyl boot laid crinkled and empty along one side of the mound, forlorn without a foot, and not one of any of them a match for any one of the others. To one side of the mound a couple of cardboard boxes with spigots and little running coffee cups printed on the side. An old man's pouring coffee from one of them into styrofoam cups on the counter before him. He's wearing a worn plaid shirt in greens and blacks with threads of yellow and his hair's a crisp circle of curls from one ear around the back of his head to the other in a white that's almost yellow against the reddish blackness of his skin. "Unleaded," says a woman in blue coveralls, holding a stainless steel travel mug, and he sets the first box down and fills her mug from the second.

"An Apportionment," someone's saying, and "since the Samani," and "not since two *weeks* before," and "a thimbleful she's promised twice now," and "you'll set up shop as a tailor if she," and "oh, a *supplier* to tailors, a veritable *thimblesmith*," and there's laughter, but it's bitter, muted.

"Yet you all keep on working for them," says the man behind the counter.

After a moment a man in an olive work shirt says, "What else is there to do?" The name tag sewn on his shirt says Turlupin.

"The work must get done," says the woman in blue coveralls.

"I think we ought to have another run at the basics of the thing," says the man behind the counter, sipping coffee from one of the styrofoam cups.

"Oh, no," says someone by the door, and they're all turning, craning to look out the window. A woman naked her hair quite short and gunmetal grey a polished silver torc about her neck is marching across the dim and empty street toward the store. Behind her hurries a man in a grimy blue windbreaker, shopping bags in either hand bounced about by his churning legs. The bell over the door to the shop rings, and someone's slipping out, walking quickly away down the sidewalk as that naked woman her pale skin splashed with something here and there that's dried in white and crusted swathes crosses the narrow median stepping into the street again without looking either way. The bell dings again, and again, men and women in work shirts and coveralls, jean jackets, paint-splattered sweatshirts and medical smocks make their studiously unhurried way to the left and the right along the sidewalk away from the lit storefront. By the time she steps through the ringing door the man behind the counter is alone, and the little trash can on the floor is filled with empty styrofoam cups.

"Good morning," says Linesse.

The man behind the counter doesn't say anything. His eyes wide staring at her and his mouth open just he's gone quite grey. "You can see her?" says Frankie, setting his shopping bags down on the floor.

"Of course I can, boy," says the man behind the counter, after a moment.

"Well, good," says Frankie, sourly. "There's three or four people and a big-ass bus driver on the number six heading downtown who couldn't at all."

"Hollow and hive, boy, she's dead," says the man behind the counter.

"Dead but not forgotten," says Linesse. "Why was your shop filled at daybreak with clods and urisks and domestics who should be about their business, Gordon? Do you mean to turn them all to rabbits?"

"You ain't come here to talk politics," says the man behind the counter.

"No," says Linesse, looking from Gordon to Frankie, and back to Gordon again. "I must ask of you one last boon," she says.

Gordon looks then at Frankie for the first time, head to toe, then shaking his head looks down at the cup of coffee in his hands. "Well," he says, "I never said no to you before." There's a smile on his face now, rueful, wistful, as he looks up to meet her still stern eyes.

"No matter that I've turned my coat?" she says.

"What's a coat to a cobbler?" says Gordon.

"What's, what are we doing here?" says Frankie Reichart.

From unseen speakers somewhere up among the maze of ductwork painted white and struts a growling voice is chanting I had money, yeah, and I had none, over a churning organ riff, I had money, yeah, and I had none, but I never been so broke that I couldn't leave town. "Another one?" says Ysabel.

"Go get some coffee or something," says Jo. She's headed for the squat grey shape of a cash machine there under the switch-back of the access ramp, by the florist stand, pulling a wad of money from her jacket clamped in a medium-sized binder clip.

"She isn't," says Ysabel, looking down the aisles of groceries at the unlit green sign that says Starbucks, down by the deli counter, "they aren't open." Jo's plucked a gold credit card from the binder clip and runs it through the reader on the cash machine. "Jo, what do you need all this money for?" says Ysabel.

Jo's running her fingers along the options listed on the screen, twenty dollars, forty dollars, sixty dollars. Jo presses the screen by the last one which says Oh the heck with it three hundred. "I'm hoping I don't," says Jo. The cash machine starts whirring. It spits out twenty dollar bill after twenty dollar bill, and Jo scoops them up, counting through them quickly, folding them, stuffing them into the duffel bag.

"Jo," says Ysabel, grabbing her hand. "Please – "

"Don't," says Jo. "Don't ask. I'm telling you."

I'm the air you breathe, food you eat, growls the voice over the speakers. Friends you greet in the sullen street, wow.

Outside in the wet grey light Jo rushes ahead across the empty intersection, Ysabel trotting behind, "Jo, wait," she's saying. Catching her at the corner. "What are we doing. What's happening."

"I don't know?" says Jo. "I need to, I've got to get some sleep, I've got to think – let's just," lifting both her hands to rub her eyes, her face, Ysabel stepping closer, her hands on Jo's arms, "let's go home, let's clean up enough to collapse. I've *got* to get some sleep."

"Whatever it is," says Ysabel, ducking her head to catch Jo's eyes as Jo looks down, away. "What*ever* it is. You can trust me, Jo. Jo, please. Jo." A hand to the side of Jo's face, leaning closer. Kissing the bruise above Jo's eye, then kissing her cheek. Jo standing stiff and still, breathing quickly, trembling. "Whatever," says Ysabel. "So you had a kid – "

"*Don't,*" snarls Jo, pushing away, "Christ, Ysabel, just, just *stop,* you have *no idea* – "

"You can *trust* me, Jo," says Ysabel. "I trust you, I, I – "

"It has *nothing* to do with that," says Jo, turning, walking away. "Oh. Oh fucking hell."

"Jo?"

Jo's pointing, down the street, toward the bulk of the apartment building, toward the cars parked along the street before it, toward the reddish brown car parked at an alacritous angle among them, a black stripe painted down its side.

"Oh," says Ysabel.

"I *just,*" says Jo, "want to get some fucking *sleep* – "

THAT STERN AND ROUGH-HEWN HAWK
EGG WHITES & ESCHATOLOGY
SKY FALLS; MOUNTAINS CRUMBLE – THREE ANSWERS

THAT STERN AND ROUGH-HEWN HAWK caged in his fingers the Duke's leaning on his cane by the glass-topped café table, still in his long and camel-colored topcoat, a red-brown derby on his head. "Was there a riot in here?" he says as they open the door. Behind him by the bulky blond wood armoire Jessie arms folded in a double-breasted pinstripe coatdress, her hair in a tight bun, her lips carefully red.

"Get out," says Jo, unshouldering the duffel bag and laying it and the narrow box on the floor. Ysabel behind her still in the little hallway kitchen.

"I came here out of concern," says the Duke, "and frankly, I'm even more concerned, now – "

"Get out," says Jo, laying a hand on the glass table-top.

"Words were said," says the Duke. "In haste. By both of us, I'm not gonna deny it, but in all that heat I had a little light in mind and I'm worried it didn't articulate in a fully appreciable manner. So maybe – "

"Get. Out," says Jo.

"Breakfast," says the Duke. "I can get us a private dining room at the Heathman, full spread buffet, we can talk, undisturbed – "

"We already ate," says Ysabel, as Jo's saying, "Dammit, Leo, get the fuck out of my apartment."

"Jo!" snaps the Duke, and he tumps his cane-tip on the carpet. "Listen to me. This is important. If you cannot keep a roof over her head then all bets are off."

Ysabel steps up close behind Jo then. Jessie's looking down at the pile of clothing by her feet. "The fuck is that supposed to mean," says Jo quietly.

"You ever stop to think why nobody's been coming at you?" Braced on his cane leaning over the table at her. "They're all wary of the special understanding between me and the Queen, as regards the two of you."

"Special," Jo starts to say, as Ysabel's saying "You don't *have* a special understanding with my mother."

"Precisely," says the Duke. "And the minute you two get kicked out of this," sniffing, looking about the small main room, "this shithole," the mounds of clothing, the broken television, the filthy walls, "the very *instant* they get a whiff of any instability in your furlough, Princess, they all tumble to that very fact. And they will come a-running for you, Gallowglas. Swords out."

"Is that how it's supposed to go down," says Jo, her voice still tightly quiet. "You graciously offer to do what you can to help us with the eviction, then do not a goddamn thing until it's too fucking late. When there's nowhere else to turn but you."

"He called," says Jessie, and the Duke thumps his cane again. "He *did* call," she mutters. The Duke's saying, "She didn't say I didn't, Jessie. We're strictly in the realm of the hypothetical, here."

"Hypothetically," says Jo, both hands on the table-top closed in fists, "it might have worked." Her eyes locked on his. "Only you went too far last night."

"Too far?" says the Duke. "When I threw a party for you? That's somehow – "

"When you raped me, you sonofabitch."

Ysabel lifts a hand but does not lay it on Jo's arm. Jessie's head snaps up, she's looking at Jo, at the Duke gone suddenly pale. The thump of his cane-tip clanks this time and rings and he tilts the head of the cane to one side in his left hand, his right twitching his longsword the tip of it in a savagely quick little circle over the carpet. "Have a care, Gallowglas," he says, "how you bandy that word about. You'll force me to name you a liar, and then we'd have to test the merits of our quarrel." Bringing his hands together again, resting them both on the hawk at the head of his cane.

"Liar?" says Jo. "You drugged me, then you fucked me. What else would you call that?"

"Jessie," says the Duke, "did you enjoy your rape of our Princess?"

"Leo – " says Jessie, and Jo roars, "I didn't know it was in the goddamn drink!"

"Jo," snaps the Duke, and then, gently, "all it does, in this, this context – I told you. It enhances, your sensations, your mood, your – "

"Turns maybe," says Jo, "into yes."

He closes his eyes, purses his lips. Opens his eyes. "It does nothing to change your mind, Jo, or – "

"I'm never gonna know that am I?" she says. "You should have just told me. You should have said something, Leo. Just, please. Just go."

"Jo," says the Duke, "I'm not about to walk out of here and leave it like this. *Listen* to me – "

"Southeast," says Ysabel, and the Duke closes his mouth, looks down at his hands on the head of his cane.

"Hawk," she says, and he looks up, eyes dark. "Hind," he says.

Ysabel puts a hand on Jo's shoulder. "My champion has asked you to leave," she says.

"Very well," says the Duke, turning, holding out a hand to Jessie, letting her looking down the whole time lead the way as he limps out past Jo and Ysabel through the little hallway kitchen. One hand on the doorknob he turns, licks his lips, says, "I take my leave of you." And then, "I wish you hadn't cut your hair."

He closes the door, gently.

"Jo?" says Ysabel, stepping to her side, both hands on Jo's shoulders. Jo's eyes are closed and she's tipping her head back slowly, slowly, her mouth tightening, her breath gone shallow and quick. "Jo?"

The kitchen yellow and cream with glossy granite counters brightly lit against the gloomy morning light outside. Standing at the counter using a fork and knife to cut an egg-white omelette into precisely tiny pieces she's wearing black, black jeans, a plain black T-shirt, a dark grey cardigan. "Well," she says, cutting the tip from a triangle of toast. "Send him in." Spearing a bite of omelette, a bit of toast, biting them both from her fork. The woman wearing the narrow black-rimmed glasses nods and turns and signals to someone in the hall.

"Chariot," says the woman all in black.

"Ma'am," says Roland. He hands a small jar half full of something viscous, milky, touched with just a hint of warm yellow gold, to the woman in the narrow black-rimmed glasses. His track suit's a pale yellow with green stripes down the sleeves and legs.

"Thank you, Anna," says the woman all in black, and the woman in the glasses nods and leaves, the jar in her hands. "How is my daughter?" says the woman all in black, slicing more strips from her toast.

"Ma'am," says Roland, "I have not seen the Princess in almost a week." His hands in fingerless bicycle gloves are clasped behind his back.

"Almost a week?"

He ducks his head. "It will have been a week ago tomorrow," he says. "Afternoon."

"And yet," says the Queen, taking another bite of egg-white and toast, chewing, swallowing, "I saw her last night." She lays her fork and knife to either side of the plate. "I managed a few hours' sleep, Chariot. Not only that, I *dreamed*. Do you dream?"

He nods. "Yes, ma'am."

"Singularly unpleasant," she says. "I was suddenly in a *filthy* little bathroom, quite disgusting. Used wads of tissue littering the corner, grime between the tiles, you couldn't begin to see your reflection in the mirror. The toilet? Was a horror. A girl lay on the floor, utterly naked, soaking wet, shivering so hard I could hear the teeth clattering in her head, and as I realized it was my *daughter* lying before me, Chariot, she opened her eyes, and she opened her mouth, and she clutched her belly," and the Queen's hands fold themselves together under her breasts, over her belly, "and it," she says, "and her, it, she – it – " She pushes her plate away across the counter, the omelette half-uneaten. "I woke up," she says. "How is my daughter, Roland?"

"She has given herself to the Gallowglas," says the Chariot. "Who has, in turn, been seduced by Southeast."

"How is she physically?"

"Physically, ma'am?" he says, looking up to meet a piercing scowl.

"Is she hale? Whole? Ill in any way?"

"She has," he says, and he looks back down, "assured me, ma'am, that she is well."

"A week ago."

"Yes, ma'am."

"Then it is not as bad as it could be," says the Queen. "Merely worse, far worse, than we feared. I'd thought to distract her, by indulging her predilections. I never dreamed the Duke would, would *stoop* to such an oblique angle."

"Ma'am," says Roland, but she's put both hands squarely on the counter, is looking at him frankly, head tipped back just, "Six weeks exactly," she says, "isn't it? He'll try on the Solstice, don't you think? It would appeal to his sense of the dramatic." Her mouth smiles but her eyes do not. "The Hawk fancies himself an oak, and for me with all I've done it's to be Gammer-hood, or worse." Her hands on the counter rippled and ridged with thick veins and dotted the left especially with liver-colored spots.

"If the Bride is well," says Roland.

"*If* she is well?" says the Queen. "You said she *is* well, all else considered."

"She *said* she is well, ma'am." His bicycle gloved hands clasped before him now, fingers fiddling with a velcro strap. "But what if she isn't? What if she is no more a Princess than, than – "

"Do you mean to say, Chariot, that she has *lied* to you?"

His hands freeze there before him. He slowly shakes his head. "What if she were wrong, ma'am?"

"She would know," says the Queen. "We would all know. It would be the end, of everything."

Roland walks back alone through the darkened house, rubbing his hands together before him. He stops to knock at a half-closed door, the room beyond lit only by a blue-shaded banker's lamp on a long library table. Sitting at it the woman in narrow black-rimmed glasses looks up from a thick ledger filled with tiny, handwritten figures. By the ledger a wide-mouthed jar hashed with lines in white ink down the sides denoting ounces, gills, mutchkins, a thirdendeal. A drift of golden dust along an arc at the very bottom of it. "My audience is done," says Roland.

"I have nothing for you, sir," says the woman, setting aside a glass nib pen.

"Nothing?"

"There is to be nothing for anyone this week," she says, looking back down at her ledger.

"What am I to tell – "

"That there is to be no Apportionment this week, sir," she says, taking off her glasses, looking up again. "This last batch was – off. No telling how, or from whom."

"I see," says Roland.

"Are you awake?" says Ysabel.

Curtains drawn sunlight thin and grey seeping around the edges. Side by side on the futon under the black and red and orange-brown blanket Jo and Ysabel neither of them eyes closed staring up at the dingy popcorned ceiling.

"No," says Jo.

"Can I tell you something?" Ysabel shifts a little, turns her head to look sidelong at Jo.

Jo closes her eyes. "Sure," she says.

"You said," says Ysabel, "you don't believe in love, and I said that was because you'd fallen out of love." She shifts back, looking up at the ceiling again. "And I said I only knew love because I'd seen it in what other people do. I'd never been in love myself before. But seeing yourself like that, seeing what you do, from outside yourself – if I *were* in love, well, I wouldn't know, would I."

"Ysabel," says Jo, and Ysabel turns on her side, "Shh," raising a hand to lay a finger against Jo's lips. Jo jerks her head to one side out from under it, "Don't," she says, and "Sorry," says Ysabel, "I'm sorry," and "Please just, let me finish." Settling on her side head on the pillow both hands folded now and tucked beneath her chin. "You're the first person," she says, "you're the only person, ever to tell me no."

Jo turns her head at that, frowning at Ysabel. "The only, what?"

"You know what I mean," says Ysabel. "The question, that I asked you. When it started to rain?"

"No, I, I," says Jo, looking away back up at the ceiling again, "I do, but, Ysabel, I – "

"Shh," says Ysabel. "Had you said yes, you would have been bound to me."

"Bound?" says Jo.

"Like," says Ysabel, "the Chariot, and the Axe, Rain, a dozen, dozen others." She swallows. "You said no. Which bound me to you, a link of toradh that will not be broken till, oh, till the sky falls, or the mountains crumble that are made of the dust of the mountains about us now."

"Bound," says Jo, shifting to look at Ysabel again.

"I am yours, Jo Maguire," says Ysabel, as Jo's saying, "That's, that's not love, that's – " and Ysabel shushes her again, presses a fingertip to Jo's lips again, "Please," she says. "Let me finish." Stroking Jo's cheek. "I knew you would say no. When I asked I knew you would say no." Brushing Jo's chin. "I am many things, but I'm not stupid. It's *why* I asked you. I knew what you would say."

"That's," says Jo, "that's insane."

Ysabel smiles. "I know." She shifts onto her back, looking up again, and takes a deep deep breath. "It's why I think it's love," she says.

Not a sob so much as a choked-off breath, a word maybe, as Jo curls over face clenching, Ysabel saying, "No, no, Jo," reaching over, pulling her close, "Jo, it's all right, I'm here, for you, whatever you need," and Jo's trembling, shaking in her arms, leaning back, wet eyes half-closed, biting her lip as the sound boils up again in bubbling yelps of laughter. "Jo?" says Ysabel, letting go, sitting up, as Jo rolls over hands to her face saying "I'm sorry, I'm sorry" in among the gasps.

"This is *important,*" says Ysabel, and Jo's laughter redoubles and helplessly squeezing herself legs kicking up under the blanket "I know," she says, "I *know,* I'm sorry, if I don't," catching her breath, "oh God if I don't laugh I'm gonna fucking break down and cry for a fucking week, oh Ysabel, oh, oh," wiping her eyes, "that was, I think that was the sweetest thing you've ever said. I'm sorry."

"I just wanted you to know," says Ysabel, arms folded in her lap.

"I know," says Jo. "I know."

"Whatever you did. Whatever you have to tell me, it doesn't matter." Shrugging in her oversized yellow nightshirt, her black curls snarled about her head. Looking down, away from Jo, a bit of a pout to her mouth. "Or not tell me, whichever."

"There's a price," says Jo.

"It doesn't matter," says Ysabel.

"Don't say that yet," says Jo. "I mean I can show it to you. It's a very concrete price."

Sitting up in her black tank top Jo plucks from the white shelf behind them a wad of money clamped in a medium-sized binder clip. She undoes the clip and rifles through the bills, teasing out a gold credit card, which she lays on the pillow between them. MasterCard, it says. Bank of Trebizond. Joliet K. Maguire. Good thru 13/99. "That bank," says Jo. "They have offices, in the Meier & Frank building, don't they, or some kind of partnership, arrangement or something?"

"That's the Duke's card," says Ysabel.

"No," says Jo. "No. I mean he gave it to me, yeah. But it's mine. All mine. The secret, that I gave them? When you sent me in there? Was worth a hell of a lot more than a couple of dresses and some underwear."

Ysabel folding her arms about herself, smaller somehow, huddled in that baggy nightshirt, looks down at the card, then back up at Jo. "Billy," she says.

"For about maybe a week?" says Jo, looking away over Ysabel's shoulder, the dark sheets of the curtains, dull light leaking around the edges. "I was going to keep him, carry him and have him. I was going to name him after my father. William. Bill, Bill Maguire. Billy." She closes her eyes. "But," she says. "I wouldn't have finished high school. And I – *tested* well. There were maybe some scholarships, there was some family money we could maybe, I had *options,* I had things, that I could do, places to go if I just, if I could just – " She shakes her head, looks down at the gold card on the pillow between them. "I made an appointment, I got an abortion."

"Oh," says Ysabel, and then, leaning forward, "oh, Jo, I – "

"I'm not done," says Jo, her hand on Ysabel's knee.

Ysabel looks down at the gold card. Her hand on Jo's hand there on her knee. She looks back up, and she nods, once.

Jo swallows. "She asked me three questions, the woman with the bank. Whether I missed him. If I still loved him. What I would tell him, if I could. And I said, I said. Yes, I said. Yes. And I'm sorry." Leaning forward elbows on her knees head down hunching in on herself. "Because it was all for nothing," she says. "Because look what all I did with all those *fucking options*. I'm sorry how *badly* I fucked it all up," and with a splintery crack the gold card splits into three sharp jagged shards. Ysabel jerks back. Jo puts her face in her hands.

After a moment, Ysabel reaches out to lay a hand on Jo's shoulder. Lays her other hand on Jo's other shoulder and leans forward, tugging Jo toward her until Jo buckles her head against Ysabel's chest, Ysabel's arms folding about her. She kisses Jo's wine-red hair, then tilts, leans down a little to kiss her cheek. Her nose against Jo's temple. "That's it, then," she says.

"Yeah," says Jo, muffled by Ysabel's nightshirt, sighing, pulling her arms out from between them, settling them around Ysabel's hips. Pulling her close, a sudden fierce hug, and Ysabel lifts her head blinking, looking down at Jo and opening her mouth a word there trembling which does not fall. She shuts her mouth firmly, closes her eyes, lays her head against Jo's.

"I got," says Jo, "twelve hundred on the way home." Sitting up, pulling back a little, leaning back in Ysabel's arms. "With what we've got here that's seventeen? Eighteen?" Looking over her shoulder at the cracked television hanging over the foot of the futon. "We sell what that thing didn't break or ruin? We can maybe clear two thousand." Leaning back further as Ysabel lets go. "It's not enough, not nearly enough. Not for first, last, security – we've gotta find new jobs – shit."

Ysabel says, "The Duke offered us a – "

"The Duke," snaps Jo, "is out of the question."

"I know!" says Ysabel. "I, I know. I'm just trying to catch up."

"Yeah," says Jo. "Yeah, he offered. Now I wouldn't be surprised if we go outside and find he's sent his boys after us again, whatsisname, the Stirrup with his sword out to take you back, for your own good."

"The Mason," says Ysabel.

"Or that scary-ass motherfucker," says Jo, looking down, then suddenly back up at Ysabel, "Oh, hell, Jessie. I'm sorry, Ysabel, I didn't even — I mean, are you gonna be, do you need to — "

"Jessie," says Ysabel, *"Rain,* well. If I need, if I want something like that, there's this — "

"A dozen dozen others?"

"Well," says Ysabel. Smiling. "Not *all* of them."

"Okay," says Jo, "that settles it. Our next place, we're definitely getting separate rooms."

Ysabel laughs. "I'd like to request a proper tub," she says.

"Why stop there? Full-on jacuzzi. Only way to go."

"Walk-in closets."

"Hell, that's a given. Underwear drawers as high as you can reach. And a fireplace."

"A ballroom," says Ysabel, laughing, "a fully stocked wet bar."

"A decent goddamn kitchen," says Jo.

"Oh yes."

"Ysabel," says Jo, her hand on Ysabel's knee. "When I find whoever it was who did this, who sicced that thing on me. I'm going to kill them."

"I know," says Ysabel, her hand on Jo's. "I'm going to help you."

A SCREWED-UP TWIST OF PAPER

A SCREWED-UP TWIST OF PAPER on the scarred wooden table before him, yellowed in a pool of streetlight from the tall wide windows. He contemplates it a moment, tilting his head this way and that, long black glossy hair slithering over a shoulder as he leans a little to one side, and then with both hands carefully carefully begins to pick it open, this corner, that fold, gently smoothing it bit by bit against the wood, careful of the spots of old grease here and there, wiping his fingertips from time to time on the thick white napkin to one side. Burger Chef, it says over and over again in pink letters under a stylized orange chef's hat. Super Shef, repeated again and again. Unfolding the last bit with a crinkle he takes up an edge of it and with a sweep of his hand turns it over. Scrawled letters in purple crayon say BILLY.

He sits back in the high wooden booth with a gentle smile, lifts a glass of water in a little salute to the wrapper and takes a sip. He scratches his cheek by a black eyepatch, tugging at the skin, and there is a glimpse of something wet and ruined underneath. "Excuse me," says a woman, and letting the eyepatch flap back into place Orlando looks up at her with his one good eye.

She's quite fat, in a black high-waisted gown and black and white striped arm socks, and her jet black hair's threaded with white ribbons and silvery spangles and gathered in two great hanks over either shoulder. Her bangs cut short and dyed a virulent pink. "You are," she says, "striking, and I just wanted, to tell you that. Because men aren't often told, that they are beautiful, and I think it would be a better world, if they knew, they were." Her eyes painted black behind thick black cat's eye glasses. Orlando leans back, looking past her, about, at a table over by the bar, three or four people dressed all in black, white collars here and cuffs there, black net gloves, a black top hat, leaning together, laughing together, looking away from him too quickly. He looks back up at her, quite still, not smiling at all, and she swallows as she meets his eye. "Please," he says. "Sit down."

"Gloria," she says, as she squeezes into the booth across from him. "You can call me Gloria. Gloria Monday."

"And I," says Orlando, "am the Mooncalfe. Why are you here?"

"Oh, the show? Bellamy Bach?" Her black and white striped hands rubbing over and over each other. "She's just, she's just fantastic – "

"No," says Orlando, "why are you at my table?" He looks over at the table by the bar again, and they all look away again, too quickly. "They dared you to come over here, didn't they. You didn't think I'd ask you to sit down."

"I," she says, "I didn't – "

"You want the world to be a better place," he says.

"Well," she says, "yes. Who wouldn't."

"Better for whom?" he says. "You may find it better that men know you think they are beautiful, but perhaps beautiful men would rather be left alone. Don't get up." She sits back in the booth. "You're here now," he says. "You might as well stay a moment. I forced my enemy to do a terrible thing tonight." He folds the crinkled wrapper carefully in half, and half again.

"Your enemy," says Gloria Monday.

"She is in great pain, now," says Orlando, and "She?" she says, and he looks at her with his one dark eye, and her black-painted lips snap shut. "She does not know who has done this thing to her. She does not know whom to trust, whom she can depend on. She will lash out. She will do many more terrible things to the people about her in the days to come. Her world is not a better place tonight. But mine is. If you are still here," he says, as he tucks the folded wrapper away in the pocket of his loose white shirt, "in half an hour's time, if you have not gone upstairs to the show with your, friends," and at that she looks over her shoulder quickly at the table by the bar and then back to him, "then," he says, "I will take you by the hand and lead you to a place where we will not be disturbed. Where you will not be heard. And I promise you this will be the best, last night of your life." He lifts his glass of water and she watches him drink it down. "When the big hand is on the three, then?" he says, setting it back on the table between them.

All we can do to comfort one another,
To stay a brother's sorrow for a brother,
To dry a child from the kind father's eyes,
Is to no purpose; it rather multiplies.
Your only smiles have power to cause relive
The dead again, or in their rooms to give
Brother a new brother, father a child:
If these appear, all griefs are reconcil'd.

—Thos. Middleton

NO. 14

MAYHEM

"You said you were going to kill me" – a Pointless rendezvous
Jo removes her Jacket – two whole Days – He's in
George's, it says – Tea & Peppers – something Pretty Special
a Taste – an Apple, peeled and cored – Talking Shop
thwarting Mr. Sogge – the Rose Garden
a Long and Narrow flight of Stairs – the Duel on the Bridge
One of her Many Names – If
the Sound of Bottles, clinking

"Y OU SAID YOU WERE GOING TO KILL ME," she says, her voice gone soft and thin.

"I might," he says.

"What is this," she says. "What are we doing."

"Magic," he says. "Take up the blade." Closing one eye, the other hidden beneath an eyepatch cupped there beside his sharply angular nose, naked on his back on the floor, his wrists bound up over his head with a sheer black stocking, tied to a pole that braces a little yellow table above them both. His long black hair spread over the grimy linoleum like a fan. In the aisle between two lines of those little yellow tables, orange plastic chairs bolted to the poles to either side, she's kneeling over him, one leg stockinged, one leg bare, black lace stretched taut about her wide round hips. Her long black hair threaded with white ribbons and silvery spangles that sweep over his narrow chest, his belly, her breasts brushing against him as her hand still in a black and white striped arm sock closes about the hilt of the long knife beside him, a slight curl to it, and no point but a sudden wedge of a tip. "It, it feels real," she says.

"Of course it does," he says, opening his eye.

"I mean, it doesn't, it isn't – "

"Don't touch the blade," he says. "Not with your hand."

"I'm sorry," she says, "I didn't mean to do anything – "

"Hush," he says, sharply. "By the hilt. Both hands. Firmly."

"It's real, isn't it," she says, the blade upright before her face. "I mean, it's sharp." The metal of it dark in the dim light, whorled with black streaks, a rainbowed shimmer floating along it like oil on water. On the wall behind her an enormous close-up photo of a hamburger, gone brown and yellowed with grime. "The wakizashi," he's saying. "The companion blade. Go on." It trembles in her hands, her fingers opening and closing about the hilt. Her face lost in the shadows thrown by the harsh light of the desk lamp on the floor away over there, plugged into an orange extension cord that snakes off into the darkness. Plywood nailed above it, a window boarded up. "Gloria," he says. "Go on."

The long knife turns over in her hands until the tip of it points at his flat stomach, at the thin dark line of hair drawn from his navel to the sudden thicket of it nestling his limply sidelong cock, that thin dark line of hair interrupted just beneath the tip of the blade by something pale, dead skin tight and shining, a ripple, a knot, scars hunched across his belly from hip to hip.

"No fear," he says, gently now. "No anger."

"No fear," she says, flatly.

"The blade comes down."

"No anger," she says.

"Empty," he says.

She swallows and clamps her hand more tightly about the hilt. "What if —"

"Empty," he says. "Those are not your hands. Those are not your eyes. Those are not your ears hearing these word I do not speak. That is not your breath, no," he says, closing his eye. "No."

The blade comes down. He grunts, head jerking wrists straining the sheer stocking toes curling spreading wide and clenching again his breath gone shallow and quick. His cock stirs, a shadow pulsing at the base of it in the dim light.

"Oh my fucking God," says Gloria.

"Pull it," he says through his teeth. He opens his eye. "Out. Now!"

She yanks the long knife up and out, a neat wet yellow cut left in its wake. "There's no," she says. "There no. Blood, there's no blood."

"Kiss it," he says, and then "No! Not the blade. No."

"Oh," she says, and "oh." Laying the long knife gingerly aside. The wedge-shaped tip of it wet with something thickly colorless.

"Go on," he says, and he closes his eye again, and her hair clatters as she stoops over him, one black and white striped hand on his chest, one on his knee, her nose brushing that thin dark line of hair, her lips on the cut. "Sweet," she says. "Like honey." She kisses it again, licks it, and he growls and yanks roughly at the stocking about his wrists. She lifts her head. "No!" he cries. "Do not. Stop." She kisses the cut once more, and opens her mouth to dig into it with her tongue. He howls.

"It's too cold," says Ysabel, wobbling along in her white heeled boots.

"Well if we're lucky then they'll have the heater turned up way too high and you can complain about how it's too hot instead," says Jo, trudging ahead of her along the side of the road. Grey-green trees over across the way and a tangle of brown and black along the ground. A demurely pocketed lot mostly full of cars and the low warrens of an anonymous office park, all brick and blank black glass.

"It is too cold," says Ysabel, "to be walking for miles through the middle of nowhere to a pointless rendezvous – "

"*Half* a mile," says Jo, rounding on her, "to the bus stop, and it wasn't fucking pointless until you made it pointless, okay?" A white panel truck that says FedEx in blue and green letters rolls past.

"He wanted us to lie," says Ysabel.

"It's sales," says Jo, snapping the sentence in half, the smoke of her breath swirling in the weak sunlight. "Lying's part of the gig."

"What I say," says Ysabel, "whatever else it might be, is true."

"Well you don't," says Jo, looking away, looking back at her, "you didn't have to, you didn't have to *tell* him that. You know?" Looking away again. "I mean, you could have."

"What, Jo?" says Ysabel. Head tilted back a little, the hood of her short white parka settling about her shoulders. "I could have what."

"Asked your question," says Jo. Shrugging, shivering in her black leather reefer jacket. "I mean you wouldn't have had to duck the thing about the extra monthly cost on the power bill or the," and as Ysabel stony-faced pushes past her, "that was how you got all those surveys, wasn't it? Wasn't it?"

"I should make people fall," says Ysabel, rounding on Jo, "for me, so I can sell them – what was it again?" And Jo looks down, scuffing the pavement with a big black boot, muttering something. "What?" says Ysabel, and Jo snaps "Yeah okay, appliance insurance, Christ. I got it."

"Appliance insurance. What on earth *is* that."

"Something you don't know you want till you need it," says Jo, pushing past Ysabel. "Weren't you paying any attention to the pitch?"

The bus stop a blue pole planted by the entrance to a sprawling apartment complex. The wooden sign in a stone-walled flowerbed by the driveway says Brookside Estates. Jo's sitting in the brown grass at the side of the road, her back against the pole. "Five more minutes," she says, stuffing her phone back in her jacket.

"I'd say it's cold," says Ysabel, "but you'd just get annoyed again." Arms folded hands tucked away she's leaning against the other side of the pole.

"Yeah, well," says Jo, looking up and back, "I'd say you shoulda put on pants, but, yeah. Let's run the list."

"The list," says Ysabel.

"Our enemies list?" says Jo. "Starting with bullet number one, Leo the fucking Duke?"

"You're wrong."

"So for weeks you're all he's bad, he's terrible, stay away from the Duke," and "I wasn't," says Ysabel as Jo's saying, "and now that I've finally come around you're all give him a break?" Ysabel shrugs. "So who's your number one?"

"Must I?" says Ysabel, sighing, and then, "Linesse, the former Helm. She's been torqued, the Dagger's destroyed, she blames us for that. And that thing, that Billy thing, that's just the sort of thing my mother's sister traffics in."

"Her with the iron nails and the nineteen names," says Jo. "Okay. So. How about the Axe?"

"Marfisa?" says Ysabel. "No."

"What if she, hear me out. What if she's miseading the situation? What if she sees me as a rival, or – "

"You aren't rivals," says Ysabel.

"What *if,* I mean what if. She throws away her sword, she walks away from, from you, from all this, she's pissed, so maybe she goes to your, ah, your mother's sister – "

"She isn't *dead,* Jo," says Ysabel, and Jo says, "I didn't say she was," as Ysabel's saying, "Those with the torc are dead. She isn't. I'd know."

"Oh," says Jo. "Okay. Okay. So who's your number two?"

"If I must," says Ysabel, "Agravante."

"Her brother," says Jo. Ysabel nods. "Okay," says Jo, "all right, I mean, we've got the mystery men to account for, and the Duke says they work for a guy who works for him – "

"So now you trust the Duke?"

"I'm gonna pretend," says Jo, "you didn't say that." Ysabel squats by Jo, rubbing her thighs, shivering, hugging her knees. Jo says, "If he's maybe linked to the guy in the skull mask?" and Ysabel shrugs. "Because," says Jo, "that would make everything awful tidy."

"We should probably put the Mooncalfe's name on the list," says Ysabel.

"You think?" says Jo. "I mean, that attack in the Safeway was completely random and spontaneous."

"He *is* the Duke's ex."

"He what?"

"I thought you knew," says Ysabel. She stands. "Here comes the bus."

Jo removes her Jacket – two whole Days – He's in

Jo removes her jacket, and "You don't have to," says Ysabel.

"I shouldn't have said anything about the damn heater," says Jo, draping the jacket over Ysabel's bare knees.

"Now you're going to freeze," says Ysabel.

"No," says Jo, wrapping her arms in her satiny red blouse about herself, "I'm gonna snuggle." She leans close to Ysabel, working a corner of the jacket up over her lap, pressing closer as Ysabel looks up, about the mostly empty bus, then leaning to one side lifts her arm up and free to drape it along Jo's side. "There," says Jo, laying her head against Ysabel's shoulder. "See? Cozy."

"You are so absurd sometimes, Jo Maguire."

"Only sometimes?"

Weakly lemon-colored sunlight dapples them, shimmering between needled branches through the windows to the right. Up behind the driver an older man sits stiffly upright facing that sunlight, a brown banker's box in his lap, a grey trilby on his head. A few rows ahead of them a woman her head down hands up fingers pressed against white earbuds. The trees thin a moment to the right and they rush past a cluster of yellow bulldozers and backhoes, a patch of earth scraped raw next to a clean new house with black shutters. "Now what?" says Ysabel.

"Which term?" says Jo. "Short, or long?"

"How about when we get back to town?" Ysabel's stroking Jo's close-cropped hair.

"I think I have to go see Erne."

"Erne."

"Yeah."

"Jo, you're not going to – you can't think you're going to just, *challenge* whoever it is." She looks down at the head nestled against her, the hair under her fingers the color of deep red wine. "Linesse, the Duke – even the Axehandle could best you. Easily."

"What did you think I was gonna do," says Jo. "Shoot them?"

"Isn't that how you people usually resolve this sort of thing?"

"No," snorts Jo, and then, "well, actually, I might could get a gun if I had to." She blows out a little laugh. "Let's just, let's figure out what to do once we figure out who it is. No, Erne – " She reaches up to take Ysabel's hand in hers. "I shouldn't have." She sighs. "I shouldn't have left it like that." Squeezes Ysabel's hand. Ysabel's looking out the window, sunlight licking her face under the white hood of her parka. "You made a promise," she says to Jo.

"Yeah."

"You're going to keep it."

"He's gonna," says Jo, letting go of Ysabel's hand, "it's two hundred bucks. For November. We only paid for October. He's gonna insist on getting his two hundred bucks."

"That was part of the promise, as I recall," says Ysabel.

"That's more than, what, ten percent of what we've got left."

"I'll trust you on the math," says Ysabel.

"So you're okay with it?"

"It's not," says Ysabel, looking down then, "it's not my decision to make."

"It's our money."

"No it isn't."

Jo shifts, looks up, sits up, wrapping her arms back about herself. "Yes," she says. "It's our money."

Ysabel almost shakes her head. "It wasn't my secret," she says, and Jo leans into her saying, "We're in this together," and Ysabel's looking away, down, out into the aisle, at the back of the seats before them, and, "I trust you," she says. "Implicitly."

"Okay," says Jo.

"Yes," says Ysabel. "It's okay."

Harsh light from the desk lamp catches here and there a curl or slice of flesh along the length of her, one leg stockinged, one leg bare, black lace still taut about her hips, tucked under a roll of her belly, bare breasts lolling. The nests of her hair undone, braids and ribbons spread out along the linoleum, spangles clattering as she turns her head, lifts a hand, the heel of it rubbing her eyes, then the palm of it her mouth, then her fingers scrubbing at the sticky sheen that's smeared about her chin and cheeks. "Hello?" she says, a shell of a word. Sitting up under that enormous photograph of a hamburger.

Over the counters the menu boards are empty and dark. Behind them she steps gingerly between rows of long-dead ovens and griddles coated with a thick rime of greasy dust. "Hello?" A wrenching croak of metal, a knock-knock-knock of pipes, a gushing splash of water. In the gloom at the back of the kitchen he's ghostly by a broad deep sink, splashing his face, his narrow chest, under his arms. Sweeping his black hair back he sees her, stops, lowers his hands. Waiting. She steps closer, hugging herself. "It smells rank in here," she says.

He reaches for a wrist, peels her arm free, pulls her to him and she lets go of herself to swallow him suddenly in a fierce hug. His hair falling over hers as he kisses the top of her head. "My phone says, it's like three o'clock? But I don't know morning or afternoon?" Her words muffled. She lifts her head to look up at him. "But it also says it's the eleventh? It's all fucked up. We haven't been here for like two days, have we?"

"I don't know."

"Dad didn't try to call. Which doesn't mean anything or anything."

"Your father."

"Yeah," she says, leaning back, her hair clattering, chiming. "Bet you, you didn't know it was, statutory." He frowns, and she says in a rush, "It's not like you care I'm sure or anything because, it's like you're a vampire, right?" His frown sharpens. "Not that you *are* a vampire, of course not, you're not. I have no idea what you are. But it's *like* a, a vampire? Maybe?"

"Should I kill you now?" he says, and she laughs wobbily. "No," she says. "You aren't going to do that. You never were."

"Stay," he says, his hands on her shoulders, smoothing her tangles of ribbons and braids.

"What, here?" Stepping back from him out from under his hands, looking about the darkened kitchen. "Josh always said this place was a shooting gallery."

"Stay here, with me." His hands on her hips now, pulling her close again.

"What about," she says, her hands on his hips now, "what about your enemy?" Looking down at her thumb, stroking the dulled scar across his belly.

"What about her." He shrugs. He kisses her, but he stops, rears up and back from her lips and he's frowning again, and then he licks her mouth with exaggerated care. "Sloppy," he says. "A sloppy, greedy girl."

"Yeah," she says. Her fingers settling about his lengthening cock. "Whatever, whatever it was, last night was the best – the best – "

"What," he says. "What is it?"

She shakes her head and squeezes him and biting her lip looks up at him again and says, quietly, precisely, "You son of a bitch."

"Oh," he says, "oh no, Gloria Monday – I am the Mooncalfe; I am motherless."

Outlandishly puffy running shoes strapped and gussetted, spotlessly white, churning the big flat pedals of an elliptical trainer, fingerless bicycle gloves on the trainer's walking poles, blue and white headphones cupping his ears. He isn't looking out at anything in particular, not the television hanging over the balcony railing, not the room below filled with the creak of cables and the clang of weights, the grunts of effort, squeaking shoes, slaps against mats. He has *no idea* how bad it is out there! yells the bald bearded man on the television. He has *no idea!* Pounding a glass table littered with paper. I have talked with the heads of almost every single one of these firms in the last seventy-two hours and he has *no idea* how bad it is out there! Stop Trading, says the red sign at the bottom of the screen, above a constant stream of numbers and acronyms. Roland leans back his pace quickening his breathing slow, regular, deeply in through his nose and out in gusts from his mouth. A red-tipped cane's lifted up by his shoulder wobbling swinging missing, poking a can of his headphones, skewing it from his ear, a soaring burst of violins leaking from it. He jerks back to one side, hands and feet stopping suddenly, a sigh from deep within the machine. The woman standing there holding the cane has a floppy black hat pulled low over her yellow hair. "Hanson?" she says. He's lowering his headphones, settling them about his neck.

"You were running backwards," she says. He steps from the pedals. His hands on his hips he tilts his head to either side, stretching his neck. She's rooting around the pockets of her rain-colored pea coat with her free hand. "You're a goddamn fool," she says.

"You'd know best."

"Was that – a joke?" Her free hand a fist tugged from a pocket. "You need to signal them better." Her fist held up between them opens with a turn of the wrist to reveal a little toy car, silver and green. "Go on," she says, the brim of that black hat lifting. "Take it." Her cheeks clench twitching milky eyes. "I won't have it on me anymore. Bad for business."

He plucks the car from her hand. "Business," he says.

"This ridiculous misapprehension of Southeast's, that we're in cahoots. No one will deal with me, Chariot."

"He's apologized for that, Miss Cheney."

"Not loudly enough." The brim of that hat dips again to hide her eyes. "Not so anyone who matters might hear."

"Who's repeating the slander?" says Roland. "Give me a name. I'll see to them myself."

Her mouth twists sourly. "Not a one will deal with me, knight."

He turns, scoops up a towel from the railing, mops his brow. "And you, naturally, assumed." He drapes the towel over his shoulder. "Perhaps no one will deal, witch, because no one has anything to deal with." He moves past her but that cane thwacks against the floor blocking his step. "Well?" he says, looking down at its red tip. "Have I told you something else you should already have known?"

"Maybe no one else is stupid enough to tell me," says Miss Cheney. She pulls the cane back, sweeps it to tock against the base of the elliptical trainer. "Something is going on," she says under the brim of that hat. "*Some*one's in cahoots."

"It doesn't concern me," says Roland, stepping past.

"No?" Miss Cheney tocks her cane again. "Well, hell," she says, as he walks away. "I'll be sure to miss you all, when you're gone!"

A steep and narrow flight of stairs. High green walls to either side painted over so many times they still seem slickly wet, all edges and corners rounded and soft. Jo on the landing halfway up in her black leather jacket, a limp buff-colored duffel slung from her shoulder, a long narrow cardboard box strapped to the side of it. She's looking up to the head of the flight, a white hall, dark double doors, a frosted glass fanlight above them lit from within.

"Jo?" says Ysabel, a couple steps below, white boots and parka.

"Looks like he's in," says Jo, and she ducks her head and goes on up.

A wide deep room the far end lost in shadows. Mirrors line one wall floor to ceiling. The dark floor's marked in a dozen spots with Xes of blue masking tape. A little man in a T-shirt and sweatpants, wiry arms and legs at odds with his barrel chest, steps smoothly from one splash of light to the next, the sword in his hand sweeping slowly a gleam from low at his side almost brushing the floor up and around over his head settling arm out gently bent hand supine at eye level pinching the hilt between thumb and forefinger. His other arm back and up for balance ends in a metal hook. Sinking slowly into a long low lunge that hook sweeping back clacking absently as he reaches his full extension. By the half-open door Ysabel behind her Jo watches as he recovers, angling his blade through precise parries to each of the four quarters, his hook lowering, feet coming together, blade upright before his downturned face, a brief salute. "Two weeks," he says, snapping the blade down, a flick of his wrist, stalking across the room to lay the sword on a rolled-up mat next to a half-dozen others, all of them tipped with blunt black rubber caps.

"Yeah, well," says Jo, "stuff happened." Lowering the duffel, the box resting upright before her. "I've got the full two hundred bucks for the month, even though, you know. Two weeks." He turns, stroking his neck under his salt-and-pepper Van Dyke. Looks at her standing there, hands folded together on the top of that box. "We have to find new jobs though," she says, "so we might need to talk about the schedule, figure out something if it's not night work, I guess."

He steps quickly toward them, leaning forward, peering at Jo's face. "You've been in another fight," he says, and her hand leaps to the yellowing bruise along her temple. "Sort of," she says.

"With that?" he says. "May I see it?"

Ysabel steps up behind Jo as she opens the flaps of the box and pulls up the sheathed sword by its beaten metal throat the color of thunderclouds. The hilt of it simple and straight, wrapped in dulled wire, quillions clean straight bars almost as long together as the hilt, and over and around them a glittering net of wire meeting in thick worked steel knots all gathered together in a single cord swooping up to the great silvery clout of the pommel.

Vincent lifts his hand, stops, looks up at Jo, his mouth open to ask a question. She nods. He takes the hilt in his hand and with a faintly scraping ring of steel against leather and metal draws the sword up and up and out. Jo holding the plain black scabbard still in one hand, the other holding the box. Ysabel her hand on Jo's.

He tilts the blade, sweeps it, swings it wide, "Nice," he says. "Well-balanced. Light, but that's good, for you. He hasn't lost his touch." Hilt up lifting the sword until the tip of it wavers just over Jo's hand guiding it into the scabbard, slowly sinking it home. "A damn sight better than that ratty épée."

"Uh," says Jo, and then all at once, "I lost that sword."

"Did you," says Vincent Erne.

"Along with my favorite jacket? I'm sorry, I'm sorry, it was stupid, I left it in the bathroom of a – "

"That's a pretty good jacket you've got right there," he says, and then he walks out of the room.

"Shit," says Jo, and "Mr. Erne?" says Ysabel, as they turn to follow him, Jo scooping up the duffel and the box. "Mr. Erne." Heading out of the wide deep room down the hall to an office next door where he's standing by a long table lost under haphazard stacks of books and piles of paper, pouring a slug of sooty whiskey into a coffee mug. A poster on the wall above him says The Loyal Subject. "For the love you bear my mother, Mr. Erne," says Ysabel, "would you consent to taking up the training of Jo Maguire once again."

"Bore," says Vincent, and he takes a drink from the mug.

"Really," says Ysabel. "The regard, then, in which I'm sure – "

"For the two hundred bucks a month," he says. "But at eleven o'clock in the morning. Now get the hell out of – what do *you* want?"

A confusion of turning in the doorway to the office. In the hallway a woman in navy coveralls and cap, a grey cardigan obscuring the nametag clipped to her breast pocket. Holding a clipboard and a plain white envelope. "Message for the Gallowglas?" she says.

And after a moment Jo says, "Yeah I, uh, who's it, what?"

"Who's it from?" says Ysabel.

The woman in the coveralls looks at the envelope, turns it over, looks at the clipboard. "Frank, ah, Frankie Reichart?"

GEORGE'S, IT SAYS – TEA & PEPPERS
SOMETHING PRETTY SPECIAL – A TASTE

GEORGE'S, IT SAYS, in red and yellow letters in a curve across the big front window. Shoes Repaired. A worktable behind a counter's mounded high with shoes of every shape and color. On a stool before it Frankie in a bulky green fleece pullover, dark hair washed and brushed and tied back, cheeks shadowed with soft black stubble. "Just a, just a second," he's saying, a blue and brown running shoe in one hand, a square-toed black Oxford in the other. "Gordon," he says. "How's this?" Strings and woodwinds cycle through a somberly repetitive phrase from the clock radio on the worktable by the pile of shoes. The old man in a pale green chamois shirt standing next to him takes the shoes in his hands and looks them over, tilting them this way, that. Nodding. "You're starting to get the hang of this," he says. The wall behind the worktable's lined with wooden shelves partitioned into regular cubbyholes each just large enough for a pair of shoes. Running his hand along a shelf, tap-tapping, stopping to slip both shoes inside an empty slot.

"Okay," says Frankie, turning back to the counter.

"The hell, Frankie," says Jo.

"Yeah," says Frankie, "been a weird few weeks, I guess."

"Anyone like some tea?" says Gordon. Jo shakes her head without looking away from Frankie, who says, "No, thanks."

"Something herbal?" says Ysabel, unzipping her parka.

"I'll put a kettle on," says Gordon, ducking through a curtained doorway. Two voices high and rich soar from the clock radio, di-ek eni awik kher ka-ek, shesepi su ankhi yemef. "So," says Frankie, standing, leaning his elbows on the counter. "There's this guy. He's coming for you."

"Who," says Jo.

"One of the ones who grabbed me that time, for that crazy, thing? At the mall?"

"For the Duke," says Jo.

"Which of them," says Ysabel.

"He had," says Frankie, "long black hair? And," gesturing toward his face, "a patch now, like a pirate. And he was always wearing, it wasn't like a kilt, it was like a skirt?"

"The Mooncalfe," says Ysabel.

"And like he never wears shoes?"

"How did you," says Jo, and then, "I told you to stay away from this shit."

"He *grabbed* me," says Frankie. "*Again.* Right out of Timmo's fucking car. He had a *sword.*"

"What were you doing in Timmo's," Jo starts to say.

"He's after *you.* He grabbed me to talk about *you.* He took me – you know that abandoned Burger King? On Burnside, right downtown? He, I guess he lives there? Anyway." His hands scrubbing themselves, grimy thumbnail scraping at a patch of grime. "I wasn't gonna. I mean it was, it couldn't have been more than a couple of days, but it was more than a week?" Fingertips rubbing an old scrape along his knuckles. "It was weird." His hands spring apart, clench into fists, one of them beats the countertop. "He had to get you before somebody else could, but when we left it was too late? It had already happened? It was like, after Hallowe'en, and it honestly I swear it was only a couple of days. And I wasn't gonna tell him a motherfucking thing, but," and he looks away.

"Frankie," says Jo.

"I told him about Billy, Jo. That's what, he liked that. He was gonna, he *is* gonna come after you somehow with Billy. I'm sorry."

"He already did," says Jo.

"I'm so *fucking* sorry – " Frankie looks up, blinking. "He already," he says. "*Shit.*" Pounding the counter again. "I called," he says. "I swear I called and called."

"I got a new phone," says Jo, as Ysabel says, "She got a new phone."

"I even called where it was you worked and the guy there, whatsisname, told me you weren't working there and I told him to tell you how to find me because it was *important,*" his hands come up, fingers splayed, to weigh that word in the air there between them, "and he said, you know, he'd do what he could, but." Frankie shrugs, shakes his head, slumps away, looking toward the back of the little shop. "That's when Gordon said he had people who could get a message to you, any time, anywhere. At least," and he sits up, and he sighs, "at least I can do this much," reaching into the pockets of his khaki pants as a stentorous fanfare unfolds itself from the clock radio. He drops with a rustle and a clatter some wadded-up bills, some coins, a couple of quarters, a dime, some pennies. He smoothes out the banknotes, a couple of tens, a five, a couple of ones. "Here," he says, pushing it across the counter at Jo.

"This is all your money, isn't it," she says.

"I'm doing okay now," he says. "I owe you fifty bucks. Now it's, now it's twenty-two and change. Please, Jo. You can take it. I'll get you the rest."

She slowly collects the bills, folds them together, scoops the coins off the counter into her hand. "You gonna go home now?" she says, and he shakes his head. "This is like," he says, "this is like a step up, you know? Over the last few weeks. I got a place to sleep, and shower, I got some clothes, and I'm, I'm working for all this, you know?" Looking back at the mound of shoes on the worktable. "And I'm not seeing Timmo. He can't get at me here." Turning back to Jo and Ysabel. "Gordon rolls pretty fucking deep. You wouldn't know it but I bet it's almost as deep as you got, these days."

"Deeper, I'm sure," says Ysabel, as Jo leans over the counter toward Frankie, who lurches back, then, shaking his head a little leans in toward her. She kisses him, lightly, and then shaking her head when he tries to kiss her back she straightens, steps back from the counter. "Thank you," she says.

"How did you end up here?" says Ysabel. "The Mooncalfe wouldn't have left you with a rabbit, I'm sure."

"He didn't?" says Frankie. "He, I mean he, *traded* me. To Linesse? I mean, not to Linesse, to her, like her boss, for, for this – "

"For Billy," says Ysabel.

"I guess?" says Frankie. "Yeah."

"Linesse," says Ysabel. "You're sure?"

"Tall woman? Grey hair? She lives in this abandoned car by this abandoned gas station way the fuck out in the middle of nowhere by the airport." Looking back at the curtained doorway, suddenly quiet, "I guess her and Gordon used to have a thing? Anyway. She left me here."

"We should go," says Ysabel to Jo.

"What about your tea?" says Frankie.

"He didn't go to make tea," says Ysabel. Jo's hefting her duffel bag, the narrow box awkward in the little shop. "Sure he did," says Frankie, as Ysabel's saying, "He didn't want to overhear business that doesn't concern him."

"Well you don't have to," says Frankie, as they turn toward the door, the window with its curve of letters. "You'll come back, right? Any time. I mean twenty-two bucks, right?"

The bell rings as Jo opens the door. "Keep it," she says.

A cramped kitchen, the sink and refrigerator and a bit of wood-topped counter beneath a window blank and black, a couple of gleaming ovens set in the wall beside them, a butcher's block in the middle with a couple of gas burners set in the top. Jessie in a loose white men's dress shirt and grey yoga pants slices a couple of red peppers into long thin strips, her blond hair pulled back in a knot held by a couple of red chopsticks. On the burner beside her chopped onions simmer in a cast-iron pan. One of the two doors swings open suddenly and a girl all knees and elbows bops into the kitchen to the beat of whatever's playing through pink headphones printed with a mouthless cartoon cat. Jessie stops slicing the pepper to watch the girl dance around the butcher's block in her cropped white tank top, her underwear festooned with rainbow-colored ponies. The girl opens the refrigerator, bends over, long straight dark hair swaying, Jessie staring over her shoulder expressionless at those ponies bouncing back and forth. "Son of a bitch," says the Duke, limping through the other swinging door, "son of a goat-fucking bitch." Tightening the belt of his striped robe of purples and browns and golds. The girl backs out of the fridge, knocks it shut with her hip, a tall purple and blue can in her hand. Four Loko, it says on the side. She presses up against the Duke, hiking up on her toes to kiss his cheek, takes a deep swig from the can, arm up, vamping and bopping back out the door through which she'd come. "Smells great, babe," says the Duke.

Jessie starts slicing the pepper again. "Housewives," she says, "had this trick: they'd take an onion just before their husbands got home from work and chop it and start it frying in some butter or just chuck the whole thing into a hot oven. Let it make the kitchen smell like she'd been cooking all day just for him, not lying around on the chaise eating bon-bons. Then she could tart up some canned tomato soup with a splash of sherry and some chives or something. Some Mrs. Dash. Like he'd know any better." She scoops up the pepper strips and dumps them into the pan with the onions.

"I got people," says the Duke, "there are restaurants," as Jessie's saying, "I *like* to cook," and the Duke shrugs and leaning on the butcher's block steps close to her, an arm settling about her waist as she stirs peppers and onions together. "So what is it you're cooking?" he says.

"Chakchouka," says Jessie. "It's North African." She reaches for a big yellow can that says Cento San Marzano.

"I got that thing with Song Wu in about an hour."

"It'll be ready in fifteen, twenty minutes," says Jessie, clamping a can opener on the can. "You'll eat it in five, tops." Opening the can with savage twists of the key. "Does she *have* to stay here?"

"What, who, Lauren?" Stepping back from Jesse. "She can't go to Seattle, babe. Jasmine's not about to move here. What am I supposed to do, kick her out to the curb?"

"She could put on some clothes," says Jessie, slopping tomatoes from the can onto the peppers and onions.

"You're one to talk," says the Duke. "Usually."

"I get paid to do that," says Jessie. "By you. Is she getting paid?"

"Okay," says the Duke, "see, I know for a fact that this is deflection, and whatever it is hasn't got a blasted thing to do with Lauren because the very idea is fucking ludicrous and we both recognize that fact, so maybe you put down the spatula and take a deep breath and tell me what's the fucking problem."

Jessie puts the spatula down, picks up a little yellow bottle with an iguana on the label, shakes out droplets of sauce over the tomatoes and peppers and onions. "Get me some eggs," she says. "Bottom shelf." And as the Duke turns and opens the fridge she says, "Who fucked the goat this time?"

"What?" he says. "Oh. Roland. The Chariot. Shows up unannounced, picks a fight with Gaveston, bulls his way up here. Has the cheek to demand I tell him everything I know about that attack on the Princess, where it happened, what I know, has the gall, the fucking *gall*," shaking his head, "to use the Queen's name. Comes this close," holding up forefinger and thumb pinched together, "to accusing *me* outright of masterminding this thing I nearly popped *him* for. The Chariot, I wouldn't call him subtle or sophisticated, not really in the job description, but this, this is taking density to a whole new cake. Jessie. Hey. Jessie." She's scooping little pockets in the simmering tomatoes and peppers and cracking an egg into each and she doesn't look up at the Duke as she does so. "Whatever happens," he says, "with me and the Gallowglas, I'm gonna be King come the turning of the year. Ysabel's gonna be Queen. And her and me, you know, we ain't exactly what you would call compatible. Now, *you* and me," and Jessie looks up at that, the last egg uncracked in her hand, "you and me, we've got something, ups and downs, it's, I think it's pretty special." She turns away, cracks open that last egg, lets it drop in the pan. "Maybe right now you're in a place, you'd rather be with a girl than a guy, which is fine, I can definitely appreciate that, and nothing's different because of that. Not a thing has to change. Whatever happens, the next month or so, the Princess likes you. A lot. She's still gonna like you when she's Queen."

Jessie's picked up a pot lid and now she looks at the Duke and, shaking her head slowly, blowing out a fluttery little laugh, she says, "Take my wife. Please."

He turns away, rubbing his forehead. "I'm just saying," he says. "Play your cards right."

"There are no goddamn cards, Leo," she says. "That's the problem. Nobody else is playing." She twists a knob, lowering the flame. "They have to poach for like ten minutes. Go put on a shirt or whatever it is you're gonna do for Wu Song."

"The Five-Oh?" says Gloria. "With the beef."

"She'll have the vegetable patty," says Orlando.

"The hell I will," says Gloria. "Five-Oh. Beef."

"That is disgusting."

"I'll let you buy me dinner," she says, "but you can't tell me what I'm gonna eat."

"She'll have the vegetable patty," says Orlando. He tugs a napkin from the neat stack under a burger-shaped paperweight. "I will also have the vegetable patty."

"Sir," says the burly guy behind the counter, his hairy forearms dark with blurred tattoos. "She doesn't want it. I'm not about to make for her a burger she doesn't want."

"Besides, those things are totally foul," says Gloria to Orlando. "Genetically modified industrial soy paste that's been soaked in additives and preservatives." He's folding the napkin and again, closing it between palms pressed together. "Place like this," she says, "the beef's a much better choice."

"Grass-fed, hormone-free," says the burly guy. "We source it ourselves and hand-form the patties. What'll it be?"

Orlando twists one hand against the other and holds up a crisply folded twenty. "I will have the totally foul vegetable patty. She will have," and he sighs, and hands the bill to the burly guy, "whatever she wants."

"Just a veggie burger? You want anything else on that?"

Orlando says, "Ketchup," then, "Keep it," as the burly guy starts to make change.

"I totally get the thing? The vegetarian thing?" says Gloria as they step back from the food cart, white-wrapped sandwiches in hand. Dead leaves crunch on the brick sidewalk beneath her thick-soled black boots, his bare feet. A line of food carts cheek by jowl down the block in the wanly dying afternoon light, and little knots of people here and there peering at signs and menu boards that say Sabria's Arabic and Philly Cheesesteaks, La Jarochita, Bulkogi Fusion and Smokin' Pig, Real Taste of India. People sitting on benches here and there, waiting for food, poking at clear plastic boxes and cardboard boxes with white plastic forks, peeling foil from wraps and slices of pizza. Orlando in his long blue skirt and a shapeless grey jacket sits abruptly on one of the benches by a sandwich board that says Dabtong Thupka, and a heavyset man in a tweed jacket stands suddenly at the other end of the bench, a paper cup of soup in one hand, chopsticks in the other, and shaking his head walks quickly away. "I was a vegetarian sophomore year," says Gloria, sitting herself next to Orlando. "Vegan, actually, mostly. Except I could never stand soy milk, in my coffee?" Her hair done up in its two great hanks again over either shoulder, her lips once more painted carefully black, a long black coat with clear glass buttons over her black high-waisted gown. "I gained like ten pounds? Which, and I started reading about factory farming, and processed food, and exactly what is in *those* things," pointing to his burger. Her hands in those black and white striped arm socks. "So even though I mean the guy had like a heart attack, or something, I have always," and looking at her own burger she chews her lip around a laugh, "been about the excess, so I went total Atkins? Meat only, and lettuce sandwiches, and I lost like five pounds?" She takes a big bite. "But I missed bread," she says, and swallows. "I missed the carbonara which, my dad makes it, with pancetta from the City Market? Up on Twenty-first?" She looks up then, at the lights coming on in the food carts, work lamps and heat lamps and strings of Christmas lights, at the deepening shadows blue and purple from the buildings that tower behind them. "It's really Friday, isn't it," she says. "I was gone. I was gone from the world for two whole days, just – " She shakes her head. She takes another bite of her burger.

"That is disgusting," says Orlando.

"This?" says Gloria.

"Blood, and death."

"Have a taste," she says, holding her hand up, fingertips smeared and shining. He draws back. "I've tasted blood," he says.

"It isn't blood," she says. "You vampire. It's pineapple juice and teriyaki sauce and meat juice and it's very, very good. Okay." Another big tearing bite of burger, chewing, swallowing, smacking her lips. Leaning close. "A taste." And she kisses him, and shuddering he opens his mouth on hers and his hands come up to her shoulders and hold there for a moment as he kisses her back before suddenly pushing them both apart. He stands abruptly. Without looking he arcs his wadded white wrapper into the garbage can on the other side of the bench. "Come," he says, taking her free hand.

"What," she says, "where are we," as he pulls her to her feet, "going?"

"The future," he says.

AN APPLE, PEELED AND CORED – TALKING SHOP
THWARTING MR. SOGGE – THE ROSE GARDEN

AN APPLE PEELED AND CORED and split into wedges on a plain white paper plate, the peel of it in one long ragged strand looped on the rug. A fat red candle slumped in on itself on another paper plate, guttering in a pool of melted wax. A black and silver matchbox that says Boxxes in angular slashes of letters about a stylized eye. Olive pits with bits of flesh still clinging, two cheese rinds black and pale red wax, a torn heel of crusty bread. Dregs of dark red wine in a couple of juice glasses, one printed with a cartoon bear in a spacesuit, one a frog in Lincoln scarlet, holding a bow. Over the scratchy hiss of needle on vinyl from some hidden corner a chorus of woodwinds lofts hauntingly simple notes atop gently giguing strings. By the candle a threadbare little rabbit on a leash of string noses a couple of empty yellowed gel caps. "An O?" says the woman sitting on the rug. She scoops the rabbit into her crazy-quilted lap, skirts lapping skirts in wool and watered silk and taffeta and corduroy, her legs in mismatched socks splayed among the paper plates and crumbs. "None for you, Jasper," she says. Sitting back against a baroquely plump sofa, her hair rustling, her hair loose about her shoulders, tumbling in coils and curls down over her grubby orange rain shell, her hair pooling in slippery hanks along the rug and the bare floor. The woman curled in a corner of the sofa behind her says, "Q," as she takes up handfuls of that hair in rhythmic, rolling strokes, and little puffs of light spark and eddy to settle again. She wears a baggy sweater the color of flour, and on the sofa beside her a floppy black hat beside a confetti-colored patchwork cap.

"Q?" The woman on the floor leans forward, tugging her hair free in a tumble of light. "There's no little thingie." Peering at the loop of apple peel. "Is that a descender? The little thingie?"

"O for whom?" says the woman on the sofa. "Oubliette? Outlaw?"

"Out of Outlaw." The woman on the floor settles back against the sofa.

"But there is a Queen." The woman on the sofa starts stroking that hair again. If her milky eyes are looking at anything, it's the counter at the other end of the long and narrow room, the dim lamp, the beads of oil trickling regularly down the threaded curtain hanging from its shade.

"It *might* be a Q," says the woman on the floor. "If everything's otherwhich."

"Isn't it?" says the woman on the sofa. "Honey's gone sour, sugar's all but gone."

"*Don't,*" says the woman on the floor, shivering, heels kicking. "Say things like that. We're not supposed to look at things like that."

"What you mean we, kemo sabe," says the woman on the sofa. She plunges her hands more deeply in that hair, and clouds of sparks light her dour moue. "It's affecting business, yours and mine. Let's see what can be seen. We don't have to tell." Up to the elbows in all that hair. The woman sitting on the floor begins to moan, her eyelids fluttering, rocking with the strokes, and her hands shape something in the air. "The dark," she croons, "the dark of the year…"

"I'm not a rube," mutters the woman on the sofa. Then as the moaning redoubles she pulls the woman on the floor closer. "But maybe you are?"

"Oak to oak and never a fig of holly," says the woman on the floor, gasping, opening her eyes. "A summer and a summer," she says flatly, "the glory and the fall. Hats."

"That doesn't make any," says the woman on the sofa as rabbit spilling scrabbling from her lap the woman on the floor lurches for the confetti-colored cap. *"Hats!"* she says.

The sound of a gong as Orlando pushes the door open, holding it for Gloria in her long black coat twisting and turning to look at all the junk piled high in the foyer. "This way," he says, leading her through the pinched doorway to the long and narrow room beyond, lit by a candle and a lamp and what light's left to seep through tall and dusty windows. Two women side by side on a baroquely plump sofa under a gaudy tapestry, a dancer in veils and spangles who holds aloft a platter laden with a bearded head. "Your pardon, Ulyssa," says Orlando. "We can come back."

"No, no," says the woman in the floppy black hat. "Just a little shop-talk. What can we, ah," as the other woman in her confetti-colored cap leaps to her feet kicking over one of the juice glasses with a clink. "O for Orlando!" she cries, skipping over the rug past Gloria to circle about him, her hands over her mouth. "Oh of course of course of course of course of course!"

"You've met the Thrummy-cap," says the woman on the sofa.

"You clear the path! You set the stage!"

"You have a question?" says the woman on the sofa, her smile a wry small thing under that floppy brim. "Ask her. She's in a generous mood."

"Gloria," says Orlando, as the Thrummy-cap bounces before him, clapping her hands, looking from him to Gloria not quite saying something. "What," says Orlando, "becomes of us, if she stays?"

The Thrummy-cap stops dead, hands clasped.

"Oh," says Miss Cheney on the sofa.

"Such," says the Thrummy-cap, "happiness," a sprig of hair escaped from her cap and coiled along her cheek. "Such joy. Three days or a day, it's hard to say, but then!" Stepping suddenly from him to her, gripping Gloria's coat, the scarecrow colors of her skirts and cap stark against the sleek black bulk of it. "A best last night indeed," she says, and "Get *back!*" shrieks Gloria, "you little," pushing her away.

"And there's the holly!" cries the Thrummy-cap. "Sprung where it's not wanted to strangle the oak a-borning, and then it's snow in every April ever after."

"If," says Orlando, "she stays." His voice a husk.

"I'm right *here,*" says Gloria as the Thrummy-cap cocks her head, cap shifting with a slithery weight. "Don't worry," she says to Orlando, then turning to Miss Cheney, *"don't.* My sweetie's getting lunch today. It's his turn! I forgot I set it all up weeks ago. It's going to be okay!"

The city, spread over a table that dominates the conference room. A broad curl of blue river painted along one side, a little white boat between white foam core bridges. Blank white buildings jumble the bank of it, a tall cluster down at one end, lowering toward the middle, a low tower higher than the rest at the other end. A man half-bent over it, a thick shock of unruly white hair, a white sack suit and a shining white shirt and a wide white knit tie. He looks up as the glass door to the conference room swings shut, and his face is quite young under all that hair. The man by the door is short and thick, a scruff of grey beard about his chin, his white hair cropped close about the back of his head. A dark windowpane jacket over a heathery hoodie that says Oregon Ducks in green and yellow letters. "Rosie says I ought to talk to you," he says.

"I have a proposition for you, Mr. Sogge," says the man in the white suit.

"You're gonna proposition me, call me Rudy. You work for Pinabel." He stays there, by the door, and the man in the white suit folds his arms and says, "I've consulted for him, yes. But I'm not here in that capacity today. You don't like to share, do you, Rudy."

Rudy puts a hand on the back of one of the big brown leather chairs, wheels it away from the table. "Let's assume," he says as he sits, "I'm not gonna answer any rhetorical questions, so how about cutting them and any dramatic pauses and other bits of theatrical business out of the presentation, okay?" Closing his eyes.

"I-Óisqis and Iô'i," says the man in the white suit. "Pah-to and Wy'east, La-wa-la-clough, the Loowit. Tanmahawis. You have no idea who they were, of course not, why would you. They were murdered long before your parents were born, before your great-grandfather ever thought to plat out Hoffmann's Addition. These people were – *gods* is not too strong a word, I trust? The very mountains about us, the rivers, the salmon and the trees, who were yet people, that you might speak with as easily as I might speak with you." Rudy snorts at that, his eyes still closed. The man in the white suit nods. "Oh, the names live on – there's pizza parlors and blues bands named for some dim echo of one or the other of them. You might even speak with them yet, though their voices are quite dim now, hard to hear, and the effort requires years of study, and ruinous quantities of bourbon and pot." Rudy his eyes still closed begins to frown at that. "A vacuum was left, is the important point, the takeaway, as I believe you put it. And nature abhors a vacuum." The man in the white suit turns then, looking out over the city on the table. "She's been abhorring this vacuum with a vengeance for decades, now. Half this state's from somewhere else? Three-quarters of this city? And somewhere else is very, very wide. You're thwarted, Mr. Sogge."

Rudy opens his eyes at that.

"Your disastrous partnership with Pinabel in Southwest. The way he's dragged his feet on that charming ærial tram," gesturing toward a pylon at one end of the city, in the cluster of white towers there by the river. "The Perrys, in Northwest, preventing the destruction of the Lovejoy Ramp, stalling the Brewery Blocks," gesturing toward high-rise blocks by one of the bridges at the other end of the table. "The Urban Restoration Squad, and Michael Lake, though of course you won't remember him. The Fox Tower," touching a high white block in the middle of downtown, and Rudy says, "That isn't mine."

"No," says the man in the white suit, "but you'd still see the benefit if more than half its square footage were leased. Here, across this park that might yet one day be finished, your Park Avenue West," and he lifts the next tower, a tall slim thing, entirely from the table, "have you done more yet than dig the basement? No?" He tosses the block to Rudy, who catches it deftly. "For more than a year. These impediments have all of them one thing in common: a person, a singular individual. A girl. In a few weeks I shall remove her from these various considerations."

"Remove," says Rudy. "You mean, you're talking about – "

"Is that a deal-breaker?"

Rudy's looking down at the blank white tower in his hands. He pushes himself out of the chair, leans over the city, carefully slots the tower back into place.

"There will then be a vacuum," says the man in the white suit. "It will be abhorred. That abhorrence, Mr. Sogge, is something you might be positioned to capitalize upon."

"Thought I told you to call me Rudy."

The man in the white suit shrugs. "I feel it's best we keep our relationship strictly professional, for now."

Rudy says, "Okay then." Leaning both hands on the river. "What is it you want."

"I? Illimitable power, of course. Wealth beyond the dreams of avarice." He reaches into his white suit coat and pulls out a mirror-bright lighter and a clear cellophane packet wrapped about cigarettes in plain white paper. "Immortality, there's a no-brainer. But at the moment? At the moment, Mr. Sogge, I'm dying for a smoke."

"Knock yourself out," says Rudy.

"So that was a completely wasted day," says Jo swaying, one hand hanging from the strap above, one holding tightly the duffel down by her feet, the narrow box awkward in the crowd. Ysabel pressed close, holding the same strap. "You made your peace with Erne," she says.

"Only cost two hundred bucks," says Jo.

"We now know who," says Ysabel.

"And I have no idea what the fuck to do with that. The Mooncalfe?"

"I feel as if I've won a bet." Ysabel swallows and closing her eyes lays her forehead against Jo's shoulder. "I think I now see what it is you see in him," she says.

"Him which?" says Jo. "You mean Frankie?"

Ysabel nods. "He'd be the Duke, if he could."

"That," says Jo, "that is so wrong I don't know where to, I mean, that isn't *even* wrong. Shit." Something buzzes. Letting go of the duffel, leaning away from Ysabel swaying she pulls a glassy black phone from her jacket, stroking its surface with a thumb. "It's that girl, with the place off Glisan? We could, we could probably catch a bus directly from the next stop – "

"Jo," says Ysabel, wincing, clutching.

"Hey," says Jo, tucking the phone away. "Hey." A hand on Ysabel's shoulder, Ysabel's arm clung about her waist. "It's just one more errand. We've *got* to find a new place. Hey." Ysabel eyes squeezed shut lowers her head, pressing against Jo. "You're tired," says Jo, "we're both – "

"I need," says Ysabel thickly, "fresh air, I need to get off – "

"Yeah, okay," says Jo, "okay."

"Rose Garden," says a loud recorded voice, and all about them people stirring, collecting bags and packages, resettling coats and scarves, hats, nudging each other, looking out the dark windows. "Doors to my left. Puertas a mi izquierda."

A wide plaza brightly lit, a tangle of intersections, streets and rail lines, crosswalks, stoplights, off up a low rise that way past a scruff of immature trees the immensely spot-lit bulk of a coliseum and under its pointed curl of a roof a sign that says Rose Garden. There a low freeway overpass, the lights of trucks and cars at standstills yearning north and south, another MAX train at the stop under the overpass, a line of busses idling each with the same Cricket wireless minutes ad on the side. Across the street behind them a wall of silos lights flaring from the tops an enormous billboard plastered along it, hands in black and white reaching up and up, Rise with us, it says, Portland Trailblazers. Away behind that the unlit towers of a bridge over the river, looming against the red-black sky. Crowds flowing from the one MAX stop to the other, heading up along sidewalks to the coliseum, over that way to the busses, waiting at the corners here and there to cross this street or that. "Fresh air," says Jo. "You want to wait here? Not that there's anywhere here to hang out or anything. Walk home, over the Steel Bridge? How's your – "

"Jo," says Ysabel, pointing.

Looking back toward the other train small figures of people getting on and off it, the small figure of a man there among them, silver piping on his green tracksuit flashing in the streetlight under the overpass, bulbous headphones blue and white clamped over his white-blond hair. "I thought he wasn't," Jo starts to say.

"We have to go," says Ysabel, and a bell rings, and with a rising, grinding hum the train beside them pulls away, clank-chunking over a rail junction. "Now. Please, Jo. Before he sees me."

"What's he doing here," says Jo, looking back over her shoulder as she takes Ysabel's hand. Away across the plaza Roland's looking along his train, the platform, the crowds about him. "We could head down the other end, out of sight. Wait for the next train there."

"Which is when?" says Ysabel, and then as Jo's saying, "Ten? Fifteen minutes?" she says "We have to *go,*" and over away across the plaza Roland's turning, heading toward them, but looking back, of to one side, at the line of busses.

"What the hell's he," Jo's saying, and Ysabel's saying, "I don't want to talk to him right now," and "Okay, yeah, okay," says Jo, and hand in hand they're headed for the crosswalk as the light changes. Ysabel starts across the street in and among the other with Jo dragged in her wake looking back and back, Roland, there's Roland, away from the busses now, the crowds, the lights, on the grass that slopes dimly up toward the coliseum. "The hell's he doing?" she mutters, slowing there in the middle of the street. "Jo!" cries Ysabel, pulling.

Roland looks up.

"Shit," says Jo, half-laughing as they half-run the rest of the way across the street, the walk don't walk sign counting down in orange numerals five, four, three, two. "Did he, did he see us," says Ysabel on the corner as traffic grunts and snorts into motion behind them.

"I don't know?" says Jo. "I can't see him anymore. He didn't wave or anything. What's he – "

"Jo," says Ysabel.

"Eastside," says Jo. "The Lloyd Center. That's where he was, shit. That night."

"Jo, please," says Ysabel.

"This is where that train finally stopped. Remember?" Jo points back to the MAX stop they'd left across the street. "That's what he's, why? Why would he, what's he after?"

"I don't *care,*" says Ysabel. "Let's just. Go. Please."

They set off across the next street as the numerals count down, four, three, two, one. Blocky yellow construction equipment behind a chain-link fence, a long banner hung there saying East Side Big Pipe – Working for Clean Rivers. The rush and roar of traffic beside them, the rumbling idle from the freeway overpass. Up a low rise and around a curve away from the coliseum, traffic thinning, a flock of bicycles clattering through the next intersection. The corner beyond a park, the ground sloping to a screen of trees and beyond the towers and lights of downtown, over across the river, and there before them the looming black shapes of trusses and girders and cables, red lights flashing from the tops of its towers. "We can lose him on the Esplanade," says Jo, and hand in hand they cross the street and head into the park down one of the paths that loop away from the sidewalk toward the trees.

As they pass from sight, up and around the curve past that banner hung from the chain-link fence comes Roland at an easy lope, headphones down about his neck.

A Long and Narrow Flight of Stairs
the Duel on the Bridge – One of her Many Names – If

A long and narrow flight of stairs angles down from the grey pedestrian bridge over the railroad tracks. A wide path heads off away along the riverbank, a branch of it there floating on pontoons, the snarling lanes of stalled traffic on the freeway overpass alongside it and above. Another path heads down to the dark bulk of the bridge, the bottom deck of it low over the water, railroad tracks and a footpath under an upper deck busy with cars, busses, a truck, a MAX train rumbling away toward the towers of downtown, lit up against the red-black sky. "Where do we," says Ysabel, "Jo, how do we," as they turn about at the base of those stairs. "How are we going to lose him?"

"I don't know?" says Jo, shrugging the duffel back up on her shoulder. "I thought there'd be more people. There's usually more people. If we," pointing, "just head over the bridge – "

"He'd see us," says Ysabel wincing, an arm about her belly. "All the way across he could see – "

"Are you okay?" says Jo, and Ysabel shakes her head quickly, and "What is it?" says Jo, and Ysabel shakes her head again. Jo takes her free hand. "It's the most direct way home. You want to go back up and catch a bus or a train? It'd be no better," pointing down the riverbank, "he could see us all the way along there, too, unless you want to squat under those bushes and hope he doesn't come down looking. Hell, maybe he's just on his way to Mississippi or something – "

"Princess!" cries Roland at the top of that flight of stairs, silver piping shining in the dusky streetlight.

"Well, hell," says Jo, as Ysabel tugging her hand heads for the bridge.

"Princess!" He's taking those stairs two at a time.

"The hell," says Jo, "are we running," and a metal plate on the bridge's footpath rings under their feet. *Please,* says Ysabel.

"Wait!" cries Roland, halfway down that long and angled flight. "Lady, wait!" At the bottom of those stairs. "We must speak!" Clanging over the metal plate, beating a tattoo against the brick-paved footpath. Jo looks quickly back to see Roland running from splash of light to splash of light the flare in his hand shining in the shadows and *"Shit,"* she says, letting go, turning, clawing the duffel from her shoulder, dropping to one knee, "Ysabel, *run!"* The box thumping and clattering as she fumbles at its flaps.

"No!" cries Roland, feet scraping to a stop, left foot forward in its spotlessly white outlandishly puffy shoe, left hand empty, the sword in his right hand held behind, pointed low, at the bricks. "I mean you no harm."

"The hell with the sword, then," says Jo, kneeling, her own blade still in its scabbard half out of the box. Ysabel behind her, leaning against gripping the railing low over the water.

"Draw, Gallowglas," says Roland, gently. His legs bent just, a ready stance, under the low-hanging light. "We cross steel once, a single exchange, and then, unharmed, you lower your arm and walk away, your honor satisfied. I would take the office, and the Princess, from your hands."

"You're mad," snaps Ysabel, before Jo can say anything at all.

"I would merely accept the offer she made before the court," says Roland. "My own honor is as nothing to the danger facing you, Princess. Facing us all. I have been to see the Duke. He," and Roland's left hand squeezes into a fist, "he sent the monsters after you, that night, on the train. He means to frighten you, to drive you from any other solace, to bind the Bride more tightly to him, trusting only him – "

"You have proof?" says Ysabel, clear and cold.

His fist relaxes, his hand opening, closing again. "I would prove the merits of my quarrel with my body and my own right hand, lady. But say the word."

"So you have no proof," says Ysabel.

"You are in grave danger, Princess. You must return with me to your mother's house. Should the Duke discover what's been done to you," and he's straightened from his stance now, sword held loosely at his side, and kneeling still between them Jo looks from Roland back to Ysabel, who's let go of the railing, who's folded her arms tightly about herself, whose white parka's gone yellow-pink in the bridgelight, who says, her voice flatly quiet, "What has been done to me, Chariot."

"The, the line, lady," he says. "The line's been broken, in you. We broke it, that night, to save you from yourself." Breathing heavily as he says it, swallowing when it's done, and that and the lapping of the water are the only sounds about them. Nothing from the deck of the bridge above. Not a growl or rumble from the lights of the empty freeway behind him. "If he learns that you can never be Queen – "

"You are mad," says Ysabel, each word a shard. Jo shoves the box from her sword still in its scabbard and stands, slowly, between them.

"Lady," he says, and then, "Ysabel," and she flinches at that. "It's over," he says. "There's been no Apportionment, not since the, since before the Samani."

"That is my mother's problem, and none of mine," says Ysabel, "and you forget yourself, Chariot."

"Come with me, please," says Roland, quietly. Holding out his empty hand. "Don't you see? It's over, it's *all* over. You're *free*. Just as you always – you could, you and I could go together – "

"I could what?" says Ysabel, and his mouth snaps shut at that. "You and I could *what*, knight? Grow old? Together? In a flower-draped cottage somewhere, no doubt, North Portland, maybe." Her arms still clutched about herself, her voice tight and quiet and low. "But those low, low monthly payments – how would we afford them? If it's *all over*, and our offices and titles gone, their prerogatives with them, all of it down to dust. Would you dig ditches, for so small a life? Would you sell, insurance? Or annuities? Would you go every day to sit at a computer for hours at a stretch, and speak with strangers on a telephone? You *idiot*," snaps Ysabel, one hand leaping to grab the railing, and Jo her free hand starts to reach for her but stops. "In the few short weeks this mortal girl has been my champion she has," clinging to the railing Ysabel looks now from Roland, his expression dumbstruck, to Jo, who's blink-ing, shivering, whose hand about the throat of her scabbard's steady and white-knuckled, "she has worked such wonders as you'd never dare. She brought me the tongue of Erymathos and *you will hear me out,*" and Roland does not take that step toward her, does not say what he'd been about to say, looks away from her, looks down at the bricks, his sword useless at his side. "She brought that monster's tongue to me," says Ysabel, "and I ate it, and saw what's yet to come. I saw my banner over this city, Chariot. I saw myself in my mother's house, *my* house, and I saw my gallowglas by my side. Tell me, then, oh prognosticator, oh chopper of logic, how all this might yet come to pass, if I cannot be Queen?"

Water laps beneath them. A buzzing whine, faint, from the bulb of the lamp over Roland's head, his head that shakes, slowly. He says, "I do not know, my lady." Looking up then. "But even I can see you are not well. Come with me, please – both of you! Come, with me, to your mother's house. Let's all make sure we know what's happened to you. Or, or not."

Ysabel straightens, lets go of herself. Lets go of the railing. "No," she says. "No, we will both go home, to what is our house for now, and you, you will, go back, to skulking in the shadows. Go wait for someone else to notice how *helpful* you might be."

"*Lady,*" he says, the word bent beneath a terrible weight.

Ysabel turns away from him and carefully walks away down the footpath. Jo stoops, her sword still in one hand, and begins to gather up the duffel and the box. She stops when the point of Roland's sword presses against the bag before her, then lifts, slowly, toward her face. She lets go of the bag and stands, slowly, and his sword follows her up. "Princess," he says. "I can still defeat your champion. Take up the keeping of you, once again."

"You might try," says Ysabel. "You'll lose. I've seen it."

"Do *you* think I'll lose?" says Roland to Jo. "A month with even the notorious Erne is hardly enough to make you a creditable swordsman."

Jo spares a glance over her shoulder for Ysabel in the shadows, then takes the hilt of her sword in her hand. Steps back, and back again. "All right," says Roland, "a single pass, as I proposed," as she yanks the scabbard from her blade and settles in a stance side-long to him, the scabbard in her left hand held behind, her blade up and at an angle before. His left hand tucked against his chest leaning back just, his sword arm canted up the blade angled down a little and a little to the left and sliding his foot forward kicking the duffel to one side his sword-tip lazily swinging toward her when he flicks his wrist and it leaps up and over her blade a looping cut she catches with a jerk of a parry, clang. "There," he says, and steps back, lowering his blade. "Put up." Shaking out his left hand. "You've fought for her, and we can both agree I've won. Honor's satisfied." And then, "Gallowglas."

Jo's blade's still there between them, up, and at an angle.

"I would not hurt you, Jo Maguire," says Roland.

"You're gonna have to," says Jo. Her hand settling and resettling itself about the hilt.

"You can't win," says Roland. Lifting his sword somewhat. "Put up your blade."

"If you were in my shoes," says Jo, and she takes a deep breath, "would you?"

And behind her, in the darkness, leaning against the railing over the water, Ysabel is smiling.

Rattle and clack of cassette tapes in a shoebox. He holds one up, clear shell, black label, white scribble of handwriting. He kicks his wheeled office chair down the length of the table lost under haphazard stacks of books and piles of paper. Down by the painted-over window under a poster that says The White Divel, or, Vittoria Corombona, a Lady of Venice, he shoves a teetering stack away from a dusty black tape deck. Punching the eject button with the back of his hook he slots the cassette and twists a couple of large silver knobs. Punches play. Twiddles one of the knobs as big round rubbery bass notes tumble through the room, fluttering and thumping about. Sits back a moment, leans forward and twists another knob as those bass notes stumble into a quick-paced, strutting vamp. Pushes himself to the middle of that table where he works the cork from a bottle of sooty whiskey and pours a healthy dollop and then another into a coffee cup. Sits back in the chair as a tambourine begins to shake. A cymbal shimmies and off in the distance a trombone's blowing a sinister fanfare and he closes his eyes, the coffee cup swaying in his hand to the beat. As more horns join in his eyes still closed he lifts the mug, swirling the whiskey, and then his hand jerks to a stop short of his lips.

"That's the point," he says, and pulls the cup toward himself, lifts it, takes a small brief sip. "Well if I thought we were gonna have an actual conversation and all I might just turn it down." He sets the cup on the table. There's a piano ringing in among the horns now, and the bass vamp has settled down with the drums. "Why!" he says, and then, "Why *did* you come all this way? What could you possibly have to say to me? It isn't enough you send your daughter to me every – *every* fucking day, with her ridiculous girlfriend –

"Don't, don't *give* me that sister-daughter crap. Sister-self, goddammit! She is every inch as much yours as – "

He stands, suddenly, the chair rolling back a little away from him. "Why did you," he says thickly, leaning his hand against the table, "what the fuck did you, what do we possibly have to *say* to each other about that! Why are you even – " His head droops, shoulders sag. "About *him*," he says, quietly. His hand closes about the cup. He looks at his shoulder, then up a little, past it, a ghost of a smile framed in his salt-and-pepper Van Dyke. He frowns, a little. "Our?" he says, and then he nods, looks back to the table. "Oh. Ha. She – " looking at the cup in his hand, "is every gesture, every curl of hair, every sniff and smirk, she's you, she's very much you. On the night we first met."

His chair rolls aside though he does not touch it. "You've grown into your beauty," he says. A smoothing ripples the wrinkles down the back of his T-shirt, wrinkles that are suddenly pressed flat as he leans forward against the table and takes in a sharp deep breath. "Don't," he says, "Duenna, please. No.

"Well of *course* I'm thinking of him. Christ, I, every day, you have no idea." His hook clacks. "I *miss* him, so much –

"Do I. Well. I *am* a selfish man."

He lets go of the cup, pinches the corners of his eyes, wipes them with the heel of his hand. Steps back suddenly, to the side, a stack of papers tumbling in his wake. "Lymond," he says, his voice worn thin and pale under the tumult of the horns and the bass and the drums. Blinking. "He means to try for the Throne," and then his head snaps to one side and he lifts his hand to his cheek. "I'm going to ask you to leave if you –

"Well he picked a lousy fucking time – *Unsettled?* There'll be war in the streets, the Count, the Duke, and the Bride out in the open with only a thoughtless slip of a –

"Duenna, she's *terrible*. And you, you've gone and given her a *sword*. How could you – Duenna – Duenna?" Shivering, tipping his head back, eyes squeezed shut. A deep breath. He sways a moment, raggedly, not at all with the music, and then he lifts the cup.

"The King is dead," says Vincent Erne. "Long live the King." And he drinks the whiskey down.

"I know this building," says Orlando.

They're standing before a big pale yellow house that comes right up to the sidewalk. Red double doors in the middle of a skinny porch, great bays to either side rising to erratic clusters of gables and dormers dotting the steep black roof, the dark green trim gone black as well in the dim light. "It's named for some old judge," says Gloria. "With enormous muttonchops." Her hands in their black and white striped arm socks fluffing to either side of her face. "There's a picture in the lobby. But it used to be called the Lawn."

Orlando nods at that, looking up at the windows above, some lit, some blank and black.

"Dad was, like, the third person to buy in, when it went condo? Been there for about, ten years. But it used to have, like twenty, thirty rooms for rent? And only two bathrooms. So it was hella cheap. Poets, and painters, and whole rock bands, and the Satyricon after-party like every other night, and when we moved in Dad told me that my closet? A junkie used to live there. And I had no idea what a junkie was. I kept imagining this monster, made of rusted pipes and old car parts, and a toilet bowl for a mouth. Scared the hell right out of me." She grabs his hand then, both his hands, and pulls him close, and he leans his forehead down against hers as she swallows him in a hug. "Stay," she says. He shakes his head. She kisses him, her arms about his neck, then her hands cupping the back of his head, kissing fiercely, both of them, his hands cupping her hips, her ass. "I can't," he says against her lips.

"Come upstairs. Now. Don't think about it. Just follow me."

"What would you tell your father."

She laughs a sniffly little laugh. "Are you kidding? He'd give you a fucking medal. I'm fat and I dress funny and I never come home. I bring home a boy? Suddenly it's like a problem he can deal with. You know?" Stroking his hair. "Though you are the strangest thing I think I've ever called a boy. Stay. Stay with me. You can live in my closet. My junkie lover." She laughs. She's crying. "My junk. They said," she says, "they said I'd die if *I* stayed with *you.* That was what you asked. So stay with me instead."

"You can't," he says, "have one, without the other." Taking a step back, leaning back, until she grips his head again, pulls him close. "So fuck it," she says. "Fuck it. You can't, ethically you can't *force* me to save my own life. If I want to, if I want to *die,* it's my life. I can, I get to decide, whether it's worth saving or not."

"I can kill you now, if you like," says Orlando.

She crumbles against him then, the whole of her sagging, staggering him back another step. "I want," she says, a whisper in his ear, "what I want's three days or just a day of what it was we did."

He kisses her, gently, and then he says, "It's not just you. If I stay, if you stay, if we are together, something happens to – everyone I know."

"Snow in April," she sniffs. "Christ, it barely snows in *January.*"

"If," he says. "If, if, if. I never met a vision of the future but was couched with an if." He wipes a tear from her cheek with the back of his hand. "Blast," he says, "and rot all ifs. I *will* see you again."

"Give me your hand," she says.

"Where did you get that knife," he says.

"There's a lot you don't know about me. Give me your hand." The blade of the knife is short and black as ash except the moon-bright edge of it, and the wood-grained handle's stained with reds and yellows and purples. He opens his right hand there between them, and she lays the edge of the blade against his palm but before she can cut or even take a breath he snaps his fingers closed about it and hissing jerks his hand away down its length. His face creased with the pain of it he opens his fist there by her cheek, her lips, the long clean slash through the meat of his palm slowly weeping thick tears of yellow and white. She kisses his hand, and he hisses again as she licks it, once, pressing his hand to her cheek as he strokes her jangling hair. Then he pushes her away.

"I lied," she says, as he walks away across the street. "My name. My name isn't Gloria Monday."

"But I know where you live," he calls back to her.

He walks past a parking lot taking up a whole block behind a low stone wall, around the corner and down under big green highway signs that say 405, 26, Right Lane. Past Italianate townhouses, a great red brick apartment building, a low yellow building painted with cheerfully stylized flowers and a sign that says Antiquities and Oddities. He stops in the middle of the bridge over the freeway cut into a gully below and looks at the cut in his palm still slickly wet. He grabs the tail of his white dress shirt and with the long knife in his hand he slices at it, ripping off a long strip around the bottom all the way back around to the other side, and he wraps it over and over tightly about his palm. On the other side of the bridge, he raises that hand in a little salute as he passes a low red building that says Allen's Radiator Shop in white script letters just below the flat roof. And as the rumble and growl of the freeway traffic fades away behind him, an odd sound can be heard ahead, growing louder – a rushing, clinking sound, the sound of glass on glass.

THE SOUND OF BOTTLES, CLINKING

THE SOUND OF BOTTLES CLINKING in the distance. Ysabel tips back her head the hood of her parka slumping. She doesn't so much blow the smoke from her mouth as let it drift, tugged back as she walks on down the sidewalk. A little parking lot beside them before a pale building that says West Bearing & Parts over dark awnings. She hands the glowing cigarette to Jo, who says, "Feeling better?"

Ysabel shrugs, nods, blows the last of the smoke from her mouth. "How do you feel? Besting the Chariot, two for two?"

Looking down the empty street Jo takes a drag and shrugs. "Does that one even count?" she says, and they cross, against the light.

"You touched steel, this time," says Ysabel. The corner before them blocked with flimsy orange fencing and a sign that says Construction Sidewalk Closed by City Permit, and up and up behind the fence a thicket of naked girders and beams. They jog across to the opposite corner as a red hand flashes, stop, stop, stop. Jo says, "Do you think he's right, about the Duke?"

"Do you think he's right about me?" says Ysabel. A sleekly low-slung chair isolated under a spotlight in the store window behind her.

"I don't know," says Jo. "What's with the cramps?"

"I just needed fresh air, and a walk. I told you. I feel so much better now." As Jo glaring turns to walk on, Ysabel grabs her arm, pulls her back. "I did, I really did see what will be, Jo. I saw myself as Queen. I saw you and your sword at my side."

"So, when? Next year? A couple years from now? Five or ten?"

"I don't – "

"I mean, it changes a thing or two, you've got some kind of peephole to the future. Who's King?" and as Ysabel's saying "I don't know" Jo says, "There's usually a King in this sort of thing, right?"

"I don't know," says Ysabel again. "I didn't see. But, Jo, you have to *trust* me. I *did* see us, together. It will be."

Jo drops the cigarette butt to the sidewalk. "It's not a question of," she says, grinding it under her boot. Cocking her head.

"Not a question of, what? What is it?"

"That sound. The bottles." Jo heads back to the corner. "The hell with the bottles?" Looking around down Twelfth instead of back up along Everett. "Ysabel, what the fuck?" The next block down a couple of blankly blocky buildings sheathed in corrugated white metal to either side and up between them crossing high over the street a slender conveyor belt, railed with metal, clanking empty green bottles from one open yellow-lit hatch to another. "The fucking brewery," says Jo. Stepping out into the empty street. "It, they ripped this out. Tore it down. They're putting up those," and Ysabel's saying "Jo" as Jo's saying "condos, I don't," sniffing, "what the hell?"

"Jo," says Ysabel, over the loudening clatter of glass, "Jo, it's all, it's all gone quiet – "

But Jo in the street's standing stock-still. A dark shape a block or more away against the light splashed from those bottles, a jacket shapeless about the shoulders, a long skirt, long hair lofted in an aimless gust. "Of course," calls Orlando, his voice quite clear. "Of course she couldn't stay. Of course I had to take her home. Of course I had to be here, now, to meet you, one last time."

"Why did you do this to me," says Jo.

"Why?" He's walking toward them slowly, his left hand on the hilt of the sword he's pulling like a curl of light from the air. "I didn't want to deny the Axe her satisfaction, but I had to do *something*. Sending you to your death as you lamented again the death of your son?" He whips the sword before him. "It might have been amusing, had I not been too late. Still. Couldn't let all that *work*," and another whip of a cut, his jacket snapping over the clink of glass, "go to waste."

"Why *me*," says Jo, the word caught in her throat.

"I don't *like* you," says Orlando, stopping there, less than half a block away. "If you try to run again," and he points his sword at Ysabel, "I will cut her down, first."

"Remember your duty, Mooncalfe," says Ysabel at that, and his laughter's high and wild. "Duty? Not a quarter of an hour's passed, Princess, since I saved us all by saying no. I've done my duty for the night. I trust, Gallowglas, you've remembered your sword this time?"

Jo's dropped the duffel, the box upright before her. She's opening the flaps at the top. "Jo," says Ysabel, her eyes wide.

"I know," says Jo, and she shucks her leather jacket. Her satiny red blouse quite dark in the dim light. She reaches into the box and draws her sword.

"Mark this, Princess!" calls Orlando, holding up his right hand wrapped in white. "I'm down an eye, and a hand. Let no one say this was an unfair fight." Slinging his sword up and back over his shoulder head down skirt flapping he's running headlong at Jo who says "Shit" and leaning stepping left foot back she swings her sword her hilt high a parry catching his savage one-handed cut with a shrieking scrape turning just as he runs past pushing his sword and hers up and up and out as he plants his foot and *stops* suddenly juddering his arm his blade turning down, back, ducking under her arm recovering from that wild parry as he *pushes* back against her and the wedge-shaped tip of that blade –

Ysabel's hands leap to her mouth.

Jo trembling lowers her arm, her sword as Orlando turns there to face her. She looks down stupefied at the rip in her red shirt fluttering about the blade of his sword stuck there through her belly. Looks along it to his hand there on the hilt. Looks up. Tries to look up. She can't quite lift her head. With a grunt he yanks his blade free and her blood splatters to the pavement as he steps back, throws his arms up, "La!" he cries. Jo's leg buckles under a step she wasn't about to take and leaning back she topples to her knees. He's slinging her blood from his sword with a whipping jerk. Ysabel her hands trembling violently tries to catch a scream that just won't come. "This, this isn't," says Jo, falling back, her head clopping against the pavement.

"You're mine now, aren't you," says Orlando. Rubbing his right hand with his left.

Wavering a little her hands still trembling Ysabel walks past him to stand over Jo, trying a couple of times to kneel there beside her without falling. "Quickly, quickly," says Orlando, as she smooths Jo's wine-red hair. Kisses Jo's lips once. Stands, a scrape of metal as she turns, Jo's sword in her hand.

"Really, Princess," says Orlando.

"Mooncalfe," says Ysabel thickly, "I would no more have you in my court."

"*Your* court?" he says, and then, "She's off the field of battle, that will no more hurt me – " and he steps to one side as she lunges at him, and snatches the blade with his wrapped right hand. Wrenches it from her grasp. Catching her hair in his left hand, hauling her back against him, and the sound of bottles has since stopped. An engine coughs to life, an orange car rumbling past, down Everett. "Let's go," says Orlando. He pushes Ysabel up onto the sidewalk, stepping after, Jo's sword in his hand. "We'll ask your mother what I'm to do with you."

Yo, my mood is real rude, I lay you out
Show you what steel do
Mobsters don't box, my pump-shot obliges
Every invitation to fight you punk hazas
Like Pun said, "You ain't even en mi clasa."

—Nas

NO. 15
FRAIL

STANDING THERE in the middle of the intersection a white paper sack in one hand his other shoving long dark hair a thin curtain from before his eyes frowning "Hey?" he says, soft and deep. A growl of engine an orange car lurid in the dim light swerves around him but he doesn't look away after it. He doesn't look up the street where it came from at the big man in a black suit walking at a fast clip up to the corner and around it. He's looking along the other street, at the man in the long dark skirt, at the long straight sword in his hand, at the woman in the short white parka he's pushing ahead of him. At the body they've left crumpled on the pavement. "Hey?" he says again. The man in the skirt, the woman in the parka, neither of them stopping or turning or noticing at all as grunting, sobbing, they make their way to the corner and around it and they're gone.

"Jo?" says the man still standing there in the middle of the intersection. He's wearing a black down vest over a black T-shirt. His arms are bare. The T-shirt says Ted Kord & Maude in white letters. The body crumpled on the pavement one leg kicked to one side asprawl the other folded up under one arm jackknifed to the side hand over belly fingers adangle the other upflung beside the canted head one eye staring whitely up at nothing. He steps closer, closer still, and a siren somewhere blocks away whoops up into stuttering bleeps and stops with a strangled blurt. The stoplight in the intersection behind him clicking and all the blood about the body's lit up yellow and orange, gold. He stops short. "Jo?" he says, again. The stoplight clicks, clacks, the blood lost again in all the red and black.

A rustle, a plop, the paper sack drops to the pavement there by the body. He squats by the sack, one hand up over his mouth. His other hand not touching her shoulder, her face, rough-knuckled, black-nailed, glittering with silver rings, an ankh, a skull, a pair of dice, snake eyes. "Hey?" he says, looking up, about. "Anybody?"

The stoplight clacks. His dark hair's splashed with green.

He folds his hand gently about hers there over her belly, turning it palm up as his other hand drifts down to settle over it pressing it between them over the rip in her shirt shining wetly skin and the blood those reds all smeared into one uncertain color by the light. He's pressing his thumb along her wrist hands shaking and then "No," he says, "no, no, not the thumb," lifting his hand away, shaking it out, pressing his fingertips, forefinger and middle pressed together against her wrist as her head lolls a bubble of spittle bursting on her lips cords jumping in her throat and he's rearing back, "oh," he says, "oh, okay," sitting back on his heels. Letting go, dropping her wrist. Rubbing his hands together. Looking about the dark block of the converted warehouse to one side, the unlit windows of the wine shop to the other, the silent construction sites past the empty intersections at either end. A duffel bag there by her foot, a long narrow cardboard box strapped to it. "I need," he says, "to find, a phone?" A rumple of black there on the pavement behind her a leather jacket. He stands, a little unsteady. "You'll be okay, right? Powell's is just, Powell's is right over there. Somebody's still got to be there. Right?" Stooping to pick up the jacket. "I'll, why am I even *talking,*" and then he freezes, looking down where the jacket had been, the jacket dangling from his hands. "Shit," he says. He starts to lay it back down, and then he says *"Fuck* the evidence," and shakes it out, steps back to Jo. "You'll be okay," he says. "I'll just be a couple of, a few minutes. You won't, bleed out. While I'm gone. Right?" Hefting the jacket in his hands. Frowning. Patting it down, reaching into the pocket on the side of it that's dangling a bit lower. Pulling out a glassy black phone.

"Oh," he says. "Right. Yeah."

He thumbs a button, pokes the screen until he gets a keypad. Punches in nine, one, one. Stares at it there in his hand, no earpiece, no microphone.

"Nine one one emergency," says a tinny little voice.

He yanks the phone to his ear. "Yeah," he says, "hello, can you hear me?

"Yeah, I need to report a stabbing? Someone's been stabbed. With a sword? I think?

"I don't know, it isn't, I think he took –

"Northwest Twelfth between, ah, Everett and what's the, the, F? Foster? Flanders.

"Yes, she's, yes, there's a pulse, and, uh, but there's a lot of blood. *Shit.*

"No, I mean, uh," he picks up the white paper sack the bottom of it soaked through dark and wet, "I got, it's all over the burritos. Ingrid's gonna be *furious.*"

"So," says the Duke. Looking out the window at the passing lights. "There nothing to be worried over." His jacket brown with wide blue stripes, his shirt a creamy gold, buttoned up to the collar without a tie. "Ready?"

Beside him in the back seat she's looking out the other window, at the traffic. Her hair cut quite short, wine red. A buff-colored bolero jacket spangled in red and pink and orange over a severely simple gown the color of old bone. Her arms folded in her lap.

"Jo," says the Duke.

"What do I say?" says Jo Maguire. "How do you figure I'm ready for this?"

"We could go back," says the Duke. "One word, this car stops. We get sandwiches from Eastside, we watch some television, we get out of these clothes – "

"You're only saying that," says Jo, "because you know I'll say no."

"You think?" says the Duke. A sign slides past out the window behind him as the car slows. Fred Meyer, it says. "I mean I've got a copy of that Canadian thing, about the guy. Wrote those plays?" The car stops, the click-clack of the turn signal. "But maybe another night, huh. Because you won't say yes." His hand on her knee, squeezing. "Anyway. Offer's on record. Okay?"

Jo says nothing.

The car pulls into a right turn. The lights from traffic and shops give way to dark sidewalks, parked cars, windows lit here and there, a glimpse of books on shelves, a canvas on a wall a great slash of red and yellow dripped, a candle on a sill, someone face in shadow sipping something from a martini glass. Streetlights here and there blurry in a drifting mist of rain. They park by the side of a big brick apartment block, across the street from an old green house up behind a low stone wall, a neatly narrow garden, big white columns of its shallow porch in the glare of tasteful spotlights. Jessie shuts off the engine, sets the parking brake. Her grey chauffeur's cap wrapped in clear plastic, a clear plastic raincoat over her grey chauffeur's jacket. Climbing out the driver's side door, levering the front seat forward, unfurling a clear plastic umbrella. Leaning in to offer a hand to Jo. In the palm of her hand a piece of paper folded and tucked into a triangle that says Is.

"Let's go," says the Duke behind Jo.

Jo looking up at Jessie nods and takes the triangle from Jessie as she climbs out of the car. "We'll be, ah," says the Duke, shifting along the back seat, planting his cane, taking Jessie's hand. "A while, actually." Settling a brown porkpie on his head. "I honestly don't know. Go have a drink, go dancing." Taking the umbrella. "Heck, go to Goodfellow's. I wouldn't even worry about starting to wait until after midnight, so – "

"I'll call," says Jo. The Duke frowns. "I have a phone?" she says.

"Oh," says the Duke, "that, right," and then Jessie steps between them, up against him, presses a brief kiss to his lips. "For luck," she says.

"Not a factor," he says, and he smiles his crooked little smile. "But I'd never turn it down." He kisses her, a longer, softer kiss, and then, stepping back, looking over at Jo, holding the umbrella up as she steps next to him, as Jessie heads off away down the sidewalk. "What was that she gave you?" he murmurs in her ear. "A note?"

Jo nods.

"For the Princess?" says the Duke. "Good thing for her I'm not a jealous god. Well." Tapping his cane against the pavement as rain patters on the umbrella above them. "Let's get this done."

They set out, across the street to the old green house behind its narrow garden, its low wall, its wrought iron gate.

ONE EYE BROWN, ONE EYE BLUE – HAND HELD HIGH
HIS REWARD – NOT A MARK

ONE EYE BROWN AS A FOREST FLOOR, ONE EYE PIERCING CLOUD-LESS BLUE, both blinking thickly, heavy-lidded. Pinkish orange hair crisply stiff crackles against the pillow as he looks to one side, then the other. Bars, a rack of equipment, digital numbers brightly fuzzy in the dim light. Tubing. A yellow catheter taped to the back his hand. More tubing up along his neck, his cheek, feeding into his nostrils. Beige sheets, a fuzzy blue blanket rumpled about his hips. "Hey," says somebody, off over that way. "Limeade. Welcome back to the land of the living."

"What," he says in a voice scratched thin. "Did you call me." Smacking chapped lips, licking them.

"Oh, hey," says a skinny man in pale pink scrubs, his hair a fuzzy bush of tightly kinked black curls. "Nickname. Wasn't thinking." Peering at the rack of equipment, checking the yellow catheter with sure and careful hands. Shaking out the blankets. "But what did you call me," says the man in the bed.

"They brought you over from Hooper a bit ago. Said you were ranting and raving before you passed out, lime to the lemon, lemon to the lime, lime soda. You remember any of that?"

"Limeade," says the man in the bed.

"Nickname," says the nurse. "Like I say. Had to have something to call you."

"Reynard," says the man in the bed, "Reynardine. Raynaud. Reynolds. Raymond."

"Pick one?" says the nurse.

"Ray," says the man in the bed, struggling to sit up. "Raymond. Call me Ray. Something – I have to get out of here."

"Hang on, hang on a minute, I'll help you to the bathroom. You probably got a – "

"*Out* of here. I must *leave.*"

"Hold *still*, Ray." The nurse gently pushes him back to the pillow. "You don't just walk away from a coma. Patience. We gotta check you out, there's these tests, and man." He smiles. "You're gonna *love* the paperwork we got picked out for you."

"I need," says Ray, "something to drink."

"Water I can do."

Ray shakes his head, pink hair crackling. "Wine," he says. "Whiskey."

"Whoa," says the nurse, shaking his head. "Not here, man. Not in here."

"I need to get *out* of here," says Ray, fighting back up on his elbows. "If you won't let me leave – "

"Calm, man." Not raising that soothing voice but his hand firm on Ray's chest, not letting him up. "It's okay – "

"I'm stripped raw as if I had no," says Ray, "someone's *coming* that's what woke me," his hand flapping by his shock of hair, "like a *pressure,* a pressing on my – "

"Headache," says the nurse, both hands on Ray's shoulders now, steady, fixed. Ray's breathing heavy, fierce. "Bet it's a king-hell doozy – "

Ray claps the heel of his hand over one eye and roars, a deep rumble torn and echoing in the dim room, rattling the IV stand, the clear plastic tubing, the clanking safety bars up on either side of the bed, the nurse steps back, the lights flicker, those numbers blink and change, wink out, flash back in bursts of random nonsense.

And then Ray sinks back against the pillow with a ghost of a smile.

"What," says the nurse, as loudspeakers crackle, "was that?" An Emergency Department lockdown is now in effect, says a tinny, staticky voice. Emergency Department lockdown, now in effect. "Ray. Talk to me, Ray. Tell me what just happened."

"I need," says Ray, barely a whisper, "liquor, I need to go away, I can't be here, not yet, not yet," and then blinking, finding the nurse, "lucky," he says. "Lucky. He isn't going to, he isn't coming here. He's looking for something else. Some*one*. But he might," sighing, closing his eyes again. "I must be dulled," he says. "I need a bushel. Booze," drawing out the word, savoring it, and then with a little laugh, "no more limeade – "

Huffing, puffing, "Make a hole," she bellows, and the four or five men and women in purple and blue scrubs flatten against either side of the hallway as keys jangling, boots thumping she barrels through them and around the corner. Far end down there a couple men, three men holding, dragging a fourth, the only one in scrubs, green scrubs under a white lab coat bunched in the hand of the big man yellow shirt flapping open over a bare broad chest. She stops crouching a little reaching for the handle of the blocky plastic gun strapped to her belt –

"Wilberforce," says the second man, the one in the tweed jacket, to the third, the tall one in the long black coat.

– the blocky plastic gun in her hand with its bulbous yellow snout coming up free hand cupping the butt of it finger tense against the trigger as that tall man spins coat swirling a loud slapping crack filling the hall her hand jerked up and back the blocky gun pinwheeling away. That long black coat settling, his arms crossed before him, black-gloved hands poised by his hips, over the pearly white handles of the revolvers holstered there. A puff of smoke floating before him curls of it tugged down toward the gun slung to his left. "Like to see it again, ma'am?" he says, a smile somewhere under his enormous grey mustache. "Stand down? Please?"

"Through there," says the man in the white lab coat, and the man in the tweed jacket says "Luys, with me," and pushes through a swinging set of double doors. The man in the yellow shirt lets go of that white coat and follows. The man in the long black coat lifts a gloved hand to the brim of his soft pale hat with an absurdly high crown, punched in on one side. "Sir," he says, to the man in the lab coat, "ma'am," to the security guard still staring at the broken plastic gun halfway down the hall, "just a minute or two more to get what we came for. Then we're out of your hair."

The room beyond is brightly lit. A cluster of people anonymous in blue and green scrubs and white surgical masks about the high table, and "Watch it" someone's saying, muffled by a mask, and "There, right there" and "It's dropping" and "God *dam*mit" and "Crashing" and "Flanagan, Security, *now.*" The man in the tweed jacket holds up one hand burning, flaring like a torch too bright to look upon. "Ladies," he says, "gentlemen." In his other hand a clear plastic bag swollen with glittery dust. "The Hawk thanks you for your service and bids you take your leave." Luys beside him, the tip of his longsword brushing the floor.

"We can't, we can't *leave*," says one of the be-scrubbed people, and "Don't, don't" and "Still dropping" and "Another clamp, if you would."

"Doctors!" he cries, stepping closer. "Nurses. You have done all you can and more besides and it will not be forgotten I assure you," and one and then another steps back, falls back before him. "But this is what she needs," his hand in all that searing light clenched in a fist, "and it's not for you to see." And he opens his mouth around a short sharp breath, then lets it out in a word, *"Go,"* and the passage of that word ruffles scrubs, aprons, flutters caps and masks, ripples the cloth spread over the body that's been laid upon the table.

The Duke lays the plastic bag on a side table by a rack of stainless tools, a dish, neatly folded squares of gauze. With the hand that isn't burning he whips sheets back, knocks aside a tented frame, exposes her there, pale, limp, naked, the red ruin of her belly peeled open, laid back. Yanking plastic tubes from his path a long needle from her arm heedless of the blood. "Shut that down," he says as beeps and buzzes sound, and Luys shrugs and heads for the station behind the table where most of the alarms seem to be sounding. The Duke carefully pries a hissing mask from her face with his free hand, working it off over her wet red hair. "Jo," he says, under the buzzing, the bleeps. "Please." His other hand drips fire over her breast, her belly, white-gold light that sizzles against her skin.

By the wall Luys lifts his sword and brings it down in a shower of sparks and the bleeps squeal and shriek and stop and the buzzing dies.

The Duke dips his burning hand into the plastic bag and the whole room lights up, a sun shining there on that table. Squinting he drags it through the air over along her body and again and in its wake her pale skin blooms with color and with warmth. Again, and as that light passes over a third time her belly's smooth, unmarred.

"Jo," says the Duke, leaning over her, taking her head in his hands, that sun gone dim, just ripples now, the reflection of light on water somewhere licking at his fingers. "Come back," he says, a whisper, and Luys looks away. "Jo," says the Duke, "come back to me," and he kisses her lips, and her chest rises with a breath, and then another.

As he wipes his eyes an unbuttoned green striped cuff falls away to reveal a watch, heavy and gold. "Thank you," he says, his voice a rasp.

"Not at all," says Mr. Leir, brushing cinders from his shirt too brightly white in the harsh glare of the arc light. "You earned it."

"It's, I just," says the man in the green striped shirt. "Words. It's, they're inadequate."

"Of course," says Mr. Leir, pulling on his white jacket. "Your coat?"

As they leave the cavernous room, Mr. Keightlinger steps into the glare with a broom, sweeping ash from the unfinished wood floor. Mr. Charlock's at the edge of that circle of light, one hand cupping his eyes, peering out into that darkly empty room, the shadowy suggestions of columns, glints from the glass of the windows lining the far walls. "You hear, like, a laugh?" says Mr. Charlock. "Weirdest damn thing." Mr. Keightlinger shakes his head.

"What news of the Bride," says Mr. Leir, in the doorway to the room.

"Unchanged," says Mr. Keightlinger, stooping for the dustpan.

"Hadn't left the house in days," says Mr. Charlock, turning, squinting in the light. "We're growing moss out there."

"And tonight?" Mr. Leir's frowning at the soot-streaked toe of one of his white bucks.

"Dinner," says Mr. Keightlinger. "You called us in for this shindig," says Mr. Charlock.

"You'd rather grow moss?" says Mr. Leir, tugging a handkerchief from his pocket. "Mr. Kerr," bending over to rub at the toe of his shoe, "deserved his reward. Six months ago, Killian wasn't going to run." A last wipe at his gleaming shoe, he folds the handkerchief carefully and again. "Today, he's the clear favorite over Beagle."

"Well her mother's got a big dinner party tonight, so hey, good timing on that reward."

"And the new guardian?" says Mr. Leir.

Mr. Keightlinger, dustpan in hand, stumps over to a bulging garbage bag, empties the ashes into it. "What's to know?" says Mr. Charlock. "He's the worst possible choice."

"Worse than the Chariot."

"The Chariot was a machine," says Mr. Charlock. "Predictable. This guy? He's," and he shrugs, hands wavering, looking for a word. "Nuts."

"That's an excuse?" says Mr. Leir.

"There's a girl," says Mr. Keightlinger.

"A girl?"

"There might be a girl," says Mr. Charlock. "That he's, I don't know. Seeing. We're doing what we can."

"Do more," says Mr. Leir, turning away.

Mr. Charlock rubs his eyes, blinks, steps further into the shadows. "So you didn't hear it, huh? High-pitched, like a giggle? A girl, I don't know – "

"Mr. Charlock?" says Mr. Keightlinger, by the door. Away across that circle of light the little guy's a hint of shoulders, a gleam struck from his bald head drooping, kneeling there in the shadows. "What is it?"

"Huh?" says Mr. Charlock. "Nothing." In his hands a pair of underwear, bikini underpants with blue and white stripes. He wads them up, stuffs them in the pocket of his jacket, stands, turns, steps back into the light. "I'm hearing things. Let's get back to it."

The fireplace cold and dark, two wing-backed chairs drawn up before it empty, the reading lamp on the thin-legged table there unlit. On the bed pillowed in a deep down comforter Ysabel on her side wrapped in a short white robe, black hair heavily damp. Feet crossed at the ankles, white nail polish chipped and dingy, no rings on any toes. Calves shaded with delicate black hair. On a flowered saucer on the nightstand a cigarette wrapped in brown paper, burned down to a feathery twig of ash, a thread of smoke still tugging at its smothered cinder. "You will dress yourself for dinner," says the woman standing at the foot of the bed in a simple black sheath and sheer black stockings. Her glasses narrow with black rims. Ysabel does not respond, or move, or even stir. "If you do not, don't think you won't be taken down in that."

"Don't *encourage* her," says the old woman by the door.

"God*dam*mit, Ysabel," says the woman at the foot of the bed, "don't make me call the Mooncalfe," and "*Anna,*" says the old woman by the door, quite stern, and then, quite softly sweet, "leave her to me, dearie. Guests will be arriving at any moment."

Anna looks back at her, nods once, crisply, turns and takes her leave. The old woman flips a switch by the door and the fixture in the middle of the ceiling fills the room with too much light. Her hair is long and glossy white, hanks of it gathered in braids that wrap about her head like a crown and hang down before her shoulders to either side. Her plain grey dress blushes pinkly iridescent as she sits on the edge of that bed. "Well," she says, with a heavy sigh. "A lot just keeps on *happening,* doesn't it. And none of it due to you."

Ysabel burrows more deeply into the pillows.

"Oh dear," says the old woman, "oh dearie dear. Have you given up so," and "Don't dearie me," says Ysabel, muffled by the folds of her robe. "So quickly," says the old woman. "Did you think it would be easy?"

"Don't ask rhetorical questions, either. I don't need a lecture, Gammer."

"What do you need, child." She strokes Ysabel's wet hair, her cheek, just visible. Ysabel lifts her head and looks the old woman in the eye. "A different dress," she says.

The Gammer leans back on an elbow to look over her shoulder. Hanging from one of the half-open louvered doors there the other side of the bed a froth of white lace draped over a satiny ivory slip. "That will look lovely on you," she says.

"It'll look like a wedding dress," says Ysabel.

"You are the Bride."

"The King comes back tonight, then? During mother's ridiculous dinner?"

The Gammer smiles. "Something's lit your fire," she says. "I've missed that, these past few days. Your mother's many things, but I'd never say she was ridiculous. What's got you so frightened, child?"

Tucking the folds of her robe under her chin, Ysabel says, "Am I broken, Gammer?"

"Broken?" says the Gammer. "And what's put that idea into your head?" Sitting up. "Ysabel?"

From behind her fingers Ysabel says, "I tried a turning."

"Did you," says the Gammer, softly. "And how'd you go and do a thing like that? Without the King to hold your hand, and me still here in the world."

"Wild queens once lived in the mountains," says Ysabel, "and spun straw into gold the livelong day, and nary a king in sight."

"The Soames told you some stories," says the Gammer. Her lips pucker. "A jar of rabbit was it, then."

"I drank it down," says Ysabel, and "Ut," says the Gammer, shaking her head. "I drank it," says Ysabel, shifting on the comforter, sitting up, "and it *did* something, inside – "

"Dearie, don't," says the Gammer. Ysabel's undoing the belt to her robe. "Jo found me," she says, and "Never should have left you," mutters the Gammer as Ysabel says, "Jo *found* me, lying,

140

lying in my own, *vomit,*" and she opens the robe, "and Roland cut it *out* of me, and, and," her words stumble over a sobbing breath.

"And not a mark on you," says the Gammer, brushing Ysabel's belly with the back of her hand.

"It *hurts,*" says Ysabel.

"Oh, it will," says the Gammer. "But not because of any cut or spew." She stands, steps over to the bay window, looks out into the street. "It's not to be drunk, child."

"Then how."

"Wait for the King."

"But why."

"It's what is done," says the Gammer, pushing the curtain open a little more. "The Duke's arrived."

"The Duke," says Ysabel. A cough, to clear her throat. "Who's with him? The Mason? The Cater?" The Gammer shakes her head. "Who?" says Ysabel. "Not Greentooth, surely."

"No," says the Gammer. "Not Greentooth."

Ysabel kicks her feet off the bed, hurries to the window, heedless of her open robe. Throws another curtain back. Her hand leaps to her mouth. There below in the rain under a clear umbrella the Duke in his brown and blue striped suit, and beside him Jo in a long straight gown the color of old bone, streetlight flashing from the spangles on her jacket, pink and orange and red.

"She's come," says Ysabel. "She's come for me."

A SEAMLESS SKY grey-white floats over an ocean milky green like well-worn jade, the yellow white sand rippled, wind-swept, empty. The big picture window specked with dead raindrops. She sits in a recliner angled back, staring out at it all, legs wrapped in a rug made from rags in colors from old magazines. A cardigan buttoned up to her chin, her head leaned against the heavy shawl collar. Every now and then she closes her eyes as if she has finally fallen asleep, but sooner, later, they blink open again, she shifts a little in the recliner, folds her arms about herself more tightly, tucks her hands back under her elbows, or under the rug, stares out at the ocean through mud-colored eyes.

A huge figure of a man comes into the airy little room, soft blue denim shirt and a moleskin vest, his face a couple of dark eyes, a daub of forehead in an explosion of wiry hair all grey and peppery black and coiling sprigs and shoots of white. In one hand a thick yellow mug that he sets steaming on the tray table by the recliner. His other's not a hand but a hand-shape, cast in bronze and beaten with whorls of puckered dots. Standing there a moment he watches her as she does not lift a hand for the tea, and then with something like a shrug he turns to walk away.

"Wish we could open the window," she says.

He stops there by the low shelf buried under a great bouquet of chrysanthemums, heavy heads of yellow and gold and bronzey orange. "Yis builden," he says, a roughly woven voice, "it'd fall. Yon light's'll can be mannered." Over his shoulder a portrait of a jowled and scowling president from many years before.

"I can almost smell it," she says, closing her eyes. "And the *sound…*"

"Ull, that," he says, tching. "That'll be, n'manner when nor where, and naught's to lay by any's name. Old as ever, it is." And then that gap in his hair about his eyes narrowing he steps back up to her, lays his metalled hand on the back of the recliner. "Ut," he says, and she opens her eyes.

Out there struggling against the wind a woman, her grey houppelande too heavy to billow, her hair hidden away in a wimple, both hands on the arm of a young man short and limping beside her, wrapped in a heavy bearskin, on his head a simple round cap of the sort favored by bankers. Bent under the weight of an iron bound chest he's balanced on one shoulder, steadied with his free hand. Black padlocks clamp the face of it to either side.

"I'll see to the kettle," says the huge man, pushing away from the chair.

"Coffey!" cries the Duke, coming through the door in his camelhair coat. Behind him Jessie in her chauffeur's jacket, a sack of groceries cradled in either arm. "Your grace," says the huge man gruffly, directing Jessie with his metalled hand toward a swinging door at the other end of the room. The Duke coming around to kneel, wincing, his weight on the arm of the recliner. "Jo," he says. "How are you?"

"Cold," she says, the yellow mug steaming in her hands.

"You know, I think he likes you?" says the Duke. His chin resting on the back of the hand draped over the arm of the chair, his other hand wrapped about the stern hawk at the head of his cane. "They're pretty much done at your place," he says. "You might want to look it all over before it's moved. Just in case. Not that there's gonna be any problems. And, you've got time. Days if you need them. So you don't have to, it's not like I think you should be worried about any of it. Just – whatever you need, Jo." She looks at him, then, his brown eyes sparked with green and gold. "For as long as you need. I'm gonna take care of you, Jo, I – " She's turning away, thumping the mug down on the tray table. "I'm sorry," he says. "Poor choice of words. I didn't mean."

"Let's go," she says. "Leo." Lifting the rug from her lap. "Let's go."

In the little hallway kitchen cabinet doors left open drawers pulled out empty, all empty, the refrigerator door ajar and dark inside. A cardboard box full of garbage in the doorway to the bathroom, dust and shards of glass and crumpled paper towels. The window on the far wall of the main room of the apartment stripped bare, no curtains, no shade, outside the skinny white faux balcony weirdly sharp in the flat grey light. Folded as a couch the bare wooden frame of the futon, pillows stacked ungainly to one side. A steamer trunk on the bleach-stained carpet, a couple of wooden crates beside it, both of them nailed shut. The glass-topped café table with a couple of spindly wrought-iron chairs set legs up on top of it. In the corner the bulky blond wood armoire stands open, empty, a contraption of thin metal tubing hanging from one side that racks nothing at all.

"Not much, all packed up like that," says Jo, her black leather reefer jacket buttoned and zipped to her chin.

"You want any of the furniture?" The Duke nudges the refrigerator closed.

"That was all," Jo waves a hand at the armoire, the glass-topped table, "that came with her. Guess she didn't want it." Her hand coming to rest on an upturned chair leg. "The futon was mine, but it's a piece of shit. I guess they chucked the mattress?"

"Probably?" says the Duke. "There's a, it's like a queen-sized bed, it's all – "

"No," says Jo, "but the blankets, I mean, there's this one blanket." Toeing a bleached spot on the carpet with her big black boot.

"Probably in the crates. Want to check? Jo?" She looks up, over at him. "If there's anything about this you don't like," he says.

"What else am I gonna do?" she says, with an unsteady laugh.

"Is it the loft?" says the Duke. He limps into the main room. "Is it too close? Too soon? I'm not, it doesn't, it's just a convenient," and Jo's saying "No, no," as the Duke says, "Give me a couple of days. We'll find you an apartment somewhere, a house, whatever. Or." He pulls something from a pocket, an envelope, unsealed, fat with bills. "I was gonna give this to you anyway, but you could – "

"The hell's that," says Jo, her hands in her pockets.

"Walking-around money," he says. "It was gonna be. Go on. Should be enough in there, you could call a cab. Get a hotel room. Call me in a week or two. If you want."

"This is real?" she says, riffling through the bills.

"As any promissory note," says the Duke. He's smiling when she looks up sharply. "Every piece of paper in there passed through a printing press, if that's what you mean. And did time on someone's hip. Except maybe some of the fifties, those were pretty new." His smile softens. "Anything you want, Jo. Anything you need."

She steps away from the table, envelope in hand. "Anything," she says, looking out the window, out over the little parking lot across the street, the gullied freeway off to the left, the towering arc of the great bridge far off over the rooftops ahead. The dark hills green and black, draped in gauzy shreds of cloud. "I need to talk to her."

"That," says the Duke, "that's not going to happen."

"Anything."

"Within reason!"

"Christ, Leo," she says, turning away from the window. "Does she even know I'm alive."

He looks away at that. "No one's," he says, "I don't, ah, she hasn't left the house. Not since he took her. But there's to be a dinner, for the court. Tomorrow night. I'll see her then. I'll tell her whatever – "

"I need to *see* her."

"That's not – "

"I could go with you."

"*Jo,*" says the Duke, his cane-tip thumping the carpet. "You *lost.* Your office was forfeit and he took the keeping of her. He took your *sword,* Jo. You aren't a knight," and as Jo's saying "That, that doesn't" the Duke says, "You have no *place.* Without a weapon, you're no more a knight."

The envelope crinkles in her hand. "So that's," she says, and she turns toward the trunk, the crates. "That's it, then. It's all over."

"You lost," says the Duke again.

She turns back, tossing the envelope onto the table, between the chairs. "So that's," she says, "what, the payoff?"

The Duke, blinking, twitches his head as if shaking off a fly. "Excuse me?" he says.

"She said," says Jo. "The Queen said. When she, when Ysabel tired of her dalliance. That would be the end of it. That I was out. That's what this is."

"Now why," says the Duke, quietly, "would I pay anyone off for her majesty, when I could have saved myself a season's worth of owr."

And then he's the first to look away. "No," he says. "That was rude."

"*I* was – "

"We were both rude," he says, shoulders hunched, scuffing the carpet with an oxblood wingtip. "I could care less what the Queen said, or wants. What *I* want," and those shoulders lift and relax as he straightens with a sigh, "I want you, with me.

The Princess? Any fool could see she isn't done with you. Let me, let me go to this dinner. Find out how things stand, before we," and then he frowns. "Jo?" he says. "What's that?"

Leaning against the bit of wall hiding the refrigerator a long black spear-haft angled, the head of it like a mirrored leaf resting the tip of it touching there the corner where the ceiling meets the walls.

"Shit," says Jo. "We never could get it out of the way with all our stuff in here. Kept tripping over the damn thing. It's, the Dagger's spear," she says. "From the hunt. Remember?"

"If it were the Dagger's spear," says the Duke, "it would have been destroyed with him. No, I gave it to you." His smile's gone slyly sidelong. "You still have a weapon. Come over here. Take it up."

"What?"

"Just go take it in your hands," says the Duke, and Jo heads around the table past him, puts a hand on the black spear-haft. "Go on," he says.

"What are we doing here," says Jo.

"Do you trust me?"

"About as far as I could throw you."

He shrugs. "Okay. Fair enough. Offer it to me. Offer it now, before one of us realizes how monstrously stupid this is."

Careful with the heavy thing, ducking under it, she turns and pushes it still angled between floor and ceiling at him, the head of it up there winking in the flat white light from the window. He grips the haft of it there between her hands. "Joliet Maguire," he says. "Gallowglas." His voice gone gentle now, and his smile is almost gone. "Do you swear before us all, to withstand oppressor's power with arm and puissant hand? To recover right, for such as wrong did grieve? To battle guile, and malice, and despite? To kick ass and take names for me, your liege?"

And with a shake of her head, blinking, a laugh, "Sure," says Jo, and then, "Yes. I do."

"The Hawk," says the Duke, letting go the haft, "welcomes the Squirrel."

"The what?" says Jo, leaning the spear-tip against the wall again.

"The T-shirt? You were wearing? At the restaurant that night, when we were, never mind." He scoops up the envelope from the table. "Welcome to my company."

Clear plucked notes a chiming descant over spidery strumming all from a big-bellied guitar wrapped up in the arms of a kid with a blue streak dyed in his bleached white hair. "Weave a circle round him three times," he's singing in a rough high voice, "you have to plan your moves at these times. Our hearts are breaking; one more song to go." Jessie in her grey chauffeur's jacket, bottle of soda in her hand, clear glass that says Dry Rhubarb in a splotch of red, at the edge of a crowd in the low back room, wool and lycra, satin and fleece, painted cheeks, drooping feathers, a long cardigan vest and a T-shirt and shorts, a lurid sari glittering with colored glass and bits of mirror, sagging jeans and a dinner jacket. "We had some good machines," the kid's singing, "but they don't work no more. I loved you once. Don't love you anymore."

She sees him as they're all applauding politely, as the kid's ducking his head over his guitar, as she's lifting the soda for a swig. His face all cheekbones and nose and eyebrows jutting, a white watch cap rolled down over the tops of his ears. A tight ringer T-shirt with a flying contraption printed on the front, all bat-wings and spiraled screws. His bare arms strung with wiry muscles and veins. He smiles at her, nods, as the kid starts picking out a new song on the guitar. "You look," says Jessie, leaning toward him, "familiar?"

"Sorry," he says, shaking that head of juts and angles.

"Or not," says Jessie, shrugging.

"Lough," he says.

"Lough?"

"My name."

"I'm Rain," she says.

"How can it hatch," the kid's singing, "if it didn't get laid. Well there's Vera Lynn, on the violin, Elvis Costello, well he's playing the cello…"

"A generous shot of heavy rum," says the old man, "something fermented from the third boiling of the sugarcane, with a good Jamaican dunder." Ivory hair like a wild crown about his pink head. "To that," he thumps his four-footed cane against the rug, "a third again of Fernet – the Jelinek, if you have it – and the same of John D. Taylor's Velvet Falernum." His pale blue suit baggy over a pink shirt, a white tie loosely knotted. "A dash of bitters, Angostura if you must, stir with ice and let it sit, this is very important! Let it sit a half-minute before straining."

"Very good sir," says the tall man, his chin nodding behind the high white gateposts of his upturned collar.

"Soda water," says the young man, a hand on the old man's shoulder, "and a straw." His pale pale hair just touched with gold hangs in tangled dreadlocks to his shoulders. "The same for me," he says, "but with ice, and orgeat, and cream. No straw."

"Indeed." The tall man all in sombre black walks softly across the dark wood-paneled room, loomed over by enormous oil paintings of dour men in rich black suits. Here and there high-backed chairs with elaborately carved wooden frames and jewel-colored cushions, little tables with barely enough space for their nests of knick-knacks. On an ornate sofa the Duke slouches in his blue and brown striped suit at one end, Jo in her bone-colored gown stiffly upright at the other. "Negroni," says the Duke.

"More of a summer's drink, isn't that, sir?" says the tall man.

"Is it?" says the Duke.

After a moment, the tall man turns to Jo. "Miss?" he says.

"I, oh," she says, "water?"

"Just water?"

"Try the soda," says the young man with the dreadlocks. "Water and fizz, cream, flavored syrup." His suit's a deep rich blue over a white shirt shimmering like silk. "No alcohol."

"What he said," says Jo.

"I am touched," says the young man, helping the old man to sit in a comfortably overstuffed armchair, "to see someone so committed to the ideal of second chances."

"Sorry?" says the Duke, leaning forward at that.

"Merely complimenting what must be your new knight, Hawk."

"How's your sister?" says the Duke. "Viscount."

"Louder," says the young man. "His hearing's not what it was."

"Pinabel!" calls the Duke, to the old man in the chair. "Hound! How goes the war?" and as the old man looks up and barks, "As expected!" the Duke lurches to his feet, says in a voice pitched low, "That's twice you've presumed in as many words, Axehandle. In the Queen's own parlor. Have a care; my second is a gallowglas."

"We've forgiven what might be forgotten," says the old man to the room, his head bobbing. The young man, smiling, murmurs "Threats, your grace?"

"That's the best you've got?" says the Duke, still low, still fierce.

"And we've forgotten," says the old man, faltering, "what we can forgive."

"But Excellency," says the Queen, in the doorway at the other end of the parlor. "That's nothing." A black high-waisted gown, her shoulders bare, her long black hair swept back. The Count smiles broadly, his bobbing head settling in a nod. The Duke steps back. Agravante's dreadlocks rustle as he wryly shakes his head. "Gentlemen," says the Queen. "How good of you to come." Ice clinking as a man in a trim black uniform moves among them, offering drinks.

"Nonsense!" bellows the Count.

"Nonetheless," says the Queen. Beside her a man whose sunbrowned head's quite bald, his cheeks grizzled with a dusting of white beard. The wide knot in his yellow tie at odds with his trim tuxedo. In his hands a delicate flute of some clear liquor, much the same as in the Queen's, and he lifts it as she lifts hers in a toast. "We salute you," she says, and all about the room their drinks are raised, then sipped. Jo looks at the thinly milky stuff in her glass, shrugs, downs some more. *"That* was bracing," the Duke mutters.

"So who's her escort?" says Jo, leaning close.

"He's no escort," says the Duke. "That's Welund, the Guisarme. A shark."

"Welund?" says Jo. "Where's Roland?"

"Not the best time for questions. Just, keep up. You're doing fine." And then, looking past her, "Hello," he says.

"Leo," says Orlando, and Jo whips around, steps back, out from between them. A white shirt open at the throat, a dark blue sarong stippled with little white flowers. There's no glass in his hands. "The Queen has sworn," he says, his dark eye bearing down on Jo, "never again to have another gallowglas in her house." She blinks but doesn't look away.

"And she does not," says the Duke. Over away behind him Agravante's laughing at something Welund's said. "She has me, and I'm the one has her." Laying his hand on Jo's spangled shoulder. Jo twitches. "A nicety, perhaps," says the Duke, "but merely one such as the many we depend on every day. Captivity suits you, Orlando."

Orlando's expression doesn't change as he shifts his gaze from Jo to the Duke. "I am my own man yet," he says.

"Then be so good as to assert yourself!" says the Duke. "Call down your charge. Let's launch whatever this is to be and steer it toward the table. I'm famished."

"But one guest yet remains," says Orlando, "though I think he's just arrived." Bare feet whispering over the rug he moves past them toward the Queen and Agravante and Welund, and Jo sags, closing her eyes, her breath gone deep and quick. "Drink some soda," says the Duke, and she scowls at him. "Just three or four more hours to go," he says, and then, "Well. I guess tonight *is* a night for bruising a few precedents."

In the doorway to the parlor the Queen inclines her head, just, to a man in a charcoal-stripe three-piece suit gaping over a sunken chest. A polished silver torc clamped about his knobby neck, his bald head bare and streaked with old grime, his shoulders damp with rain. "We are pleased and honored," says the Queen, "to welcome our sister's ambassadour."

"Forgive my graceless demeanor," says the man with the torc, and "Chazz?" cries the Count still sitting in his chair, peering about the backs of the men before him. "The invitation came to my attention at the most penultimate of moments, and any resources of which I might avail myself to freshen, as it is said, up, are thin upon the ground." He takes a heavy limp of a step. One foot's bare, the nails of his toes quite long and jagged sharp. The other foot's a wad of mud-soaked bandages, and the leg of his suit hangs in shredded tatters. "A bit of which, the ground I mean, I fear I've tracked across your lovely floors."

"A passel of gimps," mutters the Duke, and "What?" says Jo. "If that ain't a metaphor," he says.

"Gentlemen," calls the Queen, then. Beside her a woman in a simple black sheath leans close to murmur something in her ear, and she nods. "If you would join me here in the hall to raise our glasses, once again." And Jo looks down to see her hand in the Duke's, looks up to see those brown eyes sparked with green and gold. He squeezes, once, and lets her go.

The Queen stands at the foot of a sweeping flight of stairs in marble, carpeted with a runner like a neatly trimmed waterfall of white and gold. "It gives me," she says, raising her glass, and they all follow suit, Jo behind the Duke, her tall glass half drunk held up in her hand, "such pleasure as I cannot adequately express," and there's a rustle up there, a lick of white lace flashing past the bannisters above, a click of heels on marble, "to bid you welcome back once more," and there she is, at the top of the stairs, in a long ivory slip under a draped and gathered froth of white lace, her black and tangled curls held back with a simple band, and she's restlessly looking over all those bald heads looking up at her, smiling at the Duke's flopping brown locks, and then at Jo wine-dark behind him, looking back at her. "My daughter, Ysabel," says the Queen, and glasses are hoisted, lowered, sipped, as smiling the Princess takes one slow deliberate step after another down those stairs.

"GENTLEMEN!" – CHANGE & TRADITION – INTENT
A FINE ENOUGH DISTINCTION

"GENTLEMEN!" bellows the Duke, and he pounds the hood of the car. The muted conversations, the laughter from the big man in

the bulky sweater, all of it rumbles away to stillness. "Thanks,"
he says. Maybe ten of them in the little parking lot to the side of
the big brick temple, steaming cups in their hands, here and
there foil-wrapped burritos, a paper boat loaded with quesadilla.
Paper bags, ripped sauce packets, shreds of foil scattered over the
hood of the reddish-brown car. "You all know Jo Maguire." The
Duke in his camelhair coat and a snap brim tan fedora, Jo beside
him in her black leather reefer jacket, her wine-red hair bright
in the thin-stretched morning light, a cigarette smoking wanly
in her hand. "Jo, here's, well, some of the boys. Anybody know
where's the Shrieve?"

"Milwaukie," says the one in the peach and blue check jacket.
The one in the long black coat says, "The Couve." The Duke
shrugs. "Busy man. The Cater," pointing to the check jacket, "the
Mason," the big man in the sweater beside him. "Stirrup," is the
man in the brick-colored car coat, "the Kern," a man in a black
jumpsuit a-dangle with pouches and loops, "the Harper," a big
blond beard and a sheepskin jacket, "the Shootist," the man in the
long black coat, who tips his pale grey hat and says, "Pleasure to see
you up and about, miss." The Duke's moved on to a man in a dark
green work jacket. "The Axle," he says, "and that's the Spadone,"
a man in a brown and black ski jacket, a grimy white apron
stretched over his belly. "Don't listen to a word he says – "

"Yeah, boss, fuck you too," says the Spadone.

"The Buckler," a man in grey sweats, a cup of coffee in either
hand, "and the Cinquedea," a man in safety orange coveralls and
a long red coat puckered with intricate embroidery. "There will
be a quiz," says the Duke, looking over the litter on the hood of the
car. "Didn't I ask for donuts?" he asks the boy behind him,
slouched against the brick wall in a brown bomber jacket. The boy
shrugs. "Anyways," says the Duke, turning back. "The Gallowglas
has given up her banner and sworn fealty to ours. So give it up for
the newest member of the crew. She's getting the Helm's streets,"
he says, "full stop," as eyes avert, heads duck, shoulders shrug,
fingernails are closely examined, coffee's sipped. "Chilli," says
the Duke to the big blond beard, "Medoro," to the work jacket,
"Astolfo," the grey sweats, a coffee in either hand, "this is name

only. Y'all keep up the rounds as you have been. Also! Tonight. The Queen's dinner. Jo's my companion, another full stop. Do we have a problem here, gentlemen?"

Not a word or gesture from anyone until the Shootist hikes up his belt, the butts of his pearl-handled revolvers twinkling. "Nossir," he says.

"Hart and Hive, boys, can I get a fucking hello here?"

And "hello" and "hey" they say, and "hi," and "Salud!" cries the Spadone, and there are nods, and paper cups of coffee hoisted. Jo looks down, drags on her cigarette.

"Anybody worried about change? Tradition?" says the Duke. "In about a month, this whole damn city changes. Get used to it. Okay," clapping his hands a sharp pop in the little lot, "let's settle up." He heads around to the back of the car, prising a single key from the watch pocket of his brown jeans. Opening the trunk he leans in to wrestle a box to one side and drag another closer, to haul up a glass jug sloshing something viscous, white, frothed with a sheen of bubbles, a hint of warm yellow gold. Balancing it with one hand against the bumper he reaches up for the trunk and as it thunks home yelps, jumps back, catches the jug as it teeters over the pavement. Jo's standing right there, her frown slipping quizzically from the trunk to him, huddled, clutching that jug. "Startled me," he says, straightening.

"You don't need me for this. Right?" she says. "I'll just head back upstairs."

"Put that out first," he says, and rolling her eyes she flicks the half-smoked cigarette away. At the door, her hand on the knob, she turns, looks at them all watching her. "Thanks," she says, to all of them. "I, ah, yeah. Thanks." She opens the door, she steps inside.

The Duke leans over to the boy in the brown bomber jacket. "I thought I told you to – "

"You also said not to fucking let on. She stepped right the fuck up, I shoulda fucking tackled her?"

"Yeah," says the Duke, sucking his teeth, "well." Carrying the jug around to set it down before the car. "Okay, boys," he says, un-screwing the cap, and they're setting aside coffee cups, swallowing the last bit of burrito, producing bottles and jugs of their own, the Buckler cradling a plastic bag in his hands, quiveringly full of yellow-white frothy stuff. "One at a time," says the Duke, "let's go, let's go," and the first of them, the Mason, steps up to empty his bottle carefully, carefully into that big jug there on the pavement.

"Jo?" calls Jessie down the airy white room lined to her left the length of it with tall and narrow windows one after another. To her right in the corner a sofa bed's unfolded, a nest of white sheets and tangled blankets below a big flatscreen television set. A girl asprawl on her belly all elbows and knees and knobby ankles kicked up in the air her big feet dangling, wearing underpants with a mouthless cartoon cat printed across the seat, a video game controller in her hands. On the screen a figure in a scanty purple cheerleader outfit swings a chainsaw in a roundhouse swoop at a shambled knot of zombies, grinding snarls and moans from little black speakers scattered about. She shoots an ugly look at Jessie and jerks her pigtailed head, further back, further in. The cheerleader's running down a darkened hallway lined with lockers.

Past the sofa bed a long table under the windows, some high-backed chairs, four plates still set out bits of pasta and tomato sauce clinging here and there, an empty wine bottle, a couple of glasses. Past the table a red jacuzzi, over there a sink bolted to the wall opposite the windows by a white door paned with frosted glass half-open on a cramped bathroom. Well past that down a length of empty white plank flooring a queen-sized bed in a pool of soft light from the corner windows and beside it a ladder up to a dark corner of a loft under the high unfinished ceiling. At the foot of the ladder a steamer trunk, a couple of crates nailed shut, and leaning there by the ladder the black haft of a spear. "Jo?" says Jessie, peering up the ladder.

"Down here, sorry," says Jo, from the floor over on the other side of the bed. On her back, hands folded over her belly, a white V-neck T-shirt and black jeans and her big black boots. A wineglass redly full by her hip. "I can get up," she says, but she doesn't.

Jessie in her dark brown cardigan sits on the bed all crisp white sheets and fluffy comforter, an orange God's eye afghan neatly folded. "It's okay," she says. "How's, how are you – "

"It hurts," says Jo. "And I'm still getting," she swallows, "nauseous like, in waves – "

"Nauseated," says Jessie, and then, "No, don't, nothing. Never mind. Did, did Leo tell you about – "

"What," says Jo, flatly.

"Somebody, Karen, from this shop up the street, she's coming by with some dresses for you to try on. For tonight. Not for a couple of hours. I'm telling you," leaning forward, elbows on her knees, "I'm telling you this because Leo, he, he moves fast." Jo snorts. "What I mean is, he decides something, like this, and then he's, well, up and on to whatever's next."

"No followthrough," says Jo, hands tightening on her belly.

"He's got people for that," says Jessie. "Me, mostly. Ever since, for the last couple months."

"Okay," says Jo, and grunting she sits up. "You told me." Picking up the wineglass. "I got a couple hours? I'll just head upstairs, maybe take a nap or maybe another shower – "

"Jo," says Jessie, and Jo sets the wineglass back on the floor. A power cry from the other end of the room, the revving of a chainsaw, roars of pain. "I'm glad you're here. I know this is kind of a, I mean it *is* a weird situation, but he really, he cares for you. A lot. So I'm glad you're here."

"Weird," says Jo, "situation, what I don't need, sorry, no offense, what I don't need is the girlfriend telling me how *cool* he is."

"I am not – "

"Let's play this straight, okay? The two of us?" Jo's knees up, her arms about them holding on. "I'm not here because I want to be. I'm here because this is all I've got." She swallows again. "This is how I get her out of there. So that's how far I trust him and abso*lute*ly no further. Okay?"

"I was never his girlfriend, okay?" says Jessie, as Jo climbs to her feet, scooping up the wineglass. "He's my employer. I do a job for him, he pays me. This is me being straight with you, okay? He's a good man."

"I told you," says Jo, headed for the ladder, "what I do not need – "

"Did you mean to kill Tommy Rawhead?"

Jo stops at that. "I didn't kill – "

"No?" says Jessie.

"The fuck does this have to do with – "

"Intent," says Jessie, leaning back on the bed, tucking a yellow lock behind her ear. "Did you mean to step out in the street when Roland struck him with the sword?"

"I didn't know how it worked," says Jo. "When that happened."

"I was here that night," says Jessie, "when they brought in, it was a *bone,* was all that was left. I saw the *look* on his face, Jo. I know what he's forgiven you. He's a good man. He didn't *do,* what you said he did."

"I didn't mean to kill Tommy," says Jo. She starts hauling herself one-handed up the ladder, careful of the full wineglass. "But still. He's dead."

He leans against the fender of the reddish-brown car, a black stripe down its side, parked across the street from an old green house up behind a low stone wall, a neatly narrow garden, columns brightly white in a tasteful glare. It's raining harder now. He doesn't seem to notice. He wears no hat or coat, just a track suit, green, with silver stripes, and darkly splotched with rain. Rain glistens in his close-cropped hair gone pinkly orange in the streetlight. He wears a pair of sunglasses the lenses like jagged pieces of green bottle-glass, and blue and white headphones cup his ears. His hands in fingerless bicycle gloves clasped before him. His face expressionless.

And after a time, though the rain falls much as before, he pushes himself up off the fender of that car, and shakes his head, and slowly walks away.

The soup's brought out in a gilt tureen held up by a man and ladled out by a woman, both of them in trim black uniforms, and it's smooth and thick, a brightly golden red in their wide white shallow bowls. Jo reaches for her spoon and the Duke beside her lays his hand on her wrist, barely shakes his head. Another man in a trim black uniform's got a little cast iron skillet sizzling in his oven-mitted hand, and he scoops a couple-three croutons into each bowl, and the woman following him in her trim black uniform crushes a pinch of herbs over the croutons and sets a dry dead leaf, an oak or a maple, to float atop the soup. Jo reaches again and again the Duke shakes his head, more perceptibly. At the head of the table the Queen's lifted her spoon. She tastes the soup.

"A passata de ceci, ma'am," says the Majordomo standing behind her, his chin tucked behind his upturned collar. "A soup of chickpeas and tomatoes, flavored with fresh sage, peppers, saffron, and wild fiori di finocchio."

"Delicious," says the Queen, and up and down the table the clink of spoons taken up and dipped into the soup. "Dang," says Jo, scooping up another spoonful, and then she picks up her glass, looks back for the attention of one of those black-suited figures, "Excuse me," she says, quietly, as the Duke's saying "Jo, just – "

"Is something not to your liking, Gallowglas?" says the Queen.

"No. Ma'am," says Jo. "It's really very good."

"Another drink, perhaps?"

"Well, I, ah – "

"Speak up."

All about her the clinks and discreet slurps of soup assiduously ladled up to mouths. "I was going to ask," says Jo, "whether there was any maybe orange flavor? I mean, this is, this good, but with orange it would," she sets her glass down. "It would taste like a creamsicle."

"A creamsicle," says the Queen. "Well, Majordomo? Might we fulfill her request?"

"There is a blood orange syrup flavor, ma'am."

"Oh," says the Queen, looking back with a smile at him, "do whip up a batch. One for everyone, that we all might sample this delicacy." Looking down the length of the table now at Ysabel sitting at the foot of it, her hand on Jo's, Jo staring tight-lipped at her soup. "Creamsicle," says the Queen. "How marvelous. You must tell us, Hawk, how this trick was accomplished."

"Without more context, ma'am," says the Duke, leaning forward to catch her eye, "I'd have to fall back to my usual response." The Queen's still fixed on Jo.

"Which is?" says the Gammer sitting across from him.

"Clean living," says the Duke.

"The last we'd heard the Gallowglas was dead," says the Queen, and Jo looks up from her soup as Ysabel squeezes her hand.

"*Left* for dead," says the Duke. "A fine enough distinction indeed, but there we are – "

"Won't happen again," says Orlando, sitting across from Jo.

"Mooncalfe," says Welund, a warning, there on the Queen's left. "*Blood* oranges?" says the Count, alarmed, to her right. "Hush, Grandfather," says Agravante beside him.

"I had hoped," says the Duke, opening the fists he'd clenched to either side of his bowl of soup, "not to broach the subject until later – "

"Yes, tell us, Hawk," says the Queen. "Why have you brought a gallowglas in my house?"

"She is now a member of my company, ma'am, and she has been wronged, by someone you have let into your house."

"Go on," says Welund gruffly after a moment.

"He means me," says Orlando.

"They all know whom I mean," says the Duke, an aside. "Five nights ago he drew on her without warning or quarrel – "

"I *have* a quarrel," snaps Orlando.

"Even if you had," says the Duke, "even if he had, ma'am, it's a quarrel long since settled by an earlier duel, a duel he lost, as his eye bears witness."

Spoons jump. Orlando's pounded the table. "I will not put up," he says, and Welund says, "Let him finish."

"This is absurd," says Orlando.

"Any quarrel he might have is not with her," says the Duke, "but me." He picks up his drink, a finger or so of sticky red liquor clinging to melting ice, and he tosses it back, sets the glass down. "And before you all assembled, I say he is a coward for attacking her in my stead, and I demand the return of her sword, which he is not fit to bear." Looking away from Orlando up the length of the table to the Queen with a sidelong smile. "Ma'am."

A clink from Chazz there next to the Duke, chasing the last of his soup.

"That's all?" says Welund. "The sword?"

"It's all I ask of him," says the Duke.

"This is tedious," says the Queen, waving at Orlando. "Produce the weapon."

"I am my own man," says Orlando, quietly, his hands unmoving on the table before him. "No ties of toradh bind me."

"You have the keeping of my daughter," says the Queen, "and I'll not risk your losing her to the likes of him in yet another blasted duel. Produce the weapon."

His chair scrapes as he pushes it back, tossing a plain black scabbard to the table, with a throat and chape the color of thunderclouds. In his hand the bared sword long and straight, the guard of it a glittering basket of wiry strands that meet in thick round worked steel knots. "I don't know why I bothered," he says. "It's not a terribly good sword."

"The Anvil," says Agravante, leaning back away from Orlando, "is the finest smith of this or any – "

"Oh, I know," says Orlando, spinning, lunging, thrusting. "I mean," he says, head cocked, "the design of it." The man in the trim black uniform confused looks down at the blade piercing his jacket, pinning him to the wall behind. "Only good for poking things," says Orlando, straightening, leaning close to the man to plant his hand on his chest. "I don't know," he says. "Maybe her heart's not in it? No anger," he says, absently, "no fear…"

Jo eyes wide her left hand fingers knotted with Ysabel's pressed to the lace of Ysabel's gown.

Orlando wrenches the sword free from the man's chest. "You see," he says, over his shoulder to the Duke, "it's lousy at cutting – "

"No," says Jo, working her hand free as the sword sweeps back. The man against the wall looks up from the hole in his trim black jacket in time for it to meet his neck in a clean quick cut straight through.

Agravante pushes his chair back and Jo leaps to her feet and as the man's body slumps to the floor the man and woman waiting to either side of him step back along the wall to make room. The Queen her elbows on the table her face in her hands. Welund stepping away from the table, a cell phone to his ear. "Like chopping wood," says Orlando, turning back to face the Duke. "Do you still want it?"

"Jo," says the Duke. "Leave." In one hand the stern hawk head of his cane, in the other the heavy pommel of his longsword.

"I'll," she says, shaking her head, "I can take care of – "

"Go," says the Duke. "I'd not have the lesson I'm about to impart made permanent."

"I," says Jo, and then, "oh," and then, *"oh,"* backing away from the table as the Duke lurches to his feet. "I'll be along presently," he says. "With your blade."

Ysabel's hand's found hers. Jo looks at it, looks at Ysabel's eyes shining, her hurried nod, and hand in hand they turn away. A woman in a trim black uniform holds the door open for them as they stumble out into the hallway to the sound of ringing blades and the Queen's voice bellowing, *"Enough!"*

"Leo, dammit" – Getting Ready – with All her Heart

"Leo, dammit," says Jessie, hands up, blocking his way, and "Oh for pity's sake," he says, "it's my fucking office." In his blue and brown striped pants and a shirt of creamy gold, open at the throat, a very pointed pair of Persian slippers on his feet.

"She isn't done," says Jessie. The room behind her empty but for a big flat wooden desk on four stout legs and a shoulder-high rack on casters hung with dresses in colors that come from flames and dawns, sunstruck bricks, and leaves, just before they fall. A song is playing softly, guitar and piano and a big rubbery bass, on the black Fellini sails, tattered rags that hangs on nails reminds me. A woman in a navy pantsuit's bent over at an awkward angle, tugging at a zipper in the back of a severely simple gown the color of old bone.

Jo's wriggling her shoulders from the straps, letting the front of it peel away from her chest. "What's to do?" says the Duke. "That looks fantastic. Like whatshername. With the hair." He diddles his fingers in front of his face. Jo shoots a look at the Duke, an arm across her breasts. The song's soaring into a chorus, she had one long pair of eyes, she had one long pair of eyes between her. "Real nineteen-thirties Hollywood glamor thing," the Duke's saying.

"There's a jacket, a bolero jacket with that one," says the woman in the pantsuit, tugging the gown over Jo's hips.

"So why are we still talking about this?" says the Duke. "Karen, thanks, I'll have Sweetloaf run the rest back in a bit, now, if you don't mind? I need to talk to Jo here, alone."

"Leo," says Jessie, curtly, as Karen nods and heads for the door, and "What," says the Duke. "Is that dress not fantastic?"

"That's not – "

"And is five-fifteen not allotted in my schedule for helping Jo to see the light? And am I not already running ten minutes late?"

"Twenty," mutters Jessie, and "All *right* then," says the Duke, gesturing toward the door.

"Actually," says Jo. "Jessie. If you could stay." In her black boxer briefs, tugging down her white V-neck T-shirt. Her feet bare.

"I, ah," says Jessie, and the Duke's saying "You didn't, but, okay, sure. Why not. Fine."

"So this light," says Jo, and Jessie rolls her eyes, shoving her fists in the pockets of her cardigan, stretching it down and down.

"The light," says the Duke, sucking his teeth. "Okay. Tonight ain't what you think it is."

"What is it I think it is?" says Jo.

"The night you walk out of that house with a Princess on your arm."

"That's not," says Jo, "I wasn't," and "*Come* on," says the Duke, "tell me. Look me in the eye and tell me. If she takes your hand, if she kisses your cheek and she says to you, Jo, she says Jo, take me with you – what are you gonna do?"

Jo one hand gripping the rack of dresses face hot says, "I made a promise."

"And so it will be kept," says the Duke, gently. "Safe and sound, warm and hale. Jo." A shuffling limp, leaning heavily on his cane, and she looks down. "Jo, look at me." His hand on her chin, hesitantly, gently tipping it back up. "I could just," he says, and she lifts her head away with a little jerk and he lets his hand drop, "I could tell you it suits my purposes for you to go, and expect you to put on that dress without another word." Jessie snorts at that, and the Duke favors her with a sour, sidelong glare. "But I am doing you the signal honor," he says to Jo, "of explaining myself, a courtesy I rarely ever extend. If she were to walk out of that house with you, tonight. If," he takes a deep breath, "if the last bond between the Bride and the Queen were broken, and no King were there to take her hand."

"You're talking about the coup," says Jo, and Jessie looks up at that.

"No, no coup. Far worse," says the Duke, and "Yeah, but, but the stuff," says Jo, "the turning, the, the," waving her hand, looking for the word, "the owr. It stops."

"It's stopped already," says the Duke. "We squeeze ourselves dry week after week and nothing but dust comes back. No, I'm talking about it ending. Forever. No more Hive, nor Hawk, nor Hound." He looks away, a bad taste in his mouth. "It's started already. I have, Jo, with you, I have nineteen knights gathered beneath my mighty wings. How many came with their bottles to this morning's Muster?"

"I, ah, so, the King," says Jo, letting go of the rack, looking over at Jessie, who's shaking her head. "When does he come back?"

"Once I have sat upon the Throne," says the Duke, "and stood back up again."

"Well, okay, so this Throne then," says Jo. "We have to go find it?"

"It's not like that," says Jessie.

"It's not time," says the Duke.

"When, when is it gonna be – "

"I've sworn that by the turning of the year I will be King."

"So that's, what, a month? A month and a half?"

"Sooner, perhaps."

"Well what is it we're waiting for?" says Jo. "What has to happen?"

"Jo," says Jessie, "just, don't," as the Duke says "I will know it when it's time."

"*It*. What it. What are you talking about here – "

He pounds his cane-tip against the floor. "I'm *not ready*, Gallow-glas."

"Leo, we'd better," says Jessie, but Jo's saying, "You're not," as she makes her way down the rack of dresses away from him, one hand brushing their shoulders, straps, hangers clink-clinking against the rail, each other. "Ready." She stoops, picks up her black jeans, looks at them a moment in her hands. "All of this," she says, "All, the stoppage. The squeezing. Her being," shaking out the jeans, *"cooped up* with her mother, this, *all* of this, because, Christ." Looking up at him now with those mud-colored eyes. "You'd better *get* ready."

"I swore an oath," he says. "Before the turning of the – "

"Your oath!" she cries. "Her wish! Her, vision, or whatever. Herself as Queen. We know it's going to happen. Why are you even bothering with, she's – Leo, shit, let's go. Get it over with. Tonight."

"Herself as Queen, and you by her side. Is that what she told you? Is that why you flung yourself against the Mooncalfe? You thought for sure you wouldn't lose? Because of that?"

"I'm here," says Jo. "I survived."

"Let's go, downstairs," says the Duke. "You jump out in front of a bus. I want to see how her vision saves you then. If we go, tonight, to get it over with, best bring a broom with you, to sweep what's left of me from the seat for the next candidate."

"Who's next?" says Jo, and he laughs. "How quickly I'm thrown over," he says to Jessie, spreading his arms wide, the cane jaunty in one hand. "Do you see – *anyone* – else!" he bellows, and drives the cane down to crack against the floor. "Put down those pants, Gallowglas. Take a shower. Have Jessie do something with your hair and your face. Put on that dress. Do these things because it suits my purposes. We leave in an hour and a half." And he turns away and limps toward the door.

"How?" says Jo, and he stops. "How does it, why risk it? Me?"

"I think you'll make a decent catalyst," he says, "provoking and, clarifying, certain actions and reactions. We'll see how the Queen might back her daughter's new champion." His hand on the doorknob. "And I will keep a promise that I made to you: that you might see the Bride, and speak with her." He opens the door, he nods, he steps through, and pulls it shut behind him.

Jo lets out a sudden blast of breath, shaking her head. "Arrogant," she says. "Son of a bitch."

"He's a Duke, Jo," says Jessie, scooping back her yellow hair. "What did you expect?"

"Still," says Jo.

"Where's the car," says Ysabel, heading for the front door in a rustle of lace, a clatter of heels, and "Wait," says Jo, padding after in her slippers, a glitter of spangles, grabbing Ysabel's arm. "Wait."

"We're just going to walk home?" says Ysabel, turning, her hand on Jo's elbow, her hip, pulling her close, Jo's hand still on her elbow, her other arm awkward behind Ysabel's back as Ysabel hugs her tightly, cheek to cheek, her eyes squeezed shut, "Oh, Jo," she says, then leaning back a little and blinking quickly "They didn't, they didn't tell me," and then as Jo's saying "I didn't think so" Ysabel kisses her, quickly, firmly, and then, her hands coming up, Jo's awkward arm about her waist, she's stroking Jo's hair, her forehead against Jo's, her cheeks wet, she says, "I missed you so much."

"Yeah," says Jo.

"You look so, so lovely tonight," says Ysabel.

"Ysabel, we need to," says Jo, and Ysabel says "Yes of course" and turns stepping out of the embrace toward the door again, and again Jo catches her hand, "No," she says, "wait."

"We should go, now, while they're distracted," says Ysabel.

"They're, they're done fighting, I think," says Jo. A muffled bellow from somewhere down the hall behind them. "With the swords, anyway. There's nowhere to go, Ysabel. I took the

Duke up on his offer. I'm staying in his loft, until, I don't know. Haven't thought that out."

"I can stay with you – "

"Ysabel," says Jo. "Tell me. All of this. It was about becoming Queen, wasn't it."

Ysabel takes in a short sharp breath, then letting it out she smiles just a little and says, "Not at first."

"Who was gonna be the King?" says Jo, looking down at her hand in Ysabel's. Their fingers twined. "It wasn't the Duke." She doesn't see Ysabel's frown, the look she darts sideways, her swallow just before she says, "No one. I don't need a King."

"You don't. But – "

"There hasn't been a King for years."

Jo lets go of Ysabel's hand. "Yeah, but," she says. "They seem to think you do."

"I seem to think they're wrong. Jo." She grabs Jo's hand in both of hers. "All I need, Jo, is a bit of medhu to turn. Once I've done it, that's it, it's done, and all of mine, and none of hers. We could walk out that door and find some, tonight. Jo, we could try it tonight!"

"I don't know," says Jo, "if I could go through that again. If it didn't work."

Ysabel pulls her close. "I will be Queen, Jo. I've seen it."

Jo closes her eyes and lays her forehead against Ysabel's. "Maybe," she says, "maybe me saying no, maybe waiting for the King to come back, maybe that's how it is you get to be Queen."

Ysabel's grip tightens on Jo's hand pressed there between them. "You wouldn't. You've just come back to me. You wouldn't leave me."

"I don't *know,*" says Jo, and Ysabel says "Don't you trust me? Don't you believe me?"

Jo's nose brushing Ysabel's she opens her mouth to say something, but she doesn't, she presses it instead against Ysabel's in a briefly single kiss. "I believe that you believe," she says, "with all your heart." Leaning back, stepping back. Letting go. "But you could be wrong."

"So could *they,*" says Ysabel.

"I can't," says Jo, stepping back again, "I can't *make* this decision."

"You have. You already have."

"Ysabel," says Jo, as heels click-clacking Ysabel heads past her down that hall toward the stairs. Jo reaches for her, her sleeve, and Ysabel stops, and turns, her eyes so green, so cold and dry. "Let me go," she says.

"Here," says Jo, holding up a piece of paper folded and tucked into a triangle that says Is.

"Is?" says Ysabel, taking it from her.

"It's from Jessie," says Jo. "I don't think she knows how you spell your name."

"So it's my consolation prize?" says Ysabel, as she unfolds it, reading it, and her hand starts to wave the note, shake it at Jo, and she says, "She loves me, for what that's worth. That whatever I want, whatever I decide," and Ysabel lets the creased note fall to the floor. "She won't stand in my way," she says.

"Fuck," says Jo under her breath as Ysabel walks away, and then, "For what it's worth," she says, taking a step after those click-clacking heels, "I'm gonna do, everything I can, anything, to get him on that Throne as soon as fucking possible. I'm gonna – "

"Imagine my gratitude," says Ysabel, trudging up the stairs.

"I really don't want to talk to you," says Jo around the cigarette in her mouth. She's sitting tailor-fashion on a little fire-escape balcony high above an empty street, a susurrating patter of gentle wind-blown rain on the awning above her. Across the street a big tan building, windows dark, only the red letters saying Fred Meyer lit up on the sign that hangs down the front of it. She leans forward to tap ash onto the sidewalk below. Wrapped in a puffy white comforter, one foot still in a sequined slipper peeking out there by the railing. Laid beside her on the grated balcony floor a sword in a plain black scabbard to the table, with a throat and chape the color of thunderclouds.

"Mostly I wanted to make sure they got this put in while we were out," says the Duke, leaning against the sill of the open window behind her, in his dressing gown crowded with paisleys of purple and maroon and gold and brown.

"So this *is* new," says Jo.

"Can't have you traipsing all the way down through this pile to the parking lot every time you want a damn cigarette," he says. "You really should quit those."

"Yeah? Anything else I can do, to suit your purposes?"

He's rubbing his forehead under a flopping lock of brown hair, looking away, down through the grated balcony at the street below. "You could," he says, "accept an apology."

Jo shudders then, under the comforter, closing her eyes. "Fuck that," she says. "I made the decision I made. I'm not about to blame you for it."

"Was it rough?"

"She hates me now," says Jo. "I told you. I don't want to talk about it."

"Do you mind?" says the Duke, on foot in a sheepskin slipper up on the low sill, and Jo shrugs, scoots over, "It's your place," she says, pulling the comforter more tightly about herself, careful of the cigarette.

"Yours too, now," he says, climbing out the window, folding himself grimacing to sit beside her, rubbing his thigh. "What I meant was," he says, after a moment, "I did a stupid and a foolish thing, to you. I," and he takes a deep breath, *"presumed,* upon a trust we didn't have, a trust that, because of what I've done, we may never have." Looking at his hand, wrapped around the railing before him. "And I'm terribly very sorry for that."

After, after a gentle pattering moment, Jo leans over to let the half-smoked cigarette fall from her fingers. Tucks her hand under the comforter. "All right," she says. "Yes. I accept."

He nods, once. He says, "She'll get over it." He looks out at the drifting scrim of rain, looks at her beside him, huddled under the comforter. Wincing, he hauls himself to his feet. "I like it out here," he says, stepping over the sill, back inside.

"Hey," says Jo, and he stops there in the window. "One thing. Coffey's place. Why'd you take me there? How'd you know that's what I needed?"

He's smiling his crooked, sidelong smile. "Who doesn't find sea air restorative?" he says. "Goodnight, Jo."

MUFFLED VOICES

MUFFLED VOICES on the other side of a door or a wall and she opens her eyes slowly, a richly periwinkle that almost seems to cast a bluish light upon the sheets. Only a weird words that I couldn't no idea what she was. Stoned out of her mind on something. Gorgeously model tall like a different language, one of the Russians? He's gonna fucking usually sell it, or living beneath this? With the stuff from the truck.

She sits up. And immediately puts a hand to the side of her head, there under the spill of clotted yellow-white curls. Both hands to her face now pulling it, stretching, breathing heavily through her nose. Frowning. A generic little room, beige walls, two queen-sized beds side-by-side, the one over there mounded high with, with stuff, duffel bags and paper shopping bags and nylon drawstring sacks stuffed full, balls, soccer balls and footballs wrapped in clear plastic, tubes of tennis balls, on the floor before the chest of drawers with a television on top a ziggurat of shoeboxes. Quickly but carefully on hands and knees she moves to the foot of her bed, there the ruins of a brief red dress, torn, mud-stained, wet. She lowers a filthy bare foot to the carpeted floor, follows it down in a crouch. In there, says the one voice, crisp and clear.

Yeah, says the other, high and wobbly. From behind not the main door up the short dark hall that way but the flimsy communicating door, flat in the wall by the television set, the panel on her side propped open with a doorstop that stretching across the floor she reaches for but a click, a clatter, someone's hand on the knob on the other panel in the other room swinging open.

"Why did you even put her in here," says the guy pushing this room's panel open into the room, a tangle of blond hair and a big blond beard and a sheepskin jacket hanging open, and "There was room on the bed," says the other guy, and "No, I mean in here *at all,*" says the first guy, frowning, stepping into the room. "You put her where?"

"Shit," says the second guy, swarming into the room, his hair black and spiky, his jacket grey with lots of little pockets and straps and and the sleeves pushed up to his elbows. Heading around to the far side of the bed. "I swear she was in here, I swear."

"Maybe she's in the bathroom?" says the guy with the big blond beard, and as he's turning there's a squeak and a clack and the door to the room's pushed shut. She's standing there so tall, curly hair wildly white in the light, one shoulder back against the wall, one hand up, trembling, those bright blue eyes blinking rapidly. "Porth?" she says, or something like, and the second guy, the one in the grey jacket, he comes back around the bed, "There she is," he's saying, "hey, baby, it's okay – "

"You mother-defiling moron," says the guy with the big blond beard. "That's the Axe."

The eyes harden, fix, the trembling melts away as the shoulder comes off the wall her hand there lifting from behind her leg the wooden baseball bat she's holding choked up high in a vicious short swing that catches the second guy in the side of the head and as he's struck there wobbling, blinking, loops around to thunk against his chest and send him crashing to the floor. "Not. Anymore," she says, her voice rough.

"Forgive me," he says, "this far east, news of the court sometimes doesn't – "

"You're," she says, and she coughs, "Harper. The Duke. Took me."

"No, no, absolutely not. This little turd," kicking the guy on the floor, "took you. Found you asleep by the dumpsters out back. He thought you had – *potential.* You can kill him, if you like."

"Yes," she says, shaking her shaggy hair out of her face. "Draw."

"I will do no such thing," he says. "Southeast knew nothing of this. I swear it."

"Draw," she says.

"No," he says, and she shrugs, and swings the bat again.

Slumped at the foot of the bed he shudders as she's pulling off his jacket and he opens his eyes. Watches her as crouching there she pulls the jacket on, buttons the top two buttons, one hand on the bat, her eyes on him, all the while. Patting her way through the pockets she stops, suddenly, softens a little, maybe a smile as she lifts out a little plastic baggie twisted shut around a thumb-sized wodge of golden dust.

"This," he says, thickly, licking something milky from his lips, *"this* the Duke will hear of."

"Fine," she says, and she kisses the little baggie once, and tucks it away again. "Your pants."

Bless you, Jack, an inch of steel in the right place
will do wonders. Man is a pitiably frail machine.

—*Dr. Stephen Maturin*

NO. 16

PLENTY

4:59 WITH A CLACK FLOPS OVER TO BECOME 5:00 and the radio pops and crackles and hacks up a reedy synthesizer, an electric harpsichord, a programmed handclap, a woman cooing was it the kind of records that you played that made me think, was it just the way that you kiss kiss kiss kiss kiss kiss kiss kiss kissed me, that showed me, but he's sitting up in the sleeping bag, he's rolling over, he's found the off button. A croak, a burble, wings fluttering, settling, a droning, a chirruping, a ringing chime, a crackle of weight shifting on straw, on seed, a twisting creak as Frankie Reichart bundled in a heavy sweatshirt that says Sheep Rock Trails hunkers down to make his careful way through the dark room under cages heavy with drowsy birds.

Rattling down a flight of stairs bolted to the back of the old brick building, stumping across an empty, tuffeted lot high fences to either side, steaming breath lit up by the bloated moon glowering just over the roof behind him. The gate at the back of the lot hangs drunkenly from a single hinge and he steps over and through it into a narrow unpaved alley lined with tall dry grass that crunches underfoot. Across the alley a small garage, light leaking under its big main door. He opens a smaller door to the side and slips through.

Inside the walls are tiled with old album jackets, duotones in blues or greens of agonized men blowing horns, women in fanciful hats cupping enormous microphones to their lips, whole bands in matching dinner jackets against featureless backdrops of beige or pink or powder blue. There's a big round table covered in green felt out in the middle of the room, a deck of cards stacked neatly, a plastic tub that says Aunt Ruby's Peanuts in faded letters, filled with hex nuts and square nuts and round grey washers. He pushes through a herd of mismatched armchairs and recliners about the table toward one off to the side laid almost flat where a man lies sleeping in a rumpled brown suit much too big for him. Frankie fishes something, a penny up out of the pocket of his sweatpants and lays it with a dozen others and a couple of nickels in a blue glass ashtray on the arm of the recliner, then heads for a blank white door in the corner. A tiny room just big enough for a toilet and a sink. Shaking his head his long lank hair, pushing down the sweatpants, smacking his lips, working something loose from his teeth, he takes a long piss leaning one hand against the yellowed wall.

On his way out he stops by the sleeping man's recliner, looks down at that still and shriveled face. His hand hovering over the ashtray. An eyelid blotched with pale pink spots twitches and there's the ripping snort of a snore and Frankie's hand leaps up and back, he shudders, he hurries away.

Back across the alley and the harshly moonlit lot but not up the stairs, instead, he opens a back door on a kitchen, scarred linoleum, darkly looming cabinets, a yellow electric stove with only two eyes. Sitting at a small table topped with glittery teal formica a pale woman, her hair a close-cropped cap of gunmetal grey, a polished silver torc clamped about her neck. She doesn't look up as Frankie washes his hands in the red plastic tub of the sink, splashes his face. A bell rings somewhere further in past the kitchen. He's filling a cloudy glass with water and drinking it down. Her hands are folded in her lap.

A rattle of a beaded curtain and an old man steps into the kitchen, rubbing his shoulders, stamping his feet. "Nippy out," he says. He's wearing a black and red plaid barn coat. His hair a crisp circle of white curls almost yellow against the reddish darkness of his skin. He tosses a ring of keys on the counter. "Coffee in the front seat," he says. "Donuts in the back." Frankie scoops up the keys, wipes his mouth with the back of his hand. The woman stands, holds out a hand to the old man, and he takes it and says, "We got a little while. He'll be fine up front by himself a bit."

She shakes her head. "No roof over my head," she says, softly. "No floor beneath my feet."

"At least you stayed to say good morning," he says. Stroking the back of her hand with his thumb. She pulls him to her, pushes herself inside his coat and kisses him, and his arms about her hands splayed over the small of her back, cupping a pale bare buttock. "Hollow and hearth, woman," he says, breath smoking over her lips. "You're *cold.*"

Out of the kitchen down a tight hall through the beaded curtain into the main room of the shop, past shelves partitioned into regular cubbyholes stuffed here and there with mismatched pairs of shoes, past the worktable mounded high with more shoes of every shape and color, at the counter Frankie's opening a couple of pink boxes of donuts, unwrapping a sleeve of styrofoam cups. Something spiky, electric guitars playing the same phrase over and over chiming in and out of synch, pokes out of the clock radio by the pile of shoes. The bell over the door to the shop rings and a widely compact man steps in, worn jeans over longjohns and a bulky blue cardigan, his bald head ruddy. "Hey, Dogstongue," says Frankie, and the bald man nods, jerks a thumb at the music in the air. "Frasca?" he says.

"Beats me," says Frankie around a mouthful of cruller.

The bell rings again, and again, a woman in a long puffy coat over a taupe dress, a white apron, a nameplate that says Iemanya, a man in worn blue coveralls and grey leather work gloves and a long red toolbox that he sets down with a clank. Frankie's pouring coffee, offering donuts, saying hello. Three men and a woman come in together, heavy coats over trim black jackets unbuttoned, formal white shirts open at the throat, black pants with glossy black ribbons down the leg. Two of them wrangle a wide flat tray with a roundly crusted loaf under plastic wrap. They heft it up on the counter, "Whoa, hey," says Frankie, and the wrap comes off. A wedge has been cut from the loaf to reveal layers of cheese and twirly pasta with tomato sauce and pesto and olives and slices of egg and more besides. "Timpano!" cries the woman with a flourish, and the bell rings again, a fifth of them in that trim black uniform working her way through the door, a dingy red cooler in her arms, "A little help please?"

"Dang," says Dogstongue, picking at the filling of the loaf. "Compliments of the Queen," says one of the men, and "Dinner interruptus!" cries the first woman, taking one handle of the cooler.

"They fell to blows over the soup," says the second woman, opening the cooler on a jumble of bottles of soda and wine.

"Well not because of the soup," says one of the men, and "During the soup," says another.

"So," says the first woman, repeating her flourish, "leftovers!"

"There's a big old roll of tin foil in one of the cabinets back there," says the old man from the back of the room by the beaded curtain.

"Okay," says Frankie, handing off another cup of coffee. "Hey, where's Batswool? Isn't he usually," but the laughter dies, they're looking away, the three men, the two women, the trim black uniforms. "Hey, what," says Frankie, frowning.

"Go on, boy," says the old man, gently. "Fetch the foil."

"I HAVE TOLD YOUR GRACE" – A MOST DANGEROUS OPPONENT
HE'LL COME – NORTH IT IS

"I HAVE TOLD YOUR GRACE," says Vincent Erne, a towel in his hands, "as I have told her, repeatedly: I cannot teach someone who will not learn."

"It's a poor craftsman," says the Duke in his camelhair coat, tugging an oxblood leather glove from his fingers, "blames his tools, Mr. Erne."

"I'm not talking about tools," says Vincent, turning a pointed look at Jo there by the mirrors that reach from floor to ceiling, épée in her hand, mismatched Chuck Taylors on her feet. "I'm talking about material."

"Then let us test that mettle," says the Duke, slipping out of his coat, looking about a moment, then laying neatly on the floor by the front wall. He starts unbuttoning his dark red shirt. Vincent tosses the towel to Jo. "I'll get jackets and masks," he says, headed for the door. "Foils are – "

"No," says the Duke, laying his red shirt atop his coat. Smoothing the front of his white T-shirt. "None of that, and none of your stoppered toys, neither. I said we'd test the mettle." Pulling his gloves back on, he takes the cane he'd tucked under an arm and lets it fall on the shirt and the coat, leaning now on the heavy pommel of his unsheathed longsword.

"Not here, your grace," says Vincent.

"You'd rather we took it to the street?" says the Duke. "Your sword, Gallowglas."

She's already crossing the room to set her épée down in a serrated row of practice swords laid out along the floor. Wiping her hands with the towel, her face, blotting sweat from her chest. At the end of the row her leather jacket's haphazardly flumped and beside it another sword in a plain black scabbard, the hilt of it simple and straight, wrapped in dulled wire, the guard a glittering net of wire and worked steel knots. "It ain't talent or skill that's in question," says Vincent. "At the current moment." He clacks the hook at the end of his prosthetic arm. "It's discipline. It's respect. It's not making promises she forgets the moment she walks out that door. It's not disappearing for weeks at a time and going over my head to your grace in the hope of avoiding difficult questions. Do not pick up that sword."

Jo looks up at him with a shrug. "That sonofabitch is my liege," she says. She picks up the sword.

"Your, you," says Vincent. Clack.

She draws the sword from its scabbard. The Duke's limping into the middle of the room, his sword in both hands at an awkward angle before him, the heavy pommel braced against his belly. "I don't see the problem, Mr. Erne," he's saying. "I won't hit her. She can't hit me."

"An untrained amateur," says Vincent, "can be the most dangerous opponent in a duel."

"A wonder, then, that anyone manages ever to become proficient," says the Duke. "Whenever you're ready."

"Watch your stance," mutters Vincent as Jo marches past him. "Strike him, not his blade." She plants herself shoulder toward the Duke, blade up at an angle before her, free hand tucked up against her chest, almost under her chin. "You're annoyed," says the Duke. Turning his back almost to her, his sword still braced awkwardly both arms tight against his torso.

"You said you were gonna go for a walk," says Jo. "Leave us alone. Let us work. Hadn't even been ten minutes."

"I got bored," says the Duke.

"We're two blocks from Powell's," says Jo.

"I'm gonna go to Powell's, it's gonna be my Powell's," says the Duke. "You can't hit me from all the way over" as she takes two quickly scuttled steps and a third kicking into a shallow lunge sword arm up blade-tip down thrust at an angle the Duke turns to catch hilt up blade down over his shoulder the thrust aside a clang and a scrape. She shuffles back. He lurches around, facing her, pommel braced again against his belly, arms in tight. "It's more than that," he says. She lunges, thrusts high and to the right, rolling the tip over his blade to come in suddenly low and to the left but with a flick he knocks it aside. "You had a mad on for me all morning," he says.

Another thrust, parried. "I woke up at eleven," she says. Darting in low and outside, rolling under to jab up at his chest, he torques his wrist hair flopping blade spinning around and down to swat it away. "I have no idea," she says, "if I slept ten hours," another thrust, another whipping parry, his shoulder to her now, hilt in one hand pommel braced against the other, head down, and she's saying "or if it was five in the morning when I went to sleep" as she swings at his head and he ducks with a sidestep. "I don't," her blade wavering, he steps back as she leans in for a thrust, another parry, clang! "I don't have *any* idea what the fuck day it is," she says, a feint, a thrust, a parry and the Duke steps forward with a bellow as she's trying to swing her sword back, up, trying to catch his thrust before it whicks over her shoulder past her ear.

"That it?" he says, wincing, hobbling back.

"You didn't kill him," she says.

"Wednesday," says the Duke.

"What?" says Jo.

"November sixteenth," says Vincent. "If you actually feinted *at* him, rather than *near* him – "

"Christ," blurts Jo, turning away, her blade coming down with a whipping snap of her arm as something ugly masks the Duke's lips curling nostrils flaring brows crashing together he wrenches his sword up over his head steps limping the blade brought down a heavy chop as Jo's shoes squeak her arm-snap carrying her tottering around turning sword twisted up to just catch his like a falling bell.

Vincent lets out the breath he'd taken in.

"All right," say the Duke, stepping back. Jo's sidelong to him, free hand back against her chest, sword settling between them, before her, at an angle. "Mr. Erne totally telegraphed that last."

"I was paying attention," snaps Jo.

"Indeed," says the Duke. Smiling. Clapping his hands together. "One step at a time. Our first goal was only ever to get your sword back." Nodding as she lowers her sword, pulls her foot back in toward herself. Wipes her mouth with the back of her free hand. "You're useless to me without it."

"For what," says Vincent.

"Five weeks remain," says the Duke, "until the – "

"For what."

" – the turning of the, please, Mr. Erne, the year. Our next step – "

"Oh, no," says Vincent.

" – is to, Mr. Erne, please."

"Hell no, you son of a bitch."

"Why do you think that to be such an insult?" says the Duke.

"Leo," says Jo.

"Oh, *Leo,* is it," says Vincent.

"Five weeks remain," says the Duke, "but there is something, *next* week, we must prepare for."

"It's Shakespeare," says Becker into the phone.

"What is," says Jo in his ear.

"His old accustomed feast. That's like Romeo and Juliet."

"I don't think he was quoting Shakespeare. If anything I think maybe Shakespeare was quoting him. You know?"

"He what?" Becker's frowning at a spreadsheet on the computer screen, entering numbers from a handwritten column on the piece of paper in his lap.

"Never, never mind. Anyway. Are you, do you already have plans?"

"For Thanksgiving."

"Yes, for Thanksgiving."

"You call me up for the first time in weeks – "

"Since you fired me."

"Since I laid you off because we had no work, and you're asking me whether I want to come to your new, your friend's place, for turkey and trimmings."

"No turkey," says Jo.

"No turkey?"

"He's kind of a, I mean he's a vegetarian. Maybe there'll be turkey. There might be turkey. Is that a deal-breaker? Is this too weird? Is that what you're saying, this is too weird?"

Becker sits back, phone clamped between shoulder and ear, one hand still on the piece of paper in his lap. A low murmur of voices, four or five backs hunched here and there in the couple dozens kelly green carrels set up atop the long folding tables along the indecisive cream walls. Out the two tall windows across from him the last outriders of downtown's tall buildings, mostly older brick, a refurbished hotel, a stark new-build apartment block hanging over the highway's gully, and past all that the hills, black and green and lost in a low grey fog of cloud. "It's weird," he says. "But I wasn't gonna, I didn't have anything." He sighs, runs a hand through what's left of his hair.

"So you'll come?"

"What the hell."

"Cool," says Jo. "You guys were there at the start of this whole thing, I mean, you know? He said I could ask whoever I wanted, but there's not, I mean, anybody else, really, that I'd want to bring into this, you know?"

"Guys?" says Becker. "What whole thing?" The door behind his desk opens, a woman steps through, "Our phone bank," she's saying to someone, a man behind her. "We're running a bee-to-bee, a business to business right now, it's a little quiet, but there's thirty-six stations we can fill with a day's notice."

"You know," Jo's saying, "it's, ah, don't worry about it. A thing. Thirty-ninth and Hawthorne, there's a, it's the old Masonic temple? With the Indian restaurant. Upstairs. There'll be signs, or lots of people, I'm sure. Like five o'clock?"

"While I've got you," he's saying. The man who's come through the door, he's tall, his shirt striped blue and gold with crisp white cuffs and collar, a yellow tie, his hair an untidy mop of shining black curls. "We've got a, a thing, a political thing starting up. So it's residential work. Finally. I could use you and Ysabel on this." The man in the striped shirt's looking away as the woman's saying something about rigorous training and quality assurance protocols, he's looking down at his wrist, at the heavy golden watch there. He looks up, his dark eyes meeting Becker's, and Becker blinking looks away, at the computer screen.

"Yeah, well," says Jo, "that's, that's great, but. The situation's changed."

The man in the striped shirt's smiling to himself. "So that's a no," says Becker.

"Sorry," says Jo.

"And Ysabel, too? You guys still a package deal?"

"Like I say," says Jo. "Situation's changed. Thanks, Becker. See you for turkey or whatever."

"This is Arnie Becker," says the woman as he's hanging up the phone. "Our Lead Field Supervisor. He has a great deal of experience running surveys of, ah, all different sorts. Arnie, this is David Kerr, who's overseeing the survey for the commissioner."

"The committee to elect," says the man, smiling broadly. "An important distinction. Good to meet you, Arnie."

"Call me Becker," says Becker. "Everybody does."

The parlor's dark, the paintings high on the walls lost in gloom. A shadow moving through it, only the wide white collar at her throat the dimmest blue suggestion where she is, where she's going. The collar, and a squeak of a floorboard, there under a rug. She freezes. A faint rustle of hair against that collar, the shadow of a head turning a little, tilting, listening. Light scuff of a shoe on the rug, a popping tock from the floor as her weight shifts. Another scuff, a step, the floorboards silent now, and another, another, headed for the broad doorway, the open foyer beyond steeped in murky streetlight from high thin windows to either side of the broad front door, light that sparks a moment as she steps into it, snagged on the lenses of narrow, black-rimmed glasses.

"Anna," says Ysabel, ghostly by the front door in that light, white coat, white turtleneck, dark hair tied back. Holding out a hand. The woman all in black takes it, presses something into it, a crinkle, an envelope. "You'll want to put that somewhere," she says, opening Ysabel's coat, "safe, it's about five hundred – "

"Don't," Ysabel's saying, "it's, I'll – "

"It's all I could get on such short notice," says Anna, stepping closer. "She won't notice. She wouldn't ever notice." Her hand inside Ysabel's coat. "I checked the bus schedules. There's a fourteen every half hour till about one thirty. It'll drop you right in front of the Duke's place. Just get down to Madison on the Bus – Mall – " Frowning she reaches up to adjust her glasses. "You aren't going to the Duke's," she says.

Ysabel gently plucks the glasses from Anna's face. "I'm not telling you where I'm going," she says, folding the glasses, leaning close, kissing Anna, gently, and Anna squeezes her eyes shut, opens her mouth to kiss Ysabel in turn, and her hand falls away out of Ysabel's coat. She opens her eyes as Ysabel steps back and looks down to see her glasses in her hand.

"It never occurred to me before to tell you," says Anna, putting her glasses back on, "how beautiful you are."

"I never asked, before tonight," says Ysabel.

Outside on the sidewalk before the old green house up behind its low stone wall Ysabel alone shuts the gate, pulls her white coat tightly about herself, then slowly begins to step around in a tight little circle, one hand up, a pinkie to her lips. Lights here and there in the apartment block across the street, a guitar hollowed by distance, an echoing thump and pop of drums and what's maybe a chant from the ramshackle house over across the intersection behind a low screen of trees, lit up with candles and Christmas lights. A smile stealing over her face she shuts her eyes spinning faster now until a laugh leaking out she spreads her arms wide and stops, suddenly. Opens her eyes. The music, the ramshackle house behind her, the green house unlit to her left. Ahead only deep shadows, lines of parked cars, dark houses.

"All right," she says to herself. "North it is." And she sets out along the sidewalk.

A shadow shifts ahead of her, detaches itself from the shadowed line of cars, only the little white flowers stippled along the pleats of his skirt the faintest suggestion who it might be on the sidewalk there before her. "Mooncalfe," she says, stopping suddenly, and then, "I thought you were asleep."

"Always with one eye open," he says, stepping closer, a blacker shadow in the darkness ruddied by a streetlight back at the corner. "I am a conscientious guardian. It's much too dangerous for you to be out here by yourself."

"Dangerous for whom," she says, and she starts past him, but he puts out a hand to stop her. His long black hair loose, framing the pale mask of his face, slithering over the shoulders of his shapeless grey jacket. "Where are we going," he says, his hand sliding down one side of her coat. "Downtown's back that way." Sliding up the other side, stopping at a crinkle. She steps back, thumps against the side of the suv parked there at the curb, but he's already got the envelope.

"Give that back," she says.

"Your mother's far too generous," he says, thumbing the bills stuffed inside. "All this for a night on the town? I'll keep it safe for her."

"You won't need to," says Ysabel, holding out her hand. "I find I've lost my appetite for an evening out."

"But you stepped out almost every evening, when you were with your gallowglas," he says, reaching past her hand to take her arm by the elbow, tugging her more deeply into the shadows. "One might almost think you didn't like me."

Ysabel plants her feet, tugs her arm free. "Tell me, Mooncalfe," she says, "and tell me true. Why do you hate the Gallowglas so much?" A step toward him, and then another, head down, tilting, tipping to look up at him. "Can it be you, want me? That you find me," lifting her head, looking him squarely in the eye, "beautiful?"

He leans back from her, dark brows pinched together over his dark eyes. "In this light," he says, absently, his thready voice still clear, but then a smile quirks the corner of his mouth and he looks away, just, and his laugh is a silken thing, and he closes his mouth on it and it shakes his shoulders, his chest, his throat jumping as he tries but not too hard to hold it in. "Forgive me, lady," he says, swallowing. "I am a terrible romantic." Taking her hand. "I have a friend. You must come meet her. Ask her your question. I want to see what happens."

"Yeah, so, anyway" – the Nine varieties
"press Seven to delete"

"Yeah, so, anyway," says Jo, "I just figured, I mean, you and Becker, you were there at the start, you know?" A drag from the cigarette in her hand. "Maybe you got something going on, I don't know. Give me a call, okay? I, ah, I promise, I'll stop leaving messages."

The phone in her hand is little and glossy and black. On the screen a photo, herself and Ysabel cheek to cheek, Ysabel's hand at the upturned collar of her white coat, black curls trapped lopping over it, looking sidelong smiling almost at Jo eyes crinkled smiling wide and directly into the camera she's holding up before them, her arm blurrily out of focus at the bottom of the shot. Her hair

short and brown and tufted up every which way. Streetlight behind them a dark building somewhere outside at night. The
phone's clock over their heads says 27:29. Monday, November 21.
She thumbs the power button on its face and it goes dark. Sits back
on the little balcony, looks up at the featureless grey-white sky
past the awning above. In the empty intersection below stoplights
click from yellow to red, red to green. Dark windows in the big
tan building across the street, only the letters saying Fred Meyer
lit up on the sign that hangs down the front of it. One last pull at
the cigarette, then she leans over, lets it fall from her fingers
through the grated floor of the balcony to the sidewalk below.

In through the window. She leaves her leather jacket
sprawled over the mattress on the floor, drops the phone on it.
At the foot of the mattress a yawning steamer trunk, rumpled
clothing, jeans, T-shirts, most of them black, spilling over the
sides. A couple of wooden crates, one upended, more clothing,
shoes, a pair of big black boots. The white-painted floor ends
abruptly on two sides, opening out into the airy white room beyond, tall and narrow windows one after another down the
length of it. No railing about that edge, just the uprights of a
ladder leaning there against it, leading down into the room. By
the ladder a scabbard plain and black, throat and chape of beaten
metal the color of a thundercloud, the hilt of the sword within
simple and straight, wrapped in wire, the guard of it a glittering
net of wire and worked steel knots. Jo toes off her shoes,
peels off her sweatshirt, goes to unbutton her jeans but stops
a moment, her thumb, her palm against her belly bare, pale,
unmarked between navel and waistband.

She comes down the ladder in sweatpants and a black tank top,
barefoot, sword in hand. Down the length of the room past the
red jacuzzi she draws the sword, lays the scabbard on the long
dark table, takes up her stance, right foot before her left, sword
up at an angle before her, free hand pulled in close against her
chest. Stepping up, stepping back, swinging the blade slowly in
parries up, to the left, low, to the right. A long low lunge, a slow
thrust, that free hand dropping back in a fist, pulling herself
back upright, blade up again, free hand once more tucked

against her chest. Again the parries, bare feet shuffling and thumping on the white plank floor.

"That's wrong."

Jo straightens, shakes out her arms, works her head back and forth. Behind her one hand on a high-backed chair a skinny girl barely wrapped in a brief brown towel, dark hair a wet rope slung over a shoulder. "I didn't know anyone was up here," says Jo, taking up her stance again.

"I was taking a bath," says the girl. "I like long baths."

"You weren't," says Jo, looking back at the jacuzzi, "there's no tub in there." Past it the sink bolted to the wall, the white door paned with frosted glass.

"Sure there is," says the girl, with a smirk. Jo shrugs, turns to her blade, her feet shuffling, thumping, parry, parry, lunge and recover. "Sometimes," says the girl. "Your other hand's supposed to be up and back when you do that."

"You're a fencing coach, is that it?" The sword held straight out before her now. "That's why," her wrist rolls whipping the blade to the right then snapping back in line, "the Duke's keeping you around?" To the left. The tip of it trembling, just.

"It's how they do it in the movies," says the girl.

"Movies," says Jo. Whip and snap, whip and snap.

The girl's walking along the other side of the table, squeezing water from her hair. "You're jealous," she says, looking back over a bare shoulder.

"How *old* are you," says Jo, "like, fourteen?"

The girl undoes the towel and says, "Older than you, child," sweeping it off. "Older by far." Catching up her wet hair in it, twisting it deftly into a turban, patting it into shape up atop her scrawny neck. "You shouldn't worry about the Duke," she says. Jo snaps the tip of the sword to the left and trembling back. "He's far too in love with shades of grey for the likes of me. I'm all loud colors and bright noises and I need a heart as cold as a deep black tarn that's only fed on snow – "

"*Jesus*, Lauren, do I look like I care!" snaps Jo. Throwing her foot forward into another lunge, free hand flung back. Wobbling as she straightens, free hand tucked against her chest. The girl raps her knuckles on the table, turns, hand on her hip, walks away toward the unmade sofa bed off in the corner. "I don't know why you bother," she says. "Six weeks, six months, six years," pawing through a tangle of sheets and discarded clothing she comes up with a pair of underwear. "It wouldn't be enough." Yanking them up her legs. "Six *decades* wouldn't be enough."

Jo parries to the right, high, then low, sweeps the blade to the left, parries high, then low again.

A chanted chorus over organ chords from the speakers to either side of the monitor, all I've done and all I will do, all I know and all I want to, dissolves into buzzing strummed guitars and over them notes plucked clean and bent in an aching descant. The desk lamp the only light left in the narrow office, except what's splashed from the half-open door to the break room. Becker shuffles up a stack of handwritten notes, taps them on the desk to even them out. His flannel shirt a faded blue, open over a waffled undershirt. "First thing I don't get," he says, "is why you're bothering to run a poll at all. Everybody knows Beagle hasn't got a chance."

"Everybody who's paying attention," says Kerr. "And who's that, in November?" Sitting across the desk from Becker in a chair pulled over from one of the carrel workstations. "A lot can happen in six months. What else?" His shirt brown with wide white stripes, his caramel tie with polka dots in silver and gold.

"Well, I mean, that right there. It's six months out and you're spending a fortune on this thing, and it's, well, it's," Becker's pushing aside a stack of paper, fluttering his fingers over another, tugging free a bundle of typescript bound by a corner staple. "You're asking about the CRC – "

"You don't think that's a big issue."

"I don't see what the mayor's got to do with it," says Becker. "It's all down to regulatory agencies and lawsuits now." Flipping through the script. "Streetcar spurs, the Yellow line, congestion on I-5, you think it's transit but then there's the Timbers and the

Trailblazers and major league baseball, the Indigo, the Cyan, the Ladd, demolishing the Lovejoy Ramp, what you think of the NoLo nickname, which, is stupid, by the way – " Kerr shrugs " – capping the Tabor reservoirs, how well SoWhat is doing – "

"So what," says Kerr.

"South Waterfront," says Becker. "It's what they're calling South Waterfront."

"And see, I did not know that," says Kerr. "I'd quote Sun Tzu on the advisability of studying the terrain if I could remember something appropriate."

"This is one hell of a lot of advisability," says Becker, tossing the script back onto the desk.

"Sun Tzu," says Kerr with another shrug. "You have any idea how much money gets spent even on school board elections these days?"

"Well good," says Becker, "because there's all the overtime Barshefky Associates gets to charge for going over the survey results every other night with a busybody from the commissioner's office – "

"The committee, please, it's important," says Kerr, "and are you charging me for this? This conversation? Really?"

"I'm at my desk," says Becker. "I'm behind a computer."

"Then by all means let's decamp. I'll buy you a drink in lieu of time and a half."

Becker leans back in his chair. "You mean the committee will buy me a drink."

"No, me. Cæsar's wife and all."

"I – right," says Becker. "Well. I'd love to, but I'll have to rain-check. It's past ten, I'm a fucking pumpkin." Rubbing the corners of his eyes with a fingertip, pinching the bridge of his nose. "For whatever reason." Getting to his feet.

"Well tomorrow I have to go to Salem," says Kerr, pulling on a dark coat, pausing with it bunched up around his arms. "It's a long shot," he says, and then he settles the coat on his shoulders. "What are you doing Thursday?"

"Thanksgiving," says Becker, pulling a heavy raincoat from the coat tree.

"Because, because Huber's, they do a turkey dinner thing. It's really, ah, if you've never been – it's the oldest restaurant in town, you know? It's pretty old skool."

"Sounds, sounds lovely – "

"I know, I know, a restaurant on Thanksgiving. But if you're not going anywhere else, and if you are, I mean, this is maybe the one occasion where I could say, I understand, and genuinely, honestly *mean* it – "

"Well, I am," says Becker, zipping up his coat. "But it's kind of a party thing?" He leans in to shut off the break room light. "Friend of mine, something to do with her new job. I'm pretty sure I could plus-one you."

"But it's me who's supposed to buy you a drink."

"Open the door to the lobby," says Becker, and he snaps off the desk light as Kerr pushes the door open, letting the dim light from out there into the now-dark office. "Let me check," says Becker. "It's, I guess it's a big deal or something. Her boss, I guess he's this eccentric, rich guy or something, calls it his old accustomed feast."

"So he's a Capulet," says Kerr.

"Okay," says Becker, as they head into the lobby.

"You know, she really got a raw deal, Juliet?"

"What, with the suicide and all?"

"No," says Kerr. "Her name. Juliet Capulet. Must've teased her mercilessly on the playground. No wonder she couldn't wait to get married."

The black T-shirt he pulls on says The Secret of Madeleine Wool in white letters. "I don't know." He gathers up his hair in a tail at the back of his head but lets it fall away through slackened fingers. "I don't know." Rings glitter there, an ankh, a snakehead, a skull, some dice. Black paint on the nails, chipped and worn.

"She says don't bother," says the woman sitting tailor-fashion on the rumpled bed, a chunky green phone pressed to her ear. "She says you're fired." Thick blue legwarmers over neon pink fishnets over lacy black stockings over pale pantyhose, stretched-out underpants in a sort of peachy orange, a red strap riding up over one hip, and her fuzzy pink sweater bunched up by an old stained corset loosely knotted. On her head a bulging patchwork cap the color of confetti.

"Erase it," he says with a sigh.

"Okay," she says, taking the phone from her ear.

"Press seven," he says.

"Right," she says, and she does. "Okay," she says, listening, "okay, the next one's from, it's from Jo," and a look passes over his face, pinching his lips, hoisting his cheeks, squeezing his black-rimmed eyes, a look she doesn't see hunched over on the bed, phone pressed to her ear. "She says," she's saying, "she says the Duke's having a feast," and "We know, we know," he mutters, and "she says you're invited, it'll be a big thing, maybe a lot of people, maybe you don't want to come, but you should, no, it's not like you have to, that's not what she means, yeah, so, anyway, she just figures you and Becker were there at the start, maybe you have something going on. Call her. She promises to stop leaving messages." She looks up at him. "That's it," she says, and he sighs again. "Seven," he says.

"Seven?"

"Erase it."

She does.

"Do we go?" he says, kneeling on the bed beside her. The bed is low and wide and takes up most of the little room, jammed in a corner under a window full of rain, all too brightly lit by bare bulbs in a ceiling fixture.

"You're the one she invited."

"I'm supposed to go by myself?" He leans down on an elbow there beside her.

"The Duke's door is open to any and all that night."

"So," he says, lying on his side beside her, "we both go? But separately?"

"We could," she says.

"You still don't know," he says, and he covers his face with his hands.

"There's a lot I don't know."

"Like whether or not if I go or not I'll keep somebody else from getting killed or not."

"What I do know is the lights," she says.

"The lights," he says, looking up from his hands.

"In about five minutes," she says, "maybe four, Mrs. Theodorakis upstairs will try to run her disposal again, which shares wires with these lights in our room in this building that should have been torn down long before now." Her voice toneless, staccato, stilted. "The circuit in the basement will break again, which will be enough this time to send a flux of power through a grid that will blow up a grey canister on a pole on the corner, which will stop the flow of power to most of this neighborhood, including the stoplight on Burnside. In the confusion, a milk truck with a cartoon cow painted on the tank will plow into a minivan, instantly killing Piper Dupree and her two-year-old son, Noah – "

He's shut off the light. Slumps there by the light switch, forehead against the white wall. "The circuit box isn't in the basement," he says.

"It isn't?" she says brightly.

"It's in the cabinet in that weird little nook off the kitchen." He turns around, shoulders against the wall. "I bet the little old lady upstairs isn't named Mrs. Theodorakis, either."

"If it isn't part of the story it gets muddled," she says. "I told you that. Maybe I made whoever it is that owns this building sleep through the meeting where they were going to sell it to whoever it was who was going to put up the big glass tower instead because I knew we might get to stay here a while and I wanted that to happen. Maybe I haven't done that yet but I'm going to because I don't want this place where we were once to be torn down. Right now I just wanted the lights off." She lies back on the rumpled bed, pink fishnets faintly glowing.

"What are you wearing," he says.

"You like it?" she says. "I wanted to look sexy."

"All of that?" he says.

"Really, *really* sexy."

And he laughs then, and crawls into the bed with her, and kisses her as she hikes a leg over his hip and kisses him right back.

"Why are you still here," he says.

"Stupid," she says, kissing his nose. "I said your part of the story was over." Reaching up for her cap. "I didn't say your *story* was over."

TRIPPING OVER SOMETHING IN THE DARK – HERS ALSO IN THE FOYER – HE'S WASHED DISHES OLD JOHN BARLEYCORN

TRIPPING OVER SOMETHING IN THE DARK, "Shit," she says, gruffly, and a hollow echoey thump, a clank and a stumbling clatter, a snap of a light switch and there she is, catching a mop handle as it's leaning out of the mop bucket there by the door, her with her legs bare under the oversized blue sweatshirt that says Brigadoon! Gently setting the mop back against the wall. Brushing back her wine-dark sleep-matted hair. Before her a rack of cubbies stuffed with spray bottles and cartons of light bulbs and bundles of paper towels under looped hanks of orange extension cord. "Leo?" she says, and then in a smaller voice, "Jessie?" Looking at the door behind her, simple, slender, unpaneled, painted brown, a round knob with a cheap gold finish. "I just," she says. Her hand on the knob. A sharp rush of breath in through her teeth and a jerk of her wrist and she opens the door.

Outside a hall white with sunlight from a window somewhere down the length of it right there by the doorway the buzzing red bulk of a Coke machine.

"Oh, hell," says Jo. She closes the door. Takes her hand off the knob. Rubs her mouth, her chin. Turns around and around again in the narrow little closet, brushing the overstuffed rack of cubbies, rattling, clank. "Oh hell." Her hand on the golden knob once more. Twisting it. Letting go. Flexing her fingers she leans her forehead against the jamb. Maybe she says something, muttering, head rocking back and forth until she lifts it away looking about the closet again, taking up the knob a third time, her other hand a fist in the air, laid flat on the wall, reaching for the light switch there under a shelf. She snaps it off. She opens the door.

"The name, Chilli," says the Duke, coldly. Squatting there on the floor, idly flipping through inked and painted canvasses and sheets of Bristol board stacked against the wall. "And heed its syllables, as they trip from your tongue?"

The man with the big blond beard doesn't say anything. He isn't looking at the Duke. He isn't looking at the man in the brown plaid suit standing to one side of him, rich red hair flopping from a high widow's peak, he isn't looking at the big man on the other side, thick arms folded over a broad chest bared under a half-unbuttoned yellow chamois shirt. He's looking at Jo, there in the doorway, and so are those two men, and the Duke looks up, sees her, and his scowl softens. "Hey," he says. "What's, ah, what are you doing here?"

"I was, looking for the kitchen," she says. "Coffee." Opening her hand, letting go of the knob, smooth white porcelain hung from hardware dark with age, set in an elaborately paneled door painted white.

"That way," says the Duke, pointing down the length of the room lined with high shelves, some stuffed with books and comics, some swarming with homunculi, weirdly muscled figures in bright colors roaring at each other, crowded around a little black car with jagged orange trim, a toy helicopter, blue and white, bristling with guns. "Hey," he says.

"Yeah?" says Jo.

"Close that door? There's a draft."

Jo closes the door on a dim white hallway and heads away down the long room, those jumbled shelves angling around a corner, there's an overstuffed chair striped in candy-apple reds and greens, a matching ottoman, more haphazard stacks of art. "Hattock and horse, man," the Duke's saying behind her, "how were you thinking to deal with this *quickly* and *quietly?* Hand her your own sword and run yourself at it?" At the end of the room a swinging door, pale blue, a brass plate she pushes open into a cramped kitchen, a sink, a refrigerator, a bit of wood-topped counter beneath a window filled with watery grey light, a couple of gleaming ovens set in the wall, a butcher's block there before her, a stainless steel carafe to one side. She fishes a mug from the sink, rinses it out, pours coffee from the carafe. Sips, one hand on the counter, looking at the door she'd just come through, at the other door, across the kitchen. Mug in hand she heads around the butcher's block toward that other door but stops, her hand on the brass plate. Turns back toward the door she'd come through, pushes it open, steps out into an airy white room, the long wall before her lined with tall and narrow windows one after another. Off to one side a red jacuzzi out in the middle of the white plank floor, to the other a long table, some high-backed chairs. Music playing down that end of the room, it won't make sense right now, a woman's singing over soaring keys, but you're still her friend, and then you let her down easy, and those keys are swallowed by a grinding, stuttering beat.

"Oh, hell," says Jo.

"That you? Jo?" Down the other end past the jacuzzi there's Jessie, peering around the corner of an alcove, one hand on a ladder leading up to a loft.

"I was," says Jo, looking back at the swinging door, the sink bolted to the wall beside it, the second door, paned with frosted glass. "I was just in the kitchen?"

"Dang," says Jessie, stepping out, leaning against the ladder. Looking past Jo at the swinging door. "He's been telling me he'd get that done for months." Her yellow hair undone, brushing her bare shoulders. Complicated briefs, black straps criss-crossing her hips, a small panel of sheer black lace. "Actually," says Jessie, mouth quirking in a sidelong frown, "it's a little awkward, now I look at it. Two doors right there like that."

"I think," says Jo, "I interrupted a meeting or something? And he wanted to get me, out of the way, or, I could come back? If you need to get dressed?"

"What?" says Jessie. "Oh. Sorry. Don't," waving a hand, "don't do that." Turning back into the alcove. "It's your place, too, much as it's mine or," shooting a look over her shoulder at the other end of the room, *"anybody else's,"* at the music chewing up a stuttered chorus of tell her not to get upset, up–second-guessing, tell her down easy. "Typical, how he didn't even think where he was gonna put you, just, make room, make room, we'll deal with it later."

"I guess," says Jo, following her, the burning heart in a glistering starburst of red and yellow rays at the base of her spine where black straps criss-cross together in a neat little bow, "he thought maybe, I mean, you guys would be staying together more? Or something?"

Jessie stops, a hand on the corner of the alcove. "I haven't slept with him in almost two months," she says, and then she steps inside.

"Oh," says Jo, leaning on the ladder. "I didn't know."

"I swear," calls Jessie, something rustling, a scrape of hangers, "if the two of you would just sit down and *talk.*"

"We've talked," says Jo. "Actually, he apologized."

The rustling stops. "Leo Barganax apologized."

"Yeah," says Jo.

"It must be love." Another scrape.

"It's not exactly something you just say I'm sorry and it goes away," says Jo to her cup of coffee.

Jessie's there at the corner again, half in a little black dress that hangs low and loose from her shoulders. "Are you gonna call the cops," she says.

"What?"

"Are you gonna call the cops? Because if you aren't you need to stop using that word."

"Do I."

"It's getting in the way. It's fucking you up."

"Easy for you to say."

"Is it." Jessie heads back into the alcove, tugging and smoothing the dress into place.

"Did," says Jo, stepping around the corner after her, "did he ever – "

"No," snaps Jessie. She's sitting on the edge of the big white bed, working a foot into a slender high-heeled sandal. "I sure as hell wouldn't be here if he had. Leo doesn't, he isn't," setting

194

her shod foot on the floor, "he does a lot of stupid, thoughtless things, but not anything like that. That's just not who he is."

"Did he ever ask you," says Jo, one hand on the corner, "if you loved him."

Jessie looks up, her other shoe in her hand. "Oh," she says. "I told you, it's not that kind of. No. No, he hasn't."

"Do you love him?"

Jessie works the shoe onto her other foot. "I *told* you," she says.

"What do you want, Jessie?"

"What do I want?" Intent on buckling the sandal. "A big comfortable chair surrounded by all the books." Getting to her feet she resettles the drape of her little black dress. "And nothing left to do but read them."

"When she's, when she's Queen," says Jo. "I think you should stand in her way. For what it's worth. I think she *wants* you to stand in her way."

Jessie looks over at Jo then, in her Brigadoon! sweatshirt, the yellow mug steaming softly in her hands, and then without a word steps through a narrow sliding door into the closet under the loft, and Jo looks away, an exaggerated wince, a hiss of "Shit" to herself, and then "I'm sorry" she calls after Jessie, "I didn't, she," a scrape of a drawer from the closet, a rattle, a scrabble, "she read me the, well she didn't *read* it to me, she told me what it, said, when I saw her, at the dinner, when I gave it to her, and I, I wasn't thinking. I'm sorry."

Jessie comes back out of the closet, chunks of red jade hanging from her ears, a beaded rope of rough red jade in her hands, and says "Can you" as she turns her back to Jo, the folds of that black dress open all the way down to frame the burning heart. Holding up the ends of the necklace. Jo sets her mug on the floor. "What are you," she says, frowning as she fumbles with the tiny clasp, "getting all dolled up for?"

Jessie looks back over her shoulder with a little smile. Turning when Jo closes the clasp, stepping back. "Is that what you're wearing?"

"I might get around to putting on some pants in a minute," says Jo.

"You have no idea what day it is, do you," says Jessie, and Jo's face goes slack, eyes flat and wide, mouth falling open, "You're fucking kidding," she says, grabbing the ladder, turning back, scooping up the mug of coffee, "I swear to fucking *God* yesterday was Monday – "

"Happy Thanksgiving," says Jessie, as Jo hauls herself up the ladder.

It's an odd coat he's wearing, the man on the corner, red and draped in dozens of thick pilly nodules that lightly sway as he leans back to look up at torches glowering under the low dark sky. A sign over dark windows says India Oven, and another says Jambo World Crafts, there by a row of limply dangling flags, a great peace sign stitched to a tie-dyed rainbow field, an American flag, its stars replaced by another peace sign, a hawk stooping through a vertical black bar on a tawny field. The cornerstone beyond is marked with compass and square. Up between green-capped white columns the tall windows on the second floor are filled with red and blue lights softened by gauzy curtains that twitch behind the glass to the dulled thump of half-heard music. He shivers, shoves his hands his pockets, setting those stubby tendrils bobbing as he starts up the steps to the wide white doors.

In the black and white tiled foyer another man, his coat a long one, dark, leans against the wall, watching the phone in his hand. Glancing up he nods at the man in the odd red coat who pauses, one foot cocked on the steel-plated heel of his boot. "Upstairs," says the man in the dark coat, looking back at his phone. The screen of it filled with tiny figures in ancient bronze armor tumbling through a clear blue sky.

"Yeah?" says the man in the odd red coat. A watch cap's rolled down over the tops of his ears. His sunken cheeks are dark with a couple of days' worth of beard. The music's more clear in here, breaking down the walls of heartache someone's singing, I'm a carpenter of love and affection.

"Indian place is closed," says the man in the dark coat. "I assume you're here for the, uh," looking up at the ceiling, "feast?" Outside a bus pulls up to the corner, and the man in the dark coat straightens, steps away from the wall. Three or four people getting off the bus, one of them a man in a heavy raincoat, a trilby jammed on his head. The man in the dark coat steps up, leans into the crash bar on the front door pushing it open, beckoning to the man in the trilby who shoulders through the thickening rain up the low steps and inside. "You took the bus," says the man in the dark coat.

"I took," says the man taking off his trilby, running a hand through what's left of his hair, "yes, the bus, my car, my car got stolen – "

"I would've given you," the man in the dark coat's saying, "a, stolen."

" – about a month back, yeah, it's a, insurance is being a, I mean, it was a piece of junk anyway but the guy, whoever, he totaled it, and, ah, I can't, I'm sorry, I, I don't – "

"I could have given you a ride," says the man in the dark coat. "Is all."

" – I, yeah, um," says Becker. Smiling now, a little. "Yeah."

"Shall we?" says Kerr, looking up as the thumping bass above them melts away into high sharp stabs of guitar over a rattling crash of drums. Becker's mouth twists in dubiety, an eyebrow quirked. "Hey," says Kerr. "She's your friend."

"Yeah," says Becker.

Up the stairs on the other side of a humming bright Coke machine a door painted white wedged open on an unlit hall that leads to a long high-ceilinged room hung about with dim lamps shaded blue and red. Torchlight flickers outside the high narrow windows, dappling the surging crowd, I'm hurt and I want you to know a falsetto's singing, but for others I put on a show, so loud atop the spiking guitar, the thundering drums, the hands thrown up over heads tossing in time.

"This isn't!" says Kerr, "what I think of!" leaning close, "when I hear the word feast!"

"What?" says Becker, tugging at the zipper of his coat.

"Feast!" says Kerr. "This! is not! a feast!"

Those drums drop out and that guitar smacks into a fat and loose bassline. Someone's catching Becker by the arm, "Hey!" cries Jo, beaming, a glass in her hand, a blousy black shirt, a tight white vest. "You made it! Guthrie with you?"

"What?" says Becker, unshouldering his coat.

"Guthrie!" says Jo.

"David Kerr!" says Kerr, holding out his hand for a shake, and there's bongos starting up, na-na, na-na na-na-nah, the crowd around them going wild, laughing, cheering, clapping, from somewhere spotlights swooping, shadows leaping, there on the wall at the other end of the room it's two in the morning, my beeper's going off, I'm naked I roll over, enough is enough! "Hi!" says Jo, taking Kerr's hand, giving it a squeeze.

"You don't mind?" says Becker.

"Pyrocles," says Jo.

"What?" says Becker.

Turning away from Kerr, leaning close to Becker, "He's here," she says, in his ear. "Pyrocles."

"Who?" says Becker.

Stepping back, blinking, she doesn't quite smile. Looks at Kerr again. Those shadows across the room, the cheering, the laughter bouncing over that enormous bass, a couple women with the same severe blond hair strutting arms akimbo up on a table or something, the same fierce frowns on their similarly painted faces as they waggle the enormous jellied dildos sparkling pink and purple strapped to their hips, thwapping at each other in a mock duel, what can I say they can't stay away from the best cock on the block today, it's eternally hard, "I was going for a smoke!" says Jo, waving back past them toward the hall.

"Smoke?" says Becker, and Kerr shakes his head. "Jo, I don't smoke!" says Becker.

"No, how is it outside!" says Jo.

"Raining!" says Becker, and "Terrible!" says Kerr, and Jo rolls her eyes. "I'll be back in a minute!" she says as she pushes past them, "Coat-check's over there!" Tossing a hand back toward a long open rack crowded with raincoats and jackets and wraps where that man's bundling up his odd red coat, white watch cap still on his head. Behind him there's Jessie in her cocktail dress, and she lays a hand on his arm, and he turns, and smiles to see her.

Down the wide white stairwell to the black and white foyer where Jo pauses a moment, looking out at the rain through the windows in the doors. A cigarette jiggling in her fingers, a silvery lighter winking in her other hand. Somewhere above her everybody roaring from the dee to the eye to the ell to the doe! She turns away from the closed front doors, heads back past the stairs to the restaurant beneath them, a confusion of chairs upended, resting on tables, legs in the air. Up front by the shuttered steam table a couple of tables cleared of chairs and laid with trays and dishes laden with canapés and tapas and zakuski and antipasti and amuse-gueles and a couple of figures in trim black uniforms take up this one or that in one hand or the other and "Hang on, hang on," a man in a brown plaid suit is saying, turning as they bustle past him, "wait," he's saying, "they're still, they went on early and nobody's ready for snacks, Christ, Maguire, you seen His Nibs?"

"Not since this kicked off," says Jo, "and if you see him, Stirrup," waggling the cigarette in her hand, "I wasn't here, doing this, okay?"

"Gee," says the Stirrup. "Thanks."

Off to the side under the sloping ceiling she lifts a chair from a table and sets it on the floor, drops into it, the lighter in her hand chiming as she clicks it and clicks it again before it strikes. "You look sharp," says the man behind her as she puffs the cigarette to life.

"Frankie?" she says, and she turns, the smoke winding about her face. She snaps the lighter shut. He's wearing a plain black T-shirt, black pants, he's drying his hands on a dirty dishtowel. "Hey," he says.

"You're," says Jo, "what are you – *doing* here?"

"At this party, that's open this one night, to whoever?" He looks back over at the plates, the trays, the shuttered steam table, the Stirrup trying earnestly to corral the two men and the woman in trim black uniforms. "The folks who do the catering, they come by Gordon's most mornings. They needed some help with the dishes tonight. I've washed dishes." The towel balled up in one hand now. His brown hair tied back loosely, face clean-shaven, clean. "They were at *that* dinner, the other night."

"Okay," says Jo.

"His name was Batswool."

"He what?"

"Batswool. I dunno, it's Arab or something. The guy got killed while *you* were eating dinner." The wadded towel shifts from one hand to the other and back again. "You didn't know that, did you. His name."

She takes another drag from the cigarette, then leans down, gently presses the top against the floor, breaking off the coal. Gets to her feet with the snuffed cigarette in her hand. "So what," he says, backing into the aisle to block her way, "you don't care, is that it? Why you haven't done anything?" as she steps right up close to him and low and fast says "You just don't want to pay off that twenty bucks."

"The *hell* I do!" He pushes her back with the toweled fist. She grabs his hand, shoves him to one side against a table scraped against the floor, but she doesn't move on, she just stands there, and he leans there, and "Yeah" he says, a snorted laugh, "go on, hit me. Everybody knows what you did to Marsh. You woulda put the Prick in the hospital that one time I hadn't pulled you off him and you even got fucking *Abe* to back down but this guy *kills* somebody right in front of you and you just keep eating your soup."

"You don't have," says Jo, quietly, *"any* idea, what he did to me – "

"How about what he did to *me?*" says Frankie, pushing himself upright. "I get it, I do, he's connected, it'd fuck up your new boyfriend. Right? He's the one, told you not to do a fucking thing, 'cause otherwise – I'm right, yeah?" It's an ugly little smile.

Jo walks away.

"He here?" Frankie calls after her. "The freak? Is he upstairs? Dancing?" The flutter of the towel behind her, flung at her as she leaves. "I'll fuck him up, I will! I swear!" Through the foyer, up the stairs two at a time past trim black uniforms hands full of plates of crackers and cheeses and little puff pastries. Around the corner landing up more stairs into the hall she's brought up short, there, the humming bright Coke machine, she leans against it. Pounds it, once, with the flat of her hand.

The music, the music's so loud.

There's a cup in her hand, a red plastic cup. She lifts it to her mouth but it's empty. She crumples it and lets it fall to the floor. Someone's hand on her shoulder. "Jo," says Jessie in her ear. The cup rattles underfoot as she turns. "You're going to be out here for a bit?"

"Sorry," says Jo, shaking her head, nodding. A man behind Jessie, tall and thin, a white cap on his head, a tight T-shirt printed with some baroque siege engine. Jessie's leaning forward to say "You're not going back to the room?" and he's looking with a smile on his narrow face at the small of Jessie's back.

"No," says Jo, and then, "have you seen Leo?"

"Sorry," says Jessie, reaching back with one hand, and the man in the white cap takes it after a moment without looking away from the burning heart in its starburst of red and yellow at the base of her spine. "Thanks, Jo. Thanks."

Somebody's growling a chainsaw for your birthday, all the wine you could ever drink over a chugging snarl of guitar, lay you in a bed of cold steel, cover your face with my fine white mask, you spend champagne Saturday on your knees but you'll never have to beg! It's not so loud anymore. She's in a hallway, empty, dark but for a grim red EXIT sign down at the one end. There's a cup in her hand. It isn't empty. She takes a drink. She's leaning against the wall with a door to one side of her and a door to the other, both white, hydraulic hinges folded, waiting, at their tops. Brass push plates, both of them.

The cup's empty. She looks down at it in her hand, at the singed cigarette in the fingers of her other hand. She leans up off the wall. She tucks the cigarette behind her ear. She pushes open the door to her left.

Walls lined with jumbled shelves of books and comics and toys angle around a corner up ahead where there's an overstuffed chair striped in candy-apple reds and greens under a goosenecked reading lamp, a matching ottoman, haphazard stacks of canvas and board and glossy glass and plastic frames here and there along the floor. "Now, see," says someone, the Duke, off around that corner, and Jo smiles and shakes her head and makes her way through the shelves, *"that's* what I'm talking about."

He's holding an orange behind his back, a tiny half-peeled thing dwarfed by beefy, juice-slick fingers. A leather thong tied about his wrist. His broad back bare, and dark, and muscles ripple as he lifts his shoulders, his black-haired head tipped back on that thick neck. A hiss of breath. His buttocks bare, a pale hand, someone else's, cupping as they clench, his trousers down about his knees, the wide belt lolling, and Jo stops, says nothing, takes a slow and careful backwards step into a clink of glass, a rustle, a slither of slumping, falling paper, one of the stacks of art is toppling.

That head with its black cap of hair is turning, there's the corner of a frown, but it's the Duke down there peering past the naked hip, "Jo," he says, "I," but she's turned, she's fled, she's gone.

"Laugh, Luff, Love" – Neither of them, or Both
an Other word – his Weaknesses

"Laugh," she says. "Luff? Love."

"Love," he says, the word askew. He kisses her cheek, the point of her jaw.

"The tennis score," she says. "If you're not a fan of sentiment."

"Go on," he says. He kisses her throat, her shoulder, nosing the folds of her cocktail dress aside, and she's tipping her yellow hair away from his mouth. "Luck?" she says. "Lock? Loch," she says, firmly, opening her eyes, but he shakes his head and kisses the notch of her clavicle. She strokes his head still in that white watch cap. "Lack," she says, then "Lick." He laughs around his kiss, his hands on her hips, strumming the bare skin of her back there between the artful drapes of shimmering black. "How," he says, leaning back a little, "do I get you out of this," and his hands swoop up that length of skin, and she sucks in a quick sip of air. "Let go," she says. "Take off your shirt. Go on."

He steps back bootheel chiming on the wide plank floor, bumps into, sits abruptly on the foot of the big white bed. Tugs his T-shirt free from his baggy black jeans, works it up over his head. His narrow chest asymmetrically furred, the thicker, broader patch to the left brushed with tufts of grey. His ribs c an just be made out, and the bones about his shoulders. "Take off the cap," she says, but he shakes his head. "Chilly," he says. "Your turn."

She reaches behind her neck, there under her hair, and does something, her dress slumps, slips down her arms as she lowers them, reaches around her hips and does something, her dress loosens, rolls away down her legs. She steps out of it in her heels and those complicated briefs. He holds out a hand and she takes it, and he draws her to him, one knee on the bed, then the other, to either side of his thighs. "Lick," she says, again.

"Lough," he says, the vowels weirdly out of tune, the end of it ragged and rough. He says it again. "Lauch."

"Look," she says, kissing his mouth. "Luke." He's smiling. "Lake," says someone behind them, and Lough stiffens, that smile faltering. Jessie looks back over a shoulder with something terrible in her eyes, "You little shit," she says.

Lauren's there, at the mouth of the alcove, hands on hips cocked in high-waisted gingham shorts, a matching cropped halter, her long straight hair in sloppy pigtails, dark eyes full. "You're Lake," she says, voice trembling. "You're back."

"Lauren," says Jessie, "I swear to God if you don't – " but then Lough raises a hand. "Lauren," he says, roughly. "Yallowshot."

Those dark eyes shut, spill over, she nods, jerkily, and suddenly all elbows and knees and red Keds slapping runs into the alcove leaping on the bed tackling him in a wild hug Jessie leaning back, away, one arm uselessly up over her breasts, her face knitted in quizzical horror as Lauren kisses Lough and he kisses her right back. "I don't," she says, pushing away, "I don't need this," but he's reaching for, he's caught her hand, "Wait," he says, pulling her back, and she doesn't resist. He leans away from Lauren to kiss her knuckles.

"I'm not," Jessie starts to say as Lauren sits up, grabs her other hand and pulls it toward her, "Stay!" she says. "You have to. That's the point."

Lough lets go of her hand, leans across the puffy white comforter, his lap still full of Lauren, and Jessie doesn't start any further back, she's looking at Lauren, looking at the hand Lough's lifted to brush her cheek. She doesn't set her other foot on the floor. Her hand in Lauren's shifting, no longer held but holding hers in turn, there on his black-denimed knee. "It's all right," says Lough, leaning close, tipping his head back, and holding herself very still she turns just to meet his mouth, blinking quickly. "It's why we're here," he says, and settling back on an elbow, he nods, but he's looking away from them both with something of a frown. Jessie still blinking at him says "Lake?" as Lauren pulls her close, their hands still squeezed together caught between gingham and bare skin. Jessie turning away from Lough to meet those big dark eyes right there, that mouth opening for a kiss.

It's a slow and steady thing at first but the breath Jessie catches in the middle of it's a tremble of a sigh and Lauren's hiking up off Lough's lap pushing and she topples slowly back into deep soft pillowy white and the kiss redoubles into something fierce and hungry, snarling, crushing groans from them both.

"What is she to you," says Lough when the storm has passed, stroking Jessie's yellow hair.

"How did you know," says Jessie, kissing Lauren's throat.

"He was always my favorite," says Lauren. Biting her lip, pigtails awry, looking at Lough tipped up on his side. "You made such beautiful things, did you think I'd forget?" She pushes up, pushes back, "It's going to be *so* good now," she says, sliding off the edge of the bed. Jessie hitches up a little to look down her body at Lauren's wicked grin, her quick hands busy with the straps that criss-cross Jessie's hips.

"What are you," Jessie starts to say, but Lough leans down, breathes a shush in her ear. His long hand on her breast, her nipple palely pink between his fingers. Her head falls back, her chin lifts, she takes in a breath, and in some more, and more, rising, rising. "You didn't answer the question," he whispers, as she claws up handfuls of comforter.

"Wizard," he snarls, hand the size of a dinner plate flat against Kerr's chest shoving him dark coat flapping into the wall by the bright red Coke machine. "Pyrocles!" says Becker, grabbing at a slab of shoulder bared by a sleeveless grey T-shirt. Piano rings out over a thumping beat somewhere behind them, I'm a boy, someone's singing, at an open door, why you staring, do you think you know?

"Actually," says Kerr, pushing off from the wall, "I prefer the term magician." Settling his coat, utterly black in the lurid glare of the Coke machine. Straightening his black and silver tie. "Wizard makes it sound like something supernatural's involved."

"Melanchlœnidon," spits Pyrocles, and Kerr tips back at that, an eyebrow cocked, a nod, "Yes," he says. "That's another word."

"I don't," says Becker, "I didn't remember – *anything*, Kerr, until I saw him. You," he says, blinking the sweat from his eyes, to Pyrocles, that broad chest working like a bellows, a couple of heavy beads strung from the drooping tips of his mustaches swaying with the force of his breath, tocking almost to the thundering music. "I'm sorry," says Becker. And then, to Kerr, "There's something weird going on – "

"No," snaps Kerr, and Becker's brought up short.

"Trust me," he says. "I'm standing here, telling you. This is *weird."*

"No," says Kerr again, shaking his head. "There is nothing weird in this world," he says, "nothing above nature, or beyond it, there can't be. There's just," and he taps his temple, "a failure, of your mental model, to account for something that's occurred, and I'm arguing *semantics* in a goddamn rave, Becker, are you coming."

"I , uh," says Becker, arms folded in his short-sleeved shirt, open at the throat, "I need my coat."

Wordlessly Pyrocles plucks the bundle from under his other arm, holding it out, Becker's heavy raincoat, his crumpled trilby. "Oh," says Becker. "Um. Thanks." The music drops suddenly as he takes them from Pyrocles, and the crowd off away behind them, it sounds like the whole roomful, they're chanting along with the chorus, we are not what you think we are! We are golden! We are golden! and Kerr's face crumples, he lifts a hand as he ducks forward shoulders shaking, laughter that can't be heard as the song crashes to a close. Becker looks over at Pyrocles, who's looking at the floor, somewhere almost exactly between Becker's feet, and Kerr's. Kerr straightens, quaking with an aftershock, a long sighing breath, "Well, Becker?" he says, and there's not a trace left now but the hint of a twinkle in his eye. "Coming?"

"I should," says Becker, and he's looking down now, too, at the hat he's pinching and pressing, pushing it back into shape. "I think I'll, ah – "

"Take the bus," says Kerr, with a shrug. "Okay." Holding up a hand, turning it slowly before them, the back of it, the front, empty but for a plain thick silvery ring. "Yes," he says, "I am a magician," and when he turns the back of his hand to them again with a fnap there's a business card tucked between his index and middle fingers. "Which means exactly what you think it does." He extends the card to Becker. "Go on," he says, and Becker gingerly takes it. "I'll call you."

A swirl of that coat and off he's gone, clattering brusquely down the stairs.

"Call me?" mutters Becker, turning the card over in his hand. It's white, thick paper, stiff, and blank on both sides.

"Becker," says Pyrocles, his voice a rasp.

Becker shakes out his heavy raincoat, puts his hat on his head. "I should," he says, "I really should go."

"Don't," says Pyrocles, his hand catching up Becker's wrist, swallowing it, stained knuckles burred by rough skin, old scars, wisps of grey hair.

"Don't what," says Becker, half in his raincoat. "Don't go?"

"Don't see him," says Pyrocles, letting go. Becker slips his arm into the other sleeve of his coat, tucks the card in his pocket. "Men like that," says Pyrocles, "are bad news." Becker meets Pyrocles' eyes at that. "Don't go," says Pyrocles.

"I should," says Becker, "I really should. The bus – "

"You remember," says Pyrocles. "Don't you?"

"I remember," say Becker, shaking his head, "that there's something to remember." He reaches up to lightly touch one of the beads at the ends of Pyrocles' mustaches. It's a dull and heavy pewter, irregularly shaped. "Is this, this is new, isn't it."

Pyrocles gently takes Becker's hand, presses the back of it to his lips. "Stay," he says.

"I, I can't," says Becker. "Not tonight." A step back, his hand slipping free. "Tonight's," he says, "too," his hand stirring the air, looking for a word, "too," and then he shrugs, and ducks his head, and turns, and with a heavy tread he makes his way down the stairs.

The only light in the cramped kitchen comes from a shallow bay in the door of the refrigerator, a couple of levers and a spigot, she's leaning over it, white vest shining in the glow, forehead pressed against the stainless steel, wine-red hair lost in the shadows. With deliberate care she fits the glass in her hand to one of the levers, squares her shoulders, pushes. The refrigerator grinds and chuckles and she starts back, yanks the glass away. Sets it against the other lever. Pushes. A jet of water squirts into the glass.

She drinks it down in noisy gulps, sets the empty glass in the sink. The window over the sink blank and black, scratches in the glass touched with pinkish orange. Outside that auroral streetlight's shining through a fog of oily droplets that's drifting thickly downward, softening an empty tree, a tiny parking lot two or three floors below, a single car angled across a couple of its spaces, a nameless color in this light that might be brown or red, a dark stripe slashed across its roof. Across the little lot an empty diner, a brilliant pool of indoor light trapped behind glass, red booths, plush red stools at a blue counter, Bob's Big Boy says the swooning neon sign hoisted up behind the tree. She's pulled her glossy black phone from a pocket and hiked herself up on her toes leaning over the sink, her elbows on the sill. She thumbs it to life. The photo, there, herself and Ysabel cheek to cheek, somewhere outside at night. 44:44, says the phone's clock. Louhitag, Frostarious 4.

"Oh, good," says the Duke, behind her. "You're up."

Jo turns away from the window, slipping the phone into her pocket. "Still up," she says with a cough.

He's there by one of the swinging doors, across the butcher's block from her, barefoot in his shadowy paisley dressing gown. His dark hair parted like curtains about his face, curling where it's tucked up behind his ears. He isn't frowning, he isn't smiling, his lips and brow inclined neither up nor down, his gaze open and steady upon her. "I realize," he said, "a third time under these circumstances is as charmless as it might prove useless – "

"Why did you do this?" says Jo.

" – but – this. That?" He points back over his shoulder at the door behind him.

"The party," she says. "If it's all as bad as you say it is why are you – doing this."

"This feast," he says. "I do it every year. People would talk, if I didn't."

"Oh," she says, looking down. And then, "You slept with him," she says, and she looks up again to meet his gaze. "Didn't you."

His expression's unmoved. "It's the Mooncalfe you mean," he says, after a moment. She nods. "Oh," he says, "we each slept with the other. Many times over. You aren't upset about Luys."

One of her shoulders twitches, a bit of a shrug. "Luys hasn't tried to kill me."

"To be fair to us both," says the Duke, one hand on the butcher's block, "when we were doing all that sleeping, we neither of us knew that you were even in the world."

Jo says, "So it's all my fault, then," and his brow knits at that. He says, "I get the distinct impression that we keep skipping steps in this conversation."

"Keep up," she mutters.

"Damn me for a fool if you must," says the Duke, "but dance this far in my shoes, at least: he is one hell of a thing to look upon." His smile's a gentle thing, almost apologetic. "I've always had a weakness for blonds, and beautiful boys."

"I'm not either," says Jo, her voice thick.

"No," says the Duke. "You're something else entirely." Tugging the loose gown a little more tightly about his body.

"Do you want to," says Jo, and she swallows, looking down, takes in a breath, "Yes?" says the Duke, and she looks up, "fuck me?" Leaning back, elbows on the rim of the sink behind her.

"What?" says the Duke, after a moment.

"You heard me."

"Not so sure I did."

"It's a simple question."

"Like I said." There by the corner of the block now. "I haven't been sure of my footing since I stepped in here."

"Do you want to fuck me, Leo," she says, and each word's crisply clear.

"I think," says the Duke, "what's paramount, to me at least, this precise moment," taking another step closer, "is whether you, want to fuck, me," and she's taken hold of the lapel of his dressing gown, she's bunched it in a fist, yanked him one last step to fetch up tight against her, nose by nose, her forehead against his. "Good question," she says, and she kisses him, and smiles in the middle of the kiss. "Good answer, too," she says, and he takes in a sharp breath through his nose the gown falling open away from her clutching hand, slipping from his shoulder, down his arm, baring his chest, his belly, his hip, her other hand there between them about his upright cock. His hand on her hip, his hand gripping the rim of the sink, his knee between her knees as she hauls him closer for a deeper kiss and bang that knee of his against the cabinet under the sink. "Unf," he says, and "Jo," he says, and "Maybe we should," he says, pushing back, trying, failing to get the gown back up on his shoulders. Her hands falling away from his shoulder, leaving him a-bob, set to fumbling with the buttons of her vest as she chases his mouth with hers, "I want this," she says to his lips, "you. Now." Her vest dangling open she arches her back pressing close to him as his hand slips inside along bare skin where her shirt's pulled free. "Here," she says, and she starts to unbutton her baggy white trousers. "Before I lose my nerve."

"Whoa," says the Duke, pushing back, brought up against the butcher's block, naked, the gown draped from his elbows, his hands on her side, her breast, he's shaking his head, "that's, that's what I'm – "

"What."

"That's what I'm," he says, lifting a hand to her face. She jerks away. *"What."*

"Jo, you're soused."

"I am *not,*" she says, "that, drunk."

"I don't want another stupid mistake," he says, and she leans into him, pulls him into a long and slow and tender kiss that melts away until they're standing, barely swaying, lips parted just, eyes shut. "I want this," says Jo, and he opens his eyes. "I want you, Leo Barganax." And she opens hers.

"Maybe," he says, gruffly, gathering his gown about himself, looking at the other door behind them. "Maybe we should take this to your room."

She's shaking her head. "Jessie's, she's," and Jo doesn't say what she was about to say, and the Duke nods. "Oh," he says, tying off the belt to his gown.

"What about yours?" says Jo.

"I told," says the Duke, "Luys, he's waiting there. For, ah. Me."

"Oh," says Jo. Buttoning up her pants. She grabs the Duke's hand. "You've still got the condoms? They're in there?"

"Yes," he says, frowning. "I think. Those are still good?"

"They last for months," she says as she pushes past him, past the butcher's block, tugging him after.

"And Luys?" says the Duke, following. "What do we, just kick him out?"

"Maybe," says Jo, pushing open the door, stepping through.

"Jo?" says the Duke, limping after. "Jo!"

A Bit of leather

A bit of leather tied about the wrist of the great hand flopped ruddy over the chill blued skin between her breasts. She squints at it, knuckles an eye, lets her head fall back to the red pillow, looking blearily over to one side and owling in surprise at the strong nose right there brushing hers, the closed eyes, the wide-lipped mouth half-open in sleep.

Carefully lifting that arm she worms her way out from under it finding the edge of the bed, one long bare leg slipping free from brown sheet and red blanket to dip and turn and find the floor. A snuffling, she freezes, that hand held abeyant above her. Over the other side of the bed the Duke's spooned up against the Mason's broad bare back, face turning up eyes closed to the ceiling, chewing over a rapid sequence of expressions, working something out in one long yawn of a sigh that leaves him settled, slack. Jo slips neatly off the edge of the wide low bed to crouch there naked on the floor, that arm still in her hand, and she kisses the back of the wrist there by the leather thong before she lays it gently on the pillow.

In her blousy black shirt she's stirring through discarded clothing at the foot of that bed, tugging free the leg of a pair of brown jeans from the mix, freezing as a belt buckle jangles. Carefully running a finger through the watch pocket, patting down the others, front and back, setting them back on the floor with a frown. Digging up a pair of rusty black corduroy trousers, going through the pockets. Sitting back on her heels, empty-handed. Leaning forward she creeps around the corner of that bed, her hand on a corner of paisleyed fabric, purple and maroon, gold and brown. Something scrapes lightly as she pulls it across to her, careful of the stern hawk-headed cane laid on the floor beside it. Up on the bed the Duke stirs, "Distilled," he says, "a jelly of beer," and Jo holds herself quite still until he's still and quiet again. She quickly checks the two front pockets but the weight was dragging further, higher up. A third small pocket, tucked behind the lapel. From it she pulls a single key.

She makes her barefoot way across the long high-ceilinged room littered with empty crushed red plastic cups and here and there a plate, a napkin, a fork, a high-heeled shoe. On a chair tipped back against the wall between high narrow windows the Stirrup in his brown plaid suit snores lightly, one arm dangling, fingers brushing the floor. Over there by the almost empty coat rack a woman with severe blond hair sits on a worn pink sofa, wrapped in a threadbare quilt, nodding along to something unheard through oversized headphones plugged into a welter of audio equipment. Curled in her lap, wrapped in that same quilt, another woman soundly sleeping, with the same blond hair.

Up the ladder into the loft where she throws on a pair of black jeans, jams her bare feet into big black boots. Shrugs into a leather coat the color of butter. That key pinched between her thumb and forefinger a darkly brassy bronze. On her way back to the ladder she stops a moment, looks over the edge at the big white bed below, tangled in a knot of sheets and comforter and three sleeping people, Jessie and Lauren coiled around each other, heads pillowed on each other's thighs, Lough spooned up behind Jessie, his face lost in her yellow hair, his white cap skewed, his scalp a bluish haze of stubble. Jo stoops, the key closed tight in her fist, and picks up her sword in its plain black scabbard.

Outside it's still dark, the air still an oily haze of orange and pink. A bus snorts and sighs to a stop at the corner. In the green and yellow light of the sign that says Pepino's Mexican Grill in neon letters there's a red-brown car with a black stripe painted across its roof, down its sides. Jo walks around to the back of the car, looking up at the blank brick wall of the temple, criss-crossed by power conduits, unbroken by any windows at all. Looks down at the trunk of the car. Leans her sheathed sword against the bumper, fits the key in her hand to the lock, opens it.

Inside a couple of boxes, one lined with a garbage bag holding a jug. She reaches past, pulls out a mask that could swallow half a head, white, crudely painted with thick black lines to resemble a grinning skull, a mane of long black hair that stirs as she holds it up with a wry little smile and a shake of her head.

There's something else.

Setting the mask down by the sword she reaches past the boxes again and tugs something larger, heavy, free, a soft brown leather briefcase, buckled shut. She turns about, sits on the bumper, looks it over. The brass fittings on the corner smudged with something brownish that thumbs away in flakes. Not rust. The buckle's loose, unlocked. She undoes it, pries it open, peers inside.

"Oh, holy hell," says Jo Maguire.

Be glad then, ye children of Zion, and rejoice in
the Lord your God: for he hath given you the
former rain moderately, and he will cause to
come down for you the rain, the former rain,
and the latter rain in the first month.

And the floors shall be full of wheat, and the
vats shall overflow with wine and oil.

And I will restore to you the years that the
locust hath eaten, the cankerworm, and the
caterpiller, and the palmerworm, my great
army which I sent among you.

And ye shall eat in plenty, and be satisfied, and
praise the name of the Lord your God, that hath
dealt wondrously with you: and my people shall
never be ashamed.

—Joel 2:23 – 26

DELIVERANCE

A SHARP POP – HOW SHARPER THEN – NAKED HE SITS
NO LONGER BLANK – HOW TO BE GALLOWGLAS
HER MOTHER'S DAUGHTER – "YOU'RE WAITING FOR SOMETHING"
THE OPPOSITE OF HIDING – YEARS, OR A COUPLE OF MONTHS
STRIPPED BARE – AGAINST THE MIRROR – HER EMPTY HANDS
"SHE ISN'T HERE" – THE LIGHT IS THICKER, NOW
HER BROTHER'S THINGS – WHY – A SOUND TOO BIG TO HEAR
THE HOUSE, FULL OF LEAVES

THE SHARP POP of a slap and her head rocks to one side. "Have a care, Princess," says Orlando, soft and low. "She is dear to me."

"Yeah," says the woman beside her, both hands in black lace tightly wrapped about the hand that Ysabel tries to tug free as she's saying "Let *go* of me," and as Orlando says "Princess" with a warning lilt she says "You would do well to remember your place, Mooncalfe."

"My place," he says, looking down with a flourish at his bare feet there on the sidewalk, "nor am I out of it." Folding his arms in his shapeless grey jacket. "No toradh binds me; I owe nothing, and nothing is owed me."

"You have the office of my keeping," says Ysabel, yanking her hand free. The woman pouts.

"I won a duel, is all," he says.

"You've said you are a conscientious guardian."

"I am the Mooncalfe, lady," he says, his hand quick as that on her chin. "I must do nothing, that I might do anything." Tilting her head to the side, peering through his open eye. "I left no mark."

Her white coat falls open as she steps back, her dress quite short, a slip of some dull mushroom color, her legs in sheer black stockings. She wraps the coat about herself again. "If Jo were here," she says, and he laughs. "If she were here," he says,

"I'd kill her again, and make sure it took." The woman on the other side of Ysabel chuckles at that, the bulk of her shuddering in her long black coat, hair threaded with ribbons and spangles slithering from her shoulders as she lowers her head.

They're standing the three of them before the old green house up behind its low stone wall, its neatly narrow garden, the big white columns of its shallow porch glared by tasteful spotlights. "Well I am safely home again," says Ysabel. "Whatever you would do, your duties are discharged, tonight, at least. I'm cold, and I would get out of this get-up." She turns to open the wrought-iron gate set in the low stone wall. "You should walk your lady back to her father's house."

"Not without that kiss, Princess," says Orlando.

"Right here's fine," says the woman, hair clattering as she taps a cheek with a lacey fingertip.

"She answered the question," says Orlando. "Sweetly and true."

The woman's lowering that fingertip. Her full lips painted black, her hair in all those braids, white ribbons and silvery spangles, her only color at all her bangs, a spray of pink cut short above her wide pale face. Ysabel clutching the throat of her white trench coat steps away from the gate, leans close, her red lips pressed quickly to the woman's cheek, and any trace of mirth falls from that wide face, those full black lips. Her glittering eyelids tremble and crumple as Ysabel opens the gate and closes it behind her.

"Swear it," says the woman, catching Orlando's hand, the one wrapped in a bandage, between her black-laced palms. "Swear you'll let me do it again."

"Empty, sweet," says Orlando. "No fear, no anger." He might be smiling. "Or else you'll prove their prophecies all true."

"You never let me stay," she says, looking up at that house. "I *hate* her, so *much*."

"You should never have said yes," says Orlando.

"I counted it twice, boss," says the boy in the brown leather jacket by the open trunk. "It all tallies."

"Weigh it out," says the Duke, leaning on the fender in his loosely open paisleyed dressing gown. "You won't find a grain of it missing, do it anyway, nobody's getting ideas. Get Astolfo, Medoro. Don't bother digging up Chillicoathe. She's only got the two friends back in the world, the, the telephone guy, the one shacked up with the Thrummy-cap. Get eyes on them – "

"Who, boss?" says the boy, gently.

The Duke limps slowly toward the trunk, saying, "You. Sweetloaf. Go," his free hand up striking off each phrase, "find Astolfo. Find Medoro, the Axle. Get them out there. Watching her friends. Get them some phones. She shows up, they call in. They don't engage. You come back. Weigh the bags. Tell me nothing's missing. Zip up your jacket." Leaning now against the open lid of the trunk. "It's chilly. Wilberforce!"

"Yessir," says the man in the pale pink union suit.

"To Northwest," says the Duke. "She doesn't go in that house. She doesn't see the Princess. Orlando doesn't touch her. Clear?"

"Yessir," he says, somewhere under his enormous grey mustache. Sitting on the steps at his feet a man in a rumpled brown plaid suit, elbows on his knees, head in his hands. "Gaveston," says the Duke, "get the phones, get everybody phones, help Sweetloaf roust the Axle and the Buckler. Then you go north. Wait for a call."

"Rabbits," says the man in the brown plaid suit, looking blearily up.

"Why the fuck else go north," mutters the Duke. He slams the trunk shut. Snatches the key from the lock. He scoops up his cane from where it's leaning against the bumper. *Now!* Find her!" Sweetloaf hurries past, Gaveston climbs to his feet, Wilberforce holds the door open as they head inside.

Jessie's left there, alone on the stoop, wrapped in a thick white comforter, her shoulders and feet bare. Shivering in the thin grey light as the Duke makes his way across the little parking lot. "Get dressed," he says, hands folded about the stern and rough-hewn hawk at the head of his cane. "Fifteen minutes. We're going over the river."

A steep and narrow flight of stairs, high green walls to either side painted over so many times they still seem slick and wet, all edges and corners rounded and soft. A paper cup of coffee steaming in his hand, a worn blue gym bag slung from the hook at the end of his other arm, folded newspaper tucked in the handles he's on the landing halfway up, looking to the head of the flight, white walls there, double doors, a frosted glass fanlight, dark. He's faintly frowning.

She's slumped on the floor by those doors, head back against the wall, eyes closed, feet splayed out in big black boots. Her leather coat the color of butter, her close-cropped hair a red like wine. On the floor beside her a paper bag and an old brown briefcase, soft with dark brass fittings. Across her lap a sword in a black sheath, its guard a glittering net of wire. Her shoulders rise and fall with deep, sleep-heavy breaths.

Down the hall he unlocks a door, steps into an office. After a moment he's back, paper cup clamped by its lip in his hook, in his hand a mug that says How fharper then a ferpents tooth it is. He squats beside her, careful of the bag, the case, the cup held stiffly upright, and waves the mug under her nose. She snorts, starts, looks up blinking. "That isn't coffee," she says, but she takes the mug.

"What are you doing here," he says.

"We need to talk," says Jo Maguire.

NAKED HE SITS — NO LONGER BLANK
HOW TO BE GALLOWGLAS — HER MOTHER'S DAUGHTER

NAKED HE SITS upright in the big white bed, back against the pillows, idly scratching his thick-furred crotch. "You left," he says. His feet tangled in the white sheets. "You took the covers."

"Get up," says Jessie, unwinding the comforter, dumping it on the foot of the bed. She ducks into the closet to one side of the alcove. He yawns, stretches, sweeps back his thick dark hair, gathering it into a stubbly little tail. Pulls on a pair of baggy black jeans, wiggles into a tight T-shirt printed with some baroque siege engine. Yawns again. "What was that all about," he says.

"You have to go," says Jessie, buttoning up a grey chauffeur's jacket, her yellow hair swept back under a grey chauffeur's cap.

"No time for coffee, I take it," he says, rubbing his darkly stubbled cheek. "Walk you to my coat?"

She's sitting on the foot of the bed, "I have to," she says, "please, just, I have to drive him somewhere," working a thick black sock up one leg. "It's kind of an emergency." Up over her knee. He kneels there before her as she's bunching up the other sock. "You're driving him?" he says. His hand on her bare thigh.

"He's very particular," she says, "about what I wear," her breath catching as his fingers slip up under the skirt of her jacket, "when I drive," and then he kisses her, straightening as she leans back, arcing over her, following her down.

"*Jessie!*" roars the Duke, somewhere a room or two away. She pushes him off, over, sits up, "Go," she says, "you have to go." Pulls the other sock up her other leg. "Please," she says, as he sits up beside her. "Come back. Tonight."

"Of course," he says, and he kisses her again.

She watches him walk away down the long and airy room, past the red jacuzzi, the long empty table. She leans down to pick up one of the shoes kicked carelessly to the foot of the bed. A red Ked, laces loose, tongue lolling. Hesitantly she pulls it on. It fits. She tugs the laces tight, ties them, reaches for the other red shoe. "Luys!" bellows the Duke, from somewhere further away. "Jessie! Any day now!"

Buzzing the phone's almost walked itself off the glass-topped table when he fumbles out a hand to catch it. Hauls it in to peer at its little screen. David, it says. He sits up on the couch and doesn't manage to catch the heavy raincoat that falls from his legs to the floor. He flips the phone open. "Yeah," he says, running a hand through what's left of his hair.

"Rise and shine," says Kerr.

"I categorically refuse," says Becker, digging at the corners of his eyes with a pinkie.

"Yeah? You headed back for seconds after I left?"

"What?' says Becker, frowning. On the low table where the phone had been a fat leather wallet, a folded booklet of bus tickets, a couple of key rings clipped to a purple carabiner, a stiff white card. "No, I went home, pretty much, right after. I fell asleep on the couch?" There's something written on the card, in blue ink.

"You know the Bijou Café? Downtown?"

"Yeah." He's picked up the card, he's kicking over the raincoat.

"Meet me there in twenty minutes."

He's feeling around on the floor. "What?" he says. "Why?" Coming up with a blue-capped pen in his hand along with the card.

"So I can buy you breakfast. Where the elite eat to meet and greet."

"You gave me a card last night," says Becker, setting the pen on the table, clicking against the glass.

"I did."

"It was blank. Which was kind of weird."

"Not blank anymore, is it."

"No," says Becker, looking up from the card.

"Says Pyrocles, doesn't it."

"It says Remember Pyrocles." Becker sits back against the couch. "In my handwriting. My pen."

"Neat trick, huh."

"How, how did you – what the hell does that *mean?*"

"Better make it half an hour," says Kerr. "You'll want a shower and a shave." He hangs up. Becker folds his phone slowly, sets it back on the table. The card beside it, fnap.

"Things keep *happening,*" says Jo in her butter-colored coat, the mug still in her hands. She's sitting in an office chair under a painted-over window, down at one end of a long table lost under haphazard stacks of books and piles of paper. She sips, then throws her head back draining the mug, sets it on the sill behind her. "I'm sorry. I don't know where to start."

"Are you drinking more," says Vincent, leaning against the table, arms folded. A black sweater vest over a loose white T-shirt. Jo squints, lips pursed, brow cocked, then shrugs, sitting back. "You're plying me with whisky before breakfast," she says. The chair creaking as she hitches over to one side, "The, the losing days," she says, "not knowing what time it is," pulling her phone from her pocket, "that's not the booze. I know what that does. I know my limits, there."

"Yeah?" says Vincent. "You smoke. What was it, meth?"

The phone's clock says 08:21. Friday, November 25. Jo looks up, her face quite flat. She blinks. She swallows. "Yes," she says.

He nods. "Alcohol," he says, "numbs your ability to notice, it, or care about how it ain't there anymore. Nicotine – lets you focus, on the task at hand, shuts out distractions – "

"It, it," Jo's saying, "the meth? The wanting the, that's, that's not how it works, it's – "

"Okay, forget, forget meth," says Vincent. "It was just, I was pretty sure you weren't the heroin type. You, you're gonna bull your way through, not shut it all out. Trouble is when it's twenty years from now and you're, you're across the world somewhere, you're in New York, you're still pushing, only it isn't there, not anymore."

"And, and," Jo's saying, "that's the other, thing, you say it's *pushing,* but sometimes it's like," her hand up, stirring the air, "sometimes somebody says something, and it's about to, it would have made it all *fit,* but I missed it – "

"Presque," says Vincent with a shake of his head.

"What?"

"Presque vu. The three vus?" His hook clicks them off. "Déjà. Jamais. Presque."

"It's not, it's not déjà vu," says Jo. "Jamais?"

"They're all related," says Vincent. "Side-effects. Symptoms. Jamais's the opposite of déjà, you know, I see this all the time, but suddenly, I don't know it. Which can really fuck you up in the middle of a fight. But presque, presque's the worst. I'm about to see something that will let me know – *everything.*" Spreading hand and hook apart, a slow shrug. "But it never comes. It passes. Or if it doesn't, if you catch it, just for a, a moment," his hook click-clacks, "it turns out there's something else. Something more. Something further on, just around the corner again, and if only – " He sighs. "So you drink. You smoke. You run away. You go mad." A snort. "Well. Mad*der.*"

"I'm not crazy," says Jo.

"You talk to people who aren't there about things that don't exist," says Vincent. Jo leans forward at that, opens the paper bag at her feet. He says, "I don't know what the technical term is for that – "

She's pulled out a white mask large enough to swallow half a head, crudely painted with thick black lines that mark out a skull's teeth, a skull's dark and empty eye sockets, a mane of straight black hair floating out in the air. "This is real, isn't it," she says. "It exists."

He doesn't reach out, doesn't try to touch the mask. Shifts a little against the table. Doesn't step back. "Where did you get that," he says.

"The Duke had it," says Jo, sitting back, the mask in her hand, her hand on her knee. "Luys, the Mason. One of his knights, he wore it, the night I got knighted. He fought Marfisa instead of me. He lost."

"She is good," says Vincent.

"This is yours, isn't it."

He looks up from the mask's eyes to hers.

"You were the Huntsman. I'm right, aren't I. I mean – I thought, Gallowglas was an office, like, like Chariot, or Anvil, but, it's just, anybody can be a gallowglas. My ex-boyfriend was a gallowglas, for fuck's sake. You just have to be at the right place at the right time."

"Wrong place," murmurs Vincent. "Wrong time."

"But the Huntsman," she's saying, as she turns the mask to face her, that mane rippling, a wake in the air, "if it does what I think it does, you'd want a gallowglas for that." The mane eddies about her knees. "You loved her," she says. "I can see it, she looks so much like her mother, and whenever you look at her I can see it. You loved her, and you were her Huntsman, and something happened, and now you're here, and she doesn't want to have a Huntsman anymore."

"She was the only woman I will ever love," says Vincent, hoarsely, "and he was the best friend I will ever have."

"He who," says Jo. "The King?"

"John," says Vincent.

"King – John? Her father's name was, was John?"

"No," says Vincent, "he wasn't her father. That's not – "

"*You're* her father?" says Jo, blinking, and he smiles and lowers his head, shoulders loosening, "No," he says, looking up again. "No. I'm Lymond's father."

"Who?" says Jo.

A grey box on the bottom shelf of the refrigerator says Diet Coke, a smattering of withered lemons beside it. A skinny jar of olives in a cloudy yellow paste. A tiny loaf of what the label says is rye and a half-dozen individual plastic cups of yogurt, all French vanilla. She plucks one up, peels it open, digs in with a spoon as she's shutting the door with a hip, turning, jumping back, startled. The man who's standing there's quite tall, his narrowly sombre face lit by extravagant gin blossoms. His suit is crisp and black, his white shirt collar turned up about his chin. "You're to dress," he says, "and see your mother in the parlor. Immediately."

"I *am* dressed," mutters Ysabel, looking down at her oversized yellow T-shirt, her yellow and pink plaid pyjama pants.

The parlor, paneled in dark wood, loomed over by enormous oil paintings of dour men in rich dark suits. The Queen all in black sits on an ornate framed cream-cushioned sofa, her hands folded in her lap. In a high-backed chair pulled close by her a man in a brown pinstriped suit, his bald head brown with sun, a wide yellow tie loosely knotted under his grizzled chin. On the table to one side of him, the one crowded with knick-knacks, faint steam floats over a teacup on its matching saucer. On the other little table, between him and the Queen, nothing at all but a round aluminum mixing bowl and a small knife with a slim bone-colored blade. "What is that," says the Queen.

"Breakfast," says Ysabel, taking another bite of yogurt.

"You were out late yet again last night," says the Queen. Over across the room there's a young man in a rose-colored suit, his pale hair knotted in dreadlocks that brush his shoulders. "At the Duke's? His — feast?" The young man's looking up at one of those dark paintings, a man all in blacks and browns, an antique suit of clothes, frowning in an elaborate frame of muttonchops and mustaches, pointing across his body to where, far off in the distance, a little cabin can be made out in the murk.

"No," says Ysabel. "No, your champion wouldn't – "

"He isn't here, you'll note," says the Queen. "The Duke. Nor our sister's ambassadour, neither."

"Your sister has no part in this," says the man in the pinstripe suit, his attention on the teacup he's lifting from the table.

"And the Duke knows his place," says the Queen. The young man in the rose-colored suit coughs once, lightly, without turning from the painting.

"This isn't necessary," says the man in the pinstripe suit, teacup delicately pinched between his thick fingers.

"We agree, Guisarme," says the Queen. "Withdraw your question."

He sips. "Surely," he says, "even you can see that's not an option."

"Ysabel," says the Queen. "Remove your shirt."

The teacup clinks quite loudly as the Guisarme sets it back upon the table.

"What," says Ysabel.

"Majesty," says the young man, turning from the painting, and the Queen stands abruptly. "You question our fitness," she says, "by questioning hers. We would have it out for all to see. Take off your shirt."

"I will not," says Ysabel, turning to leave, but there in the foyer stands the Majordomo, his cheeks and nose quite red, his eyes downcast. "You can't possibly," says Ysabel, turning back, the Queen right there before her, the bone knife in her hand. "Mother," says Ysabel, and the tip of that slim blade dimples her yellow T-shirt just below the collar of it. The little cup of yogurt falls to the rug with a plop.

The Queen grunts. With a whick the knife's cut through the T-shirt's collar and Ysabel jerks back and the Queen snatches a loose flap of cloth a sudden whipping tear Ysabel flailing tangled in the remains of her shirt tripping over her own foot unable to catch herself headlong falling the Queen in her black skirts ballooning sinks to her knees alongside, leans over to slice the last of the shirt away, stripping it from Ysabel's arms as they curl closer, tighter, her breath gone quick and ragged. The Queen sits up, wipes her mouth with the back of the hand that holds the knife. Ysabel trembling looks out from her hands folded over her face.

"Pants," says the Queen.

Ysabel flinches. "Why are you," she says, "doing, this," each word a husk. The Guisarme's picked up his cup again. Agravante's resumed his study of the painting. The Major-domo unmoving, hands behind his back. The knife drops with a thump to the rug and the Queen's grabbed those pink and yellow pants by the waist, holding tight as Ysabel kicks up bucking the Queen leaning over her against her pressing her back against the floor saying "Ysabel *Perry*. You may be, the King's Bride," yanking the pants over her hips, "but you are, *my daughter,*" down her legs, "and you will hold. Still," whipping them from her feet skirts rustling. She tucks haywire tendrils back into her carefully arranged hair. "Turn over," she says, with one last look to Ysabel curled on her side. "Gentlemen. Gentlemen, look!" A flourish of that bone blade. "She is whole, unblemished. *Look*. The bond remains unbroken. We are yet Queen."

"It was not in doubt," says Agravante, still there by the painting. "But weeks will turn to months." The Queen's dark eyes on him. "Ma'am."

"The mood of this city is bitter and foul," says the Queen, and the Guisarme's cup clinks against the table again.

"Of course," says Agravante soothingly. He flicks an arm out, shooting his cuff, holding up his hand to undo the link. "It's why we asked to have the knife brought."

"And the bowl," says the Guisarme, bunching up his jacket sleeve, folding back the shirtsleeve beneath to bare his forearm.

"You would have me *perform*," says the Queen.

"We merely wish to help you," says Agravante, "to *isolate* this poison. To be certain."

"It takes some time," says the Queen. "Even for something so small as this, it could take," and she spreads her hands, struggling with what she might say next, but Agravante's stepped around the sofa, he takes her hand in his, he takes the knife from her hand. "We've no pressing obligations, ma'am," he says.

The Guisarme's squatting on the rug. "Get up, Princess," he says, patting her bare foot. She sits up on an elbow, looking down herself at his gently grizzled smile. "Get dressed, lady, and go."

A sharp "No" then from the Queen. "No, she will attend us."

Still squatting the Guisarme looks up to her. Agravante pauses, his bare forearm over that aluminum bowl, the bone blade against his forearm. "Surely you have someone for that."

"We did, but had to let her go," says the Queen. "The mood, of this city. Ysabel. Get up."

"You're waiting for something" – the Opposite of hiding Years, or a Couple of months – Stripped bare

"You're waiting for something," says Kerr.

"Yeah," says Becker. "Breakfast."

"It'll come, it'll come," says Kerr. His elbows on the blue-checked tablecloth, his chin in his hand. "Take off your hat, stay awhile." Gold watch heavy about his wrist, dark hair slicked straight back. Becker takes off his trilby, bends down to tuck it under his chair. Sits up, one arm hooked over the back of it, fingers laced together in his lap. Still in his heavy raincoat, unzipped over a soft flannel shirt, a plaid of indigos and old reds. "And I have to ask myself," says Kerr, "why you didn't go to hang it up," looking over at the wall of coat hooks weighted with coats and jackets and hats and scarves. "Is it you're prone to absent-mindedness?"

"Maybe I just didn't want to get up," says Becker.

"Maybe you just didn't want to deal with all that." Kerr's looking again at the wall of coats, at the people crowded beneath in yet more raingear, sitting on the benches, standing as much out of the way as they can, waiting for tables. "Keep everything close, contained. Ready to go at a moment's notice. One foot always out the door."

"You're reading a lot into how I took off my hat," says Becker.

"You can read a lot by how much somebody does almost anything," says Kerr, as a waiter sidles up to the table, sets a cup of coffee by Kerr, an empty cup and a little glass pot of steeping tea by Becker. "Trick is whether it's by, or into." Kerr pours cream into his coffee, scoops up some packets of sugar. "You're still hourly, aren't you. What is it, fifteen? Sixteen?" He rips open three or four at once and empties them into his cup.

"I get production bonuses," says Becker.

"Sure you do," says Kerr, stirring his coffee. "And I bet you hit those numbers every time, or you know the reason why. Still." A sip. "Are those something you negotiated, or just what they'd give anybody had your job? You're waiting, for something. Husbanding yourself. Are you a vegetarian, Becker?"

"What?" says Becker. "No, I just, I don't like meat, for breakfast."

"That's what she said," says Kerr, and at that Becker snorts, leans over, quaking with silent laughter. "And see?" says Kerr. "You can laugh at my appalling jokes. Very realistically, I might add."

"It wasn't, it wasn't the joke," says Becker. "It was the timing."

"It's never anything but the timing," says Kerr, leaning over, looking up, hand out to grip the hand of a man in a grey sweatshirt blazoned with a yellow U and O. "Morning, Rudy," says Kerr.

"David," says the man in the sweatshirt. "Out for a bit of Black Friday bargain hunting?" A scruff of grey beard about his chin too carefully trimmed to be forgotten stubble, his white hair cropped close about the back of his head.

"If any of you people was smart," says Kerr, "you'd take a pass on this whole mess, wait until what is it, Epiphany, do the gift exchanging then. Take advantage of all those post-holiday sales. Rudy, this is Arnold Becker." Rudy turns and Becker works his hand up from his lap, offers it for a quick grip and shake. "Becker's doing some work for the campaign, on our, the big survey."

"Oh," says Rudy. "Numbers man, eh?"

"Ah, sort of?" says Becker. "I'm in a, supervisory capacity – "

"Becker's a generalist," says Kerr.

"Good to meet you," says Rudy, turning back to Kerr. "Listen, Rosie's been trying to set up a thing. Could you maybe give her a hand?"

"She's at home?" says Kerr.

"Wherever she is, she's got her cell."

"True that," says Kerr. "Consider it done." Leaning over the table as Rudy pushes his way off through the close-set tables toward the wall of coats. "Big supporter of George's," he says. "You have any idea how much of the city's business gets done in this room?"

"What are we doing here," says Becker, pouring tea into his cup. "You and me."

"Thought it was obvious," says Kerr. "This is a job interview."

Becker sets the teapot down, looks up to meet Kerr's smiling eyes. "How'm I doing," he says.

"Not bad," says Kerr. "Not bad at all."

"Not one damn thing, it's another," she mutters, tugging the string that leads between her wrist and the threadbare little rabbit nosing a chipped and cloudy brick of lucite. Trapped inside the goggly-eyed corpse of a fish, a little mouth lined with sharp and ugly teeth. A gong sounds, the scraping squeak of hinges, "We're not open yet," she calls out, hefting the rabbit, careful of the clutter, setting it down behind the counter.

"Horsepuckey," says the Duke, limping into the shop.

"That's a new look," she says, her milked-over eyes fixed on the floor, the edge of the counter. She winds her yellow hair into a knot at the back of her head and slips a knitting needle into the knot. He's thumping toward her, leaning against a long black spear-haft, the blade of it wavering up there shaped like a leaf, mirror-bright. "She's gone," he says. Back there by the doorway Jessie's waiting in her short grey chauffeur's jacket, her bright red Keds. "I need to find her," says the Duke, resting the spear-haft against the counter, hiking himself onto one of the stools, wincing as he settles his leg, rubbing it. "That's hers," he says, nodding at the spear. "She has her sword, but that, I gave her in battle. She swore her oath to me on it. It's through and through hers."

"She broke her oath," says the woman behind the counter. "She left it behind."

He slumps at that, hunching in his tweed jacket. "I have a plan," he says. "It's a *good* plan."

"She doesn't trust you," says Miss Cheney. Turning a typewriter ball over and over in her fingers, running a thumb over its punched-out alphabet. "You don't trust her. I told you to get rid of that bag."

"I did," says the Duke. "I hid it away. It was safe."

"That's entirely the opposite of getting rid of it," says Miss Cheney. "It's nonsense, Leo. An accident, a byblow. A loose thread bedeviling your hand. Mud in your eye."

"You're just saying that," says the Duke, "because you don't know where it came from, or who made it."

"Don't know," she says, the typewriter ball clattering like a die from her fingers. "I don't need *that* to know," knocking the spear-haft back to crash to the floor like a felled tree. "She's in the last place you'll look," she says, rubbing the back of her hand.

He rears back, opens his mouth as if to say something, lets it out in a sagging sigh. "Vincent Erne," he says. "Oh, that's, that's not good."

"Look at you," says Miss Cheney. "Listen to yourself." Her words are clipped and harsh but her hands settle tenderly about his and squeeze, gently. "Fear," she says. "Uncertainty. This is not the grace I know."

"What's going to happen?" he says, and her head tips back at that, her milky eyes staring up and up at the ceiling. "Same old," she says, distant, distracted, "you'll carry on," gathering strength, "as if nothing could possibly change, until one day, everything does."

"That's how you lost your hand?" says Jo.

"What?" says Vincent, laying a page limply heavy on the floor with the others.

"The duel."

"No," he says. "That had already happened, a long time before." It's a centerfold. He tugs it open, smooths it flat. A woman removing a yellow bra, otherwise naked. The neatly trimmed line of her pubic hair like some obscure punctuation mark. "The hand I lost to a guy with these, *teeth.*"

"Yeah?" says Jo. Sitting away across the wide deep room, back against the mirrors that line the one wall, floor to ceiling. The paper bag on the floor beside her, and her sword in its sheath. "Little guy, right? Lay-lay-lay-loo?"

He dips his hand into the briefcase sagging open beside him, rummages a moment. "That's it," he says, climbing to his feet.

"All the naked ladies?" says Jo.

"Quite a few of them, anyway." Spread out on the floor before him a collage of pinks and peaches, blushing beiges, buttery wet roses, slick oranges lurid with purples and greens. The detail lost in sheens and flares from reflected light, in shadows seeping from the dark far end of the room.

"So, wait, he names you Huntsman, that very night you sleep with the Queen, she gets pregnant, he challenges you to a duel, but you'd already lost your hand a long time before?"

He spares a dark look for her, then turns back to the pages on the floor. "That's not how it happened at all," he says. "I'm telling it wrong. These things," waving his hook over all those pictures, "there's usually a, a shape to them. A rhythm. Repetition, rhyme – "

"You deal with a lot of bags full of porn?"

"Can you stop being a smirking middle-schooler for maybe five minutes?" he snaps. "This is not a joke." She looks down, hands on her upraised knees. "Where'd you first see this," he says. "Who had it."

"On the MAX, a couple months ago. After the hunt. Eastside, we were coming back from, well, from where it was we fought the boar." She leans forward, pushes herself upright. "They came outta nowhere, they, they weren't real, you know? These men just, popping up, one after another, saying the most, these, just, *vile* things." Stepping over to one side of those pages on the floor.

"So you jumped them," says Vincent.

"So Ysabel could pull the brake. The train wasn't stopping. They weren't *real,* it was – "

"This is real," says Vincent.

"Yeah, well," says Jo. "One of them had it. Bald guy, older guy, trench coat, tie, a salaryman, I don't know. They're all white."

"What?"

"The – models," she says, waving at the pages. "They're all white. The rhythm or whatever."

"Oh," says Vincent, with a nod.

"The men weren't. On the train. I don't know if that's part of it. There's no, well, I guess she's blonde, and her, up there, with the snake? And there's a redhead, looking really chilly there in that river, but otherwise they're all, they've all got, dark hair – " Vincent's squatting, reaching into the middle of that spread. "This isn't his," says Jo. "Is it. Leo's. He didn't." He's plucked up one of the pages, a woman in a tight orange jacket unzipped lying back her dark hair a thicket, gartered stockings, striped underwear stretched taut about her knees. He lays it next to a centerfold, a woman in only a pair of brown leather boots, chin perched on the post at the foot of a bed, black hair in long straight sheets about her face. "The makeup," he says, "the hair, it's hard to say, but I think it's the same girl. Only they're years apart."

"It wasn't *that* long ago the whole retro seventies thing was in, you, you think that's really from the seventies."

"Or a couple months ago," says Vincent, still squatting.

"Her, too." She's pointing at a thickly lipsticked mouth a sneer at an anonymous white-gloved hand aiming a tattoo gun. "The chin. I mean, it's not, it's not – "

"No," says Vincent.

"Her eyes are blue."

"The cheeks are wrong."

"I mean, sort of, but – "

"It's not her," says Vincent.

"Looking at it, it's eerie," says Jo. "Which vu is this, huh?"

"You need to go," says Vincent abruptly, shuffling together a row of pages, stacking them up against his hook.

"I need to," says Jo. "What about, what's – what was he *doing* with this?"

"I don't know," says Vincent, stuffing pages in the briefcase, ruffling up another handful. "And unless you want to ask him yourself, you have to go. It's no great mystery, figuring out you'd come here."

"I need help," says Jo.

"Yes," he says. "You do."

"You've been here, before, you're, you're the only person I know who's – "

"I can't *help* you, girl. I told you, I tried to tell you every step of the way, get out, get away, walk away from this shit, it ain't worth it. You shouldn't have fucked with this."

"Yeah," says Jo, "well, you're such an inspirational example there."

"Which is *my* problem. Wait here," he says, headed out of the room. "I'll be right back."

Jo spins there on her heel, throwing her hands up, fingers curling into fists. Catches sight of herself in the mirrors, all in black, black jeans, black boots, the collar of her baggy black shirt sprung up on one side. She flattens it, turns away, hands to her face, a deep and ragged breath drawn in, blown out. Fingers lowering, eyes shut, her bottom lip in her teeth. "Fuck," she says, more a sigh than a word. She stoops to gather up more glossy pages.

When Vincent comes back he has her coat draped over his prosthetic and he's holding something out to her, bills folded and folded again, tucked between his fingers. "What's that," she says, snapping the briefcase shut.

"Refund," he says. "November. Go on, take it."

"That's more than two hundred bucks," she says.

"No it isn't," he says. "Count it out if you don't believe me." She takes the money and tucks it away. "Now get that thing," he says, hook clacking at the paper bag over by the mirrors as he holds out her coat, "get both those damn things outta here."

Jo takes her coat, pulls it on. Heads over to pick up the bag. "Where," she says. "How? What's next, what do I do?"

"I'd tell you to throw them both away and buy a one-way ticket to Paducah if I thought it'd do any good. Hey. Hey, girl. Look at me." Jo looks up as she slips her sword between the handles of the briefcase. "Where are you," says Vincent Erne.

"What?"

"Where are you, girl."

"Right here," says Jo.

"What's around you? What's coming at you?"

"I don't know," she says. "Every damn thing."

"Well figure it out," says Vincent. "See what's coming, decide what you're gonna do about it, then *do* it. Okay?"

"What am I gonna do?" says Jo, picking up the bag and the briefcase. "I'm gonna walk out on the street with nothing but two hundred bucks and a sword, that's what I'm gonna fucking do."

"Well," says Vincent, "empires have been built with less. Now go on, go. Get out of here."

"It's all your fault," says the Queen over the water splashing into the tub. She sets a copper tray down on the white tiled dais, careful of the mixing bowl. "If you hadn't interfered, with poor Anna," she says, reaching up and back to undo clips that let fall coiled locks of long black hair, "we wouldn't have had to let her go. Come here." In that mixing bowl a viscous puddle the color of milk in the light of a late afternoon, its surface sheened with bubbles like lace. "My bra?"

Ysabel in a short white robe, her feet bare, a wisp of gold threaded about one ankle, a simple golden ring on the little toe of her other foot, clicking as she walks across that grimy white-tiled floor. The Queen's hauled all her dark hair over one shoulder. Ysabel unhooks the clasp of her black bra, letting it sag from the Queen's shoulders, down her arms. The Queen drops it on a neatly folded stack of black clothing there on the dais by one of the tub's claw feet. "Off with the robe," she says, leaning on the rim of the tub, shutting off the faucets. The rustle of terrycloth loud in the echoing silence. The Queen dips a hand in the faintly steaming water, "Blood," she says, and then, "Sit." Pointing to the dais.

Naked, Ysabel perches on the edge of it there at the head of the tub, the pipes to drain and faucets a dingy chrome frame behind her. "Your foot," says the Queen, kneeling before her. Undoing the thread of gold and laying it on the dais. "We must be completely bare," she says, taking Ysabel's other foot in her lap. "Shorn of all – adornment – " Wincing as she tugs the ring from the toe. "You are a beautiful girl," she says, sitting back on her heels.

"Of course you'd say that."

"Doesn't make it any less the truth. Sit up straight." A flash there as Ysabel does so, a bit of clear crystal at the end of a golden pin piercing her navel. "I can," says Ysabel, but the Queen knocks her hand away, "No," she says, sharply. Leaning over Ysabel's lap, pinching the pin open. "You must understand. I am not angry with you." Dropping the pin to the dais by the ring and the thin gold chain. "But we are far past the point of any games." Her elbows on Ysabel's knees, Ysabel leaning back, hands planted on the tile behind her. "There's nothing anymore between us," says the Queen.

"All right," says Ysabel.

"Tell me who it was," says the Queen, and Ysabel's brow pinches. "He is no Prince," says the Queen. "He'll never be King. But I must know who it was."

"I don't know what you," Ysabel starts to say, and "I'm not," says the Queen, quickly. "I'm not angry. You needn't worry about that, sweetheart." Stroking Ysabel's cheek. "Whoever he is, he has nothing to fear from me. But I would know his name." Sitting back, black curls rustling as she tips her head, trying to catch Ysabel's downcast eye. "It isn't Southeast, or we'd've swept his ash from the Throne by now. It isn't the

Mooncalfe; I'm certain it happened before he took you up. It couldn't possibly have been the Chariot. Roland would never – would he? Did he?"

Ysabel manages just to say, "No one."

"Of course there was!" snaps the Queen. Her hands on Ysabel's knees. "It's the only answer that makes any sense of it all. You've been wed." Ysabel turns away, black hair falling like a curtain over her shoulder. "Without a King, to guide you, to've done it properly, the turning's had a hard time passing between us." Catching Ysabel's chin, turning her face to look her in the eye again. "Can it be you didn't even realize? *Think,* child."

Ysabel yanks her head back from the Queen's grasp. "I told you what I saw," she says, cold and clear. "When I ate the tongue."

"Don't be absurd," says the Queen. "We have allowed you your dalliances, but – "

"There were wild queens," says Ysabel, bitter and low. "In the mountains. That never needed kings to do what they might do."

The Queen pushes back, gets to her feet, a creak in her knee. "Old wives' tales," she says, "which you must hope are true. Get in the tub."

Ysabel's green eyes wide she says, "Mother?"

"Get in the tub, child," says the Queen through her teeth. "You're no fool. Every drop of medhu brought into this house for two months' time's gone foul at my touch. If you can't turn their offering to dust, then all is lost." Holding out her hand.

"I can't," says Ysabel.

"You *can,*" says the Queen. "You must. They'll think it came from me and go back, satisfied. I'll still be Queen. It will buy the time we need for the King to come back."

"I don't know how," says Ysabel, taking the Queen's hand.

"You do," says the Queen, steadying Ysabel as she lifts a foot to step into the tub. "In your bones you do." Ysabel winces as she lowers herself into the steaming water. "Sit back." The water's quite deep, lapping her shoulders, her upturned knees low islands. Her black hair floating. The Queen holds up that bowl and tips it, and the milky stuff within rolls slowly to the edge of it and gathers there, gorging itself into a great drop that sags then falls with a plop to the water between Ysabel's knees, blooming there into airy clouds that slowly begin to sink as the last of it unspools a thread from bowl-rim to tub, a pattering chain, a last few clinging drops.

"Mother," says Ysabel.

"I'm here, child," says the Queen, setting the empty bowl on the dais, by a stack of fresh white towels.

"Mother, I'm frightened."

"Hush," says the Queen, leaning over the rim of the tub.

"What if I'm broken?" says Ysabel, as the Queen lays a hand on her shoulder, her other hand brushing a clinging lock of hair from Ysabel's forehead. "Don't talk nonsense," says the Queen.

"But," says Ysabel.

"Hush," says the Queen, pushing Ysabel's head under the water. Holding her there. Leaning her weight over the water, locking her arms, lip bitten as Ysabel thrashes, bucking, her arms, a foot kicked up, shredding those milky clouds.

AGAINST THE MIRROR — HER EMPTY HANDS
"SHE ISN'T HERE"

AGAINST THE MIRROR shoulders pressed to shoulders looking over at himself in the mirror opposite, a big guy in a black suit, the knot of his skinny black tie lost somewhere under a beard the color of mahogany furniture, shoulders back against his shoulders looking over at himself in the mirror further back, a stainless steel thermos in his hands, leaning back against himself in the mirror after that, looking over at himself through black sunglasses, one lens written over with spidery white words. Down the hall the ding of an elevator. He tips his head to one side, the other, working his neck.

She wears blue and yellow running shoes, dark stockings, a pink skirt and jacket under a tan raincoat, one hand dragging a pink rolling backpack by its extended plastic handle, the other gripping a net sack bulging with miniature gumball machines. She doesn't even look at the thing he's studiously avoiding there in the middle of that low and narrow room, the great block of crumpled chrome-plated steel higher than her head, a statue planted on the dull brown carpet, dividing the room into two narrow aisles on either side of itself and all its reflections full of weird shadows, too-bright ripples of cold yellow light, the shapeless shifting blobs and pink and tan, black and rich dark brown.

She stops, suddenly. Shifts to toe a rumple of black pants, black jacket, white shirt inside the jacket, skinny black tie still looped under the collar. Black shoes gleaming, thin black socks slopped out of them. She turns, slowly, looks back at him against the mirror in his black suit, and he lifts a hand, fingers crooked, a gentle wave, move along, move along. She shrugs, hoists the backpack, steps over the empty suit, past the reflection of the little naked guy, and trundles on down the hall out of the narrow room.

The shadows and colors in the rumpled chrome are still moving, turning, a slow churn resolving about two points chest-high, about where the reflection in the mirror across of the naked guy is pushing against, against something. The chrome's started to bulge, there and there. The big guy steps over, careful of the suit, unscrewing the thermos. The chrome bubbles and bursts, a fist opening a hand, another, coated in gleaming roiling quicksilver boiling away in the air. The reflection opposite's gone blurry, smeared, the hands, the arms, its head ducking and whittering away as a forehead slick and bare breaks free from the rumpled chrome, his wide eyes empty, silvered, that stuff strung dripping from his chin, his bulging cheeks. The big guy stoops to hold the thermos under his lips and gut heaving, shuddering, the little guy vomits up a wisp of thin white smoke, blowing it into the thermos. The big guy slaps the cap on, screwing it tight. "Okay?" he says, stepping back.

"Cwicemuk," says the little guy, shaking his head, annoyed, climbing into his pants. "Hleahptein," he says, a cough of a word, cinching his belt under his hard round belly, worming his way into his mostly buttoned shirt.

"Quickly," says Mr. Keightlinger, eyeing the hall.

"Fuck," says Mr. Charlock, rolling upright, "you." Kicking his bare feet into his shoes. Stuffing his socks in the pocket of his jacket. Standing his hand working a moment still in the pocket, jerking, looking back at the statue, the rumpled chrome gone still again, blobs of his reflection black and fish-belly pale, skipping and pooling from ripple to ripple as he steps back, orange, a flash of blue and white.

"What," says Mr. Keightlinger.

"Who puts a thing like this down here."

"Timber barons," says Mr. Keightlinger.

The elevator dings, the doors open. They step out onto the floor of a parking garage, dark shadows soft relief from the chill grey daylight washing in. "There's never a right time of day to pull a stunt like that," says Mr. Charlock, putting on a pair of sunglasses, a feather tied to one side, "but it is too damn early in the day for a stunt like that." He heads off down the aisle of parked cars.

"Shouldn't've mentioned your Army buddy," says Mr. Keightlinger, following along.

"And of course he wants this shit right the fuck now," says Mr. Charlock. He squeezes between a white panel van and a luridly orange low-slung car with a dusty black ragtop.

"We can drop it on the way," says Mr. Keightlinger, coming around to the driver's side, unlocking the door.

"Don't see how," says Mr. Charlock, opening his door, climbing into the car, "what with the gallon of coffee and the two dozen bagels we need to stop and get before we go sit outside that goddamn house all day again." Settling himself on the broad bench seat, Whipping around, hand braced on the back of the seat, two fingers curled back against his palm, two fingers extended, thumb cocked. "Told you we shoulda painted this fucking thing by now."

"Huh," says Mr. Keightlinger, leaning against the driver's door.

The man in the back seat yawns hugely and stretches out a languid hand to push Mr. Charlock's fingers to one side. "You would still be as conspicuous," he says.

"Not what I meant," says Mr. Charlock. "What do you want."

"You do not pretend not to know me." His white shirt half unbuttoned, his jacket grey and shapeless, his long straight hair a black curtain about his narrow face. One eye glinting there behind it. "Refreshing."

"Not now," says Mr. Keightlinger, looking up over the roof of the car. Mr. Charlock points his fingers one more at the Mooncalfe's face. "The fuck. Do you want," he says.

"I'm bored." Orlando sighs, then smiles. "I have a proposition."

Her cuff buttoned she strokes the veins blue-dark along the back of her hand, takes up the last of the folded white towels and rubs it, rubs both her hands, scrubbing, blotting, dropping the towel to the floor with the others, crumpled, damp. Smooths her black blouse, her black skirt. Pushes her tangled black hair back from her face, off her shoulders, leaving it loose, undone. She steps into her black pumps there by the door.

In the parlor the Guisarme looks over a pile of green and white fanfold printout spread open on the couch beside him, circling something with a fountain pen, scratching a note in the margins. Agravante stands up from where he's been sitting on a flowery overstuffed chair as the Queen totters into the room. He coughs, lightly, as she lays a hand on the elaborately carved frame of a high-backed chair. The Guisarme looks up.

"Your hands are empty," he says.

"My hands," says the Queen, "are empty, yes."

The Guisarme looks down at his printout, ticks something off. "You must write, as we discussed," he says, ruling a careful line through a cluster of numbers, "the Court of Angels, the Court of Engines – "

"It wasn't so much a discussion," says Agravante.

"They have the likely candidates," says the Guisarme. "My people have drafted letters. You need merely seal them and have them delivered. We'll still need a King."

"That, we *have* discussed," says Agravante.

"I will not have Southeast upon the Throne," says the Guisarme.

"If we had more time," says the Queen then. "Gentlemen."

The Guisarme screws the cap onto his pen and sets it aside. "Have your people pack your things, whatever you would take," he says to the Queen.

"Take," she says, "where would we take anything."

"We cannot maintain this house any longer. You, your daughter, your mother will be provided for – "

"Even if a Bride proves true," says Agravante, "it'll be a full round of seasons before she's established – "

"Or two," says the Guisarme. "We will be stretched to the very limit."

"You will do no such thing," says the Queen, letting go of the chair. "We will not leave this house." But Agravante's raised his voice, "We have *time,* is my point," he says. "We won't need to sit someone right away – "

"We cannot go cap in hand without a King," snaps the Guisarme.

"I will not sit the Throne, Welund!" says Agravante, just as hot.

"This is insurrection, gentlemen," says the Queen, a question almost to herself. "You have a knight you'd vouch for, who might stand it in your stead?" the Guisarme's saying. She turns away then, walks away out of the parlor. In the foyer the Major-domo stands waiting, hands behind his back. "Ma'am," he says, as the Queen sets foot on the stairs.

"Sluice," she says, stopping there, a hand on the newel. "Sluice the tub," she says. "Into buckets. Do not let the water into the drains. Cragflower will know where to dump it. Burn the towels, the robes. I must."

"Ma'am," says the Majordomo. And then, "The Princess, ma'am?" But she doesn't seem to have heard him, her eyes on her feet as they step carefully, deliberately up the stairs.

The water placid, coated with a thinly pale grey grease that's here and there congealed in frothy clots. Hung below it cloudy cobwebs of milk but also smoke, strands of stuff the color of old blood that drift from her nostrils, her mouth limply ajar, that shadowy coil about her breasts, her arms, that lighten the tangled darkness of her hair.

The pad of bare feet, the click of a ring perhaps against those tiny hexagonal tiles. A smooth slim hand held over the still water, the middle dipped, dimpling that scrim of grease, a sudden hiss, "Ice," says someone, surprised. Those clouds like blown smoke roiling away from the fingertip. A glimpse within the water of a blinking green eye.

Both hands plunged in the water, that sheen melting away dissolving mixing with those torn clouds in a dirty haze, a grunt of shock, of effort, splashing thumps and a squeak of flesh against enamel, an arm about a slippery torso, a squall of water falling free hand catching lolling head tipping it up against the dead weight of all that hair. A gentle kiss pressed to slack lips and a gush of air's sucked in through nose and retching, she's coughing hacking wetly catching herself against the rim of the tub as that arm slips way.

"Of course you'd say that."

Kneeling by the tub the woman's a splattered mess of dark wet stuff that streaks her skin and clings in gobs to her long dark hair. Her smile is crumpling into something that can't hold back the onrushing tears.

"But that wasn't the question," she says, thickly.

Ysabel chest heaving water sloshing wet hair slapping the side of the tub as she fights to clear her throat, to clear her eyes of slime with the heel of her hand, shivering violently, clinging to the side of the tub, reaching over it for a towel. Wrapping the towel about her shoulders. Rolling over the edge of the tub to fall with a grunt in a crouch on the edge of the dais. "Mother?" she says with a cough that echoes in that empty room. The grimy tile floor smeared with water, littered with rumpled wet white towels. Her white robe puddled there, by the sink.

"Gallowglas!" bellows the Duke as he lurches up the stairs, tweeded shoulder bouncing off the slick green walls.

"In here" comes the call from somewhere above, maybe behind those dark double doors standing open at the top of the stairs. The Duke looks back down at Jessie all in grey on the landing below. "Wait there," he says.

"What, in case she makes a break for it? You want me to trip her or something?"

"I want you should maybe yell or something. Alert me? Let Luys know? You think you could do that?"

She flumps back against the railing, head tipped back against the wall.

"*Thank* you," says the Duke.

The whole of the wide deep room is lit up brightly, all the lights in the ceiling switched on blazing, cardboard boxes piled at the far end, U-Haul, say some, and Iron Mountain, and Loch Dhu and Redbreast and Casa Noble. A wheeled clothing rack hung with padded white jackets and a cluster of mesh-faced masks. Standing there his wiry arms and legs at odds with his broad chest in that black sweater vest Vincent holds in his hand a sword, a long and straight and slender thing, pointed like a needle, the hilt of it wrapped in white leather, its simple guard just quillions bluntly flared.

"That's not one of your toys," says the Duke.

"No," says Vincent, striding up the dark floor marked in a dozen spots with Xes of blue masking tape. He holds the sword lightly upright before him, a finger curled above the quillions, crooked about the tang. "It's not."

"Been a while," says the Duke. "Okay. Where is she."

"Not here," says Vincent.

"Come on," says the Duke.

"She isn't here," says Vincent, stopping there before the Duke in the doorway, right foot before his left, angling the blade before his body. The Duke sucks his teeth, turns away, "Shit," he says, pounding his cane once against the floor.

"She's been gone over an hour," says Vincent.

"Wrack and ruin upon all oracles," says the Duke. "Ash and smoke in their eyes. You'd think I'd know by now."

"Ask me where she went," says Vincent.

"The last place I'd look," mutters the Duke. "You'd think I'd remember, when it mattered."

"Ask me," says Vincent, forefoot stepping toward the Duke, rear foot sliding after.

"This," says the Duke, eyes narrowing, "what is this?" Cane tocking he limps into the room around Vincent to one side watching the blade-tip as it tracks him. "Okay. I'll bite. Where's she gone?"

"You wanted her to find that mask," says Vincent.

"I wanted," says the Duke, rocking back as he rolls his eyes, "I swear, if I were half as crafty as everyone seems to think, I wouldn't be standing here asking you a second time. Where did she go."

"I'm not going to tell you," says Vincent.

The Duke biting his lip thumps his cane against the floor and turns away, shoulders shaking, a laugh bubbling up out of him, "You want to *fight,*" he says. "Oh, that's, that's," headed for the door, "she left, what, five minutes ago? Ten?"

"Dammit, Barganax, I can *beat* you," snarls Vincent, shuffle-stepping one-two closer an angled thrust the Duke catches with his cane, thwock, and they stand there a moment. The Duke still smiling. "With a sword, yeah, probably," he says, lowering his cane. "Today's not your lucky day. Or I don't know, maybe it is."

"Why did you keep that thing," says Vincent, not lifting his blade, not stepping forward.

The Duke shrugs. "A King must have his Huntsman," he says, and he hoists his cane in a salute.

"Hawk!" roars Vincent, leaping after him. "Dammit, get back here!" The Duke's laughter echoes up from those green-walled stairs.

THE LIGHT IS THICKER NOW, the clouds a blank grey haze tinted with a wash of blue hung high above. It isn't raining anymore. The sign over the storefront she's walking past says 4 Wheel Parts Performance Center. The next sign down is orange and says Aaron Motel in white and yellow letters. Color TV, Air Conditioning. Wifi and Phone. Weekly Rates. Micro Refrig. Slung from one hand a paper bag, a briefcase the other, sword in its sheath laid flat like a furled umbrella through the handles. Smoke streams back like a banner from the cigarette in her mouth.

Into the motel parking lot, past a couple of pickups, a purple minivan with a set of stickers in the back window, white cartoon stick figures of a zombie family, a mother zombie and a father zombie and two zombie kids and a dog chewing on the leg of one of the kids. The motel's a single storey, long and low, another set of units detached at the back of the lot. Red doors, curtained windows, dark maw of an air conditioning unit beneath each window, over and over and over again. She's checking numbers on the doors, crosses over, steps up on the sidewalk by the one that says 109. Sets the bag down, shifts the briefcase from the one hand to the other. A last drag on the cigarette and she flicks it away. She knocks.

A minute or two before the door's jerked open, a burst of music, skittering percussion and keyboards, thumping bass, "What?" snarls a big man in cargo shorts and a big black T-shirt printed with the image of a thickset man in a dark hoodie backlit by blue-white fog. Ghost Dog, it says. The Way of the Samurai. He squints. "Shit, Jo? Damn. You doing pretty well."

"Can I come in?" says Jo. Night is cool, a voice is singing. Night is calm. Nothing's missing, nothing's wrong.

"How'd you find me? Dammit, Abe," he yells into the room, "turn that down."

"You're a creature of habit, Timmo," says Jo. "You only got like five joints you stay at. Zach out at the Nordic says hi."

"That fucker?" says Timmo. The music still as loud behind him.

"So can I come in?" says Jo.

"Like I say," he says, eyeing her hair, her leather coat the color of butter, stepping back. "You doing well."

The only light inside's what makes it through the clouds and curtains and what shines from the screens of a handful of laptops, a couple on the empty bed, over on the dresser by the dead television set, one on the other bed where a tall guy's lying on his belly, bare feet dangling off the edge, enormous chin on the keyboard.

Little speakers dot the pillows, a big one hulks on the floor between the beds. "Abe!" bellows Timmo. Nothing's missing, nothing's wrong. Tell us what you want. Abe looks up, his small eyes wet and red. "It's all a lie," he says. "It's all a goddamn lie."

"Well turn it *down,*" says Timmo.

"They tell you in the name of it, man," says Abe, stabbing the screen with a blunt finger. "Something's Wrong. That's what it's *called,* man."

"Well maybe work it out between you and the headphones," says Timmo.

"Headphones, yeah," says Abe, scrabbling through the cables on the bed, coming up with a stainless steel oversized set he wraps around his neck. "Sit," says Timmo, propping himself against the other bed.

"What?" says Jo, and the room's plunged into silence as Abe jacks into one of the speakers on the pillows, even the tinny dregs of music sealed away as he settles the headphones over his ears. "What can I do you for?" says Timmo, his scraggled hair, his wispy beard a pale halo about his leer.

Jo's looking over the two beds, the one chair in the room piled high with plastic shopping bags stuffed with clothing. She sets the briefcase and the paper bag down, leans back against the dresser by the dead television. Rubbing her one hand with the other she looks up at Timmo. "I need a gun," she says.

"I don't deal black jack clips!" says Timmo, loudly.

Jo says, "What?"

"I don't deal that kind of product," he says.

"Sure you do," says Jo.

He sniffs, scratches his cheek. "The hell you need a piece for," he says, and then, "no, wait, I got it. You need it so's you can rob a bank to get the money to pay me for it."

"I've got a hundred bucks in my pocket," says Jo.

He snorts. "I don't even peek at Craigslist for less than one seventy-five."

"One fifty," says Jo.

"One sixty, and I'm cutting it to the bone because I like you so much, girl."

"One fifty," says Jo, bending down, tugging the sheathed sword free of the briefcase, "and I'll throw this in." She nudges the briefcase across the carpet with her foot. Abe snorts and swipes at the mousepad of his laptop, one hand on the headphones. Punches the spacebar a couple of times, and again. "The hell is that," says Timmo.

"A decent briefcase," says Jo, "full of porn."

He cocks an eyebrow elaborately at that, leaning down to pick it up. Unbuckling it, pulling it open. "Paper!" he says. "Damn, that's kicking it old skool."

"Vintage," says Jo. "We have a deal?"

"Keep your money," says Timmo. "Give me that sweet machete. I can get you one fuck of a lot of gun for – "

"You don't touch the sword," says Jo.

Timmo blinks, lips working. Swallowing his grin. "The hell you fixing to do, girl," he says.

"Go hunting," says Jo.

He sets the briefcase down. "Okay," he says, "okay. Don't tell." Picks up a laptop. "No skin off me."

She wraps the shirt about herself, winds the two ribbons at its bottom about her waist, ties them in a lop-sided bow. Hooks the black and gold vest from where it's slouched at the foot of the bed whipping it up over her head, letting it shimmy down her arms in a tidy twirl that leaves the vest settled on her shoulders, the heels of her hands pressed to her forehead, her eyes closed. A deep breath. Her hands all blotched and smeared with filth fumble the loose buttons down the front of the vest heavy with gold embroidery, fighting to seat each one in its buttonhole, working down to the bottom to discover she's done it up wrong, off kilter, and she jerks each button back out again.

"Your brother's things," says the old woman by the door.

More slowly now, with trembling hands she's redoing the buttons of the vest, mouth quirked.

"Why do you have them out," says the old woman. Her heavy pink robe with a tangled garden of tea-roses embroidered about the thick shawl collar. Glossy white hair gathered into a thick braid draped over a shoulder.

"You brought them out for Jo," says Ysabel. "The night she was here. You burned her shirt." She sits on the edge of the bed and slips a foot into a high black moccasin boot. "Whoever brought my things back from her apartment didn't know to hide this away in the attic again, or wherever it was it was."

"Take it off," says the old woman. "We'll put them back now. You shouldn't wear that."

"Should," says Ysabel, lacing up the other boot. "Shouldn't. Who cares."

"Ysabel."

"I'm not the Princess anymore, Gammer," says Ysabel, looking up. Her hair hangs loose in clotted, crusty hanks about her filthy face. A streak of something dark has dried flaking from her nose to the corner of her mouth, along her chin. "I'll never be the Bride. Who cares what I wear. It's all gone to hell."

"Ysabel!" A jerking step into the room at that.

"I couldn't turn the medhu!" She springs to her feet. "You were wrong, Gammer. Wrong. I am broken."

"You are not broken, child," says the Gammer. "There's no King yet for you. That's all."

"Mother can't, either," says Ysabel. "It's all gone to hell. All of it."

"You shouldn't *say* that."

"It *has,*" snaps Ysabel. "It's been hell. For a long time. A very long time."

"Ysabel. Please."

"Since my brother was killed. At least. And the King went mad. And mother, she," stepping around the bed, toward the Gammer. "No. It's been longer than that, hasn't it. Since he was born. And mother, her sister – " and the Gammer slaps her.

A laugh, a sob, a catch in her breath, "Hell," says Ysabel, and the Gammer lifts her hand again, "damned here," says Ysabel, straightening, the Gammer stepping back, eyes wide, nostrils flared, "all this time. No more."

The Gammer lowers her hand then, lays it absently on her breast. Pulling her robe more closely about herself. "I came to ask," she says, chin dipping as she swallows, "if you knew what they were doing, downstairs."

"No," says Ysabel, spreading her hands. "I don't. I've just come from my bath, you see."

The Gammer presses back against the open door as Ysabel steps out into the hall. "Wait," she says, reaching after her. "Child, wait. A few days more! It will all be set a-right when the King comes back. He will. He will!"

"Why," says Ysabel, with a glance back over her shoulder.

"Hell of a view," he says.

Past the open reception area, the little nooks of pastel armchairs, past the glass walls lining a couple of conference rooms and their empty leather chairs arrayed about identical broad wood tables, windows open on a dizzying height above the river, a dull sheet of old steel under the high blank haze of the sky that loses itself in the rumpled wooded folds of hills to the left, dotted with pockets of houses, lined here and there with little shelves of condominiums along this ridge or that, the swoop of the freeway bridge across it so far below, so small, the grain towers along the riverbank, the container ship anchored alongside a toy that might be picked up dripping with one hand, the pits dug here and there among the warehouses and the parking lots, the skeletal cages of red-black iron rising under the white and blue and yellow stalks of cranes. Another building going up there, a bulky rambling thing, its frame of wood, the color of it raw and bright. A flicker of movement, a white fuselage, a plane lumbering down from the oceanic sky, falling for the lights of the airport winking far off to the right.

"May I help you?" says the receptionist, her black hair pulled back in a simple bun, a small but ornate brass telephone headset clipped to one ear.

He cranes up his worn black leather jacket creaking, his shock of pinkish orange hair bobbing, peering past her at the letters hung on the wall, precisely serifed things cut from some heavy, leaden metal that say Welund, Rhythidd, Barlowe & Lackland. "I'm here to see Welund," he says.

"Mr. Welund has no appointments this afternoon," says the receptionist.

"Perhaps he's left something for me? An envelope?"

"Your name, sir?"

"Perry," he says. "Lymond Perry." Leaning close, brow crinkled in apology over his bulging eyes. "It might have been quite some time ago."

"I'll ask," says the receptionist.

"Disgusting," he says, and the ringing whine of steel on leather.

The Guisarme looks up at that. "Mooncalfe," he says. Nodding away the woman next to him in a houndstooth skirt and white blouse, pince nez perched on her nose. She takes the little plastic baggie from his outstretched hand, scoops up the bulging plastic shopping bags at her feet, and hurries away, careful of the boxes here and there, the trunk its lid ajar, the little tables empty now of knick-knacks lined up before the sofa. "Where have you been."

"About my business," says Orlando. His shirt is white and open at the throat, his long skirt blue and wrapped with a black sash. His bare feet whisper over the rugs.

"If it's for the Queen, or the Princess," says the Guisarme, holding up a hand to caution the man in the green coveralls behind him, "you may speak with me. You should speak with me. There's much to talk about."

"My business is my own," says Orlando. The man in the green coveralls is looking from the meagre few of plastic baggies left on the table by the Guisarme's side to Orlando's sword, the long and gentle curve of it, the hilt in both his hands, rough black cloth wound about the yellow-white of bone. The man in the green coveralls takes a step toward the table and the Guisarme waggles the fingers of his forestalling hand. "There is no threat," the Guisarme says. "Put up your blade, sir."

"I disagree," says Orlando.

"Name it," says the Guisarme. "We'll face it, together."

"I think not," says Orlando, and with a long smooth step his blade whicks up, snaps down, splintering the table, scattering the baggies in a cloud of glittering dust. "The threat, you see," he says, his sword up over his head, turning just to face the Guisarme, "is me. Draw your sword." The man in the green coveralls has left.

"We have no quarrel," says the Guisarme, the bundle of fanfold printout clutched to his chest.

"You're disgusting," says Orlando. "I finally resolve to take my best last night, only to find you here before me, paying off the help, and rummaging through couches for loose change. Draw your sword."

"We cannot maintain this house," says the Guisarme, stepping back. Bumping against the chair behind him. "Changes must be made if we're to keep the court intact – "

"What do I care for the court?" The blade lowers, angles, the tip of it scraping the bundle of paper. "I will not ask a third time."

"I cede the field to you, sir," says the Guisarme. With a wrench of Orlando's wrists the blade-tip digs and whips the paper up and away unfluttering tumbling to the floor. "You've won whatever you imagine this to be! Now, please, *speak* with me!"

"No," says Orlando, and he slashes open the Guisarme's chest. The Guisarme sits heavily in the chair behind him, catching an arm of it, managing not to fall. Looking ruefully down at the slit in his pinstripe jacket, the vest, his yellow shirt beneath, blotted by a sluggish trickle of something pale. He looks up, at the painting hanging on the wall above, a roughly bearded man in a long black gown, a blanket over his shoulders, a red cravat about his throat, sitting on a stump in a dark wood. His black-gloved hand on the stock of a long rifle leaning butt against the ground. A shapeless fur cap on his head. "This was my favorite suit," he says, rolling his head over to watch Orlando stalk away, blade up again, "Ysabel!" he's roaring in the foyer. "Princess! Duenna Queen of Roses! Show yourselves!"

"Shut up," says Ysabel Perry. Halfway down the stairs above him in her black trousers, her blousy white shirt, the gold vest.

One hand on the railing, her hair all wilding threads and clotted hanks about her face and shoulders.

"Well," says Orlando, his sword still in his hand. "A Prince now, not a Princess. Where's your mother?"

"Neither," Ysabel's saying, then, "Indisposed." A step down, and another.

"Fetch her."

"No."

"I warn you," he says, pointing his sword at the front door behind him. "Waiting on the sidewalk is a gallowglas of my own. I'll call her in, she'll dog my heels. We'll see then what my blade might do."

"I will go with you, Mooncalfe," she says, "but you must go with me, and leave your monster at the gate."

"I *warned* you," snarls Orlando, swinging his sword to point at her as she takes another step, and another. "Shut up," she says again. "There's nothing for you here, not even me. Leave them all alone. There is no Queen, not anymore, and there will never again be a King in this city."

He nods, at that, and says, "Not Prince, nor Princess, then, but prophet." She lays her hand against the flat of his blade and pushes it aside, coming down the last few steps. "Very well," he says, and he wrinkles his nose. "You reek."

"You'll not have me?"

"Oh, I'll make what use of you I can." He offers his arm. She takes it.

"Ysabel?" The Gammer's querulous voice cuts through the silence of that house. Above them, behind them, she's clinging to the curling rail of the staircase, still in her heavy pink robe shawled with roses, her long white braid dangling over one shoulder. "Go back," says Ysabel. "See to mother."

"Stop," says the Gammer. But Ysabel's hand is on the knob. "Don't say such things," says the Gammer. "Don't leave. The King will come back. There is hope."

"No," says Orlando, as Ysabel opens the door. "There isn't."

"Ysabel!" cries the Gammer, as they step out onto the shallow porch between the thick white columns. On the sidewalk outside the gate waits the big woman in her long black coat, leaning back against the gleaming bulk of a white SUV, her hands in white lace gloves, her wide lips painted white. Orlando shuts the front door, smiling in turn under his one good eye. "You have no idea what I will do to you," he says to Ysabel.

She looks sidelong at him and shakes her head. "You have no idea if it will work."

He's taking the first step off the porch when a sound too big to hear blows the front door open, staggers Ysabel, sends him askew to his knees on the steps. The blinding flash. Car alarms going off up and down the street and the sound of broken glass, falling. Her face terrible in the harsh light shining from the greatsword in her hands the Gammer's striding across the foyer and her voice too loud and deep she cries, "You will *stop* – "

Gathering himself Orlando springs from the steps his sword up and out slashing before him and it's suddenly gone quiet and dark. Crouching in the doorway he looks back to see nothing behind him but the neatly cut white braid falling limply to the porch, and Ysabel, back against one of the white columns, her hands over her mouth. "You," she says, "you – "

"Quiet," he says, his hand on her arm, pushing her down the steps before him.

The sound of the gun cocking is quite clear in all that silence.

Still on the steps above her Orlando stops. "This is hardly fair," he says.

In the street the dark figure of a man wearing a pale hat with an absurdly high crown. One hand up, an enormous pistol cocked and pointed at Orlando. The other holding up a little phone so he can eye the number he's thumbing. "Nothing to be fair," he says, from somewhere under his enormous grey mustache. "Ain't no duel. It's justice. I seen you take our Gammer's head, and you will answer for that, to the Duke if no one else."

"You forgot one thing," says Orlando, and then, "Gloria?"

Grunting the woman on the sidewalk's pushing herself up from where she's fallen by the wheel of that SUV, and as her head crests the hood the Shootist sees her, phone dipping, gun pulling up and just to the side, and that's when Orlando leaps –

White shirt blue skirt fluttering over the gate the sidewalk the parked cars sword a curl of light in the greyly shadowed street turning in his hands to come down a pop of a gunshot whine of a bullet the Shootist crumpling to the pavement. Orlando pushing himself up black hair hanging like a curtain. The Shootist coughs, and something dark and wet spatters from his mustache.

"Wow," says Gloria, leaning against the fender of the suv.

"It seems she didn't like you," says Orlando, climbing to his feet. His hands empty. A sudden gust of wind lofts the pale hat, skimming it away down the street. The whooping of the car alarms is back.

THE HOUSE, FULL OF LEAVES

THE HOUSE IS FULL OF LEAVES, piled in corners, drifted against the walls, orange and dead dry brown maple and oak, yellow alder and locust, dull silvered myrtle, crunching underfoot. In the parlor the sofa's collapsed to one side, stuffing sprung from old stained cushions. Splintered wooden frames and broken glass scored with dust sprinkled over moldering rugs. Canvases black with smoke glower from the walls above, nothing but a hand, a bit of shirt, the edge of a face, an eye to be made out through the murk. In one hand the figure holds a sheathed sword, gripped about its fitted throat of beaten metal. In the other a flat black pistol, pointed with jerks to the side, the front, the side again. "Mooncalfe?" she says, her voice muffled by a mask, a blocky skull that swallows half her head. The rustle of the stiff black mane that floats behind is louder almost than the crackle of her footsteps. "Ysabel? Anyone?"

More leaves in the hallway beyond, and a hole in the floor, a rusted pipe thrust up at an angle. She edges around it, gun pointed ahead, then back across her body, then ahead again. In the kitchen the linoleum peeling up, torn away from the mottled sub-flooring in great swathes. The refrigerator door hangs open. It's dark inside. The stove an avocado-colored thing, orange with

252

rust and black with ancient grease. Beyond the house opens up in a big back room, the far wall lined with French doors, panes empty in the gloom. Somewhere far off a floor or two away a creak, a groan, a long slow settling fall of something, paper, cloth. There's someone sitting before that blank black glass.

"Majesty?" says Jo.

In her black skirt, her black blouse, the Queen sits on the floor against one of the doors, her knees drawn up. Weeping soundlessly she clutches a glossy white braid neatly cut to her breast. On the floor before her the withered corpse of a little brindle cat.

"Ma'am?" says Jo, lowering her gun. "What happened?"

The Queen looks up, blinking. "Vincent?" she says.

"What?" says Jo, then, "no, no," dipping her head, working off the clumsy mask with the hand that holds the sword. "It's me, ma'am. Jo." The gun still in her other hand, pointed at the floor. "Your daughter's gallowglas."

The Queen looks away.

"Where *is* everyone," says Jo, coming down the shallow steps into the back room. "What, what – "

"My lover," the Queen's saying. "My son. My husband. And now my mother and my daughter. Gone, all gone – "

"Ysabel," says Jo, stooping, kneeling by the Queen, laying the sword and the mask on the floor, the gun in her hand in her lap. "Ysabel's not – gone?"

"Orlando took her," says the Queen with a shudder. "Orlando Mooncalfe, sneak-thief and scuttle-sneer. Murderer. Had I the breath, I'd render such a curse upon him – tie that hair of his in knots, and wreathe it about his neck, then pull, and pull, until his head popped off – "

"Where did he take her? Ma'am, please. Where did they go? When? How *late* am I?"

"Why?" says the Queen. "Would you just shoot him, like a gangster, with that?"

"I can't beat him with the sword," says Jo. "But please. Ma'am. I will do it. I will make amends, I swear. I will save her. Please. Please tell me."

"Even if I knew," says the Queen, "it would do no good. She's gone, she's gone, it's all gone and done. We're done."

"No ma'am," he says, stepping carefully down the shallow steps, and Jo yanks the gun up to point at him, and he smiles, eyes big and bright under that shock of pinkish orange hair. "No," he says, "it's not."

"Who," says the Queen, a breath of a word, and Jo says, "Ray?" The gun drooping.

"No," he says, kneeling before them, his worn leather jacket creaking. "Not anymore." Taking the braid from the Queen's limp hand, pressing it to his lips, then laying it back on her lap. "It's me, mother," he says. "I'm back."

when you're blinded to
the moon
and its rise
how can you know
the planting times
streetlights
tell lies

—*Robin Holcomb*

NO. 18

DAZZLE

A GLASS OF WATER, A GLASS OF DARK RED WINE on the formica table between them. "I know what this must look like," says the woman who picks up the glass of wine. Cradles it in both hands elbows on the table. She doesn't take a sip. She's draped in a brown and yellow striped serape and her hair is short and black in the dim light.

"What's that," says the woman across from her, a hazy cloud of curls the color of clotted cream tied in a thick spray of a tail at the back of her head. A sheepskin jacket slung over the back of her chair. They're up by the front windows, high dark narrow panes behind a slender wrought iron grill. The woman in the serape says, "When one person asks the other person out to a public place to talk about something important so the other person won't make a scene when they get dumped or whatever, that's not – " She sips her wine then, cupping the glass in both hands. "I'm not kicking you out. I'm not asking you to leave." Another sip. "But it's unfair. It's unfair to me, it's unfair to Jason and Grace, it's certainly not something we can ask them to – "

"What is."

Carol sets her glass back on the table. "I found your dope."

"Dope."

"Your drugs, Mar, I found your damn drugs when I was cleaning up the – "

"I don't have drugs."

"Don't!" Carol's hands clench on the table, "try to, brazen your way out of this, okay? Don't tell me it's just glitter. Glitter doesn't numb your gums."

Marfisa drinks down half her water in a couple of deep slow swallows. "I don't have drugs," she says.

"I don't know whether this has to do with your breakdown or what — "

"Carol," says Marfisa.

"Sorry," says Carol. She takes another sip of wine. "It's just," she says, "it's such a waste. You know what Streak did, the little shit?"

"Carol," says Marfisa again.

"He uploaded a couple of tracks to I guess YouTube or something. Sent them around. The Mask Song, and that goofy King Arthur Star Trek thing you had us do?"

"Deedee's Song," says Marfisa.

"The Mercury linked to them. People are listening to them. People are talking about them, about us. What happened. Where'd we go. Is there an album, where's the album."

"Carol," says Marfisa, firmly this time, and Carol bites her lip and sits back in her serape. "It's over," says Marfisa. "Even if I were willing. Even if I *could,* you would never get Otto or Wharfinger in the same room with me again."

"Anne Thorpe," says Carol. "From Anodyne? Is sniffing around. Wants to do a story."

Marfisa drinks the rest of her water, sets the empty glass upside-down on the table between them. "You're right," she says, "it is unfair, to you, and Jason, and Grace. Your holiday." Standing, pulling on the sheepskin jacket. "I've taken a week. I'm back on my feet. You've been." She looks down. "Very helpful," she says. "But. It's not drugs." Somewhere, outside, there's a fluttering pop of drums, a thin and distant whine of flutes and whistles. "It's more like," Marfisa's saying, stepping back, away from the table, looking out the windows, stepping toward the door. Carol stands. "Mar?"

Marfisa opens the door. A little bell chimes.

Under the blue and orange neon sign that says Alberta Rexall Drugs a little crowd is knotted all in raingear, dark wool and fleece, gleaming nylon and gore-tex and leather against the seeping rain. Flutes whirl around the ache of a melody over a growing growling drone as drums rattle and clatter closer and closer. Down the middle of the street through the haze of rain hung blushed by streetlight in the air a procession almost outnumbering the little crowd, at the head of it two young boys and an even younger girl in knee-length frock coats, the boys strutting with snare drums, the girl struggling with a clear bass drum strapped to her belly. Next a figure enormous in a crude suit of wicker armor, head hidden away behind a woven barrel of a helm, in one hand a long rattan pole. To one side of him a woman in a blue-black cloak over a gown of watery mail, her short hair gunmetal grey, and beside her trudges a clattering man, ducting and foam insulation clamped stiffly about his legs, a great stainless-steel pot lid hung over his chest, colander rakishly topping his head. Children the smallest barely a toddler wind laughing about their legs in rags and tatters, worn footed pyjamas, a filthy bib, a sodden wrap of fake blue fur. And behind them all a trundling black hulk of a car headlights dark the pavement beneath it lit up blue and green and purple the sides of it crusted with, with a teeming horde of dolls, doll heads, doll arms, jaggedly broken torsos and legs, all of them roughly painted black and glued and welded, bolted to the fenders, the hood, the doors, a coat of stiffly bristled fur combed back and up along the lines of the car, reaching toward the throne that squats on the roof, where's slumped a black sack of a cloak topped by a tangle of dead black hair hung low, twined with dull white streaks.

"Some Last Thursday thing?" says Carol.

Marfisa's eyes widen as that tangle of hair shifts, turns, tips back. She looks away quickly, down at the sidewalk, Carol's heeled brown boots. "But it's Friday," she says, a crack in her voice.

"It's November?" says Carol. "Last Thursday – yesterday – was Thanksgiving, right? Our holiday?" The drummers with flourishes drag their beat to a halt and the little procession stops just past the intersection at the other end of the block, those flutes and whistles still, for a moment only the seep of the rain. "So they do it on a Friday," says Carol. She's pointing. "They've got something going with Clown House, anyway."

There in the street they're all turning to face the house on the corner, peeling pink siding and mud-red trim, a welter of bicycles along the edge of the lot, tipped over onto the sidewalk, people spilling from its cramped front porch, coming out the side door gawking, wildly colored hair and faces painted white, a straw hat, a green and yellow cheerleader outfit, a grey uniform with red stripes, overalls and a plaid jacket, a ruddy round man in a leopard-print bikini and a purple feather boa his thin beard caked with white paint, and pushing to the front of them all is someone wearing a rabbit head with a metallic, skull-like face.

On the side of the car a bony man in a pinstripe suit is standing on the running board he's reaching up careful of the dolls to take the hand of the woman slumped up there on the throne. He's singing, a cold keen countertenor slicing through the murmurs of the crowds on the sidewalk, by the house, "Ní dhéanfaidh an ghealach solus d'éin-neach," as the woman in that dark black cloak rolls out of the throne and he catches her, hefting her down from the roof of the car to the street, and all of them, children and toddlers, motley knights, drums still and flutes quiet, all of them singing along, "'S ní bheidh éisg ann air muir nó air tír – "

"Is that," says Carol, "damn, that's Danny Boy. Spookiest arrangement I ever – Mar?" Marfisa isn't beside her. "Mar?" Turning, looking back, the sidewalk, the street behind her empty, just the lights from a restaurant, a couple of shops a block or more away.

THE HAT IN HIS HANDS – THE NICETIES OF DEBT
HER BUSINESS – HIS MESSAGES

THE HAT IN HIS HANDS a soft pale grey, its absurdly high crown punched in on one side. The brim of it wide. Gold dust shivers away as he turns it over, sparks that flash and fall to the pavement. "Easy enough," he says. "He got struck a mortal blow, and a gallowglas on the field." He hands it to Luys beside him, tall and broad in a brown shortwaisted jacket. "Jo?" says Luys, but the Duke's limping away down the street, cane-tip tocking loudly in the hush.

"Leo?" says Jessie, there by the reddish-brown car, slewed to a stop in the middle of the street.

"She didn't do that," says the Duke, turning, pointing up to the old green house on the corner behind them, dark, lower windows boarded front door ajar, big columns of its shallow porch once white now grimy, scored, stripped, all behind a forbidding tangle of bare branches, a narrow garden overgrowing a low stone wall, threatening the sidewalk. "Get Sweetloaf on the horn. Tell him, have him pull everyone in. Batten the gates, bolt the hatches, hunker on down. I'm gonna see what Goodfellow knows." He limps on, out across the empty, rain-wet intersection, camel-colored topcoat blown out in the glaring haze of pinkish-orange streetlight. "I'll just be a moment." Cater-corned from the old green house a big white ramshackle house, its windows all alight with flickering, winking Christmas lights and candles.

A short straight sword, the hilt of it wrapped in white leather worn and yellowed, the blade two fingers wide down to the floorboards where it's been thrust, the wood there singed about the upright blade. The Queen's black pumps primly together there at the edge of that neatly charred ring, her hands clutched to her breast, trapped within them a loosening braid of glossy white hair and Jo's hand, Jo in her butter-colored coat beside the Queen, arm out at an awkward angle, sword slung over her other shoulder, in her free hand a crudely blocky mask, its mane of black hair lazily floating in the still air. Somewhere far off from the back of the house the plink and clank of an amplified harp. Jo's looking about the big front room in fits and starts, the stairs, the dim hallway leading away beneath them, the front door, the bay windows with candles melting on every sill, always back and back to the bright doorway, the kitchen beyond the color of toothpaste, and Robin Goodfellow all in black, shaking his head. "I could not allow," he's saying, "someone of your stature to become so indebted to me."

"So damn my stature," says Ray, says Lymond, one hand clamped to the top of his head as if to keep his wild pink hair from springing away.

"Highness," says Robin, stiffly.

"No, damn it, damn the niceties, I have come too far today to be held up by this. Forget," he says, "what has just happened, forget it all, who we are, focus on this. I am someone you have never seen before."

"Highness," says Robin, again, and "You have never seen *me* before," says Lymond, "and I am asking, you, Goodfellow, if my mother, the mother of someone you have never met before, might not find herself a place to stay, here, for a time."

The Queen's reached out with one hand toward the plain pommel of the sword but doesn't touch it, quite. Robin's leaning an elbow against the doorjamb, forehead against the heel of his hand. "When one is owed a favor, highness," he says, "sooner or later those in one's debt expect one to need something in return." He straightens, hand turning a fillip there by his frown, a flutter of a shrug. "I can't afford that."

The Queen's hand closes in a fist she draws back to her breast. Squeezing Jo's hand there in hers and Jo looks over with a wince of a smile. "I didn't know," murmurs the Queen. "If I leave you without a choice?" Lymond's saying.

"Then by all means," says Robin. "If coerced, then nothing's owed." The harp has twinkled to an end, a patter of applause. "How long were you thinking you'd be?"

"Not hours but days," says Lymond, "days but not weeks. Mother." He holds out a hand to the Queen. Jo's saying, "Is that it? Are we done?" as Lymond says, "We must be off, away over the river as soon as – "

"A moment, highness," says Robin. "How do you mean, then, to leave me without a choice?"

Lymond hand still outstretched turns back to look at him. "Niceties?" he says, and Robin shrugs. The unseen harp has taken up a slower, more contemplative air. "Gallowglas," says Lymond. "The gun."

"What?" says Jo, her hand still trapped in the Queen's.

"Take the gun from your pocket and point it at Robin Goodfellow," says Lymond, his bulging eyes quite serious, and Robin takes a step back, into the kitchen.

"The hell I will," says Jo.

"Gallowglas, please. We haven't any time to spare."

"Ray," says Jo, "unless your next step's helping me find Ysabel, *we* don't have a goddamn thing at all."

"Jo," says Lymond, stepping toward her, "I need your help."

"I don't need yours," says Jo, jerking her hand free, and the front door bursts open, the Duke sweeping in, stomping his foot, "Goodfellow!" he cries, looking about the big front room, frowning, eyes widening, mouth opening, "The last place I'd look," he says, half to himself.

"Leo," says Jo, over the dripping of the harp.

His cane dropped clatters to the floor. His derby hat whipped away into the darkness on the stairs. A heavy step, the scraping drag of a limp, the flop of his long coat opening. Step and scrape and the ringing whine of steel on wool. "Draw," he says, a gutted croak, longsword in both hands held out before him, pommel braced against his hip.

"No," says Jo, gone pale.

"No duels," says Robin, "not in this house, not tonight," and *"Silence!"* bellows the Duke. Away off in the back of the house the harp stumbles, stops. "You stole from me, you left me," he says, "you *ruined* me," step and scrape again, "you sent my Tommy and the Shootist now to dust, you *broke* your *oath* – "

"No," says Jo, stepping away from the Queen, her sword bumping awkwardly on her shoulder, the mane trailing a wake from the mask in her hand. "I only took what was mine," she says. "And the only oath I swore was to do right, and good, and all that – "

"For me!" cries the Duke. "You broke your oath to *me*, Gallowglas, and I will have it proved. Draw your sword."

"No," says Jo, and the Duke with a twist of his hips flap of his coat wheels his longsword back and up, over his head –

"Look to your peers, Hawk," says Lymond.

And like that the blade stops, droops at an angle, and the Duke turns to look on Lymond, pop-eyed, pink-haired, in his black leather jacket. "Who are you," says the Duke, "that address me so familiar."

"It was them that did for my mother," says Lymond. "Guisarme and Axehandle. Look to them."

"You," says the Duke, flat-faced, "your," and then bursting up out of him a snapping bark of a laugh.

"It's marked me, hasn't it," says Lymond. "Same as it's marked you."

"You're next," says the Duke, turning back to Jo. "Unless?" Looking over his shoulder at Lymond again. "You'd stand as her champion? No?" Grunting he hauls his blade back up, and Jo standing there before him one hand in her coat pocket one hand still holding the mask, mouth set, her eyes the color of mud blinking rapidly.

"Hawk!" cries Lymond.

"Enough," says the Queen, lifting her head. *"Enough.* She has the right of it, Hawk. Put it down," and she steps between them, steps right up to him, "put it away," and he steps back and back again, sword swiveling in his hands, ponderously lowering down and down until it rests blade-tip squeaking on the scratched wood floor as he leans against the pommel. "Ma'am," he says.

She walks past him, over to the front door, stoops and picks up the Duke's cane. "Please," she says, returning, holding the cane out to him. "Not here, not now. If there is to be a fight," and she looks across the room, to Lymond, "let it be a fair one."

The Duke takes his cane from her hand. "Of course," he says, "we are thrilled your, son, has returned, from wherever it was he went. And we welcome him," thump of the cane-tip on the floorboards, creak as he leans his weight on the rough-hewn head of it, "with open arms."

"The Perry have always looked warmly to the support of Barganax," says Lymond. Beside him in the doorway to the kitchen Robin is quite still, arms folded across his chest.

"Jo," says the Queen then, and Jo looks down, thumbs her lip, looks up to meet those dark eyes. "Jo Huntsman," says the Queen. "We have kept you long enough. We would – I would, have you be about your business." The rustling of the mane of the mask in Jo's hand in the utter silence of that room. "The Mooncalfe takes bread and salt and oil from no one, but tonight. Tonight he murdered my mother and stole my daughter and for that." Her voice snagging on the words. "I would have you find him, Huntsman. Find him, and shoot him, like a gangster, and send him down to dust."

"Yes ma'am," says Jo with a deep breath. Lymond, his goggle-eyes watching as she nods, the Duke his eyes on the floor as she shifts and settles the sheathed sword a little higher on her shoulder. She walks to the front door, opens it, steps through, and pulls it shut behind her.

She's down the steps and under the trees that line the street when the front door opens again, slams shut rattling glass, "Jo!" It's the Duke, crashing down the stairs from the porch.

"Fuck you," snarls Jo, stalking away down the sidewalk.

"Jo!" Wincing, hissing as he hop-lopes after her. "Jo, wait!"

"After that?" she says. "After all that? *Fuck* you," and then, marching back toward him, "I *trusted* you, you sonofabitch. I trusted you and I waited and I *left* her. With him." One hand up churning the air mouth open head shaking from side to side, *"Fuck* you," her hand tossing the words at him, the mane of the mask in her other hand whipping, an echo. "You were gonna cut me down in there!"

"Steel's to be answered with steel," he says, and she shoves her free hand in the pocket of her coat and tugs it out, the gun, flat and black and pointed at him. "Try it," she says. The mane shivering, stiff, upright. "If she hadn't stopped you," says Jo. "I would've blown you away. You stupid motherfucker."

"Maybe," he says. "You can put it away, Gallowglas. I think we're done now."

"Huntsman," she says, the gun still pointed at him. "I got a promotion."

"Only till the King comes back," he says, looking back, away at the reddish-brown car parked on the side of the street now, in front of that green house cater-cornered. Luys on the sidewalk beside it, his hand on the roof of the car. "And I don't think I like the way it looks on you."

"Tough," says Jo.

"Jo – "

"Jo what. Jo what! Put the gun down? Get in the car, go back and wait and wait and wait," her trembling arm she crooks her elbow gun dropping pointed still at his belly, "for you to grow a pair and sit on the fucking Throne already?" Her arm snaps straight again, hauling the gun back up. The mane quivers about the mask in her other hand. "No," the Duke's saying mildly, "no, that's not what I was gonna, by all means, go. Get him. I just," and he sighs. His eyes on the barrel of the gun. "After last night." He looks up. "This morning. We're done. Yeah?" And her arm crooks again, gun hitching up, away. It tips over, pointed down. "Where're you gonna go with that," he says.

Her fingers opening the gun lying there not much longer than her hand, the dull black barrel, the letters Kel-Tec stamped in the pebbled metal, grip of it wound about with glossy black tape. "I don't know," she says, looking away from him, away from the white house, down along the street dipping under the trees toward a brightly lit intersection where a car drifts silently by. "Nobody knows where he is. Where he would've gone. Ray, Lymond, he kept saying it was okay, we'd find him, she'd be okay, but." She stuffs the gun back in her pocket. "There's somebody I know of who knows – stuff." The mane of the mask drifting languidly as she turns back to him. Blinking quickly. "It's not much, but."

"Do you love her?" says the Duke.

"I don't love anybody," she says.

"Horseshit." And then, "Burnside and Broadway. That abandoned burger joint. Start there. It's where he's been, living, the last little while."

"Oh," says Jo. "Leo, I – "

"Go."

"Thank you," says Jo.

"Don't ever," says the Duke, turning away, "say that to me again." Limping back up the sidewalk into the darkness under the trees, toward the car, Luys leaning against. A blaring horn behind her, the squall of tires, some music playing somewhere worn away to nothing but an insistent thump. She heads away down toward the brightly lit intersection, sword on her shoulder, mask in her hand.

A beep echoing harshly off the flat walls stark in the only light from a desk lamp set on the floor, two rows of yellow tables and orange plastic chairs, the enormous close-up photo of a hamburger brown and yellowed with grime, menu boards empty and dark, cold ovens lined up behind the counter in the darkness. A squawk, a recorded voice distorted by volume fills the air, "Yeah. Okay. We're in. Place and time as suggested." Rattle and click bounce from the walls, around corners. Plops of water dripping and a high-pitched whine of water rushing somewhere in the pipes, a grinding clank of flexible metal hose being pulled, yanked in the darkness there at the back of the kitchen, a wide shape all in black hauling the spray head out of the broad deep sink, holding it up by her shoulder. Squeezing open the big clamping valve there's a croak, a knocking of pipes, water erupts and she grunts as she struggles to hold the hose up, blasting Ysabel's back, soaking her hair slapped against her face as Ysabel turns away braced against the counter. Another croak, water's gone, just plopping drips again, the whine in the pipes. "God you're filthy," says Gloria all in black, opening up the hose again, aimed at Ysabel's legs, her buttocks, Ysabel hunched over the counter on her elbows. Croak again. Ysabel dripping, shivering violently, there's a blurt, a babble loud and shrill, "Kay. We're in. Place and time as." Clack. "Who the hell has an answering machine anymore," mutters Gloria, a rustle of something in the darkness, something thrown at Ysabel, she catches in awkwardly, cloth, a pair of pants, sweatpants, the blurting babble again. "Dry off with those," says Gloria. "And time as suggested," and then the rattle again of a phone dropped somewhere else, some time before.

"I need my clothes," says Ysabel.

"They're soaked. Ruined," says Gloria. "No time." More rustling, the blurt and babble, "Okay. We're." Clack.

"I have to have something," says Ysabel.

"I tried to tell him. All my stuff's too big for you. Try this." Snapping flutter, something white, Ysabel drapes it over herself, a T-shirt. "This is enormous," she says. Letters scrawled in black ink across the front say The Gloomadon Poppers.

"Put it the fuck on," snaps Gloria.

A phone rings, a loud slow clang of a ring, a metal clapper hitting metal bells, and again, and again, as Ysabel and Gloria stand there, listening, dripping. Clack and the harsh beep, a voice then, too loud as before, but higher, drier, the Duke's voice, "You stupid sonofabitch pick up I know you're there. Pick up!" Fumble rattle of phone in hand. "Get in," he says to someone else. "You've finally made it. You're way out beyond the horizon, over the pale, you're getting your fucking showdown and when the two of you are done with each other, if there's anything left of you," a breath too loud, too harsh, overwhelming, "look up, look to the west. That shadow's me, coming down off the Throne to grind you into dust." Click-clack.

Ysabel holding the T-shirt, Gloria's eyes glinting in the darkness, an eruption of babble and then the voice again, "The horizon, over the pale, you're getting" clack and tumbling squawk, "Know you're there. Pick up! Get in. You've" clack-clack. "Who," says Gloria looming, "who the fuck, you know who that is. You – you – " Another glint down low leaning in there she is wide face pressed close her hand in black lace there between them. Jutting from it a short wide blade ash-dark but for the very gleaming edge of it. "When the two of you," the loud voice says, "are done with each other, if there's" clack. "Who *is* that," says Gloria, "who's he talking about." Ysabel against the counter leaning back eyes on the knife pressed close. "Each other, if there's anything left of" click. Babble.

"You don't know what I can do with this," says the woman, pressing the blade a crease in Ysabel's cheek. "If I'm angry." Voice stretched taut. "And I hate you." Pressing hard enough to turn Ysabel's face to one side. "Thing left of you," that enormous breath, "look up, look to the west."

"Who is that," says Gloria. "Who's coming."

Ysabel blinking says, "You don't hate – "

Her shriek raw piercing there's a scramble and that recording dies in a crunch of shattered plastic. Around the corner between the rows of yellow tables he's crouching low feet fast under his dark skirt shirtless sword held up before him short blade back against his forearm leaping onto the counter beneath the dark menu boards. At the back of the kitchen light's fizzing in the air Gloria's falling back Ysabel's slumping falling to her knees hand to her bright face. He leaps again, kicks off the face of an oven, leaves a swipe of a footprint in the grease-rimed dust on the griddle, alights by the sink between them Ysabel on her side clutching her cheek with both hands floor about her flooded in a shock of white light moaning and he turns blade whipping about in his hand to point at Gloria tipped over a couple of paper bags spilling clothing black and white. "What have you done," he says, his voice gone quiet and cold.

the Only light – what Needs doing
Summing up – into the Woods

THE ONLY LIGHT from the desk lamp kicked over, the only sound a single distant plop of water dropping and she jerks the gun in her hand jabbing back the way she's come, ahead again, shadows blotting the enormous close-up photo of a hamburger behind her, weird crawling nets of shadow from the long black mane that snakes about the mask she's wearing.

Around the corner the light cut off the counter there the menu boards above it blank and dark and the blank blackness of the kitchen yawning beyond. Not quite blank. Gun over the counter wavering tilting she works her wrist resettles her fingers hefts the sheathed sword slung from her shoulder. Tips back the mask, blinking. Free hand up against the harsh light streaming behind her. Somewhere at the back of the kitchen a suggestion of light low on the floor faintly sketches the barest edges of ovens and grills, the hooded bay of the fryer.

Another plop of water. She jumps.

She steps through the gap at one end of the counter fully into shadow now she's pulling out her phone, thumbing it on, holding it up, faint haze of light from its screen enough just to show where she's putting her feet. The light ahead is brighter now than what seeps from the phone, enough to pick out the shapes of itself, splashes and splatters, a bit on the floor there, a swipe of it along the edge of something, again a plop of water, a sink there at the back of the kitchen. She stops. Looks down. Her foot tangled in, in cloth, glossy black, a glimmer, spangles. She scoops it up. A vest, heavy with gold embroidery.

The first patch of light there on the floor, a dollop no bigger than her palm, the sullen glimmer of it not enough to sheen the metal of the gun in the hand she holds over it. Unhooking her pinkie from the butt of the gun she dips, brushes the stuff, a brittle crust collapsing into glitter, dusting her fingertip with gold. More dripped along the floor there and there, the swath of it along the edge of the sink, the strings of it hunched up and over a pile of something indistinct, black, black clothing, black lace about a pale arm a boot Jo's turning standing slowly gun up pointed at the woman lying on her back the swell of her belly hiding her face.

Phone up by the gun white haze struggling with smoldering gold to light up something, anything, the splatter of gold on her breast the shape of maybe a hand, streaked and cracked by something black, head there at an angle a tangle of braids and ribbons black and pale the phone light glimmering in an eye there that blinks, and Jo steps back.

"Are you Death?" says the woman lying there on the floor.

"No," says Jo, after a moment, lowering the gun. "Can you move?"

Rustle and shift, clatter and jangle, the woman's rolling over on her side, pushing herself up, gold shivering and falling away, her hand a black shape eddying clouds of it. She grunts. "You okay?" says Jo.

"There was all this blood, I saw it – "

"Yours?" says Jo.

"Yeah," says the woman, after a moment. "You're the one he was talking about, aren't you. The one who was coming. The showdown."

"The, owr," says Jo. "The glitter, the gold dust. Where'd it come from."

And the woman says, "I cut her."

"Did you."

"Her face. And it all, and then it – I fell, and he – he sliced right *through* me. He *killed* me." Shifting, rustling, she's rolling on her side as glitter soughs and settles about her. "Why am I not dead?"

"You got lucky," says Jo, a shadow against shadows now, the phone switched off or tucked away. "She took pity on you. Where is she. Where'd they go."

"It was so *fast?*" says the woman all in black. "I don't know. He never told me, where, where he was taking her. To meet somebody, I think, I didn't ever get what he was doing, we only," hissing, gasping as she pushes herself further upright, "wow."

"That's gonna hurt for a few days," says Jo. "You got somewhere to go? Somebody who can keep an eye on you?"

Leaning on her elbow on the floor, indistinct in the splashes of dim light, peering into the shadows, she says, "You're going to kill him, aren't you."

"Go home," says Jo. "Don't come back." Walking away out of the kitchen.

Jessie shuts off the engine. Looks up in the rear-view mirror at the two of them in the back seat. "We're here," she says.

"I think," says Luys, slowly, carefully, "yes. It's what we should be doing."

"You think," says the Duke. "How about you," he says to Jessie. "What do *you* think we ought to be doing."

"I don't know," says Jessie.

"She doesn't know," says the Duke, and then to Jessie again, "Open the door." Jessie undoes her seatbelt and climbs out of the car and the Duke says to Luys, "One night? That's all it took? One night."

"That isn't why we should help her," says Luys, his hands, knuckles rough, dark fingers twined together on his knee. "It's the Princess. We should be – "

"Yeah?" says the Duke. Jessie's opening the passenger door, levering the front seat forward. "Get out of the car." He plants his cane on the sidewalk, braces himself against the seat back.

"Your grace?" says Luys.

"Get out," says the Duke, hauling himself up, "of the car. You know what to do. Go. Do it."

"Your grace, I – "

"Get out. Of the car," says the Duke, and Luys opens his door. "Go. Find her. *Save* her."

"Who?" says Luys, climbing out of the car. "Jo? The Princess?"

"Whichever!" says the Duke. "You're the one knows." Luys is looking about, wet trees climbing the hill to one side of the street, houses close by the other, beyond them the lights of the city, the curl of the river far below. "Walk," says the Duke, "catch a bus, I don't care. Go on, Mason. Do what needs doing."

Luys looks to Jessie, back to the Duke, nods stiffly, once. "Your grace," he says, and he turns, hands in the pockets of his short brown jacket, and he walks away down the dark street. "What the hell, Leo," says Jessie.

"Wait in the car," says the Duke. The house behind him a towering Queen Anne lit up by spotlights, gingerbreaded in sherbet pinks and blues, each window with its white lace curtain artfully bunched and tied off in the middle. "This'll only take a minute."

The front door set with an arc of frosted leaded glass. He raps it sharply with the hawk at the head of his cane, and again. A creak of floorboards, a rattle of the knob, the door's opened by a narrowly somber man, his nose and cheeks appled by extravagant gin blossoms, his chin tucked by behind his high white collar.

Raised voices somewhere behind him, someone yelling, the words indistinct. "Barganax for the Viscount," says the Duke, pushing his way in. "I'll announce myself." Thump of his cane-tip, squeak of his footsteps, "Handle!" he bellows, and the yelling breaks off. "You puling, knock-kneed, milk-livered giglet of a craven, puling, tangle-boweled shit!" Ringing thump of the tip of his longsword on the floor, one hand on the pommel of it, one against the newel post of the long straight staircase there in the narrow front hall. "I would have words with you!"

Rasp of a sliding door and there's Agravante at the end of the hall, pale dreadlocks brushing his shoulders, soft blue shirt open at the throat. "Barganax," he says. A cut glass tumbler in his hand. "Grandfather sleeps."

"I'll tip-toe," says the Duke, hauling up his sword both hands braced against his belly, taking a long creaking step down the hall. "Is that the Guisarme with you?" An older man in the doorway behind Agravante, bald browned head and grizzled cheeks. "Excellent. Saves me a trip."

"You'd have him as your second?" says Agravante.

"I'd have him next," says the Duke.

"Not again," says the Guisarme. His yellow shirt unbuttoned over an undershirt slashed across his chest.

"But a moment, Welund," says Agravante, tossing back half of what's left in his tumbler. In his other hand a long-bladed dagger, the hilt wrapped in blued wire.

"It will *not* be a moment," says the Guisarme. "It is *never* but a moment. One of you will stick the other and we'll call it done but it will fester and seethe and pull us apart precisely when we must work in harness. The time is out of joint, gentlemen – "

"Says the butcher," and the Duke swings at Agravante's head, "the cleaver still wet," Agravante catching it with the dagger, and the Duke hauls back into an underhanded thrust at Agravante's belly, "in his paw," and again with a clang it's parried, Agravante holding his glass up high out of the way. "How dare you," the Guisarme's saying. The Duke's levered around a cross-body cut, Agravante steps back, leans in, dagger hooking the sword on the followthrough, pinning it against the plaster cracking wall and

"Shit" says the Duke tugging the blade held fast by Agravante's dagger. Agravante hurls his tumbler into the air arm windmilling around and as it comes back up there's another dagger in his hand about a hilt wrapped blue the long blade pinning the Duke's jacket there under his arm sinking home, the Duke grunting, Agravante letting go, looking up, reaching up his hand, catching the falling glass.

Stumbling back the Duke's breath caught on his teeth the blued hilt rising and falling there under his arm. He grips it, tugs, works it scowling back and forth, slowly, trembling, pulls the long blade free. Drops it clattering to the floor.

"The matter's settled?" says the Guisarme, absently scratching the slit in his shirt.

"I concede it," says the Duke with a cough. Holding himself up against the bannister. "The Axehandle's no craven turd, his knees do not knock." Leaning down for his cane discarded there at the foot of the stairs. "His liver and lights as fine as could be hoped. Nor," cane in hand he sits suddenly there on the floor, cupping the hole in his jacket, "does he pule. But." A deep shudder of a breath. "He does dabble, in insurrection."

"Hawk!"

"You are both traitors to the court. This was *not* the argument disproved, and I will see it published."

"Don't be a fool," says the Guisarme as Agravante's saying "Would you be King of an empty city?"

"Better a city dispersed, than a city usurped," says the Duke.

"The Perry line's played out," says the Guisarme, his eyes gone sidelong at Agravante. "We merely seek a new Bride, a new Queen for the King come back."

"Merely seek," says the Duke. "You evicted the Queen tonight."

"We can't afford her extravagances," says the Guisarme, "not until we know we're once more safe and secure." Agravante quickly drinks what's left in his tumbler.

"Tonight," says the Duke, "the Princess was abducted by her guardian."

"He went through me to do it!" says the Guisarme, a hand to his chest.

"Yet here you stand, and speak – so utterly unlike the Queen's mother, or my Shootist."

"That was none of our – " says Agravante, and the Guisarme holds up a hand, and Agravante bites his lip. "One word more, your grace," says the Guisarme, "and it's war you'll have, not a duel."

"Really," says the Duke, looking over to Agravante. "Is that what I'd have, Viscount. The Queen's named the Gallowglas as her new Huntsman."

Agravante turns to the Guisarme who's hand's still up. The Guisarme says, "Mortals are fragile."

"So are bankers," says the Duke, pushing himself to his feet, cane tucked under his arm, hand still clamped over the hole in his jacket. "The Perry line's played out? I'll be sure to tell Lymond you said that, next time I see him."

"Lymond," says the Guisarme, with an odd half-laugh.

"You didn't know?" says the Duke, his hand on the doorknob. "Hair's different, and the eyes, but that was most assuredly the Prince, delivering his mother," and a heavy clonk of Agravante's glass hitting the floor, "to the tender care of Robin Goodfellow, but an hour ago." The Duke opens the door. "I'll show myself out?"

Jessie opens the door of the car and hurries up the sidewalk as he limps toward her, cane still tucked away. He lifts his free arm and she ducks under it, bearing him up, and he looks down at his cupping hand, shining wetly against the hole in his jacket. "Are you okay?" says Jessie. "What happened?"

"Well I didn't lose," says the Duke. He nods toward the car and they make their halting way back to it. "So we're going home?" says Jessie. "We're gonna go find Luys and go back home?"

"What?" says the Duke. "No." He takes his arm from her shoulders, leans against the fender. She opens the door. "We're just getting started. I'll – sit up front. Tell you where we're going. It's, it's tricky."

Ragged hum of a lone bass note held under hissing breath echoing over the speakers and feedback fluttering and whooping like some frantic birdsong and a voice buzzing against a microphone, "From her lair in Devil's Point Mary's is proud to present the Starling." Kisses, a woman's moaning over the speakers now and a rattle and thump of a single run on the drums as the bass note shifts and drops, kisses like a girl, and Orlando rubs his one good eye. Ysabel's sitting across the tiny table from him, her back to the stage that's not much bigger, a figure wrapped and hooded in a dark cloak standing there, starkly lit by tiny white-hot spots hung from the low ceiling, fog spilling across the floor into the laps of the few men and a woman sitting close to the stage, looking up. Ysabel's face shines in the darkness splashed with glitter along her cheeks, her throat, daubed across her forehead, spangling the sagging white T-shirt she wears under a thin black coat trimmed with white fur. Ring of cymbals and the feedback becomes strummed notes over that drone fading slowly away, all of it, everything waiting, and Orlando isn't looking at her, he's looking past her, over her shoulder, and Ysabel almost smiles.

The music crashes into a beat, I, that voice is singing, I've got to get out of the palace, and the little crowd's cheering. Ysabel leans over the table. "You're frightened," she says.

Orlando's head tilts, tilts back, shakes slightly. He's still looking past her. "They'll be here soon," he says. "Time and place, as suggested." He isn't looking at the door. He's looking at the stage.

"You shouldn't have killed her," says Ysabel, hands on her bare knees splattered with more glitter, shining in the darkness under the table.

"She shouldn't have cut you," says Orlando.

"That's what has you so frightened," says Ysabel. Leaning closer to him, speaking into his ear. "You and I are the only ones who know what's happened. Let me go, now, and I swear to you." Pulling back away from him, still leaning over the table. "No one will challenge you." He's still looking past her. "You will be free to go from this place."

Again a distracted shake of his head. "They'll be here soon," he says.

"Who," says Ysabel. "Who am I to be given to." Leaning over, trying to catch his eye. "Do they have any idea what they're getting?"

His eye flicks over to meet hers, and the corner of his mouth crooks. "No," he says, and he looks away again. Seems like, the voice is singing, honey you're always, mad at me, and I wonder, what have I done.

"You've never been here before," says Ysabel then. "Have you. Why. Why are we here, now?"

"You often come to places like this," says Orlando.

"I prefer places where everybody dances," says Ysabel, turning in her seat as the loud song crashes to an end, that bass note droning once more, feedback whooping, "but yes. I've been here before." The cloak's gone. The woman on the stage breathing heavily kneeling black fishnet stockings and a sheer white négligée held shut by a single bow. She's untying the bow. The crowd's cheering. Dollar bills litter the stage about her. Black hair glossy in artful tangles swings as she throws off the négligée, baring her breasts. Rakish atop her head a silvery white tiara. The drone's shifted from a bass to an accordion, a sinister wheeze that pulses too quickly as new instruments gather themselves beneath it and the woman on the stage grabs the pole to one side and pulls herself to her feet spinning about it, the moon was unsteady, a new voice high and thin is singing, the woods looked so dark and oh so deep. "You shouldn't have brought me here," says Ysabel, over her shoulder to Orlando, smiling now, shining. "And you shouldn't have killed the girl. She could've helped you."

"Can I get you something from the bar? Honey." The woman in the tight T-shirt, a tray in her hand, leans over them both, her hand on the table between them. "That glitter is phenomenal. How'd you get it to glow like that?"

"You like it?" says Ysabel, as Orlando says, "Nothing."

"It's so New Wave," says the woman in the tight T-shirt.

"Ysabel," says Orlando, and Ysabel says, "Do you think I'm beautiful?"

"What?" says the woman in the tight T-shirt, "Yes, I," as Ysabel's pushing her chair back, standing, and "Sit down," says Orlando, I've been on this job now, that new voice is singing, for a thousand years, and Ysabel says, "Do you want to kiss me?"

"Sure?" says the woman in the tight T-shirt as Ysabel's arms go around her white fur flowing about her cuffs and the tray clatters to the table as Orlando chair scraping stands abruptly music crashing about them the woman on the stage one hand on her tiara spinning upside-down about the pole, I'd like you better if you'd just go away, the woman in the tight T-shirt stepping back mouth smeared with light blinking one hand to her face Orlando trying to push past her, and Ysabel's leaning over the shoulder of the man sitting at the next table, his mustache waxed and neatly curled and his frown lights up in a smile at her that folds into another frown, puzzled, looking from her to the woman on stage and back again. "That man," says Ysabel in his ear, pointing back at Orlando, "with the eyepatch? Is trying to kill me," and the man with the mustache leaps to his feet as Orlando fetches up before him and Ysabel's already at the next table over, Orlando's hand on the hilt of his sword but the woman in the tight T-shirt's grabbing at it, and the man with the mustache throws a punch. Ysabel's making her way not to the front door but the back, toward a brightly lit glass door at the far end of the little club under a sign that says Food. Orlando's roaring. The music's pounding. Orlando's roaring. More people swarming about him, seizing his arms, his hands, "Get him!" they're crying. "Stop him!" Ysabel's running.

"Remarkable, the likeness" – a Sudden spark
bright Lights & Lefse – the Long shot

"Remarkable," says Mr. Charlock. "The likeness." Her chin in his hand he tilts her head to one side, the other, hot white light rolling over her cheekbones, gleaming her green eyes. Artlessly tangled black curls stiff with hairspray rustle over bare shoulders. "Flawless."

"Mr. Charlock," says Mr. Keightlinger, out in the middle of the club. He's wearing his sunglasses, the left lens painted over with spidery white words. In one hand a Japanese sword, long bare curl of a blade shining, bone-white hilt wrapped in rough black cloth. The crunch of broken glass as he turns, looks to the front door, the back door, the overturned tables, the little knots of people crowded together by the bar, the private booths where someone's groaning on the floor. "Sweep," he says to himself, "something. Couple more minutes."

Mr. Charlock reaches into the pocket of his black suit jacket. "Let me ask you something," he says to the woman sitting before him, on the folding chair on the little stage, draped in her sheer white négligée. Fog roiling about her ankles. She nods. Her hands folded together, tucked between her knees. He pulls out a pair of underwear, bikini underpants with blue and white stripes. "These yours?" he says.

After a moment her head begins to shake from side to side.

"You know them? Seen them before?"

Again her head shakes quick jerks back and forth now "No?" she says, the edge in her voice burring the whisper.

"Long shot," he says, with a shrug. He tucks the underwear back in his pocket. Stands, turns, hops off the stage. Shaking out his hands. He kicks a chair leg out of the way and curls two fingers back against his palm, two fingers extended, thumb cocked. Pointed at Orlando sitting on the floor legs askew in his blue skirt arms up wrists pinned to the wall, eyepatch yanked to one side, wet ruin of an empty scar there leaking yellow tears that stain his loose white shirt. Mr. Charlock hikes his hand up dropping the hammer of his thumb and something hits the wall above Orlando, cracks and a shiver in the air, glass rattling, wood creaking, shrieks and shouts from the people by the bar, by the private booths. "Where is she," says Mr. Charlock, those two fingers pointed at Orlando again, Orlando who shakes his head, who coughs, who spits. "I don't know," he says.

Mr. Charlock steps close and presses those fingertips against that wet scar, Orlando's head pressed back against the wall. "Had a deal," says Mr. Charlock.

"She tricked me," says Orlando, "and bewitched them all, and walked out that back door." He's smiling. "If you hurried, you might catch her."

"You expect me to believe that," says Mr. Charlock.

"No," says Orlando.

"Mr. Charlock," says Mr. Keightlinger once more, and Mr. Charlock steps back. "Bring that," he says, nodding at the sword in Mr. Keightlinger's hand. "We'll want to find him, later."

"We need an out," says Mr. Keightlinger.

"Quick," says Mr. Charlock, "and dirty," and then, "Ladies! Gentlemen!" he calls out. "I must apologize." His free hand plucking a pair of sunglasses from a pocket. "There's a chance not all of you will make it out of this." Looking about the dark little club. "And a Portland landmark will be gutted. Can't be helped." Settling the sunglasses over his eyes, the feather tied to one side stirring against his ear. "So take a moment, think back, this wonderful Friday night you were enjoying, the drinks, the music, the ladies," and he points those fingers thumb cocked at the tiny white-hot spots hung from the low ceiling, that shine on the fog streaming over the lip of the little stage. "Cover and ready," Mr. Keightlinger's muttering, "them, them," as Mr. Charlock says, "Because suddenly there was a *spark* – "

"A taxi," she's saying, up through the payment slot in the door, "a telephone, please," glitter spangled over her face, her hair winking and flashing in the colorless fluorescent light, and the man inside behind the glass is waving her away, "No," he says, "no, go! Hotel! Go!" Somewhere a couple of blocks away a flat whump that rattles the glass under her hands. She steps back, stricken. "Go!" says the man behind the glass, pointing this way, "Benson!" that, "Governor, go!"

"Don't you," she says, "aren't I," and he yells "Telephone!" pointing past her at the blue hutch of a payphone on the corner, and a block away behind it a silhouette against the bright-lit busy street, a big man, a dark suit, headed toward her. "Don't you think," she says, turning back, but the man's stepped away, behind the big white sign in the window that says Park & Lock $10.95 a day $5 an hour. Ysabel pulls up the hood of her thin black coat, steps away from the kiosk, forcing her feet to keep themselves at a quick walk fringe pattering on her moccasin boots, white fur trailing from her cuffs.

Across an empty street at an angle past the mouth of a garage up wide low steps into a park, flat pebbled concrete terraces and here and there trees in little plots and patches of dirt, benches, a figure prone in a sleeping bag glossy with rainwater. Peering through empty branches back and down away there's two men in black suits large and small maybe half a block away and headed quickly toward the park. "Roland," she says, and then, crying out, "Chariot!" Running down into the middle of that little park, spinning around, dark buildings high on every side, a siren wailing somewhere blocks away, another whooping suddenly much closer. "Chariot!" she cries again. The sleeping bag doesn't stir.

"It's all right," comes a man's voice, out of breath, "you're frightened, I know. We're here to help." Footsteps rapidly slapping the concrete behind her. She runs for the corner where the next block over and up opens into another parking lot, and three white semi trailers one after another along one side, rear doors open, dim lights shining on racks of cable and equipment packed into each, and a soughing rumble of slumbering engines, threaded with the thin chugging whine of a generator, all dulling those sirens blocks away. She slips between two of the trucks, ducks to one side, looking around at the food carts lining the sidewalk before her, all of them shuttered now, dark. She squeezes between the one that says Homestyle Indian Dishes and the one that says Cuba Libre! Empanadas, Croquetas, Frituras.

The lot's half full of tightly parked cars and over there another kiosk, colorless light and big white signs. More food carts line the lot, on all four sides, facing their sidewalks, all dark, all of them shuttered and dark but for a couple-three halfway along to the left, under the trees, lit up starkly by great lamps hung about on poles and a rickety scaffolding. She squats low, weaving her way toward the light through the rows and aisles of cars.

"Again," says a disembodied voice over a loudspeaker, and there's a flurry of activity around those lit-up carts, a big piece of equipment hoisted smoothly up and back on a crane and to either side of the lights little crowds in suits with umbrellas and yellow and orange raincoats and big flannel shirts and fleece pullovers are waved into place by a couple of people with clipboards and headsets. A plastic orange sign taped to a lamppost says s.u. wtf in big black letters.

"Go," says that disembodied voice.

The little crowds start walking one or two at a time toward each other, past each other along the sidewalk before the food carts as that big piece of equipment floats down and in slowly, slowly, toward two men standing by the open lit-up window of one of the carts, both of them in trench coats, both of them in dark suits and ties, the older one, taller, his tightly curled hair dusted with grey, his dark skin splotched with darker freckles over his cheeks and nose, his shirt open at the throat, his tie loose, says "Viking soul food?" as that piece of equipment hovers to a stop before them. The younger man smaller and slender and buttoned all the way up, tightly knotted, his brown hair thickly tumbled over a face that's all eyes and cheekbones hefts the wrap he's holding in one hand. "Been running on nothing but sugar all day," he says. "Wanted to lay down a more substantial base." He takes a big bite, chewing ostentatiously.

"I'll buy you whatever you need, so long as that overclocked cranium of yours can crack this case," says the older man.

There's a moment then, hanging, the younger man still chewing, older waiting, hands in the pockets of his trench coat, little crowd milling about, that piece of equipment hovering.

"Again," says the disembodied voice.

The crane hoists smoothly back and up over the heads of the crowds being waved back into place. The younger man leans over, spits his mouthful of food into a bucket there at his feet, dropping the bitten wrap in after it. Someone, a woman with a camera slung from her neck, hands him another wrap, then whisks the bucket away. "Beto," says the disembodied voice, "we need you to swallow."

"That's what he said," says the older man.

"This gets picked up," says the younger man, "I'm gonna put on twenty pounds by midseason."

"Ready," says that voice, then "go," and the crane floats smoothly, slowly down over the crowd jostling to life, and the older man cocks an eyebrow and says "Viking soul food?" as the younger man hefts his fresh wrap, and "Excuse me, I have to ask you to move along," murmurs the man in the black fleece pullover, leaning over the hood of the parked car behind Ysabel. She jumps. "I was just," she says.

"You can watch from across the street," he says, pointing. His black meshback cap says WTF in blocky white letters. "You're too close." In his hand a stubby little cell phone that crackles and echoes that disembodied voice, "Okay, reset for twenty-one. We go in fifteen."

"Don't you find me beautiful?" says Ysabel.

His brows pinch. He looks her up and down, her boots, her thin black coat, the worn T-shirt that says The Gloomadon Poppers in scrawled black letters, the glitter splashed over her, catching the bright white lights. A shudder wriggles up out of him and a smile quirks the corner of his mouth. "Girl," he says, "you look like you had yourself one rough damn night."

"I'm being followed," says Ysabel, "two men, in suits," looking back over the rows of cars. There's no one there. "If I could just stay here – "

"Don't make me insist."

"They won't," and she wipes her eye with the heel of her hand smearing glitter up along her temple, "I don't think they'll try anything, with so many – "

"You got to move it across the street. Let us do what we're here to do," he says.

"But," she says, glitter runneling down her cheeks, "am I, aren't I," and "What," he says, "what."

"I got this," says someone else, a woman, the woman with the camera slung about her neck.

"Yeah?" says the man in the meshback cap. "You know her?"

"She owes me a cup of coffee," says the woman with a camera. Her dark hair short in back, long in front, her glasses with thick black frames.

"Powers that be ain't happy," says the man in the meshback cap. "Delays. The rain, those sirens – "

"Bull never has to know," says the woman with the camera.

He shrugs, stepping back. "Okay," he says, a warning lilt, touching two fingers to the brim of his cap.

"Coffee?" says Ysabel, thin and querulous.

"Venti vanilla latte, right?" says the woman with the camera.

"Yeah, well," says Jo leaning her shoulder against the doorframe flaking glossy white.

"What I got to do," says Guthrie sleepy and slow on the other side of the door open only as far as the chain will allow.

"It's not you, so much," says Jo. "It's your girlfriend, your friend, does she, ah – "

"Hey," says Guthrie.

" – does she stay here? With you?"

"Hey," says Guthrie again. Forehead against forearm braced between door and frame. His black T-shirt says Face Holding Embrace in white letters.

"I was gonna come here first, but I heard where Orlando holes up so I went *there* first, only it was a bust, and, and," she straightens up away from the doorframe as Guthrie's saying "Hey, what do you want with," and Jo says "It's all gone to hell, Guthrie. Orlando? The Mooncalfe? He took her. Ysabel. I don't know where, nobody does. I have to find her, I have to, Guthrie – " He's closing the door. "Guthrie?" The chain rattles, the door opens, wide, he's stepping back, making way for Jo in her butter-colored coat, her sword slung from her shoulder, in her hand the mask, the mane of it restless, rustling.

"What do you want with her," says Guthrie, a shadow in the dark cramped hall.

"She *knows* stuff?" says Jo. "She knew, you and Becker had to go to the church, that time. Right?" Guthrie stops. In the room ahead of him a light flickers on, overhead, too bright, and he's silhouetted against a blare of color, pinks and yellows, oranges, reds. "Maybe she knows where he's taken her?"

"I don't know," says Guthrie, turning.

"I mean, it's," says Jo, "a long shot, I know. But it's the only thing I could think of. It's all I've got."

"I don't know," says Guthrie again, there in the dark hallway before her.

"I just, wanna ask her a question," says Jo, the mask rustling in her hand.

"Blood," says someone, a quavering voice from that lit-up room. "Blood on the snow. Blood on the burritos. That's what I saw."

"Blood?" says Jo, stepping closer, and Guthrie with a sigh steps back, out of her way.

"Blood," says the voice. "Snow. She stayed. He went back to her. Do you already have the gun?"

Jo's pushing through the gauzy stuff curtaining the doorway into a bright small room overwhelmed by a bed shoved into the back corner heaped high with blankets and quilts and afghans in a mad mound of color, rich purples and a poisonously bright green and dirty red and yellow stripes and the same beige flowers over and over and over and rows of pink and black robots, grappling, and wrapped up in the middle of it all peering out through a small wadded hole a face blue eyes and a sharp nose shadowed and pale lips bitten before she says, "Do you?"

"The gun?" says Jo in the doorway. "Yes."

"I'm sorry," says the face, ducking back under the covers.

"No," says Jo, stepping into the room, kneeling, sword rattling in its sheath, "please, tell me, can you tell me, where's," and a wail erupts from the mound, "Ysabel," says Jo, "where'd the Mooncalfe," but the wail's become words, "No! No! I can't, I can't look! I can't look!"

"Please," says Jo. Leaning close. "Please. Can you try. You're my, only – hope – "

"No," the wail, "no, it's not allowed, listen, listen!" and a hand, shaking, held up out of the mound of blankets fingers splayed, and Jo gasps, jerks back, leans back away from it, her breath harsh and quick and the only other sound a rustle, from the floor, the mane of the mask in her hand squirming over the clothing strewn over the floor, reaching, yearning up the side of the bed. "You would have to take my *head*," says the voice from the mound.

"Jo," says Guthrie, behind her, as Jo's scrambling back, climbing to her feet, tucking the mask away under her butter-colored coat. "I'm sorry?" she says. "I'm sorry."

That face worms its way back to another opening in the tangled mound. "Maybe the junk shop?"

"What?" says Jo.

"Ninth and Flanders. You could try there?"

THE FIENDISH LITTLE BASKET-BOX
HOW MANY PLANETS, AND HOW LARGE – HER GEIS
HER SITUATION – "YESSIR"

A FIENDISH LITTLE BASKET-BOX, carved from a single chunk of dark red wood, sits on the desk by a loose stack papers, covered with rows of closely written figures, by manila folders with neat labels that say Riverkeep, Cassino, the Moretti, the Elkins. He sets the cut glass tumbler empty beside the box, under the blue-shaded banker's lamp, and gingerly strokes the knurled and seamless faces of it, the pips carved into each, simple shapes, a stylized flame, a cloud, a raindrop, a quartered circle. He sighs. "I didn't hear you come in," he says, the words thick, and roughly ground.

Behind him in a chair by the door ajar Marfisa curled her feet up on the cushion arms about her knees. "What is that," she says.

"A boon," says Agravante.

"For the Guisarme?"

"Don't be ridiculous." He steps around the desk, smoked glass, thick metal frame.

"What was he *doing* here? Where's Grandfather?"

"Asleep," says Agravante, sitting in his chair, a woven contraption of black leather straps.

"Do you know what I've seen tonight, brother?"

"I did not even know that you were yet within the city, sister mine."

Wrapped tightly in her sheepskin jacket she leans her forehead against her knees. On the floor by her chair a knapsack, stuffed full. "The Loathly Mór," she says, "came with her people openly down the street, and they sang the aisling, and they stopped outside a house, and I swear, brother," looking up at him then, "she did beg sanctuary there."

"The Queen," he says, picking up the empty tumbler, putting it down again, "has been set aside." He gets up and kneels to open a small refrigerator in the credenza behind the desk.

"By – whom?" she says. "You? The Guisarme?"

"The Duke was here as well." He stands, a blue glass bottle in his hand, and pours water fizzing into the tumbler. "I believe that's a quorum."

"He agreed."

"He did not disagree."

"Then," shifting in her chair, one foot lowering, "Ysabel, is – "

He shakes his head. "That spark's blown out, sister love." A sip of water. "Evermore no Perry shall be Queen, no Queen a Perry. Letters have been sent, to the courts of Engines, Angels, Nickels, asking after – "

"Sent by whom," she says, both feet now on the floor.

"They went out under the seal of the Hound."

She sits back in the chair, looking up at the shadowed ceiling. "So," she says, with a sigh. Looking back at him. "You would be King."

He turns, stoops, drops the bottle with a clank back in the refrigerator. "You really think that to be my goal."

"How should I know?" she says. "Tonight you sigh, you moan like Fénius, agonizing over which words to leave behind. Just a month before you leered like Lothario when you came to urge me into the arms of the Princess," and "That," he says, standing abruptly, turning back to her, frowning, "that wasn't," and then he sits, heavily. "A lot has happened, this past month. More to the point's what hasn't happened."

"The boon," she says. "Whose is it. Tell me."

He leans forward, elbows on the glass, his shadow looming up the wall behind, hulking shoulders, matted dreadlocks, "I swear," he says, "by the stars above us both. It has *nothing* to do with this."

She pushes her hair a ghostly tangle back out of her face, slumping, leaning against the arm of the chair. "Do you know," she says, "what they can do now, brother, with their telescopes? They scrutinize the stars, much as you might a candle on the enemy general's desk, across the field, the night before a battle. From the, slightest waver, the least flicker, they can tell – the star has planets. And how many planets there are, how large, what they're made of, how long their years might be – "

He's waving a hand dismissively, "This is just one of your spaceship stories," he says.

"No, brother," she says. "It's real, and very true."

"So this candle, then. It – "

"If the stars have planets, worlds of their own to look after – what do you think they care, really, about you, or me, this city, your pathetic little empire of, apartment buildings, and mortgage payments?"

He smiles, then, shifts back, his face slipping out of the light. "It would have kept us safe and secure, for years to come," he says, gathering together the papers and the folders on his desk. "A bulwark against the Guisarme, and his damnable bank." He taps them against the desk into a tidy pile in his hands, leans down, opens a drawer. Tucks them away. "He'd never have done to Pinabel what he did to Perry today."

"What *he* did?" says Marfisa. Agravante's holding out an envelope, shining white under the desklamp. "What's this?" She leans forward, into the space between them, reaches over the desk to take the envelope in her hand. He doesn't let go. "Money," he says, twisting his wrist, turning the envelope over to reveal a neat label that says Bus Fare. She lets go. "Take it," he says, letting it drop to the desk. "Go on. It'll never be missed. Get out of here."

"I did," she says, still leaning against the desk, "try, to leave." Her hand still over the envelope.

"Do it," he says. "Don't look back. If – when," and he sits back, out of the light again, *"if,* I sit the Throne, in three weeks' time, I'd be nothing but a fading memory before the year's half done. Go on."

Her hand closes on the envelope, crumples it, her other hand reaching across the desk, closing on the placket of his soft blue shirt, hauling him close, into the light. "And now I can't tell," she says, "if you want me to take it, or throw it back in your face."

"To be honest," he says, the words a rasp, "I've no idea myself."

She kisses him then, fiercely pressing her mouth to his, then pushes him back into his chair. Stoops to gather up the knapsack, then yanks the door fully open, storms out into the hall, pounds down the stairs.

He sits back in his chair, lets out a pent-up sigh. Smooths the crumpled envelope against the smoked glass. Picks it up, opens a drawer, drops it in. "That works, too," he says.

Gong-sound as she pushes open the door to step into a foyer filled with junk. Pinched doorway to the left. Through that past a mannequin dressed as a letter carrier, stuffed wolf's head on its shoulders, into a long dark showroom, hurricane lamp flickering on the counter at the far end where a figure's slumped a head on folded arms dappled by colored light trickling from paintings hung on the wall behind, spaceships on black velvet rigged with blinking bulbs, a shimmer suggesting a waterfall by a tumbledown mill, tinny whine of its motor the only sound until the rattle of the sword in its sheath as she shifts it slung from her shoulder. The figure stirs, lifts the floppy brim of a dark hat, croaks "Nice coat." Bit of shadow breaks away from the silhouette, a little rabbit nosing some greens a-sprawl on a plate. "You were briefed? You know how this works?"

"Where is she?" says Jo Maguire. The mane of the mask in her hand hangs limp and still.

"In the back of a truck," says Miss Cheney. "Think a moment before you – "

"Where's the damn truck?" says Jo.

"Not where it will be when you get there," says Miss Cheney, and she pounds the counter with the heel of her hand. The rabbit's head jerks up. "Think! You're down to one!"

"I don't *want* to think! God*dam*mit!" Boots clomp the worn plank floor. *"He took her.* He took her." Striding the length of the showroom, mask shaking in her hand. "And already tonight he's killed the Gammer, he killed the, the Cowboy, and he, his – "

"Destroyed," says Miss Cheney, and Jo stops at that, there before the counter, "What do you," she starts to say, but Miss Cheney speaks up quickly, firmly, "You don't just kill something like the Gammer." Milky eyes fixed on her own hands folded before her. "Now," fingertip tapping a burl of a knuckle, *"think.* Yes. Why did you come here? What's it you're after? Ask, for that. I'll do what I do."

"He didn't kill the girl."

"Girl," says Miss Cheney.

"His, I don't know. Groupie? He didn't destroy her. In his lair." Jo's laying the mask on the counter. The rabbit's gone back to its lettuce. "He tried to. He sliced her, open, but, she, she'd *cut* Ysabel – there was, there was *owr* everywhere – "

"Owr," says Miss Cheney.

Jo, who's trembling, says, "The, gold dust stuff – "

"I know what it is," says Miss Cheney, and without looking up she covers Jo's hand with one of her own. "Are you sure. Are you certain."

"It's why she wasn't dead. The girl. Ysabel had, put it on her, healed, or, I don't know," a sob, "maybe it just, splashed, and she's, and she's," and Miss Cheney shushes and says "Please," she says, "this is terribly important," but Jo pushes back, whips her hand away, the rabbit scrabbling a frightened click of claws, "Why can't I just get a straight damn answer, where she is, go there, deal with it, once and for all – "

"You went to the wrong one first," says Miss Cheney, turning away, reaching after the rabbit. The tinny whine of the waterfall up behind her.

"What?"

"You went," says Miss Cheney, carefully placing each word, "to the wrong one, first." Sitting up, the rabbit in her arms.

"What does that even mean?"

"I just answer them." She pushes the rabbit back onto the counter. "Interpretation's well outside my wheelhouse."

"Where do I go," says Jo, "to see her again."

"Three to a customer only, I'm sorry. Nature of the geis," but Jo brings her hand down a fist to thump the counter, scattering a handful of emptied sugar packets, knocking over a little plastic pony, pink and orange with a tangled purple mane. Miss Cheney jumps. The rabbit's gone. "I," says Jo, and then, a blown sigh, "I," slumping, "have been running, since, before dawn, from somebody, after somebody, and every time, every time I take a minute to look around I'm further behind with farther to go than I was before. No." The sword in its sheath the belt of it slipping in jags down the pale leather sleeve of her coat to catch at the crook of her elbow. "I was supposed to keep her safe," she says, letting it dangle. "That was the deal. Even though he beat me. I could've gotten her out of there and, I didn't, and now he's taken her, he took her, and I don't know why, or where, or for what, or, or," and she abruptly turns away.

"He took her," says Miss Cheney, "because he could, because nothing kept him from taking her. You could've taken her. If you know the right people," those milky eyes downcast she pats around, finds the pony, sets it upright. "Unscrupulous, informed – *wealthy.*" Her smile crooks. "You'd never need to work another day in your life."

"The owr," says Jo, the word quite small.

"Of course," says Miss Cheney, and with a flick of her finger she knocks the pony over again, "the ones who *know,* who are wealthy, and without scruple, are never ever right."

"Who," says Jo, turning, hefting the sword back up on her shoulder.

"If it were so simple as the telling of it," says Miss Cheney, with a shrug of the brim of her hat.

Jo reaches out then, takes up the mask once more. "She's on a truck," she says. "It's on the move. I went to the wrong one first. Three more steps back." She heads toward the door.

"Perhaps," says Miss Cheney. "But one step forward, too."

Jo looks back, over her shoulder.

"The Queen's been passed," says Miss Cheney. "Long live the Queen."

The light seems bright enough inside the semi trailer but it's pale, washed out, shining only here and there in white-hot spots, on a rack of tools all shining silver and worn black grips, a patch panel festooned with rainbows of cables. Wrapped in the thin black coat she sits on the floor her arms about her moccasin boots, black hair lopping the white fur trim of the hood that's down about her shoulders. Cheek to bare knee smudged with gold, glittery gold dusting the folds of the coat, the fringe of those boots, the grimy floor of the trailer about her.

Clang of footfalls on a stepladder, a creak, a bustle of black, slick black jacket, black jeans, black hair quite long in front. A black lace choker about her throat, glasses with thick black frames, a camera slung about her neck from a wide black strap. Steaming jacketed paper cups in her hands she holds one out to Ysabel who takes it, smiling just, sips, puckers abruptly, looking away, her smile soured.

"Yeah, sorry," says the woman all in black. "Out of vanilla."

"I don't know vanilla would help," says Ysabel.

"So it's possible to get lousy coffee in Portland. Who knew."

Ysabel says, "No, no, it's, it's warm, and that's," and then the woman all in black laughs, and Ysabel's smile's unpuckered. "That's enough, for now," she says, both hands wrapped about the cup held close. "Thank you, Petra B."

"I was wondering," says the woman all in black.

"Of course I remember," says Ysabel. Ducking for another sip.

"I'm gonna be blunt," says Petra B, sitting back on her heels, "and I'm not gonna apologize because, well, blunt." A sigh. "You have the look of someone escaping a situation."

"A situation," says Ysabel.

"With a capital S."

Ysabel sets her coffee down, turning to one side and leaning, knees on the floor, tugging as she does the bottom of the T-shirt down, the white-furred hem of the coat over her hip. "What is all this?" she says, taking up her cup again, looking about the trailer, looking outside the trailer at the white-lit night. "What's going on? What are you doing here?"

"Okay," says Petra B, rolling the word through her dark red lips, tipping forward, knees to the floor now, hands on her knees. "They're shooting a pilot."

"I don't," says Ysabel, brows pinched. "Who?"

"I think it's Fox?" says Petra B. "Shadow Unit. Another paranormal procedural. You know, they solve crimes, they fight monsters. Like Grimm. The fairy-tale cops? Though usually I work for the Leverage boys, when they're in town. They solve crimes and con people."

"You shoot. Pilots."

Leaning forward a little more, frowning, smiling, "No," says Petra B. "They shoot. I take pictures." A hand on the camera about her neck. "Usually. Officially. They like documenting these things. But, you know. A lot of the actors are from out of town. The staff, some of the crew. So unofficially, I arrange things? Help find things. Like actual, decent, genuine boiled bagels." She sighs. "Jimmy Kelly and his fucking bagels. The ones from LA are worse snobs about it than the ones from New York, you know?"

"No," says Ysabel.

"Well they are," says Petra B. She's shifted, leaning to one side, mirroring Ysabel, one hand brushing a tendril of glitter dusting the floor. "Anyway. A fixer, you could say. The local who knows the lay of the land."

"When you aren't selling coffee at the grocery store."

"When I'm not selling coffee. I also do some modeling, I check coats at a club, couple-three nights a month, I used to sell comic books. Girl's gotta hustle. Was it," she says, fingers stirring the glitter, "is it the blond guy?"

"Is what," says Ysabel. "Who."

"Your situation. The one who tried to buy your coffee? Too chilly to be cute? He struck me as the strict type. I'm gonna press on this," and as Ysabel ducks away Petra B lowers her head, tries to hold her gaze, "hey, you, you look like you need help. And I need to know what from if I'm gonna do something, and, and," looking away now. Ysabel's looking at the floor. "I want to do something," says Petra B.

"That's, sweet," says Ysabel, lifting her cup for another sip. "It's not Roland. It's not him." Sitting up. Her other hand a fist clenched in her lap.

Petra B's down on one elbow, frowning at her shimmering fingertips. "This," she says, "it's almost, it's like it's wet, what," looking up, "what *is* this stuff?"

"My matrimony," says Ysabel.

"Your," says Petra B, "you're married? You're getting married?"

The fist in her lap wadding the thin stuff of the coat fur rustling, "I don't," says Ysabel, "even know how to answer that." Shivering. "No," she says then, "don't," setting her cup down, "stop," as Petra B says, "Sweet," her fingertips shining there be her shining rich red lips. "What," she says, and then "whoa" or maybe "oh" as Ysabel grabs her hand, leans close, careful of the camera a weight between them as she pulls Petra B's hand down to her lap, down to her trembling fist balled in her lap. Petra B's eyes wide behind her glasses, her lips parting a sudden hiss of breath at Ysabel's delicate kisses there and there, top lip, bottom lip, licking the glitter away.

"I don't," says Petra B, but Ysabel's opened her fist, pulled open her coat, she's pressing Petra B's hand to her thighs, up under the sagging hem of the T-shirt between her thighs, kissing Petra B and kissing her again, Petra B's free hand coming about Ysabel to draw her closer still as Ysabel jerks against her, her mouth sliding away from Petra B's mouth, her shuddering slowing, hitching. Stopping.

Petra B looks down at Ysabel crouching before her, down at the mess of light between them, at the glitter that spangles her jeans, her jacket. "What," she says, and she swallows, "do you need," sitting up, "a doctor," but Ysabel's shaking her head, drawing tighter about herself there on that bright floor, "No, no, I need," looking up, pushing herself up, "I need to get it *out* of me, I need to get *away* from this," clutching at Petra B leaning back, "I need, I need you."

"I," says Petra B.

"Not here," says Ysabel.

"I have a car," says Petra B, looking out the open trailer doors.

"Do you have a bed," says Ysabel, gathering herself, pulling herself unsteady to her feet. Reaching down for Petra B who says, "Yes," who's careful of her camera, holding it with the one dark hand away from the other, splashed with shining gold, the one she holds out gingerly for Ysabel to take. "I don't," she says, "even know your name."

"That's okay," says Ysabel, a shivery little laugh. "That's all right."

"Yes," he says, and then, "Yessir." Handset tucked between ear and hunched shoulder mouthpiece swallowed by his enormous mahogany beard. Peering out from behind the scant cover of the corner payphone there by a shuttered yellow foodcart, a banner that says 808 Grinds, at the two figures arms about each other staggering down the sidewalk past a line of three white semi trailers, rear doors open, dim lights shining. "Not a, no." He's pulling a black notebook from his jacket, big as the palm of his hand, thumbing the elastic band off the cover. Opens it to a page that says FRI 26 NOV at the top. "There's no indication." Under some notes headed WASH-9TH he adds, BLACK JEANS, then JACKET = BLACK / PLEATHER. "We will, of course." He scrawls a question mark after PLEATHER. Down by the last trailer under the shadows of the trees the figures have stopped, tumbled together in a clumsy embrace, streaked and splattered with glowing golden light. "Subdued," he says. He closes the notebook. He hangs up the phone.

Parked behind him a luridly orange car with a dusty black ragtop, a complicated sigil crudely painted on the hood in black. He opens the driver's door, smoothly, quietly, settles in the driver's seat behind the wheel. "Pissed," he says.

"Oh," says the little guy in the passenger seat, "I'm fucking *livid.*" Empty sleeves of his black suit yanked tight around and tied behind his back, wound about over and over in orange electrical cord. The side of his jaw mottled by a darkening bruise.

"Noise," says Mr. Keightlinger. "Uncertainty. Property destruction."

"*Who cares!*" roars Mr. Charlock, spittle flying. "We had her! In our hands!"

Mr. Keightlinger plants a finger in the orange cord and pushes, nailing Mr. Charlock back against his seat. "Observe," he says. "Do *not* engage."

He turns the key. The engine rumbles to life.

No sitting or sleeping in Front of the Windows
Snow

No Sitting or Sleeping in Front of the Windows say the signs taped over and over and over again to the sweep of glass along the first floor of the grand old building to one side of the little cobbled plaza. Across the plaza a freestanding colonnade, gold letters pitted and stained along the top that spell out Ankeny Square. In the center a dead fountain, a low octagonal pool, two caryatids back to back, a great basin held over their heads. Sitting on the edge of the pool in her black jeans, her leather coat the color of butter, her sword laid flat across her knees, Jo has one hand on the scabbard, one hand on the stony edge of the pool, a cigarette smoldering between her fingers. On her other side the mask, the mane of it coiled and still. Laughter, a couple blocks away down the alley, two men leaning together on their way to somewhere else, one of them a pink box in his arms, and "Goddammit," she says to herself.

She takes one last drag, letting smoke plume from her mouth as she stubs the cigarette out on the edge of the pool by another crumpled butt. Leaning to one side her other hand roots in the pocket of her coat, coming up with a crumpled orange pack. Only a couple-three cigarettes left inside.

"Goddammit," she says again.

Yanking the hilt of the sword then she bares a foot or so of the blade. Knuckles white about the hilt of it, the throat of the scabbard. Fists shivering. "I'll do it," she says, and slams it home. Leaps to her feet spinning to look up at the caryatid, "If I have to," she says. "I'll beg if I have to."

That stone face looking down at the empty pool, arms up, bent at the elbows.

Jo shifts the sword, ducks through the loop of its belt, settles it slung from her shoulder across her back. "It worked before," she's saying. "It'll work." Worming a hand into the pocket of her jeans, frowning, fishing in the one pocket of her coat, the other swaying heavily, grimacing as she plucks the gun from it, digs through that pocket. Holds up a coin pinched between fingers and thumb, a penny almost black. "Okay." Tucking the gun away again.

She sets one foot up on the edge of the pool but stops there leaning on her upraised knee, looking down at the mask laid out there by her boot.

The mane of it stirs as she slips it over her head and when she tugs it home the stiff black hairs loft in some unfelt tremor of wind, pulled up and out behind her to undulate lazily. She turns the empty shadowed holes where eyes should be to look then at the caryatid and from beneath the crudely chiseled mask-teeth her voice rasps, "I am Jo Gallowglas, the Queen's Huntsman. I want to make a wish."

A clang then from somewhere inside the fountain. She steps into the pool to a rising gurgle from the spout up in the basin trembling. She reaches for the caryatid's upturned arm, stepping onto its plinth as water burbles into the basin above. Another clang, a run of knocks as she pulls herself up and close and the mask tips and looms in close to the caryatid's ear. The spout above her coughs and that chuckle of water seizes and stops.

Her one hand in the crook of that elbow she reaches with the other around and up into the basin, feeling about, and starts suddenly, freezes, then pulls her hand back down. That penny still clenched between finger and thumb. Turning it over, her hand. Caught in the fine hairs on the back of it a single snowflake glittering faintly in the shadows, already melting.

That mask turning to look out at the snow gently wisping all about, pink and orange in the streetlights, white and grey and blue in the shadows, thickening, gauzy curtains of it falling now, and she laughs, holds out her hand to catch more of it falling in clumps now, a froth of ice cupped in her palm.

Pulling close to the caryatid again she presses the penny to its expressionless lips and tips the mask again to whisper "I wish" into its ear, "I wish Ysabel was home and safe and sound, I wish, I wish I didn't fuck this up," and then the mask knocking against the upturned arm she tucks that penny into the stony drape of scarf across the caryatid's impassive breast. Presses her wet red hand there a moment. It flares under the sudden light too white too bright she lifts it mask turning away red lights now and blue lights twirling, spinning across her white-lit back, her shoulders, the fountain, the falling snow picked out against the night beyond so suddenly dark. A fuzzed squawk of a voice too loud, "Step down," it says, "step away from the fountain," and "Shit" says Jo, wrenching the mask from her head. Falling back from the caryatids stumbling in the pool and "Freeze" says the voice but Jo's catching herself turning in the snow a bumbled step another up over the edge of the pool she's running, running, under the colonnade, a whoop of siren and pounding footsteps behind her she's running, head down sword bouncing on her back mask in her hand mane like a banner snapping behind her running past the dark end of the plaza into a crosswalk headlights blaring "Shit" she says again, siren whooping again, scaling up to a sudden alarming chatter, a short sharp squeal of tires.

Under a pavilion between booths draped in anonymous tarps white and blue a low dark hulk of a building behind a chain-link fence draped with a long red banner that says Festival of the Last Minute. The sky a rusty black beyond, over the empty river. "Stop" from behind her a bellow now unfuzzed, "or I will shoot" as she's running away down a loop of sidewalk toward the shadow of a bridge high above a cracking pop a chuff a zinging twang behind her, past her, a clatter dropping away as head down pelting into the shadow of the bridge, out from under the snow, boot-thuds on the pavement echoing flatly high and far away among the criss-crossed girders stretched out over the river, then back out into a wall of snow whirling hands up against it running a welter of black and white and grey, blue and rust and black tumbled together with the sudden silence, only her gasping breath now, footfalls dulled by the snow on the sidewalk, the grass, and under it only the sound of the snow itself hissing through the air.

She nearly falls up a low swell of the ground turning back a hand on a boulder between two long low aisles of gnarled trees sweeping along the riverbank, bare branches clawing at the snow, and turning again head down to run her foot snags something and hands up she sprawls headlong.

Rolling over scrambling in the snowfall back from the body half-buried in snow, snow drifted against green legs laid flat, green arms folded under snow-mounds over a green chest. Her grasping hand finds the mask flung limp and still there in the snow ahead of her, drags it close, clutches it to her as she leans over the body brushing snow from a forehead, from white-blond hair cropped close and stiff with ice, from cheeks rimed with old snow, brushing the drifts from blue and white headphones clamped over ears. Looking up, looking out, she looks back down.

"Roland," she says.

He opens his eyes.

Dazzle! It's a glittering prize.
Dazzle! It's a glittering prize!

—*Siouxsie Sioux*

NO. 19
MOON

"**F**rom this position**," says the fat guy sitting in the chair, "there's six, from this position there are six defenses." He's holding a soft brown briefcase in his lap, buckle clinking as he fondles it.

"There are seven working defenses from this position," says the tall guy standing behind him, scissors in his hand wavering over the fat guy's scraggly hair.

"And one of 'em *hurts*," says the fat guy with a guffaw. He's wearing a khaki-colored T-shirt printed with a faded picture, a bearded man holding up a pistol. Damage my calm, it says.

"Hold still," says the tall guy, snipping a wisp.

"Man, they don't, they just don't make comics like that anymore, do they?" He sighs. Wraps his arms more tightly about the briefcase. "All blood and thunder. Goddamn. Not too short, right?" He leans forward, looks back, the tall guy rolling his eyes as he lifts his scissors up and away. "Not too short, okay, Abe?"

"Not too short," says the tall guy, nodding.

The fat guy sits back. "Just, neaten it up a bit," he says. "Make it look good, though." Wrapping his arms again about the briefcase. "But quick, quick," he says, leaning forward again, looking back again, and again the scissors lift away. "She could be here any minute. Queen of the fucking world, man." Sitting back. The buckle clinking again. "Queen of the fucking world."

"Timmo, hey," says Abe. "Hold still." Snip, and snip.

"Any minute now," says Timmo. "Come on, man, come on."

"Hold," says Abe, snip, "still."

"It's gonna be incredible," says Timmo. "You don't mind, do you? Stepping out for a bit? When she gets here?" Undoing the buckle with a click, snapping it shut again. Open, close.

"I'll just go get another key from Zach," says Abe. Snip. "Hardly nobody here anyway."

"Because it might, she might just," squirming in the chair, and the scissors lift up and away again. "She might just, I mean, right out of the gate, you know?" Clink. Snap. Open, shut.

"You think," snip, "you think I want to stick around for," and then there's a knock at the door.

Abe looks up, Timmo sits up, briefcase clutched to his chest, "Shit," he says, and "Yeah, yeah," says Abe, stepping back, swatting wisps of hair from Timmo's shoulders, Timmo shrugging him off, batting his hands away, briefcase in his other hand now, by his side. The knock again becoming a pounding, a muffled Hey! Timmo!

"She knows your name, man," says Abe.

"Of course she knows my name," mutters Timmo, heading past the two rumpled queen-sized beds for the door there by the picture window, curtains drawn. Undoes the chain lock and the deadbolt, the briefcase still in his other hand. Opens the door.

"God damn man can I come in? It is fucking *crazy* out here." Stomping the snow from her running shoes sweatpants a long green coat a hoodie under it throwing it back from her head her hair scraped down to patchy stubble around a floppy mohawk. Snow caught in the parking lot light, bright white and pink and orange out there swirling, dissolving the rusty black parking lot behind her. "Timmo? Hey? It's fucking *Arctic* out here." A fluttery laugh. "Global warming, right?"

"So is that her?" calls Abe from inside the room.

"Mel," says Timmo, and she says, "So can I come in?"

"Hey," says Abe, coming up behind him. "That's Mel."

"Yeah," says Timmo.

"That's not her."

"No," says Timmo. "It's not."

"Who," says Mel, and then "Come on, aren't you freezing?" and then, frowning, "What's with the briefcase?"

A House that looks Much Like the Others
Tango milonguero – What matters, and what Doesn't
Respects

A HOUSE THAT LOOKS MUCH LIKE THE OTHERS all along the one side of the street, low, demure, set close to the curb. "Pull in there," says the Duke, pointing out the shallow curl of driveway before a closed garage. "Just get it off the street."

"Yeah, okay," says Jessie, spinning the wheel, backing and filling. "So we're here?" she says. "Leo?" He's opening his door, planting his cane, hauling himself out of the car. "I guess we're here," she says. She shuts off the engine.

Flakes of snow light on the brim of his red-brown derby hat, the shoulders of his camel-colored topcoat. Catch the edges of paving stones set in a meander across the scrap of yard, dead leaves and dying grass. Climb in lacy drifts against the front steps, cling to the panels set in the yellow door. "It's always years between snows," he says. "You ever notice that? Proper snows. I miss them." He takes in a deep breath through his nose and lets it out, a ragged cloud lit up white by the harsh bare bulb there by the door. "This one will be proper. Can you smell it?"

"I don't like it," says Jessie.

He turns to look at her back by the car in her grey chauffeur's jacket, her long black socks, her red Keds dark against the feathery snow. "It mislikes me," he says.

"What?"

"You," he says, and then "Nothing. Never mind. Too chilly?"

"Depends," she says, arms about herself. "We going inside?"

He stoops, grunting, leaning heavily on his cane, free hand peeling up a corner of the doormat to find a key, small and coppery. "Not sure the heat's on," he says, pushing himself back to his feet. "But the view's amazing."

Echoing footsteps down a long hallway, sharp pops of floor-boards and creaks in the dark, the drag and thump of the Duke's limp, his cane. "Should be a light switch," he says. "Back by the door?" Muffled swipe of a hand along the wall, sudden thick click of a switch, his back's lit up, yellow-tan against the blackness ahead. "And another one up here," he says, lurching drag and thump into the shadows. The echoes shift and open, deepen, flatten. She follows, creak and pop down the hall. Clank of his cane-tip against something, then the clinking scrape of a pull chain, a lone bulb, clear glass, the filament glowing amber hotly dangles above him, above an overstuffed armchair, a low table beside it, out in the middle of an otherwise empty room. Reflections hang dimly in the air beyond, that filament glowing again out in the blackness, a wall of glass, a great window stretching up and around before them. "Give it a minute," says the Duke.

"I've," says Jessie.

"Yeah?" says the Duke.

"I've, I, uh," says Jessie, staring at the overstuffed armchair. Behind her, far off down the dark hallway, the yellow light by the door. "No, it's," she says, "stupid. It's just, it's. Weird. Déjà vu. Is that," she's pointing, "the Throne?"

"Yes," says the Duke.

"Oh," says Jessie.

"Go on," says the Duke. "Sit." He's undoing the buttons of his topcoat with his free hand.

"Don't," says Jessie, an edge in her voice, "don't fuck with me."

"It's just a chair," he says. "Go on." Leaning against an arm of the chair he lays his cane on the floor beside it. "Probably the only stick of furniture in the joint." Working the coat off his shoulders. "Sit."

"What am I doing here," she says, words quivering under a weight.

"You mean," he says, taking off his hat, "why you."

"Why me."

"Do you trust me?"

"It's not that."

"It's not."

"You don't always seem to know," she says, "what you're doing," and he chuckles and says, "Ability, and intent," he says, and then, "I *mean* well. I swear to you, Jessie Vitaly, that nothing in no wise might happen in this house that will ever cause you to be harmed." Letting go of the chair, taking her hands in either of his. "There is nothing on this earth or under the sky that could make it otherwise." Then he grins, at her wide eyes. Lifts her hands to his lips for a kiss. "How's that for an oath?"

"You always," she says, "fuck it up, at the end." Stepping close to him, pressing against him, her arms go about him, his about her, her face to his shoulder, knocking her grey cap loose, and he fumbles for it, misses, it falls to the floor. "Jessie," he says, "Jessie. My beautiful girl. My California girl." Stroking her yellow hair. "Bikinis," he says.

"What?" Lifting her head, pulling back to look him in the eye.

"I should've had you wear more bikinis," he says, hands on her hips. "Should've had a house, with a pool. Let you lie out in the sun. Made you mojitos. Rubbed coconut oil all over you." He kisses her, lightly, and she catches his head in her hands and kisses him back. "Maybe in Laurelhurst," he says.

"This is what I'm talking about," she says. "Should'ves and ought to haves. Like something's over."

"Isn't it?" he says. "Hasn't it been?"

"What are you doing here, Leo?"

He lets go, steps back. Leans again against the chair. "What are *we* doing here," he says. "It takes two to tango." Limping away, off toward the big dark window beyond, his reflection there before him and above, the curl of the glass, hers behind him picked out in light and past them both and through them more lights now, like stars, and he turns, saying, "I've already doffed my coat. My shirt's next, my pants. Shoes, of course. Socks." Stars that glint in the glass behind him, fixing themselves in rows and lines now against the blackness. "You, you take off that cunning little jacket. Or maybe it'll all be vicey-versa? The particulars don't so much matter." Stars limning blocks, buildings, towers, stars caught in the corners of windows, a thousand thousand of them. "We're going to enjoy each other, you and me, and when the moment's right," and he lurches back toward the chair, and out there swooping arcs and nets of light define bridge after bridge marching away along the river far below, and each is far grander and more glorious than the one before. "When the moment's right," he says, "I'll sit the Throne, and either vanish from this earth, or be made King of all that's at my feet." He shrugs. "Not sure just yet if we'll be able to tell the difference, honest," he says.

"It's been a while," she says. Fingers at her throat, unbuttoning.

"Since Tommy," he says.

Her hands stilled there, at her breast, what might have been about to be a smile folding itself away.

"What," he says.

"Tommy?" she says.

"What would you have said," he says. "What did you think."

"I would've," she says, "since, since the, since your leg. You broke your leg."

"My leg," he says, leaning on the chair. "You think my leg could keep me away from you."

"Something did." Her hands, falling away.

"Do we actually have to talk about this?" he says. "You and me, we actually need to talk?" She reaches up, pulls the collar of her jacket closed. "You have any idea, the slack you picked up?" he says. "When he died?"

"I didn't come with you to pick up slack," she says.

"I *need* that," he says. "I depend on it, far more than I – you didn't, you don't begrudge me Luys. Or Chrissie, or Laúru, or the adorable little moppet that *you*, I might add, picked up from behind the counter of that comic-book shop – "

"Leo."

"The Princess," he says.

"Well of course I wouldn't," she says, "I couldn't, she's your – "

"I don't begrudge *you* the Princess." He's stepping around the chair between them.

She says, thickly, "I gave her up."

"One does not simply," and gently strokes her cheek, her hair, "give up, the Princess Ysabel." Undoing the bottommost button on her jacket, then the next one up. "How's your wizard."

"Wizard?"

"Locke," he says, "Luke, Lake – "

"He's not a," she says, stepping back, "not a wizard – "

"Nice shoes," says the Duke, looking down at her Keds, a rich red in the pool of light. "Little kiddie for you, but it works. When'd you get them?"

"These?" she says, clutching her jacket closed again. "I've always, they were – my sister's – "

"And see?" he says, a heavy step toward her. "I did not know you had a sister."

"Leo," she says. "I know. Okay? You were straight from the start. This has never been more than a job, for either of us. That's always been very clear. It's just," and she undoes the last button. Lets her jacket hang open, loosely, over bare chest, bare belly, bare thighs, the plain white underwear, low about her hips. "It was a different job, before."

"I was clear," he says. "I told you, that night. Dancing there on the stage. Rain. The most beautiful girl that ever I saw."

"I was the most beautiful girl you saw that night," she says.

"That night a year ago. Almost a year ago." Limping back, away, turning away, sweeping an arm wide back toward her. "And here you still are." Her hand on the chair. "It is really coming down out there," he says.

And then she says, "It's not the Solstice."

"No, it's not," he says. "It might be, though, by the time we get out of here. Wouldn't that be something." Turning away from the window. "Did you have somewhere to be tomorrow? Next week? A pressing engagement?"

"Leo," she says.

"Sit," he says. He's begun to unbutton his shirt.

"Why are you doing this," she says, her hand still on the chair. Another sweep of his arm, pointing past her now, back, at the yellow light down the hall by the door. "Lymond, Prince, returned," he says. "The Hound's whelp and a shove from the Guisarme. Jo Huntsman, leading whosomever she might by the nose and the Queen cheering them on. When they've made their hash and settled their play, come the Solstice, or tomorrow morning, bright and early, to take the Throne, they must come through that door and when they do." Lowering his hand then. Rubbing his thigh with a wince. "They will find here me, King before them, or gone at last from this world. Now, please. That we might, while away a pleasant interlude, until I work up the nerve. Sit you down."

She steps around the chair, her hands on the arm of the chair, leaning forward her jacket lopping open, she's perching herself gingerly on the cushion. Letting out a sigh. "Okay," she says. Sitting back. Looking about. "Now what," she says. "You gonna give me a lapdance?"

"I might," he says. "I might just, rabbit."

"Take off your shirt."

"I'm working on it," he says, undoing buttons, lips pursed in a wry smile, teeth worrying his bottom lip he sways his hips, tock tock, wincing. Hands stilled there about his belly. "There is," he says, "no conceivably sexy way for a man to untuck his shirt."

"Sure there is," she says, a black-socked knee hooked over an arm of the chair, red Ked dangling. A hand in her lap, fingers idly stroking white cotton. "Just, you know. Rip it open. Tear yourself free."

"Which, I'd have to button it all the way back up for that," he says.

"Chicken."

"It just doesn't *feel* sexy."

"Like that matters," she says. "*Work* it, baby."

He yanks at his half-open shirt, there's a rip, a button clattering away in the shadows, and she laughs with a clap of her hands. Shirt billowing he falls to his knees before her with a grunt, catching himself hands on the arm of the chair, her knee, slipping under her thigh, hands on her hips, hooking the waistband of her underwear. She isn't laughing. She's shifting herself, lifting her leg up over his head, knees together as he tugs up and up her thighs, jack-knifing her legs she reaches to help him pull them down and off and she grunts as he levers her legs apart, hands on her thighs, forearms on the cushion of the chair, her underwear hanging from the one hand dangling over the arm of the chair, her other hand clamped to the back of his head curling into a fist full of his hair when he opens his mouth.

Striped sheets clenched in her shivering hand a rough growl climbing from her chest, through her throat, breaking open in a shapeless howl. She lifts her head black hair flopping curls unspooling along her shoulders, down her arced back heaving as that howl collapses into harshly ragged breaths that wind up in a groan, her head lowering, a grimace, her hips jerk, "Hah," again, "hah," and her quivering arms fold abruptly at the elbows, she drops, back between the upraised knees, one wrapped in a soft black fabric brace, one bare, a pale smear in the darkness.

There's a light, growing, in that darkness.

"Oh," she says, "Petra," muffled, those elbows popping up, "are you," pushing herself up, over, falling back to the striped sheets rumpled, lit up now with a brightly golden warmth, a steady shine that flickers shadowed only as she draws her legs together, sits up, eyes wide, a hand to her mouth. The woman beside her, on her back knees up, one arm flung up over her head, hand dangling limply from an upturned wrist, the face of her, hair, breasts and throat, the pillows beneath her, the sheets there covered, caked, soaked, matted with golden light.

"Petra?" she says, leaning over, trembling hand a shadow brushing at the stuff about the nose, the mouth, not dust but sludge, clumps of it crumbling wetly under her sweeping fingers, "Petra!" Scooping it up, flinging fingerfuls to the floor with bright heavy plops, clearing, darkening the mouth, the nose, the closed eyes rimmed and lashed with gold. "Wake up," she's saying, "wake up, wake up, don't be, don't be – "

Petra's hand wobbles, the fingers clench. Her chin jerks. Her mouth opens, her shoulders hike her throat and breast drawn up and up as she sucks in a ragged whoop of breath and the light trickles and runnels down her belly and her flanks. Her other hand coming up to slap against Ysabel's shoulder, Ysabel's arms about Petra dimming the light, shadowing the room as she covers her laughing weakly. "Wow," says Petra, the barest stroke of a word, before Ysabel crushes her mouth with a kiss.

Petra's hand, falling away from Ysabel's shoulder.

"Petra?" says Ysabel, pulling back, sitting up, the room brightening again, that light spread over the high wide bed, the littered nightstand, the blank black glass of the window gleaming. "Don't," says Ysabel, "don't you dare," shaking Petra's shoulder. Petra's head lolling over in that puddle of light.

Pushing back scrambling back bare foot finding the edge of the bed tumbling over it to stand there shivering, looking about, the door there, ajar, and she takes a step and then another and leaning forward another, catching herself, clinging to the doorframe. Looking back. The shape of her still and limp in all that gold.

The hallway's dark, but she is not, gold splashed along her thighs and belly, smeared over her breasts, her mouth, her one hand soaked in it. She holds it up, peering as she takes a step and another down the dark hall, a closed door in the wall ahead of her, beyond the darkness opening up, the empty suggestion of a room. Turning, turning back, back past the bedroom door the hall ends in another door, and she falls against it, clings to it, the doorknob rattling in her hands as she opens it, staggers through, the knob left wet with light. Her dark hand and her bright patting the walls about her. The sudden thick click of a switch and there she is, blinking, naked under the harsh white light from the ceiling, leaning against a sink in a white-tiled bathroom.

Fumbling the taps hot and cold hands shoved under the sudden rush of water hissing, scrubbing, scrubbing them one over the other, cupping them, filling them with water, leaning over to splash her face, and again. Rubbing her face, her eyes, lifting herself back up to meet herself in the mirror, wild black hair, red eyes, gold streaks. She takes a deep breath that hitches, caught, her trembling suddenly stilled. Behind her a tub, the pale translucent shower curtain drawn closed. Through the curtain a grey shape dimly, a shadow, someone. Standing in that tub behind her.

She lets the breath out, shaky, slowly, lowers her hands to lean again against the sink. "Are you here for her?" she says.

"No," says a voice, "I am not," lugubrious, as chill and grey as old concrete.

"For me, then?"

"In a manner of speaking. Do not turn about. You should not look upon me, not yet." In the mirror the shadow shifts, what might be the inclination of a head. "I am here to, pay my respects. To your majesty."

She chokes on the laugh, bites her lip, closes her eyes. "What," she says. "Just like that?"

"There is no Throne for you to sit," says the voice. "No banner to seize. One day, you are not the Queen, and the next? You are."

"Who did you say you were?" – any Rule
Investiture – Ecclesiastes, chapter 10

"Who did you say you were?" The door ajar, the security chain taut, a slice of face behind, a frown, a gingery mustache.

"A friend," says the man in the hall, pressed close. "Your daughter's. Gloria." His hair is long and black and wet, his shapeless jacket grey. His bare foot red and raw, jammed between door and frame.

"That's, not," says the voice behind the door, "her name, isn't," and "I know," says the man in the hall. "It's what she's called."

"Daddy?" says someone, someone else.

"She's dead," says the man in the hall, lifting his head, cocking it, an ear to the gap. The faintest creak, the door, a floorboard. He wears a black patch over one eye. "I killed her."

"You need to go," says the voice behind the door. "I'm calling the police."

"Daddy, what is it?" says someone else.

"Suzette, get back, go to your room," says the voice behind the door, and "Suzette," says the man in the hall, delicately. He brushes the security chain with a fingertip. A pop, a dull red spark, the chain snaps two ends leaping apart to clink against jamb and door. He throws his shoulder against a meaty thud, a grunt, the door shivers, comes unstuck swinging into an open room, wanly yellow, a thickset man fallen back against a leather couch, bare legs kicking slippered feet for purchase beneath the sprawling skirts of a satiny white robe, "Get back," he's saying, pushing himself upright. Scrape of the couch against the floor.

The man from the hall, two quick long steps, leans in hand snapping about a thick throat, lifting, turning, smack of shoulders against the yellow wall. Heels kicking. A slipper, falling. He leans back away from a swatting hand the back of it freckled. The white robe's printed with kanji in thick black strokes. "Please," says someone else.

Still holding the thickset man against the wall Orlando turns his head. Over across the room past the couch the coffee table the low shelf neatly lined with books she's standing, jet black hair unbound, unribboned, bangs bright pink, hands clutched one above the other about her belly in a big white T-shirt. "Put him down," she says, her voice quite small, her eyes rimmed black and red. The T-shirt says dem toten Hasen in big purple letters. "I went," she says, "I went home," and her voice finds itself under that word, lifting, stumbling, "how, how did you even, how could you – "

"Home," says Orlando, turning back to the man he's holding against the wall. Those freckled hands trying to pry his away. Cheeks and forehead blotching red about jerking eyes. "What's home to such as me. I break every rule." Under the ginger mustache the mouth opens on a gurgle as one hand falls away. "Any rule," says Orlando.

"Don't," she says.

"Don't what." He opens his hand. The thickset man drops knees buckling to collapse unstrung behind the couch. Her hand to her mouth she takes a step out toward him and another but stops, dead, when Orlando says, "They took my sword."

She looks from her father sitting on the floor hauling in a wheezing breath to Orlando over him, both hands clasped behind his back. "The one I killed you with," he says.

Her father coughs. Tries to clear his throat.

"It still hurts," she says.

"She ran away," says Orlando. "She tricked me, and she ran away, and they did not like that, not one bit. Place," he says, "and time. They took my sword."

"Get out," says her father, rubbing his throat, "of my house," and she says, quickly, coming around the shelves, the couch, "I'll go with you, I swear. Let me get my coat."

"But we both know," Orlando's saying, "I have another."

She shouts, she lurches toward him crashing into the arm of the couch his hand's leaping out away from her lifting as he falls to a knee coming down a short and shining arc her father grunts. Her hand on the back of the couch. His hand about a bone-white hilt wrapped in rough black cloth, the heel of his other hand on the butt of it pushing a soft wet sound, her hand slapping his shoulder, shoving, knocking him to the floor. He looks up at her, blinking blood from his eye. The long knife left upright in her father's belly.

"It's snowing," says Orlando, climbing to his feet as she gropes for the narrow table against the wall, knocking a bowl away, scattering coins. "What?" she says, stepping back, a phone in her hand.

"It's snowing," says Orlando, turning, heading out into the hall, away. "You're welcome, Gloria."

In this washed-out streetlight at once too bright and pale the marmalade cat is difficult to see, fluttered by falling snow. Leather jacket creaking the man squats, "Tch-tch," he says, holding out a hand. "Puss puss." Pink hair bobs, dulled by that thin light. The cat hikes up on its rear legs, bumbling against the wheel of one of the bicycles parked at the edge of the yard. "Not usually so skittish," says the man up on the cramped front porch.

"What's he called?" says the man on the sidewalk.

"Don't know," says the man on the porch. Lit by tiny white lights strung along the railing he's draped in a dark sagging jumpsuit. "Tim?" His hair slicked with sweat or gel and a thick dark line smeared under each of his eyes. The cat's weaving away through the welter of bicycles, pausing to daintily shake snow from a paw. "Tim," says the man on the sidewalk, pulling himself to his feet.

"You're Ray, right?" says the man on the porch. "Pretty much missed the to-do. Been a while, hasn't it? How's it doing for you?"

The man on the sidewalk's tipped his head back. "Yeah," he says, blinking, shaking his head, looking down to thumb flakes of snow from eyes one pale, one dark. "I'm here to see the Devil," he says.

The man on the porch lifts a cigar in a white-gloved hand. "The Devil," he says. "I didn't know you played guitar." On the railing among the tangle of lights a mask, grey fur, limp rabbit's ears, the face of it an ugly metallic skull.

"The Oxys, maybe," says the man on the sidewalk. "The Bull-beggar? Wicht?" To one side of the porch a figure in shadow leans against peeling pink siding, a crude suit of wicker armor, snow filling the corners of its warp and weft. "Even the Frittening Boneless," says the man on the sidewalk, "if you could," and then he shrugs. "You aren't dead yet." Those eyes bulging over a snaggletoothed grin. "You're just a clown."

The cigar comes down, comes away, "Just?" says the man on the porch in his furry grey jumpsuit, and smoke curls around the word.

"It's not a *bad* thing," says the man on the sidewalk, a gust of snow swirling about him. Up on the front porch the dull red front door opening, swinging back into shadow. "But really, the Devil, or the – "

"There is no Devil," says the woman stepping out on to the porch. Close-cropped gunmetal hair almost black in that light. The clown's shrugging, "Or the what," he says, as the man on the sidewalk says, "Helm?" His smile gone, his eyebrow climbing. "Aren't you cold?"

"Not really," says the clown.

"There is no Helm," says the woman, light dappling her bare skin, sheening the polished torc about her throat.

"Was, though," says the man on the sidewalk. "Will be again."

"You're, tipping toward the obscure, here," says the clown.

"I'm back," says the man on the sidewalk. Squeezing one eye shut, then the other, back and forth. "We're not all in it, are we," he says.

"Like I said, you missed the to-do," says the clown, and "Who are you," says the woman, "that being back," as the clown's saying, "but if you want to come in out of the snow," that cigar waving airily, and the woman says, "being back means anything at all?"

"You just want to be quiet," says the clown. "Going in."

"Linesse, wasn't it? Isn't it?" Lymond steps off the sidewalk, across the yard, up toward the house. "Pledged to the Hawk, you rode with, the Dagger, the Harper, the Shrieve – "

"Dagger's no more, neither," says the woman. "People are sleeping it off," says the clown.

"It's okay," says Lymond, one foot on the bottom step. "It's all right. I'm back." Snow slithers down the creases of his jacket as he reaches for the zipper at his throat and yanks it down, with a flourish. Working one shoulder free, the other, "Here," he says, leaning forward. Holding up that jacket hung from his hand. "Take it. But know," he says, "that when you do," tightening a fist now about the collar of it, "you take also from this our hand, these, our Northeast Marches."

She pulls back. The clown's looking from the foot of the steps to the head of them and back, Lymond in his purple T-shirt in the snow up along his bare skinny arm to that black jacket heavy and still. "There's this whole story," says the clown, wreathed in smoke, "you got going on here, isn't there."

"Highness," says Linesse.

"There is no highness," says Lymond. The clown snorts.

"You can't possibly," says Linesse.

"You heard what we have said."

"You are too generous."

"Oh," says Lymond. "This is no gift."

Her hand on the jacket then. The clown pushes away from the railing, straightens, watching the jacket loft into the air as Lymond's hand drops away, "You," says the clown, the jacket swinging around to settle over shoulders, the arms of it wriggling, inflating with the weight of arms, "how," says the clown, hands slipping from the sleeves to grab the bottom of the jacket, tug it closed about hips, "you weren't," says the clown. "How."

Lymond's springing up the steps. "She is within?"

"She is," says Linesse, and the sound of a zipper.

"And with her?"

"But three remain." She smooths the jacket's collar over polished silver.

"So few," says Lymond. And then, "Come Marquess! You've made your choice." He sweeps a hand toward the dull red door ajar. "Lead on."

Dark inside, and close. She takes his hand. A hall butler mounded with coats and scarves that overlap a speckled mirror, boots and shoes piled over and around its low bench. Stumble and thump the clown behind them, "Shit," he says, wrestling the rabbit-head under an arm. To one side a wide doorway, a ruddy, high-ceilinged room, a long dining table, a woman sitting at it lit up starkly blue and white by the laptop open before her. Lying the length of the table asleep among a litter of glasses and mostly empty bottles a round little man in a leopard print bikini, his thin beard curded with white paint. A hiss, the red light and yellow throbbing about the room, past the table a man's crouching, poking at the stone hearth, blowing, coughing. Over him a narrow figure untouched by the firelight until it turns, yellow and red like embers edging her nose, her cheek, unveiling the white streaks twined through her mad black mane. "You're ugly," she says, and there's rust in her words.

"And you," says Lymond, "are beautiful." There in the wide doorway, Linesse behind him, and the clown. "A great many things are turned about from where they ought to be. You, hiding behind walls, sending flunkies to answer the door that I pound. You, bootlessly drunk," his voice rising, stepping into the room, "and I am at last quite not. A great," and then he stops, his hand resting on the table. "Many things." The woman across from him's shutting the laptop, changing, dimming the light in the room, pushing back her chair. Her cheerleader outfit green and yellow. "Wait," the clown's saying, reaching for her arm, "you gotta, Ray, he just, he pulled the most amazing trick, out on the porch, she just, out of nowhere," and the cheerleader pats his grey-furred shoulder. "You're an idiot, Glenn," she murmurs, and she leaves.

Lymond says, quietly, "I don't want to fight, Mother."

The man by the hearth straightens, wiping his bald head with a filthy hand, the poker still in the other. His suit unbuttoned over a bare and sunken chest. Polished silver gleams about his throat. Shuffle and step the narrow figure before him with a rustle of tattered cloak a hand emerges, and pale and rough-nailed fingers brush the top of the table. The man lying the length of it stirs. The clink of glass. "What does it matter," she says. "What you want. You will be fought."

"I've already won," says Lymond. "I am returned. I will be King. Your daughter, Queen. We will all go on. How," and his head shakes slowly, side to side, "how is this not a happy day?"

"You are *not mine,*" she says.

"Yet you are as much my mother as she," he says.

"You *left,*" she says.

"He left," says Lymond. "I only went ahead, a little ways. I saw –"

"*Nothing!*" she cries, and a glass falls shattering to the floor.

"I saw," says Lymond, "where we're going. Every street a corner, every corner a tower, every tower ten thousand windows and in every window a lamp. And every lamp was lit, and every street was empty, and it was all so quiet," he's leaning over the table, over the man lying asleep on the table, "so quiet, you could hear the snow stop falling."

"You saw nothing," she says.

"If we go on," he says.

"And you." She lifts her nose, her chin, looks past him to Linesse behind him. "All it takes to turn your coat again's the gift of another?"

"I was cold," says Linesse, and Lymond lifts a hand, "Chazz," he says. "A King needs his Devil."

The bald man chuckles, lowers the poker in his hand to thump the tip of it against the floor. "Further be it from me than anyone else of us in this room to so thoroughly embody an aphorism, but," and thump again of the poker-tip, "the temptation's too delectable. For if the spirit of the ruler rise up against thee, leave not thy place; for yielding pacifieth," and he hefts the poker up in his hand, "great offences."

Lymond nods at that.

Scrape of a chair and that narrow figure rustling sits, heavily. "I do not know what you thought to gain, by coming, here, but you have not," and she coughs, bends over, wheezing, Chazz a hand on the back of the chair leaning over her. "You," she says, bracing herself against the table, bottles shivering, "you don't even look like your – "

"A clown," says Lymond, and "What?" says Glenn behind him. The man on the table lifts a hand, knuckles his eye. "We have a clown, now," says Lymond. "We have a peer. And we have already won. This house, Helm," and he looks up, turns about. "This house." Up in the shadows licked by firelight along the picture-molding lines of faces, of styrofoam wigstands and mannequin heads clumped in crowded lines all around the room and each of them painted, thick lines and curls and calligraphs in red and black and blue exaggerating eyes and mouths, cheeks and chins, fixed rictuses of joy and wonder and delight and here and there a glum recrimination, and no two of any of them alike. "It is subject to an agreement made with the King before us, and much like Goodfellow's house across the river, or, or the," frowning as the man on the table sits up abruptly, and a bottle thumps unbroken to the floor. "Where we left our mother," says Lymond. "A free house, and open, where she might be safe. Within your demesne, Marquess, but not your purview. And when she smelled the first hint of snow in the air, she came straight here." Crackle and pop from the hearth, and Chazz turns to it, poker at the ready. The man on the table snorts, and shivers. Her leather jacket creaking, Linesse looks from the figure at the head of the table to Lymond there at the other end. "She hopes," says Lymond, "but cannot bring herself to ask, that I hew and cleave to that agreement."

"Snow," says the man sitting on the table, tugging the top of his bikini back into place. "Dammit, Ray, did you say snow?"

"Well hell," says Glenn, "I was only telling everybody half an hour ago and nobody wanted to go out and look at it."

"What *time* is it," says the man on the table, blinking owlishly, scooting to the edge of it, clink and chime and another bottle falls, smash. "Shit." Glenn's stepping forward, shuffling side to side as Lymond's turning this way, back about, "Ah," he's saying, "it's Saturday, Saturday morning," Linesse reaching past him to offer a hand to the man hopping down from the table. He's tugging his bikini bottom up about his hips. "Very early Saturday," says Lymond, turning about again. Down the table those pale, pale hands cover the sharp-edged face, and the white threads tangled within the thick black hair are stained red and pink by the light. "And the next day is Sunday," he says. "A Zoobomb day. And, snow or no snow, we shall have," and he spreads his hands, and his snaggled smile beneath beaming, bulging eyes, "the greatest, grandest, most astounding Zoobomb ever."

The clown in the bikini's still blinking, rapidly, scratching the back of his neck. He shrugs. "Yeah, sure," he says. "We could do that."

"Now," says Lymond, and he clasps his hands together. "We have what we had come for. Marquess? Glenn? Attend me," and he turns to leave the room.

"Sunday, the Sun's day," says Chazz, "the day we all might rest. But not, that day, the Solstice. The sun will not stand still for you, tomorrow."

Lymond stops, there in the doorway. "Has it really been so long, Chazz," and he speaks that name quite carefully, "since you have spoken to a King?"

"There is always a King, boy," says Chazz.

"Then you must know," says Lymond. "The Solstice is not the day the King comes back. The day the King comes back, is the Solstice."

The snow's falling more thickly now. In his purple T-shirt Lymond wraps his arms about himself, ducking pink hair bobbing as he heads out into it, down the steps. "Majesty," says Linesse, at the top of them. Glenn behind her, the rabbit's head still clamped beneath his arm.

"The cold," says Lymond in the yard, speaking over the stuttering snow. "You feel it, now."

She nods, shivering in her jacket, looking down, her bare legs, her bare feet. Lymond says, "And you would know what we're about," and her shivering stills, and she looks up, and nods once, crisply. "Yessir," she says.

"I will always speak my mind to you Marquess," says Lymond. "You have but to ask. One peer alone does not a quorum make." He turns away west, speaking into the teeth of the snow. "We go to call another banner to our hosts." Looking back to them up on the porch, and his grin is back. "It's not far. But I'm sure we'll find something along the way to keep us warm."

"Are we, uh, so, we're walking?" says Glenn, following Linesse down the steps.

"Do you see a car?" says Lymond, away off down the sidewalk.

GENTLY BRUSH THE DUST – SO SMALL A LIFE
HOW DIFFERENT, HE LOOKS – "IS THAT IT?"

GENTLY BRUSHING DUST from that sleeping face, fingertips dredging a crumbling pile from pillow to palm, both hands together now cupping the fitful glow, lifting to lips pursed to blow, gently, dust that lofts in great slow billows that do not fall, that coil and glitter, a thousand thousand golden stars, a galaxy of atomies that lights them both lain on the high wide bed, bodies shadowed shapes atop striped sheets drifted with more dust. "I kissed her, once," says Ysabel. "For a cup of coffee. And tonight, she, she," a heavy hank of curls dislodges with a shrug.

"She wanted you. She did not know what having you entailed."

"*I* didn't know," she says, thin wisps of words. "I had no idea." A gold-flecked hand strokes a shining, sleeping cheek, brushes spangled short black hair. Her other hand laid across the bare gold-dusted breast, fingertips against black lace still tied about the throat. "Will she wake?"

"She will wake." Past the yawning door in the lightless hall a shuffle, a change in posture perhaps, a shift of clothing. "She will wake, when day has broken, and if she does not see you here she will wonder why her bed is full of sand. She will curse the need to sweep her floor, and wash her only linen, and she will scour herself in the bath, and at brunch with her friends when stray specks yet catch the light at her cheek or the corner of her eye she'll make empty jokes about glitter and glue and grade-school art. And in the days and weeks to come she will find herself from time to time to've been staring at nothing at all, and her chest cracked open, and the heart of her cored right out, and nothing to hand but stones that might fill the hollow ache, and she will not know why. But these will pass; they will come to her fewer and fainter and further between, as time passes. But they still will come, till the end of her days."

Bending down she presses a simple kiss to those sleeping lips, then sits up. "I should go," she says. She pulls at sheets and blankets to free them, drape them over the body beside her, sloughing more glimmering clouds.

"You might. But where?"

Tucking blankets about shoulders she doesn't look up, doesn't turn around. "With you?" she says.

And a hiss of intaken breath from out in the hall, and the light all about the room quivers. "Not yet." A sigh, and the light begins to gyre. "Not for some time yet."

"How," she says, but the next word's just a shape of her mouth, and she swallows, and starts again. "I have nothing," she says. Turning on the bed, light swimming about her. "Not a thing." Lowering a foot to the rumpled shadows strewn along the floor, but she does not stand. "Even my clothes are someone else's."

"I hope the coat is warm, majesty."

She looks up, into the darkness, arms around herself.

"It snows. Do you not hear it? An inch or more already, while you were," and another hiss of breath then, colder, softer, "otherwise," as she says "Fucking" sharply. "While we we were fucking. Say it. It's a perfectly fine word, for what we were doing."

"Majesty. This is unseemly," but she's turned away again, stirring the syrupy light with a dismissive hand. "So this is the great mystery?" she says, her voice rising. "This is how Queens might be quickened? Because the wonder then is that it hasn't happened a hundred times over already." Leaning over the body asleep beside her, hair falling a curtain before her face. "Is this woman, then, Petra B, does this make her King of Roses? And am I now her Bride?" Pushing her hair up and back over her shoulder, a gesture that sets off another glittering pavane in the air, she looks up and past it all into the darkness. "Or is it to be the cocktail waitress I kissed tonight, or the dancer? The Starling? And a fine return on the Duke's joke that would be." Up then and unfolding herself by the bed to stand in an awful slow collision of light, knotting sparks that flare and pop about her, here and there, and there. "Or that appalling girl who cut me, laid me open and started it all, welling up. Who's dead now, but no matter! All hail her! All hail the King, come back." The light's settling, glittering in her hair, limning her shoulders, her breasts, her hand on her hip, her knee cocked, so. "Or must," she says, "the King be a king? Is it then to be the Mooncalfe? He did sweep me so adroitly off my feet. Will *he* now sit the Empty Throne? Is *that* where this all ends?"

A creak, a floorboard, perhaps. "Your brother," says that voice, slowly, and lugubrious.

"Wait for the King," she's saying, "wait for the King, wait for the King to take my hand and gallantly lead me to my wheel. My wheel; my burden, my guí and toradh; his hand. My brother? He," but the next word stumbles, and she closes her eyes. Bites her lip. Sits back again, against the edge of the bed. "Ys, he said, Ys, there once were queens, wild queens, in the mountains, who spun whatever gold they liked from straw. If we might only learn their secret, that mystery, why, you can be Queen, Ys, and I can be your King, and you, you will *never*, have to take, anyone's, hand..."

"He loves you, very much."

"He left me."

"Majesty – "

"Do not call me that," she says, quietly, and calm.

"But you are now the Queen."

"Because of this," she says, scooping up a handful of dust. "What do you think, a firkin? Or more?" Letting it shimmer through her fingers. "A Queen's ransom," she says.

"Or a city's."

She flings the dust then, toward the open door, but it blooms in swirls and useless puffs of light that do not reach the shadows. "You'd leave it here, like sand, for her to sweep," she says.

"You will make more."

The light sifting out of the dimming air. Sullen glows lick the edges of things, the blankets hillocked behind her, the crowded nightstand there, wineglass and plastic tumbler, bottles and jars of lotions and creams, an alarm clock topped by little bells, a dull pale fluted phallus, a jumble of keys on a ring. The artless tangle of her hair as her head bows. The bare slopes of her shoulders. "I broke," she says. Arms folded in her lap, elbows cupped in her hands, feet on the gilded floor crossed one over the other. "I need a," and then she shivers, shakes her head, fending off what might have been a laugh. "I don't even have any cigarettes," she says, and then, "I saw, today, what I hadn't seen, that morning. When I ate the tongue." Looking up now, up and up in the darkening room. "I've told anyone who might listen that I'd seen myself, as Queen. And Jo, at my side, and, and no King at all, that I was mindful of." She's closed her eyes. "But," she says. "I was not sumptuously dressed. Jo wore, one of her T-shirts. One of those awful T-shirts. And it was, a glorious day, a blue sky, and only one great cloud, white and gold, and," she opens her eyes. "It was shaped, it was a shape one might've taken for a Hind, for the banner, of the Bride. But it was just, a cloud, and her hand, I held, her hand. And all about us," and she takes a breath, and looks down, back out into the shadowed hall. "All about us people, just people, went about their business, and took no notice." A hand to her forehead now, her eyes. "And I hadn't noticed, until, it hadn't occurred to me, before. I was just, we were just." Another breath, deep, shaky. "So small a life," she says, "but still. And now — you've come, to tell me I am Queen. And she will wake. And I must go." Both hands in her lap again, and her head hung low. "I need a cigarette."

"I — can't help, with that."

"Then what use are you," she says, and pushes herself back to her feet. Dust kicked up from the floor glimmers over the shapes of discarded clothing. She stoops, to snatch at something.

"But little enough, except at times. When I might pass on some scrap of message, or such little news, as might, for instance, be about your brother."

"Petulance does not," she snaps, "become," but then she looks up, a T-shirt pale in her hands, and "you," she says, a sliver of a word. "Lymond?"

"Even he. He has returned."

"You let him go."

"I never held him, child. He's none of mine."

"No," she says, looking down.

"He is about the city, gathering banners to his own. He would be King."

"I would," she's saying, "he would've found me. He would've come for me. I would, I would be, he, he promised."

"Whatever I might think, he will be King. And you, his Queen. And everything you wanted, everything, despite all our misgivings. It will come to pass."

"No," she says, and she lifts the T-shirt up above her head, working one arm then the other up and into and through the sleeves.

"It snows, but snow will melt. We will go on."

"No," she says, tugging the T-shirt down about herself. A thump from out in the hall then, a step toward her, or away. "Ysabel."

"No," she says, and then more loudly "No" and "No" and "*No.*" A rustle of blankets behind her, a bedspring's groan, a snort, a snoring sigh. She tugs her black hair from the neck of the T-shirt, and light fluffs into the air. "No," she says, quietly, again. Letters scrawled in black ink across the front of that shirt say The Gloomadon Poppers.

"We must go on."

"I *broke,*" she says. "Today. I," and then, "for as long as I can remember," she says, "I have held above my head this crown, and waited, patiently, until the day that I might put it on. But, today." Kneeling in that sagging T-shirt on the glowering floor. "Today. This," and a hitch in her breath before the next word, "terrible, day, I, I put it down. And I'm, you can't see it. But I'm trembling, with such, such *relief?* It was too heavy. You must know. Far too heavy. And I can't take it up, again." Looking out once more through the empty doorway. "No one could."

"Ysabel. Child."

"I think," she says, "I've changed my mind. I'd rather you showed the deference you think I'm due."

"But you have just said you refuse it. You would not take it up again."

"You would have us want it."

"You can no more not be Queen, Ysabel, than not – "

"Not spin your straw to gold," she says. She blinks, and then looks down, at her hands, lain flat upon her knees.

Another rush of breath sucked in, and when it's let out bright dust skirls in flickering devils, a dozen candles or more, wavering, guttering, dying, stripping away what little light is left. "Why then did you flee?"

Her one hand crosses over the other and wraps about it.

"Why did you run from the Mooncalfe? If you'd stayed, let him take you with him to whatever hell he's planned – it will all end much the same."

"For the city, perhaps?" she says. "But not for me."

The room is dark, now, almost as dark as the hall outside. The window in the wall past the bed's no longer so blank, so black, a sense within of something falling, softly, gently. Or else the whole room floating, rising dizzily, up into the air. And a feathery scratching, faint against the glass.

"Then, majesty, we have returned to our impasse. And there is nothing left for me to do but hope the coat you have is warm."

"Wait," she says, looking up, pushing up, to her feet, a groan and a pop from out in the hall, floorboards, a footstep. She heads for the wall there by the doorway, whick and whisp of her hands on the wallpaper, the sudden thick click of a switch. Light blares whitely from naked bulbs in the fixture in the middle of the ceiling. The walls are suddenly all pink arabesques and faded bouquets, the tangled bedclothes striped dull brown and beige, the clothing on the floor still black, the window harshly glazed now with reflections, and everywhere the drifts of yellow dust. And out in the hall the floor a ruddy wood, the walls of it painted white some time ago, a man, and his pants the color of gravel, and his shirt of ash, and his face is cold and colorless in that light caught wide eyes black a mouth held open under a shapeless nose, jaw set, fixed, a word unspoken, held back with great effort.

"You look," she says, a hand on the door frame, "so, different..."

And, he closes his eyes. His mouth. He opens his eyes and that face has softened, his shoulders in that ashen shirt pulling back, lowering as he straightens, and his hands held empty, useless, at his sides. He says, in that voice grey, and drear, "You will see me twice more yet."

"Twice," says Ysabel, "once, two three – if I, do this," and the light switch clicks again, the light's gone, snuffed in ink, "does it count," she says in the darkness, and click again, the light, too bright, returns, beaming, "as a second time?" But the hall is empty now. There's no one there.

She takes her hand from the switch, her face quite still, and sere.

Behind her a rustle, and a creak of bedsprings, a hoarsely sleepy voice, "I just had the strangest," and a cough. "What time is it? Ysabel?"

Ysabel doesn't answer, doesn't say anything, doesn't turn, doesn't move.

Petra B sits up in her bed, dust sparkling in the harsh light as it falls from her shoulders. "Are you leaving?" She reaches over to the nightstand and finds a phone and thumbs its screen to life. "It's not even almost three," she says.

When Ysabel doesn't say anything again, "Hey. Beautiful. Come back to bed. Stay a while?"

And then, "Ysabel?"

Lurching buttocks clenching spasms tremoring up to jerking shoulders slap and again of flesh on flesh and he barks, the heel of his hand on her hip thumbing the burning heart at the base of her spine and she groans, her hands braced against the other arm of the overstuffed chair and "greh" she says as blowing out he pushes back a single unsteady step reaching out to catch at the back of the chair, his other hand about his cock, her yellow hair heavy with sweat she pushes grimacing the cushion rolling onto her hip on the arm of the chair as he barks and "hanh" he says, a strangled yelp and pale stuff gouts across the chair-back falling to glisten on the cushion and another stream of it jetting from the darkly swollen head of his cock over the other arm of the chair to patter to the floor beyond and she's off the chair entirely half-falling to a crouch before it looking up at him in that ruddy amber light, head back, braced, clenched, a yowl, and one last dollop, plopping.

"Leo?" she says.

Slumping, buckling, clutching the side of the chair as he sags to his knees, hauling air in, shoving it out, "Nothing," he says. Shivering.

"Leo," she says, wincing as she shifts herself a closer crab-wise step.

"Not a thing," he says, looking up, pulling himself grunting to his feet. "All right." Reaching down a hand to her. She takes it shaky in her own and lets him pull her up. "Maybe it wasn't, whatever. That's it. It's time." The words a mutter he's pushing her backwards before him around to the front of the chair. "Forget the car, they're gonna come looking for the car. Forget the money. Don't go back to the hall at all. I should've thought of that."

"Leo," she says, a third time.

"You can't trust them. You can't trust anybody."

"Not even you?"

Pulling her into his arms tight about her, his forehead to her shoulder, "Especially not him," he says, muffled. Then he leans back to say, "Leave the city," and she kisses him. "Go," he says, turning his mouth to one side away. "Plane, train, automobile, gravel barge by dead of night. Get out."

"I'm not going anywhere," she says, and lays her cheek against his chest.

"You will," he says, stepping back from her embrace, turning to face the chair. "Give it a minute." Leaning forward, bending over, both hands planting on the ends of the arms of the chair.

"Hey," she says.

"Blood and milk, and jism," he says, "and honey, and not a mark," breathing in as he straightens slowly unrolling his spine lifting his shoulders, his head, letting go of the arms of the chair, and then turning his back to it, and facing her again. "Don't," she says.

He opens his eyes. Out there past the dim reflections in the great sweep of window the lights of the city spread out below, and the snow, falling. "I am King," he says, "or I am nothing," and he lowers himself to sit upon the chair.

And naked before him she shudders violently as he does.

"Huh," he says.

Naked before him, shivering, arms wound about herself, fingers to her lips, she's looking down at him naked in the chair, armrests gripped by hands unclenching, bare feet crossed at the ankles. "Is that," she says, "is that it?"

He looks up from himself his brown locks spilling back from his face and there a slyly sidelong grin, an eyebrow cocked, "Is that it," he says, "Your majesty."

A gasp of a laugh from her and she looks away, a jerk of her head, fingers falling, and laughing himself he snatches her hand and pulls her, stumbling, into his lap, a tangle of knees and elbows, and he kisses her, and she squirms about settling herself, folding her legs together to stretch them out over an arm of the chair, and she takes his face in both her hands and kisses him back.

"You know," he says.

"What," she says.

"I am, un*utt*erably hungry."

"Am I not enough," and a giggle, "for his majesty?"

"Ah, ha ha," he says, "supping my fill of you's what's left me ravenous."

"It's, what time is it." She sits up, pulls back. "Three? Four?"

"Or noon, or tea, or quitting, who knows?" he says. "Who cares? There's one place in town that's always open."

"You want hot cakes," she says, getting up off his lap.

"I could go for some hot cakes," says the King.

Orange doors, wide segmented overhead doors set one after another down the white walls either side of the alley, all of them that color too luridly deep for the milky light, and a couple of them lifted opened on unlit storage units packed with boxes, furniture, the bulbous rear of a midnight-blue sedan, and the trunk lid's up, and climbing from it a confusion of pastel taffetas, a striped sock, a plaid plimsoll delicately crushing the snow that's drifted over the threshold. Straightening a fluff and crinkle of skirts beneath a large black hooded sweatshirt leaning over the fender to offer up a folded bundle soft and grey to Linesse, in her black leather jacket, in a folding lawn chair, legs draped in an afghan, pink and yellow, blue and green.

Squeak and crunch of snow, a man in a knee-length parka and a knit cap, thermos in one ungloved hand, fingers of the other threaded through the handles of mismatched clinking mugs. He offers up his mugged hand to the woman in the skirts, her face still hidden by that hood, and she takes a yellow one that says Is It Friday Yet, and then he swings to offer them to Linesse bent over, she's unfurled that bundle, sweatpants, and now she looks up, tucks herself back under the afghan, takes a white mug printed with a drooping cartoon mustache. He sets the third on the fender, a black mug that says I'm Not Lost, I'm Locationally Challenged, and pours something richly red and steaming from the thermos into each. He lifts his, and the woman in the skirts lifts hers, and then with the slightest tic of her gunmetal head Linesse lifts hers, and then a nod, and she drinks, and they drink.

At the one end of the alley a pickup truck, and Lymond sitting on the rear bumper in his purple T-shirt, his pinkish-orange hair laid back, dark with sweat, or melted snow. Over the edge of the truck's bed lopped a couple of shaggy rabbit ears, Glenn's curled up back there, asleep under a tarp. A creak, a rattle, a bang and another orange door is hoisted, opened, a woman in a pale blue quilted robe shuffling from between a wall of cardboard boxes and a glass-fronted cabinet. A sludgy drone of pipes erupts, counterpointed by bass, and drums, someone's set an old boom box on a crate, clamoring with the rattle and bang of another door thrown up, someone else stepping out, here, and there, a nod perhaps, a wave.

A short and heavy man climbs out of the cab of the truck, shapeless green coveralls and a battered tweed jacket, a blue meshback cap that says Vanport 15. "He's here," he calls out, and Lymond peers around the back of the truck. Trudging down another alley quiet and still, the orange doors all closed and locked, an old man in a pea coat his dark head bald and bare, bent under the weight of an olive duffel. Lymond nods, then sits back against the tailgate. "Gordon," says the man in the meshback cap.

"Soames," says the old man with a nod. "That this Prince?"

A brisk nod from the Soames, a jerk of his thumb. "But it's her," he says. "Down past Biscuit."

The pipes and the drums and the bass climb to and end and a guitar jigs out from under it all, a clattering bodhrán, and voices in a harmony distorted by those overpowered speakers sing they're changing the guard at Buckingham Palace. A man in a worn barn coat's doing a little dance, there's a laugh, and a clap, and a whoop. The man in the knee-length parka's headed back toward the truck, thermos in his hand, and back behind him there's Linesse in her black leather jacket, her grey sweatpants, one bare foot in the snow and the other lifted to rest against her cocked knee, a tree, her back to the truck, and her mug held up in both her hands.

Gordon stops, dips his shoulder to let the duffel fall, then leaning in lowers himself first one knee then the other beside it.

"She needs shoes," says the Soames.

"I know what she needs, Tommy Tom," says Gordon, opening the duffel, digging among a jumble of shoes to pull out a long boot, grey wool and brown leather straps and a buckle, chiming. "Fetch the bolt cutters."

The Soames Thomas says, "What?"

Up to the shoulder in that duffel Gordon scowls. "Every tool known to man in that truck of yours," he says. "So reach in and fetch me out a set of bolt cutters." And then, "You think anyone else of you is gonna do this."

Around the back of the truck Lymond's gotten to his feet.

Thomas opens the driver's door, leans in, working something loose. Up in the back Glenn in his furry jumpsuit sits up as the truck rocks, rubbing at eyes slitted against the thickening light. Thomas pulls out all long dinged yellow levers and snubbed pincers brown with rust and holds them close to himself, frowning at Gordon, who's pulled the mate of that boot from the duffel. He reaches for the cutters, and Thomas lets them go. "You're still wearing that hat," says Gordon, and then he heads off down the alley, past Biscuit, toward Linesse.

"Forgive him, highness," says Thomas. He's taken off his cap, smoothing his thick black hair. "It's been an extraordinary time." Biscuit's putting the thermos in the cab of the truck. "This weather," says Thomas, putting his cap back on, favoring Biscuit with the briefest look, the merest shake of his head. Biscuit shuts the door, leans back against the truck, blowing on his hands.

"It snowed," says Glenn, up in the back of the truck. "It *never* snows."

Down the alley in their heavy coats and coveralls, their loose black rubber boots, wrapped in blankets and one of them a sleeping bag all splotchy camouflage of pink and red and white and dirty grey, they keep their distance but still, circling about, as Linesse turns to see Gordon there beside her, and his head bowed. She lifts a hand but he stoops away, sets the cutters on the pavement, kneels, heavily, there before her, the boots in his hands, and the music's now a ringing, chugging guitar riff, a fusillade of drumbeats, a wailing harmony, true love, true love, true love. "And here you are, nevertheless," says Lymond then, "up with the sun, to see to the needs of your people."

"My, people?" says Thomas. "Domestics, who can't keep a hearth? Mechanicals without a purpose? Highness, these, they — these are *no* one's people."

"But," says Lymond, "when our little band is once more on its way, you'll have Biscuit open up the truck, and you'll bring forth the last of my sister's gift to you, and dole it out to them."

And Gordon's buckling a boot about Linesse's calf.

"Give me your rabbits, Twice Thomas," says Lymond.

"My rabbits," says Thomas, toeing a frozen rut.

"The Hare, then," says Lymond. "A fine emblem it'll make, on a banner, in the sunlight."

And Gordon's tugging the other boot up over Linesse's foot.

The Soames Thomas, still looking down, hands in the pockets of his jacket, says, "You can't give us the North, highness."

"Can't?" says Lymond, lightly.

"You can't," says Thomas, "make a gift, of what we already hold."

"A point," says Lymond, "a fair point," and Thomas nods, "Highness," he says. Gordon's leaning away as Linesse steps back from him in her new boots. He's climbing slowly to his feet, waving away the hand she offers.

"What you don't have," says Lymond, "is a place at court," and Thomas starts to say, "We'd never," but Lymond's speaking over him, "What you don't have," he says, "is a full share in the Apportionment."

Thomas looks up at that. Over to Lymond. "There must be a Queen," he says.

"Yes," says Lymond. "There will."

The cutters in one hand Gordon's saying something with great force, holding up his free hand, throwing it to one side, and he repeats himself, redoubled, shaking the cutters at her, and when he's said what he's saying she reaches out and lets the mug in her hand drop. She unzips her jacket just enough to pull aside the collar and reveal there polished silver. Black Betty, Black Betty had a baby, that wailing harmony's chanting around itself, Freddy's dead, that's what I said.

"It's not for me," says Thomas. "It can't be for me. We won't allow it. We'll send who we send to court, and divvy up our share as we see fit."

"A Count, a Duke, a Marquess," says Lymond, watching as Gordon levers the cutters open, bites the polished silver with those snubbed brown jaws. "Why not a President, too? The office is yours to fill."

"I was just thinking," says Glenn, up behind them, "I mean, are the busses running today? With the snow? We should probably try to figure that – "

Flare of light and a hollow roar almost a voice and a thump of impact rattling the orange doors in their frames, sending more than one of them clattering crashing closed and closed, and the crowd turns ducking falling away, hands up, shading eyes, and Gordon bellowing staggers back, dropping the cutters smoking to the snow, as Linesse with a slow twist peels the silver torc from about her throat.

"Shit," says Jessie, working the gas and the clutch, one hand gripping the steering wheel, one hand the gear shift, the car slewing left, juddering, whipping back and settling as speed's picked up, engine snorting climbing down from its redline howl, snow popping under the tires rolling under the traffic light, past the palatial movie theater on the corner, Bagdad says the big sign in ornamented letters. Careful, says the unlit marquee. Twilight of the Ice Nymphs 1030. Cowards Bend the Knee. "Leo," she says, both hands on the wheel now to steady it through a shudder. The roar of the heater swallowing her voice. "Leo. Almost home." He's slumped over against the passenger door, eyes closed wobbling with the car as it whines over another slick patch.

She brakes in stages approaching the snow-draped temple, those high mullioned windows up between white columns capped in green, and turns with a crunch of snow, gunning up into the little lot between the temple and the glass-walled restaurant, and noses to park at a sloppy angle under the blank brick wall. She shuts off the engine, keys clinking in the sudden thunderous silence. "Leo," she says, and then she's overtaken by a mighty yawn. He's blinking, still slumped, thumbing the corners of his eyes. "Time is it," he says.

"I don't know," she says.

"Sun's up," he says. "I think?"

"Took a while to get across town," she says, "what with the snow," and he's leaning over, "Hey," he says, "that's not what I was getting at." His hand in her lap. "Leo," she says. His eyes squeezed shut, his shoulder leaning heavily against her. "I feel," he says. "Weird? All bloated and starving at once."

"Given what you ate," she says.

"Not talking about food." He frowns at his hand on her thigh, fingers on bare skin between sock and jacket-hem. "You're cold," he says.

"I'm *freezing*," she says. "I want to get inside and climb into bed and sleep for two days."

"Only two," he says, and then, "okay," and lifts his hand away.

"I like it when it's snowing," he says, opening his door, pushing himself to his feet as she opens hers. "Not so much when it *has* snowed." Leaning on his cane, limping a step or two away from the car. "What time is it?"

"Leo." She's looking over the top of the car at him. "You feeling okay?"

"Something *hurts*," he says. "We got something wrong." Turning about in the empty lot, lifting his cane, "Nineteen," he says, with a sweep of his arm, "eighteen – *seventeen* knights, and who's here the break of a Saturday dawn, jars and bottles in hand?"

"The snow," she says.

"*Fuck* the snow." He stomps around the front of the car. "Sixteen."

"Sixteen."

"You think Luys is coming back? You think *any* of them are coming back?"

"Your grace?"

There at the corner by the sidewalk a man in a puffy cream-colored coat, rich red hair flopping from a high widow's peak, and in his hand a cloudy plastic bottle with a bright red lid, and Leo leaning into it cane-tip squelching in the snow swarms up to him, "You will address my *majesty*," he snarls, slapping the bottle away.

"Leo!" says Jessie.

"Sir?" says the man in the cream-colored coat.

And he draws back, both hands on the head of his cane now, looking from the one to the other, biting his lip. "Let's go inside," he says, the words clipped, small, and when the man in the cream-colored coat steps over to reach for the bottle, "Leave it."

Around the corner then, and up the steps, and through the double doors.

Through the double doors, and across the black-and-white tiled foyer. Up the wide white-painted stairs. She leans against, presses herself against the buzzing red bulk of a Coke machine as his hand on the faceted glass knob he leans close to the plain white door and says, "And Farquahr will be two."

Down the dark hall, past the big room washed in thin light from those high narrow windows, through an odd little corner and into the cramped kitchen, where she stops, looks back. "Leo?" she says. By the sink a single glass turned upside down.

Through a swinging door into the airy white room, the small round table there in the middle of it, the three absurdly high-backed chairs about it, the white ridge of a sectional sofa down at the one end, the plain translucent shower curtains lining the other, and slowly a hand up before her she walks up to them, and parts them, and steps between racks of clothing, dresses, jackets, a phalanx of skirts, a platoon of jeans, clouds of lingerie. At the end of it all she sits on a low stool before a three-way mirror, in her grey chauffeur's jacket, her yellow hair swept back under her grey chauffeur's cap, reaching down her black-socked leg for the laces of her red shoes, those bright red Keds, but her hands fall away and up to wrap about her knees, and when she looks up, her eyes screwed shut, her mouth a twist, her cheeks shine.

Squeal and a scrape of rings as she pushes through shower curtains, clear but rippled with triangles in loud colors. She's wearing a long white sleeveless T-shirt, and her eyes are clear, and her feet bare. There before her a queen-sized bed in a pool of soft light from the corner windows, piled high with white comforters and pillows. The man in the bed sits up on one elbow, and his smile is rueful, and he says, "I'm sorry. I had nowhere else to go." His dark hair brushes his shoulders, and his new beard's neatly trimmed. His chest a thicket of lush dark curls. His eyebrows cock, his smile quirks, "You did ask me to come back," he says.

"I haven't slept," she says, climbing into the bed. "I have got to sleep." Settling on her side, her back to him. Folding a pillow under her ear.

"So sleep," he says. "I've kept the bed warm for you." He leans over her, kisses her shoulder, and when she closes her eyes and doesn't lift her face to him he leans over even more to kiss her cheek. "Kings die," he says. "They die; it's what they do." Stroking her shoulder once more, then rolling over on his back. "Magicians don't."

Some time passes before she says, "Lake," without opening her eyes. "I don't have a sister."

His hands clasped together just beneath his chin, those dark eyes gazing up at the unfinished ceiling, he sighs. "Tell me about her," he says. "Whatever you like. Just until you fall asleep."

"Certain ancient megaliths," says Mr. Charlock, "were said to go down to the nearest stream for a drink, at astronomically propitious times of the year." He's stretched out the length of the back seat, empty sleeves of his black suit yanked tight around and beneath him, and wound about with orange electrical cord. "Their dead were buried upright, facing west." He's looking up, working his shoulders, his neck, trying to see out the window above him. His shoelaces have been tied together. "It is suggested," he says, straining, "the experimenter, face himself, to the east."

"East," says Mr. Keightlinger, stirring from behind the wheel, leaning down to look up and out the passenger window. Outside the snow's steeped in pale blue shadows, but light sharpens up behind the big house across the trackless street. A broad porch, there, and four front doors each set one right next to another. "Okay," says Mr. Keightlinger.

"He didn't sing," says Mr. Charlock. "They sing, in the snow." Wriggling against the cords. "He didn't beat his wings against our shields."

"Keep still," says Mr. Keightlinger.

"Low, keep low," says Mr. Charlock, "hell yes I did, like a worm in the," and he frowns, shoulder rolling as he pulls against something, "snow," wriggling again, "all those wings, and eyes." Jacket bunching up under the orange cord and there where his white shirt's showing his hand, twisting about. "He didn't *see* us, but he wasn't even *looking*. He was, he – was."

"What," says Mr. Keightlinger.

"Sad," says Mr. Charlock.

"Sad."

"Sad. Still. As near a *miss,* as I'll, ever *want.*" The car rocks as he kicks, jerks, kicks again. His hand down by his hip clawing at a loop of cord.

"Stop," says Mr. Keightlinger, leaning even further down. "Be still."

Out there the third of those four front doors is opening and stepping out there's Ysabel, black moccasin boots and thin black coat, white fur trailing from the cuffs, white fur about the hood of it framing her face. Mr. Charlock kicks again, hand wrenching free enough to flop against his belly. *"Stop,"* says Mr. Keightlinger, crouching along the front seat. Ysabel's turned back, facing the woman wrapped in a long heavy robe the color of wine, her black hair short, and tied about her throat a strand of fine black lace, and the air glimmers about them as she reaches out for Ysabel's hand. Mr. Keightlinger clucks his tongue.

"What," says Mr. Charlock, kicking, rocking the car. "What!"

Ysabel says something, lifts her hand away, and Petra leans forward abruptly to snatch a kiss at her fingertips. "Burgundy," says Mr. Keightlinger, and a jingle of keys. "The hell does that even *mean?*" says Mr. Charlock. Ysabel's taken Petra's face in both her hands and leaned in for a long swallow of a kiss, and light blooms in the shadows about them, and a burning limb of sunlight crests the roof far above. "Around the block," says Mr. Keightlinger, ducked below the wheel, slotting a key in the ignition. "Get some distance."

"From *what?*" Flicking the fingers of his free hand, crossing them index and middle, pinkie and ring, Mr. Charlock twists it about and curls it into a white-cornered fist. Mr. Keightlinger turns the key, and nothing happens. Ysabel lets go of Petra, steps back, steps back again, and Petra B reaches after her, clutching her parting robe, saying something, pleading. "Let go," says Mr. Keightlinger.

"Where," says Mr. Charlock, fist still tightly curled.

"Wait and watch," says Mr. Keightlinger, turning the key again, and again, pounding the wheel with the heel of his hand. "Let *go.*"

"She's *alone,*" says Mr. Charlock, rocking the car with another kick. "She has *no one!* Grab her and be *done* with it!"

Ysabel's coming down the steps. Still reaching out her face crumpling Petra sinks to her knees, and light falls from her hand as it closes on nothing. Ysabel careful of her booted feet in the stiff snow, looking up to see the low-slung orange car parked across the trackless street, snow falling from its faded black ragtop as it rocks from side to side.

"We coulda had her *last night!*" says Mr. Charlock, and Mr. Keightlinger's muttering "Bind, bind and stop." Mr. Charlock's rolled over on one side, his other hand squirming there at the small of his back, fighting free of his rucked-up jacket, fingers jabbing, rigid, a sizzle, a long slash ripping through the vinyl seat-back, and old yellow foam rubber popping from the slit. "We coulda been back in *Schenectady* by now!"

"Never been," says Mr. Keightlinger, leaning over the front seat, raising a hand.

"It's a *figure* of *speech!*" shrieks Mr. Charlock, and someone's tapping on the window, and they freeze.

"Well?" says Mr. Charlock, after a moment.

Mr. Keightlinger ducks back down, peers up through the window. Ysabel's squinting through the scratched and dirty light-struck glass.

"Go on," says Mr. Charlock, relaxing his fist, stretching out his fingers.

Mr. Keightlinger leans across to roll down the passenger-side window a couple of inches. "Do you have any cigarettes?" says Ysabel through the gap. "I could really use a smoke, and I don't, I don't have any," and she shrugs. Mr. Keightlinger shakes his head. "No," he says.

"Okay," she says, looking away, blinking at the light. "You've been following me."

And a single loud flat bark of a laugh from Mr. Charlock.

"All this time," says Ysabel, looking back into the car, at Mr. Charlock sprawled across the back seat. "The two of you. All this time."

Mr. Keightlinger doesn't say anything. "She's got us, dead to rights," says Mr. Charlock.

"And that was you, last night," says Ysabel. "And on his machine. Place and time. The club. He was going to sell me to you."

Mr. Keightlinger doesn't say anything. "Give, more like," says Mr. Charlock.

From behind her across the street a plaintive cry, "Ysabel!"

"Show me," she says, and she opens the passenger door. Mr. Keightlinger presses himself back against the driver's door, "Wait," he says, as she climbs into the car. "Show me what would've happened," she says, "if he had. If I hadn't."

"Observe!" cackles Mr. Charlock. "Wait and watch her climb right in!"

"Ysabel!" wails Petra B.

She pulls the car door shut, and glitter settles on the seat about her. "Go," she says. "Before that woman wakes the whole neighborhood."

"Do not engage," says Mr. Charlock. Mr. Keightlinger turns the key. The engine rumbles to life. And the Queen leans over, punches a button, twists a knob, and the heater roars to life. She holds her hands over the vent in the dash. "Come on," she says. "Show me what I'm for."

"Just watch," Mr. Charlock's chanting, as Mr. Keightlinger puts the car in gear, "Just watch, just you watch – "

Clank, and up

Clank and up he sits, owlish, fuddled. Puts out a hand bang against the side of the tub and clatter the ducting clamped about his forearm, the pot lid cupping his shoulder, wound about with grubby grey tape. The colander rakishly precarious on his head tilts over the bridge of his nose and his running shoes squeak on the enamel and the ducting and stove pipe crimping his filthy jeans a kitchen cabinet spilling into a sink. Scrape and thump. One hand bare finds the edge of the tub and grips it, the other a club in a thick hockey glove bats the colander, knocking it back, there's his dark unfocused eyes, his unwashed hair that lankly shines, the stubble blotching his chin.

Leaning over the toilet rush and splatter of piss that bulky gloved hand braced against the wall. Scrape and jangle. Red plastic cups lined up along the back of the toilet and a couple of cans that say Wild Turkey Kentucky Straight Bourbon Whiskey and Cola, Real Kentucky. Pushing back wavering from the wall both hands gloved and bare pawing at the fly of his jeans "Shit" he says and hisses and then frustrated shakes the glove loose, flings it thump to the floor and catches himself from falling. Buttons himself up.

"Fucking hell," says Frankie Reichart.

Clamor and clunk down a flight of stairs too many at a time, wrenching himself to a stop before the bottom, leaning out over the railing, the dark hall below, to one side a wide doorway, high-ceilinged room, a ruddy flicker struggling with daylight muted by drawn shades. At the foot of the steps is sprawled a woman in a green and yellow cheerleader outfit, dozing with a laptop on her chest. She doesn't stir as he gingerly steps over.

In that room past the long dining table littered with dirty glasses and mostly empty bottles a fireplace, and crouching before it a bald man all sharp corners draped in a charcoal-stripe suit. He doesn't look up as Frankie crashes to a halt. Keeps poking the dying fire as Frankie says "Hey," and *"Hey"* and "Where is every-body." Clanking further into the room, and all those painted faces up along the picture-molding, just beneath the ceiling, looking out upon each other. "The party's over? You got me all dolled up like this, marched me half across town, now what."

"She's left us here, arreared, to join herself to the Changeling's court," says the bald man by the fire. "Yourself is free to go, or not." On the pale hearth by his knee in a splash of char a tarnished snake of silvery metal, not much longer than two hands laid one after another.

"What happened," says Frankie, "what happened to your – "

"Stay, or go," says the bald man, "as you'd prefer." Levering up a log with the poker, he blows into the gap he's made, and sullen flames lick out from underneath. "You'll find it makes no difference."

A hand up against the brilliance of the white outside, the seamless snow, the faintest blue tingeing the cloudless sky. "Christ," says Frankie Reichart, looking back through the door stood open on the darkness of that house. A gassy snort, a climbing whine of a rumble dropping suddenly to climb again and the clinking of chains, a bus bulling its way down the street, and wet black ruts in its wake. A peal of laughter from somewhere, a block away, or two, and water ticking, dripping, a plop and splash from the eaves. "Well, hell," he says, and yanks the colander from his head, whips it skimming out into the yard. "It'll all be gone by two, anyway." Banging a stumble down the steps from the porch, and way up above, the ghost of a crescent moon, looking back toward the rising sun.

It's funny, now
I should remember – still
The sight, the smell, the sound
And how it feels
But up above
Could it be
The same moon

—*Lea Krueger*

NO. 20
SUN

There's a tree now, towering above the snow-swept plaza, the green of it overwhelmed by lights hung all upon it, by blues almost white, reds almost pink and orange, by greens almost yellow and blue, a rift of light opened in the unearthly blue climbing all the way up to a pale slice of moon, and if that spread of sky above is all of it brighter than the tree, soaking up the coming day in pearly yellows and whites shining even now behind the unlit bulk of the courthouse, it's still dark on the plaza, the snow blued by the shadows of the buildings all about, the darkened signs of banks and restaurants and jewelers, and the lights of that tree are enough to tamp down those shadows beneath it, and play fitfully over the man stood there, tall and broad in a shortwaisted jacket, his hair a dark black cap, looking over the base of the tree, wrapped in a hinged red box, printed with snowflakes. Welcome to Portland's Living Room, it says. Be Merry. "Mason!" cries someone, somewhere up behind him, and he turns.

She's coming down the great sweep of steps that walls that end of the plaza, careful of the drifts and pockets of snow, wrapped in a sheepskin jacket, and a knapsack on her back, her hair loose and wild about her head a creamy glow against the darkness behind her. "I had not thought to meet you here, again," she says. In one hand a baseball bat.

"I hadn't thought to see you again at all," he says. His hands in the pockets of his jacket.

At the bottom of the steps now, she's walking up the slight slope toward the tree, the bat loosely idle at her side. "I beat you, the last time."

"A near-enough thing," he says.

She's there beside him now, under the tree, a step or two more than a sword's length between them. Without shifting his feet, without moving his hands he looks up, along the trunk looming over them. "You can see," he says, "where they've bolted on extra greenery. To fill out the bottom of it."

"Yes," she says, without looking up, or away from him at all.

"My lord," he says then, "the Duke – he asked me to wear the mask."

"And you'd do anything, if asked?"

"I'm but a knight, lady."

"Then it was but the form, of a question," she says, and he inclines his head, lifts a shoulder, something of a shrug. "She has it now," he says. "The Gallowglas."

"A proper Huntsman, once again," says Marfisa. "So set her on my heels! I'll make a proper sport of it, I swear."

The frown that steals over his face is hesitant, even tender. "The Queen," he says.

"The Queen," she snaps.

"Has set her," he says, "to hunt the Mooncalfe."

She looks down, then, and the tip of the bat in her hand thumps the brick at her feet. "Well," she says.

"Coming down from the hills," he says, "I'd thought to see fires, pillars of smoke, that I'd hear trumpets. The Queen, unhoused, and the Duke, the Count, the Prince now, vying for the Throne, the Bride taken, and the Shootist and our Gammer cut down," his eyes on his boots as he says this, his black hair shot with red and green and blue from the lights above. "But it's all so, so *quiet.*" Sighing. He looks up to see her frozen there, breathless, eyes wide, mouth set, so still she almost trembles. "I," he says, "you, I thought you must've known – "

"Which," she says, the word a crack.

"Which, what – "

"Which of them has *taken her*," she says, "the *Duke*," she says, "the, the Prince?" Turning away from him. "My brother," looking back over her shoulder, up the sweep of steps. "Who has, it seems, neglected," she says, "to mention, some, aspects – "

"None of them, lady," says the Mason. "The Mooncalfe."

The bat thumps the brick again. "Orlando," she says. Then, "And a telephone salesgirl's sent to bring her back."

"My lord, the Duke," he says. "Told me, go, do, what must be done. But I don't – I came here, because I don't know where to find her, or how to go about it, and I must confess, Axe, that when I saw you coming down those," and then he says, "oh. I must apologize, for that."

"Don't," she says.

And when she does not go on, he says, carefully, "When I saw you coming down those steps, I thought, at last, someone else, to help." He's holding out a hand to her, and a bit of leather tied about his wrist. "Together, we can – "

"My lady broke with me," she says.

"But she is still your lady," he says.

The sound she makes is not a laugh. "I broke with the court, I left my sword," she says. "The Gallowglas, if we find her, might harry me to the ends, of the," and she shakes her head. "I went," she says, "to the bus station, a week after I came back to myself. I went and I bought a ticket to some, other place, with a candy wrapper, and I actually got my foot on the steps of a bus, I stood there, about to pull myself aboard..."

"But," he says, his hand held out to her, "she is still your lady."

Just two blocks away or so a man stands outside the entrance to a tiny shop, little more than a booth behind a window plastered with advertisements for Repair and Unlocking and Prepaid Minutes and Handmade Wooden Cases for Your Phone, All Sizes. His long dark coat unbuttoned over a blue silk shirt open at the throat, his shoes severe and black and highly polished, and in one hand a heavy ring of keys. His cheeks red-blotched, his puffed eyes ringed with purple. He isn't looking at the keys, or the notice taped to the door, a single sheet of paper different from the advertisements about and under it. He isn't looking at the thick yellow chain wrapped around the handle, held by a great padlock, wrapped in a red seal. A slice of snow, drifted up in the corner of the step before the door, an unblemished lune of blue. Off to his left the street dips between high buildings toward a burning edge of dawn away beyond the river. To his right the street climbs toward a skelter of trees, a church spire, the hills, steeply black on black. A gust of wind lifts his thin and colorless hair in a single shellacked wing, holding it even as the sound of it fades, and in the silence he looks up.

Not an arm's length away a tall man, thin, his long straight black hair settling as the gust dies. His jacket grey and shapeless, his long skirt a dark and nameless blue, his feet bare in the snow. The man in the coat starts, scrape of shoe, jangle of keys. "Tut," says Orlando. Something dark's been splattered along the sleeves of his jacket, something dark, and brown, and up his neck, and the side of his face. He leans in abruptly smiling now, a wide-eyed reckless smile as he brings his hands together up above his head, the man in the coat stumbling back, and with a jerk Orlando lunges after him, bringing those hands down, "Gah!" bursts the man in the coat as those hands stop pressed together touching his chest the dark hair curling there where his blue silk shirt opens. Orlando steps back, throws his arms up, "La!" he cries.

The man in the coat falls against the door frame floundering arm clunking the chain keys falling to splash in the snow. Orlando twirling away, arms spread, skirt flaring, smiling, smiling. The man in the coat coughs, hawks, leans over to spit. Straightens his coat, his shirt, his shoulder brushing the notice taped to the door. He hikes up his trousers to kneel and scoop up the keys, then steps out into the empty street, heedless of his shining shoes in the snow, turning about, looking up the street, looking down. At the heavy ring of keys in his hand.

A deep breath stretches his broad chest, lifts his shoulders, is blown out in a sudden deflating sigh. He drops the hand holding the keys and twists to one side, then spins back all the way around and swings that arm out and up and letting go, and the chiming keys arc up and away down the street, the spark of them lost in all this morning light.

SWINGING THE BLADE – HALF ELEVEN
WHAT HAD BEEN PLANNED

THE BLADE SWUNG slowly parries up, to the left, low, to the right, and then a long low lunge, a stately thrust, a gleam slipping down the edge of it to splinter in the glittering guard about the hilt. Her free hand dropped back in a fist pulling herself back up, and tucks up close against her chest again.

"No," he says.

Jo all in black shakes out her arms, works her head back and forth. Takes up her stance again, blade upright before her again, and again the parries, the lunge, the thrust.

"I can hear you *thinking*," he says.

"I'm not," she says, pulling back, *"trying,"* and the parries to all four quarters again, "for *fast* – "

"I don't mean speed," Roland says, "it's," his hands in fingerless bicycle gloves reach up, grasping, closing into fists about nothing. He claps them together, pushes himself up from the base of the engine hulking quietly idle, the housing of it painted an industrial pea-soup green, the great nest of gears racked vertically behind, waist-high and higher, glistening with grease. "The flow," he says. The sword he's holding is long, and straight, with a heavy golden pommel bright in the shadows. He plants himself before her in the narrow aisle, right foot forward, off-hand loosely curled against the small of his back, and he's already moving, swipe and step and cut and back and down into a lunge, his off-hand swinging down and back, extending, pulling him up again, the sword returning, "Just so," he says. "Again?" Falling forward into a lunge, pulling back, the sword licking at this parry, that. "You see?"

"Ever been stabbed through the gut?" says Jo.

Pulling his foot back, lowering his sword. "That's how Orlando took you."

"Yeah," she says. The tip of her blade looping a figure eight there by her boot. "He came at me, swinging this hellacious cut at my head, and I," she hoists the hilt, torquing up, around, *"blocked* it," the blade above her upturned face, "but I had to turn?" A twist of her waist. "And when his cut slid off he just somehow *stopped,"* a boot-stamp as her sword continues the twist, blade-tip arcing over and down and back, her off-hand cupping the hilt of it, pushing. "And that was it."

Roland nods. "His Fool's Mate."

"It has a name," she says.

"He defeated me with that move, once," Roland's saying. "The Guerdon, too, Linesse, the Wulver, that I know of. He tried it on Marfisa; she stepped to the side," his white shoes hop, "and," miming a low quick cut, "hamstrung him as he passed. He limped for three days, after."

She's smiling as she kneels, taking up her discarded scabbard. "So at least once," she says, fitting blade-tip to mouth, sliding it home.

"Three times, that particular wound." He picks up the butter-colored coat from the concrete floor and holds out the weight of it dangling from his hand. "You're the only fighter ever to defeat me without landing a blow. His lips purse, his eyebrows rise, a judicious smile. "Which you've done twice."

"You gave up," she says, putting on the coat, passing her sword from the one hand to the other.

"I never did."

"You gave up!" she says. "I found you *sleeping* in the damn *snow."* Laying her sword at the base of the engine, there by the blue and white headphones atop a portable CD player, by the crudely painted skull-mask with its long black mane. "And don't think I don't know why you hauled us up into *this* bridge, over the damn river." He turns away at that, looking down the length of the great axle shining in the chill grey light, the light seeping from the end of the room there, the curling stairwell caged behind chicken-wire. "Burnside," says Jo. "The middle of it all, nowhere, no North, no South, no East or West, and not a fucking thumb to be seen."

"I was, waiting," says Roland.

"For what?" she says. He's turned abruptly, he's walking away, down toward the end of the room. "The King," he calls back.

"The King," she says, starting after him. "You were gonna, what, sleep? In the snow? Till he came back?"

His hand on the latch of the cage. "Yes," he says, and he opens it, and steps through.

"There's a," says Jo, reaching the cage as he starts up the tightly spiraled stairs, "there's a Queen?" His feet clanging up and around and out of sight. "There's a Queen!" She starts up after him, around and up, up into thin grey daylight, a cramped hexagon of a room, high-ceilinged, the stairs turning on to the next floor up. Narrow sash windows in each wood-paneled wall look out on an emptiness of grey cloud. Roland leans against a sill, and past him and down, through that gelid haze, a suggestion of weight, of lines, edges, a railing, the paved deck. "Beneath our feet," he says, "there is a forest. Nearly four hundred trees sunk in the cold mud, bearing up the weight of this end of the bridge." He looks back to her, over his shoulder. "Stripped of leaves," he says. "Shorn of branches. She may have granted you an office, Gallowglas, and charged you with a duty, but she is no more the Queen, nor has been, for many months."

"I don't mean her," says Jo. He's looking out into the fog again. "Roland, that girl was dead."

"You're mistaken," he says, quietly.

"She brought her back to life!"

"She is not the *Queen.*"

"There was owr," says Jo. "Everywhere."

"We *broke her!*" he roars. And then, a knuckle knocking the sill, flatly, "I broke her."

"No," she says, letting go of the curled rail, stepping off the staircase. "We didn't. Roland. Roland, what does the Queen do."

"She," he says, "she is the Queen."

"She makes owr."

"That's, that's not – "

"She turns the, the stuff, into owr. The Queen, the, her, her mother, Ysabel's mother. She does everything else, everything but that, and you – "

"Jo, you don't – "

" – she can't turn the owr, and you say she's no longer Queen – "

"There is no King!" he cries. "The King did not come back! And without a King, to take her hand, she cannot turn the owr."

"That burger joint," she says. "It's not five blocks from here. You can go scoop it off the floor."

He's shaking his head. "You tried," he says. "No one can deny. You've done," he says, "everything that could have been done, but." A gesture, toward the window. "It's too late. It's over." That gesture folding, into a fist. "No King, no Queen, the Gammer cut down, by the Mooncalfe, who's stolen the Bride, and this snow, and," the fist opening, "the city," his fingers spread wide there by his face, "melting away... Gallowglas," he says, looking over to her. She's digging through the pockets of her coat. "Jo," he says, tenderly.

"Too late," she's muttering, pulling out her black glass phone, thumbing it to life.

"It's not something you should expect to understand," he says.

"Half past eleven," she says.

"What?" he says. He steps away from the window. She's holding up her phone. "It's eleven thirty," she says. On the screen of it a photo, Jo and Ysabel cheek to cheek, Ysabel, her hand to the upturned collar of her coat, looking sidelong at Jo smiling widely and directly at the camera, the blur of her arm at the bottom of the shot. At the top of the screen the clock says Half Eleven. Seventh Groosalugg. "We don't know what time it is, out there," says Jo. "We don't have any idea what's going on right now. So don't – " She stares a moment, not at him, not past him, then turns the phone back to herself. Pokes and swipes at the screen.

"Don't?" he says. "Gallowglas?"

"The wrong one first," she says. She's scrolling through the call log.

"Yes," says Roland. "That, *burger* joint. When you followed the Duke's counsel, instead of your own, and went to the wrong – "

"That's the wrong wrong one," she says, standing, tucking the phone away. "I know what she meant," she says. "I figured it out." She's started down the steps. "The wrong one, first." Stopping,

looking back. Coming back up, a step or two. "I don't know how
yet," she says, "or why, but. We can get a direct answer, we can
find her, he, how would he, I," she shakes her head, quickly.
"Roland," she says. "We haven't done everything, not nearly, not
yet. And we, I – she, she needs your help, Roland." Holding out
her hand. "Please." A sudden twist of a smile. "I mean, even if I'm
wrong. He might have, I don't know. Breakfast?"

The desk is broad, the pale leather top of it empty but for a silver
pen, an ivory-handled knife, a banker's lamp with a white glass
shade. Behind the desk a glass cabinet of shelves crowded with
dolls and figurines, a swordswoman in scraps of chainmail and
elaborate boots, a cowgirl guns cocked sitting her chapped legs
spread on a bag of money, a slender schoolgirl in a tight orange
jacket and long dark stockings, tossing an arch salute. A man
bellows, full of pain, edged with fear, the sound of it dulled by a
wall or two. Her hand tentative, Ysabel reaches in, careful of the
ball-jointed woman leaning on a plinth, panels on her naked
arms, her thighs, her belly and breast popped open, pulled aside to
reveal intricate circuitry, pipework, armatures. She plucks up a girl
in a furry pink bodysuit, furry pink booties on her feet and a hood
with rabbit ears pink and furry, and above her head an enormous
rainbow-swirled lollipop held like an umbrella, or a balloon.

"Do you like them?" says the man in the white suit. His vest is
white, his tie a white of alternating stripes, glossy and matte,
woven in a complex knot between the spread collar of his spotless white shirt. His white hair thick, unruly, his face beneath it
unlined, and quite young.

"One notices a theme," she says.

His head inclines. "If there's anything you find you require."
His eyes are almost grey. A room or two away, someone yells, a
stammering, bubbling sound that isn't quite a word.

Ysabel lays a hand on the desk, dimpling the leather. Her hair
in clumps and tangles about her face, thicketing her shoulders.
The sleeves and neck of her oversized T-shirt sagging, loose.

"Some answers," she says. Letters scrawled in black ink across the front of her shirt say The Gloomadon Poppers. Glitter hints along her cheek, her throat, has spangled the fine hair on her arm.

"To any questions in particular?" he says.

"I," she says. "I could use a cigarette."

"Of course." He reaches over a corner of the desk to open a drawer. Pulls out a clear cellophane packet of unmarked cigarettes and a clean glass dish and a mirror-bright lighter, and then busies himself with freeing a smoke and holding it up for her to take, opening the lighter, striking a flame. "Strong," she says, blinking, after her first drag.

"A custom blend," he says, putting the lighter and the packet away. "Burley, and a Macedonian leaf. Not to everyone's liking. Please, sit. You must be exhausted."

She reaches back to find an arm of the chair behind her, dark wood framing glossy tufted leather, and she lowers herself, carefully, into it. In that white suit he's kneeling before her, and his fingers smooth and slender, the nails cut close and neatly shaped, pick at the knots in the laces of her moccasin boots. "The office has a shower," he's saying, "and a cot, if you would nap. Fresh clothing will be fetched, but later, later." Laying the empty boots one atop the other, his hands, the pale backs of them rumpled with blue veins, wrap themselves about her bare feet worn, creased, reddened and stained from those black boots. "Coffee?" he says as he strokes them, holds them, warms them. "Tea? A pastry, or an omelet?" Brushing with a fingertip the silvery gold-tinged ring about a toe. "Liquor, cocaine, hashish?"

Ysabel lets out a smoke-wreathed laugh, and leans forward to tip ash into the glass dish. Sitting back she lifts a foot from his hands, swinging it out and up, hiking up her knee to hook it over the arm of the chair. Leaning on the other arm she tips her matted hair out of her face. "What would you have of me," she says.

"Oh my lady Bride," he says, and he lets go her other foot. "What I would've had of you, had you not," and then, sighing, he stands. "Had things gone according to plan." Stepping back. "The King was to have," and his eyebrows lift, "returned, in three weeks' time. The turning of the year, when the sun is passed from archer to goat, and the wheel turns from sun to Saturn, and up comes a man, dancing, his body all over hair like a boar's, and his teeth like roof-beams; he holds a cattle-goad, and catches fish." He half-sits on the corner of the desk. "And at that moment, with you quickened, but not yet realized, I'd've stepped in and bound you about in such a ceremony," spreading his hands, a shrug. "A ring, a dress as white as snow, and flowers, mountains of flowers, in this dead of winter. Pale roses," he says, "pinks and yellows, and white, of course."

She leans forward, to tip more ash into the dish. "White roses," he says, "and then four walls, and a daily routine, a career, if you'd needed one. Real estate, perhaps. You could have been kept on the cusp for years. Decades." He brushes nothing from his knee, then stands, steps around to the other side of the desk. "But it seems," he's saying, "the rules are less stringent than I'd been led to believe. They always are, of course;" he stands there, his back to her, arms folded before him, "the question's always whether the other players are also aware of this fact." He looks down, not quite back at her. "I blame myself, you must understand. I miscalculated. There's no other word for it."

"The wedding's off," says Ysabel, her voice a flatly cautious thing.

"Oh, there'll be a small ceremony. A few close friends. Business associates. Tonight, of course; it's Saturn's day, after all." Turning, smiling. "Short notice, but they'll take my calls. For this, they'll rush to pick up the phone. We'll settle on some mutually agreeable location, a well-appointed room, we'll say a few words, then lay you out upon the table, take up our forks, and eat the very essence out of you." He picks up the ivory-handled knife from the desk, bounces it once, in his hand, "So," he says, slipping it into a pocket. "Fresh clothing, soon, new shoes, and in the meanwhile, if there's anything you need – Mr. Charlock and Mr. Keightlinger should be done, by now. Let them know."

He opens the door, stops there, a hand on the knob. "I take the fact you haven't asked me what I'm to be called as a sign that, you understand – this is strictly business. Nothing personal to it, at all."

He closes the door. The sound of the lock, turning. It's some time before she leans forward to snub out the half-smoked cigarette, and then sits back, in that chair, behind that desk.

Sunlight, bright & clear – his First, his Second his Particular end – the Least little Thing

Sunlight bright and clear pours through snow-dusted branches, through leaded glass, through venetian blinds lowered but louvered open, striking sharply from the silvery coffee pot, the spoons, the fork laid on a pristine white plate, the untouched glass of tomato juice, the upright console of the telephone, silver and black. Black cords plugged here and there wound together into a single hank that dangles over to the bulky headset clamped about his ears, over the unruly dreadlocks, a dully fuzzed white touched with gold. "I've no doubt of it, Welund," he says. Somewhere in the room a toy piano's tinkling a line of a fugue beneath a sticky chorus of saxophones. "But do recall," he says, "this career as coinsmith and debt-minter's but a hobby? You serve the court as lawright, first and foremost. Forge me a thing of clauses and parentheticals that I might use to cut away this ludicrous guarantee." His crisp shirt salmon-colored, with collar and cuffs of smooth pale blue. His fitted boxers blue printed with a pattern of little dogs and fishes. "Nevertheless," he says. Sipping black coffee from a thin bone china cup, careful of the microphone. His other hand he's pointing to the map pinned up over the sideboard, touching an intersection in Northeast, sliding west and north, up and along the horn of the city above the river, stopping just short of St. Johns. "I understand that," he says, "I do." The slender man standing next to him wears a blue suit tight over broad shoulders, and his pink tie's so pale it's almost white, and he reaches past Agravante, over the river, to tap another intersection, in Northwest, near a little blob of color that says Civic Stadium, not more than a block from the long clear line of Burnside.

"Our situation," says Agravante, leaning over the table then, the platter of scrambled eggs, the dish of salsa picada, the tortilla warmer, "is, to use your word, fluid. Liquidity is called for." He lifts a thin tube from a rack of them, each capped with cork and sealed with dark blue wax, each sparkling with threads of golden dust. He hands it to the man in the tight blue suit, who nods, then leaves, stepping past another man, younger, his pale hair elaborately braided, his sweater a pattern of jagged, angular blues. "Hold a moment, Welund," says Agravante, tilting the microphone away from his mouth. "Well?"

"Returned to his temple with the last of the snow," says the man in the sweater. "Since dawn. Hasn't left."

"But where was he between here and there?" says Agravante, quietly.

"We don't yet know."

After a moment Agravante tilts the microphone back. "Welund?" he says. "I need to – I must go.

"Yes, they've been sent. All three. If there's a response –

"If there's a response.

"And a good morning to you." He presses a button on the phone, then opens a green binder there by the rack of glass tubes, and the fiendish little basket-box, carved from a single chunk of dark red wood. He takes up a pen. "Forget the Duke," he says, scribbling an amount on a check, signing it with a broad flourish. Folding the check precisely along its perforations and ripping it neatly loose. "This to the American bank," he says, "not the Trapezuntine. Exchange it for fiat money."

"But the snow," says the man in the sweater, taking the check.

"Find one that is open," says Agravante. He plucks up another tube from the rack. "Then take the valuta to a store, and purchase bicycles."

"Bicycles," says the young man.

"As many as that will buy. At least a dozen. You'll need the truck."

The man in the sweater takes the tube, and nods, and leaves. Agravante turns back to the phone, punching in a number. "Tell me you've found her," he says, into the microphone, and then, looking toward the door, frowning, he bellows, "Where are my trousers?"

The crash of a gong as he opens the door. He holds it open so she might push past him, knapsack slung from her shoulder, bat in her hand, into a foyer stacked with boxes. To the left a pinched doorway, more boxes and stuffed garbage bags piled up to either side. He follows her into a showroom lit by what daylight makes it through the dusty windows lining the one wall. More boxes yet line the other, and more garbage bags, and a rolled rug set on one end and a plump sofa piled with coats and other clothes, a stool leaned against it, a table upended, and laid against them a stack of paintings, the foremost a sheet of black velvet in a baroque frame, pricked with unlit stars, smeared with spaceships in a blur of battle. And the floor before them empty but for scraps of paper, a blue silk rose, a scatter of tickets, all of them red and not one torn in half, the remains of an orange clay bowl smashed there, under the window.

"This doesn't," says Marfisa, turning about in her sheepskin jacket, and "I know," says the Mason, rubbing the back of his neck. "It looks like," she says, and "I know," he says. She strides to the front corner, pulls from the window a sign, holding it up. Orange letters on black say For Rent. "So where's Miss Cheney?" she says, putting it back.

"Your questions," says a sour croak of a voice, "I don't have to answer." She's there, by the counter at the back of the showroom, a fleecy pullover the color of plaster dust, her yellow hair held back by a black band, and cradled in her arms a little rabbit.

"Why?" says the Mason.

"She broke her bond," says Miss Cheney. "To city, brother, court and Queen. Your questions?" She's nodding. "That was your first."

The Mason opens his mouth, looks away, snapping it shut. "You're breaking your bond," says Marfisa, and a gesture toward the boxes, the bags, the furniture stacked. "Where do you mean to go?"

"I'm breaking nothing," says Miss Cheney. "I'll still take the questions of those who care to find me. Case in point."

"Jo was here," says the Mason. "You gave her answers."

"Can't answer what isn't asked," says Miss Cheney.

"What did you," says the Mason, and "Luys," says Marfisa, and he holds up a hand, "when you spoke to her," he says, "to Jo, what did you see?"

"I didn't see anything," says Miss Cheney. "That was your second."

"That's not what he meant!" snaps Marfisa.

"You think I *want* to leave?" cries Miss Cheney, squeezing the rabbit rigid to her chest. "Is that it? I *love* this city. You dolts." Turning away, letting the rabbit scrabble from her arms to the countertop.

"Then help us," says the Mason. "Please."

"We all want the same thing," says Marfisa.

"Do we," says Miss Cheney.

"What did you," says the Mason, and *"Luys,"* says Marfisa, quickly, "think. Carefully. Ask her – ask where we must go, to find Ysabel. Today! To find her today."

"What did you learn – "

"Luys!"

" – from answering the Huntsman's questions that has frightened you so?"

And Marfisa closes her eyes.

"The Mooncalfe," says Miss Cheney, stepping away from the counter, "has taken the Queen, and means to sell her to the highest bidder he can find." Her hand out, brushing the wall of boxes with her fingers.

The Mason smiles, relieved. "Then somehow, this once, you are wrong, Miss Cheney. The Queen is safe at Goodfellow's; her son, the Prince, is returned, and took her there himself. The Duke – "

"She doesn't mean Duenna," says Marfisa.

"But," says the Mason, "the Queen," and then, a hand to his mouth, "oh."

Miss Cheney says, "Even if I might answer a fourth question, or a fifth, about where or who or when," the sound of her fingertips sweeping down cardboard, "don't think for a moment I could. The geis only goes so far."

"Melanchlœnidon," says the Mason.

"There can't," says Marfisa, "there can't be that many wizards in the city. We could – "

The gong sounds, and as they all look to the pinched doorway framed in stacks of boxes and bags "Hail me!" cries a voice. "Hail and blast me, in a breath." From the foyer steps a figure in a shapeless grey jacket, a long dark skirt, and his black hair long and straight, and his feet bare. "I went back to her," says Orlando, the Mooncalfe, "I let her stay, she stayed, and I killed her," marching the length of the showroom, "I killed her, and she would not die." Past the Mason, past Marfisa staring. "I slew her father, and the snows came, just as you said, so tell me," the Mason lunging after him, "where do I," the Mason grabbing his arm, his shoulder, hauling back, to the side, the Mooncalfe stumbling swung into the wall of windows shivering crash.

"Hold!" cries the Mooncalfe, arms up before his face, the Mason pulling a flare of light in that dim room his sword back for a thrust and Marfisa grabbing his elbow, "Luys!" she shouts. He holds. She doesn't let go. "He knows," she says.

"By my troth," says the Mooncalfe, "I do not."

"You all want the same thing," says Miss Cheney, and then, stalking back to the counter, "One blow lands and I'll *find* a goddamn King to exile the lot."

"Where is the Bride," says Marfisa, her hand still in the crook of the Mason's arm still cocked, the tip of his blade aimed squarely for the Mooncalfe's throat, that's bulging in a swallow. "I let her go," he says, the one eye blinking.

"Just like that," says Marfisa.

"You said you killed her," says the Mason, his voice gone rough.

"Gloria," says the Mooncalfe. Shaking his head. "Suzette. Don't worry. She's fine." He reaches out to push the Mason's blade aside. "If I might be about my business," he says.

"You," says Miss Cheney, comforting her rabbit, "you have questions."

"Oh, I do," says the Mooncalfe. Marfisa's let go of the Mason's arm. "Orlando," she says. The Mason's lowering his sword. "Will I ever see my blades again?" says the Mooncalfe.

"No," says Miss Cheney.

"Barely a knight," murmurs the Mooncalfe. "Down to my spurs."

"Orlando," says Marfisa. "Please. Ask about the Bride. The, the Queen."

His bare feet whisk him aimlessly out into the middle of the room. "Will I," he says, then, "no – I'll raise the stakes. Will anyone in this room ever kneel before another King?"

"Not a one," says Miss Cheney.

The Mooncalfe lifts up his smiling face, and the Mason looks down at his empty hands. "Orlando," says Marfisa, once more. "Ysabel. Please. You let her go, you left her, alone? Your third. Please. Ask – I beg you. Ask where we must go to find her. To help her."

"Help," says the Mooncalfe. "The Princess. Surely," turning his back to her, "surely she might help herself. My third!" Sweeping away from them down to Miss Cheney, the little rabbit in her arms. "I've closed the door on the King, all Kings. I've cut the last rose from its cane and left its petals in the snow. I will not be forgotten. So. Answer me," and he closes his eyes, "where must I go to meet my particular end?"

And Miss Cheney, the rabbit clutched rigid to her chest, opens her mouth to speak.

A mechanical cursive, the letters slender, spells out Crown Imperial between two simple windows above and below in the buff-colored wall. The window above festooned with Christmas lights blinking red and red and green. The building's a long and shallow U-shape enclosing a parking lot rutted and marred by sludgy dikes of melting snow, and in the shrinking shadow of the stubby eastern wing a litter of snowmen no higher than a knee, or a shin, some with the twigs that were their arms already fallen to the ground, one with a top hat askew on its slumping head-shape, and water dripping everywhere, from eaves and steps and sills. In the middle of the lot stands Jo her hand up against the brightening sunlight, peering at the numbers next to doors shadowed by walkways and awnings. "Over there," says Roland, pointing across and up. "Okay," says Jo. Sword slung from her shoulder, mask in her hand, she sets off across the lot boots crunching and splashing to mount the sidewalk and then one of the long lines of stairs. Roland follows, his steps long swoops from one island and bank of snow to another, careful of the meltwater.

Jo presses a yellowing plastic doorbell taped to the frame under black metal numbers, 1917, and when Roland catches up to her she presses it again. Clack of the handle under her thumb, croaking wrench of the hinge as she opens the screen door, props it with a boot, leans in to rap on the front door, and there's footsteps on the other side, rattle and thunk of locks. The mane of the mask in her hand shivers and ripples. The front door opens. Becker's wrapped in a maroon robe, over pyjamas in a Stewart Dress tartan. "Jo?" he says.

"I, ah, tried the bell," she says.

"It doesn't, yeah, I've been meaning to replace that," he says.

"I tried to call," she says. "Before we, headed over here."

"We, well, I guess I was busy," says Becker. Taking in the sword she's carrying, and the quivering mask. "Am."

"Can we, oh, this is, Roland," nodding over at Roland beside her. "Hi," says Becker, without stepping back, without opening the door any further. "Can we come in?" says Jo. "It's important. About Ysabel. You, remember Ysabel. Right?"

"Of course I remember Ysabel," says Becker.

"Okay," says Jo. "It's hard, sometimes. Knowing what you remember."

"I remember Ysabel."

"But you remember forgetting, right?" she says, and he shifts at that, a short step back, a quick look back over his shoulder. "You remember the party? Thursday? Thanksgiving?"

"The old accustomed feast," he says, and then, "I think, it's not a good time, really, so, if you could," and Roland's putting a bicycle-gloved hand on Jo's shoulder, there by the hilt of her sword, "Jo," he says, as Becker's saying "I'd really appreciate" and then she says "Pyrocles," and they all stop.

"Pyrocles," she says again.

And Becker asks, "What does that have to do with Ysabel?"

"Can we come in?" says Jo.

He steps back, and opens the door wide.

The living room inside is coolly dim, blue carpet, white walls blued in the light that drifts through gauzy curtains drawn. A piano ringing softly from little speakers on a low shelf, and if they ask if I've seen Casablanca, someone's singing, I'll answer a resounding no. "Ysabel's missing," says Jo, "and, we're looking for her. And I got this clue, this, which," and she stops, hand to her head, and takes in a deep breath, "it was, I went to the wrong one first. And I thought meant I listened to the Duke when I shouldn't have, because I went where he said to go first, but that doesn't make any sense because then I went where I would've gone first if he hadn't which was Guthrie's, to talk to his girl-friend, who couldn't have helped me even if I *had* gone there first because she can't see this stuff anyway, and you have no idea what it is I'm talking about." The mane of the mask in her hand lashes out, the ends of it pattering against the low glass-topped coffee table there by her knee. "It's been the two of you, all this time, is the thing," Jo's saying, "even before all this, before you got promoted, but then, that night, it was both of you who went with us, me and Ysabel, to Goodfellow's house, and then the boar hunt, and the church, and when the Duke said to ask whoever I wanted to his, to that feast, I called you, I called both of you, just the two of you." She looks at Becker then, his robe gone darkly purple in the dim room. "But it was Guthrie's I went to first, last night, and that was the wrong one. I should've come here."

"I don't," says Becker, eyes wide, mouth pinched.

"It could be anything," says Jo. "Something you saw, some-thing you remember. Something you're about to say." He doesn't say anything. She's looking about. "Something in this room." On the glass tabletop, a phone, two coffee cups, a white paper bag, the bottom of it translucent with grease. "The least little thing. Could be enough to, to get us to. The next step." Becker blinks, looks down, away. "To finding her," says Jo. "Ysabel."

"I," says Becker, and his jaw trembles. Roland a dark shape in the open doorway, sunlight behind him, and the drip and trickle of melting snow. "Jo," he says.

"Wait," she says, a crack running through the word.

Becker lets out the breath he's holding, blinks quickly, eyes shining, and asks, "What's Pyrocles?"

"I think I can help," says someone else, and they look up, look around, turn. He's there in the passageway leading further back into the apartment, tall, grey dress slacks and a blue and white striped shirt half-open over his blackly furred chest, his hair an untidy mop of black curls. "Sorry," he says. "I overheard a little of that. Well. Most of it."

"Help," says Jo, and "David?" says Becker, his voice gone far away.

"That call, I had to take?" says the tall man to Becker. "The day job. Well. The twenty-hour hour a seven-day job." He sucks his teeth. "I don't know where the Bride is," he says, to Jo, "but," and he holds up the phone in his hand, a platter of black glass in a white frame. "I'm pretty sure I know where she *will* be. Tonight."

"Bride?" says Becker.

"She's the Queen, now," says Jo.

"Even so," says David Kerr.

A SUIT OF WORSTED WOOL – HE IS AS HE DOES
THE GIRL IN HER HAND – COMPANY

A SUIT OF WORSTED WOOL, grey sheened through with threads of black, and a crisp white shirt, there by the front door. He's looking at the watch on his wrist, a heavy silver nest of gears and dials, the numbers and hashes picked out in something that gleams like mother-of-pearl. His sun-browned head's quite bald, his cheeks dusted with white stubble. Out in the middle of the big front room a sword upright, the hilt of it wrapped in leather yellowed with long handling, and the floor where it's been thrust is singed in a neat black circle. The window's empty, the fireplace dark and cold, swept clean. From somewhere further, deeper in the house, a tumble of plucks and picks, flurried strums, mandolin, banjo, a guitar or two. He's looking at his watch again.

A door swings open over across the room, a glimpse of kitchen beyond as Lymond steps through, wide eyes and maybe a grin, plain white T-shirt and bone-colored chinos and his shock of pinkish orange hair, wiping his hands on a floury towel. "Good afternoon, my lord," says the man in the suit, but Lymond says sharply, "Welund," and his maybe grin is gone. "We must find a way to live together, or we won't."

The man in the suit purses his lips. "If it regards your mother's house," he says, "once the question of succession's settled, we might discuss what must – "

"There's nothing to discuss," says Lymond.

"It is possible, perhaps," says Welund, weighing each word, "your highness does not realize the monies needed to keep such a house – "

"I've seen the house," says Lymond. "What's required's some brooms and buckets, lumber, some plaster, some paint, knowledge and time, and hands. Money's but one way this stuff is put to work."

"And the owr you'll need?" Welund spreads his hands, inclines his head. "Everything I've done was for the good of the city, and the court, without a King for so long – and now, with every conceivable respect to you, to your mother, your – sister, but. The line is broken. I saw it myself. We have no Queen."

"You're wrong, Welund, and everything you've done, was wrong." Lymond drapes the towel over his shoulder. "There's always a King, and always, always a Queen. You must have faith."

"Faith does not fill coffers," says Welund.

"How useful, that excuse," says Lymond. "What we wouldn't do to fill those blasted coffers." Turning toward the empty fireplace, there by the sword in the floor. "And if the coffers prove inconveniently full, well. All that must be done is tip one over yourself, to call upon its power." That music's stopped. There might have been a patter of applause. Welund's frowning, there by the door, "I don't," he says, "take my lord's meaning..."

"This peace, Goodfellow treasures;" says Lymond, careful of the charred floor about the sword, "I've nothing but the utmost respect. And this sword! You know the story? How Marfisa struck it here, a single blow, threw everything away – the court, the Queen, her love," and his hand closes lightly about the hilt of it. "Merely to keep my sister safe from any hint of insult." Looking up, to Welund there by the door. "But that's not it, either." His grip shifts, tightens. Feet braced. "But one thing stays my hand, Welund. From ripping this sword from the floor and striking your head from your shoulders. And that's that I do not know, to a certainty, that you were the one to unleash the Mooncalfe."

"Highness," says Welund, as he tries to settle on an expression, "I can assure you, I would never," and he catches his hand from reaching for the door. "The Mooncalfe, my lord!" That hand lifted to his shoulder, his chest, pressed flat. "He is as he does!"

And Lymond says, "It's interesting, Guisarme, to me, that you haven't drawn a weapon."

The hand on his chest now a fist, Welund, "Nor you yours."

Lymond says, "My hand is stayed," and he lets go the hilt. "Would you like some bread?" And there under his bulging eyes a flash of teeth, his grin.

"Bread," says Welund.

"Baguettes," says Lymond. "For tomorrow? I thought, a light repast, crostini or bruschetta. Maybe just some olive oil, and good sea salt."

"My lord is baking bread."

"Well." Lymond's grin slips wryly sideways. "Mostly I'm staying out of the way. They say," he holds up his hands, "I don't have a feel for the kneading. I will see you there?"

"Of course, my lord," says Welund, and now his hand's on the knob.

"Good," says Lymond. "Good."

Wrapped in glass, in steam, in streaming water, lilting slightly, side to side, one hand held up and out, and the crusts and streaks that glitter her arms, her breast, her belly, that filigree her thighs and knees are crumbling, darkening, melting away, and the water splashing about her feet's a cloudy grey, larded with ropes of black. She leans back to let the shower soak her hair, that one hand still held up out of the water, a hand still spangled with gold that warmly gleams in the wet white light, burnished, dazzling, a shape of light too bright to look at as flashes pop and spark in her hair, yellow and gold and orange, pink and white along her skin, stars that shining burn and one by one flicker and dim and die. She's turning under the water, holding that hand under it, and the last of it washes away, the water running grey and gritted black along her arm.

A thick white robe about her, her hair done up in a towel. Behind her the door closes, and the sound of the lock, turning. Clothing's draped over the desk, drifts of white that shine under the stark light of that white-shaded banker's lamp, lawn and lace and satin, taffeta, a cloudy hillock of crinoline, and there on the floor a line of shoes, slender foot-shapes balanced tip-toe on delicate heels of various heights, thin sandal-straps of white and silver and grey lolling emptily. She nudges them aside with a foot, reaches into the pile on the desk with a clink of hangers, a crinkle of paper and plastic wrap slitherly settling as she tugs something free, white fur ivoried as she pulls it from the circle of light, a long coat of it, the skirts lopping softly from desk to floor, the lining of it a chilly grey.

The light from the desk lamp's washed away when she yanks open the heavy curtains. The fogged glass filled a richly blue that shades through white to yellow and red and an orange, and only a simple latch at the top of the sash. She turns it with a solid thunk, and presses up against the frame, and with a shudder the window lifts, a suck of air in the gap and she hisses, then hoists it up with a rattle in the frame, counterweight scraping inside the wall. Ducking her head she leans out, seven storeys up or eight, the street below gleaming wetly in the shadows, and beads of snow strung along the gutters. The face of the building off to the left of yellow brick glowing and glass ablaze in the sunset torching the hills off to the right, the block ahead across the street a parking lot nearly filled, and lining the sidewalks on all four sides of it carts and kiosks, placards, sandwich boards, the steam of cookpots and griddles, the smoke of grills, and lights strung in the bare branches of the trees here and there, and knots of people bundled in coats and hats, scarves, stocking caps, at the corner, before this stand or that, and laughter, and a cry, someone calling someone else's name. She opens her mouth, as if to say something, to call out, but only the tattered wisp of her breath, a sigh. She leans her elbows on the sill, her face flushed in the light, shadows staining the robe. "Any more than the sun is the sun," she says to herself. She shivers, and the shiver becomes a shudder. She pulls herself back inside.

The thick white robe in a heap on the floor below the window. The white fur draped over the pale leather top of the desk, and the rest of all that clothing pushed to the edge of it, and over, and "Each of each," she's singing to herself, a whisper, if that. "Exactly where." Sitting on the fur, hands on her knees, head hung low, damp hair a pendulum, drifting. Hands on her thighs now, goosefleshed. The window before her's still opened wide. She lifts her head, her shoulders, eyes closed, her lips moving around a word, words she doesn't voice. Lifting a foot to plant a heel on the fur, a hand on her upraised knee, the other between her thighs, thumbing the sprigs of black hair there, her other hand to her mouth now, her lips, her teeth against her lip, her breath quick in and out through her nostrils now and her lips parting, her finger drawn between them wetted, slicked with spit. Lowering her hand her jaw set, shoulders set, rocking now back and forth to the beat of her heart, the squeeze of her lungs, a hiss, a grunt, rocking and a slap of flesh, her mouth in what might be a snarl, a sneer, her eyes opening on that window full of deepening sky.

The window, open, dark, the lamp at an angle, the bare desk. The piles of clothing fallen softly over the tumbled line of shoes. A tongue of white fur there, crumpled to the floor, over around behind the desk she's kneeling on it, slumped to one side elbow on her knee, fur clenched in one hand, dangled hair brushing the broken glass about her. The cabinet's sagging broken against the wall. A scatter of dolls, figurines splayed, a woman with a cabled mechanical leg red-lensed goggles and a sledgehammer balanced on her shoulders, a schoolgirl arm akimbo on her kilted hip and black boots and a patch over one eye, a swordswoman fixed mid-lunge in fiercely tangled ribbons and her own long yellow hair, a cowgirl guns cocked chapped legs spread as if to sit on something that isn't there. A shiver tremors down the length of her, ending as an absent tic of her foot. The girl in her hand wears a cat-eared helmet and a silver maillot and her long-socked leg's kicked high as if to climb onto something. She sets it down precariously next to a blocky toy scooter and picks up another, a schoolgirl weirdly slender in a tight orange jacket and a flippy little skirt, and dark stockings stretched along elongated thighs, tossing off an arch salute. A thump at the door, the lock rattling, turning. She tips the doll over, fingering a long brown plastic ponytail. The door bangs open, "The hell," says someone, and then "Shit!" and a bustle into the room, it's the little guy in the black suit, feet catching in the clothing strewn and a crash into the desk, "Shit" again, and he's reaching for the open window when he sees her there, and stops dead. "What happened," he says. The tuft of hair between his brown and the top of his skull uncurled, standing up and out. "It's *freezing* in here." He shuts the window. She rolls onto her back, a clink and crunch of glass. "That was stupid," he says, rubbing his forehead.

"It's not as if I could fly away," she says.

"You can, you could fall," he says. The doll in her hand. Her hand on her belly. Her wet hand, the edge of it gashed shining yellow and white, and her forearm webbed to the elbow in glistening trickles. "You need a bandage," he says.

"I won't run dry," she says. "Besides. It's not what he wants. This?" Sitting up, holding up her hand. "This he could get from any of us."

"Does it hurt?"

"Of course it hurts," she says. "But it's the last time it ever will. Let me enjoy it."

The doll, dropped to the fur. "Do you," he says, and then, "I," and then, "We're leaving soon. You, you'll need to put something on."

"Why?" She rolls over onto her knees. "Why put something on," pushing herself to her feet, "only to take it all off again shortly thereafter?"

"It's – cold?" he says.

She takes up the fur and shakes it out, a tumble of dolls, a clatter of shards. "I'll wear this," she says, slipping an arm into a sleeve, settling it about her shoulders, the skirts of it twirling about her calves. Opening it, holding it open, the grey silk shining behind her. "What do you think?"

"You really," he says, "made a mess of things."

"I didn't like the way they looked," she says.

He squats, he reaches out for the weirdly slender doll, her orange jacket, her arch salute. "It's kind of a weird thing to ask," he says, sitting back, without touching it. "But can I ask you a question?" In his other hand something wadded, a bit of fabric, blue and white.

"If I can ask one first," she says.

He laughs. "You know," he says, "I know how that works."

"Do you," she says. Hands on her bare hips. "Well?" she says.

"Mr. Charlock," says the big guy in the doorway.

"I might," he says. "I might just."

"Mr. Charlock." Black suit, bush of a beard the color of polished mahogany. In his hands a stainless steel thermos. "The car. It's time."

"Yeah," says Mr. Charlock, stuffing the wadded cloth back in a pocket. "Okay." Reaching out to her. "I might've let you," he says. She's shaking her head. "I wouldn't," she says. She takes his hand. "I gave my word. I told you. I've given up."

"Right," says Mr. Keightlinger, in the doorway. "Check."

"Uh," says Mr. Charlock, as they step around the desk. "You might want some shoes."

"No," says Ysabel.

The walls tiled with old album jackets, duotones in yellows and reds of elaborately coiffed women sitting at pianos, smiling men snapping fingers, whole bands at feverish work on darkly crowded stages. Out in the middle of the room a big round table covered in green felt, and little stacks and piles of nuts and washers here and there about the edge of it, and by each pile two cards face down, and the rest of the deck there by a plastic tub that says Aunt Ruby's Peanuts in faded letters. Out in the middle of the table more washers grey and dull red and hex nuts, square nuts, wing nuts all in a heap by four cards in a line face up, the six and jack of diamonds, the five of clubs, the ace of spades. "The hell you been boy," says the old man in a rumpled blue suit much too big for him, sitting up in the recliner there laid almost flat. His face blotched with pale pink.

"Out," says Frankie. "Dragged all the way across town, suited up to march back, and then I fell asleep in a tub in a house full of clowns." He's standing in the doorway there to the side of the closed garage door. "And then I had to fucking *walk* back." The old man yawps at that. "Sorry," says Frankie. "I couldn't find a, a bus, because it *snowed*. And I swear, sorry, I was halfway here, before I even thought to take the kit off? I mean it's basically garbage, right? All those fucking stovepipes and shit." Picking at the shreds of duct tape still glued to the shoulder of his jacket. "Sorry. Where is everybody? Where's Gordon?"

The old man's lying back down in the recliner. "Company," he croaks, waving a careless hand.

Across the alley steeped in evening light, the crunch of dead grass and ice, the squonk of the single hinge, the gate hung drunkenly. Up the tuffeted lot high fences to either side of the old brick building there, and there at the back door Frankie stops. A muffled chug of drums, a piano rattling up to a ringing hymn of an anthem, voices raised a shout and an impact that shakes the wall, the door in its frame, the knob in his hand, a smash of falling crockery. He throws open the door. A kitchen, scarred linoleum and darkly looming cabinets, a scuffle, the mouth of a pitcher underfoot edged in jagged shards and a grunt, one man bare muscled arms pushing an older man back, "Gordon!" yells Frankie, leaping into the fist at the end of one of those muscled arms swung to catch him knock him gasping to the floor. A heavy knife in the other fist, forearm against the chest of the older man grunting, another scuffle there by the yellow stove, "Frankie," calls the older man over one of those pale broad shoulders, reaching, and "Chill and still, everybody," says the big man in the tank top, turning the knife by Gordon's cheek. "Limpid." His cheeks dark with stubble, his hair slicked back.

"You let him alone," says Gordon. The radio on the shelf above his head's gone quiet, piano contemplative, the drums dropped away. Frankie's sitting up. A hand's offered, and he takes it, pulls himself up, careful of the small formica table, and the fourth man in the room, short and wide and bald. "Dogstongue?" says Frankie, looking from him to the man in the tank top and back again. The hand he took's about his wrist, and doesn't let go when he tugs.

"Hey, Swift," says the bald man.

"Due time," says the man in the tank top, and then, "Cobbler?"

"I give no drop," says Gordon, leaning away from that careless knife. "I take no pinch. Everyone knows this."

"Everyone's upended," says Swift. "He's come back, the King. We're passing the hat. The Hare's to be a banner now, and Tommy Tom will not go empty-handed to take it up."

"And domestics?" says Gordon. "Will you take your knife to knock at every cupboard door?"

Swift pushes close, the stove behind them scraping the floor, "The hell," says Frankie, yanking, as Dogstongue grabs his other hand and says, *"Swift."*

"Nothing's changed," says Gordon, "not anything real. Nothing at all. You want more than spit from me, you best get ready to cut."

"Domestics," says Swift, "clods and hobs," and stepping back turning the knife in his hand arcing up, "Swift!" cries Dogstongue one more time as Frankie tries to pull away again, as the knife comes down a thunk and Frankie jerks, looking down at the hand on the hilt of the knife in his chest. "Let 'em give," says Swift, "if they would get!" Muscles bulge, he twists and rips the knife free. The blade of it dark with blood. "I," says Swift, face falling.

"He's not," says Dogstongue, struggling with a sinking Frankie knees buckling jacket lapping open over his yellow shirt welling blood.

"I didn't," says Swift. "I thought."

"He's mortal," says Dogstongue, letting Frankie slump. "Was."

"I had no," says Swift, waxy pale beneath his stubble. "Idea," he says to Gordon. Beads rattle. The piano's found its footing again, banging up a fanfare over the bubbling bass. Dogstongue's gone. Gordon shaking steps away from the stove and Swift leaps back, over Frankie's legs, catching himself on the doorframe, ducking through the beaded curtain pattering, away. Gordon kneels, reaching for Frankie's face, his open eyes. The DJ's saying something about the weather.

SKY BRIDGE, THEATRE, ACCESSIBLE ROUTE
THE SECOND SIGN, & THE THIRD – "LOOK, BEHOLD" – EXIT

SKY BRIDGE, THEATRE, ACCESSIBLE ROUTE, white letters on a blue sign hung in a counterbalanced assemblage of white poles leaning away from each other on the brick-paved corner. He's wearing a trench coat over a black suit, bow tie crooked beneath his chin, dark curls shellacked, he's looking along Second and then up and down Salmon, then at the watch on his wrist, heavy and gold. Behind him a couple of escalators rise to the glass-walled lobby that ceils this little plaza, this bit of garden, and over there on a plinth a great homolosine map of the world unfolded, stylized continents shaped in chrome, and the letters beneath it say World Trade Center. Enormous snowflakes of yellow-white lights dangle among the white poles and columns that brace and frame the glass above. He steps away down the sidewalk, past signs in dark windows that say Washington Federal, Invested Here, Right-size your Loan, and a green sigil of a long-tressed woman, crowned with a single star. A block away across the street a couple of figures, pale coat, green jacket and a flash of silver. He lifts a hand to beckon, once. Absently shaking his head.

Jo leads the way as they come over, in one hand her sword in its scabbard, in the other the mask, the mane undulating gently behind her. Roland's gloved hands are empty, his head bare, his blue and white headphones down about his neck. "You're cutting it close," says Kerr, shooting his cuff to show his watch. "Less than an hour left. There's already some caterers or something setting up."

"Okay," says Jo, looking past him along Second, the other corner there, the snowflake lights, then over down Taylor. Her breath a ragged banner. "Where do we go? Where they coming in?"

Kerr says, "You're probably going to want people watching all three blocks – " but Jo says, "Where's the theater? The, auditorium or wherever, that this is going down?"

"Building Two," say Kerr, pointing down Salmon. Roland nods. "Okay," says Jo. "There's a front door?"

"You go up over the skybridge, the escalators back there," and Jo's saying, "A back door? Any other way in?"

"I," says Kerr, "don't know, there's a parking garage? A couple of elevators, some staircases – "

"Shit," says Jo.

Roland says, "You are the Huntsman; I'll be your mastiff and lymner, at once." He points down toward the escalators. "Station yourself at the front doors. I'll circle the blocks on the street, and sound the rechance when I spy them."

"The phone, you mean," says Jo.

"On the phone," says Roland.

"Hey," says Kerr.

"Okay," says Jo, "I don't like it, but okay." And as Kerr says, "Can I just," she heads off, toward the escalators, and Roland nods once, crisply, and jogs away across Salmon, ahead of a trundling white van. "Hello?" says Kerr. "Still talking, here?" Eyes rolling, he sets off after Jo. Off a couple of blocks away somebody whoops, ah-yi-hee, Shaw*nee!* "Hey," calls Kerr, "hey!" Jo stops there at the foot of the narrow escalators tocking quietly, regularly up and down. "You have any idea," says Kerr, "how far out on a limb I am for you?"

"Sure, thanks," says Jo, turning back toward the escalators, "but that's hardly my" and "Dammit!" he snaps, lunging for her arm. "You half-ass this thing and you'll get yourself killed, or worse. And your Queen."

"Let go of me," says Jo.

About and behind them white columns depend aslant from the glass canopy above to meet butt ends braced against each other atop stubby concrete pedestals. The snowflake lights among those boles hang still in the still air. "You think you know something," says Kerr, letting go. "You heard something, something the witch told you that makes you think you're going to win, no matter what. That's what this is."

"What?" says Jo, her sword in its scabbard held between them.

"That's not how it works," he says, and she's saying "What are you" as he says, "Prophecy! That's not," and both hands up to his forehead pressing his hair back. "The first duty of prophecy is to be true, no matter what. Ibis redibis nunquam in bello morieris, okay? So whatever you think you heard, it's not – "

"What I heard," says Jo, "is what you said. You got the call from the guy who said to tell the mayor he's got the Perry girl and it's time to do what he said. Here. Tonight. Which means Ysabel's gonna be here. In about an hour." The mask dangling from her other hand, the mane of it straining back, past her, toward the rising steps. "That's what I think I know," she says. "That's what this is about. Did I hear wrong? Misinterpret?"

He's looking at his shoes, narrow and gleaming black. "I don't," he says, "it's not the mayor." Looking up. "I work for a commissioner – "

"Whatever," says Jo, turning away, stepping onto the escalator, a scuffle as he leaps after her, grabbing for her again, her coat, "Dammit," he's saying, "that *guy*," and a squeak of metal on leather, Jo's drawing her sword, he's stumbling back staggering down and away from the blade swiveling tip toward him, "he's a *sorcerer*, that guy," says Kerr, hands up, backing unsteadily down the rising steps, turning to hop off as Jo steps down behind, her sword-tip following him as he backs away, the mask dangling from her sword hand, the mane starkly black against her pale coat as it winds lashing about her arm. "You can't just – "

"You're a sorcerer, too," says Jo.

"More of a," says Kerr, "a tregetour, really – "

"So do some magic," she says, stepping lightly off the escalator, elbow crooked up, blade level, mask staring. "Stop me. Change my mind."

"That's not," he says, looking down. Shoulders hunched. "That isn't how it works."

"Okay then," she says, and sheathes her sword. The mane relaxing, falling about the mask a-dangle as she steps back onto the escalator.

"You're gonna Butch and Sundance this," he says. "And you'll die. She'll die. And he gets exactly what he wants!" She doesn't look back. "For fuck's sake," he says, "call Southeast! You're tight, you only have to *ask* and there'd be a dozen knights – "

"We broke up," she says, rising away.

The hand he's reaching after her curls in a fist, bobs there a moment, slams into the crawling handrail of the escalator. Turning away, shaking out his hand, he digs up the headset for a cellphone and clips it to his ear. "Hey," he says, walking away. "It's me. This thing tonight. I'm waving you off." Waiting at the corner as an SUV stretched to limousine length wallows by. "I got one of those bad feeling you pay me for," he says.

At the top of the escalator a blue sign hangs from one of the white beams there beneath the glass canopy. The numeral one's to the left, numerals two and three further on ahead, and a glyph of figures seated at a conference table, and two simple masks side by side, one smiling, one weeping. On ahead the airy lobby narrows to a bridge, glass walls tipped to lean against each other above, braced by angled files of white poles, lit by streetlight from below.

On the other side another sign, the numeral two to the left now, and three to the right, over another bridge. The lobby here's a low but open space, glass-walled, glass doors to the left, the room beyond but dimly lit, low steps, a baleful sign that says Exit, a dark conference room behind a floor-to-ceiling pane of glass. Movement in there, a shift of shadows lost in a welter of reflections and shadows. Jo walks on by, her pale coat, her sword in one hand, the mask in the other, and her wine-dark hair. Across the open lobby folding chairs grey and brown and tables unfolded, one of them strewn with the remains of a paper cornucopia, plastic vegetables, fake flowers, and then the leaning glass wall, more white poles criss-crossed and braced, the plaza below and the trees here and there strung with tiny white lights, the street and the river beyond. The mask in her hand is still, the mane hanging limply, rustling as she turns it over. The empty shadowed holes where eyes should be. The tooth-shapes crudely chiseled, lined with thick black ink.

She leans the sword in its scabbard against the railing.

The mane shivers, stiffening as she settles the mask on her head, then relaxes to float weirdly behind her, undulating as she turns, looking about the glass-walled lobby, then back out over the plaza, the street, the river. "Your banner, over the city," she murmurs, under those mask-teeth. "Me, by your side."

"Excuse me," says someone. The mane jumps. She turns with a jerk, reaches up to tilt the mask back, clearing her eyes. The man there under the blue sign's short and thick, his black tuxedo blocky, his necktie plain and bottle green, tied in a wide Windsor knot, the boutonière in his lapel a tiny yellow rose. "There going to be a floor show?" he says. The scruff of grey about his chin too carefully trimmed to be forgotten stubble.

"I, ah," says Jo, and then, "you're, are you the mayor?"

A curt laugh. "No," he says.

"They'll," she points toward the glass doors, "let you in, I'm sure – "

"I know," he says. He nods at her hands. "No smoking up here."

She looks down at the crumpled orange pack she's holding, the lone cigarette within. "Yeah," she says. Her phone's ringing. "I know." She turns away, hauls the mask off, the phone up and out, "Hey," she says.

"They're coming," says Roland. "On foot, down the street. Three men and the Bride, and they're going to come up the escalator."

She tucks the phone away. The man's gone. Nothing's moving in the dimness past the glass doors. She lifts the mask, sets it back on her head. Takes up the sword in its scabbard and strides across the lobby to the mouth of the skybridge.

Movement, down there at the other end. A white hat clears the floor, rising with the escalator, white shoulders, a long white coat over a white suit, white shirt, white tie. Behind him rising as he steps off a little guy, black suit and a skinny black tie, and in his hands a stainless steel thermos. His hair thinned to a single curl between his brow and the top of his skull, an owl's feather dangling from one side of the classic black sunglasses he's wearing, and looming behind them both now a big guy, black suit and a skinny black tie swallowed by his bush of a beard, and the one lens of his classic black sunglasses swarming with spidery letters written in white ink. And leaning against him in a white fur coat, her head against his chest, stumbling as they step off the escalator, "Home, and safe, and sound," says Jo to herself, and she sets foot on the bridge.

Striding toward her Mr. Leir doffs his hat, his face quite young beneath that unruly white hair. "And who might you be," he calls.

"I am the Queen's Huntsman," says Jo, planting her feet, and Ysabel looks up as Jo draws her sword, letting the scabbard fall to the speckled grey industrial carpeting. "You need to let her go," pointing her sword at Mr. Leir, "and walk away," and Ysabel straightens, pushes a little away from Mr. Keightlinger, his arm still about her. Mr. Leir laughs and waves his hat at Mr. Charlock. "Look, behold," he says, "a whirlwind in a bottle, a great cloud and a fire infolded from before the world was the world. Cold and empty and utterly inimical. If loosed it will swallow whatever it touches until it's sated, and eat up even the hole you leave when you're gone."

"Let her go," says Jo again.

"Jo," says Ysabel, ducking out from under Mr. Keightlinger's arm.

"Drop your sword," says Mr. Leir, "or he anoints your Queen, and pours what's left down your throat." Mr. Charlock, holding the mirror-bright thermos up, starts to unscrew the cap of it. The tip of Jo's sword wavers, shifting from Mr. Leir to Mr. Charlock and back again. "I'd rather do it myself," says Mr. Leir, "but eaten by us or this she will be done away with." He puts his hat back on his head, caressing the pinch, the curl of the brim. "You've lost, Jo Gallowglas," he says. "Drop your sword, walk away," and the rattle and clunk of Jo's sword hitting the carpet, and Mr. Leir nods. "Save yourself," he says, and then his head rocks back.

His head rocks back, his hat flies off, his arms flop up, unstrung. The dull pop an echoless crack enormous, the flash too quick, an afterthought. The smoke rising from the mouth of the flat black pistol in Jo's hand as it shifts to point to Mr. Charlock, the feathers bristling brown and black and white about his eyes, his mouth ajar in a wordless howl as torn pages gush into the air from the white coat flapping open beside him, fluttering, falling to the bridge in drifts about an empty pair of white and ivory brogues and with a flump behind them a glossy white wig, the acrylic hairs yellowed with old sweat.

Mr. Keightlinger stock still, Ysabel leaping forward through the falling pages, Mr. Charlock roaring lunging after her catching her arm hauling her up short between him and the gun. She swings a white-furred arm, thunk, "I will *eat you,*" he's screaming, "grind your bones to *salt,*" and the pistol in Jo's hand sweeps away from Ysabel struggling, wavers, fixes on Mr. Keightlinger holding his sunglasses up between his wide-open eyes and Mr. Charlock, whose face is wreathed in feathers. He's locked a hand on Ysabel's arm, the thermos loose cap rattling in the other. "This can still," he says, as if two or three voices are fighting for the words in his mouth, and then he roars. Ysabel hits him again pulling away, and feathers rustle as he looks down, frowning, at the blade-tip that's ripped a hole in his white shirt, knocking his tie aside. A good two inches poking out of his chest, just to the left of center.

A twist, and a jerk, and Roland pulls his blade from Mr. Charlock's body.

"Jo," says Ysabel. The pistol in Jo's hand is following Mr. Charlock's body as it slumps to the carpet. "Gallowglas," says Ysabel, there before her, reaching up to take the mask in her hands, the mane of it slumping as she lifts it from Jo's head. Jo lowers the pistol, blinking. "Kilo," says Mr. Charlock, a cough of those awful voices. On his hands and knees on the torn pages, feathers falling. "Kay," he says, and his arms buckle, and he falls to his side. Roland's swiveled his sword to point at Mr. Keightlinger quickly walking away, stuffing his sunglasses in the pocket of his jacket.

"Ysabel," says Jo, and the mask drops to the bridge, and Ysabel's arms around her white fur about her pulled close together, shivering.

Lights flickering on behind the glass doors, the jingle and clink of keys against glass, "Princess," says Roland, and then, "Majesty. Huntsman. We must go."

The top of the thermos, unscrewed, falls without a sound to the roughly speckled carpet. The stuff that seeps out hissing in wisps of white smoke crawling, curling, hard to make out in this light, roiling up suddenly, surging a gout of it sloshing into the rippling thickening air uncoiling reaching for Roland as he turns, frow

ickening rippling air as it whitens, flashes. Ysabel looking up, Jo stepping back, "The hell," she says.

On the other side of it Mr. Charlock crowned in feathers looks down at the uncapped silver thermos in his hand. "I didn't mean to," he says, turning away, "Keightlinger!" he calls. "Kay!"

"What *is* that," says Jo.

"Old," says Ysabel. "We must go."

That stuff swells and lops and spills more smoke into the air and "Dammit, Phil!" yells Mr. Charlock, and when he tries to step back he falls, his leg is caught, his foot already gone and he screa

ivering glass falls in sheets the cracking of it loud as gunshots shattering below that fills the street a wave of crashing sound pops sparks and flying lights that flicker and go out as Jo sits up Ysabel in white fur sprawled and coughing. "We've got to go," says Jo over the din, gathering herself.

"What *is* that," says Ysabel, taking Jo's hand, pulling herself up.

"Run?" says Jo. The boiling shape of smoke, yellowing, reddening, filling the space from carpet to glass to where the glass had been. Hand in hand they're stumbling running Ysabel looking to the closed glass doors across the lobby Jo pointing leaning toward the door ajar there, a glimpse of stairwell, a booming crash the floor thrumming wobbling knocking them Ysabel down to her knees and Jo tipping forward brought up short, falling back, rolling over the red smoke and black there filling swallowing the lobby and "Jo!" cries Ysabel white fur billowing hand wrenched away from hand and scrabbling to her feet pushing kicking lunging into the smoke screaming reaching for the last glimmering flickering scrap of white and her hand closing about, the lobby, dark, turning about in the, the glass walls leaned against each, and the white poles, the skybridge, and the, the columns, the streetlight from below, the stretch of speckled grey industrial carpet, the glass doors closed, the red glare of the Exit sign, the clear air quiet and still, the, the, the, she, and she, she stops.

A ways down the skybridge her sword, in its scabbard. There before her the skull-mask, the mane spread about in limp coils. In the hand she lifts with a jerk a pistol, the dull black barrel, the grip of it wound about with glossy black tape. She drops it in a pocket of her pale leather coat. Her other hand pressed to her chest rising and falling with her quickening, shallowing breath, her mouth, opening –

"Ysabel?" says Jo Maguire.

LAUGHTER, A WHOOP OF DELIGHT – SUNDAY MORNING

LAUGHTER, A WHOOP OF DELIGHT as they come across the darkly silent intersection, black parka, big green coat, hoodie over a nightgown leaping boots to clomp the last bit of snow in the gutter. On the wedge of sidewalk there across from the pizza place a mound of bicycles, tires fat and white, and skinny buff, ape-hanger bars over a comically tiny front wheel, banana seats glittering silver and gold, stumpy kid's bikes in medicinal pinks and blues. Wound about and through a thick chain and also lengths of yellow plastic tape printed with bold black letters, CRIME SCENE – DO NOT CROSS. Hung on the front of the pile by chain and tape a door ripped from a car, white with letters that say ND POLICE and a rose stenciled near the bottom. The woman in the nightgown bangs a tattoo on the door, whooping again, as the man in the parka finds a padlock on the chain and fits a key to it. The man in the green coat leans over to catch a loosening hank of chain. The woman in the nightgown takes the weight of the car door, helping it down the pile clatter and scrape.

Backing out of the cabinet under the sink he's hunched over rubbing the small of his back, grumble and whoof, settling on his knees on the lemon-yellow floor. He pulls from the cabinet a yellow tin that says Clabber Girl, and a white tin that says Guardsman Professional Strength, and a handful of rags. Reaching deep inside, thump and rattle, he pulls out a little red handheld vacuum cleaner, and then pulls himself to his feet, yawning, scratching himself under his loose blue shirt. He reaches a knobby bare foot into the cabinet to drag out a pair of salt-stained espadrilles, working in one foot, then the other, and taking up tins and vacuum and rags in his wide hands he shuffles out of the dark kitchen, down a long unlit hall creak and pop into a big room empty but for an overstuffed armchair, and a low table beside it and through a wall of glass the lights of the city beyond, below. He sets his stuff down and with a muttered growl reaches up to yank a pull chain and a low bulb flares above, banishing the city. Leaning down he takes up the yellow tin and tut-tutting, shaking his head, he sprinkles cornstarch over the stains that blot the cushions of the chair.

Eight people in the train car, all clustered there in the open space near the doors, each of them with a bicycle, hung from the racks, upended on back wheels, a sturdy mountain bike and a low dun brown recumbent, a couple of battered minibikes their frames gleaming under chipped and scored paint, a delicate ten-speed with drop handlebars. The clack and chunk of wheels on rails as the walls of a tunnel rise up and over them, and they pick up speed, and the woman with the recumbent bike opens her mouth to let out a low rumbling note. The man with one of the minibikes laughs and joins her, and the man with the luridly purple wheelie bike, the note becoming a syllable, the syllable a word, "Uncorrected personality traits," they're singing, a ragged, jagged harmony, "that seem whimsical in a child," and another joining in, and another, "may prove to be ugly in a fully grown adult," as the walls of the tunnel rush past.

Parked at an angle in the shallow curl of driveway a white panel van, the tail of it tucked under the open garage door, and light spilling out onto the shadowed scrap of yard. She opens the rear doors, then tugs her black vest down and back into place before with a scrape startling loud pulling a tray from the rack, lifting a corner of the towel draped over it to check the loaves, flat slipper-shapes darkly crusted. Careful in both hands she carries it up a short flight of steps into the kitchen, brightly lit, the lemon-yellow floor, the gleaming white cabinets. "One more of these," she says, wrestling it up onto the countertop, "and the butter into the fridge," and the man in the black vest and the bow tie just like hers nods and hands her a paper coffee cup. "Thank you," she says, and she turns to fill it from a great silver urn as he heads out the door to the garage.

"Here he comes!" someone cries, and the cheers go up across the parking lot, knots of people with their bicycles, and clustered around this pickup truck, that unmarked van. Men in suits of sky and Carolina, periwinkle, denim and Oxford, midnight, navy, all about the tailgate of a dark blue suv, reach up for the bicycles being handed down, all of them pink with the same swooping frames, and dotted with the same appliquéd flowers, yellow and white. Down there, past the closed dark gates, the cabin that says Oregon Zoo in letters up on the gable, up the arc of sidewalk along the lot a lone man in a long dark coat, his head bare, and his hair a pinkish orange pompadour. The sky above a pearly grey, and all the colors lurking within.

Flights of bicycles kick off skirling toward him, he waves, he nods, stepping into the lot and across it toward the crowd, toward the woman there in the black leather jacket and the long silvery dress of sequins, like mail, toward the man beside her in green coveralls that say Thomas Thomas over his left breast in neat black embroidery. "Marquess," says Lymond, and "Soames," shaking their hands, turning to find the Viscount there in a suit of Prussian blue, pale dreadlocks tied back neatly, and a pink bicycle up on his shoulder. "You must not think of me as a rival," he says to Lymond, and offers up his hand. "I'm only sorry you've been pushed to this extremity, and without a Queen." Lymond, slowly, takes his hand, and shakes it. "The Duke's sent no ambassadour?" says Agravante.

"No," says Lymond.

"If only your mother had ever managed a Bride," says Agravante. "To wed to him, and heal this rift. It'd be him to take this terrible risk today, instead of you."

Lymond turns away, lifting his hands, to face the crowd. "Thank you!" he calls to them, and they all fall silent, mechanicals and bikers, knights and clowns. "Thank you. For coming on such short notice, and so early in the morning. It's not far, and there's a little something at the end of it, tea, and coffee, and fresh-baked bread." And he turns abruptly and starts away, up the switchbacking length of road out of the lot, up the wooded slope still dusted with snow, soaking up the chilly early light.

"The Viscount's rude," says the Soames Thomas, marching close beside Lymond down the quiet winding street, "but he's right." The bicycles winding behind them, and the trundling pickup and its hangers-on.

"You'd rather a Duke, not a Prince, for King," says Lymond.

"I'd rather a Queen," says the Soames. "I was promised a Queen."

"You expect wonder hard on the heels of miracle," says Lymond. "I am the only Perry, and the last of them. Let's first see if that's enough."

Heading to the edge of the street, across the sidewalk and the scrap of dying grass, up to the yellow front door, followed by the Marquess and the Soames and the Viscount, and clatter and clank and ticking spinning as bicycles tumble to stops behind them. Lymond pulls a padded envelope from inside his coat, and from the envelope he pulls a gold credit card. Letting the envelope fall he works the card into the gap between door and frame, slipping it down, jimmying it as he leans against the door. The Soames frowns at the Marquess, and the Viscount smiles behind his fingers. A click, a clunk, and Lymond opens the door. "My house," he calls out to them, "is yours," and he steps inside, and down the long hall, followed by the thunder of dozens of footsteps out into the big room, empty but for the overstuffed armchair and the low table beside it, and that great window, and the shapes of the city uncertain in the shining haze, and beyond the mountain a pale shadow of blue and rose against the first rays of the rising sun.

"Well," says Lymond, as the footsteps settle, and the rustle of coats, scarves and gloves, blue suits and green coveralls. All of that motley crowd under the window, uncertain whether to look at out the view, or at Lymond there, his back to them, his hands on the arms of the chair. "Let's see," he says, and turning, sits him down.

Prepare your selves; for he is comming strayt.
Set all your things in seemely good aray,
Fit for so joyfull day:
The joyfulst day that ever sunne did see.

—Edmund Spenser

NO. 21

GALLOWGLAS

A SCREAMING – EASING HER COAT – STUPID STUPID STUPID STUPID
PROPHECY – SALT FOR A JADED PALATE – THE GREY MAN – BAD DREAMS
SO MUCH, LEFT OUT; SO MUCH TAKES SHAPE – HER CERTAINTY
WRENCHED – "DO YOU SEE?" – FALLING WILL FALL, FELL
UP AND UP AND UP – STEPPING INTO JOCKEY SHORTS
THE WEDDING GARMENT – NOT THE GUN
THIS TIME, MAYBE THIS TIME – FALLING
IF EVEN THIS

A SCREAMING cuts the silence of the car, right through the engine's rumble, the hum of tires, the tocking turn signal. She's kicking digging her feet into the backs of the seat ahead fighting to free her arms from the men on either side the car lurches, a grind, a thunk and to her right Leo winces, sparing a glace at the front seat, "Don't *do* that," he says. Streetlight flickering, flashes lighting his camel-colored coat, lost again in the gloom.

"Out of practice," says Luys, up behind the wheel.

"Jo," says Marfisa, leaning over the back of the front seat.

"Take me back," says Jo, her quickly heaving breath.

"Jo," says Marfisa again, reaching back and down for her hand, her knee, and "Look," says Leo, and "Take me *back*," says Jo, "right the hell *now*," and Orlando's hand snaps up to backhand her, she growls, kicks again, wrenching her arm from Orlando's grasp, Leo's holding grimly on, buffeted by blows as the car wobbles, wavers, Orlando's hand coming up a fist and Marfisa lunging to grab at it, "Don't!" cries Luys, gripping the wheel, ducking a flap of her sheepskin coat, and Jo's screaming again. *"Why,"* bellows Leo, and the car is quiet, again. Engine-rumble, tire-hiss. Jo's panting breath, too quick. Orlando's hands, in his lap. "Why," says Leo, "must we," looking at her, past her, to Orlando, "what in blazes," he says, and then, *"what happened."*

"I was not told what happened;" says Orlando, and Jo's saying, a burr in her breath, "You, you know," as Orlando says, "merely where to find her."

"And why were you asking where to find her," says Leo, as Jo's saying, "You know, she, she was," and Orlando snorts. "Again, this," he says.

"Let her speak," says Leo.

"Ysabel," says Jo, and then again, finding her voice, "Ysabel. The – Queen. Princess." Faltering. "The Bride," she says.

Loudly, getting louder, Leo says, "There *is* no" and Marfisa says *"Leo"* and he breaks off, glaring, "Sit," he says. "Buckle your seatbelt. Jo," he says. "Gallowglas. There is no – "

"No," says Jo, shaking her head.

" – no Bride," says Leo.

"No," says Jo.

"Our curse, all this time. We knew this day was coming, but – "

"No," she's saying, "no, no, no," her face screwing up around the word, and Marfisa's leaning over the back of the front seat again, reaching once more for a knee, a hand, "Please," she's saying, "Jo. For the love I bear you, if nothing else. Please."

Jo looks up to fix on Marfisa, her wildly white-blond hair, "The love," she manages to say, "you bear," before the words are strangled in a sob and she kicks again, and Leo's grabbing for her, Orlando falling on her, snarling, Luys yelping, and "Mooncalfe!" cries Marfisa. "Harm her and we *will* come to blows!"

"I await," says Orlando, struggling, "your pleasure." Jo screams again, elbows his gut, clips Leo's chin, the car wheeling right, left, lurching leaning forward lifting and settling on its haunches Marfisa banging against the dash Jo piling into the seats before her Orlando grabbing at her pale coat and Leo his face in his hands. Luys shuts off the engine, and silence swallows the car, the rustle of cloth, the squeak of leather and jingle of metal, the ragged edges of breath.

"We're here?" says Luys.

Leo leans forward, a hand on Jo's shoulder, her forehead against the back of the seat. "Jo," he says, gently. "Jo. Can you."

Leaning close, stroking her wine-red hair. "You need," she says, her face hidden. She sniffs. "You need to take me back."

"Can you get out of the car," he says. "Come inside. Please."

"I can't," she says. "I can't lose."

"Jo."

"I can't lose her," she says. "Please. Take me back."

Easing her Coat – stupid stupid stupid stupid Prophecy – Salt for a Jaded palate

Easing her coat the color of butter from her shoulders, down her motionless arms. Pausing as he takes the weight of it dragging the one side down in his hands. "What have you in your pocket?" he says. She doesn't respond. He folds the coat over, careful of the weight of it, and lays it on one of the folding chairs there by the wall. "If you were to sit," he says, "I might remove your boots."

"Luys," she says then, looking away from nothing to meet his eyes.

From out in the hall there's Leo striding into the high-ceilinged room, white T-shirt tucked into houndstooth trousers and a paper cup in either hand. "Since dawn," says the squat man following behind, a black leather vest over a black T-shirt, his long dark hair in a gleaming braid.

"So," says Leo, gesturing with one of the cups at the lightening windows high and narrow that line the opposite wall. "Since now."

"An hour or more. The first train got there at twenty of."

Leo's still looking out at the blue-grey light. "I have got to stop coming home so early," he says.

"It's the Prince, m'lord," says the man in the vest, and over against the other wall Jo falls into one of the folding chairs, staring at him. "He means to sit the Throne. I'd stake your hoard on it."

"All that?" says Leo, and a sip of coffee from one of the cups. A shrug. "Let him stand back up, Tommy. Then we'll have a ball game. Gallowglas!" Coming across the room to her, kicking away a crumpled red plastic cup. Luys is kneeling before her, busy with

386

the laces of her boot. "Leave us," says Leo, and lips pinched Luys pushes himself to his feet. Jo catches his hand, the one with a bit of leather about the wrist, but does not try to hold it as he steps away.

"We need to talk," says Leo.

"Here?" says Jo.

"You gonna," he spreads his hands, both cups steaming, "start screaming again? Damage any more upholstery?" He hands her one of the cups. She's shaking her head. "I'm safe," she says, "for the moment."

"The two of you," he mutters, and sips. "He's in the library, he's sworn to stay put. But he's determined to fight you. What is this, what. Jo. What is it." She's scowling at her cup. "It's really, really sweet," she says.

"It's just," he says, "it's how you like it. Sweetloaf!" he bellows. "Black, four sugars," he says. "Just like you like it."

"I," she says, "I don't," and from the hall there's a boy in a brown bomber jacket and his matted hair swept up and back. "Yeah?" he says.

Leo's looking down at Jo. "You want, what do you want. You want a different coffee?" She's shaking her head. "You want my coffee? Never mind!" he bellows. Sweetloaf shrugs and heads back out to the hall. Leo says, "I don't know what I'm gonna do, the two of you," and then, "the Mooncalfe. Orlando."

"Yeah," she's saying. She's set the cup down. She's pulling the boot from her grubby foot. "Is this over me?" says Leo. "This can't be over me, not now. You're actually stupid enough to go through with it, you need to find a pretext. The three of them, together, pestering Miss Cheney," and he trails off as he leans over to tug something free of the weight of her folded coat, a mask, its eyes empty, the chiseled teeth crudely inked, the mane dangling. "The hell did you dig this up," he says.

"I," she says, tugging off her other boot, "you," and then, "you had the party, on Thanksgiving? Your accustomed feast?"

"Yeah?" says Leo.

"The next morning," says Jo. She's looking off past him, at the man in the black leather vest, there by one of the windows. "I went to see Vincent," says Jo.

"Erne? Had this?" Leo tosses the mask back onto Jo's coat, flump. "I know what he's said, Gallowglas. How much he means to you, but we talked about this. You can't be my Huntsman. It's not the image I need to project. Not now." A thoughtful sip. "But connect the dots for me here, between this and the Mooncalfe, because I'm not – "

"The hole you leave when you're gone," says Jo.

"What?" says Leo.

"I need a shower," she says, the words half-strangled.

Pipes knock, water chugs and gurgles, resumes, under its stream lilting slightly side, to side, one hand held up and out against the grimy tile festooned with suds, the other a fist against her breast, knuckles to sternum as soap slides around them, down her arm, her belly, her thighs to her knees, dripping to the bottom of the tub where the water about her feet's a rusted foaming brown. Leaning back her head to let the water as it slows to a trickle soak her hair, shaking it out when the stream once more resumes, her one hand still pressed to her chest, over her heart a fist, and water dripping soapy from her elbow.

Wrapped in a towel, holding it closed, her other hand scrubbing her dark wet hair. The only light the wide-screen television hanging over the wide low bed, a Technicolor desert, yellow sand, white sun, a muscled buttock floured with dust, a brassy plate strapped to a delicate hand deep brown, a pink cord trailing away, humming over the dust, sloughing it to reveal the clean skin red and brown of thigh, of hip. My lord. You *are* filthy.

In the gloom at the edge of the fitful light a dressing table, and her reflection in the mirror atop it, the ghostly towel, her shoulder, her cheek, the sheen of her eyes. Leaning over the table, the jackets laid across it, the snarl of neckties, she peers at herself in the glass, dark eyes to either side of her nose, that nose, her mouth a thin flat line, her fist holding up the towel at her chest white-knuckled. Having someone give you a clean-up like you were a little kid is the most sensuous thing in the world, I think, says the television. Does it feel good?

Yeah, says the television.

She closes her eyes. She lets go, lets the towel drop to the floor. With your back to me, says the television. No, like that. Her fingers caress the skin over her sternum, over her heart. Wait a minute. Eyeing her reflecting, turning to present this angle, that. Fingertips, then the heel of her hand, pressed between her breasts.

Stupid, stupid, stupid, stupid, stupid, stupid, the television filled with a rough brown hand wrapped in a glove of black ribbons, stupid, stupid, stupidity, a process, not a state, a new voice is saying over the stupid, stupid, stupid, she steps over, a human being takes in far more information than he or she can put out, stupid, stupid, she reaches up to the television, turns it off.

"I was watching that," says someone from the bed. A low white lamp on one of the nightstands clicks on and there, nestled on the brown sheets, the mounded pillows, naked from painted toe-tip along to the arm draped languidly above a head of yellow hair severely straight. "It *was* you got him out of bed." Sitting up, stretching, yawning and a dainty laugh, "Oh, mon poussin," as Jo grabs at a shirt from the table, "how delightful." The woman's sitting on the edge of the bed now. "Shall we surprise him? He'll be back." Head tipped winsomely. "Though I don't know *long* he'll be, mon chouchoute. Do you?" And Jo leaves off trying to button the rest of the shirt, heads off, into the gloom, followed by a pealing laugh. Finding a door she pulls it open on a short white hall too brightly lit, and a silence that muffles the door-slam.

A moment there, hand to her forehead. The door behind her, painted white and a shining nickle knob. The shirt she's taken a warmly iridescent grey. She buttons another button. Her fumbling hands. She tugs it down, ripples of orange and red hinted in the light, and the door at the other end is blue, and a gleaming brass push-plate, and her hand to her mouth, her chin, her hair.

The blue door opens on a cramped kitchen, butcher's block in the middle of it, and a squat man drying a plate by the sink there under a window filled with grey-pink light. "Jo," he says, mildly surprised. "Something wrong?" A black leather vest over a black T-shirt, his long black hair in a shining braid.

"I," she says, the door swinging shut behind her. "I," she says again, hands at her sides, empty, still.

"Is something wrong? Leo," he sets the plate down, "was gonna bring you some clothes. Did he," watching her face, tilting his head, "he must've got distracted."

"Tommy," she says. "Tommy Rawhead."

"Yes," he says, the edge of a question in his voice, hoarse from hard use. He takes down a couple of glasses from the cabinet above. "Jo," he says, "I know it's been hard." He heads around to the refrigerator, and she shifts a jerky step to the side, keeping the butcher's block between them. "Past few days. But I'm real glad you're back." Filling a glass with water from the spigot in the door. "He loves you." Filling the second glass. "Very much." He sets one down on the butcher's block and says, "He's a better man when he's with you." Pushing the glass toward her, her hands, empty and still. "He'll be a better King."

"I need to get," she says, "some sleep?" Stepping back.

"Of course," he says, setting his glass down, "sorry," he says, "dragging this out when you're so obviously knackered. We'n talk when you wake up," as she's blundering back through the swinging door into a long, high-ceilinged room painted a lurid red, and black trim about the tall and narrow windows set one after another in the wall before her. The plank floor under her bare feet slowing, stopping the color of dark chocolate. Off to one side white sheets draped against the walls soften a corner, and great lights and silvery reflectors and a camera or two on stands and tripods, waiting. To the other a square of sofas, brown leather strewn with madly clashing pillows and cushions about a low wide table littered with empty bottles and glasses, mugs, plastic cups, a pizza box and a couple of cardboard sandwich boxes and a plastic tray with a veggie roll left in a corner and some shrimp tails battered, congealed, cigarette butts here and there and an ashtray mounded high, and in the middle a hookah. And beyond it the other end of the room an alcove, a huge sleigh bed tucked away back there, and bare arms in an embrace about a sheepskin jacket, a wild cloud of hair. "Marfisa?" says Jo, and then, quietly, hesitantly, "Jessie?"

"Jo?" says Marfisa, turning. The woman her hand on Marfisa's hip, athletically heathered grey tank top and briefs, yellow hair, straight, severe. "Hey, killer," she says.

"You," says Jo, "you're," and then, mouth pinching, looking away, "your sister."

"Oh," says the woman in the tank top, and "What's she done," says Marfisa, stepping away, and then as Jo heads toward them, past them, "Jo? What did Ettie do?" But Jo's climbing the ladder, up to the dark corner of a loft under the high unfinished ceiling.

"Let her sulk," says the woman in the tank top, her hand reaching for Marfisa's. Marfisa shakes it away. "Jo," she says, at the foot of the ladder. "It's Sunday. You were gone for two whole days. Jo?" Marfisa starts to climb.

Breasting the loft there's Jo, on her knees in the middle of the dust-furred space. Down by the milky window scabbed over with brown paint a length of two-by-four worn grey, askew on the floor by a cracked cinder block. Marfisa stays there, on the ladder, "He was out of his mind," she says. "The Mason went to ask Miss Cheney where you were, for him. *I* went because," a deep breath before the next words, "I had to know. I was worried." Silhouetted in the haze Jo hasn't moved, doesn't respond. "He interrupted us, Jo, the Mooncalfe, to ask a question of his own. He'd come to learn from her where he'd meet his, particular, end." She leans over the top of the ladder toward Jo. "He was told where to find you," she says. "Don't you see? You will *win.*" She raps the dusty floor before her. "You will end him, and his hold over the King. Jo, this is – "

"Her banner over the city," says Jo, "her gallowglas by her side. She was Queen for a night, and a day, and I was there for a minute?" The shadow of her head shifting, turning. "*Fuck* prophecy," says Jo. "You loved her so much you left the court for her and now you don't even know her name."

"I left the court for *you,*" says Marfisa, but Jo's on her feet, headed hunched over for the ladder, and Marfisa jerks back, leans to one side out of the way as Jo grabs the one upright of the ladder and kicks over the edge of the loft, dropping to the floor in a crouch and a whuff of dust. "Jo?" says Marfisa, coming down after. Jo's around the corner, in the alcove, and the woman in the tank top's saying, "Wait, Jo, hey – "

"Where's my stuff," Jo's saying, "my clothes, my boxes, my fucking *futon* – "

"Maybe your room?" the woman in the tank top's saying. She's put on a pair of jeans, she's grabbed Jo by the arm, Jo her other hand to her chest, in that warm grey shirt, in the doorway of the closet there under the loft. "My, room," she says, looking around, looking up, at the loft, "this isn't," and then, "the, the *balcony,* that he made, that he had made, for – "

"Jo," says Marfisa, and "Balcony?" says the woman in the tank top, and "Jo," says Marfisa again. But Jo isn't looking at either of them, she's looking past them both to the brown leather sofa out in the long high-ceilinged room, the bundle neatly folded at the foot of it, leaned against it, her sword, her mask, her coat the color of butter. "You left it in the ballroom," says Marfisa, seeing what she sees. "I was bringing them to you, Jo," she says, stepping toward her, but she's shivering, Jo, and the hand to her chest's a fist, and "Hey," says the woman in the tank top, letting go, "Jo – "

She's pushed past Marfisa, she's there by the sofa, she's scooping up the coat, knocking the mask aside, she's reaching in a pocket to pull out not much bigger than her hand a dull black barrel the grip of it wound about with black tape and the letters Kel-Tec stamped in pebbled metal. "Jo," says Marfisa again, and "Jesus," says the woman in the tank top, and a rustle, a scramble, Jo's up, past the mess, over there by the swinging door a sink bolted to the wall and another door, white, paned with frosted glass thrown open into a cramped bathroom where she swipes at the shower curtain hanging stuck she yanks, "Shit," and down it comes curtain rings and rod into the empty tub, she staggers back, half in, half out, catching the doorframe, face caught there in the mirrored door of the medicine cabinet, her face and shoulder, warm grey shirt as she pulls herself up and in, as she lifts the gun, as she points it at the reflection of her breast, as she points it at the reflection of itself.

"Jo?" says Marfisa, still back there by the sofas, by the table laden. "Jo – "

A bang. Splintering glass and something falling, a shelf, brass dancing across the floor and the echo still a wave that founders endlessly on far-off rocks, the next room, receding, Jo lowers her arm, her hand, the gun. Blood welling to trickle drip from the gash along her brow. Marfisa's saying something, hands up, pleading, Jo's walking away unsteadily down the length of the room, red walls, high narrow windows filling with clouded morning light. She opens the door down there by the waiting cameras, the dark lights on tripods. Out into the hallway, bare feet on a white-painted floor, down a skinny switchbacked flight of steps, wiping at the blood with her free hand. Into a room lined with high shelves stuffed with books and comics and here and there a shelf swarming with homunculi, brightly colored figures roaring at each other or nothing at all, and a murmur of voices somewhere away around a corner angling past an overstuffed chair in tufted oxblood leather and painted canvasses and sheets of Bristol board stacked against an arm of it, and someone's saying "on a Monday," Leo's saying, his back to her draped in a gown of paisleys, purple and maroon, gold and brown. "Dubbed on a Tuesday. Wedded on Wednesday. She's coming, Lando. On the Empire Builder. Two days by rail."

"An eternity, mortgaged," says a voice highly pitched, rich and bitterly smooth. "Roses fed to Engines, evermore." A hand, lifted from the paisleyed shoulder, fingers stroking Leo's cheek, his hair. "Needs must," says Leo, taking the hand in his own.

"Need I must then be kept rustically? Stalled up with your other oxen?"

"Keep yourself where you like," says Leo, tilting his head for a kiss, and there's the long black hair, the thin nose, the black patch over an eye. "As you would," says Leo, "if she weren't," and another, "on her way."

"I mislike a bed so crowded," says Orlando, unpatched eye opening, glinting. Jo's hand tightens on the grip of her gun. "Dancers, jugglers. Freaks."

"Who doesn't like a circus?" says Leo.

"And your biting something of fragility, Ieraks?" says Orlando, with the slightest smile. "The bitter draught you pour to salt your jaded palate?"

"My," says Leo, drawing back, "are we still on my bed? Because – "

"He means me," says Jo, raising the gun in both hands, and Orlando steps back, and Leo between them turning and turning about again "Wait" he's saying, "wait," and Orlando his hand on the lacquered scabbard of his sword says "But a word, m'lord. Before she pulls the trigger I'll have her gutted."

"No!" cries Leo, both arms up, hands out, stop, stop. "You'll do no such thing. Either of you."

"The worst is the shit that hasn't changed," says Jo, shifting to keep the gun on Orlando. "How's your leg, Leo?"

"Which one?" snaps Leo, and then, "You're bleeding. Gallow-glas." Gentling. "What have you done." She's stepping to the side, and again, Orlando his other hand on the hilt of his sword, rough black cloth wrapped about a bone-white grip. "Give me the gun," says Leo. Her back's to the shelves, now, and he's still between them. "We'll go back to our room – "

"I don't," says Jo, "want to sleep, alone, or with any, I don't," she says, "I'm not hungry, I'm not thirsty, I don't, God help me," lowering the gun, "I don't want to hurt him. I could care less if he stubbed his fucking toe."

"Your head," says Leo.

"I just want to go back, Leo. Can you do that?"

"Where," says Leo. "Go back where."

"Ysabel," says Jo, and Orlando with a jerk bares an inch or so of blade.

"I don't know what that means," says Leo.

"I know," says Jo, and she turns and heads for the door. Orlando's hand is stopped by Leo's, he's looking after Jo as she's leaving and in the doorway past her, in the hall outside, a grey flicker, the heel of a mole-grey shoe, stepping, gone, "Jo?" he says. She's left. He lets go of Orlando's hand, and the rasp and thock of the sword driven home as Leo steps out into the hall, unlit but for the buzzing red bulk of the Coke machine. Down the wide white-painted steps dressing gown floating purple and gold as he doubles back down and into the black-and-white tiled foyer. It's empty. The door to the bar is locked, and the vegan diner, and he throws open the front doors and out, onto the brick steps, the street beyond filled with thin light, a truck snorting to itself in the intersection, a cartoon on the side of it, a muscular, mustached man with a guitar. Dave's Killer Bread, it says. Someone's inside the bus shelter, leaning against a shopping cart loaded with empty bottles and cans. She isn't there. She isn't anywhere.

THE GREY MAN – BAD DREAMS
SO MUCH, LEFT OUT; SO MUCH TAKES SHAPE – HER CERTAINTY

THE GREY MAN's standing in the black-and-white tiled foyer as she makes her way down the wide white-painted steps, his mole-grey shoes, his gravel trousers roughly flecked, his ashen shirt, his rumpled face like old oatmeal. "Tell me you know who Ysabel is," says Jo, "or I'm blowing right the hell past you."

"The Queen in her folly," he says, "who refused her crown. Put the gun away."

Jo says, "She's here?"

"One thing at a time. Put the gun away. Put it down. Then open your shirt."

She's stopped on the third step up, the gun in her hand at her side. "There's something there, isn't there," she says.

"We must make certain," he says.

"I can't touch it," she says, sitting on the steps. "I can *feel* it. It's cold, a little. Numb." The weighty clink of the gun as she sets it down. "But no matter which way I turn, or the light," as she undoes a button, and another. "I can't see anything there." He hitches up his trousers to squat before her, her bare knees pressed together. "Who are you?" she says.

He looks up, his eyes grey blue a-swim in yellow grey. "My name is John," he says, his voice lugubrious, "and once I was King of the City of Roses."

"Oh," says Jo.

That hand parts her shirt and within what might be a soapy blur. When his fingers press there her eyes go wide head thrown back shoulders hunched and she howls, and falls back, against the steps.

"Quicksmoke," he's saying, sitting on the steps beside her. Her elbows on her knees, her head hanging down. "Echoes of the world before, its last foul airs and vapors."

"There was," she says, "the sorcerer had a thermos, and the thermos – there were two of them." A drop of blood from her brow splats between her feet. "One in black, one in white? And one of them had a thermos."

"Mirrors hold it," he says, "and certain chambers, far underground. It can be, directed, by lenses, or sound, or, if one is obscenely careful, the breath."

"Or me," she says, sitting up.

His grey head slowly, back and forth. "It makes a shell for itself, of what it takes from the world. It makes a shell, of scales, and when it's done, it plants itself." He looks down then, from her mudded eyes, to her chest, her shirt hung open. "It will slumber there for months, or even years."

"I was thinking," she says, blotting her brow with the heel of her hand, "it was, that maybe it got me, too. That all this was like, my life, flashing, my brain misfiring, just before – like a bad dream." Her hands, one blooded, one not, folded over her breast. "And when it stops?" she says. "When it wakes up?"

"It will," he says, "bloom. Things, and people, you'd thought were long since gone, forgot forever, will begin to return to you – " Her shoulders rise, shuddering, she's closing her eyes, swallowing a sob. "Ghosts," he says, and before he lays a rope-veined hand on her knee he closes it in a fist and puts it back in his graveled lap. "Bad dreams," he says.

"But," she says, opening her eyes. Looking over at him. "You remember her."

His grey head lifts, and drops. "She shouldn't be here," he says. "Not yet."

"But, she is," says Jo, "she's here."

His head lifts again, and his shoulders, "An hour ago," he says, "or a day, a star," and his fingers draw a line in the air, from his eyes down to his lap, "fell. I can show you where."

Unsteady she climbs to her feet, "Then what are we waiting for," she says, and shaking she kneels on the steps, a click and scrape as she picks up the gun.

"You need clothing," he says, standing beside her. "Shoes."

"I've got," she says, wincing, wiping a bit of oozing blood away from her eye, "stuff, upstairs," turning, a gesture with the gun. "Not here," he says, stepping down, stepping out onto the black-and-white tiled floor.

"Not here?" she says. Slowly, gingerly down the steps, following. "John?"

"It's cold, outside," he says, his hand on the crash bar that opens the front door. "If I had a coat." He pushes it open. "But it's not far. What I have in mind. Three blocks away." And he steps through.

Night outside, but not dark. "Jesus," she says, forcing her bare feet out onto the frost-rimed brick of the porch drifted in the corners with snow. More snow blankets the sidewalk where the grey man waits by the bus shelter, and snow stretches deeply soft unbroken by tire-track or footprint up and down the street, and all of the snow shines with reflected light where it isn't an eerily luminous blue. Across the street the building on the corner climbs floor by floor up fifty or seventy storeys or more, and the building behind her, and behind them and around them more buildings, the regular, edged trunks of some cyclopean forest, eighty storeys, a hundred, two thousand feet, twenty-five hundred or more, the tops of them lost in the shining bellies of the clouds above. And every storey lined with windows, in every window a lamp, and every lamp is lit.

"Him, I loved," says the grey man, slowly, wearily, "as my hand; her as my very breath." His arms folded he leans on a glass-topped counter, the shelves within lit up, laden with piles of dice in lucite and bright chrome, a couple of silvery hip flasks, a hollowed-out book safe whose tattered jacket says Bright Orange for the Shroud, a neat little silver and black crossbow pistol, uncocked, tilted to one side. "He could give her, something I could not," he says. "That's all."

"Is this, what, a son thing?" says Jo, from over there, a line of louvered saloon doors one after another past the racks of clothing. The one there at the end, lit up yellow and red. "Daughters, don't count?"

"It could as easily have been a daughter," he says, a crease shifting the rumples of his forehead. "As I understand it."

"But Ysabel," says Jo, her head appearing over the top of the saloon doors, red hair dark in that light.

He looks up. "The Bride?" he says. "The mysteries of Bride, and Queen, have nothing at all to do with, *birth.*" He pushes back from the glass. "Her belly, distended;" his hands shaping a curve before him, "the sweats, the sickness; the changes to her tongue – she could no longer bear the taste of fennel, or of tarragon. The sight of, eggs, revolted her. She, *demanded,* roasted peppers, in yogurt. And the pain." That face of his twisting itself into an expression, trying it on, a grimace that falters, into a snarl, and then is smoothed away as he heads down the length of the counter. "The body, feeling what it will; doing, even saying, what it would." Past a mechanical cash register with an elaborate cameo painted on the back of it, a display of knee socks printed up the sides with slogans that say Whiskey, Bacon, Kosher, Brooklyn. "When she was delivered of the boy," and he steps around the end of the counter now, to the other side, there by the electric cash register, its dark monitor, the oblong little card swipe, "she could once more stomach eggs. The whites of them, at least. With tarragon." He's looking over a set of shelves there in the shadows behind the counter, untidily stuffed with boxes, baskets, redwelds of papers and folders. "But as the boy grew – at first, I thought, perhaps, she'd merely become – subdued? The stress of it all." He pulls from a shelf a wooden box, shallow and wide, the top of it inlaid with pale ivory and fitful gleaming gold. "But as the years turned themselves about, it became clear: Duenna's joy. The mischief, that led her once to ask my Huntsman for a dance, so long ago. Echoes of them yet ring in Ysabel – how could they not? – but in my Queen they were not, muffled; they were – not. Gone, and never to return." He sets the box on the counter, tink of wood against glass. "And then the stories, from the Northeast Marches, of a loathly lady all in black, who entered houses, hurt women, who brought trouble upon children, whose eyes were like stars, whose hands of iron. And her laugh, and the nails of her fingers, like sickles."

"She has nineteen names," says Jo, stepping through the doors of her fitting room.

"She has but one name," says the grey man, "and it is no more her own."

"But, I mean," says Jo. She wears a shirtwaist dress, in black and grey, with pink and white dots here and there, over black leggings and black boots. "I've seen them both, together. The Queen, and the lady." Pushing one arm and the other into a heavy black jacket with a wide hood to it that lies back, crumpled about her neck like a scarf. "At the same time."

"And the Gammer," says the grey man, and the crease has returned to his forehead. "And the Bride, also."

She's come up to the counter opposite him, her hands on either side of the box there on the glass. "They're," she says. Then, "She's." Under a curl of her wine-dark hair there's a couple of white butterfly bandages, holding shut the red gash across her brow. "I," she says, "I didn't know – "

Bang his hand comes down on the glass, and she jumps at the sound. "There is so much," he says, "left out, when one word is chosen, instead of another, over another, but – also, as well, so much I had not," both hands folded together atop the box, the irregular honeycomb picked out in white and gold on the lid, "considered, takes shape, risks rushing in to overwhelm, the more I speak of this – " and "John" Jo's saying, "John. Please. Pull it back. What does it, what does this have to do, with finding Ysabel, with bringing her back – "

"You must understand," he says, and he's taken her hand in his. "I do not know, what it is, to father a child. I could not tell you, what it would have been, to have loved him as he were my own." He lets go, and she pulls her hand back to herself. "It was to Vincent that he turned, as he grew, to find a father. It was in Vincent, my true friend, that he found a bitterness, to brace the sweetness of his boyhood."

"John," she says.

"Vincent," he says, "my good right hand, who could find no more trace of the Duenna *he* had loved in my Queen, in her loathly shadow. It was Vincent, my Huntsman, who told him of his mother, that Duenna, so long since gone."

"Sir," she says.

"We *lost* him!" cries the grey man, and Jo takes a step back, blinking. "He left us, to find her!" Those big grey hands hovering uncertain, settling over his face. "He ended," he says. "He ended. Up. Here." Lowering, shaking, to press against the glass. "Here. Here. There was no here. Not then." A breath drawn sharply in through his nose, and, "Then," he says, a slow stone of a word, "then, in my grief, my towering rage, I dropped a glove at the feet of my bitterest best of friends, and, I lost, myself."

And when he doesn't say anything more, Jo says, "John," and then, "majesty. Where are we?"

He looks up, at the dark ceiling close above. He lifts his hands, spreads them, a benison for the dark racks of clothing, the framed posters unseen on the walls, the windows full of mannequins in outlandish costumes looking out over the snow, the great stuffed tiger lounging on the shelf above the doors. "A place," he says, "where we might come to rest, when we are done with the world."

"So I'm," says Jo, "am I, are we, I'm, I'm not done, I'm not done with anything – "

"Do you love her, Gallowglas?" says the grey man.

She looks down, leaning against the glass. Looks up, meeting his gelid eyes. "With all my heart," she says.

"Then there is yet a chance," he says. "Open the box."

And Jo lifts the white-gold lid.

The inside lined with yellow velvet here and there worn a darker almost orange, and it's filled with a jumble of things. She looks up at the grey man, lifting the first of them out, a telephone headset with a single earpiece, the microphone askew, the cord of it only a few inches long, and copper wire peeking from the frayed end. She sets it on the glass. Next a bottle cap, silver, that says Snapple on the top of it, Made From the Best Stuff on Earth. She turns it over. Real Fact no. 95, it says, The red deer inhabits most of Europe, the Caucasus Mountains, Asia Minor, parts of Western Asia, and Central Asia. A slender pack of cigarettes, the label of it orange, Djarum, it says, Sigaret Kretek. A ticket stub that says SE-CRET SHOW, Sept. 30. "That was," says Jo, setting it by the bottle cap, "that was a good show. That was the night we killed the boar."

"Erymathos," says the grey man.

Jo plucks out a bus transfer, and then a folded page torn from a magazine some time ago, and careful of the delicate creases she opens it up. "The hell," she says, smoothing it flat against the glass. A photograph fills the page, a woman lying back, her orange jacket opened, dark stocking gartered halfway along her thighs, under-wear striped blue and white stretched taut between her knees.

"What's in the box is yours," says the grey man. "You've seen it before?"

"There was a," she says, "a satchel. A briefcase. One of the, we were attacked, on the MAX, by some – guys. One of them had it. The Duke ended up with it somehow, and it was full of," she flicks the page with a fingertip, "this. And I," and she lays a hand on the glass, a finger on a corner of the page.

"Yes?" says the grey man.

Jo reaches into a pocket of the jacket she's wearing and pulls from it her gun. Cradles it a moment in both her hands, and then, care-fully, sets it snugly in the yellow velvet lining of the box. She closes the lid. She pushes the box back over the glass to him, and gathers up what she's taken out, the transfer, the ticket, the bottle cap, the headset, into this pocket or that. The page, folding it back up again.

"You're certain?" says the grey man.

She nods, then stops, the folded page in her hand. "Can I," she says, "could I, ask for one more thing?" She's looking down through the glass at something on one of the shelves.

"You might," he says.

She points. "The gloves?" she says. By one of the flasks a pair of fingerless cycling gloves, grey and black. He stoops to pull them out, then lays them on the glass before her, flat. As she works her hand into one it's clear they've never been worn before.

She tugs them both home, tightens and closes the velcro about her wrists. "Okay," she says. "Let's go." The grey man nods.

"None of this," he says, lifting a grey hand, "was here when I first came." His shoes, her boots squeaking in the blue-white unmarked snow that blankets the street. "And now," he says, "look," lifting his grey face. The skeletal branches an empty canopy above and up and up beyond them behind the dark trees thronging the sidewalks buildings loom, darkly shadowed blue, pricked with windows lit up weakly white and yellow. "All of them, every one, ready and waiting for someone I might save, someone I've caught, kept, held fast."

"But not," says Jo, "not Duenna," the word a tattered fog of breath blown back from her hood.

"When her time comes," says the grey man. His hands clasped behind his back. He wears no coat, and his ashen shirt's still open at the throat. "Lymond – is still very much a boy. He is, impatient. He certainly was, when he brought himself here, and when he refused all that I might do to help him home."

And then, a block or so later, he says, "How he managed that remains a mystery, to me."

They're at the top of a ridge now, and at the next intersection the trees thin out, fall back, and the buildings about them drop with the street down and down to the cluster of overpasses there at the edge of the river, and rising over across it towers, more towers, towers climbing a mile or more into the thinning eddied clouds, and the thousand thousand sparks shining gleaming flickering in the windows of them. Coming down the slope of the ridge the view opens even further, swooping arcs and nets of light, the bridges there, and there, marching along the river, each grander and more glorious than the one before. There to the right, where the clouds thicken, stained with color, a smoldering yellow edged with red in all that blue-black and blued white, the buildings below shining reds and oranges and even mirroring silvers, reflections and refractions, and Jo slows, she stops there in the snow, staring at the lone tower a mile or so away, higher than everything about it, the amber glass of it glaring in the too-brilliant light framed by bright pink stone flaring white as the sparks, the drops of yellow-white light, fall and splash and splattering bounce from the top of it gone, the corner of it broken, eaten away, a crater there at the top of the city, a bowl overflowing, too bright to look upon.

"Christ," says Jo.

"A star, fell," he says. "See what it's done." And then, "I will go no further."

"But," she says, looking to him, the buildings about them, "what do I, I just," the river, the burning tower, him again, "so I walk up there? By myself? And find her? And then we just, what, leave?"

He's pointing to her breast. "This," he says. He's pointing to her but he's looking away, to the burning tower. "This, and what's been built here," and his hand sweeps now, his gaze to encompass the buildings all about, "these were enough perhaps to catch her, to hold her, to keep her from melting away." The grey of his face unwarmed by the far-off light. "What you found in the box should be enough to bring the both of you home. But. Little enough's the stock to be put in shoulds." He's holding out to her a small silvery coil of a horn, the bell of it oval, and dented, the finish scratched. "Sound it, if you must," he says. "If you absolutely must, I will come then, and see the both of you home."

"Why don't you come with me? Make sure?" she says. "Why don't you go yourself?"

"It is given that you might see me but three times, only," he says, still holding out the horn. "You might see me twice more, yet. She's seen me once already."

"Oh," says Jo, and then she takes the horn from his hand.

"Jo Gallowglas," he says, as she tucks it away in her jacket. "Jo Maguire. You are not what I would have chosen, but." Looking her up and down, from her hood to her boots and back. "But you are, I think, what is needed."

"I, ah," says Jo. She nods. "Okay."

She turns away, sets off, down the middle of the snow-filled street. Traffic lights click above the next intersection, blinking blue over the street she follows, white over the cross street. As she passes under them she looks back, over her shoulder. He can't be seen, against the dark trees, the dark ground floors of the buildings left behind.

WRENCHED – "Do you see?" – Falling will fall, Fell
up and up and up

WRENCHED away from hand and white fur billowing "Jo!" she cries, slap of her bare feet now on tile, click of a ring about her toe. Small white hexagonal tile, lapping a low dais before her, and on the dais a white slipper tub that rests on clawed feet, and a silver bowl on a copper tray, and a slim knife with a blade the color of bone, and she stands beside them, naked, a hand on the curl of the rim of the tub, her black hair glossy swept up, pinned back to fall behind her shoulders in artful tangles.

"Mother?" says Ysabel, clutching her white fur closed.

"Perhaps?" she says, stepping down from the dais. "It's hard to say, in here, which way you've turned." Holding out a hand. "You, yet to come?" Fingers, brushing white fur, matted there, an ivory stain, sticky, wet. "Oh, my lady," she says, "my girl," taking her hand in her hand, turning it over, the ragged gash torn in the edge of it, weeping milky gold. "You're hurt," she says, and she presses her lips to the wound, a kiss, and Ysabel with a gasp closes her glimmering eyes. When she lifts her mouth away her hand is whole, the cut a smooth faint line.

"My lady," says Ysabel, opening her eyes, and "Yes," she says, her hands on the fur. "Lady," says Ysabel, "what's happened? Where are we?"

"Hush," she says, parting the fur, baring her shoulders, her breast, a hand to her breast, slipped up along her throat to her cheek, the nails of it cut short and painted a creamy honey color.

404

"Where's Jo?" says Ysabel, and then she kisses her mouth, lightly, gently, and the slither of that white fur down her arms to crumple about her feet.

Down and down the hill, and as the buildings close about her again they block off the view of the bridges and the river and all but the most immediate towers ahead and about her, but all of it's touched by that light now, the glare of it in the sky. Another intersection, another traffic light, clicking, and again the lights are blue this way, and white the other. Jo looks up and down the empty streets, the snow about her only marred by the path she's made.

Up ahead past the next intersection the street climbs, a ramp up onto a bridge over the streets below to the whirl of off-ramps and on-ramps feeding the freeway by the river. She crosses it at an angle, making for the sidewalk, which splits here, one line of it running up along the ramp, the other down, along a narrow branch of street that ducks under the bridge, into the darkness there. At the point of the split, bolted to the guardrail, a warning light, two white lamps set one over the other, blinking, blinking, click and the snow's a bright white field about her, click and it's gone, blued shadows steeping into black.

She takes the left fork, up and onto the ramp, up onto the bridge.

The windows now in the towers she's passing are three and four storeys off the ground, and in each window a light, and the walls through the glass of each are blank and white, no shelves, no art, no photographs or television sets, no cabinets, no shadows. A movement – there? She stops, a silhouetted head, an arm, falling. She waits there, on the sidewalk, but whoever it is doesn't get back up.

Ahead off to the right an off-ramp from the bridge, feeding into the snarl of freeway to the right, to the north. and there, just before the mouth of it, a staircase leads down to a pedestrian underpass, the steps of it clear of snow except the corners, drifted over. On the other side of the ramp another staircase leads back up to the sidewalk that continues on beyond. She's standing, one hand on the railing, looking back at the empty streets, ahead, over across the river to those impossible towers, and the glare of the highest of them, burning, a torch.

As she descends the steps a stillness closes over her, there beneath the deck of the ramp, and it's clear how noisy the quiet had been before. Footsteps somewhere below, the clap of a hand, the crisply snap of a fire burning. At the bottom of the staircase the girders and concrete beams of the bridge and the ramps loom above in the space under the deck. The railing's a concrete rampart well up above her waist. The underpass itself a narrow span, choked with garbage, snow drifted over a pile of clothing there, filthy sweatpants and a grimy pink T-shirt, food wrappers crusted, a single flip-flop grey in the darkness, one of its plastic straps sprung. The way is mostly blocked by a shopping cart filled with swollen garbage bags and all of it swaddled in a blue plastic tarp. Jo's leaning up against the rampart, feet still on the last step, to look past the cart, there's a roll of industrial felt tucked flat against the inner wall of the underpass, a sleeping bag laid out atop it, a ghostly smear of hair, poking from a dark stocking cap.

Jo leans out, looking down through interstices of column and beam and truss to the street below, and train tracks, a bonfire burning under the bridge, red and orange, yellow and white, striking gleams from the polished rails. A handful of figures, someone small there directly before the blaze, a slight silhouette even in a bulky coat, scrape of gravel tock of heel another figure stepping away from something, bulk of white rock shaped a hint of an eye, a beak, a wing fixed, spread in the firelight. That figure's long coat swings open, head bare, hair a mop of artful tangles, black, bobbing as he lifts a black-gloved hand to forestall anyone from following, he's looking up, peering up, stopping as he sees her there on the underpass.

She pulls back, against the rampart on the other side of the stairs. The steady crackle of the fire below. She looks over the shopping cart barricade, the makeshift bed, the figure asleep, the garbage, fingertips pressed to the butterfly bandages on her brow. And then stuffing her hand in her pocket she heads back up the stairs, into the drifted snow, the stulted air.

At the sidewalk she looks back the way she's come, and then she leaps out into the mouth of the on-ramp, plunging across it, kicking up snow, grabbing the railing on the other side to stop herself, swinging about. Shreds of breath flying from her hood.

She trudges across the mouth of the next on-ramp, the one that feeds from the freeway into the city, and up and onto the empty bridge. The snow that swallows her boots is blushing now, pinks and pale gold and then a strident orange chasing the blue into hollows and backsides. She looks up. The tower's closer, higher, the cauldron of light atop it bubbling over, the air about it hazed, the faces of the buildings about it too bright, all whites and light-struck chromes, the rest of them flung into blackness. Along the river the trees the river itself lit up like day, and each long shadow starkly drawn. She looks back then, there at the top of the arch of the bridge, back past the tangle of freeway ramps, the buildings looming stretching off to the east and the south and the clouds above streaming away, breaking against them, the starless night sky opening up beyond, and there far away to the east at the edge of it all the pale tooth of a mountain, the snow of it mottled only here and there with dark bare rock scraped clean, and the western slopes of it even now warming with sunrise colors, pinks, pale gold, the merest edge of orange, so far away.

She steps back, letting go of Ysabel's hand. "Do you see?" she says, and wiping her lips with the back of that hand she neither nods nor shakes her head. "Yes?" she says, after a moment.

"Until it's done, it can't be spoken of," she says. "And once it's done," a shrug. "Why speak of it?"

"I thought I'd broken!" she cries. "I was told. I'd broke."

"And you were told you hadn't. Yet until you knew, how could you know?" She lifts a hand to her cheek, to brush at the tear that trembles at the corner of her eye. She leans back from the hand, blinking, sniffing. "It was so hard," she says.

"It always is." She steps back, away, toward the dais, the tub.

"Where's Jo?" she says.

"Who?"

"Jo. Jo! Don't pretend you do not know her. She was right beside me, just before I ended up in here."

She lifts a porcelain lever on the faucet, and water spits and splashes into the tub. "Why," she says.

"She came back." Stepping away from the fur, toward the tub. "She was there, on the bridge. She slew the sorcerer. She came back, when everyone else had left, to *save* me."

"No one left you, lady," she says, sitting against the rim of the tub.

"Mother," she says. "Walked away. When I didn't turn it quickly enough, she left me to *drown.*"

"The last thing we could ever do, is drown," she says.

"The Gammer hurled herself on the nearest blade," she says, and she says, "She was coming to your" but she's saying, "just as Father, in his duel, so long ago."

She snorts. "And what do you care for that vain and jealous man."

She says, "Lymond left. To go find him."

"No one *left!*" she cries, standing, a hand pressed to her belly, and a scowl on her face. "*You* walked away. You leaped after your doom. You slapped at every offered hand and smiled as you ripped yourself out of the world. And now," she says, "here," and she swallows, "we are."

She says, "Marfisa – " and she cries, "*You* – " but her knees buckle and she falls one arm catching the side of the tub ringing a muffled bell-thump, she heaves, doubled over, retching, a choke and a bolus of slurry slithers glistening from her lips to plop to the tile. She's coughing, she's hauling in breath. She's leaning over her, an arm about her, catching her as she falls back, trembling. Holding her. She's scooping up a handful of water from the tub, she's splashing her face, wiping her chest, sluicing away the dregs of muddy gold. She's relaxing, settling, her breath slowing. Shivering. Reaching up and back, her arms about her, the two of them dark heads together clinging to each other at the foot of the plashing tub.

"Jo," she says.

"She isn't here. Look up."

She does. She closes her eyes. There is no ceiling, no roof above them, and the wheeling sky is full of stars.

She stands as she slumps against the side of the tub, and steps around her to the faucet. "How many rounds of the year," she says, "have we kept this city, Kingless, balanced between petulant Dukes and senile Counts. Waiting."

"Father says our brother has returned," she says, pushing her hair back up out of her face, behind her shoulders.

"Father, brother," she says, lowering the lever, "husband, son," shutting off the flow of water. "Our wait is over. The King's come back. Take up the knife." And when she does not move, "Pick it up, or I will. Only one of us might leave this place."

She looks up at that, startled. She's smiling serenely, sitting on the rim of the tub. "How did you think it all began," she says, lifting one foot, then the other, over the edge and in. A spark falls, hissing, popping when it strikes the water, blackening, sinking, and another, cracking when it strikes the tile, flaring, skittering away. Chiming pop as a spark hits the copper tray. She picks up the knife, the handle of it polished wood, the blade the color of bone. "I'm dizzy?" she says, standing.

"We fell," she says, holding out her hand. "We're falling." She takes her hand. "We will fall," she says. The light a steady rain now, pattering, sizzling, flaring in her black hair loose, undone, her black hair pulled back, a tendril of it worked loose, crackling like a fuse. "Tell me this is the end of it," she says. Light brightly the edge of the blade dapples her arm steadied against the edge of the tub, light splashing to dapple her thighs as she lowers herself into the water, light snuffed to mottle with soggy cinders a-float about them, hunched over knees to her chest at the one end of the tub, the knife in her hands, sitting at the other end leaning forward away from the faucet, legs outstretched, her feet tucked one on either side of her hips. "This doesn't end," she says.

"Tell me we will go back," she says. "Tell me we will be Queen."

"We were already Queen," she says. "We can't go back."

"We can only go on," she says, and "I can't," she says. Her forehead against her hands about the hilt. "We will," she says. Water sloshing as she leans close, and a kiss for her fingers. "Look," she says. "Look at us." The crackle and hiss of the falling light. The blade lowering, between them now. Hands on her shoulders, foreheads pressed together, green eyes blinking green. "What we do is wrong," she says.

"Magic, is wrong," she says, her hands about her hands.

"I'm frightened," she says, and "I'm terrified," she says. "Look me in the eye," she says, "look me in the eye and ask yourself this – "

"Do you love me?" she says.

And in her hands about her hands about the hilt the knife turns and, pressing together, with a sigh, sinks home.

Down the long mall of a lobby her footsteps echo from empty storefronts to either side, cut metal letters over the doorways spelling out Freddie Browns, Plaza Teriyaki, Players Zone. Pink granite columns under the mezzanine almost brown in this dim light. An enormous poster, a woman akimbo, West Side Athletic Club. The mall opens into a lobby, the hulk there of an abandoned security desk, dark halls beyond leading to the banks of elevators, Floors 18 – 30, Parking, say letters gleaming above each in the polished stone, Floors 30 – 8, Floors 1 – 17. A television monitor, blankly cerulean, under a sign that says US Bancorp Tower, and a poster beside it, Portland City Grill it says, On the 30th Floor, and the glass over it cracked, trembling. The floor under her boots shivering, a growing hum, a moan, a rising, scraping groan as the building all about her and above begins to thrum, a bell struck, a note plucked from one great steel and granite string, and "Oh, shit," says Jo, pitching forward scrambling to grab hold of something, the desk, things are falling sparks and pops and the rattle and slither of falling dust as it all slows, it all stops, it all begins to settle. She lets go of the desk.

"Hello?"

Light's moving, shifting, shining the walls and the floor down the hall of the middle bank of elevators, light crawling, falling still as the rumbles die away. She heads across the cracked floor, past a broken plaque popped loose from the wall, US Green Building Council, it says, LEED Silver. A bang and she throws up a hand, a sudden flood of brightness burning down the length of the wall washing all the colors away to white and gold and the shadow of something, a door burst loose, pirouetting, falling as the light shades to orange now, reddens to a sullen glow that steeps the walls, the floor, leaks out over the browned pink granite and Jo there, rusting her black jacket, light spattering from the gaping mouth of that last elevator, flares bouncing, wobbling, pooling on the floor there, formless white and shaded just with yellows, oranges, and gold. She steps into the hall, and shadows shift, take flight about her as more light falls from the shaft to strike the roof of the fallen elevator car, the confusion of cables and wheels, and slops out onto the floor. She kneels there, at the edge of that sluggish lake of light, and the buckles and seams of her boots, the folds of her jacket, the hood lowered over her shoulders, her chin and her nose and those bandages, the wisps and sprigs of her hair, all of her limned in yellow and orange and coruscating red. She holds a gloved hand out over the light and it streams up over her spread fingers, thickening the air, flaring as she lowers it and the shape and shadows of it swallowed in that brightness. A hiss, a sizzle, she gasps, lifts up her hand out of the light to her mouth, and her fingers drip with glitter. "Okay," she says, lips shining, smiling, "yeah." She rubs her wet eyes with the grey-gloved heel of her hand, she's sagging, almost laughing. "Okay," she says.

Another rumble building, and more light splashes down, in curds, in gobs, dollops plopping audibly into that settling heap of itself, oozing over the wreckage of the elevator car, flowing treacly out over the floor, over her boots, and everything's gone yellow-white, her hands ripping sharp black shadows as she pulls her hood up, ducking, the brilliance fading, the rumble dying. Boots squelching she steps toward the gaping elevator shaft, ducking her head, peering up. The light surging up over her ankles now. Somewhere far above a speck of what might be an opening. She wobbles, clutching at the warped and broken jamb of the elevator door as with a sucking schlorp of a sound a boot lifts free of the light, then the other, lifting and tipping her forward and over on her side soles shining, blazing as her feet lift up and faster up, "Shit," she says, and a grunt as her hip hits the top of the elevator doorway her feet swinging up to thunk against the ceiling one hand gripping the frame her feet scrabbling slinging light about, and glitter, "Shit" she says again as she's slowly rolled, "oh shit stop, stop" one foot kicking bumping down and through the elevator doorway momentum turning her over her other leg swooping faster and through and up in the shaft yanking reaching wildly both hands catching gripping the frame, "Oh, God," she says, echoing up the shaft, and light still falling behind her from above to below. Her hands straining. Grip shifting grunting and heaving she's levered a forearm under the top of the frame and there's her face eyes wild as she pulls herself down her elbow slips, her hand slips, her face is gone again, just the one hand clinging, slipping, "Oh hell," she says, and she's gone, up and up, and up.

Stepping into Jockey shorts – the Wedding garment
not the Gun – this time, Maybe this time

Stepping into grey jockey shorts with thick white seams he pulls them up and snaps them into place below his hard round belly, furred white like his thighs, his forearms, dashed with black. Sheer black nylon socks with garters snapped about his calves. A shirt of fine white broadcloth, and he fastens the lowest three buttons up to its pleated bib already smudged with ash. The trousers black, simply cut, the outer seams masked by plain black satin ribbon, and he climbs into them, tucks in his shirttails, wrestles the braces up over his shoulders, does up the fly. He fishes silver and black enameled studs from a little bowl on the dressing table and closes up his shirt, leaving the cuffs undone. And then from the table, careful of the ash that dusts the top of it, he lifts a black silk tie, slender but for the butterfly bulges at either end.

"Shit," says Mr. Charlock, Mr. Leir, weighing the tie in his hands.

"You think she let you skate with a clip-on?"

"You ain't here," says Mr. Charlock, lifting his collar, draping the tie about his neck.

"Here as you. How here is that? Doctor Charley fucking Leir."

"You're dead," says Mr. Leir, intent on crossing the one end over the other. "I shot you."

"Whole damn time it was you. Whole damn time, and you, sitting in the car, next to me."

"It was so obvious," says Leir, lifting his chin to tuck one end under and through, "I couldn't even let myself know. Shit."

"Turn the fuck around."

The man behind him wears a grey suit and a white shirt buttoned all the way up to his throat, and three neat black-edged holes punched through the front of it. He grabs the ends of Leir's tie and saws it back and forth, deftly passing over and under, tucking it through, pulling it tight. "Never could take care of yourself," he says.

"How's Phil?" says Leir. "Okay?"

"Phil?" says Bottle John, adjusting, neatening. "The fuck is Phil?"

"Mr. Kay," says Leir. "Dr. Kilo."

Evening out the ends of the bow he checks the width of it with his finger. "Now why you think," he says, "I know anything about your Dr. Kilo."

"You're a figment of my imagination," says Leir. "I can't keep track of everything myself. Figured you maybe saw something, in the confusion."

"A figment," says Bottle John. "You know what I been asking myself, ever since, what I been trying to untangle?" He steps back. "How it is a wisp a smoke buried in ice since the dawn of time gets such a hard-on for Charley Wentworth Leir, outta Fugate Fork Kentucky."

"I get around?" says Leir, sitting on the stool, taking up a silvery shoehorn and working it into a black patent leather pump.

"What you gotten yourself into this time," says Bottle John.

"What, this?" Leir slips his foot into the shoe. "Nothing I can't get out of." He picks up a pair of sunglasses from the dressing table as a flaring, dying spark drifts down. "The rules are always less stringent than you think." Blows ash from the lenses, the feather tied to the arm of it fluttering. "Fucking phantasmata." Puts them on.

Reflections in the gold-mirrored panels of the elevator walls, a hundred hundred Leirs one behind another all about. They lift hands to brush back grey tufts of hair almost precisely midway between brows and tops of skulls, and wind those strands about their fingers twisting, helping the curls along. "Now although many apparent byways shewed themselves, yet would I still proceed with my compass, and not budge one step from the line it set before me. Motherfuckers." Each Leir takes off his black sunglasses and all of them squeeze their eyes shut, rubbing at them with fingertips and thumbs. "But they made light of it, and went their ways, one to his farms, another to his books, and the rest closed up about the messengers, and slew them." Heads dip, look up again. "And he sent forth his armies, and destroyed those murderers, and burned up their city," he says. "The wedding is ready, but them which was bidden weren't worthy. Friend," he says, "how camest thou, in here, without a wedding garment?" Those sunglasses lifted in a hundred hundred hands, and hands take hold of all those feathers, rip them free. "I am as without speech," he says. A rumble, a shudder, the sound of the elevator changing pitch, speeding up, thinning out. "Woman, what have I to do with thee? – mine hour is not yet come." Those hands open, those sunglasses drop, fall below the mirrored panel, a single pair there on the carpet at his feet. "Piker," says Leir, and he stomps them, shattering the lenses, snapping the frame in two. Another shudder, the grinding slows, clunks, stops. "For Art is but the Priestess of Nature," he says, "and Nature the Daughter of Time, and Time?" The Leirs before him split down the middle and withdraw, as the doors open. "Fuck time," he says, light pouring over him, "there is no time, but now, and now, and now," and lifting one of those patent leather pumps over the threshold he steps out.

Crunch of glass underfoot, cubical nodules of powdering amber, silvery white, sheets of it sagging from frames there and there, pink crazed mirror-white and orange with heat, webbed by tremendous blows, past them a ruddy black emptiness and a buffeting wind, and light, all about light, a confusion of brilliance, shadows leap and climb and skitter over jagged drywall, bare steel struts, sprung cables, wrenched pipes. The ceiling's gone. The floor above is gone. The walls upreaching distended, twisted, broken, gone. He holds up a hand, the feather pinched in his fingers, against the punishing light. A crater before him, above him in the wreckage of the building, a seething caldera, light slopping over the edges of it, sloshing, starspume tossed by the wind, the howling, the roaring, sobbing wind.

"I ascend!" he cries, and sets his hand and foot to a gap in the wall, prying himself up, higher into the wreckage. "The form of a man," he says, careful of a sharp prong of broken rebar, "armed in a coat of male." Testing his footing on a sloping bit of concrete floor scraped clean. "I hold in my hand," he's pulling something from the pocket of his jacket, "a naked sword." Working his way about the crumbling wall at the edge of the floor there, braced clumsily, feather in one hand, cloth wadded in the other, squinting down at all that light below, thrusting both hands up, the feather, the scrap of underwear striped blue and white. "My operation!" he bellows. "Is for boldness! Malice! Liberty!"

Within that shapeless light a shape, a curl, a curve. A back. An arm, about a folded leg. A shadow there, hair, black hair.

"My lady," says Leir, lowering his hands. "You are mine."

Behind him a rustle, a thump, crackle and drag, "Fuck," says someone, someone else, "oh fuck," and he looks back, careful of his perch. Movement there in the ruined elevator bank, a glimmer in the shadows cast by all that light, nodules of glass clinking as she claws herself on her belly out of the hole in the floor, dripping light, smearing it into the carpet. Her boot finds solid purchase and she stops a moment, breathing deep and slow. Gathers herself, pushes over on her back blinking, looking up into a night sky cloudless blazing full of stars everywhere except the black slash looming, the blocky silhouette, him leaning over her, holding out a hand to her, pointing his hand at her, two fingers curled back against his palm, two fingers extended, thumb cocked. "Don't move, chickie," he growls. "Don't even breathe."

"Okay," says Jo.

"This is serious," says Leir.

"Okay."

"This will fuck you up."

"I believe you."

"Okay," says Leir. "Okay." Squatting, those two fingers pointed still at her face, her throat. Not too close. His face, his shoulders and arms, his smudged white shirt lit in harsh slashes shifting as he looks her over, her clothing soaked in light. "God damn," he says, looking away, off toward the edge of the floor. Those fingers unwavering. "You're covered in the stuff." Looking her over again. "How'd you get up here?"

"I don't know," says Jo. "I fell."

"Up."

"Yeah."

"Okay." His hand lifts, those two fingers still pointed at her. Clutched by the fingers curled back against his palm a single feather, dark in the uncertain light. "Here's what's gonna happen. You pick a hand. You reach up nice and slow with that hand, you unzip your coat. You open it up for me. I see the slightest twitch I do not like, I'm just gonna have to learn to live with the agony of never knowing what it was you thought you might've done. We understand each other?"

"I think so," says Jo.

"Pick your hand," says Leir.

Jo slowly, carefully slides the zipper of her jacket down, the click of each tooth clear, distinct until at the end she disengages it with a tug. She's reaching up to pull it open when he bats her hand away, jabbing her cheek with those extended fingers, cocked thumb straining, feather trembling as he pushes. His other hand wrapped in something, a scrap of fabric, striped, flipping open her jacket, careful of what he touches. "What is that, some-body's," she says, and he leans on her, pressing the side of her face to the carpet. "Asking questions," he says, "that's moving, that's breathing. What is this. This isn't the gun." In the hand wrapped about in stuff striped white and blue he's holding the small silvery coil of horn, the finish scratched, the bell dented. "Talk to me. You got a special dispensation to answer this one."

"A horn," says Jo, wincing as he presses again. "It's supposed to, supposed to get us back home – "

"Back?" He jerks upright with a laugh, taking those fingers with him. *"Why* on *earth* would you *ever* want to go *back?"* He hurls the horn into the air, "Wait," she says, but he's tracking its arc with those fingers, dropping the hammer of his thumb. A throaty exhalation, a tinny crump, the horn, smashed flat, falls away out of sight. "In case," he says, smiling down, "you were thinking I was maybe crazy. With the fingers. And all."

"No," says Jo, and the merest shake of her head. She's looking at the other hand, the striped hand, then away, blinking. "Where's," she says, "what have you done with," and she swallows, "Ysabel."

"Done with," he says, and those two fingers stroke his chin. "Always important, chickie-babe, to get it straight who it is who's gone and done zoomed who. It's what *she's* done to *me."*

"You're still here," says Jo.

"For which I will ever eternally grateful be. Come on, get up." Those fingers pointing at her again. "Get up! I figured out how you can help me." She rolls onto her side, her hands and knees, pushes back and up a little, into a crouch. Light flaking and drifting from her. "Kinda bridesmaid type a deal. Maid of honor." Shadows crawling over him as light erupts and falls about. "Wedding at the end of the world." His grey tuft jerking, caught in the gusting wind. He closes those fingers into a fist, working it back and forth with a grimace, then waves the feather at her, pinched now between index finger and thumb uncocked. "Come *on,"* he says. "On your feet."

Past the elevators, out to where the floor ends abruptly, cracked and jagged concrete, rebar yanked, walls and what once were walls angled around them, the floor below a lake of incandescence that banishes the stars, that surges in the wind, slops out broken windows, through doorways, that falls in showers of sparks, and there in the middle of it, Jo's hand to her mouth, "Ysabel," she says, the curve of a back, the arm about the folded leg, the shadowed curl of hair.

"Thus, my dilemma," says Leir, and Jo looks from the light to him. "That," he says, and a gesture of the hand wrapped in blue and white cloth. "I ain't about to go wading out into that shit."

"It's owr," she says. "It's just owr."

"Just." He looks down, head shaking, shoulders shaking, a chuckle. "Just. That much, this close, to the source? It'll drown a body out, shuffle it off to the choir ineffable. But." Looking her over, her light-scummed boots, her spangled hair. "Maybe not. So go on." Waving the feather out over the blaze. "Hop to it."

She says, "Hop what?"

"Climb down there," he says, "and go, and get her. Bring her back. Play the hero, girl. You don't make it, I'll just have to think of something else."

She says, "And if I do?"

He sucks in an exasperated breath. "I kiss her, I wake her, and I join myself to her in wedded bliss." The feather tilts back to her. "You've got to see this as a win, however limited. I *was* gonna eat her." Looking back out over the simmering light. "Get all of that inside me. Can you imagine?"

She says, "What if, what if she doesn't, want to get, married?"

"You think she has *any* idea what she wants? What she can do? What she's for?"

"And," she says, and she shivers, "and you do?"

He closes his eyes, tips back his head, "You smell this?" he says. "This is what gods breathe." Lowering his head, looking over at her, eyes pale over his dimpled cheeks. "Wait till I open my seventeen eyes." And then he laughs, loud, percussive barks, "Don't," he says, "don't even, Joliet Kendal Maguire." Another laugh. "I swear. You'd jump in front of a semi truck to save a damn ice cream cone, because this time, *this* time maybe Mommy or Daddy might notice. I *know* you!" She's staring at him, hands in her gloves at her sides, out where they can be seen. "I followed your very waking move for three damn months, girl. I kicked the tires of your dreams. You're going down there, and you're fighting your way to her side because you will cling to the slenderest hope in hell you can find that maybe, just maybe you might see some way of turning this back on me, and saving the goddamn day. Because who knows. This time, maybe this time, it'll bring your brother back."

"I don't," says Jo, not lifting her hands, "I don't," and a swallow, "I don't *have* a brother – "

"Right!" he snaps, leaning close. "Your little never-baby boy. *I know you!*" Rearing back as she takes a step away, unsteady on the broken floor. "So I see you start to do the least little thing I didn't know was gonna happen, I bite the top off this fucking building. *Do you hear me.*"

"I," she says, "yes, I," looking down, "I, could I," hands opening, closing, a shudder, "do you smoke?"

"What?"

"Just a quick," she says, "cigarette. To steady, my nerves?" Her hands, carefully not moving. "You, ah, do you want one?"

The two of them, limned and cloaked by that tumult of light, his white shirtfront streaked with ash, her grey skirt dotted white and greyly pink, snapped and rumpled by the wind.

"Yeah," he says. His hand curling about the feather, tucking it against his palm. "Yeah, sure." Two fingers extending. His thumb, cocking. "Okay."

"They're in the," she says, lifting a hand, slowly, "front right pocket, I'll just," crinkle of plastic and a twitch of his hand, "Cigarettes," she says, "cigarettes," in her hand, trembling, a slender orange pack. "I have to," she says, "it's a new pack, I have to open – "

"I almost wish you *had* tried to what's that," he says. In the hand that's holding the pack as she's ripping at a corner of it something else, a piece of paper crumpled, folded, a page torn from a magazine. "That's a," he says. She's taken the pack into her other hand, she's holding up the folded page, just above her fingers a cartooned figure, a sketch of a woman, opera gloves and stockings. "That's a femlin," he says. "Why do you, what are you doing with a centerfold in your pocket?"

"I found it in a briefcase," she says. "You want it?"

"Unfold it," he's saying, "you unfold it, open it up, now, now dammit, show me," and she's carefully peeling the corners away and shaking it out, turning it over to hold it up, the photograph filling the page, the woman lying back, the orange jacket, the dark stockings, the blue and white underwear, stretched taut. "What is this," he says, his voice gone quiet, flat. "A joke, what is this. You think this is funny."

"No," says Jo. "No, I don't."

"You're mocking me," he says, as if two or three voices are fighting for the words in his mouth, and lifts his hands to sweep the feathers from his face, the great mane of feathers brown and white and black and dull brick red, and smoke is curling from the bottom of the page. She lets it go, lets it flaring fall, she turns as he opens his eyes, all of them, she lunges away a step full-tilt and another out past the jagged edge of concrete leaping as he opens his mouths, all of them, roaring, bellowing, and a throaty punch of a sound. Cartwheeling over herself she screams, falling, plowing a wake in all that light.

Rolling and tumbling coated in dripping with caked-over glitter, sodden with light, gasping shimmering spittle the waves of it sloshing about her elbows, her knees and behind another, soaring splitting howl and all around the wind, and everything's starting to shake. "Ysabel!" she screams, up on her feet in slurry, waves of it building breaking brilliant slush of it drifting the wreckage and ahead the figure still on its side, black curls strung with light. A howl rises to a screech and everything drops a foot or more to hang there one long frozen moment Jo pitching forward before it all of it falls again and under she goes the crashing surf of light that slops and rolls and settles as stone falls, as glass cracks, as flames rip and climb.

There by Ysabel she surfaces shoulders heaving clinging her arms about her, looking back at the rim of the floor above, the wings spreading there like thunder, the fire, and all those eyes. "Ysabel," she says. "Wake up. Ysabel. We've got to." Another shrieking chorus and she hunches herself up over Ysabel's back as everything drops once more, and a sob as it's all brought up short again, a boom.

"Ysabel," she says. Ysabel's head cradled in her arm. Wiping light from closed eyes, slack mouth. "I'm here," she says. "The sky's falling," she says, and a laughing sob as another howl climbs up above them, "but I'm here," she says. "I'm here."

A flash of green, as Ysabel opens her eyes

That flash of green, as she sits up in Jo's arms, and reaches out a hand. Reaches out a hand, and catches there a moth between thumb and forefinger, a moth, wings spread, and the spots on its wings like eyes. That moth, trembling when she crushes it.

The green, shining, as the flames close in and she pulls Jo close, and everything drops once more but all the light about them, rising

FALLING – IF EVEN THIS

FALLING slumping shoulder fetching up she jolts awake, she blinks. Out there lights flash, red and red over a line of parked cars, a pickup truck, a minivan luridly purple in that light. She sits up, and a rough grey blanket slips away. There in her lap her hand, bare, and in her hand a hand, Ysabel's hand, Ysabel wrapped in a rough grey blanket and Jo's black hooded jacket. "Hey," says Jo, softly.

Stirring Ysabel smiles before she opens her eyes. Squeezes Jo's squeezing hand. "Hey," she says, sitting up, leaning over, tipping together the two of them, shoulder to shoulder, wine-red hair spangled with gold against glossy black curls streaked, here and there, with white.

Red lights still flash. The ambulance is parked at an angle in the lot, right up by the long single-storey line of motel units. Jo drops out the back of it, black boots heavy splashing a runnel of melting snow, her shirtwaist dress, black and grey, white and pink, arms pulled in tight for warmth, tugging a glove onto her hand, grey and fingerless, wrapping the velcro about her wrist. Looking up at the blue-black sky, featureless in the glare of worklights. Over there at the back

of the lot, by the corner of the detached set of motel units, a
reddish brown car, a black stripe along its side, the driver's
door open, a man sitting there, his feet on the pavement, and
a woman leaning against the trunk of it, wrapped in a sheepskin coat, her wild hair yellow-white. "How is she," she says,
as Jo slowly approaches.

"Sleeping," says Jo. "You should – " but Marfisa shakes her
head, lifts her chin, a gesture back toward the main building of
the motel. "He's in there," she says, and then, as Jo turns to
look, "Gallowglas."

Jo turns back. In the front seat Luys leans against the doorframe, head hung low, looking at his shoes. Marfisa traps one of
Jo's hands between both of hers and holds it a moment, looking
her wordless in the eye. Jo's free hand comes up, laid gently atop
Marfisa's, and Marfisa nods, once, and lets go.

That long low line of motel units, red doors, curtained windows,
the dark maw of an air conditioner under each, over and over
again until that room there, just past the hood of the ambulance the
frames about the shattered window and the missing door scorched
black, the dregs of snow before it stomped into sooty puddles that
flash red and red and red. In the doorway, leaning on his cane, Leo
in his camel-colored topcoat, and no hat upon his head, looking at
something inside the room. "Where is everyone," says Jo.

Smiling he reaches a hand for her, the small of her back, her
hip, pulling her close there in the doorway, leaning in to kiss
her mouth. "Hello to you, too," he says.

"No, I mean," says Jo, and then, gloved hands up on his
shoulders, she kisses him, lightly. "It's so, quiet."

"We have some little time," he says, straightening. Letting
go. "Welcome back."

"This," says Jo, she's looking into the room, "Timmo and
Abe, they were staying here."

Leo points to the one bed, a spavined, cinder-furred hulk under
a frozen wheel of smoke-stain printed over the wall, the ceiling,
dripping with grimy water. What once was a laptop at one end,
warped, the screen of it burned white. "He was holding what was
left of a, ah, briefcase," he says.

"But we were, on, top of Big Pink," says Jo, looking back, out into the glare. "And then, the – tub?" Looking inside, a shake of her head.

"Probably saved you from the blaze," says Leo.

"No, I, what I, what I'm – how – how did we, how did we end up," and she takes a deep and shaky breath, "how the hell did you *know?* How?"

"That's the thing," says Leo, looking out, to the ambulance. "Or, at least, a thing." There in the shadow of it, leaning against the side of it, Orlando in his long dark skirt, his white shirt, his feet bare.

"You," says Jo, starting forward, "you get away from there – " and Leo's hand on her shoulder, "Jo," he says, gently. "He knew where you'd be, and when. He knew there'd be a fire. If he hadn't told us – "

"What do you *want,*" says Jo, and Orlando, pushing up off the ambulance, says, "Dust or blood, my nemesis."

"Jo?" says Ysabel, there at the back of the ambulance. Marfisa behind her. "A brief affair, my lady," says Leo. "Over quickly, and done."

Ysabel looks from Jo, to Leo, and the briefest inclination of her head. "I *won,*" says Jo. "I *beat* you, two out of three, however you want to count it, we're *done,*" and he laughs, and taps the patch over his eye. "A blow to each, but we both yet stand," he says. "And our first, of three? A technicality. You really want to've won on points? My *blade* was in your *back,* Gallowglas." His hands spread, smiling mildly. "And you took my love, and I took yours, but now he is King, and she is Queen, and for us there's nothing left but blood, or dust."

"I will *not* fight you," says Jo.

"Why then is your sword there in your hand?" says Orlando.

She looks down, to see her hand in its glove about a plain hilt wrapped in dull wire, within a glittering net of wiry strands that meet in worked steel knots, twining down to the great silvery clout of a pommel, and stretched before her straight and true the shining blade. "I," she says, and no scabbard in her other hand, nor at her hip. "I didn't, I," lowering the sword, and the tip of it chiming against the charred sidewalk.

"I'll need a blade myself, Ieraks," says Orlando. "Careless, I know, but one of mine's held by a wizard, now, and the other by the father of my latest inamorata."

"Leo," says Jo as he limps sourly past, hefting a longsword by the strong of its blade, "If it must needs be done," he's saying, extending the heavy-pommeled hilt of it toward Orlando's waiting hand, "it were best to get it done."

Orlando takes the hilt and swings the blade away from Leo, a high sweeping cut, and another, settling into his stance. "Are you frightened?" he says, looking to Jo.

"Yes," she says.

"Good," he says. "I'd hate to be the only one enjoying this." And then, when she doesn't lift her sword, "Your cue, Gallowglas."

She's looking from Leo beside her, hands on the stern hawk at the head of his cane, to Ysabel there at the back of the ambulance, wrapped in blankets and her black jacket, and Marfisa's hand on her shoulder.

"Think of your anger," says Orlando. "Those senseless murders. The Gammer, the Shootist. The Soames. Gloria, and her father. You, perhaps. Almost. Think of Billy, Gallowglas. Little Billy Maguire."

She opens her eyes. She lifts her sword up at an angle before her, slides her left foot back, tucks her free hand up against her chest. Waiting.

He sighs. "Fear alone will have to do," he says, stepping forward, leaping forward blade coming down a hammer blow Jo catches and throws off, rocking Orlando back. A peal of blows then, his wild swings met by jerks and yanks, her sword moving only enough to catch and block and catch again as he falls back and strikes and falls back, with each pass turning a circle like a ratchet that carries him away from the back of the ambulance, away from Ysabel. One last overhead cut parried by Jo settling back in her stance as he lifts his sword up and away, pointedly leaving himself wide open. "*Strike* me!" he cries. "Are you not the Huntsman? Were you not tasked?"

Her blade at an angle before her, her free hand over her heart.

His shoulders slump. He shakes his head. "What will it take," he says. His one eye catching hers as she looks up from his lowered blade-tip.

He says, "I wonder if even this."

"Jo – " cries Ysabel, and "Mooncalfe!" cries Marfisa, and Jo breaks screaming into a run blade up hilt back for a thrust, and "Lando?" says Leo, looking down at the sword. Looking down at his sword. At the strong of the blade of it there between the lapels of his camel-colored topcoat, at the torn edges of the hole it's made in his soft shirt of some nameless harvest gold. At Orlando's hand on the hilt of it, and the look in Orlando's eye, the sweet smile on his face as the tip of Jo's sword punches through his throat, and at the lacy darkness falling all about, like ashes.

"You'd rather a Duke, not a Prince, for a King," says Lymond. The sky above them a softening blue grey.

"I'd rather a Queen," says the Soames. "I was promised a Queen."

"You expect wonder hard on the heels of a miracle," says Lymond. And then, "But do you think me the only Perry?"

"Ysabel, the Bride?" says the Soames. "Your Bride?" Frowning as he marches along, close beside Lymond down the quiet winding street. "Then the line's not broken, as we were told." The bicycles winding behind them, and the trundling pickup and its hangers-on.

"We shall see," says Lymond.

Heading to the edge of the street, across the sidewalk and the scrap of dying grass, up to the yellow front door, followed by Marquess and Soames and Viscount, and the clatter and clank and ticking spin of bicycles. He pulls out a padded envelope, and from it a gold credit card, and he works the card into the gap between door and frame, jimmying the lock, a click and a clunk and he opens the door. "My house," he calls out to all of them, "is yours," and he steps inside. Down the long hall, the thunder of dozens of footsteps, out into the big room empty but for an overstuffed armchair, a low table beside it, a great window, the shapes of the city uncertain in the shining haze, and the mountain beyond a pale shadow of blue and rose against the first rays of the rising sun.

"Well," says Lymond, as those footsteps settle, the rustle of coats and scarves and gloves, blue suits, green coveralls. All that motley crowd beneath the window, uncertain whether to look out, or in. His back to them, his hands on the arm of the chair, "Mark this," he says, and turning, sits him down.

The silence, as everyone in the room takes in a breath.

And then a rustle once more, of heads lowering, of hands lifted to hearts, to brows, as here, there, there and there again, and again, a knee is taken, as the King stands up from his Throne.

"There is much to be done," he says, smiling under his bulging eyes, one brown, one blue, his pinkish orange pompadour a-bob. "Let us begin."

The Gallowglas succeedeth the Horseman, and he is commonly armed with a scull, a shirt of mail, and a Gallowglas axe; his service in the field is neither good against horsemen, nor able to endure an encounter with pikes, yet the Irish do make great account of them.

—*Barnabie Rich*

NO. 22

MAIESTIE

WHEN THE PHONE SINGS I want trumpets and violins to play over thumping drums and piano and chugging guitar the rumpled blankets jerk and twist and spit out a hand. It fumbles about and finds the phone, cutting it off mid-revolvers and adrenaline. A head drifts up, sleep-matted hair wine-red, cut short. Jo opens her eyes.

Starkly white, walls, ceiling, wider at the one end than the other, windows blotched with old paint about the mullions, two or three storeys up. Over across a narrow street an unfinished apartment complex, welter of scaffolding, plywood draped in green paper printed over and over with logos that say Regen Homewrap. Under the windows three or four blond wood crates filled with clothing neatly folded. She swings her feet off the futon and standing almost trips over discarded black jeans, black boots flopped emptily beside them, a brown glass growler wrapped in a plastic garbage bag. On the wall by the door a sword's slung from a leather strap, the scabbard of it plain and black, the simple hilt swaddled in a basket of wiry strands. Above it from the same nail a painted skull-mask, teeth crudely chiseled, black mane falling, motionless, long enough almost to brush the floor.

A bathroom, white tile, windows of frosted glass, the tub an enameled slipper up on clawed feet. Against the wall by the tub a lidded white bucket, a stainless steel tureen covered with foil, a plastic milk jug, a blue bottle sealed with pink wax. Jo skins off her tank top, leaves it puddled blackly on white tile. Over the sink the mirror's an artfully jagged oblong set in the wall, and caught there muddy eyes to either side of the nose, that nose, the mouth, thinly pale-lipped. Red line of an old and faded wound across her brow. Her hand to her breast, fingertips pressed against, dimpling the skin, whitening, trembling. A hiss of breath, her eyes squeezed shut, her hand yanked away.

The kitchen's airy, white and blue and stainless steel, thin grey morning light. Wrapped in a robe of buffalo plaid, feet bare, hair wet, Jo picks a glass up out of the sink and eyes the bit of milk ringing the bottom before rinsing it out. Opening cabinets she finds a shelf of mugs, pulls one down. Over on a counter between the kitchen and the open room beyond a stainless steel carafe, there by a bouquet, a profusion of orange and gold sunflowers overtopping a slender glass vase. She thumbs back the lid of the carafe, sniffs, pours herself a cup of coffee. On the other side of the carafe a neat stack of paper, maybe an inch high, held at one corner by a fat black binder clip.

Down three low steps into the open room beyond, windows to the left and right in walls that narrow to a point, where Jo sits herself in a great maroon chair. Sipping her coffee she flips through the pages littered with little plastic flags brightly yellow and red marking this line, that box, and she sets to signing here, initialing there, JKM, JKM, Joliet Maguire, JKM. The window behind her looks out over a hatching of bare branches, a wedge of sidewalk below shimmed between two angled streets, a theater marquee across the intersection that says Brazil 700, Long Kiss Goodnight 945. Back along the length of the apartment past the kitchen down the hall beyond a door opens, quietly. Jo looks up. A silhouette down there, carrying something, a mass of tangled curls that lighten paling as she steps into the kitchen, a cloud the color of clotted cream. "Marfisa," says Jo.

Marfisa starts, looks down into the open room. Sets her knapsack down, and the wooden baseball bat, leaning it against the door to the apartment. Shakes out her sheepskin coat. "Congratulations," she says, slipping it on.

Jo sets down the pen. "For what?" she says. "The hell is that supposed to mean?"

"She loves you, Gallowglas," says Marfisa, taking up the bat again, the knapsack. Jo stands, pages falling a rustling thump to the floor, "Look," she says, stalking over to the steps up into the kitchen, "You do what you're gonna do, don't do it, I don't care, but if you *hurt* her, *again* – "

"I never," says Marfisa, but Jo's up the steps, *"If,"* she's saying, hand raised, and then "don't," she says, "don't hurt her. Or I'll hurt you."

"As I said," says Marfisa, opening the door to the apartment.

The door, closing behind her. The papers splayed on the floor below, in the sunlight. The dark hall ahead.

In the white room kicking the black jeans out of the way Jo kneels by the growler, yanking the plastic garbage bag down and off. Inside the bottom of it slicked with something viscous, white, frothed with a sheen of bubbles, a hint of warm yellow gold. Both arms about it hefting the weight of it wadding out into the hall, the bathroom at the end. Careful of the slippery floor, lowering with her knees, she sets the growler by the bucket and the tureen. Re-belts her robe before heading back out into the hall, where the door to the left is open now, on a room painted yellow and white, and Ysabel, leaning in the doorway, arms folded in a bulky fisherman's sweater, a cigarette smoldering in her hand. Her hair's been cut quite short, little more than sleek black fuzz. She opens her reddened eyes. "So," she says, and she lifts the cigarette to her lips. "Shall we do this?"

"Sure," says Jo. "What the hell."

Night, and the sky above an overcast rusted with city light, blotted at the end of a long busy street by the black hulk of a hill. In the lap of it there the street ends at the colonnaded porch of a big yellow house awash in pinkish orange light, and climbing up behind it isolated blooms of streetlight scratched by bare branches, the startled green of conifers, and there, and there above, the light's pooled about fences, low stone buildings, and zigging and zagging up that hill, winding from there to there a line of embers, sparks just bright enough, flickering, to hollow out the shadows about them, marking a slow and stately passage back and forth and up, and always up, and in the lulls of the traffic's rush, when engines idle and tires roll to a stop, when the door swings shut on the noise of the bar, when the busker at the corner strikes the last chord from her guitar and stills the strings with a hand, looking up, cocking her ear, just faintly, floating down from that hill, what might be a hundred voices or more that lift, lilting something like a song.

WATER, CRASHING – WEDNESDAY MORNING
JO, UNEXPECTED

WATER, CRASHING into the tub. Jo tests it with a hand, adjusts a knob, fetches the stopper from a chrome rack over the nozzle and leans in to sink it home. She's headed for the bucket, the tureen, when Ysabel says, "First things first."

"Oh," says Jo. She undoes the belt of her robe, but turns her back before opening it, shrugging it off to hang it from a hook there by the tub.

"I would not have expected modesty," says Ysabel. She's sitting on the closed toilet seat, smoking the end of her cigarette. Jo turns, head cocked, hands spread, a gesture of display, before stooping by the bucket. "Any time you're ready," she says.

Cigarette in her mouth Ysabel works the sweater up over her head, down her arms, to drop to the floor. She lifts her foot to work a gold ring from her little toe. "Your tattoo's gone," she says. Setting the ring on the windowsill. Jo's working to pop the seals that hold the lid of the bucket in place, but one hand strays to her belly. "I guess," she says, "it, he, couldn't put it back. Or didn't bother."

"It never suited you," says Ysabel, stubbing out the cigarette.

"It was a warning," says Jo, but Ysabel's hand is on her back, sliding up to her shoulder as she jerks upright, turning to find herself in an embrace, Ysabel pulling her close, shorn fuzz against wine-colored locks.

"This is weird," says Jo.

"Of course it is," says Ysabel. Letting go, stepping back. "We've never done it before." Hoisting a leg into the tub, pulling herself in after. "Properly," she says, and sighs as she settles in the steaming water. "Wait," she says, when Jo turns back to the bucket. "Wait."

Jo sits on the edge of the tub, and takes Ysabel's dripping hand in her own, and Ysabel pulls it close to press a kiss to the palm of it. Jo closes her eyes. "Let it fill a bit more," says Ysabel.

Abruptly up, mouth open, a word unsaid, beige blankets, white sheet wound about her legs. Grey daylight leaking past the edges of a heavy curtain drawn, incandescent light seeping under a closed door, and the howl of a hair dryer, and she draws herself up, elbow on knees, hand to her forehead, the neat white bit of gauze taped there, under her rumpled wine-red hair. A second bed beside her, comforter turned back, pillows in disarray. Grey suit laid out neatly at the foot of it, and a yellow camisole. "Ysabel?" says Jo, but softly. Clink of glass as she sets her feet to the floor, an empty bottle or two. Black tank top, black briefs, she makes her gingerly way past the low dresser laden with ravaged take-out boxes, an empty bottle of wine, white shopping bags that say Meier and Frank in red letters. A sword, blade bare, the hilt of it guarded about by a net of wiry strands. She lifts an edge of the heavy curtain and squints out, washed over in thin grey light. The wall over across the street paneled in squares of colors from old photographs, dull orange, pale grey, dull greenish grey, the brick building beside it painted over in a mural, a camel, an oasis, M.E. Dinihanian and Sons, it says. Rug Cleaning. Rug Repairing. The hair dryer stops.

The bathroom door opens. There's Ysabel, smoothing the artful tangles of her long black hair, shot through with occasional curling threads of white. "Did I wake you?" she says.

"Time's it," says Jo.

"After nine," says Ysabel. "In the morning." She picks up the yellow camisole. "Wednesday morning," she says, slipping it on.

"I *know* what," says Jo, and then, catching herself, "it's tomorrow."

"The Apportionment, yes," says Ysabel, fingers busy with buttons. "Tomorrow evening. So plenty of time, *oceans* of time, to gather the medhu, turn the owr, see to my mother, reassure the gentry," reaching for grey trousers, smokey stockings.

"Is there, anything you need?" says Jo. "I can do, to help?"

Ysabel looks up. Lays the trousers back over the foot of the bed. "Don't go," she says. "Don't do this to yourself." Taking Jo's hand from the curtain, letting darkness fall again. Jo pulls her close, a sudden embrace. "You don't have to go," says Ysabel, her chin on Jo's shoulder.

"Yeah, I do," says Jo, leaning back from all that hair.

"Then I will go with you," says Ysabel, kissing her, softly.

"Everything you got going on?" says Jo. "And you didn't know him. Really, you don't have to," and another kiss. "Yes," says Ysabel. "I do."

Letting go. Ysabel dressing, crisply, quietly, stockings and trousers, jacket. Jo lays a hand on the curtain again but doesn't lift it. "Is there time for breakfast?" says Jo. "I could maybe make myself presentable, you give me a minute."

"I must go now to secure a tub," says Ysabel, slipping on a lemon and grey spectator pump. "For the turning. You get back in bed. We'll try for lunch."

"Okay," says Jo. "Lunch. Where."

"I'll let you know," says Ysabel, putting on her long white topcoat. "A surprise. My treat." A white slouch hat on her head. "All right?"

Jo nods. When the door closes, when she's alone, she looks down, picks up a bottle that isn't yet empty. Jim Beam Honey, the label says.

Wandering through a grocery store a featureless silhouette, down a city street. He isn't watching. He isn't looking at the other monitor either, the one filled with columned numbers, rows highlighted in yellow and green. Something burbles, chimes, a notice appears, floating over the numbers, Andy Hornbeck's office calling, Answer, Answer with video, Decline. He looks up, runs a hand through what's left of his hair, fits a tiny black headset to his ear and taps it. "Mendlesohn Associates," he says. Past the monitors a glass-walled office, inside a man looking out at the cityscape, dark hills, soft grey rain. "Mr. Mendlesohn's in conference," says Becker. "I can take a message, or he can – that's – yes. He can. Any time before two? Yes, I'll, I'll let him know. Thank you." Tapping the space bar, setting the tiny headset by the keyboard, a sleek aluminum thing with spotless white keys, unburdened by any cords.

A woman comes around a corner of those glass walls, studiedly graceful in nosebleed heels, a slender pinstripe skirt. "Arnold," she says.

"Becker, actually," he says, adjusting the knot of his tie, a burnished brown with muted polka dots. "Everybody, ah, calls me, just, Becker."

She nods once, and says, "Is there any way to possibly, *rearrange* the entries, in the Pink Cloud and White Cloud reports, by admittance date? And print them?" Her makeup precisely invisible, blond hair swept back, pinned up. "Sure," says Becker. "If you click the column," pointing to the spreadsheet, "then use the sort icon, you can – "

"Excellent," she says. "And printouts. Of each. Thanks."

Becker says, "Sure."

She heads off into the glass-walled office, and he presses a key. Watches the rows and columns shift and rearrange. Stands when the printer over on the credenza whirs to life. Pages in hand, he knocks once on the glass door, then steps in, "of the under-thirties," the man's saying, "lock, stock, and barrel the crosstabs," and then he looks away from the rain to see Becker, there, in the doorway. "Here," says Becker, holding out the pages to the woman perched on a corner of the glass-topped desk.

"Both reports, Arnold," she says.

"It is," he says. "It's both."

"Five copies?" she says. "I need five copies. Of each."

And Becker says, "Sure."

In the bathroom he bangs open a stall door, leans against one red-painted wall. Loosens his tie, undoes the top button of his shirt. Swipes and thumbs the screen of his phone, holds it up to his ear. "We have got to talk about this situation," he says.

"I have been here three days," he says, "and I don't know what I'm doing or what they think they're doing but I don't think they know either –

"What? David, I'm not talking about lunch! We have to –

"I – I don't, I didn't – " He sighs. "Red Star. Six o'clock. Drinks, whatever." Leaning his head back, closing his eyes. "Sure," says Becker.

At the top of those wide white steps the Coke machine hums to itself, bright red, and on the front of it a photo of a bottle of soda, a thickly blackish brown that's hoared with ice. In the ruddied shadows beside it a nondescript white door, the knob of it faceted glass. Up from the lobby below comes Jo's voice echoing, rising, "my stuff! Every goddamn thing I had left in this world!"

"But there's nothing there, milady," says the man in the brown tweed vest.

"Bullshit," says Jo all in black, black jeans, black boots, the hood of her jacket back over her shoulders like a crumpled scarf. The neat white dressing at her brow. She moves to step past him, and he scrambles into her path. "Lady, *please.*"

"The *hell* with this lady shit," she says.

"I merely wish," says the man in the vest, and "Stirrup!" says a deep voice, over there. "Gallowglas." Jo whips around, catching herself. A man there in the doorway, under a hanging bouquet of tie-dyed T-shirts, his shoulders broad in yellow chamois, his hair a neat black cap. "What seems to be the matter in dispute," he says.

"I just," says Jo, "want to go upstairs, and get my stuff?"

"There's nothing up there anymore," says the man in the doorway, and he holds up a hand as Jo snaps, "Luys!" and he says, "so there's no harm, in letting you see that for yourself." A bit of leather thong tied loosely about his wrist. "Mason!" cries the Stirrup, but Luys turns his hand from forestalling to an offering with a gentle smile. Jo doesn't take it.

"We weren't told to expect you," says the Stirrup, stepping aside with a scowl.

"I can't just," says Jo, headed for the wide white steps, "*sit,* all the damn day in that hotel, while she's off, doing, *God* knows what." On the landing she pauses, her hand against the wall, and Luys hurries up after, taking her arm. "My lady," he says, quietly. "You're drunk."

"The hell I am," she says.

"You've been drinking," he says.

"Call me lady again," she says, yanking herself free, marching on, up the steps. "I'll deck you."

The buzzing Coke machine. The white door beside it. Jo rips and resettles the velcro closures on her cycling gloves, black and grey. "The password," she says.

"There's no one inside to give it," says Luys. "Go on."

Jo closes her eyes, her hand on the knob. "Farquahr will be two," she murmurs, and she opens the door.

The room beyond is little more than a closet. To one side a mop bucket. "Wait," says Jo. A rack of cubbies stuffed with spray bottles and cartons of light bulbs. "I've seen this before." Wrapped bundles of paper towels and looped hanks of extension cords. She closes the door. "If I just." Opens it again.

"It's gone," says Luys, as she's saying, "The rooms, all the rooms, his, my things, they were," and he says, "You didn't come for your things, Gallowglas." Her eyes closing, lips clenching. "You came alone," says Luys, quietly, "on the bus, didn't you? With liquor on your breath, and only half the morning gone." He takes her hand in both of his. "You loved him, didn't you." Her eyes open abruptly. "Or you might have," he says. "Come to. But he's gone. Jo. He's gone."

"Did you?" says Jo. "Love him?"

He looks away. Lets go her hand. Reaches past her to close the door. "Come along with me," he says, and he heads back past the Coke machine to the steps.

"Where," says Jo. "Where're you going?" Stepping after him. "Where are we going?"

"To get the car," says Luys. "To take you to your things."

Under the trees in a ragged file they move, having left street-lights behind, a hundred of them, and another, and more, and each of them holding up a shining hand, and gleaming tendrils of a summery haze drift like smoke down and down in their wake, and fall about the brims of their hats, the crowns of their hoods, the shoulders of their heavy coats and leather jackets, nylon rainshells and fleecey pullovers, and their mouths open, singing, a nameless vowel to eddy that sluggish fog of light, and the sound of it rising slowly until it slips all at once in a dizzying ululation that winds about the trees around them. Light falls more thickly now, on roots and gravel, mud and the thin grass, pine needles and mushrooms, and the boots and shoes and muddy feet of those that come after disturb the fallen light as they pass, kick it up like dust as they move on, singing, and yet more light falling, from all those upraised hands.

THE STUFF IN THE BUCKET – A SURPRISE
THE MEN ABOUT THE CITY – HOW THINGS ARE DONE

THE STUFF IN THE BUCKET'S thick, frothed with iridescent bubbles around the edge of it, creamily flat in the center, and all a milky white that's warmed with hints of gold. "I just," says Jo, "pour it in?"

In the tub Ysabel nods, steaming water up to her chin, droplets shining silvery in the darkness of her short short hair. "All at once?" says Jo. "Or slow and steady, maybe drizzle it around?"

"It'll be slow," says Ysabel. She opens her eyes. "Which do you have?"

"Uh," says Jo, her hand on the bucket, "this is North's. The, I guess the Hare, now?"

"Pour yours first," says Ysabel.

"Mine."

"Yes," says Ysabel, closing her eyes. "Yours."

"Okay," says Jo. "Okay." Shifting the bucket to one side she reaches for the growler, unscrews the cap of it with a fluted pop. Heaving the weight of it up in her arms she sidesteps back to the tub and a boom as she sets it on the edge, balanced at an angle in her hands. "Okay," she says. "Here we go." Tipping the growler, leaning it scraping the edge of the tub, "whoops," and a sucking oozing glug of a sound, a drop, gathering itself in the mouth of the jug, swelling and sagging, distending, slipping the lip of it falling reluctant paloop to the water where it unfolds, clouds of white, billowing open, shreds and tatters spreading, over Ysabel.

"Gallowglas?" says Luys, a down vest over his yellow chamois shirt.

Above him Jo's stopped on the landing, a hand on the railing of the next flight up. "There's only two storeys," she says. "This building only had two storeys, outside."

"Three one two," says Luys.

"I don't think," says Jo, scowling past him to the ground floor below, "this is a storage unit."

"No," says Luys. "It isn't."

That next flight ends in a narrow landing, just large enough for them both to stand before a plain brown door. Black numerals, a three, a one, a two, hung above a peephole, the rim of it pitted with rust. Jo lifts a hand knuckled to knock, lowers it, looking over at Luys. He shrugs. She lifts it again when someone inside, Ysabel, calls out, "It's open!"

Jo opens the door.

The room beyond an airy kitchen, white and blue and stainless steel, and on the counter there a mound of roses, yellow, white, pink and orange, mottled red and white, striated, a deep rich red that's almost black among the dark green leaves. "Ysabel?" says Jo, stepping in, followed by Luys. Past that counter down three low steps an open room, windows to the left and right in walls that narrow to a point and there stands Ysabel in her grey suit, smiling. On a sofa to one side a man in a brown suit coat, and on the cushions beside him a briefcase veneered in some lightly colored wood. He gruffly pushes himself to his feet as Luys inclines his head, a bow, "Majesty," he says.

"You've gone and spoiled the surprise, Mason," says Ysabel.

"The hell," says Jo, as Luys says, "She came to us, quite upset, ma'am. It seemed best."

"Very well," says Ysabel, her gesture offering up the room about her, the roses, the kitchen and past it, behind them, the hallway strung with yellow lights, the open doors there, and there. "Welcome home," she says, and Jo turns about there by the door to the apartment, taking it all in, "What," she's saying, "you said," and then, "I'm sorry," to the man in the brown suit coat, "you're, who are you? Who is this?"

"You hadn't met the Shrieve?" says Ysabel.

"I don't, I'm sorry, I don't know the Shrieve," says Jo.

"Bruno, lady," he says, with a nod, quite short, standing next to Ysabel. He wears no collar or tie, and his pants are rumpled corduroy.

"What do you think?" says Ysabel, and then, bounding forward, up the steps, "come on," into the kitchen, taking Jo's hand, dragging her along, "come and see." Down the hall, under the lights, two doors left, and right, "I thought you were," Jo's saying, as Ysabel says "Separate rooms, see? Like we said," and through the one doorway yellow and white, and white on white through the other, and "you were getting a *tub*," says Jo. Under the window in there a row of crates made from polished blond wood, a steamer trunk, "Wait," says Jo, "is that," but "Oh," says Ysabel, pulling Jo down to the end of the hall, the door there open on gleaming white tile and frosted glass and "the *tub*," says Ysabel, the great enameled slipper of it. "It's not a jacuzzi," she says, taking both Jo's hands in her own, "but," letting go to open the last of the doors, ducking under a dangle of yellow lights, pulling Jo in after. In the kitchen Luys looks after them, looks back into the open front room, tucks his hands away in his pockets. Bruno with a shrug sits himself back on the sofa, there by his briefcase.

Through a narrow dark room, the blank glass portholes of clothes dryer and washing machine, "Out here," says Ysabel, opening the door at the other end on a trickle and seep of rain, stepping out under a low canopy, a little wooden porch, a single step down to a pocket of yellow grass and low green scrub out to the low parapets to either side, and here and there islands of the building's infrastructure, a ventilator hood, chimney pots, the boxy bulk of a fan. Wooden tubs there and there that hold small leafless trees, a raised bed filled with bare earth waiting, a couple of unpainted Adirondack chairs before a patterned bronze chiminea on spindly legs, and everywhere strung from branches to poles more strands of little yellow lights. "We have a garden," says Ysabel.

"You," says Jo, turning about, a shadow in the dim light, "you moved," fingers flashing as she waves back into the apartment, "my *stuff.*"

"*You* were supposed to sleep in," says Ysabel.

"I got," says Jo, "antsy. I wanted to do something." And then, "You didn't *tell* me!" and Ysabel steps back, blinking. "I wanted it to be a surprise," she says.

"Well." Jo looks away, looks about. Wiping her eyes. "Hey. That worked."

"Tonight, after you, said goodbye," says Ysabel, stepping close again, "I would have brought you here. Home. To this." Jo ducks her head, shoulders settling her arms about Ysabel, and Ysabel's about her. "And tomorrow, together, we turn the owr, and tomorrow night we give it out again. To everyone." Pulling them together, tightly. "We've made it, Jo. We did it."

Jo nods. She leans back, in Ysabel's arms, "So what are we," she says, and a sniff, "what are we talking about here, this apartment. It's ours? Or just the tub."

"Oh," says Ysabel, a chuckle, "it's more than *that.*"

Thumbing open the locks of the briefcase in his lap, lifting the lid, a manila folder, a calculator, a scatter of pens, a foolscap pad, he takes out the folder, careful of a couple of not quite empty glassine envelopes that he tips back into the case. Closing the lid he rifles through a number of stapled documents, "I've had to take some decisions," he says, "given mandated outlays, dispensations, remittances, the portfolio could not I'm afraid remain, ah, intact. But." His smile's a flash, there and gone again. "There are options."

"For, what?" says Jo, on the sofa beside him, a panini in her hand, greens, tomatoes, soft white cheese. "What is all this?"

"Your fortune," says Bruno, laying out the documents he's selected.

"My," says Jo, "what?" Plucking up a page. "That's a quarterly projection," he says. "I cast a number of them, under differing," that smile again, on-off, "assumptions?"

"Quarterly," she says, the sandwich drifting toward her mouth. She doesn't take a bite. "This is what comes in every, every three months."

His brow pinches, a frown that doesn't flit away. "There are," he says, "more aggressively liquid postures to be taken," shuffling through the pages in his hands.

"I don't," says Jo, looking up, to Ysabel there in the kitchen, "understand. What is all this?"

"Let the Shrieve explain," says Ysabel, white coat in her hands. "He's very good with all these rituals and incantations, and, unlike some," slipping her arms in the sleeves, "eminently trustworthy."

"Your majesty is too kind," says Bruno, and then he lunges after the pages slipping to the floor as Jo beside him leaps to her feet, hand to her chest, "You're leaving?" she cries.

"I must," says Ysabel, sweeping her hair back, settling her white hat on her head, "now see to my mother. Another appointment. I should be back in plenty of time."

"This, is," says Jo, headed across the room, "you can't just," up the steps to the kitchen, and "You'll be fine," says Ysabel.

"Ask your questions of the Shrieve, heed his advice." She catches Jo's free hand in hers. "Nothing needs to be done right away. We'll talk, about it all, tonight, tomorrow – "

"If I might, ma'am," says Bruno, gathering pages, "some signatures are required, resolutions, power of attorney," but Ysabel says, "Which might wait, until tomorrow, or the day after," and Bruno, looking up, nodding, says, "Of course." Stacking pages together. "Yes, ma'am." Binding them with a clip.

"Do you need me with you?" says Jo.

"It's my mother, Jo," says Ysabel. "If I end up running late," and she opens the door to the apartment. A woman's waiting on the landing, powerfully built, thick arms folded in a yellow track suit with white piping. "Majesty," she says with a nod, unfolding her arms, "your grace." Her close-cropped hair's been dyed a virulent chartreuse.

"Ysabel?" says Jo.

"If I'm running late," says Ysabel in the doorway, "I'll meet you there. Mason? Can you be at the Huntsman's disposal, should she require a driver?"

"Of course, ma'am," says Luys, sitting at the counter by the mound of roses.

"There," says Ysabel, stepping out onto the landing. The woman in the track suit leans in to pull the door shut.

"There," says Jo, as footsteps descend the stairs outside. "Okay," she says. Turning, to look at Luys, at the counter, at Bruno, down there on the sofa. The pages on the briefcase in his lap. "Okay," she says, again. "This, this fortune. Those numbers. Ten words or less. Where's it come from."

"It," says Bruno, hesitantly, feeling his way, "has, always been, Southeast's, milady."

"But what *is* it," says Jo, setting her sandwich on the counter, stepping down into the open room. "Where does it all," and then, frowning, she turns, looks back at the door to the apartment. "Rents, mortgages," Bruno's saying, "real, fixed properties and their associated monies," but "Lady," Jo's saying to herself, *"grace,"* turning about again, there in that room, "Southeast," she says, looking up at Luys, who's looking down at his hands.

"Holy shit," says Jo Maguire.

"A pretty speech;" he says, circumspectly, "airy words on the honesty of labor, the filthiness of lucre. I believed he meant them, at the time." His sun-browned head's quite bald, his cheeks grizzled with a dusting of white beard. "Then that son of a bitch walked away and left me holding the paper." The lips of the man beside him pinch at that, and he smiles, pointing with his glass for emphasis, "Such delicacy, Pinabel," he says. "I use the term advisedly – she whelped him, did she not? Or must I now take care, in how I speak of Gammers?"

The man beside him shakes his head, white dreadlocks brushing the shoulders of his pale blue suit. "Only when our host's so free with wine," he says, looking over the long and heavy table that dominates the room, and the city laid out atop it, blank white towers cut and shaped from foam core lining a broad blue curl of river crossed, here and there, by the delicate spans of bridges. "Also, you're left a house," he says.

"A wreck," says the bald man, "a ruin. A slap, to my face." His suit like most of the others in the room is dark, a navy subtly flecked with grey and back. "As if he'll accomplish anything without my bank."

"Then he'll be back, when he's something to accomplish," says Agravante. "And he may well slap you again, Welund. Kings never love their creditors."

"Gentlemen," says a man at the front of the room, and conversations still, attentions turn. He's short, thickset, the scruff of beard about his chin too neat to be an afterthought. "No need for introductions," he says. A baggy tweed jacket over a bottle green sweatshirt blazoned with a brightly yellow O. "We all, each share a, concern, for how this city," waving his hand, a distracted benison over the towers, "is grown?" He turns to the man beside him, tall, sharp-chinned, sharp-nosed, narrow black glasses like a constant squint. "Mr. Killian here," says the man in the sweatshirt. That sharp-featured man's leaning over to hear what's murmured to him by a man who's pointing to the heavy gold watch on his wrist. The sharp-featured man nods. "I wanted you," says the man in the sweatshirt, turning back to all those dark-suited men, standing about the city, "to hear what he has to say."

"Thank you, Rudy," says the sharp-featured man, stepping up to the head of the table, adjusting his glasses. His high-buttoned suit's a lighter grey than most of the rest in the room. "I'd like to think," he says, "most of you already know of me; certainly, I know of all of you. But it's the first time many of us have met. My name is George Killian; I will be the next mayor of Portland. I'd like to tell you what that means, for you."

A meander of paving stones across a scrap of yard, dead leaves, dying grass, black boots clomping, brown work boots following, hurrying, "Milady," he says, and she stops so abruptly he almost runs into her, "Do *not*," she says, "*call* me that."

He nods, he swallows, big hands open to either side of her. "Jo," he says. "Are you certain," but she's up the front steps, she's pounding the yellow front door, "Ray!" she yells. "Lymond!" Rattling the knob, it clacks, the door pops open. "Lady," says Luys, wincing, and then "Jo, wait – " but she's already off inside.

Inside, a long hall, the chugging whir of an air compressor, the chunk chunk, chunk of a nail gun. Jo in her black jacket bursts out into a high wide room, one great curving wall of glass and black trees falling away outside, into a formless chasm of cloud. The air compressor whines away down to silence, and the flap and snap of translucent plastic sheets draping a frame of two-by-fours built around a great square hole that's been cut in the floor to one side. A man in buff coveralls studiedly checks a level. Jo calls, "Lymond!" again. To the other side an armchair under a blue plastic tarp, a low table beside it, the only furniture other than the table saw, the compressor, the stack of lumber. A second man steps around a corner of the frame, his hair a pinkish orange, his sweater soused in sawdust. "Huntsman," he says. "Mason. A pleasant surprise. And as good a time as any, for a break?" The man in the coveralls sets his level down, dusts off his hands as Luys ducks his head, "Majesty," he says, and "God*dam*mit, Lymond," says Jo. Lymond pinches off a smile. "Jo, come," he says. "Walk with me. Mason, if you'd let Scuppernong show you to the kitchen?" He lifts a corner of plastic to reveal the top of an aluminum ladder, leaned against an edge of that great square hole. "After you?" he says, a fillip of his hand in a bulky work glove.

Down through the floor, under the house, the ground falling steeply here, sturdy squared stilts rising up from concrete pilings to meet rough-edged joists and beams, criss-crossed bracings, all of wood the color of old coffee. The ladder rests on a platform built of new yellow lumber, cantilevered out over the vertiginous drop, the house above, the clouds below, the wet roofs of the other houses, black trees all about and the drip of fallen rain. "Tell me you're not this stupid," says Jo, as Lymond steps off the ladder. "I wanted a deck," he says, moving past her carefully to the edge of it all. "I didn't want to spoil the view."

"Southeast," she says.

"Yes," he says, his back to her, straightening, sighing. "You are to be created a Duchess."

"Just like that."

"There'll be a ceremony, tomorrow, at the Apportionment — yourself, Linesse, Twice Thomas." He's looking down. He's smiling, to himself. "Ours is a terribly new court. But yes," he says. "Just like that."

"And you, you're, you were maybe gonna *ask* me?" and *"Jo,"* he says, sharply. She recoils. "What say you, to money?" he says. "Power?" Looking over his shoulder, turning to face her. "Never a need to worry again about the roof, over your head? Your next meal?"

"That's not, what I – "

"You saved the Queen, Gallowglas. You saved the city. We're not ungrateful."

"That's not!" she cries. "That isn't why I did it."

He cocks his brow over those bulging eyes, one brown, one blue. "Then tell me why," he says.

"I," says Jo, and a sudden shivering shake of her head, she looks away, "it was," she says, "the right thing to do. She needed – someone, had to do it."

"And she needs you yet," says Lymond. "We're all a long way off, from happily every after."

"Me," says Jo.

"Southeast," says Lymond, looking back out over the drop, the trees, the rain, "the largest, richest fief in the city; without a clear and certain succession it will fall, to infighting, and take the city with it." His hands in those bulky gloves clasped behind him. "But a hero? Loved by the city? Closely tied to the King, and his Queen?"

"*Me,*" she says, a squeak, a gasp of a laugh.

"The Hawk was your liege, Gallowglas. You fought for him and when he was cut down, you took a vengeance swift, and terrible. No one will," and she punches him, a stiff-armed blow to his shoulder, "Is this how it *works,*" she cries, and he rolls with it, and pulling up from the follow-through she grabs at him, clinging to his dusty sweater, "is *this* how things get done?" She pushes away from him, "I can't," she says. Unsteady, the both of them, there at the edge. "Do this. I can't."

He grabs a stilt, grabs her jacket, "You can," he says, easing her back, letting go. "You will. You're not alone, Jo."

She snorts. "Alone," she says, "the hell I'm not alone," but he's stripping a glove from his hand, "what are you," she says. He tosses the glove to the platform between them. "Whoa," she says, "hey, I didn't," and then he thrusts his bare hand at the stilt, the splintery edge of it, hissing when he hits it. "We're in this together," he says, holding up his hand, and the gash torn in the heel of it an ugly color, red, dark red, blood, red blood oozing over his palm, down his wrist.

Climbing the hillside, under the trees, crossing and crossing again a neat little roadway doubling back, looping the shoulder of a rise, they come out under an open sky starless, moonless above, a small empty parking lot before them, and the orange haze of streetlight shifts, yellows, warming in fitful flickers from the light they carry in their hands, swelling as their voices swell in a ringing, chorused shout. At the one end of the lot a railing, and a ramp that leads down the side of it to a round of greensward, a slope to a low stone-fronted stage, a stretch of black gravel before it, and all about rise crumbling cliffs of black rock clutched in knuckled tree-roots. They come down that ramp, silently now but for the rustle of their coats, the patter and tramp of their feet. More of them spill over the red clay basketball court at the end there, pushing back shadows with their light, merging and mingling into a crowd that stands, waiting, looking toward the bare stage under the blank sky far above.

"I will," says Ysabel — the Last he has
How, and Why

"I will," says Ysabel, sitting back, water sloshing milkily about her, "in a minute, I'm going to." She sighs. "Go. Under. Until it's done. The owr." Reaching up out of the water she takes Jo's hand in her own, slickly shining. "It might take some little while."

"Define while," says Jo.

"Minutes?" says Ysabel. "A few minutes. Nothing more. You mustn't worry."

"Underwater," says Jo.

"Just don't let go," says Ysabel. The water trembles about her, the surface of it wrinkling, and already in the thick white clouds below sparks flare. "Ysabel," says Jo, shifting her grip from Ysabel's hand to her wrist, and "I'll be fine," says Ysabel, "Jo," she says, "Jo, trust me," and "I do," says Jo. "In this," says Ysabel, "trust me."

"I do," says Jo.

"Do you," says Ysabel. "Do you," but she bites off the next word, turns away, and her other hand breaks the water's skin a billow of steam lifting to wipe at eyes and cheeks sheened with water, sweat, with tears, "it's never, I always, I always *knew*, before," she's saying. Looking up, those green eyes immense, the black fuzz of her shorn hair.

"Ysabel," says Jo.

"Now, I don't," says Ysabel.

"Yes," says Jo.

"Do you," says Ysabel, water lapping her chin, and "Yes," says Jo again, as Ysabel says, "love me?"

"Of course," says Jo. Looking down. Swallowing. Her other hand pressed between her breasts, fingers flat against her skin. "I love you," she says.

Ysabel ducks her head again, a sniff, a smile. "I love you, too," she says, and she hikes up a deep shuddering swallow of air and cheeks bulging, eyes shut, plunges suddenly under the water. Her hand the last of her to slip under, and Jo's with it, into the whitely swirling mirk.

A short straight sword, the hilt of it wrapped in white leather yellowed with long handling, quillions and pommel heavy and plain. The floor where it's been thrust is singed, scratched wood black and rough as charcoal in a neat ring about the blade. Ysabel stands with her back to it, long white coat colored by Christmas lights blinking in the window, white hat in her hands. Her hair spilling down, over her shoulders, black curls tangled here and there with sprigs of white. She looks expectantly up the flight of stairs that descends into this big front room. By the front door there a woman waits, powerfully built, yellow track suit, white piping, and from somewhere further back in the house, brittlely slippery guitar chords rise and fall.

Footsteps above, a murmur, a floorboard groans. Black sneakers, black jeans descending carefully, leading a tic-thock, tic-thock of polished black heels, long black skirts swaying like a bell. The man in the black jeans steps aside as the woman pauses, gathering herself on the last step, hand on the newel post, hand on her hip. Long black coat buttoned up to a hint of white collar at her throat. Long hair glossy, almost entirely white, twisted into a ruthless coil of braids. "Chariot," she says, and the woman in yellow nods. And then, "But where's your brother? Has the King not come to see me to my exile?"

"Don't be so dramatic, Mother," says Ysabel.

"It's to be the end of me, you realize."

"Have you packed?" says Ysabel. Her mother gestures absently, and Robin Goodfellow all in black sets the small black bag he's carried on the step beside her. "I have so little left, you see," says Duenna says.

"Your health," says Ysabel. "Family. A city, restored."

"I see," says Duenna, chin lifting, lips moued. And then, "Majesty suits you."

"The car's waiting, Mother," says Ysabel, sweeping her hat up onto her head. The Chariot all in yellow opens the front door.

The noise in the bar, the crowd, the piano and bass somewhere above it all, so Becker leans close over the standing table between them, the drinks, what's left of his martini, the other darkly red in a squat glass, a curl of lemon peel. "I told you!" he says. "I don't have any idea what I'm doing!"

"Who does?" says Kerr across from him, hair a dark untidy mop, his shirt striped red and brown, a gold watch heavy about his wrist. "You're making more than twice what you were for less than half the work. What's to understand?" He sips, he shrugs, he sips again.

"But *why?*" says Becker.

"I like you?" says Kerr, and he grins, and he laughs. "You have talents!" he says, laying a hand on Becker's. "A keen eye, a cool head, and who but me's seen that?" He swallows the rest of his drink.

"I'll get you another," says Becker, of a sudden, pushing away from the table, and Kerr looks after him, quizzical, bemused.

"Gin martini," says Becker, when he can get the bartender's attention, "and a Sazerac." She nods, she's reaching for glasses, bottles, and he taps his fingers on the bar, takes a paper napkin, folds it over, and over again. "Do I know you?" he says, to the man at the bar beside him, who's looking down, the mustaches drooping to either side of his mouth, the ends of them gathered and weighted by heavy irregular beads of dull pewter. "That," says the man, his voice pitched low, "is a question you must answer for yourself."

"Okay," says Becker, unfolding the napkin. "Do you know me. Every time I look up you're staring. At me."

"It isn't only that." He wears a blue jacket, tight across his shoulders. "No," says Becker, smoothing the napkin flat. "No, it isn't."

"My name is Pyrocles," says the man in the blue jacket. He lays a hand flat for a moment on the napkin, between Becker's hands, and when he lifts it away a clear plastic baggie is left behind, almost empty but for a pinch of dust, twisted into a corner of it. "The hell," says Becker, looking up, blinking, "drugs? I don't – "

"Not medicine," says Pyrocles. "Magic. The last I have. Tip it into a glass of water tonight, and drink it off before you take yourself to sleep. And tomorrow, then, if you remember," his hand on Becker's shoulder, and Becker doesn't start, or shy away, "come to Mount Tabor, midway between sunset, and midnight. The reservoirs, on the southwest slopes."

"Martini," says the bartender, setting a glass down. Becker nods to her, takes it, and when he looks back that blue jacket's pushing off away through the crowd. He turns about, looking over the crush of people to see the standing table by the window, Kerr leaning an elbow on it, phone to his ear. Becker sips his drink, and tucks the baggie into his pocket.

"Wait," says Duenna in her black coat there on the sidewalk, by the bicycles parked in a jumble at the edge of the yard.

"Mother," says Ysabel, in her white coat on the steps, a foot on the cramped front porch.

450

"Three weeks remain, until the Solstice. Three whole weeks. Why do we not wait, and do it properly?"

"Tomorrow night we hold the Apportionment," says Ysabel.

"But," says Duenna, agog, "you, you must rally the peers, you must gather up a whole new offering! You've no time to put me off like – "

"It is all," says Ysabel, "well in hand, Mother." Coming down a step. The house behind her, the peeling pink siding, the tiny lights strung along the railing of the porch. "So soon," says Duenna, and "Needs must," says Ysabel, tightly, and "No!" cries Duenna, hands raised against Ysabel before her.

"Mother," says Ysabel, again.

"Why can we not stay, the both of us, either of us on either side? Why can't you and I just, go, back across the river? As we were?"

"It's time," says Ysabel.

"As we have been for so long?"

The front door of the house opens and the man who steps out's tall, in a charcoal stripe suit. "Majesty," he says, and a bow to Ysabel, who nods in return. Duenna's drawn a hand back to her face, her lips. "Chazz," she says, softly.

"Ah," he says, with a smile. "My lady. I am better." One hand to his chest there, just below his throat wrapped about in a black turtleneck. "The Devil, you know." His trousers rolled at the cuffs, feet laced into stiffly shining black wingtips. His hand floats a gesture toward the front door opening again, the people stepping one by one out onto the porch, all of them in black, black shirts, black sweaters, black jackets and coats, and all their faces crudely blotched with reds, blues, yellows and black, rictuses thickly drawn on ghastly white. Shoulder to shoulder along the railing, silent, still, as behind them one last figure, stooped, tump and thock of the stick in her hand, shuffle and rustle of her tattered black cloak, and her white hair unbound, drifting lightly in the air. "You are," she says, "you have," and Duenna bursts into tears.

The woman on the porch lifts her stick, gnarled and grey, dull as driftwood, tossing it down to clatter before Duenna. One careful step at a time she comes down past Ysabel leaning back, out of the way, a bare foot nudging from under her cloak to kick the stick aside, and Duenna lifts up her head, sobbing, wailing wordlessly. She reaches for Duenna's cheek and Duenna twists away, her own hand coming up to catch, to grip, to hold. "You're here," she says, and a gulp, a hiccough.

Ysabel looks away, up to the Devil, the clowns, waiting, expressionless.

Ragged tatters, straight black coat, white-haired heads leaned together, tangled and braided, nodding in unison. "Seize her," says one of them.

The Devil nods, steps back, as two of the clowns push their way over to the steps, one little and round, one taller, head wrapped in a black scarf. They stop there to either side of Ysabel waiting patiently on the steps below, and they look from her to each other, to the Devil, to the figures on the sidewalk, draped in black, crowned in white. *"Seize* her!" cries the other of them, and with a shrug Ysabel lifts both her hands up and out. The clowns, gingerly, tenderly, each take hold of a wrist.

Up the ladder, out into that high wide room, the glass wall blankly black, down the hall, boots loud. She grabs the frame of one of the side doors jerking to a stop, a kitchen brightly lit, white cabinets gleaming, lemon yellow floor. Luys, sitting at a table in his yellow chamois shirt. Standing at the sink the man in buff coveralls, washing his hands. "You coming?" snaps Jo, and Luys looks up, startled, nodding, stooping to gather up his brown ski vest from the floor at his feet.

She's already in the car by the time he makes it out the front door, her head tipped back, eyes closed. The dressing on her brow a pale flash in the dark. He sits himself behind the wheel, pulls his door shut.

"Still no answer," she says, her hand on her knee, her phone in her hand.

"Jo," he says, but she looks over at him. "Did you know?" she says. "I mean, did you have any idea?"

His hands on the wheel. A bit of leather thong tied loosely about one wrist. "I had my hopes," he says.

"Hopes," she says. "Okay." Stuffing her phone back into her jacket. "So," she says. "I have somewhere I need to be."

"You have but to tell me where," says Luys, starting the engine.

Spitting wine poured into her mouth, black in the darkness lightening to a red that slathers her cheeks, her throat, purples her yellow camisole, coughing, she laughs. Shadows pass over, a hand reaches in, green clumped on two fingers pressed to her eyelid, smudged, the other, another hand red thickly across her mouth, brighter than the wine that's stained her chin. She ducks away, shaking back her hair, curls of it heavy, wet. A figure backlit squats before her, haloed in white frizz tangled, harsh light slopping over a bare shoulder, blue-veined breast brown-nippled. Knobby fingers grip her chin, her cheeks, pointed grey nails dimpling her skin, turning this way, that. Another figure behind her, bare flesh stooping stark in the light. Knobby flat-nailed fingers take up the weight of all that hair. "Memento," says the one. "Godhvydh!" the other.

"Yes," she says. "I know."

Pulling that hair into a sheaf, tugging, jerking her back she pulls forward, wincing, "Nakoirano," says the one, and "Riaghail," the other, and "Yes," she says. "Yes."

"Mer, mr-no. Murnan, Mimir."

"Caw. Cwo cwi caw. Fetch them."

A rustle, a step. "Th'art," says the one, and "Thou rul'st," the other. "How, thou art," and, "Why, the rule." Black sleeve, a hand holding by the blades a set of shears. Her eyes widen. The figure before her takes the shears by the joint and passes them handle first to the figure behind. "No," she says, struggling against her jacket tugged down, binding her arms, "this stops," she says, but her head's yanked back, her hair pulled taut, "Remember!"

"Thou art."

"Know this."

"Memento."

"Remorse."

"I am," she says, "you must, wait," but those grey nails dig into her cheeks again, "Thou art regal, daughter mine."

"Thy rule, my Queen."

"Memento."

"Regere."

"How."

"And why."

"I am," she says, again. Indistinct about them, painted faces float in the darkness. She nods. She says, "Yes, I will." She says, "I am."

"Thou art regal," the whisper in one ear. "Thou art regal," the whisper in the other. Shears lifted, blades spread with a scrape of metal. Hair lifted, wound about once, the hank of it fitted between. The flat-nailed fingers, squeezing. Her eyes, closing, as the blades bite.

Waiting under the blank sky far above, stirring as here and there someone, someone else, moves through the crowd toward the bare stage, off to the side there, stepping up onto it, a man in a pale suit glimmering blue in the light, and he lifts his shining hand to them all, his hair white, touched with gold, hanging in dreaded locks down to his shoulders. Behind him, a tall woman in a gown of sequins glittering like water, like starlight, like mail, her arms and shoulders bare, her close-cropped hair a gunmetal grey. Over there, mounting the steps on the other side of the stage, a short man, heavyset, tweed suit brown and green and a meshback cap on his head, and when he holds both his hands up shining there are cheers and whoops and whistles from the crowd. And there, hoisting herself up in the middle, black jeans, black jacket swinging open as she stands on the stage, turning, her T-shirt red, and in her dark-gloved hand a mask, a skull of white with empty eyes, teeth crudely drawn, a long black mane brushing the stone floor of the stage. The noise of the crowd falters, fades, back to that rustling stillness, and the light, growing now even as the crowd parts, shuffling, turning, looking back, to where that light is breaking. In a yellow raincoat over a plain white shirt, his pink hair washed out in the brilliance, the King, Lymond, waving to them all, shaking hands as he makes his way down the aisle they've made, and at his side, in her long white coat, Ysabel, the Queen.

JO, CRUMPLED – GOD BUY YOU – KISSING, AND KISSING AGAIN NO PROMISE BROKEN – BLOOD; SWEAT; TEARS

JO CRUMPLED to white tile dusted over all about with gold, hand pressed to her breast clenching, relaxing, lifting, as she opens her eyes, "Ow," she says. Reaching for the rim of the tub, and the skin between her breasts left clean, pale, dust falling as she pulls herself up, dust crunching under her fingers, squeaking under her thigh, her knee as she shifts, crusts of it clinging, wetly, dropping in darker clumps. The tub filled with dust, wet, a shoreline rippled, trembling, crumbling up as fingers wriggle free, "Ysabel," says Jo, a croak, grabbing the hand, pulling, a chin appearing, lips spitting, working, eyes blinking, arm pulled free, shoulder, chest and throat a spilling hiss of dust that slithers under around behind her as she sits up shaking, sobbing, laughing soundlessly. Jo's brushing dust from those eyes, those cheeks, the glinting stubble of that hair, that mouth, and Ysabel presses a kiss, triumphant, to the tips of her fingers.

Unsteadily Jo makes her way through buttery summer light to the robe that's hung from a hook on the wall, the wall of white tile splattered, spangled in a great jagged bloom of gold all about the tub. Gold, shaken from plaid folds as she digs into a pocket of the robe, pulling out a crumpled orange pack of cigarettes, a book of matches.

Pop and spark Jo lights a cigarette, sits on the rim of the tub. Shakes out the match. Offers another to Ysabel straining against that softly golden weight to take it in her lips. Jo holds out her own, touching the bright coal of it to Ysabel's, and Ysabel puffs until with a crackle hers is lit. Tips back her head, both hands resting limply on all that gold.

"We're gonna need a bigger tub," says Jo, and sputtering, coughing, Ysabel begins to laugh.

Signing her name, Jo Maguire, her hand hangs a moment, pen above the heavy, gilt-edged page. Three names written, above hers, "Thomas Thomas?" she says. Luys beside her looks back along the hall, flocked yellow wallpaper, brass chandeliers brightly lit, a spray of flowers atop an old mahogany hutch, lilies pink and white, spears of pale green gladiolus, there by the flashing lights of a cable modem. The doorway before them hung with red curtains, and light glaring from soffits all about the room within, green-cushioned pews in tight rows facing a white-draped catafalque. The casket softly taupe, with coppery fittings, lid of it propped open, laid within a man in a sober grey suit, his long hair brushed to a dark gleam over the pillow. Pale hands folded at his breast, just so.

In the second row a woman, hunched in a puffy winter coat, head ducked, short hair the color of iron. At the back of the room the only other figure in a green jacket zipped up to his chin, a maroon meshback cap that says Freightliner over the bill, and he's looking out from under it directly at Luys, who nods, crisply, turns back to Jo, to the body resting before them. His brow lifts, his lips purse. "I know him," he says, quietly, but his deep voice carries in the hush. "The Duke's jape." Whispering, now.

"Frankie," says Jo, quietly. "Reichart."

Luys steps back. "I," he says, "I'll just," and another step back. He turns. He makes his way down the aisle, he sits at the back of the room, across from the man in the green jacket, who leans over to say, quietly, "A good evening to you, sir." Jo's holding a crumpled orange pack of cigarettes in her hand.

"Your grace," whispers Luys. The man in the green jacket shakes his head. "Address me direct, sir, if you please. It's only myself, and the union, after all."

"Soames," says Luys. Jo's reaching into the casket, tucking a cigarette into the breast pocket of that suit.

"Uncanny," says the Soames. "How they linger, when they've gone." Luys doesn't nod at that, or shake his head. Jo's stepped into the aisle, she's kneeling now, creak of her boots, hand up on the pew as she says something to the woman hunched there, unmoving as Jo leans in, looks up, repeats herself.

"She must understand," says the Soames. "Her grace, I mean. It was an accident. He thought to defend his friend; Swift thought only to defend himself – when he saw the blood, red, on his blade," and he shakes his head. "There's no retaliation to be called for," he says, "is what we'd have her understand." Jo's stopped, in the middle of what she's saying, as the woman begins to speak, lifting her iron head to make a point, and another, and only a few words can be made out of her brittle voice, "didn't," and "you," and "fault."

"Mrs. Reichart, please," says Jo, standing, stepping back. The woman in the pew looks away with a shake of her head, and Jo leaves, abruptly, red curtains flapping in her wake as Luys pulls himself to his feet.

Barreling out the front door of the funeral home head down hood up hands jammed in her pockets Jo heads down the front steps into the mostly empty parking lot. The front door bangs open again, there's Luys, coming after her, and she quickens her pace, around the corner of the big brick home, where she stops, suddenly. Behind a screen of hedge the reddish brown car, the black stripe down the side, and parked beside it now a white suv, gold trim, tinted glass, the back of it opened, a woman there in a yellow track suit, and a man in blue coveralls, handing her a white plastic bucket. Skirting them Jo makes her way around to the other side of the suv, the rear door open there, demure interior lights, a grey-trousered leg, a lemon and grey pump, "You're late," she says, heated, a hand on the doorpost, and her eyes wide, her face slack, "Jesus fucking Christ," she says.

"I do apologize," says Ysabel, sitting back in the white leather seat, her cheeks, her forehead still blotched with traces of color, her jacket rent, her camisole stained. "I promised I would be here for you."

"You cut off your hair," says Jo, a hand to her chest.

"I had it cut," says Ysabel, her green eyes immense. "How was," and she shakes her head, "how are you," she says.

"Oh," says Jo, looking away. Luys is out there, by the corner of the home, waiting. "My ex-boyfriend's mother just told me to go to hell, at his funeral. But hey," lowering her hood, turning back to Ysabel, the flash of the white dressing taped to her brow, "apparently I'm running half the city?"

"A fifth," says Ysabel, but Jo's shouting, "Why didn't you say something! Why didn't you *tell* me!"

"I wanted," says Ysabel, and the suv shakes as the tailgate's closed. Out there, at the edge of the shadowed lot, the Soames half-listens to what the man in the blue coveralls is telling him. "I wanted you," says Ysabel, "to have a chance to say goodbye, before you were caught up in all of this."

"You should've *asked*," says Jo, stepping back.

"I didn't think I had to," says Ysabel, closing her eyes.

"Where do you wish to go?" says Luys, signaling a turn, working the clutch and the gear shift with some concentration. And a block or so later, Jo says, "I don't know. What does a Duke do, time like this?" And then, "Duchess." And then, "What do I do."

Luys signals another turn.

"Will there be anything else, ma'am," says the Chariot all in yellow, setting the bucket down by the tub.

"No, Iona," says Ysabel in the hall. "I'll see myself to bed."

"Of course," says Iona. "I'm right downstairs, should you need anything."

After a moment, Ysabel nods.

458

"Hell of a view," says Jo, leaning back against the hood of the car. Past the fence a dizzying fall of steps to an inky reservoir below, and then the lights, house lights and porch lights, signs and storefronts, streetlights an awful grid broken, gentled here and there by blank dark clusters and thickets of tree-shadow, all of it lipped by a dark low line of a ridge, blocks and blocks away. Past all that the glowing downtown haze, clusters of light piled up under the blank black sky, and there a lone tower off to the right, a silhouette dotted with windows irregularly lit, and lined at the top bright red and green. "We need to talk," she says, and she drops the spark of her cigarette to the sidewalk. "I can't," she says.

"Milady?" says Luys, sitting beside her, work boots up on the bumper.

"I am never gonna get you not to do that, am I."

"I will," he says, big hands on his knees, a bit of leather thong tied about his wrist. "Withstand oppressor's power, with arm, with puissant hand. Recover right, for those that wrong has grieved." Looking up, at her. "Battle guile, and malice, and despite." Those eyes, big, darkly brown. "And I will show my liege the respect that she is due." One of his hands on the leaden pommel of a very long sword, the hilt of it and the ricasso wrapped about in leather, the tip of it against the sidewalk, and he bows his head, tilting the weight of it toward her, and trembling Jo lets out the breath she's holding and leans over, leans down, gently to kiss his knuckle.

On the counter by the mound of roses a blue glass bottle sealed with pink wax, a white card propped on the counter before it, a simple drawing in blue ink of a hound's head. Ysabel lays the card flat, shaking her head at it. Stepping out of her pumps she picks up the bottle and carries it off, padding down the dim hall to the bathroom shining white at the end of it, where she sets it on the floor by the lidded bucket, the plastic milk jug, the tureen, wrapped in foil.

Skinning off her camisole she leaves it maroon and yellow on the white tile. Leans against the sink, green eyes blinking in the jagged oblong of mirror set in the wall. Fingers to a delicate chin, lifted to brush sleek black fuzz. She looks out suddenly, into the dark hall, blinking. Waiting a moment. Says something, a barely shaped breath, not even a whisper, "Jo?"

White coat about her shoulders, clutched to her throat, past the blank glass portholes of washer and dryer, through the door out under the low canopy. A fire's burning in the patterned bronze chiminea, and someone's sitting up in one of the Adirondack chairs, long legs gathering themselves to push up a shadow, a silhouette haloed blazing white and gold in the firelight. "My Queen," says Marfisa.

Kissing him, and kissing him again, his breath catching as she reaches a bare arm out from under her white coat parting, gripping her arm, pulling her close, and he grunts, her gloved hand under his down vest, inside his shirt, gripping his wide brown belt as she kisses his throat, as she presses a delicate kiss to her shivering lips, uncertain what to say.

"Yes," he says, when she looks up at him, and then, thickly, "please," as she falls heavily to her knees in the dying grass, sheepskin coat draped over stockinged feet, and he's hiked himself up on the hood to give her room, leaning back on an elbow as she undoes his jeans, belt lolling in her hand, her hand in that white-gold hair as she kisses her there, at the top of her thigh, "Yes," she says, "yes, please."

"Oh hell yes," she says, wrenching the car door open as her white coat falls from her shoulders, gasping as she's caught in arms laid back along the grass, sitting heavily in the back seat as he looms in over leaned against the front seat levered up, hands at the buttons of her jeans she kisses him once more before rolling over on her hands and knees, kisses that skim her belly, that lick at a nipple, that meet her mouth left slack and a weak laugh rolling over in the grass, kicking free of trousers tangling

460

her legs as he helps her tug her black jeans over her hips, as she reaches down to pull her up, "It's cold," she says.

Her hand on his between her thighs, his boot scraping pavement as she skips away laughing, as she lunges to her feet, he hisses, she bites her lip, her cheek grinding digging the heel of her hand in the vinyl as one door crashes open and the next, thump and squeak after slithery whick and the car rocks, his hips pump shoulders arm spread out against the roof head wedged at an awkward angle, "Wait," she's saying, and a whoop of delight as slap her hand catches her arm, "hold it," she's saying, panting, he falters, whirling about in the hall to spin to crash together, "there," she's saying, "try," then she groans, she lets her turn her about, leaning back as she reaches around the sheepskin coat, and his face is set, his hand braces her hip, grunting, her fingers unzipping her pants, worming under, in, her cries, muffled by the seat, her sigh, in her arms.

The screen door croaks, he holds it open with his foot, he's patting his coat, his pants for his keys. The hand on his shoulder, the heavy gold watch. "I, could," says Kerr, a small sly smile.

"You could," says Becker, looking down, and that hand shifts, lifts away, as he says, "but."

"But," says Kerr. Leaning back against the siding weirdly pale in the streetlight.

"I have," says Becker, and he sighs, "this job? In the morning."

"Hey," says Kerr. A finger under Becker's chin. "There's the basic deal of this world. Right?" Becker, looking up at him. "You take," says Kerr, "or you get took," and he kisses Becker, stepping back, smile widening at Becker's smile. "Start taking."

"Tomorrow," says Becker, and, stepping back, again, "All right," says Kerr, nodding. "Tomorrow." Turning, heading away, down the stairs.

Unlocking the front door, stepping inside. There by the low glass-topped coffee table Becker empties his pockets, pants and coat, setting down a wallet, a phone, a ring of keys, a plastic baggie, a handful of change, he stops, quarter twirling down to clatter flat against the glass. Picks up the baggie. Looks at it, there in his palm.

"It is what's within," he says, leaning over her, yellow shirt unbuttoned, her boot in his lap. "What we weep, what we sweat, what we bleed," and "I know," she's saying, "I get it, I do," laid out across the back seat, jeans lopped open, "I just," she says, shivering, arms wrapped about herself, "I didn't, get it."

He shifts, closer to her, jangle of belt buckle, slur of his down vest against the vinyl. The one hand held over her, two fingers crooked, sheened with something glimmering in the darkness. "It fades, rapidly, unless it's fixed," he says.

"Turned," she says, shaking with something that might be laughter.

"Yes," he says. "But." Gently nudging aside the bit of gauze askew on her brow, the tape peeling away. "Freshly spilled," he says, intent on his fingers, dabbing at the wound there, ugly, open, darkly red. "It's as puissant as any pinch of dust," he says.

She fills the glass up to the brim, then sets the bottle of milk back in the refrigerator, closing the door, shutting out the harsh white light of it. Leaving the full glass there by the sink she takes up the tray and heads back down the hall, glasses clinking, into the flickering yellow and white room, the curls and pools of light from serried ranks of candles aflame along the dresser there, the windowsills, and she sets the tray on the bed by Marfisa on her side, propped up on an elbow. Shucking her bulky sweater Ysabel clambers naked under the blankets, careful of the tray, "This cordial," she's saying, "you must try. An eau de vie," plucking up one of the high narrow glasses of something faintly in that light just barely green, "infused," and Marfisa takes it from her, "with an essence of fir."

"Fir," says Marfisa, dubious, and then, "what is this supposed to be," with a gesture of her glass over the rest of the tray, the heel of bread, the cheese, the dish of olives, purple and black and grassy green. "I thought," says Ysabel, "you might, perhaps, be hungry."

"Lady," says Marfisa, and she drains her glass, and carefully sets it back on the tray, by the wooden salt cellar. "I didn't come here to come back."

"But you haven't left," says Ysabel, her glass in her hand.

"I tried," says Marfisa, and Ysabel closes her eyes. "I did try. I walked out into the woods until I forgot my words," and her hand on Ysabel's still hand. "I woke up in a Gresham motel. I thought about, flying – I set a foot on the steps of a bus. My brother, my own Handle, gave me money to go." Her hand, pulled away. "I threw it in his face."

"You tried," says Ysabel, the words half-voiced, lifting from a whisper, "and you failed. And now the King's come back. And you, you might kiss me," and she's smiling, "in the street, for all to see," reaching over the tray for Marfisa's hand. "And not a promise broken."

"Your brother can't be King," says Marfisa.

"He sat the Throne," says Ysabel.

"What does that matter, lady, when he's sat a mechanical at your deliberations! With my brother, and faithless Linesse, and Southeast's empty chair – "

"The Gallowglas," says Ysabel.

"As?" says Marfisa, and then she looks away, slumping at Ysabel's nod, white hair a cloud, massed on the pillows. "Speak your mind," says Ysabel, sipping her cordial.

"You will not hold this city long," says Marfisa. "Even if you might turn the owr."

"I can," says Ysabel. "I will."

"They will turn on you," says Marfisa. "My brother has written to other courts, seeking any spare Princess – "

"We know," says Ysabel.

"A new Bride," says Marfisa, looking to Ysabel, "for the King to come."

"So come you back," says Ysabel. "Take up your sword again. *Help* us."

Marfisa sits up, leaning on an elbow. "I was told," she says. "I will never kneel to another King." And then, "Lady, leave with me." Ysabel drinks off the rest of her cordial, and sets her glass down, clink. "Come away with me," says Marfisa, and then, "Ysabel," she says. "Do you love me."

And Ysabel leans over to kiss her, Marfisa starting back, and Ysabel pursues her, heedless of the tray, kissing her over, over and down.

"I wanted," she says, headed around to the trunk of the reddish brown car, "to talk." Bare arms about herself.

"Yes," he says, leaned against the open door. "You said. Aren't you cold?"

"Before," says Jo. "I wanted to talk before we, did, that."

"If we get back in the car," says Luys, "I might turn on the heater," but "Nope," she says. Holding out her hand. "Give me the keys." And then, "Luys. Mason." And stepping to the rear fender, he hands them over. "Last week," she says, jangling through them in her hand. "That night. When we, the three of us." Shivering, her other arm still wrapped about herself.

"Yes," says Luys.

"I wasn't entirely honest," she says, holding up one of the keys, darkly brassy bronze against her fingers.

"That's, a key to the car," says Luys, after a moment.

"To the *trunk,*" she says. "Jessie had the car keys, or Sweetloaf. *This* one he always kept, in a pocket, on his person, safest place, he said, in the city," and she fits the key to the lock of the trunk. "Only reason I was in that bed that night was so when he went to sleep." Looking up. "When you went to sleep. I could get it, and come down here. See for sure."

"See, what?" says Luys, his hand leaned on the trunk, and then, when she does not look away, he does, shifting, lifting his hand away. "The mask," she says. "That you wore, that once."

"I did not want to do that," he says, the one hand rubbing the other.

"Don't get me wrong," says Jo. "I'm glad you did." She turns the key in the lock. "But. I saw it, that day, when he introduced me to the crew? I saw it, or thought I saw it. I was pretty sure I saw it." Her hands on the lid. "But it wasn't till that night, last week. Frankie was there. Did you know that? Washing dishes. It was the last, time." Shivering she takes in a breath. "It wasn't, until he said – anyway. That I got up the nerve," and she opens up the trunk.

Inside a couple of boxes, one lined with a garbage bag, holding a big brown glass growler. She pulls out from between them a mask that could swallow half a head, white, crudely painted with thick black lines to resemble a grinning skull, and a mane of long black hair that stirs as she holds it up with a swallowed sob, her eyes shut tight.

"Jo?" says Luys. He leans into the car, comes out with her black coat, stands there holding it in his hands as unsteady she sits back against the lip of the open trunk, the mask held at her knee. "It was *gone*," she says, head bowed. "Lost." Her other hand a fist against her heart. "I dropped it," and the mane of it rustles by her feet, "somewhere, *else*." Looking up, looking back. "He gave you the key, didn't he," she says.

"He," says Luys, frowning, "asked me to drive, yes." Stepping closer, her coat in his hands. "To the motel. Jessie had left, unexpectedly and – "

"That bastard," she says, to herself. "He knew. How could he possibly have known."

"Milady," he says, "I don't understand," but shaking her head she's turning, setting the mask back in the trunk, coiling its spill of mane in after it. "Milady?"

"Okay," she's saying. "All right. I'll do it." She's peeling the garbage bag away from the neck of the growler, tugging at a sticky patch, and her face screws up, she draws back, "That, smell," she says, waving a hand, looking for a word, "that, sour, that's the, the," and Luys beside her now says "It's been in there a week, or more. It spoils, if it's not fixed."

"So it's, worthless?" she says, stepping back as he nods, once, and she turns about, away, "Fine," she says, and "okay, that's not a, we can just," she says, and "that's fine, I will," she says, and then she shouts, "I will!"

And standing there, her coat in his hands, Luys says, "What will you, my lady."

"Freeze," she says, with a laugh, taking her coat from him. Nodding toward the open trunk as she slips an arm into a sleeve, "We're gonna find somewhere we can hose that out," she says, "and then," and she laughs, "we're gonna go about the, the," her hand waving again, "the realm? I guess?" Headed past him suddenly, she lurches for the trunk, slams it shut, "We'll get some more!" she cries. Past the car now, up onto the sidewalk, "Somebody's got to still be up," she says. Turning back there, and behind her the fence, and beyond, below, the lights of the night-filled city, and her wet cheeks shine, but she's smiling, laughing again, "That's how it works, right? Blood, sweat? Tears? Our offering, to the Queen?"

And Luys, the Mason, nods. "Yes, your grace," he says.

All that white gold hair spread over a bent knee not so pale as her wet cheek, fingers chilly white against the warm bare belly, gently stroking a scribble of hair, black hair longer than the fuzz that sleeks the scalp between her own spread thighs, and as she lets herself fall back to the tangled blankets, spilled salt, tumbled olives, she closes her eyes, she bites her lip, gripping that upturned hip now, fumbling, slapping the sheets, knocking a delicate glass to the floor, and out in the hall Jo's lifted her hand to knock but there's a whimper, a groaning sob, she opens her hand, lowers it. In her other hand the mask, the mane of it looped about her fingers. Past the closed door a rustle, a murmur, she steps back, the lilt of a question, an answering syllable, she stoops, hauls up in her free hand the weight of the growler, wrapped in a plastic garbage bag, sloshing faintly as she steps into the room across the hall, unlit, white walls. She sets the growler down.

She stands there, unmoving, for a time.

The light, changing, shifting and returning as traffic crawls by, outside, the sound of it distant, muted.

She lifts a hand, brushes back her hair. She's smiling. She turns, hangs the mask there, on the wall, above the sword slung from its leather strap. She unbuckles, pries loose her boots, leaves them by the futon, shrugs off the black coat, wrestles her way out of black jeans that she lets fall to the floor. Pulls something from a pocket of her coat, her phone, and crawling under the covers thumbs it to life, shining a photo, Jo and Ysabel cheek to cheek, Ysabel with a hand to the upturned collar of her coat, looking sidelong at Jo, smiling widely, directly at the camera, the blur of her arm at the bottom, and at the top the phone's clock. It says 03:07, Thursday, December 1. She swipes and pokes, sets the alarm for seven in the morning, lays the phone on the crate by the head of the futon. A sharp cry from across the hall through both closed doors and she stifles a laugh with the heel of her hand, shaking under the blankets, head nestled on the pillows.

Only a few more minutes pass before her shoulder slumps, her hand tips away, her breathing gentles, smoothed, into sleep.

"MY PEOPLE!"

"MY PEOPLE!" cries the King, as he mounts the stage there in the middle, by Jo. "All of you that call this city home." Spreading his arms as applause begins to spatter below, redouble, grow. "Here we are!" he cries, into the mounting approbation. "Your Court, of Roses!" Stepping to one side, throwing out a hand toward the short man in tweed, the meshback cap on his head, "The Soames!" cries the King. "For the North!" and the Soames lifts his hands clasped over his head to the cheers and whoops. Stepping to the other, leaning, a gesture toward the woman down there in her silvery gown, "The Helm," cries the King, "for the Northeast Marches!" and she inclines her head. "The Handle!" cries the King, as the man in the pale blue suit steps forward, and the applause swells even more, deepening, thundering. "For Southwest!" And then, taking Jo's hand in his, "For Southeast!" His voice booming. "Our Huntsman!" Down there, at the end of the stage, the Queen in her white coat's climbed the steps, she's making her way to the center, past the Soames, in her long white coat, her shorn head crowned with a white slouch hat, her hand outstretched to reach for the King's other, outstretched hand. "And," he cries, "I give you," taking her hand in his own, "my sister," and the applause, the cheers are deafening now, "your Queen!"

And when he can make himself heard again, "All of you," he says, "all of you who washed up on this shore so long ago, in the light of a dawn that had never before been seen." Jo looks down at her hand in his, at his hand about hers, firm, familiar, and the red mark there, on the heel of it, an old cut long since healed. "Who gave voice to a word that had never before been said, and sent it ringing out into the day. Tonight!" And the light that's filling that little round is growing, warmer, brighter, shining up from them all, banishing the sky above, "Here!" cries the King, "And now!" And Jo looks over, past him, to the Queen, to Ysabel, holding his other hand. "My people!" cries the King. "Lift up your hands, your voices, with mine!" And he hoists his in the air, and theirs up with him, as down the ragged aisle left in the crowd before them too bright almost to look upon a cooler held up in the Anvil's broad arms, the lid of it removed, and the Mason beside him, and the Devil, the Chariot, Biscuit in his long brown coat, each of them reaching into the cooler and pulling out handfuls of light, tossing them, pellets and globules, spangles and sparks, lighting up the glowing shining hands that catch them, and the upturned faces, smiling, laughing, weeping, cheering, whooping, sobbing, roaring, as the King cries out, his words lost in the noise, as the Queen, as Ysabel, closes her eyes, leans back her head, takes it all in, as the mask jerks and twists in Jo's hand, the mane of it leaping and lashing about, and down in the city Philip Keightlinger sits up on a bare mattress, mahogany beard in disarray, and reaches for a pair of sunglasses, and Jessie Vitaly wrapped in a ski jacket and a fleece blanket looks over at the man asleep in the driver's seat beside her, Lach, or Luke, or Lake, and Guthrie turns on the light in an empty kitchen, stands there, blinking, rings a-glitter, and Petra B winds herself more tightly in striped sheets as tears spring to her eyes, and Vincent Erne his full length stretched along a spavined couch snores lightly, his face relaxed, his hook still, and in a room full of bunk beds all of them occupied, Suzette, Gloria Monday, glares at the bedsprings above her, glaring at the rustle from across the aisle, and Tim Carroll runs packing tape over the top of another box, but takes a sharp breath, looks up, blinking, at the faintest echo of that sound, and in the train station, a woman's sitting on a bench, head wrapped in a fringed scarf, and at her feet a cage with walls of gauzy nylon, and the shadows of butterflies sleeping within, and she checks her pocket watch, and frowns.

Some time later Pyrocles looks up, stands up, there by the ravaged cooler, heads across the glittering lawn, past knots of people here and there, some speaking quietly one to another and all of them looking down at the dimming light in their hands. On the ramp there, leading down from the parking lot, a man in a heavy raincoat, trilby in his hands, and what's left of his hair lofts a little in a gelid gust, and striding, not quite running, Pyrocles makes his way up to him to kiss him, and kiss him again.

"What *is* this," says Becker, as Pyrocles hands to him a plastic baggie filled with dust.

"I told you," says Pyrocles. "Magic." And then he says, "But it is late, and cold, and I should take you home – "

"No," says Becker, "not yet," and he sighs. Leans against Pyrocles, and kisses him, their arms about each other.

> If your master
> Would have a queen his beggar, you must tell him,
> That majesty, to keep decorum, must
> No less beg than a kingdom.
>
> *—Cleopatra*

The text has been set in Tribute, a typeface designed by Frank Heine from types cut in the 16th century by Françoise Guyot; specifically, a specimen printed around 1565 in the Netherlands.

Kip Manley lives in Portland, Oregon, with a cartoonist, an aspiring large and exotic animal veterinarian who loves animals, and (at last count) two cats and one hamster.

He may be contacted via email at kipmanley@yahoo.com. His general-interest website is available for viewing at www.longstoryshortpier.com.